THE COMPLETE TOBIAS FINCH SERIES

ELISHA KEMP

For information contact the author at her website elishakempbooks.com

Contents

Latent Wolf - Book One

Chapter 1

Tobias Finch

I cringe inwardly as I step off the bus. Buffalo, Wyoming is exactly as I imagined.

Small. Old. Run-down.

A dry wind gusts through the deserted main street, kicking up dirt. The rusty sign above the hunting and fishing store swings on its hinges.

Sighing, I sit down heavily on my suitcase, pulling my backpack onto my lap and waiting. The building across the street looks like something out of a bad western movie. I snap a photo of it, then send out a text.

Literally a ghost town.

A minute later my phone pings in reply.

Is that a movie set?

I snort at Greg's reply, then shoot back:

Unfortunately, no. This is home.

**Wide eyed emoji.*

And that pretty much sums it up.

I rub at my eyes, the coloured contact lenses like sandpaper after two nights of traveling cross country.

My grandparents are late. After everything that has happened over the past couple weeks, this additional proof of bad luck shouldn't surprise me.

An hour passes and I rise stiffly to my feet. Shops have started to open and the scent of bacon and eggs wafts temptingly from a nearby café. My stomach grumbles. I'm starving. Nothing new there. But I'm also out of cash.

Hefting my backpack across one shoulder, I start dragging my suitcase in the direction of my grandparents' house. John and Susan Vance. 781 Cottonwood Avenue, exactly one point five miles out of town.

No doubt the wheels on my bag will be worn to stubs by the time I get there.

Cottonwood Avenue is a gravel road. The house marked 781 sits at the end, nestled against dun-coloured foothills that match the worn weatherboards.

Hoping this is the right house, I lift my fist to the door and knock cautiously. The door opens and a frowning wrinkled face topped with a mop of grey hair greets me. I step back involuntarily as the smell of stale cigarette smoke slams me in the face.

"What do you want?" The elderly man growls, his withered body propped against the doorframe.

He looks like death warmed up – if death wore a vacant expression and was featured on an anti-smoking campaign poster.

"I – I'm Tobias Finch, sir," I babble as I rub my face to stop the embarrassment prickling my cheeks, "I thought you were expecting me?"

I must have got the wrong house after all. Of course. That would be just my luck.

"The only one I've been expecting for the past ten years is the grim reaper," the old man drawls, flashing yellowing teeth as he speaks, "and he ain't in any hurry to get me out of this hell hole."

"Oh. Okay…"

I frown, stepping back slowly to eye the numbers painted on the house. 781. Did I get the address wrong?

"You're – you're not John Vance?"

"Depends on who's askin." The old man's eyes narrow, then he adds, tone menacing: "Who sent you, boy? You one of those government agents? I told 'em to stop comin' round here. I'm not talking. Got nothing for yeh."

"Johnny, who you talking to dear?" A woman's voice calls from within the house.

"Some guy who calls himself Tobias Finch," the man shoots back.

"Tobias!" the woman exclaims excitedly.

Johnny – presumably John Vance, my grandfather - is suddenly pulled back and a smiling older woman surges forward, wrapping me in surprisingly strong arms. Short, jet-black hair frames a friendly, wrinkled face.

"I thought you were coming tomorrow," the woman says, holding me by the shoulders as she examines my face, black eyes bright and perceptive. She shakes her head. "Can't believe you're really here."

When John appears on the doorstep beside his wife, she explains patiently: "Johnny, sweetie, this is Tobias. Your grandson. Remember, Marian's son. We were expecting him."

"Well, yah, I guess we were," the old man frowns, eyeing me suspiciously. "But where's Marian? Where's my daughter?"

My gut wrenches at the question. At the sound of mom's name.

I'm back there, just like that. With that one word. I can still see the blood. Remember the exact pattern it made on the linoleum floor in the kitchen. The angle of her neck. Throat torn out. Dad howling in rage and grief.

"She passed away, dearest," the old woman says. "Remember, they had the funeral a week ago?"

The old man shakes his head, face crumpling as he gives an unintelligible gurgling cry. The sound makes my chest clench, a familiar nausea rising in my throat.

Susan gently comforts her husband, rubbing his arms and muttering unintelligible words to sooth him until the man stumbles back inside, hiccupping.

I stare at my shoes, unsure of whether I should say anything while my grandmother ushers the sobbing man inside.

When I spoke with her over the phone, grandma had mentioned grandpa's "fragile mental state" as she had called it. *The dementia is making him a little forgetful and paranoid*, she had explained.

Well, hadn't that just been the understatement of the year.

A few moments later, Susan reappears on the doorstep.

"I'm so sorry. Come in. Please, come in," she says, shaking her head apologetically. "You must be exhausted."

I nod and obey. It took me more than forty hours and five different bus transfers to get from New York to this hole of a town. I'm hungry and broke. And I've got nowhere else to go. Well, except the care of the state, I guess.

Which would be a disaster for someone like me, for so many reasons.

The cigarette smoke hits me like a wall as I step inside, completely overwhelming to my sensitive sense of smell.

Just my luck that my only living relatives are grandparents I've never met, who apparently chain smoke indoors. One of whom should probably be in a care home.

This is the least of my problems. My parents are dead. The scent of mom's killer haunts my dreams. A charcoal, pine and animal scent. Another wolf shifter, and male.

Worse than the memory of that smell is the echo of my father's whimpering as the once formidable wolf shuddered under the breaking of his mating bond. He didn't survive his human mate more than twenty-four hours.

At first, my mom's death sent me into a hot rage. The wolf inside me clawed and howled to break free. It wanted to follow her killer's scent, tear him apart, exact revenge.

Stupid animal.

It hasn't yet accepted that I am defective. A latent. A shifter who can't shift. A beast caged in a weak human body.

Although thanks to my shifter genetics, I'm still significantly stronger than your average fifteen-year-old male. Bright-side, right?

"This will be your room," my grandmother says, interrupting my thoughts. The room is faded pink with a single bed covered in a worn rose patterned quilt. I have a sinking suspicion it was once my mom's, though her apple and mint scent has long faded, replaced by the acrid scent of stale cigarette smoke.

"Thanks."

It's all I can manage around the lump in my throat. I heft my suitcase onto the bed, keeping my back to her.

"I'll leave you to unpack," grandma says gently.

I flinch at the pity in her voice.

"They'll be breakfast in the kitchen if you want it. Bacon and pancakes..."

It's a bribe, of course. A way to lure me out, force me to make conversation. I know this, but I also know it is a bribe I will accept.

I am a teenage wolf shifter after all. A fact my human grandparents will have to remain completely ignorant about. But keeping them in the dark about what I am won't be a problem.

After all, I'm used to keeping secrets.

Chapter 2

Tobias Finch

Screams rent the night air, piercing and raw, then abruptly stop. The silence that follows chills me to my core, even beneath the thick wool blankets. I cling to them, fingers frozen like claws.

"Marian! Oh gods, Marian!"

Dad's voice is a chocked sob, quickly replaced with the sounds of snarling and bones cracking and popping. Dad has shifted.

An unfamiliar growl rumbles in response, low and menacing.

And then chaos erupts.

I know the sound is dad fighting another shifter. It's a sound I heard once before when dad fought off a lone wolf who had accosted us in New Mexico on our one and only camping trip. My father's wolf – a grey and black giant – had bested the lone wolf, forcing its submission and retreat.

What is another shifter doing here, in our apartment, three stories up in the middle of New York City?

Heart racing, I slink from my bed and make my way down the dark hallway towards the kitchen. Growls have given way to low snarls met with whimpering.

Stay back son.

Dad's voice echoes in my head through our pack bond, clear and commanding. Our pack of two.

The words are full of alpha command that would have forced any other wolf to submit. I feel their force roll over my shoulders and shrug them off, like a dog flicking off water. I take another step forward, pressing my palm on the kitchen door.

Please.

There is desperation in my father's voice this time. And something worse. Despair? Reluctantly, I obey, remaining hidden in the dark shadows of the hallway.

On the other side of the door, the snarling ceases and bones pop. Someone has shifted again. Then there is a human voice, pained and panting.

"Look Finneas," the voice wheezes, "I'm sorry about your mate..."

A wolf snarls in reply. Dad.

"I submitted, I submitted, okay! Gods, I didn't want to hurt her. Your human female took a knife to me – what did you expect me to do? It wasn't supposed to go down like this."

More snarling.

"You had to know this would happen. They'll come back. You broke the law, you and Marian. They'll come for the boy."

I feel my blood turn to ice in my veins.

"He's here, isn't he?"

The snarling turns feral then, and I can hear the snapping of teeth. The man yelps, and then there is the sound of the front door opening and clicking shut.

That's when the howling begins.

I WAKE WITH A START, throat hoarse and mouth dry.

Had I been howling in my sleep? It wouldn't be the first time my father's howls in my nightmares have voiced themselves on my own lips.

I rub at my neck, half expecting to feel fur instead of clammy skin.

Moonlight pours in through the open window, illuminating the pale pink walls of mom's old room.

I take a deep breath, trying to inhale fresh night air and getting a nose full of stale cigarette instead. I shake my head, as if to rid myself of the scent that has permeated the walls, carpet and furniture of my grandparents' home. Even after two days, the smell of this place still riles my wolf.

I throw the covers aside and pad to the window, leaning to rest my arms and chin on the wooden frame. The scent of dry grass and sage caresses my senses, at once calming and invigorating. The wolf within me stirs, wanting to run in the sprawling foothills, bathe in the light of the waxing moon.

For the hundredth time, I wonder what my wolf would look like if I could shift. Would it be grey and black like my father's? Or would it be a chocolate brown to match my own brown hair?

It is a stupid thing to wonder about.

The sound of a wolf howling snaps me from my reverie. It's faint, likely coming from mountains beyond the foothills, far enough away to be inaudible to ordinary human ears.

A second voice joins the first, and then a third. I feel an inexplicable ache in my chest.

What would it be like to have a pack? To shift and run with other wolves? To join my voice with their own?

I'll never know. Honestly, given what I am, it's probably for the best.

Born alpha.

The label rattles around in my waking consciousness, like the spare part to a car engine that just doesn't fit. Wolves like me, well… we're not supposed to exist.

I can still feel the night air and moonlight on my skin though.

Soundlessly, I throw one leg and then the other out the window, landing with a light thud beside the house. The dry earth feels harsh on the soft soles of my feet, and I take a moment to spread my toes in the dirt.

I can't recall the last time I've walked outside barefoot. It feels right.

Sparing a quick glance to the house behind me, I set off across the open field that backs my grandparents' house. I will just go to the first ridge of the foothills, I tell myself. It isn't that far. I can be back before the dawn.

"YOU NEED to have a shower before we leave this house, young man," my grandmother chides over breakfast. "You've got enough dirt and twigs in that mop of yours to build a nest."

I grunt my acquiescence and shovel down another mouthful of scrambled eggs. Really, there should be a law against conversation before breakfast.

"Now it's only natural you'll be worried about your first day at school here," Susan goes on, "But just be yourself, and the other kids will take to you in no time."

I almost choke back a laugh.

There is literally no one living, shifter or human, who I can be myself around. The penalty for letting humans know about shifters? Death. And if any shifters find out I'm a born alpha? Yep, also death.

"We don't get many new families in this town. No doubt they'll want to know all about you, but they'll be friendly enough. You're a good-looking kid, just like your momma was, and a friendly face goes a long way to making new friends."

Susan pauses to flick two pancakes from the griddle onto my plate, and I respond with a muffled, "Thanks."

"Course, dear," Susan smiles, wiping her hands on her jeans before turning to pour more batter on the pan. "It's good to have someone to cook for other than my Johnny. He don't eat as much as he used to."

My grandfather grumbles something incoherent from across the table, shooting a glare at me. Right back at you, old man.

"He's not a government agent," Susan counters patiently, apparently in response to whatever her husband said. "He's your grandson, remember. Look, he's got Marian's pretty blue eyes."

I put in blue contact lenses that morning, like I have done every day of my life since I was old enough to wear them, even living in New York City.

Humans might just think the golden colour was unusual, but otherwise take no notice. Another shifter though? My eyes might as well be a flashing neon sign shouting out "Hi there, I'm a threat to your whole pack and society as you know it. I was supposed to be killed at birth, but wasn't, so you should do the shifter world a solid and eradicate me."

At least shifters are rare. Super rare.

We hardly ever came across them in New York, so it's unlikely that there are any in Buffalo. But you can never be too cautious. That was rule number one of staying alive – always assume there were shifters around and always keep the truth of what I am hidden.

You broke the law, you and Marian. They'll come for the boy.

My stomach clenches as I recall the words of mom's killer. Even with all the precautions, even with the obscurity that comes with living in the centre of a big city, they had found us.

Suddenly, the pancakes taste like ash in my mouth. We had followed the rules, and Mom still paid the price of breaking some archaic shifter law. Guilty of letting me live.

I push my plate aside, no longer hungry.

I should have disobeyed dad, should have opened that door. Seen the killer's face. Fought him. Killed him, like my father should have done. Then my dreams would be haunted with the sound of the killer's screams, instead of his chilling faceless words and his charcoal and pine scent.

My grandmother eyes my plate questioningly, but I just stand, mumbling: "Gotta get ready for school."

Lucy Stone

The new boy in Mrs. Spring's English class is undeniably a wolf shifter, and not from our pack.

I would have known that even if I didn't already know everyone in our pack by name, scent, face and wolf. There is an otherness to his scent of pine, sage and chocolate that instantly marks him as an outsider.

Something different.

I don't like different. Different is what tempted my mom away from her family when I was ten years old, in the handsome package of a lone wolf shifter. Different is the gift my mother left me, passed down from her mother and the grandmother before that.

Well at least she called it a gift. I have a lot of other names for it.

Whether it's a gift or curse, differences in the shifter world almost always mean secrets and lies. No pack animal wants to stand out. Wolf shifters, at least in the Clear Creek pack, are no exception.

I pull my phone out of my pocket and send Anton a text, making sure to keep my it under the desk so Mrs. Spring doesn't catch me.

I could use the pack link to speak to him mind to mind, but I haven't managed to do that in a way that keeps my own feelings from flowing across the bond. And right now, the stranger's scent is stirring up too many feelings for me to fully understand.

The ones I do understand, I definitely don't want to be sharing with my older brother.

There's a new kid in Mrs. Spring's class with me. Scented him as an unknown wolf shifter. You should check him out when the bell rings.

My brother Anton's response is almost instant.

I'll let Cody know. Don't approach him on your own.

I roll my eyes.

I'm not sure why my brother still insists on coddling me like I'm some little pup. I'm only a year younger than him and, thanks to my gift, I've seen more than him too. Torture? Yep. Betrayal? More times than I can count. Executions. Unfortunately, yes.

I close my eyes, pinching the bridge of my nose to fight the headache that those memories always bring. There is no point trying to forget any of it. Every year will just bring new horrors for me to witness. Maybe a pack member will break the law and be hauled in for questioning. Or a rival shifter will be caught trespassing on our territory or planning another territory war.

In many ways, shifter packs aren't that different from what I imagine the human mafia to be like, where power is handed down through generations in an organisation operating under its own laws.

In a pack, violence is both the sickness and the medicine. Violence is the only way to disrupt the power balance. It's the way a beta becomes an alpha or an alpha becomes dead. At the same time, violence maintains that structure. It is a constant battle. Even if most of the time, no one sees it.

I am my pack's secret weapon in that battle.

I'll be there to listen to an accused pack-member's testimony. Or a captive's interrogation, as the case may be. My face and scent masked from view as I weigh the truth of their statements, smell the lies on their breath.

That is my gift. The perfect gift for a beta's mate, or in my case, the beta's daughter. The gift I share with my mother. This gift is probably why my dad chose my mom in the first place, even if they weren't true mates.

Speaking of the smell of lies, the newcomer's scent is rife with them. As good as he smells – and he smells so good my wolf is practically whining to get closer to him – there is no hiding the smell of dishonesty wafting off of him. Strong enough to make my eyes water.

The only other shifter I've smelt such strong dishonesty on was the lone wolf who pretended to want a place in our pack just long enough to tempt my mother away from us. I haven't seen her since.

Needless to say, I'm on edge.

I should probably let Anton know. He's the only one, other than dad, the alpha and some of the enforcers, who knows about my gift.

The new guy smells of lies, I type out.

My brother will know what that means. The newcomer may just be a pup, but that doesn't mean he isn't dangerous.

If anyone knows how dangerous a pup can be, it's me.

TOBIAS FINCH

I take a seat at my desk when the scent hits me like a punch to the gut.

Wolf. Shifter.

I look around the classroom nervously, unable to identify the culprit. My wolf's hackles rise, and I feel a throbbing pressure start to build behind my eyes, as if my wolf is pushing to get out and sniff out the potential threat.

I grit my teeth, forcing myself to focus on the book Mrs. Spring has placed in front of me. *White Fang*, by Jack London. I would laugh at the irony of it, if the fear of meeting another shifter wasn't riding me.

Because I am afraid.

By the end of class, I think I might be sick. I linger behind, pretending to search for something in my bag until all the other students have left. Only once the class is empty do I make my way to the door.

I take two steps down the nearly deserted hallway when a hand grabs my shoulder, spinning me and pushing me until my back is pressed to the row of lockers.

The smell of wolf fills my nostrils, cloying and pungent. I look up. The teen – more a man, really – stands a full head taller than me, broad shouldered, clad in Wranglers and red plaid, the ghosting of blond facial hair along a rugged jaw line. His nostrils flare as he leans forward, taking in my scent with a distinctively lupine sniff.

"You don't belong here."

The teen's voice comes out in a low grumble. The statement is met by two growls of agreement, and I notice a boy and girl flanking my attacker. I recognise the girl from my English class, but haven't seen the two boys before.

"I'm new," I offer weakly, lowering my eyes and lifting my chin to expose my neck.

Like a submissive wolf, I have to remind myself. This is one of the rules of staying alive – act submissive, even if it hurts your pride.

My wolf protests, wanting to push back and snap its teeth.

"Like we said. You don't belong." The lumberjack leans forward, continuing in a low rumble: "We don't want lone wolves in our territory."

I'm not a lone wolf, I want to argue. But I am now, aren't I? The only pack I had was my parents, and they're gone. The silence of the pack link I shared with dad feels like a missing limb.

"I don't mean your pack any trouble," I whisper instead.

"Your being here is trouble," the girl from my English class says, grey eyes full of ice as she stares at me with her arms folded across her chest.

I think the pose is meant to look intimidating, but it only serves to make her t-shirt fit tighter, showcasing the perfect curves underneath.

My mouth goes dry, heat rising in my blood until the denim jacket I chose to wear this morning feels stifling. Its uncomfortably distracting. I need to be on my guard, not gaping at some girl.

Even the look of disgust aimed directly at me does nothing to detract from how gorgeous she is.

"I'm not leaving," I say firmly, but softly, because my life depends on acting like I'm a submissive wolf right now.

"Well, you can't stay here," the second boy snaps.

He looks close to my own age but he's shorter, with cropped dark hair and a smattering of pimples on tanned cheeks. As if in agreement, Lumberjack tightens his grip on my shirt and lets out a low growl.

I roll my eyes.

"I don't have anywhere else to go."

I hate how weak I sound. Like a submissive wolf.

Lumberjack huffs. I suspect he may have a limited range of verbal communication.

"What pack are you from?" Pimples asks.

"I don't have a pack."

"Your parents are loners?" Lumberjack asks, with no effort to hide the blatant distaste at the word *loners*.

Despite my best intentions, I glare up at Lumberjack.

I wonder what it would be like to pummel this boy. Wolf. Whatever. Sinking my fist into the pup's face would feel good. I could definitely take him. Even if he's bigger.

"Answer us, pup," Lumberjack spits.

I can feel the dominance in his command. I could shrug it off easily, but doing so would give me away. Because that's another rule of staying alive: never use my dominance.

"Yep," I grit out. "They were loners."

My lips feel dry, struggling around the word 'were' when it should be 'are'. Referring to my parents in past tense… it makes all of this way too real.

"Why'd they leave their pack?" the persistent prick questions. "What did they do?"

I open my mouth to answer. I'm ready to give the story my parents told me to tell any shifter that asked. *My mom was an artist and a human, and wanted to live in New York City. My dad left pack life to be with her. He had been from a pack in Russia.*

Relations between the American and Russian wolves are strained at best. It is unlikely that any shifter would attempt to cross-check the story by reaching out to a Russian pack.

Before I can speak, a voice rings out authoritatively from down the hall: "Anton, what's going on?"

Lumberjack – Anton, presumably - drops his arms to his sides as the newcomer approaches.

"Just questioning the new boy here," he explains sheepishly. "He's a loner."

"You think that's your job?" the newcomer asks as he cocks his head.

Black curls sweep across his forehead with the movement.

"Since when do you get to make decisions about who to question?"

"Sorry, Cody," Anton mumbles, shoulders tensing.

The dark-haired boy - Cody - gives a short nod in silent acknowledgement of the apology, then stares down the other two. Pimples shrinks visibly under his stare. The Valkyrie holds her ground.

"I scented the new boy in my English class," she explains defensively. "We wanted to catch him before lunch. Alone."

Pimples doesn't offer an excuse, but scuffs his shoes on the linoleum and stares at his feet.

"Not an excuse," Cody shakes his head, then looks at me with bald curiosity. "You're the new kid."

I nod, reminding myself to keep my eyes lowered.

"Sorry about these assholes," he says, white teeth flashing in a grin. "Come sit with us at lunch. We'll talk."

The request is tinged with enough alpha command to let me know that refusal isn't really an option. Or at least, it wouldn't be an option if I was actually a submissive wolf.

Which I'm not.

"Okay, thanks," I say, sighing inwardly.

After years of hiding from other shifters, I end up at a high school with wolves, at least three of whom probably want to tear my throat out.

Great.

At lunch, I can hardly eat the lasagne as I field the alpha's questions, giving the practiced explanation of why I lived in New York, outside of a pack. I explain that my parents died. That I moved in with my grandparents.

I keep it as close to the truth as possible. Still, there is a lot that I can't tell them.

I sure as hell am not letting on that I am latent.

It is one thing to have to pretend to be a submissive wolf. I don't need them to know I am physically defective. Unable to fight as a wolf. Unable to fully benefit from the quick healing that comes with the shift, that makes our kind so hard to seriously injure.

"How many other kids at this school are shifters?" I ask, leaning across the table in the cafeteria, keeping my voice low so as not to be overheard.

I need to get as much information about this situation as possible. And to deflect Cody's intensive questioning.

"There's us," Cody indicates to himself and the three that cornered me by the lockers. "And Summer, but she's not here today. She's on pack lands."

I raise one eyebrow inquisitively and Cody replies shrugging: "It's her heat."

Her *heat*? Did female wolf shifters go into heat?

I feel my cheeks redden, and steal a glance at the Valkyrie. She's currently sending me a death glare. I have never been around female shifters before. It suddenly occurs to me that I actually don't know anything about them.

"We're from the Clear Creek pack," Cody continues. "My parents are the alphas. Anton is the beta's pup, so he's my second here on campus."

He shoots Anton a sharp look, as if to remind him that he'd gone beyond that role earlier. Lumberjack's stubbled face is set in a glower. It's hard to tell whether the expression is aimed at Cody, or whether his face just looks like that.

"This is Anton's little sister, Lucy."

Cody nudges Lucy with his shoulder, flashing a flirtatious grin. I feel an inexplicable knot of jealousy tighten in my stomach at the playful contact. Anton scowls. Maybe he doesn't like Cody sitting so close to his sister either. Or maybe he just hates everyone.

"And this is Jason."

Cody nods towards the other boy, but says nothing about his rank or family. It's impossible to ignore the worn state of Jason's clothes, his unkempt hair.

"What's the pack like?" I ask, genuinely curious.

"It's okay," Cody shrugs. "It's the biggest in the state in terms of territory, and probably the strongest. Ranch life gets a bit boring though."

"I've never been to a ranch," I say, then huff a mirthless laugh. "Or met a pack, actually."

Because one rule of staying alive is to avoid pack territory. Given the risk of death and all.

"Really?" Cody says, surprise written on his features. The others gape and Lucy snorts derisively.

"Yup."

I force an apologetic smile.

I wonder whether they are more shocked I haven't been to a ranch, or that I've never met a pack. I'm also not sure how either of these things are surprising, given what I've just told them.

"You should visit the Half Moon ranch sometime," Cody offers.

The others shoot Cody a dark look.

"Shouldn't you be asking your parents first?" Lucy asks. "I don't think they'd like you bringing a loner to pack lands."

Cody just shrugs. "Can't say I really care what they think. Especially if they're going to be snobs like you guys."

Jason blushes at the criticism. Lucy and Anton's expressions remain cold, but they don't contradict him.

I can't help but look at Cody with a new respect. The pup is well-built, compact muscle and a frame that promises just as much agility as strength. He has ridiculous curls and a rakish smile with dimples that probably has every girl at this school falling all over him. He's cocky and one hundred percent alpha-hole, but he just stood up to his friends. His pack. One of whom is built like a line-backer.

And all for a lone shifter. A stranger. For me.

"Why don't you come 'round to the ranch on Friday after school?" Cody continues. "The pack is having a barbecue – probably the last one we'll have until spring. They'll be lots of steak on the grill."

My mouth waters at the thought of steak. My wolf licks its chops in anticipation, like the easily persuaded carnivore that he is.

"Will you come?" Cody asks.

"Uh, maybe." I bite the inside of my lip, contemplating. "I'll think about it. Have to check with my grandparents first."

It is a bad idea. A really, really bad idea to visit their pack. Completely against the rules of keeping Tobias Finch alive.

My wolf doesn't think so though. The dumb animal relishes the idea of being around other wolves. *Pack*, it practically pants. *Pack. Pack.*

Cody nods. He can see I'm reluctant, but he doesn't press.

The bell rings, and I practically leap up, slinging my backpack on in one fluid movement.

"I'll see you guys later," I say.

I need to get away from these wolves. Each minute I spend with them is a minute I am at risk of exposing my secret.

A secret my parents died to protect.

In my rush to leave, I knock into Lucy, the back of my hand brushing against the bare skin of her arm. It's soft. Warm. I feel a jolt course through me at the light contact, right to the pit of my stomach.

"Watch where you're going," Lucy snaps, grey eyes flashing silver as her wolf surges close to the surface.

Sheesh. The chick is seriously aggressive. And tall. Almost my height. Lucy crosses her arms, giving off unmistakable 'back off' vibes.

I almost want to throw my hands up in surrender and apologise, even though I've done nothing wrong.

My wolf? The dumb animal thinks we should crouch down, bat her with our paws and antagonise her into a game of chase. Or maybe just rub up against her.

Yes, my wolf is officially an idiot.

Chapter 3

Lucy Stone

"Why did you invite the loner to our pack meet?" I snap as soon as I reach Cody's truck in the school parking lot.

"Drop it, Luce," Anton grumbles.

He's still sore about Cody putting him in his place as his unofficial 'second' (whatever that means) and is trying to make up for it. He might be in line to be beta, but I'm my father's child too. And if I'm still part of this pack when Cody becomes alpha, he'll figure out pretty quick the importance of the role I play behind the scenes.

Of course, Cody has no idea about any of that now. That's how dad wants it to be. He wants to take all the credit for my hard work. 'It's to keep you safe' he tells me. Like I don't see how he basks in the pack's perception of him. The beta who is always able to find out the truth.

He can only do that because of me.

"You just don't like him because he's a loner."

Cody's grin does little to hide the poisoned barb in his words. If anything, it sharpens the sting. He knows all about mom. How I feel about lone shifters.

"And you just like him because you feel sorry for him," I counter.

Because it's true. Cody is your typical arrogant alpha. Desperate to play the white knight to any wolves that seem weaker than him. Intimidated by any true power.

Which is why Cody has never really liked me.

"You say that like it's a bad thing."

I roll my eyes.

"It's not a reason to open ourselves up to an attack. Have you ever heard of a trojan horse?"

"A what?"

I just stare at him. "A trojan horse. You know, from Homer's Odyssey."

He looks at me blankly, cocking his head to one side and letting those annoying curls fall into his eyes.

"The Simpsons?"

This, ladies and gentlemen, is the future of the Clear Creek pack. Pretty, but stupid.

I snort in disgust and climb into the back seat of Cody's truck. I don't have the patience to explain basic history or war strategy to our future glorious leader. Luckily for Cody, Jason is there to pick up the slack.

"A trojan horse refers to a trick or strategy to trick an opponent into thinking something is harmless when it actually isn't," Jason pipes up from beside me.

If he was in his wolf form right now, his tail would be thumping in excitement at the opportunity to be of use to his future alpha. Typical omega.

"The term comes from the battle of Troy, when the Greeks gave the Trojans a statue of a horse as a gift. The Trojans brought the statue into the city, but a bunch of Greek soldiers were hiding inside of it. They came out late at night and helped take the city."

Cody nods, as if to signal his brain is processing this new information. It's not.

"I think I saw that movie," he finally says, "I still don't see what that has to do with Tobias though. He seems like a good kid."

I press my forehead into my palm. I'm basically Cassandra right now.

TOBIAS FINCH

I decide not to go to the ranch after school on Friday.

When Cody repeats his invitation at lunch on Friday, I give a noncommittal response and hope he drops it. When the school bell rings at the end of the day, I grab my backpack and head to my grandparents' house.

I feel a little bad about bailing. Cody has been cool. But the others have made it clear I'm not welcome. And visiting the pack is just a bad idea.

I should just make friends with some nice, safe humans who won't have me executed if one of my contact lenses comes out. Who won't sense my dominance if I slip up and get pissed off about something. Who won't care that I can't shift into a wolf.

I'm starting to think that it would be nice to be human.

I'm contemplating that very thing while I sit at the kitchen table after school, eating a bowl of cereal and congratulating myself for resisting the temptation of barbecued steak. Which is when I hear the sound of tires crunching gravel outside. I freeze, spoon hallway to my mouth, when I hear the doorbell ring and my grandmother opens the door.

"Hi ma'am, you must be Tobias' grandmother? I'm Cody Winslow. I know Tobes from school."

I roll my eyes at the nickname. At some point over the past week, Cody had started calling me 'Tobes' because apparently the three syllables in 'Tobias' is too difficult.

"I'm here to pick Tobes up for the barbecue."

Well, what a persistent little...

"Barbecue? Wait, you said your name was Winslow? Your parents are Cooper and Cindy? They own Half Moon Ranch?" Grandma asks, sounding impressed.

"Yes ma'am." I can practically hear Cody's wide grin. No doubt he's turning on the charm for grandma. That kid has no shame. "Barbecue's up at the ranch. Mostly family, the workers and a few kids from school."

"Well, that sounds like a fun evening," grandma drawls. I swear I can hear grandma patting Cody's arm. Typical. "Come on in, I'll get Tobias for you."

"Tobias," grandma calls loudly, "you've got a friend from school here to pick you up."

I pinch the bridge of my nose and contemplate doing a runner. I could probably make it out the back door before anyone could stop me. But then, there would be questions. Lots of questions. Which would mean talking.

Sighing, I toss my cereal bowl in the sink and stalk out of the kitchen.

"Sup." I say, nodding at Cody.

"Tobias," grandma admonishes, hands on her hips, "that's not how we greet people."

I huff, because actually, that is exactly how we greet people. Unless you're Cody trying to get yourself into some granny's good books.

Cody tilts his chin in the direction of his truck. A new model with a double cab. Fancy.

"You ready to go?"

He has his usual boyish smile, but there's no missing the hard glint in his eyes. The look is all alpha. Leaving no room for refusal.

"Yup," I confirm.

Because there is no way I am getting out of this now.

"Good."

I follow Cody out to the pick-up truck, then do a double-take. A girl I haven't met sits waiting in the cab of the truck, face lighting up in a wide smile at the sight of Cody.

"Summer," Cody says to the girl, as I climb into the back of the truck, "this is Tobias Finch, the guy I told you about. Tobes, this is Summer."

"Nice to meet you, Tobes," Summer says, bright smile turning somewhat reticent as she faces me.

"Tobias, not Tobes," I grit out, flushing red.

Summer just laughs. It's a light, pretty sound, and I get the feeling she laughs a lot.

I rub one hand over my face, then nod to Cody's truck appreciatively, deflecting the conversation away from myself.

"Nice truck man. This yours?"

"Sure is," Cody replies, gravel flying as he backs out of the drive. "My folks got it for me so I could help with the ranch. No such thing as a free lunch and all that."

"Wait, are you seriously complaining about being given a truck? A new truck?" Summer elbows Cody in the ribs. "Privileged much? The rest of us have to get jobs to pay for these things." She slaps the dash for emphasis.

"I've got a job," Cody says defensively. "My parents work me like a dog at Half Moon Ranch."

"And they pay you for it. Above minimum wage too."

"It's still forced labour."

Summer raises one eyebrow. "Please. You are aware of how the other ninety-nine percent live, right?"

"Okay, okay," Cody raises both hands in defeat, letting go of the wheel and grinning sheepishly.

"Keep your hands on the wheel, you maniac," Summer snaps, but there's no ire in her voice.

I chuckle under my breath, but a pang of longing hits me like a punch in the gut. I've messaged my friends in New York a couple of times. Okay, so I've really just messaged Greg, but texting has never been my thing. Buffalo doesn't offer up much worth sharing on social media – at least, nothing my friends would be interested in.

"So, you looking forward to meeting the pack?" Summer asks. "Or you nervous?"

"Umm…" I frown, deliberating.

"Course he's looking forward to it," Cody answers confidently, "there's going to be food."

Summer rolls her eyes. "I know *you* just see these things as an opportunity to feed your face, but the rest of us actually enjoy social interaction."

Cody shrugs. "I see people all the time." White teeth flash as he grins. "Steak, ribs and brisket all in one meal – that doesn't happen every day sweetheart."

"Not your sweetheart," Summer counters in a sing-song voice, then pivots to face me. "Anyway, what I meant was, I heard Anton and Lucy were not super welcoming on your first day of school…"

"They were dicks," Cody interjects, a hard edge to his tone, "Embarrassment to the pack."

Summer wrinkles her nose. "That's probably a bit overdramatic, don't you think?" Cody doesn't answer, and she turns to face me again, giving a reassuring smile. "The rest of the pack isn't like that. They won't blame you for being a lone shifter."

They might blame my parents though. Or want to know more about my father's pack in Russia. Which doesn't exist.

They certainly wouldn't be happy to find out what I really am.

"It's all good," I shrug.

Anton, Lucy and Jason haven't been friendly, but Cody has been. Summer seems nice. The human kids at school seem okay.

Back in New York, if kids had treated me like Lumberjack and friends did, there would have been retribution. Probably in the form of pranks. Possibly violence. I try not to fight humans, since it's not really fair. But I'm not above throwing my weight around when its needed.

In New York, I only had to deal with human kids. Shifters are a different story.

The truck rounds a bend in the gravel road and Half Moon Ranch comes into view.

I wasn't sure what I had expected the place to look like, but it wasn't the view in front of me. A modern mansion that looks like it could have won architectural awards is flanked by tasteful landscaping that blends into the valley, foothills and mountains. A creek runs through one part of the property, and smaller modern cabins dot their way up the valley. The place looks more like a five-star resort than anything else.

My stomach clenches as the truck rumbles past the main house, pulling to a stop outside a large industrial looking barn. Several other vehicles are parked outside.

"This is the pack-house," Cody explains, tilting his chin at the large structure as he climbs out of the truck. "It's connected to the stables, and there's an indoor arena that doubles up as a space for pack meetings."

"You've really never been to pack territory before?" Summer asks, incredulous.

I force a grin that probably looks more like a grimace.

"Nope. Never."

Well, unless you count the hours after my birth, before my parents were forced to take me and run into hiding so I wouldn't be killed.

The front doors fly open and a giant of a man strides out, his every step advertising easy confidence. He is flanked by a woman with dark curls that fall loose around her shoulders.

"Mom, dad, this is Tobias Finch," Cody says as he steps beside me.

It's almost a protective sort of move, and I feel a mix of irritation and gratitude.

"He's the new kid I told you about. Tobias, these are my parents, Cooper and Cindy."

The alphas.

Even if I hadn't already known, it would have been obvious by the way the man moves. As if he owns the place. As if he knows any orders he gives will be obeyed without question.

"Nice to meet you," I say, as I thrust my hands into the pockets of my jeans and keep my eyes on the ground in front of me. A purposefully non-confrontational stance.

Cindy smiles, dimples identical to Cody's appearing on her face. "Welcome to Half Moon Ranch. It's so good of you to come."

Cooper grunts in reluctant agreement, expression stony as he stares at me for a long moment. My completely suicidal wolf wants to hold his gaze, but I keep my expression bland, eyes fixed on the alpha's cowboy boots. Then he says: "I understand you've never been part of a pack before. That right, kid?"

I nod, resisting the urge to ball my hands into fists at my side.

There is something intrinsically grating about being called 'kid'. Pretty sure it wouldn't go down well if I responded by saying, 'sure thing, boomer'.

"We might be more flexible than some packs, but we don't particularly like loners here," the alpha drawls, expression stony.

Given the welcome party Anton and Lucy threw for me on my first day of school, I can't say this comes as a surprise. Still, my face heats and I bite my tongue in an effort to remain silent.

"Now, Cody here has explained your situation, and has offered to vouch for you." The alpha shoots his son a hard look. "But that don't change the facts. How others in the pack might react. Especially the elders."

"Okay," I say, if only because Cooper is looking at me like he expects a response.

Seriously, what is it with these backwater wolves and their antipathy for lone shifters? Like, I get that wolves typically run in packs, but surely not everyone wants to live in what is essentially a hierarchical commune.

Cody claps his hands together, giving me an apologetic look.

"Aaaand I think this brings our little meet and greet to a close. Great chat, dad."

He hauls me towards the barn and away from his parents before his dad can get another word in. Summer follows close on our heels.

"Just ignore dad," he says, shaking his head. "He's just being… you know… old school. You know how it is."

I really don't know how it is, but I'm starting to get an idea.

Before this week, the only shifter I've really been around was dad, who taught gender studies at NYU, told me to avoid shifters and (when avoidance failed) to always pretend to be a submissive wolf. He wore wire-rimmed glasses and a tweed suit, and even if he was six foot two and built, he was about as far from being an alpha-hole as you could imagine.

"Welcome to Buffalo's hottest party venue."

Summer makes a sweeping gesture with her arms as we enter the barn. I blink, letting my eyes get accustomed to the dimmer lighting.

Inside the barn, the sand floor of the indoor arena has been covered with temporary flooring. A row of tables sits on one side, and several people bustle around carrying dishes of food, setting up folding chairs, hauling out speakers and sound equipment. The smell of horse still lingers, but with the lights and decorations, the space looks more like a dance venue than a barn. There's even a small child carrying a disco ball half his own body mass.

"A disco ball? Seriously? Is this like a school dance or something?" I snort derisively.

"Oh yeah," Cody chuckles. "Our pack takes these events pretty seriously. Shifters from other packs are invited too. Not too many from one pack at a time, obviously. But usually there's a couple delegations."

"Delegations?"

"One or two shifters representing each nearby pack. Usually there's a representative spokesperson along with a male or female of mating age."

Cody glances sidelong at Summer, and I notice the hint of a frown on his face.

"There should be about six other packs represented here tonight."

"Have you ever gone to another pack's – um…" I wave my hand at the people setting up for the evening. "Barbecue event thingy?"

A laugh bursts out from behind us, and both Cody and I turn to see Summer doubled over. Cody's eyes darken and his jaw clenches. Summer continues on, oblivious.

"Cody, go to another pack's social event? Like, for mating? Oh my gosh Toby, really?"

Great, so I'm Toby now.

Summer swipes tears from her eyes as she strains to catch her breath, holding her sides with one hand.

"Cody would be, like, a child bride. Or child groom. Whatever. He's waay too young for mating meets."

"I'm almost seventeen," Cody says defensively. "Some people recognise their mates that early."

"Maybe." Summer waves one hand dismissively. "But the pack would never send you to visit another pack in the hopes you'd meet your mate. Not yet anyway. Not when you might still be too young to recognise her."

Cody lets out a discontented grunt.

"Have you ever seen it?" I ask, unable to mask my curiosity.

I know a little about the mating bond from my parents, but mom was human. Dad would have felt the mating urge, like all shifters do if they are lucky enough to meet their mate. My mom wouldn't have, at least not to the same extent.

I'd never been brave enough to ask them how they'd dealt with that. Or to ask dad what it was like. It was always one of those subjects that made me feel a little uncomfortable to talk about. Because, parents. Gross.

Now I regret not asking more questions.

"Uh huh." Summer nods, wrinkling her nose. "It happens a couple times a year at one of these events. It's disturbing."

Cody flicks the hair from his forehead and gives Summer an irritated look. "It's biology. It's perfectly natural."

Summer snorts. "Yah, yah, I know. And it's a blessing from fate to find your true mate. Makes your soul whole and all that jazz." She gives a dramatic eye roll. "It doesn't change the fact that it is seriously disturbing to watch two perfectly sane people completely lose their minds to the mating urge."

"What do you mean?" I ask.

Cody groans. "Seriously man, don't even get her started."

Summer goes on, unfazed.

"You know those movies where the couple meet and the camera pans back and its like there's no one else in the room? Or they burst into a perfectly synchronised duet declaring their love after having literally met just two seconds ago? Think Frozen, Cinderella – anything with a love at first sight trope. Then amplify that by about one thousand and replace the super-hot hero and heroine with really ordinary and sometimes sweaty wolf shifters in an old barn, dancing under the romantic light of a disco ball, surrounded by their parents and grandparents and well… you get the picture." She tosses her hair over her shoulder. "It is very, very un-sexy."

Hmm. I have to agree that sounds pretty cringe.

Cody's brows slam down at Summer's description.

"You're missing the point. When you find your true mate…"

"When I *recognise* my true mate, I'll be in the thrall of the mating urge. So yah, I'll probably think it's the most magical thing ever." She shrugs. "But everyone watching will be like 'okay Summer, chill the crap out, it's just a male, please peel yourself off of him and put your clothes back on…'"

Her rant is interrupted by a low, animalistic growl that is most definitely coming from Cody.

Summer levels him with a look of unamused disbelief.

"Really? Did your wolf just growl at my hypothetical mate?"

Cody runs one hand over his face. "Yah. Maybe. So what if I did?"

Summer shakes her head. "You're unbelievable. You know that?"

Cody shrugs, looking unabashed. "My wolf is feeling riled tonight, okay. Full moon and all."

"Typical." Summer crosses her arms over her chest. "You males think you can use the moon to excuse just about anything. Like, 'oh, sorry I got into that fight, it was the full moon' or 'I was too irritated to do the dishes without breaking them all because it was the full moon, so I just didn't do them'." She levels him with a glare. "You do realize that is the equivalent of a female saying she kneed you in the balls because she was having PMS, right?"

Cody looks taken aback, his mouth opening and closing as he searches for the right thing to say.

I look away, pretending to be mesmerised watching a couple of kids stringing the disco ball up in the barn rafters. This is one conversation I'm more than happy to take the bench on.

"Hey guys," a familiar voice calls out.

Cody's shoulders visibly relax as Anton and Lucy stride towards us. As much as I dislike Anton, I'm almost relieved to see him. And not just because Lucy is with him, although that is probably a relevant factor.

Especially for my wolf.

Anton is dressed in his usual jeans and cowboy boots, his muscled bulk stretching the buttons of a red plaid shirt. He shoots his obligatory glare at me as he approaches, but I don't care. Hardly even notice.

Because Lucy is looking at me.

Smiling at me, actually.

Her perfect, bow-shaped mouth curving up, grey eyes crinkling at the edges. To top it all off, she's wearing this little white sundress that ties at the shoulders, exposing the smooth bare skin of her arms and legs.

And her scent. Good shifter gods, her scent. Was it always this mouth-watering? Lavender and rain and fresh grass.

I take a deep breath, and I swear for a moment I think my lungs seize up.

"Glad to see you made it." Lucy looks right at me as she says this, voice lyrical.

I blink, trying to make sense of this new reality. A reality where Lucy is speaking to me. Smiling at me. Not just to tell me to get out of her way.

"Cody more or less kidnapped me from my grandparents' place," I offer lamely, trying to sound nonchalant.

Like gorgeous girls are always nice to me and this is just another ordinary day in the life of Tobias Finch.

Actually, I never had any trouble with girls before I came to Buffalo. I know I'm a good-looking guy. Especially compared to humans. I could always get a date. Always had a girlfriend to hold hands with in the halls between class and mess around with after school. None of them ever lasted long, but that didn't matter.

But Lucy. Lucy is a different story. A different game. One I don't even know the rules to.

"Well, I'm glad he did," Lucy beams, then turns to her older brother. "Anton, I just realized I forgot the food dad told me to bring down. Can you drive me back to our place?"

Anton shakes his head, frowning. "Not a chance Luce. Just walk. It's only ten minutes."

"I can't carry everything back on my own."

"Not my problem," Anton shrugs. Then as an afterthought, "Why don't you ask Tobias to help you? He probably wants to see the ranch anyway."

There's a strange glint in Anton's eyes as he says this, and the fantasy I was riding (which might have involved the taste of Lucy's lips and the feel of that warm golden skin under my fingertips) comes to a screeching halt.

Anton doesn't care whether I want to see this ranch. I don't think Anton would consider my feelings if he was running me over with his car.

I look between the two siblings, starting to wonder if I'm being played. Because I'm a suspicious mofo, especially when it comes to shifters.

Dad's voice rings like a warning bell in my head. *Never trust other shifters, Tobias. They live in a world of power plays and shows of dominance. They're always going to have their own agenda, and they'll be playing a game that you can't play.*

"Would you mind Tobes?" Lucy asks, using the nickname Cody has coined. Strangely, it doesn't sound half bad when she says it.

I might not trust Anton. Or Lucy. But there is also no way I can refuse to help her. Not without sounding like a total dick.

"Um, sure," I reply quickly. "I can help carry stuff."

As soon as the words leave my lips, I want to punch myself. I sound like a complete idiot.

“Thanks so much,” Lucy gushes, already pulling me towards the doors.

Cody and Summer wave me off before resuming their heated debate. I see Anton tip his chin at Lucy, his thin lips curling into a harsh smile, some unspoken message flashing in his eyes.

Yep. I’m definitely being played.

I frown as I follow Lucy into the bright afternoon sun.

“Our place isn’t that far,” Lucy babbles, pointing to a pine clad house farther up the valley. “There’s a shortcut if you’re okay climbing a few fences.”

“Yah, that’s fine.” I reply, almost jogging to keep up with her.

Ahead of me, Lucy’s pale hair glints in the sun, the same colour as the dry grass floating around her calves like a golden sea. Her white sundress shifts as she moves, the colour making her lean, muscled legs look even tanner than they actually are.

Lucy talks the whole time, pointing out different parts of the ranch, explaining how many miles up into the foothills the ranch goes, describing how the whole pack works to raise the cattle and bring them down from the hills at the end of each summer.

The dry earth underneath the tall grass and sage is pockmarked from where the cattle have run. It takes all my concentration not to stumble and embarrass myself. I follow Lucy over a couple of barbed wire fences, taking care not to let the rusted metal snag on my jeans. When we end up in a hollow, close to the creek I noticed earlier, I can no longer see the pack-house or Lucy’s house.

“Shoot,” Lucy says, stopping abruptly after we have crossed the third fence, “I think my cell phone came out of my pocket when we were climbing over that last fence.”

She pats the sides of her sundress, feeling for her phone in its pockets.

"Yep, definitely gone," she sighs. "I'm just going to run back and check. You go ahead. I'll meet you at that tree up at the top of the hill." Lucy points ahead to a gnarled looking cottonwood.

"You don't want me to help you look for it?" I ask, looking at the tall grass. It will be nearly impossible to find anything in it.

Lucy shakes her head vehemently. "No, no. If I don't find it right away, I'll have my dad use the tracking app." She rolls her eyes. "They insisted I have it set up so they can track my phone location at all times. Not Anton though because 'he's a boy'. So medieval right? I mean, I'm a shifter for goodness sake. I would like to see someone try and kidnap me."

I have to agree with her. She's built like a Viking warrior, and I have no doubt she could take down any of the human boys at school in a one-on-one fight. Heck, she could probably take me down. Since I can't shift and all.

She points back at the tree. "I'll meet you there, just be a couple minutes."

I watch her trot back the way we came for a moment. I have to admit, there is something captivating in the way that dress sways, the afternoon sun glistening off of her until she looks made of gold. In the heat of the sun, the graceful movements of her body, the sweet scent that follows her like an invisible trail – it's intoxicating.

Which is my only excuse for my momentary lapse in judgement.

I turn to head up the hill. There is one more fence to climb before reaching the tree. I can see Lucy's house from the top of the hill. It isn't as close as I thought it would have been. In fact, it seems like we've hiked up alongside it, rather than directly to it. The pack-house is also visible far below at the base of the valley. Smoke rises in thin lines from the barbecues out the back, and my mouth waters at the thought of grilled meat.

"Did you find it?" I ask at the sound of grass rustling behind me.

There is no reply, just heavy breathing followed by a snort. It's not a sound I can imagine Lucy making.

I spin around, brow furrowing in confusion, not quite sure what I'm seeing at first.

Instead of Lucy's grey eyes, one big black eye meets my own. Black nostrils flare, filling the air with the scent of grass and manure. A huge set of horns lowers. And then pain explodes in my ribs. I'm flying, the world spinning, hurtling upside-down in flashes of sky blue and greys and gold, like a slow-motion kaleidoscope. The ground rushes up to meet me with a blinding crack, and then everything goes dark.

Chapter 4

Tobias Finch

"Shift. Tobias Finch, you need to shift."

I am vaguely aware of the words, the command rolling off Cody's panicked voice.

"Shift." I can feel the alpha command stronger now, the voice different, deeper. Cooper Winslow's voice, I realize. "Shift."

Within me, my wolf cocks its head to one side, studying the compulsion to obey with a detached curiosity.

"Why isn't he shifting?" A panicked voice asks. Summer, I realize through the haze.

Rough hands clasp my shoulders. Pain jolts through my body, forcing my eyes to flit open momentarily. Through blurred vision I see Cody's face close to my own, etched with worry.

"Tobias, you need to shift or you're going to bleed out."

The late afternoon sun burns my retinas, splitting through my skull like an axe. I squeeze my eyes shut against it as consciousness floods back. The earth is hard beneath my back as I curl my fingers into dry grass.

"What the hell were you thinking, Lucy? Bringing him into the bull pen?" I recognise Summer's voice.

"I didn't – I thought," Lucy stammers.

"Save it. You knew exactly what you were doing," Summer accuses.

"He should have shifted," Lucy whimpers. "It was a joke. Just a joke."

"Tobias, shift," Cody says again, his voice wavering as he gives me another shake.

Pain radiates through my back and ribs with the movement. I want to ask him to leave it, to tell him I'll be fine if he just gives me some dark and quiet. But my words come out in a garbled jumble, mouth filling with what tastes like blood.

"We need to carry him to the pack house," Cooper Winslow's voice booms out authoritatively. "Boys, you know where the med room is. Summer, run ahead and get Tricia Crow. Tell her the boy's been gored by a bull. Puncture wound, likely internal bleeding and broken ribs. Potential spinal injury. Concussion."

"Yes, alpha," Summer replies.

There is the sound of bones and tendons cracking as someone shifts, followed by the 'yip' of a wolf.

I wonder briefly if it was Summer who shifted, but I can't turn my head to see. My vision blurs, and I almost black out again as Cody and Anton lift me up, each of the males taking position on either side of me.

"He's heavier than he looks," Anton comments ruefully.

Even in my half-alert state, I tense. I go to a lot of effort to hide my muscle mass and size. The Lumberjack look-alike is more preceptive than I gave him credit for.

Cody grunts in agreement.

I try forcing my legs to bear some of my weight, to no avail. They feel cold and lifeless. When I look down, I am surprised to see red soaking my baggy t-shirt and pooling at the waistband of my jeans.

I feel a fresh rush of blood, probably a result of my trying to walk. It doesn't go unnoticed, and I hear alpha Winslow snap: "Lucy, keep compression on that wound."

Lucy keeps her head bowed as she presses a cloth to my stomach.

A joke. She'd said it had just been a joke.

She had been so friendly. Had she really tried to get me injured? Had her brother been in on it too?

I try to get a look at Lucy's face, to read some answer in her expression, but she keeps her gaze averted.

By the time we reach the pack house, the cloth Lucy has been using is soaked through and my limbs feel numb. A grey-haired female runs out to meet us.

"Tricia," the alpha greets, his tone clipped.

"You couldn't get him to shift?"

"We tried," Cooper says irritably. "He's not shifting."

Tricia makes a humming sound as she shepherds us into what looks like a small doctor's office. Cody and Anton lift me onto the table, but don't move away. I can just make their faces out through the black spots forming in my vision. Their faces are pale, expressions worried.

"Right, out you brutes," Tricia says unceremoniously. "You take up too much room and I need to work."

"I'm staying," Cody argues.

"No, you're not," the healer replies sharply. "Not unless you're going to give him a blood donation. Because that's what the pup needs. Not a bunch of onlookers breathing up his oxygen."

"You can't be serious," Cooper growls. The sound is so low I feel it vibrating in my bones. "You can't give him any of the pack's blood. He's not pack."

"I'm aware of that, alpha." Tricia's voice is calm and smooth as she bustles around the room. "Nevertheless, the pup needs blood."

"I'll donate," Cody offers without a second's hesitation. In the corner of my vision, I see him holding out his arm as if he expects the healer to jab a line into him right there.

"It could create a pack bond," Cooper hisses, pushing Cody's arm down.

"Not if it's only one way," Cody retorts. "You need a full blood exchange. And an oath ceremony."

"Half a pack bond, then." The alpha shakes his head. "We don't know what the implications of that would be with someone who isn't pack."

I try to make sense of their words, but numbness is quickly taking over. I need blood? I know my injuries must be bad. I've never felt worse in my entire life. But somehow the idea that I might need a blood transfusion still surprises me.

"If he could just shift," the alpha continues, glaring at me. As if I am somehow refusing to shift out of sheer stubbornness. I open my mouth to try and explain. To tell them the embarrassing truth. But I can't speak.

"Obviously, he can't shift," Tricia says tersely. "Small pinch," she warns, moments before sticking a needle into my forearm. I feel nothing.

"What do you mean, he can't shift?" The alpha's voice is full of scepticism.

"Can't. Impossible. Not going to happen. What it usually means." I see the healer attach a line to the needle, then wave Cody towards a chair. "Sit down then and I'll get this line hooked up to you."

"I said no." Cooper's growl carries enough alpha command to make Cody whimper.

The healer flinches, but squares her shoulders and turns to face him, eyes burning like dark coals. "Do not give your alpha commands to me here, in this room." Her voice is soft, but there is no mistaking the anger in it. "I might be blood bound to follow you, but I also have a blood oath to heal. That oath is older, runs deeper. I cannot break it."

"Let me do this, dad," Cody's begs, "Please."

"I don't like it," the alpha says.

"You don't have to like it." Tricia takes hold of Cody's arm. "Right, clench your fist. Small sting. That's it, good."

Through blurred vision, I watch as the line fills with Cody's blood, the red liquid rushing into my own veins. Moments later a rush of energy thunders through my system, a painless liquid fire moving along each limb, to my fingertips, to the ends of my toes. The black spots in my vision fades, the ringing in my ears quietens. I feel the wound on my side now, a great gaping hole where the bull's horn must have speared me. I can feel the flesh starting to knit together, a hot, itchy, restless sort of feeling. My wolf lets out a low, contented rumble.

The healer keeps her fingers on my pulse, keen hazel eyes watching me. "That should be enough." She ends the blood transfusion, then looks at me inquiringly. "How are you feeling?"

I close my eyes, silently taking stock of my injuries. Whatever healing properties Cody's blood contained has done nothing to dull the pain. If anything, it has made it worse, since I am no longer floating on the edge of consciousness.

"Like I got hit by a truck," I croak out, dry lips cracking as I force a smile.

I'm pretty sure I have blood in my teeth, going by the metallic taste in my mouth.

Cody lets out a long breath, running his hands through his dark curls until they stand up on end.

"Honestly, man. I thought you were a goner. We saw the bull take you out, but we were down at the pack house. It took so long to get to you, even after we shifted and ran." He shakes his head, growling. "I can't believe that bitch-"

"Don't call her that." I snap without thinking.

My wolf bristles protectively, and I clench my fists at my sides, fighting to rein the animal in.

"You're defending her?" Cody snorts in disbelief.

"She didn't know I couldn't shift."

I try to roll onto my side to face Cody, and instantly regret it when my ribs scream in protest. I inhale sharply, then let out a slow exhale.

"I should have told you guys I'm latent."

I nearly choke on that word. Latent. Defective. No better than human.

"That's no excuse. It was a real dick move."

"More importantly," Cooper Winslow cuts in, tapping one booted foot with irritation as he glares down at me. "Has a pack bond been formed? Or part of one?"

I look at the alpha blankly. "A pack bond?"

"From the blood transfusion."

"Um..."

I wrinkle my brow in confusion.

The only pack bond I have ever experienced was with dad. It allowed us to push thoughts to each other without speaking. Something that had been largely useless, given the existence of cell phones and the ability to talk. Normally. Using words.

The only times dad used the bond were the rare times he was in his wolf form. Like the day mom was killed…

"Can you feel anything through the pack link?" Cody's dad pushes impatiently. "Any of Cody's thoughts or emotions?"

I shake my head.

"No, sir."

At least, I don't think I can. I haven't really tried.

The alpha's broad shoulders visibly relax. "Okay." He rubs his face with one large, callused hand. "That's good." He pats Cody on the shoulder, then turns on his heel and leaves me and Cody alone in the med room with the healer. Good to know he's taking care of what matters.

"Sit up and I'll wrap your wound," Tricia orders, helping me to a seated position.

Obediently, I hold my arms away from my body as the healer wraps my bare stomach tightly in medical gauze.

"What about my ribs?" I ask. I'm pretty sure several of my ribs are broken, if the pain when I breath is any indication.

She shakes her head. "We don't wrap broken ribs anymore." I wince where her fingers brush against my skin. "However, you should stay the night." She packs the wound at my side, though it is nearly closed up now. I've always healed quickly, even though I'm latent. I guess this process has been accelerated significantly by Cody's blood. "Your grandparents are human, right?" she asks.

"Yah…" I say, not completely sure where she is going with this.

"You should be fully healed by tomorrow. If we send you home now, it will raise a lot of questions when you are healed overnight."

I nod. Of course, that makes sense. It would definitely raise questions if my grandparents noticed I had super-human healing abilities.

"I'll call them," I say, pulling my phone from my pocket, sighing at the now-cracked screen. At least the thing still works.

To my surprise, grandma actually sounds please that I'm staying the night. "They're an important ranching family in the community," she says seriously, "Very well connected. I hope you're being respectful and making a good impression."

I just tell her whatever she wants to hear. My face hurts, and talking isn't helping anything.

I end the call and turn to Tricia. "Done. She's fine with me staying here." I shoot Cody a wry smile. The movement sends pain spiking along my jaw. "Grandma seems to think your parents are a big deal."

Cody shrugs. "The ranch employs a lot of people. All shifters, and all pack, but the humans don't know that."

I can tell it makes him uncomfortable. "You should go back to the party," I suggest. "You shouldn't miss out just because I got my ass handed to me."

"I don't know," Cody says, dark brows furrowing. "That seems a bit unfair, seeing as you're stuck in here."

"Bring me back some food then." That was the part I was looking forward to the most anyway.

"Yah, okay," Cody agrees. "We'll get you set up in a guest room for the night first though."

Lucy Stone

I forgot how scary alpha Winslow can be. A giant of a man, eyes as black as a moonless night, sharp features. There is nothing beautiful about him. If there was, it was long ago swallowed up by power.

"Why did you do it?"

I find my eyes lowering, even though I know I was in the right. I was protecting my pack. I'm not even sure why Cooper cares about some lone shifter.

"Answer me, Lucy."

Dad is standing beside the alpha, his frown uncertain. I've always been the good girl. Obedient. Doing what is best for the pack. I still am. He just can't see it yet.

It's just the three of us in this room.

"He smells of lies," I finally say, giving dad a beseeching look.

Of all people, he should understand how dangerous that can be. Especially in a lone shifter.

My voice sounds quiet in the little office, all my bravado somehow swallowed up by the carpet and formica table and plastic chairs. I hate that I sound weak. Squaring my shoulders, I make myself meet the alpha's eyes.

"Tobias Finch is hiding something from us. I don't know what it is, but it has to be something big. He's lied about lots of little things, like where his father's pack is from…"

"I fail to see why you thought leading him up to the bull pen was an appropriate solution to this."

Cooper's voice is icy, lips tilting up humourlessly. Honestly, it's a terrifying expression. One I've seen too many times in the interrogation room.

I drop my gaze. "I'm sorry, alpha." I can smell the lie in the statement, even if no one else can.

I'm not sorry. I would do it again.

I'll do more if I have to. If they won't listen.

"You should have come to me or your father with the information, and left us to deal with it," Cooper continues. "You are not an alpha. You are not a beta. You're not even in line to be the beta. You do not make decisions. And you do not meet out justice."

Each word is like a whip, aimed to cut. To remind me of place in this pack.

"Yes, alpha." I bite my lip, deliberating for a long moment before adding: "I think we should let Cody know too. Since he's determined to be friends with the loner."

Cooper's answering growl sends ice to my bones. I have to resist the urge to quiver, to show him my throat in the typical wolf move of surrender.

"It is not your job to think," he says and I feel my cheeks redden. "And while I certainly don't have to explain my decision making to you, I think you know I have good reasons for not telling him."

My eyes flick up in surprise and the alpha smirks.

"I might not have your gift. But I also don't trust Tobias Finch. Having him around is the best way to sniff out his secrets and find out if they are dangerous to the pack. If he's a spy from a rival pack, don't you want to find out who sent him? If he's a rogue with an agenda, don't you want to know what that agenda is? When there's a wasp in the room, it's better to know where it is at all times."

And just like that, alpha Winslow has reduced me to a pup with my tail between my legs. Ashamed of my own bumbling inadequacies.

"You're right, alpha," I say. And I mean it this time. "I won't let it happen again."

He nods. "Good." He looks me over, but I know he doesn't see me. Not really.

He only sees my gift. The thing that makes me too valuable to share. Too valuable to let go.

"Make amends with the loner," he orders, before turning and striding out of the room, my father close on his heels.

My upper lip curls at the order. I have no desire to have anything to do with Tobias Finch. This whole situation is entirely his fault.

My wolf and I have always agreed, always moved in sync. I've always been able to trust her. Her and my gift. Until Tobias.

My gift screams that he is a liar. He lies with every other breath, lives in secrets.

Yet my wolf likes him. Really likes him. And she's not a friendly animal. Apart from Anton, she barely tolerates her own pack members.

If I was foolish, it's only because Tobias upsets my equilibrium.

TOBIAS FINCH

The guest room in the main house is seriously five-star. Just as sleek and modern as the exterior of the building, it has a massive flat screen TV, its own bathroom and a small patio that looks out at the rugged mountains beyond the valley and foothills of the ranch.

It almost makes the beating I just took worth it. Almost.

I lay down gingerly on the large bed and flick on the television as I wait for Cody to bring some food.

A reality show about ranchers is on. It's one I've seen before, back in New York. The show had seemed so far-fetched then. I couldn't imagine that people actually lived like that. Talked like that. Dressed like that. Now I see it wasn't completely off the mark. Sure, it's a bit exaggerated. It is television after all. But the world it portrays is real.

It has been little over a week, and already my life in New York feels like someone else's life. But I don't feel at home here either. I doubt I ever will. I feel like a boat whose anchor has been cut, and I am just bobbing powerlessly across the ocean.

My thoughts are interrupted by a tentative knock on the door. It must be Cody with the food. I sit up, stomach grumbling.

"Come in," I call. The door swings open. But it isn't Cody. Lucy stands there, staring angrily from the threshold, holding a plate piled with food.

My jaw drops in surprise as I pull the blankets up around my waist, suddenly conscious that I am shirtless, my torso half covered in bandages.

Lucy strides in, setting the plate down roughly on the bedside table. She looks angry. Vengeful almost. Like *I've* wronged her, not the other way around.

"Thanks?" I say, eyeing Lucy warily.

Given it is her fault I currently feel like a piece of meat that has just gone through a grinder, I can't say I'm feeling particularly thankful for her presence just now. Even if I do like looking at her.

Lucy just glares at me, grey eyes like chips of ice as she surveys my bare chest, the bandages, and then my face. The bruises are probably becoming more visible, changing from red to purple and green. I probably look like crap. Still, Lucy's blatant cold perusal makes me feel defensive. Angry. It makes me want to throw her off balance.

I force a smirk and lean back in the bed. "Like what you see?" I indicate to my bare chest, making sure to give my biceps a little flex.

Colour rises to Lucy's cheeks and she narrows her eyes down to slits. The grey of her eyes flashes an icy blue as her wolf pushes close to the surface.

"Not really," she says.

I scoff. "Sure you do. Why else would you be here?"

I know I'm good looking, by human or shifter standards. I have clear skin, a solid, muscular build, and am taller than most fifteen-year-olds without being gangly. I'm not a pretty boy, but I have my mom's high cheekbones and a strong jaw like my dad. I don't have any real facial hair yet, but that will come.

Assuming I live past this year. Which is looking less likely by the day.

I also suspect my looks don't mean a thing to Lucy, since the girl clearly hates me.

"Don't kid yourself, Finch." Lucy tosses a wave of silky blond hair over one shoulder. "They ordered me to bring you your food. And to apologise. So, *sorry*."

She draws out the last word, baring her teeth. Making it clear that while she might have to follow an alpha command, she sure as shit doesn't have to mean it.

"Mostly I just wanted to see the damage."

She lets her eyes rove over my chest, at the bandages wrapped around me. Her lips curve into a disgusted sneer, but I swear I can see her cheeks redden.

"Looks like the bull won this round. Guess that's what happens if you're a latent."

She spits that last word out like a bad taste.

I should be angry at the jab. I want to be angry. Instead, my stomach drops nauseatingly, churning with disappointment. At what, I'm not exactly sure, since I never really thought Lucy liked me. My wolf lays his head on his paws, whining and watching the female hopefully.

There is no doubt about it. My wolf is an idiot.

"This?" I gesture to my bandages and force a grin. "Just a flesh wound. I'm not dead yet."

She just raises her eyebrows haughtily, either ignoring or not getting the Monty Python reference.

I lift the plate of food onto my lap and start to cut into my steak. "I'm guessing this isn't poisoned or anything?" Before she can answer, I bite into the steak. It's a little cold, but I'm too hungry to care.

"Eat it and find out." Lucy snarks, turning on her heel and stomping out of the room.

With Lucy gone, the silence settles on me like a weight. It's the numb, cold sort of silence that I've come to know well in the past couple weeks. Like all the feeling bled out of me on that kitchen floor. I shift to bring my plate closer and pain lances up my side. A welcome relief from the numbness.

I switch the channel to MTV. It's playing *Monster* by Shawn Mendes and Justin Bieber. I close my eyes against the flickering light of the screen.

I knew agreeing to come to this stupid ranch was a bad idea. I should have trusted my instincts. Followed the rules. Now I am staying the night here with these shifters and I'll have to see them again in the morning. They will either continue to hate me because I'm a loner. Or pity me because I'm latent. Neither option is particularly pleasant.

I take another bite of the steak, then turn my attention to the potatoes. At least I'm not dead.

Yet.

Chapter 5

Tobias Finch

"Have I got the juiciest bit of gossip for you."

Summer enters the room in a whirlwind, bringing the smell of coffee and bacon with her.

"Do you want to let him wake up first?" Cody admonishes, trailing behind with a plate of food and a steaming mug.

"He is awake," Summer snipes. "I could tell as soon as we came in."

I sit up in bed, still groggy, having woken up just moments before they came in.

Before that, I had been back in that kitchen in New York, my mom's empty eyes open and staring. The blood. All that blood.

And then I woke up disoriented in a strange room, sun streaming in the window, white blankets and white walls gold in the morning light.

"Does this gossip come with food?" I grumble, eyeing the plates through bleary eyes.

"Of course."

Summer holds a plate up out of reach. It's piled with toast, eggs and bacon and I literally start salivating like one of Pavlov's dogs.

"But trust me, you are going to want the gossip just as much."

I shoot Cody an inquiring look, and he nods.

"She's actually not exaggerating for once."

He sits down on the edge of my bed, a weird grin on his face. Summer finally hands me the plate and I immediately start eating.

Maybe it's because I'm recovering from a brush with death, but I have never felt so hungry in my life. The craving for meat is unreal. I eat all the bacon on my plate in about five seconds flat, then start scoffing down the eggs. When I reach out for the coffee Cody put on the bedside table, I realize both Cody and Summer are staring at me like I've got two heads.

"You okay, man?" Cody asks.

I cock a brow, because it's a stupid question that doesn't deserve an answer. Especially pre-caffeine. Also, I don't like people watching me eat. But these guys are shifters, they've got a high metabolism too. They should understand what it's like.

I take a swig of the coffee, hoping it puts me in a better mood, then say: "So, what's this news?"

Summer smiles mysteriously. I've known this girl for less than twenty-four hours and already I can tell she's the type to draw this out. I take another long drink of coffee, setting in for a long, convoluted story about some people in their pack.

"Anton met his mate!" Summer squeals and Cody winces at the sound. I choke on my coffee, spilling some of the burning liquid onto the white quilt.

"Sorry, what?" I dab at the coffee stain, but there is no way that's coming out without bleach. "His mate? Who? Is Anton even old enough to find his mate?"

"He's seventeen," Cody chimes in, throwing a smug look at Summer. I recall their conversation from yesterday, where Cody argued that some shifters could recognise their mates as early as seventeen.

Summer waves a hand dismissively. "He's almost eighteen. And let's be honest here. Anton is not exactly normal, okay. I'm pretty sure he could grow a full beard when he was twelve." She pats Cody's face and coos mockingly. "Your little cheeks are still soft as a baby's bottom."

Cody glowers, opening his mouth to shoot out what is probably going to be a rude retort, but Summer keeps speaking.

"Anton met his mate yesterday at the dance. It was literally the most ridiculous and cringe moment I have ever witnessed in my entire life." Summer rubs her hands together with unbridled glee. "Her name is Tori Alton and she's this gorgeous she-wolf from a pack in California. I'm talking model gorgeous. Like, she actually works as a model."

I look at Cody incredulously.

"She's pretty hot," he shrugs. "If there was no mating instinct involved, there is no way that Anton would ever get a date with her. He probably wouldn't even get a smile from her."

"So the music is playing, the disco lights are spinning," Summer continues."People are eating spare ribs with their bare hands off paper plates, drinking from plastic cups, and just being super classy, as per usual. Then the Californian contingent arrives. They were like two hours late because their GPS took them down Crazy Woman Canyon, and they got a little lost. And then Anton spots his mate."

Summer pauses for dramatic effect and I raise one eyebrow. The movement hurts, reminding me that my face is probably still covered in bruises.

"Well, Tori arrived holding another guy's hand. I guess she was dating some guy from her pack, and they both came along to the party. Which, if you ask me, is in super poor taste. Why would you go with your boyfriend to another pack hoping to find your true mate?" Summer shakes her head.

"As soon as Anton noticed Tori, he completely freaked out. He didn't even say 'hi, how do you do' to Tori. He just attacked her boyfriend, ranting loudly about this girl being his mate, telling the other guy to get his paws off her. And then he shifted."

"What!?"

"Yah. He lost control of his wolf, just like that. He ripped up all his clothes in the process because that is what happens when you're an idiot like Anton and just shift on the fly without undressing first. Not that it was a huge loss, because his clothes sucked."

Summer pauses, stretching out her hand to snag a hash brown from my plate, and I resist the urge to growl at her. She just gives me a mischievous smirk, taking a bite before continuing her story.

"The other guy had to shift to fight him off. There was blood and fur everywhere. The poor girl was screaming for them both to stop..."

"It was embarrassing," Cody says darkly. "The California pack already think we are all a bunch of rednecks."

"Well, they're right where Anton is concerned," I say unforgivingly. They are probably right where most this pack is concerned, but I don't say that. I like Cody too much to want to offend him.

"I think Anton would have killed the other guy if my dad hadn't stepped in," Cody frowns.

"Yes, and then the best part was that Anton had to shift back into human form so he could heal, but all his clothes were ripped up. He was in too much of a frenzy to go out and get new clothes, and he probably didn't want to leave his new mate alone with her boyfriend. Or, ex-boyfriend now, I guess. So Anton ended up being completely naked – and covered in blood - when he introduced himself to his mate."

I burst out laughing.

"It wasn't funny," Cody growls.

"Oh, it totally was," Summer says.

"How did his mate react?" I ask. "Did she – accept him – or whatever?"

"Yah, she did." Summer scoffs, sounding disappointed. "As soon as she recognised Anton as her mate, she was a goner. She dumped the boyfriend she arrived with. Poor guy. He was really good-looking too."

"He looked like a clown," Cody snaps.

"He is probably infinitesimally smarter than Anton," Summer counters.

"I don't know how smart he is, coming to a pack event like this with a girlfriend."

"Whatever." Summer waves her hand, glittery nail polish sparkling. "I think we can all agree that the material point here is that fate is a ruthless, whacked out, crazy…"

Cody claps his hand over Summer's mouth. "Nope, don't say it."

She glares up at him, and he drops his hand. "Fate picks mates for a reason," he argues. "There'll be something that we can't see that makes Anton and his mate perfect for each other."

I can't imagine Anton being perfect for anyone. I haven't met this Tori girl, but already I feel bad for her.

"It's just biology," Summer retorts. "Plain and simple. Designed to produce the best shifter offspring. There are lots of unhappy mates."

"Then how do you explain shifters that mate with humans?" Cody argues. "There are no biological benefits to that. Half-shifter pups might be born too human, or latent. How is that beneficial…"

He looks at me then, and the blood drains out of his face as he realizes his audience.

"Sorry man. I – I didn't mean…"

I raise one hand, waving off his apology.

"No biggie."

I school my expression to hide the hurt his words inflict. It's the truth, and the truth always hurts the most. I am latent. Probably because my mom was human.

"Anyway, I hope I never meet my true mate," Summer says, artfully trying to steer the conversation away from the awkward topic of my defective wolf. "I would rather choose someone I actually like, fall in love, imprint."

She sighs, her gaze darting momentarily to Cody.

He's too busy frowning at her words to notice, but I catch the look. It's full of sadness and longing, and something else that I don't quite understand, but it makes me feel like an uninvited guest.

"I wish I could have seen Anton make a fool of himself," I say. "Did anyone film it or anything?"

"Don't think so," Summer muses. "We have a pretty strict anti-filming policy at pack events. You know, just in case something gets recorded that shouldn't get out there. For the humans to see and all."

Hmm, she has a point. I hadn't thought about that.

"What did Lucy think about it?" I ask, wondering if she was embarrassed by her older brother.

"She wasn't there," Cody says. "At least, not until the fight was over and Anton was standing there naked trying to introduce himself to his mate, barely able to put two words together."

I wonder if it happened while she was in my room, glaring at me and telling me how not sorry she was for almost getting me killed.

"What do Anton and Lucy have against me anyway?" I ask, unable to help myself.

I instantly regret it. It sounds whiny, like I'm one of those kids who wants to be popular, loved by everyone. That just isn't me.

Cody and Summer exchange a look. Summer bites her lip, clearly wanting to say something. Cody's eyebrows draw together, and he gives a short shake of his head.

I can tell they're having one of those silent conversations through the pack bond, like my dad and I used to have. I clench my fist around my fork, trying to ignore the pang of jealousy.

"Look, it's fine. I don't need to know. It doesn't matter anyway."

I drain the last of my coffee.

It shouldn't matter why Lucy doesn't like me. Because after today, I'm going to try and have as little to do with this pack as possible. I'm going to keep my head down, focus on school until I can get out of this shit-hole.

Maybe I can get my GED and enroll at a community college. Somewhere away from Buffalo. Because if I've learned anything this week, it's that staying in Buffalo is dangerous.

Chapter 6

Tobias Finch

I do a pretty good job of avoiding the pack for a couple of weeks. I eat my lunch in the library, so there is no risk of being cornered by Cody and Summer. Lucy is the only one I have classes with (Cody, Summer and Jason are in the year ahead, and Anton is a senior) and she's about the last person in the world to try and talk to me.

In fact, Lucy has mastered the art of pretending I don't exist. I guess that's better than having her pay attention to me, since last time her attention resulted in my being gored by a bull.

The downside of avoiding the pack is the humans.

It turns out, they are about as welcoming of outsiders as the wolves.

At first, it's just small stuff. Snooty looks, cold shoulders. Muttered comments behind my back about superficial shit, like my Air Jordan's and Knick's hat. They're a bunch of rednecks who think cowboy boots and wranglers are cool, so their fashion critiques are pretty easy to ignore.

I know none of them will try anything with me, or say anything to my face. I'm tall for my age, and I made the varsity wrestling team in early October, which seems to be enough to keep any overt shows of aggression at bay.

It's just not enough to win friends.

I still hear the wolves at night. Some nights, I swear they are right outside my window, calling for me.

When I asked grandma about them a couple mornings ago, she just looked confused.

"There's no wolves in this part of Wyoming," she said, patting my hand. "Haven't been for years. The ranchers killed them all. They put them back in Yellowstone a few years back, but they wouldn't have made it all the way over to Johnson County."

"But I'm sure I heard them," I muttered, frowning at my plate.

Grandma just shook her head, and got up from the table to flip the next lot of pancakes. While she was at the stove, grandpa grabbed my arm, his bony fingers digging into my bicep. I looked at him, surprised by the move and the strength in his grip.

"There *are* wolves, son," he whispered. His eyes glinted amber, like cats' eyes. For once, they were lucid and his speech was clear. "I've heard them too."

My eyes flicked towards his hearing aid. He can hardly hear when you shout at him, so I didn't find it particularly reassuring that he claims to have heard the wolves at night.

Since that conversation two days ago, I've heard the wolves every night.

I WAKE MUCH EARLIER than I usually do on a Saturday morning to find the landscape blanketed in snow.

It snows in New York, but it's an icy sort of sleet that turns to grey mush almost instantly, then re-freezes overnight.

I've never seen snow like this.

Light and thick and fluffy, coating the world like icing on a cake. Exactly like a cheesy Christmas card. Except it's October.

I'm not going to lie. The child in me goes ballistic.

I leap out of bed, throw my coat and shoes on over my pyjamas and start playing in the snow. I build snowballs. I try to make a snowman, but the snow is too dry and light to really pack together. I lay down and make a snow angel, like I've seen people do in the movies. The whole time I'm laughing like a crazy person. My wolf is in heaven, so happy that we're playing.

For a brief moment, I forget about losing my mom and dad. I forget that I live in a shit-hole town with a senile chain smoker. I forget about the pack. About Lucy. By the time I come back inside I'm soaked to the skin, so cold I probably have minor frostbite, and I don't care one bit.

Grandpa is sitting at the kitchen table smoking a cigarette when I traipse in, leaving snow to melt on the linoleum. He's eyeing me creepily, and I wonder if he was watching me through the front window the whole time.

It's still early and Grandma isn't up yet. She likes to sleep in on the weekends.

Switching on the coffee machine, I pour myself a bowl of cereal, doing my best to ignore the old man. As a rule, I try not to interact with him. Especially when grandma isn't there to temper the crazy.

Grandpa swivels in his chair to watch me as I move around the kitchen. I feel his gaze boring into me, unusually sharp and alert. When I turn and meet his eyes, he crooks one gnarled finger in my direction.

"Come here, kid."

Warily, I make my way towards him, keeping the table between us as I clutch my cereal bowl to my chest.

Grandpa always makes me a little nervous. Maybe it's because I never know if he's going to remember who I am or not. Or maybe it's because he occasionally talks to himself saying things like 'they're coming for me again' and 'they know, they know.' I know it's because of the dementia, but it still freaks me out.

"Closer." He says, narrowing his eyes.

I sigh and reluctantly move around the table so that I'm standing in front of him.

"What is it, grandpa?" I ask, keeping my voice as calm and non-confrontational as possible, using the tone I've heard grandma use a hundred times in the weeks I've been here.

Abruptly, he stands up and grabs my face with his hands. I freeze, too surprised to move. Just like when he grabbed my arm a few days ago, I'm surprised by how strong his grip is.

"Your eyes," he growls. "Your gods-damned eyes."

He looks pale and angry, but his eyes are clear and lucid as he stares into my own. I blink, unsure of what he's talking about. And then it hits me, like ice in my veins, colder than the snow falling outside.

I forgot. I forgot to put my contacts in. And somehow, I think he *knows*.

But he can't know. He's human.

"What about my eyes?" I ask, feigning ignorance.

"Don't play dumb with me boy," he hisses, looking around to make sure we're still alone. "You've been hiding them."

I shrug. "I wear coloured lenses sometimes."

"Smart," he whispers, nodding. "Very smart. If only they'd had those back in my day…" He trails off, shaking his head, then says abruptly: "Who else knows?"

"Knows what?"

He grabs me by my collar, giving it a shake with a vigour that really should not be possible for someone who looks like they're two steps from their grave.

"Who else has seen your true eye colour? Who else knows what you really are?"

My mind is racing, trying to make sense of this. This is not a normal human reaction to seeing my true eye colour. And Grandpa is human. There's no way he even knows that shifters even exist.

"No one knows," I whisper. "Just mom and dad. And now you."

"Good. That's good." He nods, a look of grim satisfaction on his face. "Come with me."

He pulls me towards the back door, then hauls me out towards the dilapidated chicken shed that sits at the back of the house. I don't think it's had chickens in it for fifty years, and now it just stores broken power tools and gardening equipment. We're standing in knee deep snow, completely shielded from view of the house by the chicken shed when grandpa starts undressing.

"Um, what are you doing?" I practically squeak, so alarmed my voice raises an octave.

I probably should be worried he's going to do something weird, or inappropriate, but that doesn't even cross my mind. My first thought is that he's going to die of exposure out here and then grandma will kill me. My second thought is that the neighbours will see and won't that just be super embarrassing.

He doesn't answer, just starts shucking off his house slippers and then his worn pyjama pants like he's not standing knee-deep in snow. I shield my eyes, embarrassed at the sight of those thin legs, bent and covered in age spots.

"Grandpa," I whimper, "what are you doing? You're going to get frostbite or something."

He ignores me and pulls off his shirt, letting it drop in the snow.

"Order me to shift," he hisses. He's standing completely naked in the snow, starting to shiver.

"Wha – what?" I stammer, not sure I can be hearing him right.

"Order me to shift, damn it."

His eyes are pure fire now, lips pulled back in a snarl. He looks frantic and a little crazed and for the first time, I think I might actually be afraid of the old man.

"I can't," I say lamely.

I'm not supposed to use my alpha command, not supposed to show my dominance. It goes against everything my parents have taught me. I'm supposed to keep it hidden, at all costs.

"You can," he bites out, rubbing his arms with his hands to warm them against the cold "And you will, or by all the shifter gods, boy..."

"I don't know how."

It's the truth. I don't even know if I can give an alpha command. The kind that other shifters would have to obey. Maybe that part of me is defective, just like my wolf. Maybe I'm a born alpha who can't even command. Wouldn't that just be the perfect irony?

"And also, you're human," I add, though I'm starting to seriously doubt the correctness of this assumption.

"Just try. Please, Tobias. Please, just order me to shift. Try."

His voice is pleading now. His small, frail frame is shaking with cold. And the look he gives me – full of desperation and sorrow. Something about it strikes me to the core.

It's wrong, and dangerous, and completely insane. But I'll try. I have to.

"Shift," I order.

Nothing happens.

I try to remember what it felt like when Cooper Winslow gave the command. The feel of that alpha power running over my skin, like it wanted to seep into the cracks of my very being and pull the wolf out of me.

"Shift," I say again.

Nothing.

"L- let your w-wolf do it," he suggests, teeth chattering as he shivers against the cold.

I'm not really sure what that means. I've never spent much time thinking about my wolf. He's like an annoying inner voice that I do my best to ignore. He's illogical and volatile. He's always wanting to do stupid shit that will get us killed, like fight Anton or chase after Lucy. I've spent so much time suppressing him, fighting him, that I can't even imagine letting my wolf take the lead on anything.

I take a deep breath, shut my eyes and feel for the wolf inside me. He's large and bristling, full of energetic anticipation. Like a caged beast, pacing and pressing against a gate. I know if I open that gate there is no closing it again. No going back.

I can feel my wolf's dominance and power. Its hectic and steadying all at once, wild and unmoving. I reach out for it. I let it wash over me until it is pulsing in my veins, prickling at my skin, uncomfortably large for my human frame.

"Shift," I say again.

This time I feel it. It's like the alpha command I felt from alpha Winslow, but in reverse, moving out of me instead of over me. And much more powerful. Like an ocean compared to a puddle. The force of it nearly makes me black out.

I hear the cracking and popping of bones and tendons. Shaking my head, I realize I'm sitting in the snow staring at a big, black wolf. His face is peppered with grey fur, but his eyes are full and intelligent, glowing amber like hot coals in soot. Large white flakes catch in his coat, glistening.

"Grandpa?" I whisper, the sound so faint it's almost swallowed up by the rustling of falling snow.

As if in response, the wolf licks the side of my face. It's rough and wet and takes me completely by surprise. Then without any warning, the wolf turns, darting off in long bounding leaps towards the hills.

Chapter 7

Tobias Finch

I stare after the black wolf until he becomes a dark speck against the white snow in the distant foothills, then disappears into the pine forest that marks the base of the Little Bighorn mountains. Even my preternatural shifter vision can't compete with the distance and the cover of the forest, and I completely lose sight of him.

And then the reality hits me, with a force equal to the bull that ran me down all those weeks ago.

Grandpa is a wolf shifter. A freaking wolf shifter.

My eyes follow the wolf prints that lead away from the chicken shed, across my grandparent's property, through the fence line and up towards the mountains.

I've turned grandpa into a wolf. A senile wolf, probably. And now he's gone.

All that is left is a pile of old clothes in the snow at my feet while he's off running around the forest somewhere.

Is he going to come back? Will he even be able to find the way home? I know grandma is always worried about grandpa getting lost if he goes outside on his own. As a human he couldn't go very far. As a wolf, who knows how far he'll go.

Can he even shift back on his own? Will he remember how?

Panic rises in me, hot and fast. I'm in so much trouble. There's no way I can tell grandma I've turned grandpa into a wolf and let him run off into the forest. First of all, she'd definitely skin me alive. Plus, I don't know what she knows, but telling humans about shifters is a big 'no-no'. The kind that would get both of us killed by anyone in the shifter community.

There's only one thing to do. I've got to get grandpa.

I dart back into the house, shuck off my wet pyjamas and put on a pair of gym pants, a t-shirt and a sweater. My coat is wet, but I yank that on over top, then jam my feet back into my boots. Not ideal clothing for snow, but I don't exactly have a lot of options.

By the time I reach the foothills, my sweatpants are soaked through. At least breaking trail in knee-deep snow is hard enough that it keeps me warm. So warm that I'm sweating beneath my layers.

"Grandpa," I call out, now that I'm far enough away from the house so grandma won't hear. "Grandpa."

No answer.

I run one hand over my face in frustration, then keep following the trail left by grandpa's paw prints in the snow.

After a while, it becomes almost hypnotic. The sound of my feet crunching snow, the feel of the morning sun on my back, the way the untouched snow around me glistens like an infinite number of tiny diamonds. I know I should feel tired, but I don't. I feel warm and - alive.

Maybe it's because I can feel my wolf more strongly now. Not as strong as when I told grandpa to shift. But stronger than I've ever felt before. It's like I really did open up a gate, or maybe I took down the entire cage because the wolf's strength is flowing into my own. Like when the healer gave me the blood transfusion with Cody's blood. Only stronger. And mine.

I reach the edge of the pines quicker than I would have thought possible.

"Grandpa!" I call out into the dark forest. My voice is swallowed up by the dense trees and undergrowth.

"Grandpa!"

There is no response. No sound of rustling or movement. Not even bird song. The forest is completely and utterly silent.

Careful. Not natural, my wolf whispers, on edge and wary of the silence.

I pause, eyeing the trail of prints that lead under the pines. I have to follow them. I have to find grandpa.

Moving through forest is harder than running through fresh snow. There is less snow under the pines, but the forest floor is uneven, with roots and branches and fallen pine needles ready to trip me at every step. Snow tumbles in clumps from the boughs above, trickling wet and cold down the back of my coat, on my face, in my hair.

I'm tired. I'm wet. And I'm totally screwed because I'm never going to find him.

"Stupid old man," I mutter under my breath.

Wolf tracks wind their way between trees in what seems like a senseless pattern. At least I think they're wolf tracks. I mean, they look the same. What if I'm just following some stray dog in the forest? A manic laugh bursts from me, the sound swallowed up by the trees.

I trudge on, eyes scanning the ground. Grandpa is a wolf shifter. That's the thing I just can't wrap my head around. How is it that no one told me this? Why would my parents pretend mom was human, when she was actually half shifter?

I stop abruptly, staring into the snow at my feet, eyes unseeing as realisation dawns. "I'm not a half," I say out loud.

If grandpa is a wolf, then I'm mostly shifter. Three quarters actually.

My latency suddenly feels more like a defect than it ever did before. Before, I could chalk it up to being half human. Now? What does it mean if I'm mostly shifter but still can't shift?

A low growl interrupts my thoughts. My eyes snap up, searching the dense forest for the origin of the sound. A pair of eyes meet mine. Gold eyes. Bright and glowing like swirling embers, contrasting against black fur. Black like grandpa's wolf, but this isn't the same wolf I've been tracking all morning. I'm facing the biggest wolf I've ever seen.

I should be terrified. Maybe I am. Maybe I'm just too surprised to feel fear. My wolf lets out a low rumble of contentment, as if meeting an old friend.

I know this is no natural wolf. It has to be a shifter. And its eyes. Gold eyes. Eyes like mine. Eyes of a born alpha.

I gape, staring directly at him. In my shock, I've forgotten the rules my parents have drilled into me – act submissive, lower your gaze, show your throat. *Don't show weakness*, my wolf insists. For once, I listen to him, keeping my chin level, my eyes locked on the eyes of the strange wolf.

"Wh – who are you?" I ask, willing my voice not to tremble, and failing.

The wolf lets out a low rumble in reply, but it doesn't move to attack. Instead, it sits down on its haunches.

"He won't answer."

Grandpa steps silently from the trees, stopping to stand beside the giant wolf. Even sitting, the wolf's head comes up to grandpa's shoulder. He rests one large hand on the wolf's head, letting his fingers sink into the dark fur.

I have so many questions. Who is this giant wolf? How does grandpa know him? Because he obviously does. Well enough to pat him like a common dog. And how did I never know grandpa was a shifter?

With all these questions burning in me, I'm surprised when the first thing out my mouth is: "Aren't you cold?"

It's probably not a stupid question, since grandpa is standing completely naked and barefoot in the snow. He doesn't look cold though. He looks happy and – alive. More alive and aware than I've ever seen him. Like the clock has turned back at least ten years, clearing the fog from his brain, restoring muscle and health to that usually frail frame.

The black wolf huffs out what sounds like a laugh, hot breath clouding in the cold forest air.

Grandpa doesn't answer my question. Instead, he turns towards the forest, putting his back to me and says: "Come on. We don't have much time. There's a lot to discuss."

He and the wolf pat into the forest, following what looks to be a worn trail. Reluctantly, I follow. The forest here is denser, darker, and soon we reach a granite cliff with a small rock overhang at its base, a burrow dug out underneath. The wolf slinks into the burrow, ducking his head under the rock entrance. Grandpa follows.

"Seriously?" I wrinkle my nose.

There is no part of me that wants to climb into what is basically a cramped dirt cave with the largest shifter I've ever seen and my naked senile grandfather. But I'm not sure what choice I have here. Not if I want to get grandpa back home in one piece. So I duck down and scramble after them.

Once inside, the wolf curls up, nose tucked beside his tail, grandpa sitting beside him on the bare earth. I crouch down beside grandpa, sitting on my heels, my back pressed against the earth wall. It feels warm compared to the shadows of the snow-covered forest outside.

"Take my jacket," I say to grandpa in a low voice, handing him my jacket as I eye the wolf warily.

Grandpa drapes my jacket over his bent shoulders and I fix him with a glare. I know I should be relieved I finally found the old man, but honestly, at this point, I'm just pissed. I've been hiking for hours, I'm soaking wet and now I'm sitting underground with my naked, senile grandfather and a strange shifter. Oh, and grandpa is smiling. Smiling. Un-freaking-believable.

"You have a lot of explaining to do," I snap. "Who is he?" I tilt my chin towards the wolf. "How is it you can shift? Oh, and why didn't you tell me you were a shifter in the first place? I mean, I get you have dementia but that seems like a pretty significant thing to have forgotten. Also, how on earth did you even walk this far?"

Grandpa's smile falls away and he lets out a long sigh, pulling the jacket tight around his shoulders. He strokes the wolf idly, a sad look ghosting across his face. For a long moment, I don't think he's going to answer.

"It's a long story," he finally says. "I haven't shifted in over forty years, and neither has he. This here is my brother, Jamison. Guess that'd make him your great-uncle."

"My great-uncle?" I gasp, eyes wide as I look at the wolf again.

His gold eyes meet mine and he gives one long blink. *Yes*, he seems to say.

"He – he's a..." I pause, afraid to voice what he is. What I am.

"A born alpha?" Grandpa gives a humourless chuckle. "Yes, that is exactly what he is." He shakes his head. "You see what has become of the mighty born alpha? The one all shifters feared and shunned? Forced into hiding for so long he's become stuck in his wolf form. More beast than man." Grandpa strokes the wolf – Uncle Jamison -

again, then says to the wolf, so low its almost inaudible, "I'm sorry it's been so long, brother."

A sick feeling rises in my stomach. Has this man really been in wolf form for so long? Alone? What humanity can even be left after all that time?

Grandpa must see the horror on my face because he says: "Yes, this is what our kind does to those born into power. This, and so much worse." He narrows his eyes at me and says, "Tell me, Tobias Finch, how is it that you are still alive?"

I swallow hard, my mouth feeling suddenly dry. I can feel my grandfather's eyes boring into me. Uncle Jamison rests his chin on his paws, head cocked to one side, watching me with interest.

"I- I don't know the whole story," I admit. "All I know is what my parents told me. They had to leave dad's pack when I was born, otherwise I'd have been killed. We moved to New York, and my parents kept me hidden as much as possible. Kept me around humans and away from other shifters. Had me wear contact lenses to hide my eye colour. Dad trained me to hide my dominance."

I frown, then add: "My parents didn't like to talk about what I was, or about our old pack, or what had happened when we left. I didn't even know mom was a half-shifter. They always said she was human."

"I'm afraid that was my fault."

Grandpa leans back against the earthen wall of the den, tilting his head till he's staring at the ceiling.

"Your mother didn't know I was a shifter. Your grandma still doesn't know. If I'd met your father, if I'd known he was a shifter, then maybe I would have told him. Warned him what could happen if they tried to have pups."

He gives me a sideways glance. "Warned them their pup could be a born alpha."

He kicks his thin legs out in front of him, letting them rest beside the wolf. His brother. Then he closes his eyes, as if giving himself over to the memories that dance behind his eyelids.

"Our mother died giving birth to Jamison. I was only thirteen years old. Our dad didn't survive the breaking of the mating bond, and died hours later."

My breath catches hearing that. I had no idea grandpa lost his parents when he was young. That he lost his dad to the mating bond, just like I lost my own.

"Our pack was going to kill Jamison," he continues, "but Jamison was all I had left. This little baby, weak and helpless. An orphan just like me. I didn't know the first thing about raising a pup. But I couldn't let them kill him. So I ran."

Grandpa pauses, running his hand over his face at the memory. Jamison nuzzles grandpa's leg encouragingly.

"The first few years were rough. So bad I can scare remember them now. We lived wild. I had just learned to shift and I spent most my time in my wolf form, only going into human form to steal things he needed. Bottles, formula, clothes and the like. It was a miracle Jamison survived my raising him. But he did. Shifters are hard to kill. Even as pups."

Grandpa shoots Jamison a wry smile.

"We moved around, but that proved to be dangerous. You can end up in shifter territory without knowing it. And there was no hiding what Jamison was from other shifters. So we came here."

Grandpa nods to the woods around us.

"Close enough to the Clear Creek pack's territory to keep other shifters away, far enough from their lands that they'd never have reason to come here. But it was too dangerous for Jamison to go into town in his human form. Always a risk of running into one of the Clear Creek pack. So once Jamison could shift, he stayed in his wolf form and stayed on this land here. It was safer that way."

Jamison lets out a huff, and grandpa nods, grimacing, as if there is some joke between them that only they know.

"Yep, I got stuck on one side and you got stuck on the other, didn't you?"

I frown, not understanding what grandpa means until he says: "After enough time not shifting, Jamison couldn't shift back into human form and I couldn't shift into wolf form."

"You see, to keep Jamison safe, I had to hide I was a shifter too. I stopped shifting into wolf form until my wolf scent became faint, faint enough that I could mask it with tobacco smoke. I picked up smoking. Or at least, made sure to keep a cigarette burning as often as I could. Truth is, I didn't much like cigarettes, though I tolerate them now."

He gives a dry chuckle.

"That's how Jamison and I stayed off the Clear Creek pack's radar. And if any lone shifters wandered onto Jamison's land well…"

Grandpa trails off, and Jamison lets out a low menacing growl. The sound goes straight to my bones.

"I used to hike out and visit Jamison every week. Least, I did until I got sick with the Alzheimer's," grandpa continues, rubbing his face. "That's a disease no shifter should get. But not shifting smothered my wolf until I was near weak as a human."

Grandpa huffs out a laugh, then says: "You know, it's funny. You'd have thought I'd have gotten lung cancer before anything else, the amount of cigarettes I go through each day. But life is funny like that, isn't it?"

"The shift," I muse, recalling alpha Winslow yelling at me to shift after the bull ran me down, so that I could heal. Now I understand why grandpa had wanted me to order him to shift.

"The shifting healed your Alzheimer's?"

"More or less," Grandpa drawls, absently patting Jamison's head.

Well, damn.

Despite the fact that I'm completely confused and overwhelmed by what grandpa has just told me, and despite the fact that I'm sitting in the den of a feral wolf shifter who grandpa has basically admitted murders lone shifters that cross his territory, I feel pretty awesome right now.

Because I've just cured grandpa's Alzheimer's.

I look at Jamison, and a thought occurs to me.

"Do you think I could make him shift back into human form?"

Jamison lets out a low growl. I'm not sure if it's at the suggestion of me compelling him to do something, or at the suggestion that he shift back to human.

"Maybe…" grandpa frowns, considering. "You're a born alpha. But so is he, and he's older, stronger. Past his prime but…"

Jamison snaps his teeth at grandpa. I think it's meant to be playful, but there's honestly nothing friendly in his massive jaws or those long yellow canines.

"What? You are." Grandpa throws up his hands. "You're no spring chicken any more, Jamison. Though I don't think a fifteen-year-old kid could best you for dominance either."

Jamison huffs, seeming somewhat mollified and grandpa turns back to me.

"Maybe if you were a wolf in your prime. And even then, I suspect it would be a challenge."

I nod, agreeing. I could barely get grandpa to shift. There's not a chance I could compel this beast to do anything.

Also, he looks like he would eat me if I tried.

Then another thought hits me. One that has the colour draining from my face.

"Umm, what are we going to tell grandma?"

Chapter 8

Tobias Finch

Late afternoon paints the foothills in reds and golds before we reach the crest of the hill overlooking my grandparent's house. There's a cop car in the driveway, and grandma is out back with the officer, shouting and pointing to where I know grandpa's clothes were left lying in the snow. As if sensing us, grandma looks up, squinting towards our figures on the crest of the hill.

"Susan is going to kill me," grandpa says resignedly, trudging down the hill towards the house. I managed to convince him to wear my sweatpants and boots along with my coat, so at least he's not naked anymore.

Of course, that means I'm hiking in the snow in my socks and boxers, looking like a complete lunatic. To make matters worse, I've stuffed my socks with dried pine needles because apparently that provides insulation and prevents frostbite. It's as uncomfortable as it sounds.

"Johnathan Leeland Vance!" Grandma's voice carries across to us on the wind. "What in God's green earth do you think are you doing?"

She's not yelling and probably doesn't expect either of us to be able to hear her, given we're still a good ten-minute walk away. But of course, we both can. There's no mistaking the emotion in her voice, or the way her lower lip trembles as she watches us approach.

Grandpa lets out a weary sigh.

"Yep, she's definitely going to kill me."

"Well, you should have thought about that before you darted off in wolf form," I snap.

After hours of walking through snow without pants, boots or a coat, I'm feeling less than charitable towards the old man.

When we draw close to the house, grandpa stops, noticing the cop standing beside grandma.

"Is that a human or shifter?" he asks, nostrils flaring as he tries to scent the man.

"Uh, not sure," I admit, "I don't recognise him as one of the Clear Creek pack, but I didn't actually meet most of the pack…"

I trail off, not wanting to admit the reason I didn't meet anyone. Grandpa immediately picks up on my reticence. Downside to him having all his mental faculties back, I guess.

"I thought you went there for one of those parties they have. Wasn't the whole pack there?"

"Well…" Just the memory of what happened has my face heating. "I kind of had a bit of an incident when I was there and missed the party. Spent the night in the infirmary so to speak…"

Thankfully grandpa doesn't push. Instead, he just shakes his head and says: "If the cop's a shifter you're going to have to make yourself scarce somehow. You don't have your contacts in."

"Okay."

I can't believe how stupid I was, forgetting to put them in this morning. It's like my brain just short circuited or something.

As if reading my thoughts, grandpa says: "You need to put them in before you leave your room each morning."

Yah, thanks Captain Obvious. I resist the urge to roll my eyes because, yah, okay, he's right. That was something my parents drilled into me constantly. That and the other rules - which I seem to be breaking with alarming regularity.

Of course, if I hadn't forgotten my contacts this morning, grandpa wouldn't have known I was a born alpha. I wouldn't have forced him to shift. And he'd still be mentally deteriorating.

I don't say that though.

I catch the cop's scent when we get closer. Definitely human. I let out a sigh of relief, watching as the cop trudges across the field and part way up the hill to meet us, one of those silver emergency blankets tucked under his arm. He wraps it around grandpa, then tries to put an arm around the old man to help him down the hill.

"I've walked this far on my own steam, I don't need you tripping me up," grandpa grumbles, shoving off the police officer and adjusting the blanket around his shoulders so it's more like a silvery cape.

Which of course means it has no warming properties whatsoever and makes him look like a wizard.

I resist the urge to palm my face with embarrassment. The cop only steps back and replies "Okay, sir," while trying to suppress a grin.

Once we cross the fence, grandma sprints towards grandpa, throwing her arms around him as she heaves with sobs.

I look away, because old people being affectionate is one of those things that is cute on cards but actually kind of weird in real life. Before I can make my escape, grandma is throwing her arms around my neck, sobbing into my chest.

"You - you found him, you r-rescued him."

Awkwardly, I place one arm around her shoulders to return the hug, her black hair resting under my chin. I give her shoulder a little pat because I really don't know what to do when people are crying.

"Well, I - um…" My eyes dart around nervously. Like maybe there is some way I can just slip away without anyone noticing. But the lady has an iron grip and grandpa and the cop are both standing nearby, so it doesn't look like that is happening any time soon.

"You're a real asset to your community," the cop says. Officer Payne, his name badge reads. "You've done a good thing here."

Before I can protest further, grandma shepherds us into the house saying,: "Get inside you two, you must be frozen to the bone."

"Yes, ma'am," grandpa says obediently, pretending to hobble up the steps to the back door before shooting me a quick wink over his shoulder.

…

Over the weeks that follow, grandpa pretends to slowly become more and more lucid. Or I should say, he pretends to be less confused, because the lucidity is very much real. His Alzheimer's is definitely gone. The tricky part is convincing grandma that he's somehow just got better.

Grandma attributes his mental clarity to the new supplements she's been having grandpa take. He complains that they taste like raw fish and seaweed, but he keeps on taking them since she's convinced if he doesn't take them, the Alzheimer's will get worse again.

My wolf feels like he's got a pack again, even if it's just one other wolf. Well, two if you count Jamison.

Whenever grandpa can get me alone, he tells me little bits about being a shifter. Things my dad never talked about, like the names and locations of different packs, shifter customs, history, mythology.

I visit Jamison once a week, and grandpa plans to start visiting him again as well, just as soon as he can convince grandma to let him hike out to the forest.

It turns out my grandpa is the best thing that's happened to me all year. Not at all expected, considering not that long ago, I could hardly stand to be in the same room as him.

Chapter 9

Tobias Finch

The icy evening air is biting cold when I step out of the gymnasium and into the school parking lot. A shock after the heat and sweat of the wrestling meet. Guys are climbing into their cars and trucks to drive home. Some of the younger students – or those with more dedicated parents – get into their parent's cars. People are laughing, talking, just milling about like it's not cold enough to freeze the balls off a polar bear.

You'd think this was one of Buffalo's prime social occasions. Who knows, maybe it is.

I shake my head as I pull my hood up over my ears, adjust my back-pack and start jogging toward the highway.

"See you, Toby," Matt Payne, one of my teammates, calls out as I weave through the parked cars.

My team are all used to this. They think I'm a fitness freak.

Really, it's a necessity. I'm still too young to drive and there is no way my grandparents are coming to watch me wrestle.

First of all, that would be embarrassing. Most importantly though, one of the Clear Creek pack might figure out grandpa is a shifter.

I lift one hand to wave to Matt, not breaking stride. My stomach is growling. I just want to get home, eat dinner, and crash.

I'm almost out of the parking lot when I hear a familiar voice amongst the chatter and idling car engines.

"I'm sorry, okay. I didn't mean any disrespect, I swear."

"I don't give a shit. You'll stay away from him, you hear?"

"I – I can't…"

There's the thud of a body against metal and I turn towards the sound, just in time to see Jason being pushed up against the side of a pick-up truck by Quentin Slade, a senior on the varsity wrestling team.

I stop in my tracks, turning to watch the scene unfold, debating whether to go and intervene.

Coach has a strict no-fighting rule in place, which means whatever beef Quentin has with Jason, he shouldn't be trying to start shit. But everyone knows Quentin is about as smart as a bag of rocks, so he probably doesn't realize 'fighting' includes body slamming.

With my comparatively higher intelligence, I'm probably under a moral obligation to go enlighten him.

"Say you'll stay away from him, you creep," Quentin hisses, his face close to Jason's. "I want to hear you say it."

Jason shakes his head, even as he's starting to tremble with adrenaline and fear.

Since getting to know the pack, I've also learned that Jason is an omega – one of the most submissive and lowest ranking wolves. He's basically hardwired to flight not fight in conflict situations.

Jason lets out a whimper that is more animal than human as his wolf presses close to the surface. I can practically feel his wolf, wild and feral and scared.

Oh man. This is not good. Not good at all.

Frantically, my gaze flits around the parking lot, searching for someone from the Clear Creek pack.

Someone needs to step in here. Not because of Coach's rule, but because Jason is one wrong move away from shifting. In front of a parking lot full of humans.

My blood burns, pressure building behind my eyes as my wolf pushes me to intervene.

Ever since the incident with grandpa, the animal has gotten more insistent, his voice louder. What used to be a faint whisper, easily ignored, is a rumbling growl filling my ears. I'm pretty sure this is a bad thing, because I'm across the parking lot in seconds, moving without thinking.

"Quentin, put Jason down," I say, wedging myself between the two of them.

"This isn't your business, Finch," Quentin barks out. "Run home." Like I'm a stray dog.

He's not far off.

Except the animal in me is getting more and more difficult to leash.

"It's one hundred percent my business."

I push him farther away from Jason.

"Coach is watching, the other team is watching. You're going to get yourself disqualified from the next meet. You know Coach's rule."

"It's not a fight," Quentin stupidly argues. The vein on his neck bulges out, pulsing angrily.

I've always wondered if he's on roids and now, with this aggression, I'm really starting to think he might be.

"He's stalking my brother."

Jason throws his hands up in the air. "I swear, that's not what I'm doing. We're friends."

"Bullshit," Quentin spits out. "You stay away from him, runt."

Jason flinches, the insult apparently hitting him harder than it should. Maybe it's one that has been thrown at him before by the pack. Still, he stares at the ground and whispers: "I can't do that."

Quentin shoves at my chest in an effort to get back to Jason. I shove him back.

"What's your problem, Finch?" Quentin yells.

"Tone it down," I hiss, because all the people who were milling around the parking lot are now wandering over, watching Quentin and I like it's the post-meet entertainment.

I really don't want to fight Quentin. He's my teammate. But I can't have him getting in Jason's space. Not if there's a risk Jason could shift.

"You tone it down," he retorts, giving another shove.

Then he reaches up and flicks my Knick's hat off. In my peripheral vision, I see it sail away, landing in a puddle of grey slush.

In this moment, it's like that stupid hat symbolises everything I've left behind in New York. The life I should have had with my parents, with my friends. My old school. A comfortable place in the world.

And Quentin, he's the embodiment of the cold Wyoming wind that has come and torn my whole world down.

It's completely illogical. But I lose my shit.

My fist crashes into Quentin's ugly mug. He reels back, trying to throw a swing back at my jaw.

It's like I see it in slow motion. I duck, and his swing goes high. I jab upwards. His head snaps back and I follow it with a second hit to his gut. He doubles over, winded.

A low growl erupts from my chest. I know it's my wolf. I should pull back. I should stop. The human part of me knows this, but the wolf is riding me too hard, full of rage and protective instinct. Quentin is a threat and it wants to end him. End him. End the pain boiling in my veins, throbbing in my head.

Quentin falls to the ground and I'm instantly on top of him, teeth bared as I pummel into his face.

Soon, it's not Quentin I'm seeing at all. It's the faceless bastard that killed my mom. It's my dad, his weakness for leaving me. It's every shifter now and in history that made my parents think the only way they could keep me safe was to run. Who made a thirteen-year-old wolf have to run to keep his baby brother safe.

If I could shift, I probably would have by now. My wolf wants to rip his throat out, use its hind claws to drag his guts out into the icy asphalt of the parking lot.

My wolf is a monster and, in this moment, so am I.

I hear someone calling my name, but it's a thousand miles away, on the other side of the red fog clouding my vision, the ringing in my ears.

"Tobias."

The sound is stronger now, and I feel the brush of an alpha command on my skin. My wolf shakes it off, as if it is no more than a few stray droplets of water on his coat.

"TOBIAS."

Strong hands are pulling at my shoulders, grabbing my arms, holding me back and hauling me up. When my vision clears, Cody and Anton are on either side of me.

"Shit, Tobes," Cody hisses through his teeth. "Have you lost your ever-loving mind? The guy's out cold."

I blink, and realize with growing horror that they're right. Quentin lays motionless below me. His nose sits at an odd angle, blood staining the ice around his head.

"What is going on here?"

A voice booms out. Coach Jenkins. His eyes survey the mess that is Quentin's face, then flick up to Anton and Cody holding me back, to my knuckles, swollen and stained with blood. He gives me a hard stare.

"Tobias Finch, did you do this?"

"Quen – Quentin threw the first hit," Jason chimes in from behind me, his voice shaky.

I lift my eyebrows in surprise at how quickly Jason lies for me. Though I suppose technically Quentin did hit my hat first…

"I don't want any excuses," Coach snaps. "We have a no-fighting policy for a reason."

Coach kneels down, assessing Quentin's injuries. Quentin's eyes flick open, blinking unseeingly and I let out a breath of relief.

Coach drags Quentin to his feet, then turns to me, as if in afterthought.

"Finch. My office. Ten minutes."

"Yes, sir," I reply reflexively, watching them haul Quentin inside, then look down at the blood-stained ice.

What have I done?

"This is what comes of letting a stray in," Anton spits out, glowering at Cody, like all of this is his fault. "Look at him. Beating up a human. He's got absolutely no control."

Cody opens his mouth to respond, but Jason cuts in.

"It was my fault."

The words are so quiet you would need shifter hearing to make them out.

Cody turns to Jason, surprise written on his face.

"He cornered me about Ross."

"Ross? You mean Ross Slade?" Cody asks, brow furrowed in confusion. "His little brother?"

Jason just nods, face turning red.

"What about Ross?" Cody's eyes narrow.

Jason swallows hard, then looks away. "He's – um – well, I'm pretty sure he's my – my…"

Anton's eyes go wide and Cody drags a hand over his face. I look between the three of them, feeling like I'm missing something.

"Oh geez, Jason," Cody lets out a low whistle. "Please tell me you haven't done something stupid."

Jason just hangs his head, looking at his feet.

"Jason," Cody says warningly, putting enough dominance into his voice to compel an omega like Jason. "You have two minutes to tell me everything."

Jason's head snaps up at the command, eyes wide. It's hard to read his expression. Anger. Betrayal maybe. But he says: "The mating urge hit me two weeks ago, at the full moon. I know he's human, but I've never felt anything like this before."

He looks at Anton, seeking sympathy from the guy who first met his mate under less-than-ideal circumstances several weeks ago.

"I've tried to be cool about it. But my wolf won't let me. Their dad drinks a lot, and I saw a bruise on his arm the other day. It looked like hand prints." Jason throws up his hands defensively when Cody gives him a hard stare. "I haven't done anything crazy! I've just been keeping an eye on things. I might have parked on his street a few nights, just to make sure nothing bad happens to him." He looks at Anton pleadingly. "I just can't stand the thought of someone hurting him. That's all. I swear."

I nod, starting to put the pieces together. "Let me guess. Quentin saw you parked outside."

Jason winces and nods.

Cody shakes his head, incredulous. "You've got to be kidding me, Jace." He sighs. "You didn't think to tell us? Or at least tell my parents? They're your alphas."

"I didn't want my dad to know," Jason whispers. "You know how he is. About humans."

Anton nods solemnly. "I get it dude."

Cody shoots him a look and Anton just shrugs.

"Maybe I wouldn't have before I met Tori. But trust me. I get it. Fate kind of just grabs you by the balls, and …"

I wince at that description as Cody looks between me and Jason and asks: "Okay, but why was Tobias fighting Quentin about all this? It doesn't involve him."

I open my mouth to answer, but Jason says: "I was going to shift." He fixes his gaze on his shoes. On the blood still pooling in the snow and ice. "I lost control of my wolf when Quentin said I couldn't see his brother anymore."

Cody follows Jason's gaze, upper lip curling in disgust at the blood. The look of disgust turns to confused disappointment when he looks back up at me.

"So you beat Quentin within an inch of his life?"

I frown, not sure how to explain what happened.

"He said some shit. I was fired up from the meet." I shrug, trying to make light of it. Trying to ignore the sick feeling of shame and guilt rising in my stomach.

There was a lot of truth in what Anton said. I lost control. Maybe my wolf is damaged. Or maybe this is why born alphas are killed at birth. Why Jamison has lived like a recluse for the past fifty years.

"I've got to go meet Coach," I say, turning back towards the school, desperate for an excuse to escape their questioning.

I deserve the looks they are giving me. But it doesn't mean I want to stand here and bear them.

"I'm coming with you," Cody says, trotting along beside me.

"Whatever," I grunt.

Cody might be Coach's favourite, but I doubt him coming as back-up is going to save me from the man's wrath. I messed up. Big time.

"And then you're coming out to the ranch this weekend," Cody continues.

"Oh yah?" I feel my lips tug up into a forced half smile.

There is absolutely no way I'm going back to the ranch. Ever. Nope. Not a chance.

"Yah." Cody's tone is hard. "This isn't a discussion. You're coming."

I thought I left all my anger on the bloodied asphalt, but it turns out its still churning around in my chest.

I turn to face Cody, hands on my hips.

"What's your game, man? I'm not a part of your pack. No one wants me there. Lucy made that pretty freaking clear when I came out last time. Even your dad pretty much said I'm not welcome."

A look of hurt flashes across Cody's face, but he masks it quickly, his mouth pressing into a thin line.

"You're wrong."

He doesn't offer any further explanation because we've reached Coach's office. I roll my eyes. Cody can take that patronising wannabe-alpha crap and shove it…

"Finch."

Coach's voice snaps out like a whip, reminding me of where I am. What I'm supposed to be doing. I swallow hard.

"Sit down." Coach points to a flimsy plastic chair opposite his desk. I sit, aware of Cody taking the seat beside me.

"How's Quentin?" I ask, my eyes fixed on the scratched wood of Coach's desk.

I honestly feel terrible about what I did to him. He didn't deserve it. It wasn't even a fair fight. Even a latent shifter will beat a human in a fight every time.

"He'll be fine. A broken nose, a concussion but nothing worse." Coach tilts his head, cracking his neck. I shudder at the sound. "But his dad is a lawyer, so you can be sure he's going to rain hellfire down on the school for what happened. Especially if Quentin can't compete for a while."

I wince, recalling Quentin's face. So smashed up, it was nearly unrecognisable.

"I need you to tell me exactly what happened, Finch."

Coach lets out a tired sigh, and I can't help but notice that Coach's face is paler that usual, dark circles under his eyes.

I take a deep breath, readying to tell him everything I can when Cody kicks my leg to silence me.

"With respect, Coach…" Cody sits up straight in his chair, using that voice he employs with authority figures. The one that gets everyone eating out of his hand, grandma included. "I can tell you what happened. Quentin was roughing up Jason in the parking lot, calling him some names which don't merit repeating in good company." Cody pauses, giving Coach a meaningful look. "Tobias tried to get him to back down, but Quentin refused. Tobias even reminded him of your no-fighting rule, sir."

I press my lips together, resisting the urge to scoff at Cody's rose-tinted description of what went down. His careful bending of the truth.

"Quentin threw the first hit, and Tobias just reacted." Cody gives me a sharp, reprimanding look. "He may have gotten a little carried away after that." Understatement of the year. "But I believe his heart was in the right place."

Coach gives me a long look. I try to look as contrite as possible. It's not difficult, with how guilty I feel.

"I've spoken with my father," Cody continues. "He's got a contact who provides therapy for some of the returned vets we employ out at the ranch. Dad has offered to put Tobias through a similar course, to help him process the loss and grief he's no doubt experiencing having recently lost his parents."

Coach's eyebrows flick up with surprise.

He must not have known about my parent's deaths. I guess the only ones I've told here are the pack. Even then, I haven't told them everything. Just said 'my parents recently died' and left it at that. Because how can I even begin to explain what happened?

I bite the inside of my lip, resisting the urge to glare at Cody. I can't believe he's brought this up, used it as an excuse. And therapy? Anger management classes? Is he serious? Not to mention, I know he hasn't had a chance to clear this with his father, since he's been with me the whole ten minutes since the fight.

"Well now..." Coach rubs his chin thoughtfully. "Anger management training, that's a good idea. If it's someone Cooper Winslow uses for the vets, they must be good."

I feel a strange pang of shame. Cody is making it out like I'm some hero who got a bit carried away. Like the Incredible Hulk or something. Really, I'm just the guy who flipped out about his Knick's hat because his inner-wolf lacks a moral compass.

Coach leans back in his chair, then says, as if to himself, "Yes, that's probably the best course of action…" He lifts one bushy brow, cocking his head and eyeing me critically. "Does that all sound good to you, Finch?"

There is no way I'm doing this anger management crap Cody's talking about. No freaking way.

I meet Coach's eyes and give a curt nod. "Yah. Okay."

"Good. Okay." Coach rubs his hands together. "Well, that's settled then. You'll be suspended from the team for the next two meets. We'll review your wrestling again once I've heard how the anger management is going." He looks at Cody. "Your dad can give me a report on that, I take it?"

I look between him and Cody.

Is Coach serious? Is he actually asking Cody's dad report to him on this, like I'm somehow under the Winslow's care? Just because Cody is a Winslow and his daddy is like some ranching mafia king-pin in this backwater town?

He can't be serious.

Cody gives a saccharine smile. "I'm sure he'd be happy to, Coach."

"Now get going. I suspect I've got a long evening ahead of me." Coach glances up at the clock on his wall.

"Yes, sir."

I'm in the parking lot as quick as possible, Cody on my heels. Almost all the cars are gone.

"Come on, I'll give you a ride home," Cody says, tilting his chin towards his truck.

"I can walk."

Cody gives me a disbelieving look. "Seriously man. It's freezing. And dark. Plus, your place is on my way home."

"Fine." The words come out through clenched teeth. When he puts it like that, it does sound pretty unreasonable to refuse a lift.

We sit in silence for most of the drive out of town. I'm running the events of the evening over in my head, trying to work out why my wolf flipped out so badly, thinking of all the things I could have done differently. I'm also trying to work out whether I'm thankful for Cody intervening, or pissed.

Right now, I'm going with pissed.

"How did you ignore my alpha command?" Cody asks, abruptly breaking the silence.

My heart drops like a lead ball to the pit of my stomach. "What do you mean?"

"When I told you to stop fighting. You didn't stop."

Somehow, that little detail had slipped to the back of my mind, overtaken by the shame of what I'd done to Quentin.

He's right. I had ignored his alpha command. I shouldn't have. If I was a submissive wolf, I couldn't have. Wouldn't have been able to.

"You're not really a submissive wolf, are you Tobes?" Cody's voice is low, as if he's afraid someone will hear us, even though it's just us in the cab of his truck.

I turn my head away, staring blankly into the darkness as indiscernible forms flick past outside the truck window.

"Look, I know you're keeping secrets Tobes." Cody's fingers flex and tighten around the steering wheel, stare fixed on the road ahead of him. "I don't expect you to trust me. But whatever it is, your secret is safe with me."

"Even from your dad?" I ask, knowing what the answer will be. Secrets can't be kept in the face of an alpha command. And my secret? My secret isn't safe with anyone.

Cody lets out a long breath. "Point taken."

"Were you serious about the anger management stuff?" I ask, changing the subject. I don't actually plan on taking those classes he mentioned, but at this stage, I'll do anything to avoid talking about my ability to ignore alpha commands.

"Completely serious," Cody replies. "Dad's got the first session lined up for this Saturday. See if you can stay Saturday night and we can do one on Sunday as well."

Oh man, this night just gets worse and worse.

"I don't think that's really necessary..." I say, then frown. "Wait - when did you talk to your dad about all this?"

Cody just taps his temple. "Pack link."

Right. Of course. That also explains how Cody knew everything that happened at the fight. He must have pumped Jason for additional information telepathically over the link.

"Look man." I rub the back of my neck. "I appreciate you talking to Coach back there for me. I really do. But I'm not down for this whole anger management thing..."

Cody lets out an exasperated grunt. "I don't think you get it. This isn't about Coach letting you off the hook – although, for the record, the only reason you aren't getting expelled right now is because of me."

I huff in annoyance. But...he's probably right.

"This is about you losing control of your wolf and almost killing a human. A human." He gives me a sharp look. "Just because you can't shift doesn't mean you don't put our entire community at risk when you do shit like that."

"It was a once-off," I argue. "It's never happened before. I doubt it will happen again." It won't happen again if I have anything to do with it.

"Once is too much."

He has no idea how right he is there. I've been living my whole life in anticipation of the one mis-step that will result in me getting put down like a rabid dog.

We're both silent for the rest of the ride until Cody pulls into my grandparent's driveway. The lights glow yellow through the curtains, and I can make out the shape of grandpa pacing around the living room.

As I climb out of the truck, Cody calls after me. "Hey, Tobes." My nostrils flare at the sound of the nickname, but I don't bother to correct him. "Thanks for looking out for Jason tonight. I know he appreciated you having his back. Even if things got a little out of hand."

I shrug. "No problem. Quentin is a dick-bag."

Cody laughs. "Yah. That he is."

I lift one hand in farewell as I climb the steps to the front porch, listening to gravel crunching beneath truck wheels as Cody drives off. Then my shoulders slump. Cody did me a solid. He probably prevented me from committing murder and he definitely made sure I didn't get expelled. He's been nice to me since day one, and I've done nothing but try and push him and the rest of the pack away.

I don't deserve his friendship and I certainly don't want it.

But I wish I did.

Chapter 10

Tobias Finch

"Horses can sense your emotions, and they respond to them. They're like a mirror. If you're afraid, they'll be flighty. If you're angry, they'll push you."

The horse in question looks like it wants to bite my face off and dance on my corpse with its hooves. I'm not sure what that says about my emotional state.

My heart is thudding wildly in my chest. I should never have let Cody pick me up this morning. I should have run to the forest and hidden out with Jamison.

My wolf, on the other hand, has been silent but alert since Ms. Crossguns put me in the arena with this creature. I think he remembers that the last time we encountered a large grass-eating animal at this ranch, he did not come out the winner.

"Keep your body language relaxed, non-threatening. Make your breathing even. That's it. Now, square your shoulders to face her and look her in the eye. That tells her to 'move on' or 'move away'. We want her to trot a circle around the arena."

Surprisingly, the horse does start to trot a slow circle, following the rail of the small round training arena. Her nostrils flare as she lifts her head defiantly, the whites of her eyes visible as she watches me warily.

"Good. Pivot with her as she moves around, so that you're always facing her. That tells her to keep moving. It's how horses exert dominance in a herd," Ms. Crossguns explains from beside me.

The horse keeps moving, lowering its head to give out a discontented snort as I keep my eyes locked on hers.

"How long do I do this for again?" I feel a bit bad, using horse-dominance to make her run around in circles. It's like being forced to run a treadmill. I hate running on a treadmill.

"Not that much longer," Ms. Crossguns assures me. "Watch her face, her mouth. See how she's lowering her head. Chomping and licking her mouth."

"Yah…"

I watch those big horse lips nervously, wondering if that means the horse is thinking about trying to make me into a snack.

"That's a horse's way of saying 'okay, I submit'. Once she submits, then you can try and approach her."

My stomach drops. "Ah… Um - approach her?"

From the corner of my eye, I can see Ms. Crossguns lips quirk in amusement as she runs one hand through grey and blond short-cropped hair. "That's right. The end goal is to get her used to being touched so she can be ridden eventually."

Great. Just great.

Ms. Crossguns explained earlier that the horse was a rescue horse who had suffered abuse. Apparently, this 'therapy' I'm supposed to be doing involves rehabilitating people and horses together.

"I don't think she really likes people," I mention. As if in agreement, the horse lets out a loud huff through her nostrils.

"So how is this good for her again?" I ask. "Isn't this kind of cruel?"

And yes. I am appealing to the woman's concern for animal welfare.

Ms. Crossguns doesn't laugh. She keeps her eyes fixed on the horse, pivoting as the horse trots around the arena, her countenance serious.

"Horses are naturally herd animals with a very complex social structure. There's a head mare, and then the other horses fall into line underneath that, some more dominant or bossy than the others." She tilts her chin at the horse in question. "Most horses are naturally submissive. They feel safest when someone else is at the helm, telling them what to do, creating order in their lives. Being told what to do, gently guided. It's at the heart of their very nature."

I go still, listening. My wolf perks up his ears.

"Their very survival depends on figuring out where they fit in the social structure of the herd, knowing who they have to listen to and who they can boss around. That means a horse will always be pushing you, checking to see if you are still going to be the one to tell them what to do." She gives a rough laugh, and the horse throws up her head in response. "But no matter how much they push, at the end of the day, the horse wants you to be the one in charge. Because it's always easier and more comfortable for someone else to take the reins."

She pauses, watching the horse a while longer, then says: "People are much the same really. Most people don't want to be a leader. Same as wolves."

I look at her in surprise. My nostrils flare as I take in her scent. She smells of human and horse and dry grass. Not a hint of wolf. An uneasy feeling shifts in my gut. Human's don't know about shifters. At least, they're not supposed to. That is the primary rule we all ascribe to.

"Keep your hat on," she chides.

I don't have a hat on, since my hat met a tragic end in the school parking lot a few days ago.

"The horses can sense it. So of course, I know."

She doesn't say what she knows though, and I'm not stupid enough to ask. I press my lips together and keep my eyes on the horse.

"The real question is not whether you're a wolf or a man," she continues, "it's whether you are brave enough to draw on what's in you to be the leader this horse needs you to be. Because she's ready for you to try and pat her now."

The horse has slowed to a walk, her head low, her mouth chomping on frothy looking saliva.

Gross.

However, the whites of her eyes are no longer showing and she seems calmer. Happier even.

"When you approach her, you need to change your body language from the 'move away' stance to the 'I'm not a threat' stance. Turn your shoulder so you're not facing her head-on anymore. Drop your gaze. That's it. Now slowly but steadily move towards her. Let her feel that you're not a threat, but you're still in charge."

I follow her instructions, wondering if the horse can hear how loudly my heart is thundering in my chest. To my surprise, the horse doesn't try to run away, though she continues to watch me warily.

"Go ahead and give her a pat on the flank. Her shoulder, that is. Not too hard, not too soft."

The horse's muscles bunch nervously under my hand, quivering as I pat her. I rub my fingers tentatively into the soft fur. I'm struck by how warm and alive she is.

"You're doing great," Ms. Crossguns encourages. "Keep patting her and see if you can move your body closer to her, so you're standing right next to her. That's it. Good."

My shoulder is leaning on the horse's side now, and I can feel the weight of the horse as she leans back into me, as if she's seeking out my warmth and comfort just like I'm reaching out for her. I feel the nuzzling of whiskers on the back of my neck, and I feel myself tense.

"It's fine. She's just returning the affection," Ms. Crossguns reassures. "She won't bite you."

The horse's nose rubs the back of my neck, then ruffles the hair on my head. It's warm and velvety, but I can't help but think about those big teeth that could clamp down on me any minute.

After several long minutes I forget to be afraid of the giant animal beside me. I can feel the horse's trust. Can feel that she does take comfort in my standing beside her, patting her. I press my forehead to her side, then wrap my arm around her neck. It's familiar and warm, like being hugged.

And then those warm feelings turn on me, melting through the walls I've built up around everything. Around my parents' death. My anger at being latent. At being a born alpha. At being so alone at school. Hot tears spill out, running down my cheeks, wetting the horse's fur as I press my face into her. The horse nuzzles my back, almost like she's offering me comfort.

Letting the tears out, it feels right somehow. Like this horse has suffered too and so she understands. She doesn't expect me to talk about things or explain things.

When I finally stop crying, Ms. Crossguns says from behind me: "That's probably enough for today. We can let Misty rest and work with her again next week."

I nod, giving Misty a final pat before I turn and walk away. Its not until I'm halfway to the ranch house that I realize something. For the first time since my parent's death, my wolf feels calm. Satisfied.

"WHAT EXACTLY ARE YOU WEARING?" Lucy's voice cuts through my feeling of calm, like the wire of an electric fence.

"Um, clothes," Anton responds tersely.

I round the corner, surprised to see Lucy and Anton in the Winslow's giant kitchen, where Cody told me to meet for lunch. They're seated around a big table along with Jason, Summer, Cody, the two alphas and a man who I guess must be Anton and Lucy's dad, the pack's beta, since he looks just like Anton down to the red plaid shirt and Wrangler jeans.

Anton, however, is not wearing his usual lumberjack attire. He's dressed in a yellow Adidas sweater with coordinated yellow tech sweatpants and matching shoes. Even in the hip-hop dance circles of New York, Anton's outfit would be bright. Here, he's basically luminescent.

The need to laugh is almost reflexive, but I press my lips together, the laugh becoming a choking sound in my throat. After weeks of the good people of Clear Creek High School commenting on my clothes, I know how annoying it is to receive unsolicited fashion critiques from people you don't like.

I sit in the empty chair beside Summer. She whispers loudly in my ear: "Anton's mate sent him some clothes. Apparently, she wasn't a fan of the flannel."

Anton's face reddens, because of course he can hear every word out of Summer's mouth. I suppress a grin.

Lucy ignores us, fixing Anton with a hard stare. "Why does she want you to wear that crap? Are you her Ken doll or something?"

"It's not crap," Anton retorts before angrily biting into his club sandwich. "It's a gift. And she asked to see what it looked like on when we had our video chat this morning. Not a big deal."

"Whatever you say, Vanilla Ice."

"Vanilla – who?"

Lucy just rolls her eyes before snapping a photo of Anton with her phone. He lunges to snatch it from her hands, but she veers away, fingers tapping furiously on the screen. "And shared." Pink lips curve into a cruel smirk when several phones in the room simultaneously *ping* an alert.

Cody and Summer both check their phones. Summer's eyes go round and Cody takes a long drink of orange juice to keep from laughing.

Anton's glares at his sister, grey eyes glowing silver as his wolf presses to the surface.

"You did not just – you little…"

"Enough you two," the lumberjack looking man at the end of the table booms out. He rakes a big hand through a messy head of salt and pepper hair.

Anton continues to glare at Lucy, who looks about as contrite as she was the day she tried to get the bull to murder me.

That is to say, not sorry at all.

As if also remembering that day, the lumberjack-beta turns his gaze to me, brown eyes narrowing. "You must be Tobias Finch." He spits out my name like it's a bad word.

"Yep." I hold his gaze for a moment longer than I should before I remember I'm supposed to be a submissive wolf, then lower my eyes to my plate.

"Jeb, he's here to work with Roberta," Cody's dad explains. "Cody thought he'd benefit from the equine therapy program."

"Humpf." Jeb frowns, shooting a dark look at Cody. "Is that so?"

Cody doesn't respond. Apparently, the sucking-up-to-adults act he pulls doesn't extend to Jeb.

"How's that going anyway?" Cooper asks, turning to look at me for the first time since I've sat down at the table.

My wolf squares its shoulders, wanting to face the alpha, hold his gaze. It reminds me of the same body language Ms. Crossguns had me use to get the horse to move away. The body language of dominance.

I shrug, making myself look down at my plate. Remembering to slump, making myself look smaller than I am, hiding the width of my shoulders.

"Okay, I guess. Ms. Crossguns is nice."

I take a bite of my sandwich, hoping that will prevent them asking further questions. I don't particularly feel like sharing what happened in that arena. The way that horse cracked me wide open. How being a leader felt so right to my wolf, even if it was just for a short moment in time.

"That she is." Cody's dad gives a cold half-smile. It's a much less friendly version of Cody's smile. My wolf curls a lip back, wanting to bare his teeth at the male.

"I've asked Tobes to stay the night," Cody interjects. "That way he can have another session with Ms. Crossguns tomorrow."

"Ugh, really?" Lucy hisses under her breath from the other end of the table. Anton turns his glare from his sister to me.

I sigh inwardly, silently hoping that the alphas say I can't stay.

"That's fine." Cody's dad gives a curt nod. My stomach sinks.

"You'll have to stay in the smaller guest room," Cody's mom smiles apologetically. "We'll need the large one for a guest that's arriving this afternoon."

Cody raises an eyebrow. "Who?"

"Lawrence Smith," Cooper drawls, saying the name like it should mean something. It doesn't. At least, not to me. "A wolf from one of the North Dakota packs. He'll be staying for a week to discuss an exchange offer." Cooper's brow contracts. "Can't say it's something we're likely to be interested in, but it would be bad politics not to hear him out."

"What kind of exchange offer?" Cody asks.

"It's pack business." Cooper shoots a meaningful look at me.

Right. Because I am definitely not pack.

There's a long silence that's only punctuated the sounds of chewing. Then Lucy sits back, smiling smugly as she says to Cody: "How is Quentin doing? Is he recovering okay?"

I can tell she's bringing up Quentin to bait me. Or maybe to remind the pack how badly I messed up. Cody seems to sense that too, because he shoots me an apologetic look as he mulls over what to say.

"Who is Quentin?" Jeb snaps before Cody can respond. The beta's broad shoulders tense under his plaid shirt and the look he gives Lucy – it's as if he is trying to see to her very bones.

"Just a human at school, Dad," Lucy assures him, injecting sweetness into her voice. "The one Tobias beat up."

"Why you askin' questions about some human boy?" Jeb growls. "By the gods, there better not be something going on, so help me, Lucy Stone."

I wonder idly which gods he is referring to, and whether he is one of those rare shifters who still believe that shifter gods and goddesses pull the strings of fate somewhere in their starry realm. That our destiny is controlled by some she-wolf – like Leto or Morrigan – and her diabolical twins.

Lucy pales. “No, there’s nothing. I don’t think I’ve even spoken to him.”

I almost feel sorry for her. Almost. But since she didn’t bring up Quentin to enquire after his health, there is some satisfaction in seeing her game backfire.

Jeb’s fist tightens around his sandwich, causing the fillings to squeeze out the sides. “That true Anton?”

“No idea,” Anton shrugs. “He’s pretty well liked though. Good looking guy. On the wrestling team.” He shoots Lucy a surreptitious smirk. One that their father completely misses.

I gape because, wow. Anton just threw Lucy under the bus. Big time, going by the expression of fury on Jeb’s face. Is this retaliation for the clothes thing? Is Anton that petty?

Lucy’s cheeks flush red and she gives Anton a look that promises a painful death. Anton just idly taps his phone, screen still showing the picture she sent over the group chat.

I can practically hear Jeb’s teeth grinding. “Morrigan’s tits, Lucy. It’s bad enough that the omega pup here has gone and fallen for some human.”

I feel Jason tense up in the seat beside me, his hands frozen as he holds his sandwich over his plate. I wonder what that is all about?

Jeb carries on, uncaring of Jason’s reaction. “Then Cody here is picking up loners like they’re stray kittens free to a good home…”

Cody’s lips curl back as he snarls in response to the jibe, but Jeb raises one hand, demanding silence as he fixes his daughter with a hard stare. “You have an obligation to your pack. To our whole species even. You’re not some low-ranking omega. I will not have you sullying yourself with some human…”

“I – I’m not,” Lucy stammers, red splotches appearing on both cheeks, grey eyes shining.

"Do. Not. Speak," her father growls, imposing enough dominance into the command that her voice wavers and she clamps her mouth shut. The fire in her goes out and I can practically feel the loss of its heat from across the table. There's no smug satisfaction for me anymore. Only anger at the male who has the audacity to smother her flame.

My wolf rises in my chest, wanting to challenge. Wanting to protect.

I push the animal down.

But it hurts. Man, it hurts. Burning like acid behind my ribs while the ringing in my ears grows to a steady drum beat, thrumming until I can't hear what else is being said. I stare at my sandwich, until my vision blurs, not trusting myself to look up at anyone. Not trusting my wolf. If I see the hurt on Lucy's face, the anger in Jeb's eyes – there's no telling what I might do.

I'M WALKING BACK from the barn late Sunday morning, after my second session with Ms. Crossguns and Misty, enjoying a moment of calm.

I know the feeling is as temporary as the warmth from the winter sun, bright but cold and distant. It doesn't prevent me from stopping to drink in my surroundings – the endless browns and beiges of the valley that stretch out to snow-capped mountains, white with hints of emerald pine.

I wouldn't say it is beautiful. There's something about the rawness of the scenery here that makes me feel uncomfortable.

But it's real.

I'm almost at the massive modern structure that they call the ranch house when I hear familiar voices coming from around the corner of the building.

"There is no way I would ever agree to go to Smith's pack," Cody whispers vehemently. "I don't care about some stupid treaty."

I freeze, listening as curiosity gets the better of me. Last night the visitor – Lawrence Smith – was holed up in some office with both alphas and Cody. Cody wouldn't say what they had discussed, but he had looked angrier than I'd ever seen him when he stepped out of that room.

"You know you're going to have to leave eventually," Summer reasons. "You know there can't be two alpha males in a pack."

"That doesn't mean I have to leave now. I don't have to worry about it until I finish college. That's years away."

"And what about bloodlines," Summer continues. "You said Smith told you..."

Cody gives a mirthless laugh. "You want me to go and mate with some female in that pack?" His voice raises in pitch even as Summer tries to hush him. "Hey, why not make it a couple females? We can see how many pups I can sire. Is that what you want? For me to be some pack's prize bull?"

"Of course not," Summer's voice quavers. "I just..."

"Then what? What is it you want, Summer? Because you know what *I* want."

"You – you don't know that yet." She says, voice is so soft I barely hear it.

"I do." His voice tapers into a low growl. "I might not be under the thrall like Anton but I know. I've always known."

Summer lets out a long sigh as Cody murmurs something that I can't hear.

My face burns as I realize that I'm eavesdropping on a very private conversation.

I could try and walk back to the barn, but they might hear me. If I stay here, they'll see me when they come around the corner of the house to go in the back door. Standing here like a mega creeper. Neither option is ideal.

Unsure of what else to do, I start humming to myself and stomp my feet a few times before walking towards the back door, hoping they'll hear me and realize they aren't alone. It seems to work.

"Oh, hey Tobes," Cody says half-heartedly when he rounds the corner. There's the distinct sound of light footsteps as Summer walks around the other side of the house, presumably to avoid being seen.

"Hey." I tip my chin in his direction.

"You done with Crossguns?" He gives me a piercing look, like he's trying to work out what I heard. If I heard anything at all.

I keep my features impassive and shrug. "Yah. Done for now."

Of course, my new overbearing and unrequited friend has signed me up for more sessions with Crossguns, so it looks like I'll be coming out to the ranch for at least a couple more weekends.

Great. Just great.

Cody is silent, waiting for me to speak. There is no way I'm going to admit to overhearing that awkward conversation.

He's not my pack member. I'm not even sure if he's my friend. Sometimes I feel more like a project for him. A stray his alpha instincts are telling him to protect.

I'm not bitter about it. Honestly, I get it. I felt those same instincts when I saw Quentin pushing Jason around in the school parking lot. I felt them when the beta silenced Lucy at lunch yesterday.

Jeb. What a dick-face.

I understand that drive to protect the weak. Except, unlike Cody, it's an instinct I can't afford to follow.

Unfortunately, it's an instinct that is getting stronger.

Being on Clear Creek land is torture for my wolf. When I'm here, my wolf's instincts rise to a fever pitch. The need to belong, to be part of a pack - it's so strong, I can taste it. So is the disappointment and inexplicable shame that come with each little rejection. Each reminder that I'm an outsider. A loner. And I'll always be one.

I'm suddenly hit with the need to run. To have cold wind cut my cheeks as my feet pound against dried earth.

I should go visit Jamison. Hang out in his forest for a bit. Give my wolf a break.

"Can you give me a lift back to my grandparent's place?" I ask.

"Yah, sure." Cody gives a smile, but it's forced.

I would bet my Air Jordan's his mind is still on the conversation he was having with Summer. On whatever went down in that meeting with his parents and Lawrence Smith.

"You don't want to stay for lunch?" he asks.

"Nah." There's no way I'm sitting down at that table with all of them again. "Thanks though."

Lunch yesterday was bad enough. I don't know why they all have to eat together anyway. The rest of the pack eat at their own houses on the ranch.

I'm half expecting Cody to push the issue, but he just shrugs. "Okay then, let me grab my keys."

Then it dawns on me that maybe he's just as eager to escape lunch as I am. Especially given his blatant dislike of this Lawrence Smith fellow who is still visiting.

We're in his truck, ambling along the gravel road that leads from the ranch to the freeway when my curiosity gets the better of me.

"What's this exchange business all about?" I ask. "Are they trying to get you to change packs?"

As soon as the questions leaves my mouth, I want to shove it back in. I'm dumb as a brick for asking. Cody made it pretty clear yesterday that he wasn't allowed to tell me anything. And now I'm basically advertising that I was eavesdropping on his and Summer's conversation.

Cody narrows his eyes at me before flicking his gaze back to the road. His fingers flex on the steering wheel, knuckles going white. After a long silence he bites out: "I'm not changing packs."

I just give him a sardonic smile because, yah. I figured that much, buddy.

He frowns. "You're not supposed to know about this stuff anyway."

I shrug. "Well, I know what I know. Shifter hearing and all."

I figure its best to leave out the eavesdropping part. The part where I stood and listened to their little lovers' spat like some nosy tween.

When Cody doesn't offer up any more information, I decide to prod a bit further. Recalling a bit of his conversation with Summer I ask: "So what, does some other pack need an alpha or something?"

"Something like that," Cody grinds out.

"So why go now? Why not wait until later?"

"Because they want more than just an alpha." Cody lets out an exasperated breath. "Look man, I'm really not supposed to tell you this. But you've been cool. And after the whole Jason incident, I think you're pretty loyal, whatever the rest of the pack say."

By Jason incident, I guess he means when I lost control of my wolf and nearly murdered Quentin? I'm not sure how that is a factor in my favour. But hey, I'll take what I can get.

Cody runs one hand through his hair, the fingers of his other hand tapping against the steering wheel, as if he's trying to communicate in morse code.

Finally, he says: "There's this pack in North Dakota that lost its alpha, and also has a shortage of young male wolves. They want to send a female down to our pack in exchange for me going up there. They'd want me to come up straight away though, because having a pack without an alpha is bad news. It creates this power vacuum, and if no alpha comes in then you start having other dominant wolves in the pack fighting each other for dominance."

Cody shakes his head, dark curls falling across his forehead. "Whatever. It's not my problem. Not our pack's problem."

"But your dad doesn't agree?"

It's a question I suspect I already know the answer to. No way would Cody be so upset unless his parents were pushing him to move up north.

"Dad thinks it's a great opportunity," Cody scoffs, then continues in a mock serious tone. "'An alpha position doesn't come up every day, son. You should seize the opportunity now or you'll risk missing your chance.'"

"Man, that sucks."

"It would, if I was going." Cody gives a dark laugh. "But I'm not."

"Can't they make you?"

I was under the impression that Cooper was packing a lot more dominance than Cody. While it's probably at least partially owing to their age difference, it doesn't change the fact that Cody's dad is a more dominant wolf, even if they both have alpha level dominance.

Cody doesn't respond, his silence telling me everything. They can make him, he's just in denial about it. Or hoping that it won't come to that.

I suddenly feel a pang of sympathy for Cody.

It surprises me, because on the surface, the guy has everything. His family is rich. Everyone at school likes and respects him – even the human kids and the teachers. He's literally the embodiment of prime teenage maleness – good looking, the star quarter-back. He gets good grades, and drives a new truck.

But at the end of the day, he's just like me. With no control over his own destiny, at the mercy of others.

There are no invisible gods controlling the strings of fate for him, any more than for me.

My wolf surges forward protectively. *Pack. Cody is pack*, the animal seems to say. *Protect him.*

I want to roll my eyes because the last thing Cody needs is protection from a lone wolf who lives with his grandparents and doesn't even have a driver's license.

But somehow, I find myself saying: "If you ever need anything – if they make you leave the pack or whatever – let me know and I'll do what I can to help you. I've got your back."

My promise thuds like an awkward present between us. I half expect Cody to scoff at it. Because I have no idea what sort of help I could offer him. Also, I'm not sure I even want to be his friend.

To my surprise, Cody nods solemnly. "Thanks man. Appreciate it."

Chapter 11

Tobias Finch

"Most the pack are a-holes."

I've run across to Jamison's forest, to spend the last of my weekend with him under dripping pines, letting my irritation with the Clear Creek pack fade with the late afternoon sun.

"I think you've got the right idea, hanging out in these woods by yourself."

Jamison huffs in reply, knocking his furry head into my shoulder. The playful move nearly knocks me off my feet.

"It's no joke. Lucy basically tried to have me killed, remember? Using a bull as her hired thug, but still."

Strangely, that doesn't bother me so much anymore. It was the worst physical pain I've ever experienced, but at the end of the day, it was temporary. Over pretty quickly all things considered.

"Yesterday, the beta basically called me a stray in front of everyone. I can tell most of the others think the same."

For some reason, that lack of acceptance hurts more than what Lucy did.

The wolf lets out a low growl.

"Yah, yah, simmer down." I shrug. "I think the beta is a jerk to pretty much everyone." Including his own daughter. "Cody's got my back though – whether I want him to or not, apparently. And Summer is nice. Jason likes me too I think, but it's hard to tell with him. He's super quiet…"

My rambling trails off. None of them would like me if they found out what I really am.

Jamison must be thinking the same thing – or maybe years of being in wolf form has given him the ability to read a person's moods – because golden eyes shoot me a sad look. Eyes that look more and more human each time I come to visit.

I've been talking to him a lot lately. There is something cathartic in being able to talk to someone who can only listen and can't respond. If he could respond, I feel like Jamison wouldn't sugar-coat things for me. He isn't one of those adults who would say "people will like you better once they get to know the real you" and "just be yourself".

He knows better than anyone what a lie that would be. How deadly it could be to be myself.

"I wish you could shift," I muse absently. He gives me a look that I can't interpret, serious and thoughtful.

"I could try giving you an alpha command, like I did to grandpa," I suggest half-heartedly. We've already tried this a few times with no success. I'm not surprised it didn't work, since neither Cody nor Cooper's alpha commands affected me.

But, it seems hope is persistent as a cockroach. Like, you can set that thing on fire, run it over with a truck, and spray it with insecticide and it will still be making its home in the cracks of your foundations.

I sit down on a fallen log near Jamison's den, rubbing my temples.

"Dad and I shared a pack link," I muse. "The few times dad was in wolf form he communicated with me that way. You know, telepathically." I tap my head.

Jamison sits up straighter, fixing me with his intelligent gaze.

"Do you have a link like that with grandpa?" I ask. He doesn't answer and I sigh in frustration. There must be a way for him to communicate yes or no. I close my eyes, thinking.

And then I remember something. I read the *Count of Monte Cristo* a while back. In that book, there was an old man who had a disease that prevented him from moving his whole body, except his eyes. He communicated with his granddaughter by blinking.

An excited grin splits my face.

"Hey, let's try something."

I rub my palms on my jeans to warm them. The early snow from October has melted, but November is still ridiculously cold in Buffalo. Especially sitting under the thick shade of a pine forest right before sundown.

"Blink once to answer yes to a question, and twice to answer no," I say.

I can't believe I haven't thought of this before. I'm such an idiot. But also maybe a genius, because this is totally going to work.

The wolf stares at me, unblinking. A feeling of dread creeps up in my gut. What if he can't really understand me at all? What if he has actually gone so wolf, after decades of being trapped in this form, and then years without grandpa visiting, that he's gone feral? I swallow the lump in my throat, and try again.

"Do you have a pack link with grandpa?"

There is a long moment where Jamison just stares at me. Then one deliberate blink. *Yes.*

I exhale the breath I didn't realize I was holding. Okay. Awesome. He can understand. This also explains how grandpa and Jamison have been able to communicate.

"How does it work?" I pause, realising instantly that he won't be able to answer that, then try again. "Can you communicate with him from here?"

Grandpa is still at home because grandma doesn't think he's well enough to go hiking out into the woods in the middle of winter. Grandpa has been calling grandma his jailor, referring to their room as 'the cell'...

Needless to say, grandma is not impressed by his behaviour.

Two blinks. *No.*

Okay, no wonder grandpa is feeling frustrated, if he can't talk to his brother.

"You have to be close to him?"

One blink. *Yes.*

"Could you and I have a pack link?

Jamison doesn't respond for so long I think he's not going to answer. Then he slowly blinks once.

"Do you know how to make one?"

I have no recollection of how dad created the link with me. It was there as long as I could remember. For all I know, we were born with it.

Another slow blink.

"Will you?" I ask excitedly. "Will you make one with me?"

It seems the obvious solution to this whole communication problem. My wolf is practically leaping at the thought, at the idea of having a pack. Me, Jamison, and grandpa.

I am surprised when Jamison blinks twice. *No.*

"Why not?"

Of course, he can't answer that, and a growl of frustration rumbles in my chest, so low I would almost think it was coming from my stupid latent wolf, not me.

"Come on," I urge.

Again, two blinks.

Seriously?

"What, do you like being alone?" I ask, disappointment stinging my eyes, catching in my throat.

I sound like a petulant child. To be honest, feel like one right now. I thought he enjoyed my coming to visit him, talk to him. He always seemed happy to see me.

Clearly, I was wrong.

To my surprise, Jamison lets out a whine, staring at me longingly before blinking twice. *No.*

I furrow my brow, trying to sort this all out. "Lemmie get this straight. You do like me visiting you?"

One blink.

"But you don't want to talk?"

Two blinks.

Okay. This blinking thing is actually super confusing.

"So you want me to visit and you want us to talk. But you don't want the pack link?" I ask, brow furrowing because this makes absolutely no sense. Maybe being alone for so long has damaged him after all.

One blink. Yes.

"Wait. So you do want the pack link?"

Two blinks. No.

Well. What in the actual - ? I lean forward on my log seat to rest my forehead in the palm of my hands.

A wet nose pushes against my hands, and I lift my head. Jamison's golden orbs are full of unmistakable apology. He likes me visiting and wants to talk with me. So why won't he form a pack link with me?

I PLAN to ask grandpa as much when I get back to the house that evening, but I can't seem to get him alone. Since grandma doesn't know about Jamison, or about shifters at all, there is no way that I can talk to him about this in front of her.

"How was the ranch, dear?" Grandma asks at dinner as she piles meatloaf onto my plate.

"Good."

Grandpa's eyes are fixed on me. I can tell he wants more information, but he's not going to ask for it. Which is good, because I don't really feel like talking about the Clear Creek pack. I take a big bite of meatloaf. Can't answer questions if I've got my mouth full of food.

"The Winslow's are nice people," grandma says conversationally. "And their land is some of the prettiest in this area, don't you think."

"Uh-huh."

"I understand a few of the kids from your school live out on the ranch, is that right?"

"Yah."

"Are you making friends with them?"

"Yep."

If convincing them not to kill me counts as making friends, then yes. Yes, I am.

Grandpa raises one eyebrow, the corner of his lips quirking into a smile at my monosyllabic responses. He knows how much I hate talking about the pack. I resist the urge to roll my eyes. I'll fill him in on everything later.

I can't even tell grandma about working with the horses, because that would lead to questions as to why I'm doing horse therapy or whatever it is. I haven't exactly been eager to tell her I beat the crap out of some kid at school. I'm hoping that little nugget of intel will stay between grandpa and me.

It's close to eleven at night when grandma falls asleep and I finally get grandpa alone. He moves with the silent stealth of a wolf now, appearing in my doorway without a sound. I sit up in bed, and he pulls my desk chair up beside me, fixing me with his keen amber eyes.

I tell him about the horse therapy, about the conversations with the pack at meal times. When I get to the information about Lawrence Smith, he leans forward, his interest piqued.

"It sounds like a traditional pack exchange to strengthen bloodlines," he muses, shaking his head in disbelief. "Even when I was a pup those were considered old-fashioned. It's basically the equivalent of an arranged mating. Not that your friend Cody would have to mate anyone specifically, but it would be expected that he'd mate with someone in the new pack."

"Yah… I'm pretty sure he's not up for that."

I recall the anger on Cody's face after he spoke with his parents, and the things I heard him say to Summer.

Then, without any preamble, I move to what is really bothering me. "Why is Jamison against creating a pack link with me?"

Grandpa's bushy eyebrows shoot up, disappearing beneath his hairline. "What on earth are you talking about?" he drawls.

I explain my pseudo-conversation with Jamison.

"You can communicate with him, so obviously you two already have some sort of pack link. He said he wants to be able to communicate with me too, but he doesn't want to form a pack link." I shake my head. "It doesn't make any sense."

Not to mention it's pissing me off. I hike out to visit this old bugger at least once a week. People don't even visit their grandparents in nursing homes that often, and you can drive to those. And they're indoors, with heating.

Making it so he could communicate with me is the least he can do.

"Hmm," grandpa rubs the grey stubble on his jaw, considering. "There might be something in it. What do you know about pack links?"

"Well…" I'm always embarrassed by how little I actually know about shifter lore. My parents tried to raise me as human as possible, believing I would be safest hidden in the human world. "I had a pack link with my dad."

"Do you remember how it was created?"

I shake my head.

He sighs, steeling himself for another lesson of all the obvious things I should know but don't.

"Pack links - or pack bonds - are made by a blood exchange with an alpha. Traditionally, a pack member would consume a small amount of the alpha's blood and give some of his or her blood to the alpha in exchange."

I scrunch up my nose. "What, like drinking blood?"

Seriously, gross.

"Exactly." Grandpa's cheeks creases into a wry smile. "That's typically how it's done, but some packs take a more civilised approach and exchange blood in a handshake or something similar. The main thing is the exchange, not the method."

I nod. Suddenly the alpha's concerns about my blood transfusion from Cody make a lot more sense. Though obviously no pack link could be formed without me also giving blood to Cody.

"Though it's not enough to just exchange blood," grandpa continues. "There has to be an oath from the alpha. Usually, it's something along the lines of an alpha swearing to lead and protect. In exchange, pack members give an oath of obedience. I mean, alphas can be compelling using dominance, but they can't require absolute obedience. They need the oath for that."

Unlike born alphas, he doesn't need to say. Born alphas can require obedience from any wolf, even wolves who aren't pack.

Which is one of the major problems with my kind of wolf. Why I am a disruption to the natural order. An aberration of the worst kind.

"Okay, so why can't Jamison and I do a blood exchange?" I ask.

"In order for a pack link to be formed, there needs to be an alpha. One shifter vowing to protect and lead his pack."

I shrug because, yah, I got that much. Thanks grandpa.

Grandpa narrows his eyes. "Tell me, Tobias Finch, out of you and Jamison, who is the alpha?"

"Jamison," I answer unhesitatingly. My wolf growls, disagreeing with my statement.

He gives a sad smile. "Is that so?"

Then it dawns on me. "I'm an alpha," I whisper.

It's a fact I've spent my whole life hiding. Alpha. Alpha. The word tastes sooty on my tongue.

"So, who would give the oath? You? Or Jamison?"

Well, shoot.

"Couldn't we both give the oath? Or couldn't one of us be more alpha than the other?" I know before I ask that both are ridiculous propositions.

"No." Grandpa gives me a look that says he thinks I'm short a few brain cells. "That's the whole point of a born alpha. Unmatched dominance. The ultimate alpha. Not to mention your wolf would never submit to another alpha. And Jamison's would never either."

As soon as he says it, I know it's true. My wolf wants a pack. To the point of obsession. But he would never accept Jamison's leadership or protection. He wants to protect. To lead.

He wants his own pack.

I sigh, flopping down onto the bed, sinking into the too-small mattress covered with the worn pink blankets that used to belong to my mom. They smell of dust and cigarettes. I wish they smelt of her, but her apple and mint scent would have faded from this house years ago. She hasn't been here for years, as far as I know. Not since before I was born.

Grandpa leaves the room as silently as he came. He knows our conversation is over.

So that's it then. No pack.

Chapter 12

Tobias Finch

"That's him," a girl whispers to her friend in the hall. I think she's a junior, but I'm not really sure. "That's the boy who beat up Quentin Slade."

"No way," her friend whisper-yells. "The new boy? He's only a sophomore."

"I know, right." The first girl sighs.

I cast a glance in her direction and she blushes before reaching up to toy with her sandy coloured hair. It's one of those gestures I've never understood. Maybe girls think it looks cute or flirtatious, but I think it just makes them look fidgety. My wolf huffs in annoyance and I quickly look away.

I start to make my way to the library, my paper bag lunch clutched so tight I'm probably squashing the peanut butter and jelly sandwich inside. The two girls trail after me, whispering and giggling. They're going the opposite direction of everyone else, walking away from the cafeteria.

They're probably just going to work on a project or something in one of the classrooms. The feeling of being hunted, followed, stalked – that is all in my head. Just my being on edge from all the wolf stuff.

I inwardly cringe when I hear their footsteps following me into the library.

"Mind if we sit with you?" the sandy haired girl asks as soon as I sit at my usual spot in the library.

I stare at her wordlessly for a long moment, then look pointedly at the two other empty tables.

"Why?" I ask, drawing out the word.

I've been coming to the library to eat lunch for almost six weeks now and no one – literally, no one – has come in here during the lunch period.

She gives a breathy giggle and shifts from one foot to the other nervously, looking at her friend for support. "Well – we just thought – you looked so alone and you're new, maybe you wanted the company."

Not sure how she reaches that conclusion when I've been hiding out in the library with the sole aim of avoiding people. I quirk a brow. "I'm good, thanks."

She giggles again and sits down anyway, choosing the chair right beside me, her friend following suit.

"I'm Vanessa and this is Sofia. We're both on the cheerleading squad, but I don't think we've seen you at any of the games." Vanessa lets out an exaggerated pout. "You're on the wrestling team, right? I bet you work out a lot." She drags out the last word, reaching up to squeeze my bicep. Fake nails drag across my bare skin and I shudder.

I stand up abruptly, chair toppling back with the movement. "I - I just remembered I'm supposed to meet someone in the cafeteria." I swipe my lunch sack off the table and practically sprint for the door.

Surprised laughter follows me, then fades when the library doors shut. I barrel down the hall towards the cafeteria, cursing the Wyoming winter weather for making it much too cold to eat outside.

Initially, I plan to enter the cafeteria unnoticed by the pack, find an empty seat, and eat my sandwich alone. Unfortunately, Cody and the rest of the group are sitting at the table closest to the doors I enter at.

Cody's nostrils flare as my scent hits his nose and the entire pack turns to look at me, with the exception of Anton, who is staring at his phone. Lucy narrows her eyes at me before flicking her blond ponytail over one shoulder, giving me her back. Cody grins with his perfect white teeth and those ridiculous dimples, looking genuinely happy to see me.

"Tobes," he calls out, "Good to see you, buddy. Grab a seat."

Tobes. Buddy.

Ugh.

Before I can come up with an excuse to leave, the two girls from the library come barrelling through the doors behind me. Without thinking, I sit down, squeezing into the seat between Jason and Anton. Anton grunts his disapproval, but doesn't take his eyes off his phone.

Curiosity gets the better of me and I glance over his shoulder, catching a screen full of chat bubbles with the words 'Mate' at the top. Not Tori. Just 'Mate'. I roll my eyes. Gross.

Summer notices what I'm looking at and must catch my expression because she presses her lips together in an effort to bite back laughter.

"How is Tori?" I ask, only to get a reaction from Anton.

The guy is so over-protective of his still unclaimed mate that he growls every time another male says her name. Which is exactly what he does now, just as he pulls his phone to his chest, as if he's hiding her from view with the movement.

Summer's laugh erupts from across the table. She knows I'm baiting him and hasn't missed a second of Anton's response. Lucy glares at me even as her lips twitch with amusement, and it hits me that if anyone's fed up with Anton's mate-frenzy-crazed antics, it must be her.

This thought makes my wolf give a little smug huff. I'm not sure if its because the animal likes that Lucy might secretly be on the same page as me, or if the deranged creature just enjoys seeing Lucy irritated.

"So, you're back to eating with us, hey Tobes? Finished up that project you've been working on?" He gives an exaggerated wink, making air quotes with his hands as he says the word 'project'.

"Something like that," I shrug, trying to ignore the hurt that flashes in his eyes as my gaze darts around the cafeteria, looking around for my two stalkers. They've found seats at a table with a bunch of other girls. Girls from their cheerleading squad by the looks of them. The sandy haired girl – Vanessa – flashes me a toothy grin when she catches me looking at her.

"How was the last meet?" I ask Jason, changing the subject. "I heard we came up on top."

"Yah, we did," Jason's eyes glitter with excitement. "But we should have scored higher. We would have, if you and Quentin had been able to compete."

I flinch.

Coach banned me from competing for three weeks after the little Quentin-beat-down incident. Three weeks is a really long time at this point in the season, and even though I'm training, I'm worried being benched for so long is going to impact on my performance, not to mention our team's ranking.

As if reading my thoughts, Cody gives me a conciliatory pat on the shoulder. "Just two weeks to go." Technically it's two weeks and three days. But hey, who's counting.

I shrug, as if being benched doesn't bother me.

"Better prognosis than Quentin," Jason chirps cheerfully. "Ross told me Quentin won't be back at school until next week at the earliest and he might be off for the rest of the season."

"What a cry-baby," I mutter under my breath. Jason furrows his brow and I quickly add: "Quentin. Not Ross."

After beating Quentin to a bloody pulp, the guilt made me feel sympathetic to the guy. Now that I know he's going to live and I'm not going to go to jail or get suspended, my animosity towards the prick has returned in full force.

When Jason doesn't say anything, I add: "I hope Ross isn't too upset about it."

Not because I really care what Ross thinks. I don't. But out of all the pack, Jason's not half bad. And obviously Ross is his friend.

"Oh, he's not that upset. At least, he shouldn't be." Jason's expression turns dark, almost aggressive. It's an unexpected look for an omega wolf.

I exchange an inquiring glance with Cody and Summer. Summer leans forward, whispering loudly: "Ross is a loaded topic where Jason is concerned."

"Ross' dad is an abusive prick. Quentin isn't much better." Jason bites out.

My eyebrows fly up in surprise, and Jason continues, tone quiet and lethal.

"Their dad is a drinker. The angry kind," Jason sneers. "Quentin doesn't do what he should to protect his little brother. He's just as big as his dad, and he sits back and lets the man hurt Ross. I think he even eggs him on."

My eyes widen in surprise, wondering how he knows this, when I remember Quentin accusing Jason of staking out the Slade's house. "Dude. You saw this?" I ask, keeping my voice low.

Jason nods.

"Shit." Quentin might be a jerk, but that doesn't mean he deserves a crappy dad. I surreptitiously glance at Ross Slade, a few tables down from us. He's short, probably barely over five and half feet, with a huge smile that radiates out from him like sunshine. There isn't a single person in the school who doesn't like Ross. Like, you'd have to be the sort of person who hates puppies and kittens to dislike Ross. I can't imagine anyone trying to hurt someone so friendly. My wolf lets out a low, angry rumble at the thought.

"I know." Jason's hands clench into fists at either side of his lunch tray. "And I can't do a damn thing about it because alpha Winslow has ordered me to stand down." His voice is laced with bitterness.

Cody lets out a long sigh from across the table, expression unreadable. Summer's brown eyes are filled with pity.

"At least you haven't been ordered to stay away from him," Anton offers unhelpfully, glancing up dazedly from his phone's screen. "If the alphas think you're going to try and mark him, or show your wolf, or something equally stupid, then you're going to get banned from seeing him. You know that, right?"

"I'd like to see them try," Jason grinds out, a red flush creeping up his pimple-reddend cheeks. Of course, we all know that they wouldn't have to try. They would just give an alpha command and that would be that.

Anton lifts his chin, looking down at Jason with an air of superiority. "You haven't told the alphas yet, have you?"

Jason looks down at his pizza, frowning.

"Told them what?" I ask.

"Jason thinks Ross is his mate," Summer whispers.

"Ahh." Jason's behaviour makes total sense now. I'm not even surprised, given with how crazy Jason is acting. I mean, sure, he's sixteen, which is super young to recognise your true mate. But stranger things have happened.

"So what?" I take a bite of my sandwich, then eye Summer's pizza enviously. Packed lunches are so not my jam. "What's the big deal?"

It can't be because they're both guys. I might not know heaps about mating, but I do recall my dad telling me that same-sex matings have been acceptable in the shifter world for a lot longer than same-sex marriage in the human world. As a gender studies professor, it was one of those factoids he found interesting.

Anton looks at me like I've just come out as a proponent of the flat-Earth theory. "What's the big deal?" he asks mockingly, keeping his voice low enough so it won't be heard by the neighbouring tables. "Are you that much of an idiot, Finch. We can't mate with humans, for one. Two, we can't expose ourselves to humans..."

I shrug. "My dad mated a human." Of course, I now know this isn't strictly correct. Mom was half shifter. But I don't think she or dad ever knew that.

"Plus, the rules on humans don't apply where mates are concerned," I recited, recalling another titbit my dad had told me. Mainly because its fate who decide your true mate. And the long-term effects of not claiming your true mate can be deadly.

"Yah, and look how well mixing bloodlines turned out where you are concerned. A latent wolf with rage issues." Anton scoffs.

Cody sits up straight, fixing his piercing gaze on Anton. "That's enough, Ant."

His voice is low, calm, but there is no mistaking the command in it. Anton bristles, then adjusts his neon green bomber jacket – another gift from Tori, no doubt - before turning back to his phone.

"You're going to have to tell them," Summer reminds Jason gently.

"I know." Jason's voice is so low, it's barely audible. He looks like he's going to be sick.

"Would they really prevent Jason from marking a human?" I ask Summer, "Like, if that's his true mate…"

It's Cody that answers. "Unfortunately, yes." He scrubs one hand down his face. "Some packs allow members to mate with humans. But not ours."

"That's messed up," I say.

I'm not a romantic, but love is love. Or mating instinct is mating instinct. Whatever. Socially constructed rules shouldn't get in the way of someone being with the person who – literally - holds the other half of their soul.

Cody frowns. "It's pack rules."

"Not all rules are worth keeping," I retort, staring at him dead on, "or worth following." I've completely forgotten that I'm supposed to be a submissive wolf. Honestly, between the horse therapy and spending time with Jamison and grandpa, it's getting harder and harder to suppress the alpha instinct, to hide my dominance.

Cody narrows his eyes at me, and I can practically feel his wolf surge close to the surface. Like it feels my dominance, and wants to respond to it. To challenge it. Or maybe to follow it? My wolf likes that thought.

I look down at my plate, but I can still feel Cody's scrutinising gaze boring into me. There's a long silence, then Cody says softly: "That might be the case, but it doesn't change the facts. If the alphas order Jason to stay away from the human, he'll have to obey." There's a tinge of sadness in his proclamation, and I wonder if he's thinking about the fallout he had with his parents after that North Dakota wolf, Lawrence Smith, came to visit.

Before I can reply, the bell rings, calling us back to class.

My wolf is agitated as I traipse down the hall to class. The animal was already wound up about Cody being forced out to some North Dakota pack. Now the defective thing is freaking out about Jason not being able to claim his mate. Not to mention worried about the human – Ross Slade – being hurt.

I give my head a dog-like shake, trying to clear my thoughts. It doesn't work.

Instead, images of Lucy sitting at the lunch table flash through my head. She hadn't said a word the whole time. Didn't even offer up her usual biting commentary. It's strange, and for some reason her silence has my wolf on edge more than anything else.

Chapter 13

Tobias Finch

"Your dad never mentioned where his pack was from?"

It's not the first time grandpa has asked me this question.

"No," I sigh. "Never."

"Hmm."

He trudges ahead of me, boots crunching the dry grass that blankets the foothills behind our house. Winter sun glares low on the horizon, even though it's nearly midday.

After promising that I'll stick by grandpa's side, grandma has finally agreed to let him out for a walk. I can practically feel the nervous energy emanating from him – or perhaps it's his wolf – in anticipation of shifting and running in the forest.

"I think it was in the mountains. His pack." I say.

The words tumble out as a memory of conversations with my dad burst to life, vivid as the pink cumulous clouds gathering above the Little Bighorns.

"We went camping once and dad talked about going camping in the mountains close to his pack when he was a pup. He said they had to store food up in trees so bears wouldn't raid their campsite."

Grandpa stills briefly, amber eyes glowing with interest at this piece of information.

"Bear country, then," he murmurs. "Did he say anything else about it? Anything about the landmarks or other pack members?"

The scent of charcoal, pine and animal. A rough voice answered by my father's growls, speaking my father's name.

"Why is it so important?" I snap abruptly.

Brick by brick, I've been erecting a wall between my now and the past. The world where I had parents, my life in New York.

I don't need to dredge up memories that chisel away at that wall. Because on the other side of it, the wound is as fresh as my mom's blood on the kitchen floor. It's there when I do the horse therapy sessions with Ms. Crossguns. It's there in that dream space at night, when the wall becomes a gauze curtain.

I don't know, maybe that sort of pain never fades. I sure as shit don't want to feel it right now. I just want to feel the winter sun on my back, the cold mountain wind cut across my bare face and hands.

At the very least, I want to be numb.

"It's important because they know you exist," grandpa replies, the forced calmness in his voice barely masking his irritation. "If there's a predator hunting you, at the very least you should know what it is, where it's attacking from."

I shouldn't have told him about that night. But he'd asked, and I only figured he had a right to know, since she was his daughter. His only child.

I hate that he's right. They will come for me. It's only a matter of time.

I shrug. "So what if they find me?"

With a growl, he rounds on me with surprising speed, grabbing me by the shoulders so tight I'm sure his fingertips will leave bruises.

"If they find you, you're dead," he hisses, leaning close to my face. "If you think I'm going to let you put yourself and Jamison at risk, you've got another thing coming, boy. Not to mention Susie. You think killers like that care if some human gets in the way? You need to start talking. Start answering some questions."

My wolf bristles, baring his teeth at the old man. I push the aggression down. Even with how pissed I am, I know the old man is right. My very presence is a danger to my grandparents, to Jamison. Maybe even to the Clear Creek pack.

It doesn't change the fact that I'm sick of his questions. Sick of him prying into my darkest memories. I narrow my eyes at him, leaning into his hold on me, pressing my face closer to his.

"Why don't you answer some questions first? Like what happened between you and mom? I know she wasn't speaking to you."

It's a question that has plagued my mind every night I've spent in that pink floral bedroom. My grandparents kept mom's childhood room pretty much intact, but I never remember her calling them. I'd never met them before my parents' death, when my grandparent's inherited guardianship over me.

I expect grandpa to deny it, or maybe lash out defensively. Instead, he releases his grip on me, his arms going slack at his sides before he reaches up and rubs his wrinkled face with one hand.

"Yah," he says after a long silence. An icy breeze whips around us, chilling whatever warmth there was from the winter sun, and grandpa looks towards the tree-line ahead of us. "I figured you'd ask that eventually."

He continues walking towards Jamison's forest in long strides, as if maybe he can walk away from the question hanging in the air between us. I keep pace beside him.

"It was my fault," he finally says, not breaking stride, keeping his face turned towards the mountains. "Though I didn't see it until it was too late. Until she was gone." The last word catches in his throat, as if his voice doesn't want to accept it. Gone. Mom is gone.

"Marian went away to college in Missoula," grandpa explains, eyes distant, as if he's staring into the past instead of the trees ahead. "It was her first year of college. Her first year away from home. She was only eighteen years old and she called us up, saying she'd met a guy. Finneas Finch." My father's name falls off his lips like a bad taste. "She said they were in love and she was getting married. They wanted to get hitched over spring break, right up there in Montana. She wanted us to come up for the wedding, to give her our blessing and all that." Grandpa huffs, shaking his head. "They were both so young." He sighs, regret sinking into the lines etched on his face, hardening his already jagged features. "I told her we wouldn't come to the wedding unless your father drove down to Buffalo and asked for her hand in marriage, all proper like you know. She said they didn't have money for the gas, and it was too far to drive for a weekend anyway. I said if he was a real man who wanted to support my daughter, he'd find a way to do it. In the end, he didn't come, and so we didn't go up to the wedding."

I wait for grandpa to continue, expecting some dramatic turn of events that could sensibly lead to my mom refusing to speak to her parents for my entire life, but there's nothing. For a long moment the only sound is the crunching of dry grass and earth beneath our boots.

Then I say: "So what, she stopped speaking to you after you refused to go to the wedding?"

For some reason that doesn't seem like my mom. She wasn't the kind to get angry, to hold a grudge. She was soft. Sweet. Forgiving. The complete opposite of me.

"No, not quite." Grandpa rubs at his chest. "After you were born, they moved to New York and she tried to get us out there to visit.

She wanted us to meet our grandchild. You. Susie wanted to go. But I said if they wanted us to see you, they'd have to bring you to us."

"Why?" I ask. "Just because dad didn't come ask for permission to marry mom?"

"Pretty much." Grandpa barks out a mirthless laugh. "I was a goddamned idiot."

I shake my head, truly dumbfounded. It sounds like the stupidest reason ever to hold a grudge.

As if reading my thoughts, grandpa says: "Sometimes we wear our anger for so long, we forget it's just a mask to hide our fears. Letting go of that anger and forgiving someone, well that's just too much like admitting how wrong we were in the first place. I was a coward, Tobias. A prideful coward."

We've reached the tree-line, and I duck my head under the thick pine boughs as I follow the trail towards Jamison's den. I'm not sure how to respond to grandpa's confession, to the pain that laces his admission. So I remain silent as memories of my parents barrage the barriers I've built in my mind.

The way they looked at each other, so full of love that it would make me cringe in embarrassment. The photo from their wedding day that hung in the hallway of our apartment in New York – two young people dressed in white against a backdrop of melting snow and rugged, wild looking mountains.

"The worst of it is," grandpa continues, "is that if I'd met Finneas, I would have scented that he was a wolf shifter. I could have told Marian about what I really was, and warned them about the risk of having a born alpha pup."

I frown. If they had been warned, would it have stopped them from having me? Is that what grandpa is saying? That it would have been better if I had never been born?

Since both my parents are dead because of me, they definitely would have been better off without me. My shoulders slump under the crushing weight of that realisation.

We're almost at Jamison's den when I pause, thinking of something, sparked by the memory of my parents' wedding photo.

"Do you think they got married near dad's pack lands?"

After meeting the Clear Creek pack, it seems plausible. The Clear Creek pack is so in everyone's business, no doubt they'd want all weddings to be held on pack land, or close by. Probably other packs are the same.

Grandpa nods. "Yes, it's definitely possible."

"Did mom ever send you any wedding photos?"

"You know, I think she did," grandpa replies, brow wrinkling in thought. "I'll see if Susan stored them somewhere when we get home."

Grandpa turns towards the rocky outcrop where Jamison's den is hidden.

"Hello Jamison," he says.

I know he's speaking out loud for my benefit. He's probably been communicating with his brother the second we reached the trees.

Jamison slinks out from behind two large boulders, his breath puffing in clouds around his face. I'm always a little surprised by how big he is, even though I've been coming to see him almost every weekend for months now. I tilt my chin at him in silent greeting, and he huffs in reply before coming up and pressing his head under against my shoulder in an unusual display of affection. I shoot grandpa a confused look.

"I told him about our conversation from a few weeks ago," grandpa explains, shrugging. "He wanted you to know that he would have liked to share a pack link with you. If it was possible."

Warmth coils around my chest like a band, a mix of longing and gratitude. I stroke the fur between Jamison's ears. It's softer than it looks.

"Thanks," I mutter, the word catching in my throat.

I sit with grandpa and Jamison under the icy shade of the pine trees until the sun starts to dip close to the horizon. It's different coming to visit Jamison with grandpa.

When it's just me, I talk to Jamison, as if the silence needs to be filled with my one-sided ramblings. With grandpa here, the silence seems full. I guess it's because the two of them are talking over the bond.

I listen to the sounds the birds make as they scratch for food in the underbrush, to the faint wind whispering in the branches above my head, to the steady rhythm of my own heart.

When grandpa finally rises to his feet, joints creaking stiffly, I turn to Jamison.

"Its winter break now, so I'll be able to come visit you more often, okay?"

Jamison blinks once in reply. I guess he means "Yes" or "okay", and I give a small smile.

I don't mention that I'm going to spend a few days at the Clear Creek pack territory after Christmas. Talking about the pack seems to make Jamison a bit edgy. I'll tell him about my visit to the pack when I come see him next.

After its happened.

…

My ears prick at the sound of Cody's truck when it turns onto our street, at least ten houses away from our driveway. Even latent, my shifter hearing has always been good, just like my sense of smell and my vision.

It's gotten stronger, sharper, since I've arrived in Buffalo. My wolf has become more vocal too, pressing himself against my will until my skin feels hot and stretched, my mind buzzing from the lupine instincts that frequently conflict with what is required of me as a human.

As usual, Summer is in the front seat beside Cody, a laughing smile on her face. Cody looks more serious than usual, with dark circles beneath his eyes and no sign of his usual dimples.

I sling my back pack over my shoulder as I trot out to meet them, feeling the weight of the extra clothes I've packed. Somehow, I've agreed to stay on pack territory for five days. Ostensibly to work with Ms. Crossguns and Misty. Though I'm starting to suspect the real reason is that Cody wants to keep an eye on me. Or his wolf does, driven by that alpha instinct to protect.

For the first time in my life, I get that. I felt that impulse when Quentin cornered Jason in the school parking lot. When the beta berated Lucy in front of the everyone at lunch. When Cody confessed that the pack might send him away.

I even feel strangely protective of Jamison, worrying about whether he's lonely up in the mountains. I even brought him some food for Christmas. I know he hunts, but I get the feeling he misses things like apple pie and roast turkey.

"Are you ready for a week of drama and intrigue with the Clear Creek pack?" Summer asks chirpily from the front seat.

"Five days," I remind her. I don't think I could last a week.

Summer just shrugs. "Tomato, tomato. It will feel like a week by the time you leave, because Tori just arrived last night. She's staying in the main house. With the alpha family. And you, of course."

I raise an eyebrow, fighting a smile. "Yah, so what?"

"She brought a whole suitcase full of clothes for Anton. No surprise there. Then this morning she woke us all up for a sunrise yoga session. She's a yoga instructor – did you know that?"

I just snort, trying to imagine Anton's bulky form bent and contorted into yoga poses.

"Lucy is not really into yoga. Or a morning person for that matter, and her and Anton have been at each other's throats since dawn. Anton went on and on about how she wasn't supportive of his mate, blah blah blah, until Lucy just shifted, right in the kitchen and took off. We haven't seen her since."

"She's probably just up at the waterfall," Cody drawls, the corner of his mouth curving up in a faint smile. "She'll come back when it's time for lunch."

"Do you think Anton will move to Tori's pack?" I ask, trying not to sound too hopeful.

Summer shrugs. "Maybe. I kind of hope so. Is that mean?"

She looks at Cody for a reaction, but his eyes are fixed on the road ahead of him.

"I know our pack needs more females, but Tori…" Summer trails off, biting her lip. "I guess I would just like someone who doesn't treat us all like we're a bunch of rednecks or something. I mean, yah, I know, Buffalo is a small town and we live on a ranch, but that doesn't mean we don't have access to the internet or television or fashion magazines. Not everyone has to be an influencer."

"Tori's an influencer?" The clothes she's been sending Anton suddenly make a lot more sense.

Summer rolls her eyes. "Oh yah. If you're lucky, she'll dismiss you as irrelevant. If she takes an interest in you, then watch out. She'll try to use you in one of her stories. Plaster your face and your personal information all over the internet."

Cold panic suddenly hits me, and I clench the seat. I've worked hard to keep a low profile, for obvious reasons. The last thing I need is my picture out there, advertising to the world where I am, that I'm linked up with the Clear Creek pack.

I shake my head. This is not good. Not good at all.

"You okay, Tobes?" Cody must sense my fear – maybe he can hear the way my heart speeds up or smell the metallic tang that accompanies a burst of adrenaline.

"Yep," I lie.

He shoots me a sideways glance that clearly says he doesn't believe me. I squirm.

"I'm just not a fan of having my photo taken," I say, opting for a half-truth.

"Uh-huh." Cody narrows his eyes. For someone who doesn't like to talk about his own personal business, or what he refers to as 'pack business', Cody is annoyingly nosy.

To change the subject, I round back on something Summer mentioned earlier. Something sure to make Cody back off.

"You said your pack needs more females? Is that why that Lawrence guy was on about the whole pack exchange thing?"

I can practically hear Cody's molars grinding. He's uncomfortable.

Good.

"Pretty much," Summer sighs, glancing nervously at Cody. "Though most packs have the opposite problem. Or at least, they don't have enough young male wolves."

"Why does that matter?" I ask.

Summer raises her eyebrows, as if to say 'Isn't it obvious?'

Maybe it should be, but I wasn't raised pack. I'm basically and outsider to my own species.

I just stare at her with a look of blank confusion.

Summer gives a strained smile. "Packs need enforcers, soldiers, whatever you want to call them. Even though packs very rarely war with each other, if one pack was to have too many young males, it would make the others nervous. They might think it was part of a bid to expand, win more territory…"

"Really?" I snort. "What is this, feudal Italy or something? And why can't female wolves be enforcers or whatever too?" I lean forward, resting my arms on the back of Summer's seat. "You guys aren't exactly weak or anything."

In fact, I am pretty sure Lucy would be a ruthless fighter. The girl's wolf packs a truck load of dominance. Plus, I'm honestly a little afraid of her after the whole attempted murder by bull attack incident.

Summer shoots me an amused look. "Only you would refer to female wolves as 'you guys'. And agreed. We are total bad-asses."

She shoots Cody a look that dares him to challenge this statement, but he wisely holds his tongue.

The amusement fades from her tone as she continues: "Unfortunately, humans aren't the only ones with an outdated system of patriarchy and gender-based oppression. A lot of packs – most packs, actually – don't let women hold positions of power or work as enforcers. Despite the indisputable fact that we are probably more capable than some of the males in those positions."

Cody gives a little scoff from the driver's seat.

"If you have something to add, please use your words Cody Raymond Winslow," Summer snaps, pivoting to face him.

He throws up his hands, momentarily letting go of the wheel. "I think it's worth noting..."

"Hands on the wheel!"

Cody drops his hands back to the wheel, letting out a low chuckle. "Look, maybe it's just because, historically, females tended to stay home with the pups. Males are more expendable."

Summer shakes her head. "That argument is not only a bunch of sexist crap, it has no basis in logic or reality. This isn't the 1950's anymore, no one stays at home playing housewife. I honestly doubt anyone did that in the 50's either. If they did, it was only because the patriarchy required women to forgo a career in favour of unpaid labour in the household…"

"Gods, Summer," Cody's shoulders shake as he tries to hold back a laugh.

"Oh, you think that's funny?" Summer pokes him hard in the ribs.

Cody grunts, but the grin hasn't faded from his face.

"You think oppression is funny?" Another jab. "You're no better than Jeb Stone, stirring up the toxic masculinity cool-aid for everyone in the pack to drink."

"The toxic – what?" Cody wrinkles his nose. "Honestly Summer, what are you even talking about?"

"Please. You saw how he treated his mate. How he treats Lucy. If he had his way, female wolves would be the property of their fathers or mates. Locked up and never allowed to leave pack territory."

I lean forward in my seat at the mention of Lucy.

"You're being dramatic," Cody argues. "Sure, Jeb's been a little over-protective of Lucy since Rachel left. That doesn't make him a monster."

Summer raises her eyebrows. "Oh really? You know Anton doesn't have a curfew, right? Never has had one. He can go wherever he wants, whenever. No questions asked. Lucy, on the other hand, has to be home by 9pm. No exceptions."

"Yah, well…"

"And she has to have a GPS tracker installed on her phone at all times."

"That's just safety…"

"Before Anton met his precious Tori, he went on dates with human girls all the time. Lucy wanted to go to the homecoming dance with Samuel Stevenson, just as friends, and guess what Jeb said?"

I frown. Samuel Stevenson is a Junior on the school football team. He's always been friendly and nice. Even showed me where my locker was on the first day of school.

Right now, my wolf is growling possessively at the thought of Samuel getting anywhere near Lucy.

"Where are you going with all of this, Summer?" Cody asks, his brow furrowing.

He's starting to look annoyed, like he did the other day when pushed on the pack's no-human-mating policy.

"Dude," I interject, looking between the pair of them, hoping to diffuse the situation, "I think Summer is just saying that things could be a little more egalitarian, you know?"

Cody looks away from the road to narrow his eyes at Summer. "Have you been making Toby read that feminist propaganda? What was that book you were reading the other day? The *Feminine Mystique* or something?"

Summer rolls her eyes, but I can tell her frustration with Cody is real, even if she knows he's intentionally goading her.

I raise my hands. "Oh, I read that long before I came here," I say with a forced laugh. "We had to take gender studies at my old school in New York…" My voice falters as I remember dad ranting about that book, how it was racist, classist, homophobic and outdated.

"Of course, you did," Cody drawls, "You're such a..."

"Townie?" I offer, then list off a few of the other names the kids at school have called me, counting the names off on my fingers. "City slicker? New Yorker? Metro?"

I look down at my clothes and shoes. They're as out of place here as the ones Tori sends Anton in her care packages, just in a different way.

I actually don't mind standing out as the New Yorker at school. None of the human boys give me a hard time about it anymore. Not since I joined the wrestling team. Definitely not since I beat Quentin Slade into a pulp.

I flash Cody a cocky grin.

"I prefer the term 'educated'. And news flash, Cody. Chicks dig feminists. It's a fact."

"Riiight." Cody shakes his head, drawing the word out.

Summer frowns and looks out her window, remaining silent for the rest of the trip to the ranch.

Cody acts like he doesn't notice, talking about plans for the rest of Christmas break. The group are going skiing in a few days, and he tries to convince me to come along. I tell him I'll think about it, but I don't find the idea of being trapped in a little ski lodge with Lucy and Anton that appealing. Not to mention the more time I spend with them, the greater the risk is that they'll find out what I really am.

Dinner in the pack house is even more awkward than the truck ride. Summer remains quiet, only talking to me and Jason, ignoring Cody completely. There's an unmistakable panic on Cody's face. His eyes keep darting over to Summer, all while fielding questions from his dad about college applications.

Cody and Anton are both seniors, and there seems to be this expectation that the pair of them will attend the same university. Cody wants to stay close to Buffalo, while Anton wants to study in California to be close to Tori.

"Coach seems to think I could get a scholarship to play at USC," Anton explains.

Tori is tucked as close to his side as separate dining chairs will allow, and he's playing with a stray lock of her long, sun kissed hair. Lucy glares openly across the table at the pair of them, that beautiful bow shaped mouth curled up into a sneer. Weirdly, the expression just makes her look hotter.

"UW has a world class ag program," Cody says, not even responding to Anton's statement. "That is where pack usually go. John and Wren are both still there."

John and Wren are both sophomores at college and members of the Clear Creek pack, but I haven't met them yet.

"If I get a scholarship to USC, I'm accepting it." Anton glares at Cody, though his voice has an almost pleading quality and he looks at Jeb, seeking his father's support.

The beta doesn't seem to notice, or at least doesn't acknowledge his son's appeal. Instead, he turns to Jason.

"Jason," the beta barks, "have you given much thought yet to college?"

"I – I don't mind going to USC or UW," Jason murmurs. "Either way is fine for me."

I'd almost forgotten Jason's a junior like Summer, so he'll be thinking about college applications now too, especially if he wants to apply for scholarships. From what I understand about his family's financial situation, he's going to need a scholarship. Or have to take on hefty student loans. He must be realising the same thing, because he adds, so quietly it's almost like he's speaking to himself: "We get in state tuition at UW. I'd need a scholarship for USC."

Nobody asks Summer what her plans are, and she visibly bristles, exchanging a look with Lucy.

Cooper Winslow surveys the boys from his seat at the head of the table. "I suggest you boys apply for both UW and USC. If Anton gets a scholarship offer from USC, we can revisit that as an option. Son," the alpha turns a hard stare on Cody, "there's no reason why you can't go to USC instead of UW, if it means helping a packmate take an opportunity like a scholarship."

"Dad…" Cody begins.

The alpha raises one hand, silencing him. "This discussion is over for now."

Cody lets out another low growl, then levels another glare in Anton's direction.

I get the feeling Cody really doesn't want to go to USC, and I find myself wondering if it's because that would mean going away from Summer, or if he just doesn't like the idea of being so far away from his pack.

"What about Summer?" Lucy's clear voice cuts through the tense silence like a knife.

The beta glares at Lucy, dark brows drawing low over his eyes.

"What about her?" he grinds out.

Lucy gives a little shrug, affecting nonchalance.

"She's a junior too. Starting college at the same time as Jason. Just thought the pack would want to ask her where she's wanting to go for college as well."

Jeb curls his lip at this speech, but Lucy just squares her shoulders, holding her father's gaze, refusing to back down.

I wonder if she's fighting for herself in this moment just as much as she's fighting for Summer, and my chest constricts.

Sure, she tried to kill me, but the girl is loyal to the core and has some serious balls. Well, maybe not balls, exactly. My cheeks heat inexplicably as I think about what Lucy *does* have, and I find myself staring at my plate to hide my face.

To my surprise, it's Cody who steps in.

"That's a good question, Lucy." Cody keeps his voice light, as if there isn't some sort of father-daughter power-play going on over the plates of roast beef and potatoes. He turns to look at Summer, his face a calm, unreadable mask.

I've come to recognise this as his alpha mask. I don't particularly like it.

Summer must not like it either, because her lips turn down slightly, even as she says, "I would go to USC, if that's where the pack was going."

By pack she means Anton, Cody and Jason.

"Thanks, Summer," Anton mumbles, and Tori practically beams at her.

I don't miss the hurt in Cody's eyes. Maybe he expected her to vote in favour of UW, since that's where he wants to go?

Meanwhile, Lucy gives Summer a barely perceptible nod, as if in acknowledgment. Or maybe, gratitude?

For how much Lucy and Anton fight, I think Lucy has Anton's back on the whole USC football scholarship thing. The girl is seriously loyal.

My wolf loves it. He's practically panting in her direction, wagging his tail like an idiot.

Honestly, I think it's a good thing I'm latent.

"We'll take all this into consideration," Cooper Winslow says, and his tone makes it clear that this is the end of the conversation.

Cody rubs one large hand through his dark hair, pushing it away from his forehead until it stands on end. After several long minutes he stands and stalks off towards his room, meal only half eaten.

Summer's gaze follows him until he's out of sight, a disappointed look on her face. The rest of us don't remain at the table much longer.

"I'll be holding a yoga class at seven o'clock tomorrow morning for anyone who is interested," Tori sings out as we get up from the table.

Summer and Lucy exchange a look.

"Tobias, you like yoga, right?" Anton asks, levelling me with a look that says I better say yes or he'll finish what his sister and that bull started.

My first instinct is to challenge him. At least, my wolf wants to.

I drop my head in forced submission as I carry my plate to the sink.

"Um, yah, I guess," I say. "I've never done yoga before, but why not."

It can't be much harder than any of the training we do for wrestling. Or any of the boxing training I used to do back in New York, when my dad thought it would be a good way for me to learn to control my strength.

After what I did to Quentin though, I'm not sure the training had the desired effect.

"Great," Tori chirps, beaming at Anton with a level of adoration that is equal parts sickening and baffling.

How any female could find the lumberjack-turned-pop-idol-wannabe attractive is beyond me.

"I'm actually training to be a yoga instructor, so having practice teaching beginners is just perfect."

"No problem," I mumble, though I suspect I'm going to regret this tomorrow morning. I had plans to sleep in.

They put me in the usual guest room. I'm familiar with it now, and my wolf feels somewhat calm in the space, like its accepted it as its den or something. Still, I can't sleep. Maybe it's the light of the full moon filtering through the curtains, bathing the room in silver. Maybe it's the whisper of nightmares that flicker past each time I close my eyes, the scent of charcoal, pine and wolf filling my nostrils.

After a few hours of sleeplessness, my wolf is pacing, almost frantic to get outside, to run. There's no point in trying to sleep when he gets like this, so I peel back the covers, slip on sweatpants, a hoodie and sneakers, and silently make my way outside.

I can practically feel the heat of the moon on my skin when I get outside.

I know that would make no sense to a human, but the wolf in me can feel the moon. Can feel the cold warmth and gravitational pull, drawing out the beast just like it pulls tides. If I could shift and run, I would.

From the far-off sounds of howls coming from the mountains surrounding the ranch, I know others in the Clear Creek pack have succumbed to the moon's pull and are out running, bathing in wildness and light.

Pulling my hood up to block out the light, I take off at a jog. There's a well-worn path that runs up towards the mountain, rutted from tire tracks and cattle hooves. I can see every dip and rock clearly, the combination of shifter vision and moonlight turning the world as bright as a colourless day.

My thoughts tumble past as I run, like pebbles caught at the bottom of a waterfall, churning around and around on repeat.

I miss my mom.

It's the first thought, the one I feel the most. It's there to greet me each morning when I wake up, when I have to remember again that she's gone. That I'll never hear her voice again, or feel the warmth of her arms surrounding me. No matter how much I cloak myself in numbness each day, that pain is always waiting for a chance to slip past my defences.

My feet pound against dirt and gravel, faster and faster, like maybe I can run away from these feelings. I know eventually the pain of muscle fatigue and the hit of endorphins will dull out everything, like white noise.

I hate my dad.

This thought comes as a surprise. I've always loved him. Sure, he annoyed me sometimes, but he was a really good dad.

Until he left me. Chose to die, let mom's death break him. Chose death over me.

What a weak coward. He could have fought mom's killer, could have taken him.

A growl rises from within me, my wolf stirring against its human cage.

I need to talk to grandpa, to find out more about my father's pack. Even if I don't want to talk to him, he's right. They'll keep searching for me.

Logic and instinct tell me that the killer was almost definitely from my father's pack.

My wolf wants to hunt him, to hunt them all. It wants to follow that charcoal and pine smell until it finds the wolf that killed my mom. It wants revenge on every wolf that drove my parents from the safety of their pack. On every wolf that would kill a baby for the colour of its eyes.

I need a pack.

I almost laugh at this thought, which clearly comes from my deranged wolf. Except my wolf's thirst for belonging has started to blend with my own. Its desire is primal. It wants to lead, to protect, to own.

I just want friendship. Real friendship, the kind that isn't premised on a lie about who and what I am.

Either way, it's an impossibility.

I'm miles away from the lodge now, well above Lucy and Anton's house, at the point where the rolling hills turn to steep granite boulders and cliffs sheltered by pine and aspen trees. I stop, taking in the moonlit scenery below me.

My eyes rest on Lucy's house, on the tree below it where the bull gored me, and I can't help but smile. She hates me. She's hated me since that first day of school. Is it just because I'm a loner? Or is there something else, something more?

I've tried to hate her too, but I can't. And it's not just because she's beautiful, brimming with quiet, understated strength. It's not just her alluring scent. That lavender and fresh rain on grass scent that makes my blood heat each time it fills my nostrils.

I feel a pull. Like she's the moon, cold and radiant, calling to the beast sleeping under my skin. I can't help but wonder if she feels it too.

My thoughts are interrupted by a wolf howling somewhere in the mountains behind me. The sound is quickly answered by a chorus of wolf song. It must be the alpha, running with the pack.

That should be me, my wolf says, wild and bristling within me. Not jealous, exactly, but certainly possessive and a little put out. Like when a waiter delivers your meal to someone else, and you know it should be yours.

Except I know there's really no meal coming to me. I shouldn't even be at the restaurant.

I lift my head until my hood falls back, tilting my face towards the moon, and let out a long breath. It's like a silent scream, a keening howl, and a prayer rolled into one.

I'll never shift, never have a pack, never get my parents back, never have Lucy. I'm a monster, a creature born to destroy or be destroyed, ironically packaged in the form of a teenage boy.

But I can have revenge. I can hunt the killer down. I can make those who wronged me pay. And in the meantime, I can protect those my wolf has informally claimed has his – Jason, Summer and Cody. Even Lucy. Especially Lucy.

I inhale, filling my lungs with icy December night air, relishing in the burn of it. There's a certain liberty in solitude. No one to answer to but myself. Only one grave to dig. Because in the end it will either be him, or it will be me.

Chapter 14

Tobias Finch

Dawn is only hours away by the time I return to the house. I manage to claim a few hours' sleep before I'm woken by the sounds of voices calling out in the hallway.

"Cody! Cody!? Are you here?"

I recognise Summer's voice through the fog of sleep. There's an edge of fear in her voice that I've never heard before.

"Have you tried calling them?" Lucy asks. Her voice is smooth as a glacier, unruffled.

"I've called Anton like a million times," Tori snaps. "He's never not answered my calls. Never. Are you sure you didn't see him at your place?"

"Uh, yah," Lucy scoffs, "I'm sure. I don't think he was home all night. Pretty sure he snuck down here as soon as dad went to go on the pack run last night."

I'm sitting up in bed, rubbing my eyes and trying to make sense of the conversation when my door is flung open and Summer, Lucy and Tori come tumbling in.

"Jesus," I grumble, pulling the blankets over my lap.

Sure, I'm wearing boxers, and shifters are relatively used to nudity, since you can't exactly shift with clothes on. That doesn't mean I feel comfortable sitting here almost naked in front of a bunch of girls. Especially first thing in the morning.

"Have you seen Cody?" Summer asks, her hazel eyes flicking around the room as if expecting to see him hiding somewhere.

"Or Anton?" Tori asks.

"What's going on?"

Jason comes trotting in behind them, dressed in athletic wear, a look of confusion on his face.

"I thought we were doing yoga this morning."

I look at my phone. It's ten past seven in the morning. I must have turned my alarm off and gone back to sleep. Oops. Is it bad that I feel absolutely no guilt for missing Tori's yoga class?

Tori waves one hand dismissively. "Yoga is postponed. Anton is missing." Her voice rises in pitch at the word 'missing'.

"What do you mean, missing?" Jason ruffles his short, mousy hair, making it stick up in all directions. "Have you tried calling him?"

"Of course, we've tried calling him." Tori stomps one foot, the sound is muffled by the thick carpet.

"Cody is missing too," Summer adds, wringing her hands. She's looking at me with a quiet sort of desperation, like this is a problem I should be able to solve for her.

I rub one hand over my face, feeling the faint roughness of stubble on my jaw and clear my throat.

"When did you last see them?" I ask. "And where?"

Lucy crosses her arms, glaring at me, but her eyes look tired and I can't help but think that at least today, her anger is a shield against the worry she must be feeling for her brother.

"He drove me home after dinner and went in his room to play video games. He wasn't there when I got up this morning and his bed was made. Like he hadn't slept in it." She narrows her eyes at Tori. "I'm pretty sure he snuck out to see you, so maybe you can elaborate on where he was last seen."

Tori blushes. "He texted that he was going to try and sneak out. But he never showed up and I fell asleep."

"Sure," Lucy drawls.

"Okay, what about Cody?" I ask, before Tori can respond.

"I didn't see him after dinner," Summer says, biting her lip. "Not after he went to his room…"

She trails off, and I know she's thinking of that awkward conversation with Cooper and Jeb about where everyone should be going to university. The more I think about it, it's pretty obvious that the real reason Cody wants to study and UW is to be close to Summer while she finishes up high school.

Lucy finishes for her.

"When Summer knocked on his door this morning, he wasn't there."

Cold fingers of dread curl themselves in my stomach. There could be lots of reasons why Anton and Cody are missing. They could have gone to the store to pick something up, or gone for an early morning run.

But something doesn't feel right, and after mom, I've seen enough to know that sometimes bad things happen. Really bad things. They come out of nowhere, without warning. There's no harbinger in the plot, no suspenseful music to warn you what is coming.

One minute, people are there. The next, they're gone.

I slide out of bed, quickly pulling on the sweatpants I wore last night, and stand up.

"What way is his room?" I ask, since this house is as big as a hotel and I've never been to his room before.

Summer leads the way, and Lucy, Tori and Jason follow behind us.

"What are you, Sherlock Holmes?" Lucy sneers, "Going to look for clues?"

I don't bother to answer her but instead turn to Jason.

"Run and see if Cody's truck is out front," I tell him.

He nods, obeying without hesitation.

I turn back to Lucy. "Was Anton's car at your place."

She nods, her face paling slightly.

We come up to a door, and Summer stops.

"This is Cody's room," she says shakily, just as Jason comes careening down the hallway, panting.

"His truck is there," Jason pants, "Cody's truck is still here."

I frown, feeling strangely queasy as I turn the handle to Cody's door. If both Anton and Cody's vehicles are here, then they would have left on foot.

Cody's room is empty, his bed unmade, windows shut.

I close my eyes, nostrils flaring as I take in the lingering scent. Cody's scent is faint, like he hasn't been in the room for hours. Alongside that is the faintest hint of some sort of chemical, metallic and foreign. I wrinkle my nose at it, then move to the window.

And that's when it hits me.

Charcoal, pine and wolf.

My eyes fly open, and my wolf comes barrelling to the surface. If I could shift, I probably would.

I take another deep breath. The scent is there, unmistakable.

I'll remember that smell until I die. A smell that brings with it the copper scent of blood, my father's cries, mom with her throat torn out, blood on the kitchen floor.

I squeeze my eyes shut against the memory, breaths coming in quick pants.

"What is it?" Summer asks, sniffing the air beside me. "I can't smell anything."

Lucy, Tori and Jason lift their noses as well, and I realize in that moment how strange we would all look to humans, a group of kids standing together with their noses raised.

"I can smell something," Jason offers tentatively. "A wolf shifter. Definitely a strange wolf. Not our pack."

"Are you sure? I can't smell anything either," Lucy frowns.

"I've – I've got a pretty good sense of smell," Jason shrugs, blushing and looking down, almost like he's ashamed of having a skill that the others don't.

"You recognised it, didn't you?" Tori folds her arms across her chest, glaring at me accusingly.

I feel like my throat is closing shut, like my chest is being crushed, and rub both hands over my face as I draw a deep breath, trying to force oxygen into my lungs.

"Yah. Yah, I recognise it."

Bile rises in my stomach, and suddenly Cody's room feels too small, too crowded.

"Just give me a moment." I hold my hand out in front of me, palm outwards. "I just need some air."

Before anyone can ask any questions, I'm out the door, sprinting down the hallway to the back doors that lead outside. The sun is just starting to rise, peeking up along the eastern rim of the mountains, bathing the valley in a brilliant red.

I take a deep breath, cleansing my lungs of that scent.

My mom's killer. He was here. Right here. So close. He probably came in while I was out running last night.

"Tobias?"

I startle at the sound of Summer's voice, surprised to see her standing beside me, her brown hair tinged red with the sunrise.

"Whose scent is it?" she asks, voice wary.

I shake my head, mind racing as I try to think how much I can say without revealing what I am.

"We should go to Lucy and Anton's place. Sniff around there before any scents fade. See if the same shifter was up there."

"We can take my car," Lucy offers from behind us.

When we've piled into the car, the five of us careening at top speed up the gravel road to Lucy and Anton's house, Summer asks again.

"How did you recognise the shifter's scent, Tobias? Who was it? Who was here?" Her voice is trembling but serious, and I know she's not going to let this go.

I sigh, pressing my forehead against the window in the back seat of the car. The glass is icy against my skin. I can feel the vibration of the wheels over gravel, but it does nothing to shake out the darkness filling my thoughts.

"You know my parents died earlier this year?" I ask her.

"Yah." Summer's voice is soft, full of pity. "Cody told me."

"Did he mention my mom was murdered?"

I get that feeling again, like I'm not in my own body, like I'm somewhere else watching myself in the car. Like it's not my own lips saying that word. Murdered. Mom was murdered.

Summer's breath hitches. "No. No I didn't know that. Oh my god, that's horrible."

I grind my teeth, refusing to look at her. Horrible. Yah, that one word seems totally insufficient to describe the wrongness of what was done to mom.

"It was a shifter who killed her." My voice sounds gravelly to my ears. "I never saw him, but I came in after and… his scent was there…"

The car is silent for a long moment. Then finally Tori asks: "You're sure it's the same shifter?"

I nod, then realize she can't see me because she's sitting in the seat in front of me.

"Absolutely sure," I grit out.

I'll never forget that scent as long as I live.

The beta's house is quiet when we roll up, Lucy leaping out of the driver's seat the moment she kills the engine.

"That's his room." Lucy points to a low window along the side of the house, eyeing me with blatant distrust.

Quietly, I make my way over to the window, trying to see if there are any footprints outside the window. I feel a bit foolish, to be honest. I'm no tracker. I'm just a city kid who wouldn't know a dog print from a wolf print, even if it were possible to make out any marks in the dry earth. Which it's not.

Awareness of my own ineptitude washes over me as I crouch to the ground, hoping my wolf instincts will serve me better.

And there it is.

Lingering against the dirt, grass and sage scents, the distinctive smell of charcoal, pine and wolf.

My stomach roils, and I sit back on my heels, vision going white with rage. I guess that's why they call it a 'blind rage'. Anger this strong really does block out everything else, focuses everything to a fine point, a dagger aimed at my target. At the killer.

Jason notices my reaction and crouches beside me, sniffing the earth like a sommelier testing a glass of wine before the first sip. He gives a faint hiss through his teeth as he catches the scent.

"Yah, it's here too," he says.

He cocks his head, looking at me in anticipation, as if waiting for me to take the lead and tell him what to do.

"Is he right?" Lucy snaps, coming to loom over us.

I haven't moved from this spot on the ground. I'm just sitting here, staring at the earth as if it will open up and reveal my mom's killer to me, like some sort of sacrificial offering.

It doesn't. Because the world is a cruel place and there are no benevolent beings waiting to offer up justice.

No. If we want justice, we have to take it.

"He's right." I whisper, eyes fixed on the ground as my mind whirs, conjuring up dark plans, still vague as shadows.

I'm going to track the bastard down. I'm going to make him suffer. I'm just not sure how yet.

There's a muffled sob behind me, snapping me back to the present. It's Tori, her fist pressed against her mouth as she stifles a cry, green eyes swimming with tears.

"What should we do?" Summer asks, voice cracking.

Her stare is the mirror of Jason's. Like I'm going to provide them with the answers on what happened. On how to get Cody and Anton back.

I glance at Lucy, but she's just staring blankly at Anton's window, face pale, lips trembling.

"We should wake up your dad," I tell Lucy, trying to keep my voice gentle, but it just comes out sounding harsh and emotionless.

In my shock, I unintentionally lace my words with a hit of alpha command, so my words have the effect of jolting Jason and Summer – the more submissive wolves - into superficial alertness.

Lucy must feel it too, because she turns to look at me, a mixture of surprise and wariness on her face. She doesn't remark on it though, just presses her lips together before stalking into her house.

Moments later, Jeb comes barrelling out towards us, face twisted, expression promising dark hell.

"Where's my son?" He bellows, spittle flying as he looms over us.

His eyes are fixed on me though, and it doesn't take much imagination to conclude he's somehow blaming me for Cody and Anton's disappearance. My wolf bristles, but thankfully Summer steps in before I can do or say something stupid.

"Cody and Anton are both missing, Mr. Stone."

Summer's voice is clear, even as she looks at the ground.

"Tobias thinks he recognises the scent of a wolf around Cody and Anton's rooms. He believes it's the same wolf that murdered his mother."

"Missing? Missing?" The word booms out like an alarm bell, loud enough to make Jason flinch.

Summer patiently explains everything we have learned so far and I watch as Jeb's face reddens with each passing moment.

"And who is this wolf?" Jeb growls, narrowing his eyes at me. "What do you know about him? Tell me everything."

I realize then that there is no way I can tell any of them what I know about the killer-turned-kidnapper.

I can't tell them his motives for killing my mom, because that would expose the secret of what I am. I assume the killer is from my father's old pack, but of course I can't tell them that either. Especially since I've told them my father's pack is in Russia. Not to mention, I don't actually know where my father's old pack is, or if it even still exists.

"We should go and let Cody's parents know first," I say, deflecting the beta's questions. "He doesn't know Cody is missing yet."

Meanwhile, all I can think is my mom's killer stood right here, right where I'm standing now.

A desperate sort of helplessness washes over me, knowing that the bastard is getting farther away from me with each passing second. That I have absolutely no way of knowing where to find him.

"Right. Fine." Jeb says, casting his gaze to Lucy's compact five-seater.

There's no way he's fitting in there with us. He must come to the same conclusion because he says: "I'll send an alert through the pack link and then meet you at the alpha's house."

With that, he strips off his pants and shirt, shifting into a brown wolf. The wolf gives a vicious snap in my direction before bolting down the hill towards the house.

Okay. Clearly, the wolf likes me even less than the man. Or maybe the wolf is just less capable of holding back.

We're all quiet for the short ride to Cody's house. Lucy worries her lower lip with her teeth as she drives. Tori stares out the front passenger window, but a glimpse of her face from the wing mirror shows silent tears running silver lines down her cheeks. Summer is hunched forward, elbows on her knees, face pressed into her hands. Jason sits in the middle, staring nervously between me and Summer, his face so pale that the bloom of pimples across his cheeks appear even redder than usual.

Cody's parents are already at the front of the house when we pull in, flanked by Jeb and a couple of wolves I don't recognise. Judging by their bulky size and aggressively vacant expressions, they're probably enforcers.

Cody's mom is wringing her hands, but her husband looks stoic and completely unmoved. Not like he's hiding his concern, but like there's never been an obstacle that he couldn't overcome. He can't imagine his son's kidnapping be any different.

Cooper Winslow moves over to me the instant I'm out of the car, Jeb standing beside him.

"Jeb has informed me you have intel on the shifter suspected of trespassing on our territory last night. What can you tell us?"

"There – there's not much to tell, sir. I recognised the scent…"

I look down at the gravel lining the driveway, hoping the show of submissive nervousness will be enough to mask the lies I'm about to spew.

"It's the same scent as the shifter who murdered my mom." I nearly choke on these last words. Murdered my mom. Mom was murdered. The killer was here. And now he's gone.

I lift my chin, but am careful not to make eye contact as I say, "I never saw him." It's the truth. Even if it masks a glaring omission.

"And how can you be sure it's the same shifter?" the alpha asks. "You're latent…"

I flush, irritated. Sure, I'm latent. I'm still not a human.

"My sense of smell is not affected by that," I say, trying to keep my voice as respectful as possible. "And I would recognise that scent anywhere."

The alpha's nostrils flare. "Do you have any idea where the killer was from? What his motives were?"

I shake my head, not trusting myself to speak.

"Could be a lone shifter for hire," Jeb suggests gruffly.

The alpha rubs his stubbled cheek in thought. "That seems most likely. It wouldn't be the first time a lone shifter took on a kidnapping job." He lets out a long sigh. "If that's the case, tracking his origins is likely a dead lead." He looks at me, the disappointment clear on his face. "In any event, without knowing what he looks like or where he is from, having a scent link to a previous suspected attack is of little value."

I am almost certain this shifter isn't a loner, but there is no way I can tell them that. Not without exposing what I am. The reason why my father's old packmate would be hunting me down.

What doesn't make sense is why that same shifter would take Cody and Anton.

"What about Lawrence Smith, that shifter who visited a few weeks back?"

It's one of the enforcers who asks this, a guy with close cropped brown hair, eyes slightly too close together, and a bland expression. "He was pretty interested in having Cody move across to that North Dakota pack."

"Black Hills pack wouldn't dare kidnap our pups." Alpha Winslow pales as he says this, like he's hoping more than believing the statement to be true. "That would be tantamount to a declaration of war."

The enforcer shrugs. "Wouldn't be the first time, sir."

"If they did, it would make sense to send a loner to do the job," Jeb muses. "We know that pack well enough that one of us would be bound to scent if a Black Hills wolf was on our territory."

"You should call Lawrence Smith." Cindy presses beside her husband, as if she's trying to draw some comfort from the contact. Her hands tremble, dark eyes she shares with her son watery.

Cooper Winslow shakes his head, giving his wife a sympathetic look. "No. We can't do that. If the Black Hills pack did take them, calling them just gives away any advantage we might have in surprise." He looks at the enforcer. "Hank, get our boys ready. We leave in half an hour." Then addressing his beta: "We need to discuss strategy. Come inside. There's coffee."

Lucy, Summer, Jason and Tori follow the alphas and beta inside, and I trail after them, heading to the kitchen. Cooper Winslow stops me before I can pass across the threshold, his lips curving down in a sharp frown.

"You need to go home, Finch."

My eyebrows flit up in momentary surprise. I only just arrived. I was supposed to stay for five days.

"You're not pack, and I can't have you on my territory at a vulnerable time," the alpha commands.

"Sure, okay. I can call my grandma to pick me up later today."

I step forward, looking past Cooper through the kitchen door at the breakfast spread on the table. Man, that looks good. Also, coffee sounds really good right now.

The alpha shakes his head, frown deepening as he moves to bar my entry.

"Now, Finch. Get your things. Lucy will drive you home."

I hear Lucy huff her discontentment from down the hall. She doesn't say anything though, just stomps off towards the kitchen.

"Okay," I say.

Truth be told, I'm anxious to get home. I need to speak with grandpa, tell him what happened. He's going to help me figure out what pack my father was from. And then I'm going to hunt down the bastard that killed mom. It might take years. Might take my whole life. But I'll do it.

"You will not speak of what happened here this morning to anyone," alpha Winslow adds, infusing alpha command into his request.

I nod, making a show of looking down submissively, but I have no intention of following his command. Not a chance.

He grunts in satisfaction, then turns on his heel and stalks into the kitchen, no doubt to meet with his beta about how to get Cody and Anton back.

A knot forms in my stomach, a mixture of fear and guilt. I doubt the Black Hills pack have anything to do with the kidnapping – not unless by some chance of fate, my mom's killer is from that pack. Or somehow mixed up with them. More likely than not, the alpha and his men will be following an empty lead. They might even start a war with the wrong pack.

Meanwhile Cody and Anton will be going farther away, becoming more difficult to find. All because of my silence about who the killer really is.

In the guest room, I make quick work of packing up my duffel bag, then cast one long look around the room. It's a small miracle the killer didn't find me here, didn't recognise my scent from our apartment in New York.

Maybe because I was out running, and because my room is at the opposite end of the house from Cody's room?

"You ready to go?" Lucy's voice cuts through my thoughts and I lift my head to see her standing in the doorway. Her keys are clutched tight in her fist, the usual hardness in her grey eyes softened by sadness and worry.

"I'm sorry about Anton," I say, trailing her out to the car.

She doesn't respond, merely slams the car door shut as she slides into the driver's seat and I slip into the passenger seat beside her.

It's the first time the two of us have been alone together since the day she set me up to get gored by a bull, and I'm suddenly very aware of how close we are. Heat flushes over my skin, an uncomfortable prickling sensation. I press my palms into my face, rubbing the heels of my hands into my tired eyes.

Twenty minutes. I just have to survive twenty minutes in the car with Lucy. That's it. I can do that, right?

The first five minutes are marked by an uncomfortable silence that fills the car as loudly as the rumbling of the engine and the crunching of gravel under tires. My mind is busy running over things I can say to bait Lucy into talking – even if it just results in her snarking at me – when she beats me to it.

"I know you're hiding something, Tobias Finch."

The words are so soft, they are barely audible over the sound of the car. Even though her voice is sweet, there is no hiding the menace in her tone.

I look at her, forcing my face to remain expressionless, even as my heart races. She doesn't meet my stare, but keeps her eyes fixed on the road, fingers drumming on the steering wheel.

"Everyone's hiding something," I reply caustically, even as my stomach drops as I consider all the secrets I hold balled up in my chest.

"Yah, well…" The hint of a mirthless smile lifts the corner of her mouth. "That might be true."

She's silent for a long moment, and I can't help but wonder what Lucy's secrets are, and what it would take to win them. It's a futile wish though, because Lucy hates me and there's nothing I can do to change that.

Of course, the wolf part of my brain disagrees. He thinks Lucy's secrets are his to keep, just like he thinks she is his to protect.

But he's defective and trapped, so he doesn't get a say in anything.

"Why are you downplaying your dominance?"

Her question snaps out like a whip, startling me from my thoughts as I'm hit with a mixture of panic and relief at this question.

No one should be able to see through my mask. But if anyone could, I would want it to be her.

"Not sure what you're talking about…" I start.

She waves one hand through the air dismissively.

"Don't give me that crap, Tobias. You might have the rest of them convinced, but you can't fool me. What is your game, anyway?"

"My game? Baby, I'm all game," I retort, leaning back into my seat with false bravado, tucking my hands behind my head, biceps flexing with the movement.

I catch her eye as she looks at me and smirk before adding. "No one has more game than me."

"You're deluded," she scoffs, but I don't miss the way her cheeks redden as she looks back at the road.

"Probably," I shrug, "What's your point?"

Of course, she's completely right. I am deluded. Enough to try and flirt with a she-wolf that probably wants to gut me. But hey, I've got to try and deflect her questions somehow, right?

"You pretend to be a submissive wolf, but I don't buy it. I felt your dominance back there. Why pretend to be submissive when you're clearly not? What are you hiding?"

Everything.

I'm hiding everything from my eye colour to how I feel about Lucy.

It's starting to feel like my life is a stage, like I'm acting out some messed up theatre performance, one where the price for failure is my death.

"How 'bout you tell me why you hate loners so much?"

"I don't hate loners. I just don't like you," she snaps.

We turn onto the freeway, and Lucy's car makes a disconcerting rattling sound as it gets up past fifty miles an hour, like whatever metal and plastic holding the thing together might come apart any moment.

"Liar," I retort. "You've been at me from day one, before you even knew my name. Prejudice isn't cool, you know."

"Liar? Oh, that's ripe, coming from you. Someone who pretends with every waking breath to be something they aren't. If that doesn't make someone a liar, I don't know what does." Her voice rises in volume as she speaks. When she finishes, she's practically panting with anger.

"Yah, okay, bigot." I wave one hand lazily in her direction, forcing myself to keep my hyper-relaxed pose in the passenger seat. "If you need to project your issues onto me to feel better, go ahead. I'm cool with that."

Lucy lets out a low growl in response, gripping the wheel and pushing the car past the speed limit until it rattles dangerously.

"I swear to God, Tobias," she hisses through clenched teeth, "if they don't bring Anton back… if I find out you know something more than what you've been saying…" She glances from the road long enough to flash me a meaningful look. "I will end you."

I feel that strange sick feeling in my gut again and my wolf paces, restless and anxious.

My parents died for my secret. Now Cody and Anton might be suffering for it too.

I turn away, unable to meet those icy grey eyes, focusing instead on the white lines of the freeway zipping past.

"Calm your tits," I drawl, "and focus on your driving. You've already tried to kill me once before. Not super keen for a repeat."

"Screw you, Finch."

The rest of the drive is full of a different type of tense silence, one that is made up of Lucy's brooding anger and my guilt.

There is so much I want to say, so many things I could tell her. The words burn like acid in my throat, then settle in my stomach, churning impatiently alongside the guilt.

I'm hit with an inexplicable sense of wrongness at the sight of my grandparent's house, the little white washed house at the edge of the foothills.

My wolf growls, like this is the last place on earth it wants to be. The killer's scent is still in its nostrils.

It wants to hunt.

I want revenge too, but I've got to be realistic here. Even if I'm a born alpha, I'm a fifteen-year-old lone shifter who can't shift, with basically no skills that would enable me to hunt down what is likely a dangerous adult shifter.

Whatever I do, I have to be smart about it. I need to formulate a plan. I have to be patient.

My wolf is not patient.

The car lurches to a stop, skidding across the gravel driveway as Lucy slams on the brakes just outside the house. Slowly, I open the door and climb out of the car.

"Thanks for the lift," I drawl.

I pause, leaning into the vehicle, feet planted on the driveway but unable to make myself close the door and walk away.

She's glaring at me – her trademark expression when it comes to me – and still I'm drawn to her. Like a moth to a flame, not caring if I go up in a ball of fire.

Or maybe I want to get under her skin?

I flash her a mocking grin and she glares at me.

"Get out of my car," she says, trying to shove my torso out and pull the passenger door shut. "You stink of lies and it's getting on my upholstery."

I wrinkle my nose because that is probably the weirdest insult I've heard.

"Just let me know if you hear anything, okay?" I ask, dropping the usual cocky asshole mask for a brief moment. "Please?"

Because I really am worried about Cody. I'm even worried about Anton.

Most of all, I'm worried about Lucy.

She looks up at me, those grey eyes unreadable, lips curved into a frown.

"I don't have your number," she says.

I smile. "Tell me your number and I'll text it to you."

I stand up to reach into my pocket and pull out my phone.

The movement brings me out of the car and Lucy takes the opportunity to slam the passenger door shut. I hear the sound of the automated locks clicking on all the doors, and then gravel is flying as she peels out of the driveway.

"Jerk." I say under my breath, but I can't help the smile that quirks at the corner of my lips.

That smile quickly fades.

My mom's killer was just outside my grasp. And now Anton and Cody are in the killer's hands.

"You're home early."

I look up at the front door to see my grandmother standing with her hands on her hips, dark hair glistening in the morning sunlight, a gentle smile on her face.

That smile reminds me so much of mom that I feel a pang in my chest. Like grief is a shard of glass imbedded there. It never heals, just waits for a moment to twist under my flesh and make me bleed again.

"Cody got sick," I lie, at a loss of what else to say because I can't exactly say 'Hey grandma, so there's such a thing as wolf shifters and the same one that killed your daughter also kidnapped my new wolf friends'.

I sling my bag over my shoulder and traipse up the stairs.

"Is grandpa home?"

"I'm here," grandpa replies from his usual seat at the kitchen table, cigarette dangling from his fingertips, chain of ash dripping into the full ash tray.

I've started to notice he doesn't really smoke the things, just uses them like portable incense. It must be expensive. Not to mention the health risks of second hand smoke.

I slump down at the table across from him as grandma slides a plate in front of me, then starts piling it with breakfast food. Her compulsion to feed every person who enters her house is definitely appreciated at this moment.

"Thanks grandma," I say, even if it feels somewhat surreal to be shovelling food into my mouth given everything that has happened.

I wonder if Cody and Anton are getting breakfast. Somehow, I doubt it. Killers-turned-kidnappers probably aren't that concerned about giving people three cooked meals a day.

The tightness in my stomach grows, but it doesn't stop me from eating. I'm not sure what kind of person that makes me. A hungry one, I guess?

"You really shouldn't drink coffee," grandma chides as she fills my mug almost to the brim with a second cup of weak coffee.

"I know."

I take a long sip, enjoying the way it burns on the way down. With food and caffeine, my brain starts to wake up and the seriousness of the morning's events move to the front of my consciousness.

“Grandma,” I say, pulling the coffee cup under my chin, “do you have mom and dad’s wedding photos? Or any letters they sent you from before I was born?”

Grandma looks surprised for a brief moment, then smiles shakily. “Of course.” She pushes up off the table to stand. “Give me a couple minutes and I can dig them out for you.”

In normal circumstances I would tell her not to rush, let her finish her own coffee. But there’s a sense of urgency driving me that wasn’t there before, so I let her go.

Grandpa raises one bushy eyebrow at me inquisitively, missing nothing.

“Cody and Anton went missing early this morning,” I whisper.

Grandma is out of earshot. I can hear her moving things around in her bedroom closet.

“I caught the scent of a strange shifter by both their windows. I recognised the scent.” I pause, biting the inside of my mouth. “It was mom’s killer.”

His eyes widen, glowing wolfishly as a burst of energy radiates from him, angry and snarling. I almost expect to see him shift right there in the house. By the time he reins himself in, he’s gripping the table and breathing heavily.

“Son of a bitch,” he growls out.

I nod, giving him a moment to compose himself, waiting until I hear his heart-rate even out. He just stares at me the whole time, jaw clenched and fingers digging into the wood of the table so hard I’m sure he’ll leave marks.

He doesn’t ask me if I’m sure, or question my ability to recognise the scent. He knows better.

“I don’t know why he’s taken them, or where they’ve gone,” I continue. “The alpha thinks the North Dakota pack has taken them – remember, the one that wanted to do the exchange.”

"That would make sense..." Grandpa's voice is so low, it's practically a growl, like the wolf is so close to the surface he can hardly speak.

I shake my head.

"Except we think that the wolf that killed mom was from dad's old pack. I don't think his pack was from North Dakota. I mean, it could have been, but Montana is more likely right? Because that is where mom was going to school, and is where she got married?"

Grandpa gives a slow nod, contemplating. "Could be working with another pack though. Or could be a loner for hire."

"It wasn't a loner," I snap.

I know I have no right to be annoyed at grandpa. Especially when I haven't spoken to him about that night, not in detail. He doesn't know everything I heard. Everything I saw.

I take a deep breath. Squeezing my eyes shut, I say: "I heard dad talking to the killer after... after mom was..."

I can't actually bring myself to say the words. *Mom was killed. Mom was murdered.*

"Dad seemed to know him. And the killer knew about me, knew what I was."

Of course, then dad had to go into shock and die from the breaking of the mating bond, so he couldn't actually tell me anything useful that might help me track down the murderer.

"I see." Grandpa rubs one trembling hand over his face.

It's at that moment grandma toddles back into the kitchen, swaying under the weight of boxes and photo albums. She lumps the stack onto the table, then takes a seat.

"I brought everything out, so we can have a look through them," she says, stroking one of the albums lovingly. "These were from when your mom was a little girl." She pulls out a white album with gold trim. "I made this one up after the wedding. She emailed me all the photos, and I got them printed out you see. Since we couldn't make it to the actual wedding."

Gingerly, I open the album. Even though I know *cognitively* what I'm going to see, I'm completely unprepared to come face to face with photos of my parents, only a few years older than I am now, surrounded by mountains and snow, completely wrapped up in the happiness of being with each other.

That is what life was like for them before you were born, the dark part of me says. *Before you came and forced them into hiding. Before you put a target on their backs.*

"I can't say I recognise those mountains," grandpa murmurs, sidling up beside me to look at the album. He turns to face grandma. "Do you remember Marian ever saying what part of Montana the wedding was at?"

She shakes her head. "Not exactly. Just that it was north of Missoula somewhere."

Pulling out my phone, I snap a few photos of the pictures in the album, focusing especially on the ones that show a mountain range in the background. Maybe I can work through pictures on google images and try and match things up or something.

I dart a glance at grandma, who is currently rifling through a shoe box full of letters. I also need to get grandpa alone and see if he knows where the wolf packs are located in that part of Montana. That should narrow things down a bit, especially if my theory of the wedding being on pack land holds true.

"Did they send a wedding invite or anything?" I ask.

That would have the address of the wedding on it, right?

"They sure did," grandma replies, shooting an annoyed look at grandpa. "Not sure where it is now though. It might be in one of these boxes."

She sets the first shoe box aside and starts methodically working through the next one.

I keep flipping through the wedding photos, pausing when I get to a photo of my parents staring into each other's eyes, a small wintery lake shimmering in the background. I take a photo of it, then pull up a map of Montana on my phone. Judging by the map, there is a surprising number of lakes in what look to be mountain areas north of Missoula. Still, knowing there's a lake will help narrow down locations too.

I work through the album, taking photos of any of the pictures with scenery in them. I pause when I come to a photo of my parents posing beside a male who looks strikingly like my dad, only younger. They have the same broad smile – the kind that almost shows too much teeth and makes you smile reflexively when you see it. Their hair colour is different though. The other male is auburn where my own dad's hair was salt and pepper, even before I was born.

I wonder briefly if they were cousins or brothers, and my chest constricts, the familiar longing for a family I never got to know.

Just at that moment, my phone flashes with a message from Summer.

They've left for North Dakota, the message reads.

It's quickly followed by another message. *Alpha said to remind you to keep quiet.*

I know, I text back.

Then, feeling slightly guilty for how clipped that response probably sounds I add: *Keep me updated on what they find, K?*

I will, she messages back, and I smile.

Times like this, it almost feels like I'm part of a pack.

Almost.

Chapter 15

Tobias Finch

I've spent the past two days methodically searching through google images, trying to pinpoint the possible location of my parents' wedding. I've narrowed it down to one of five small lakes that surround a mountain called Holland Peak, about an hour and a half from Missoula.

Now I just have to try and work out which lake the photos were taken from.

This is proving surprisingly difficult, since all these lakes appear to be pretty remote, so there isn't a large number of photos online to work with. I'm starting to think the best way would be to go to these locations myself.

Of course, this would also be the stupidest option, if my theory that they were married on pack land holds true. I would essentially be walking right into the wolfs den, giving myself up to the pack that has been gunning for my death since I was born.

I'm scrolling through pictures online and coming to the depressing realisation that my plan for revenge is nebulous at best and a suicidal pipe dream at worst, when a text from Summer comes in.

The Black Hills pack doesn't have Cody and Anton. Alphas and co leaving to come home tomorrow.

Ice spikes through my veins when I read this message, then re-read it. I guess I was holding onto the hope that they were right, that this was just a loner acting on behalf of the Black Hills pack.

I turn back to my laptop and click open the tab with the map on it, little red pins dropped at the possible locations. Cody and Anton could be at one of those locations, and meanwhile their families have no idea where in the world they are.

I know there are a lot of possible holes in my theory on tracking down the killer. The killer could have changed packs. The pack could have moved. My parents could have just chosen a random picturesque location for their wedding, so even if I find it, that could be a complete dead end. But there is still a change that one of those five pins represents Cody and Anton's location.

I can't keep this information secret. What if Cody and Anton get killed because of it? What if they are never found? I wouldn't be able to forgive myself.

I run my hand through my hair, fingers catching where the brown waves tangle. I've been so focused on my task, I haven't showered or shaved since I got home. I've only left my room to eat and pump grandpa for information. It turns out he doesn't know anything about any packs in near Holland Peak, so he hasn't been particularly helpful.

My fingers hover over the keyboard on my phone as I contemplate what to say in reply. A reckless part of me – largely driven by my idiot wolf – wants to take a screen shot of the map with the five pins in it and send that to Summer in reply. Of course, that is a terrible idea. For so many reasons.

I put the phone in my pocket and slip on my trainers. It's early enough that I could make it to Jamison's forest and back before nightfall. A run will clear my head. So will talking to Jamison, even if he can't talk back.

I SPEND most of the day in Jamison's forest. The sun is setting when I clear the ridge of the foothills that overlook my grandparents' house, golden light bathing brown earth in fire, turning the whitewashed walls of the little house red. In the distance, the snow-capped mountains gleam purple and pink in contrast against the pitch black of the pine forests.

I slow to a jog and pull my hoodie over my head, taking a moment to breath the fresh evening air, feel the cold in my lungs. The fresh taste of the air reminds me of the night I went for a run at the Half Moon ranch. The night Anton and Cody went missing.

I'm so lost in the scenery that I don't notice Lucy's car pulling up in the driveway until I'm practically in the front yard. Blind panic rushes over me and I freeze. If she gets close to me now, she'll scent Jamison on me. Quietly, I make my way around to the back of the house. I need to get in through the back door and hop through the shower before she has a chance to catch my scent.

There's the distinctive sound of a car door opening and I hear her voice call out my name. I ignore it, darting towards the back door. She swears under her breath. No doubt she'll be pissed at me, but there's nothing new there.

I sprint to the bathroom, flinging off my clothes and shoving them into the washing machine like a madman, pouring a ridiculous amount of scented laundry detergent over them before switching the machine on. My nose wrinkles at the strong chemical smell as I ignore the insistent knocking at the front door.

By the time I get out of the shower Lucy is sitting at the kitchen table with my grandmother, fixing me with a dark glare. Meanwhile,

Grandma is giving me this excited smile, practically leaping from her chair when I come in, completely oblivious to the pure hatred emanating from the she-wolf sitting across from her.

"Tobias," grandma chides, "you didn't mention the Winslows want you to come back out to the ranch."

I shoot Lucy a questioning look. She just smirks.

"Are your bags packed?" Grandma asks, eyeing what I'm wearing with a mixture of concern and disappointment.

I'm wearing clean sweatpants and a t-shirt, since I had absolutely no plans of leaving the house anytime in the near future.

Clearly not up to standards for visiting the revered Winslows on their fancy ranch.

"Um…"

Grandma shakes her head, then shoes me out of the kitchen with her hands. "Go get your things together. Don't keep Miss Stone here waiting."

I open my mouth to reply, but no words come out.

Grandma turns back to Lucy. "Your daddy is Jeb Stone, is he? I remember when he used to be on the rodeo circuit. He was the best bull rider this state has seen in a long time…"

Grandma is practically preening as she regales Lucy with tales of Jeb's rodeo day prowess. Lucy just smiles blandly, her face the polite mask I've seen her use with the alphas and even her dad on so many occasions.

Sensing I haven't left yet, grandma turns back to me, a look of warning in her eyes. "Tobias Finch, don't make me ask again."

I practically stumble to my room, completely confused. What. In. The. Actual. Crap.

Grandpa is standing in my room when I get there, face stony and cast in shadow, actually looking kind of menacing. I flick on the lights.

"Jesus, grandpa."

"There is a she-wolf in this house," he practically growls.

"Yah, I know."

His wife let the girl in, not me. I really don't see how any of this is my fault.

"Do you know the risk this puts Jamison in?" he grinds out.

I just give him a look because, of course, I freaking know.

"If she catches my scent, they'll start asking questions," he continues, stating more of the obvious. "That could lead them to Jamison."

"She's not going to catch your scent."

I feel pretty confident about this. While his wolf scent has gotten stronger since he's started shifting again, the cigarettes he smokes really do mask his scent. They also completely fry my sense of smell each time I come in the house, so it will be having the same effect on Lucy.

"You need to get her out of this house. Now."

His eyes flash wolf, and I nod, even as my own wolf bristles, wanting to rise to the challenge.

"Yah, I will. I think I'm meant to go with her, actually…"

I frown, trying to work out why Lucy is over here demanding I come back to the ranch in the first place, and if there is any way I can get out of going with her. Cooper won't be happy to come home and see me there, that's for sure. Maybe this is part of some elaborate plot to try and get me killed by Cody's dad?

Grandpa raises a questioning brow and I shrug, then start re-packing the bag I had only just unpacked, indiscriminately shoving in clothes, my laptop, phone charger and wallet. I throw in an extra pack of contact lenses, just in case.

"She told grandma the Winslows want me to come back to the ranch," I explain, zipping the bag shut. "They didn't. They're not even back from North Dakota yet, and there is no sign of Cody or Anton." I shake my head, flicking the hair out of my eyes. "I don't really know why she is picking me up."

The frown on grandpa's face deepens as he stills in that preternatural lupine way. "Be careful."

I give a curt nod.

He doesn't need to tell me twice.

Lucy might be the most fascinating, beautiful girl I've ever encountered. My wolf might be getting increasingly obsessed with her. I might want to spill all my secrets at her feet, let my walls crumble and see if she helps me pick up the pieces.

That doesn't change the fact that she is dangerous. Maybe it makes her more dangerous than anyone.

"Call me if you need anything," he adds, his voice low. "I can always come and get you."

I bite my lip. "I don't think that would be smart," I admit. "Your scent might be masked at home, but I don't think that would hold true if you were outside."

"That is my decision to make," he retorts gruffly, before fixing me with a pointed look and saying, "Give me your word."

Something about the way he says this catches my attention. "My word?"

He nods. "Your word is binding when you give it to other shifters," a grim smile flits across his face. "Didn't your dad warn you about that?"

I shake my head. This is certainly the first time I've heard of this.

"What, even outside of a blood oath? Without a pack bond?"

"Yes," grandpa grimaces. "It's one of those born alpha anomalies. Jamison recently reminded me of it."

I just gape at grandpa. Why didn't he mention this during his many discussions about packs and born alphas and wolf history? It feels like that would be a very important 'anomaly' to tell me about.

A feeling of dread welling up in my chest, my mind flitting frantically as I try to recall all the times I've promised something before.

"What happens if I break a promise?" I ask warily.

"Your wolf won't let you," he replies, his voice low. "It will push you to act, to follow your word. Your wolf is strong, even latent. It has the power to drive you mad until you follow its instincts. It can do the same to make you keep your promises."

I try to swallow, but my mouth feels too dry.

"Just give me your word that you'll call me if anything happens," he asks, his expression softening, a sad glint in his eyes. "I lost Marian before I could make things right with her. I would never forgive myself if I let anything happen to her child."

My chest clenches at the mention of my mom, at the pained expression on grandpa's face.

"I doubt Lucy or the other kids would hurt me," say tentatively.

He quirks a disbelieving smile, no doubt recalling that time Lucy tried to have me run down by a bull.

"Okay, so Lucy might hate me, but the others have my back."

He doesn't look convinced.

"Your word, Tobias."

Exhaling shakily, I say: "Yah, okay. I'll call if something happens. You've got my word."

I feel a familiar settling feeling inside of me, like the pieces of a puzzle locking into place inside me, stirring my wolf. I know instinctively this must be the binding effects of making a promise.

Unfortunately, I also know I've felt this before. Which means I've unintentionally given my word in the past. I've just never paid attention to it until now.

Great. Freaking great.

Sighing, I sling my bag over my shoulder and stalk out to the kitchen, plastering on a fake smile for the benefit of my grandma, who is now gushing about how great the Winslow family is, and how happy she is that I'm spending time out at the ranch.

"It's the sort of connection and experience that will serve you well in Wyoming," she's told me on numerous occasions. "I bet they'd give you a job over summer vacation if you wanted one."

Lucy is starting to look annoyed, but whatever game she's playing – one where she pretends to be my friend - requires her to sit and listen with feigned interest.

It would be amusing, if there wasn't a real need to get Lucy out of the house before she scents grandpa.

Grabbing Lucy by the elbow, I pull her to stand, ushering her towards the door. She shoots me a glare and I give her a smug grin. I'll probably regret the move later.

"Okay, see you later grandma," I call over my shoulder as we head towards Lucy's car.

The sun has set behind the mountains, the sky a deep blue colour that promises brilliant stars once night truly comes. At least until the moon rises to dim their light.

Once we're on the road, I recline the seat back and rest my arm on the center console, partially because its comfortable, but mainly to get a reaction from her.

"What is this really about," I ask from my recumbent position.

"Get your arm out of my space, Finch," she snaps, not taking her eyes off the road.

I snort, but do as she asks before shooting her a lazy grin.

"Admit it, you missed me."

She flicks her hair dismissively over one shoulder.

"Have you been suffering from delusions for a while? Or is this a recent development?" she quips.

"Well, I'm definitely not imagining that you've driven all the way to my place to pick me up, then lied to my grandmother to get me to come with you," I drawl. "I know I'm irresistible, but that does seem a little excessive, don't you think?"

Lucy gives an annoyed huff, but doesn't respond. I look out my window, frowning at the darkening landscape.

Why *has* Lucy come to pick me up? There is absolutely no part of me that believes she wants me in this car with her, let alone out at the ranch. I mean, obviously someone wants me there because Lucy has come to pick me up, but it's certainly not because Lucy likes my company.

Accepting that she's not going to give me an explanation while we're driving, I turn the volume of Lucy's stereo up. *Guard Down* by Claud is playing, the line *nothing like a New York summer* in the lyrics causing me to cast a melancholy smile out to the darkness as I recall what my life was like just six months ago.

The summer when mom and dad were alive and I would go to the park with my friends or get coffee or play basketball in the park.

Those days seem like another lifetime, belonging to someone else.

I hum along to the words *don't let your guard down* in the chorus, my eyes fixed on the darkening sky and the growing starlight.

I had never seen stars like this before I came to Wyoming. In New York, city lights drown out everything but the moon.

I close my eyes, letting my eyelids block out the cold starlight, since it feels too much like a symbol of how much my whole world has changed.

My daydreaming is cut short when I feel a sharp sting punching my thigh, like a wasp, but a million times more painful.

I look down, confused to see a syringe sticking out of my leg.

Acting on instinct, I pull it out, then just stare at the needle. It moves in and out of focus, my hand with it, as a comfortable warmth wraps itself around me. I blink rapidly, trying to make sense of what is happening.

Then everything goes black.

Chapter 16

Tobias Finch

"How much did you give him, exactly?"

A familiar voice cuts through the grey fog I seem to be immersed in. There's an insistent humming that nearly drowns out the voice of the person speaking. This sound is met with a thudding that I'm pretty sure is coming from within my own head, since the thudding matches the pounding rhythm of the headache pulsing like a sledgehammer behind my eyes.

"Less than what you would give a horse," another voice replies, and I instantly recognise Lucy's voice.

My nostrils flare as I try to take in the scent of who else is with us, but I just get a nose full of some metallic chemical.

"He's not dead," Lucy continues, "I can still hear his heartbeat."

I'm not dead yet, I imagine myself saying, repeating those lines from *Monty Python* in my head. The same lines I said to her in that room all those months ago.

I can't say I feel that far from dead though. Headache aside, my whole body feels like it doesn't quite belong to me and my tongue may as well be coated in sand.

"Well, he needs to wake up soon," the first voice retorts snappishly, "otherwise we'll lose our chance to question him before the alphas come back."

I recognise Tori's voice now, that peppy California accent incongruous with the angsty edge of her voice.

"He'll wake up," Lucy replies confidently.

I feel a rough pressure against my ribs before cold water splashes over my face.

I blink, trying to see through the haze of semi-consciousness and the water droplets still clinging to my eyelashes.

"See, he's already waking up."

There's an unmistakable smugness in Lucy's voice.

I reach up to rub the water from my face, only to find I can't move my arms as I'm met with a biting pain at my wrists. That's when I realize just how serious my situation is. I'm zip tied to a cheap metal chair with my wrists pressed behind my back. The air smells faintly of mildew and the metal cans of tinned food.

"Wha- what's goin' on," I slur, blinking to clear my vision.

As my eyes adjust, a dark low-roofed becomes visible. Probably some basement or cellar judging by the absence of any real windows and the rough-cast concrete floor.

Lucy's form comes into focus in front of me. Those long, jean-clad legs, the sweater hugging the delicate shape of her waist and hips, the low scoop neckline showing those perfect…

"Eyes up here, Finch," she snaps, and I can't help but grin stupidly as I look up at her face.

Gods, she's beautiful. So beautiful, with her cheeks flushed, grey eyes burning with determined fire.

"Didn't know you were into this sort of thing," I drawl, tongue heavy, words still slurring from the effects of whatever drug they gave me, as I infuse as much bravado into my voice as I can muster.

This situation should be terrifying and I'm supposed to pretend to be a submissive wolf. A submissive wolf would probably be pissing himself right now. I don't think I have it in me to do that.

Besides, I don't feel as scared as I should.

Sure, I don't feel *great* about waking from what was likely a drugged sleep, tied up in a basement, under the relentless gaze of two angry she-wolves. But one of those wolves is Lucy, so my deranged wolf just thinks this is amusing. Some sort of game.

Because my wolf is an idiot, sarcasm is the best response my half-dazed mind can come up with at the moment.

Lucy wrinkles her nose. "There is something seriously wrong with you."

"Agreed." I nod.

Even that slight movement feels awkward and jerky.

Tori steps forward, crossing her arms over her chest in attempt to hide the fact that her hands are trembling.

Good. I hope she feels uncomfortable. Nervous.

It means she's not likely to kill me.

"We need some answers." Tori's face is stony, even as her voice shakes.

I force my eyes to meet her own, hoping my expression remains a mask of bland amusement. "I'm at your disposal, ladies."

Lucy gives a disgusted snort. "Let's cut to the chase. My brother is missing. You have information that you're holding back. Spill. Now."

"I told you guys what I know." I shrug.

Annoyingly, my wolf choses this moment to push its will against me, itching to give them information. *We need to find Cody*, the idiot animal urges me wordlessly. *We promised to help him.*

Guilt boils in my stomach and I grit my teeth.

"Cut the crap," Lucy hisses, bringing her face so close to mine I can feel the heat of her breath, see the dark blue rim around her grey eyes. "I can feel your lies."

My mouth opens, the words resting on my tongue, ready to spill into this musty basement. I press my lips together, holding the words in.

All the while, my wolf is pushing me to tell. Pushing so hard it hurts.

Is this how it feels when an alpha exerts their will on you? Is this my own wolf using its alpha dominance on me? Because of some vague promise I made to Cody? That I'd have his back or whatever?

Or is this just the deranged animal's overactive instinct to protect?

I shake my head against the pressure, the movement causing the room to spin.

A high-pitched buzzing brings me back, and my eyes widen at the source of the sound. Lucy is standing across from me, her feet widened in a fighting stance, an electric cattle prod in one hand.

"Please don't tell me you use those things on your cattle," I say dryly, but I can feel my pulse pick up in panic. Surely, she wouldn't really use that on me, right? "Does that even meet animal welfare standards?"

"What, are you with PETA now or something?" Lucy snarks.

"I eat meat," I say, because, of course. I'm a wolf shifter. Therefore, a carnivore. "Doesn't mean I support animal abuse."

Lucy shrugs. "Good thing you're not an animal then."

"You're not seriously planning on using that?"

"We – we really don't want to." Tori gives me a pleading look from behind Lucy as she shifts from one foot to the other. "Just tell us what you know."

"You're going to torture me?" I ask, just to be sure.

I mean, it's pretty clear that is what Lucy is planning on. But it's just so unbelievable, I can't help the question from coming out.

Lucy just smiles, a smirk that cuts across her face in an angry red slash.

Not a friendly look.

"Okaaay," I exhale, drawing out the word.

I really can't let Lucy do this. Sure, it will hurt, so obviously there is that. But also, I seriously doubt she's ever tortured someone for information before. It doesn't seem like the sort of thing someone can easily come back from.

"I don't actually *know* anything."

My mind races as I try to work out what I can say. Without giving away my secret.

"But I do have some theories. If you untie me, we can sit down and go over them like reasonable people."

I flash Tori what I hope is a genuine smile. Of the two, she seems the most reasonable.

Lucy shakes her head. "Nope. Don't trust you. You stay where you are until you give us some information."

Tori frowns slightly, but doesn't argue.

Taking a deep breath, I close my eyes. The zip ties are cutting into my wrists, and my shoulders ache. How long have I been tied up here?

"I think maybe the killer was from my father's old pack," I finally say, deciding to offer up what information I can.

This better not come back to bite me.

Lucy's eyes widen as she lowers the buzzing cattle prod. "The pack in Russia?"

"No." I shake my head. "I don't actually know where his pack was from," I tell her honestly. "But it wasn't Russia. He was definitely American. I think maybe his pack was located in Montana somewhere. I've narrowed it down to a couple possible locations."

Tori steps forward, a look of relief sweeping across her face. "Montana. That's really close to here."

Lucy doesn't look like she shares Tori's relief. "There's hundreds of small packs in Montana." She frowns, cocking her head at me. "How do you know his pack is from Montana? And how do you know the shifter who kidnapped them is from that pack."

I tell them my theories on where my father's pack is located - obviously leaving out the details of my being a born alpha, or the reason mom was murdered.

After several long minutes of questioning, the discomfort is getting to me. Like, did they really have to tie me to a metal chair? Couldn't they have used something with cushioning?

I'm also starving, since I haven't eaten since breakfast this morning, and it's now well past dinner time.

When Tori asks for the fifth time about the likely locations of the pack, I roll my eyes and reply in a scathing tone: "I've dropped some pins on a map on my phone with the possible locations. If you untie me, I can be of more help to you."

Lucy makes no move to release me. Instead, she juts out her hip and asks: "Why did you tell us your father's pack was from Russia?"

"Because that was what he always told me to say."

I give her an exasperated look.

"And he never said where his pack was actually from. Now are you guys going to untie me or what? Also, is there something to eat? I could really use some dinner."

I've had enough of this interrogation ruse. They're clearly not going to kill me. Or torture me.

"One more question." Lucy leans down, bringing her face eye level with my own. "Why have you been lying about your level of dominance?"

I haven't been lying exactly, just pretending to be a submissive wolf. Which is totally different.

Somehow, I don't think that response is going to get me untied and fed.

I give an exaggerated eye roll, before spewing out a stream of half-truths that I hope will appease her.

"Okay. Fine. I've been downplaying my dominance. To be completely honest, it seemed like the smart thing to do. You know, make the scary lone wolf not come across as a threat. Plus, I'm latent. Dad always said I should downplay my dominance, since I wouldn't be able to hold my own against another shifter. So yah, sure. I'm marginally dominant. But Jason – or any omega really - could probably take me out in a fight. Especially if they shifted. So I'm not sure that my dominance is really relevant."

Technically, if we were in human form, it would probably be a close fight between Jason and me, even if he can draw on additional strength from being able to shift. Then again, I'm not sure if Jason could even fight me in wolf form, given how strong the omega flight instincts are.

That doesn't really matter, because I doubt my wolf would even let me fight Jason. My wolf has, for some reason or another, placed Jason into the category of 'wolves we must protect'. Along with Summer, Cody and (despite the current circumstances) Lucy.

Which is a bit unfortunate, since Lucy is currently brandishing a knife and looming over me. I can't help but flinch. Maybe killing me is on the cards after all?

Lucy notices my reaction and smirks before bending down to cut the zip tie at one ankle, then another, then moving behind me to run the blade between my wrists, cutting my arms free. My arms snap forward, relief and pain coming in equal measures as the blood flows back to my shoulder joints and arms. I try to stand, only to find my legs are still weak, either from whatever sedative they shot me up with, or from being tied to a metal chair in a cold basement for what may have been hours.

Lucy turns to head up the stairs. "Come on, Finch. Dinner is almost ready. We'll take a look at your map upstairs."

Tori casts a nervous, almost apologetic look back at me, then moves to follow Lucy up the basement steps. The two girls are nearly at the top of the steps before I manage to find my feet.

"Sure, sounds good. No hard feelings or anything," I call to their retreating figures. "Don't worry about me. I'll be fine. A little horse tranquilliser never hurt anyone."

It takes an embarrassing, long couple of minutes before I'm able to haul myself to the top of the stairs. By the time I reach the top, a familiar face is swinging the door open, brown eyes wide with surprise.

"What on earth are you doing in the basement?" Summer asks.

She peers past my shoulder, like she's expecting to see someone else in the basement with me. Of course, it's just an empty cement block with a chair and some cut zip ties.

Nothing to see here.

I shrug. "Nobody expects the Spanish Inquisition."

The door opens up to some utility shed – maybe the barn? I have no idea where we are.

Summer cocks an eyebrow, clearly confused by the Monty Python reference.

"Never mind," I say, forcing myself to smile. "Lucy said there's dinner?"

"THIS IS EXCELLENT NEWS."

I've just given Summer and Jason a recap of the information Lucy extorted from me. Even though there's nothing particularly damning in what I told Lucy – nothing that could easily expose what I really am – it is still disconcerting to hand over even the edges of my well concealed secret.

Unsurprisingly, it's much more relaxing doing so over dinner rather than tied to a chair in a basement. Especially when dinner is steak. There's also real gratification in watching Summer's face light up with hope at finding Cody and Anton. Even if it isn't quite enough to erase the dark circles that have formed under her eyes.

I frown. I don't want to dispel that hope. I'm also conscious that it could be completely misplaced.

"I could be totally wrong about what pack the kidnapper is from," I warn her. "It's just a theory. I don't even know the exact location."

Pulling my phone from my pocket, I add: "I narrowed it down to about five possible spots though."

I unlock the screen, open up my map and slide the phone across the table to her. Lucy and Tori both scoot alongside Summer to peer at the map.

"How did you work out the possible spots?" Jason asks, craning his neck to get a look at the screen. "If your dad never told you where his pack was and all."

"My parents were both studying at college in Missoula," I explain. "They got married in the mountains not far from there. I figured dad probably studied at the college closest to his pack, and he would have gotten married on pack lands, right? At least, that's what most of you guys do, isn't it?"

I wave my hand around the table, indicating at Lucy, Tori, Jason and Summer. Like they're representative of all young shifters everywhere.

"Yah. That's pretty on point actually." Jason cringes, casting Tori an apologetic look.

He's probably thinking of the awkward conversation with Cody and Anton about where to go for college.

"Our packs don't like us to go too far away from pack lands. It's risky."

I nod. Of course. Because if they stray too far from the support of the pack, they're targets for other packs. Kind of like lone shifters who inadvertently show up at a high school with a high shifter population.

"Well, I don't know exactly where my parents got married."

I twirl my fork with one hand as I eye the last baked potato. Its drenched in cheese and butter and looks really good. There's some psychological explanation about why people never want to take the last piece of cake or candy or whatever, but I think potatoes are different right? I scoop it onto my plate.

"But I dug up some of their old wedding photos at my grandparent's house. I used the images to work out that it has to be at one of five lakes by Holland Peak, north of Missoula. This is just based on the fact that you can see Holland Peak in most of the photos. I mean, I've never been there but it matched up on google images. It's kind of distinctive for a mountain. And there was this one photo of them by a lake. I've got the photo on my phone if you want to see it too. There weren't enough photos from the different lakes on google images to narrow down the exact location though. Which is why there are the five pins on the map there."

I tilt my chin at the phone and realize everyone is staring at me like I've grown five heads. Or shifted into a born alpha…

"What?" I ask cautiously, a fork-full of cheesy potato frozen in front of my mouth.

"You were really trying to help us." Summer's lips quirk up into a smile, easing some of my panic. "Like, you put some serious time into all of this." She gives Lucy a pointed look. "I told you he wasn't hiding things from us. He just wanted to work things out first." She looks back at me. "I totally get it."

"Is this your way of apologising for Lucy and Tori drugging me, tying me up and interrogating me?" I tease.

Summer and Jason have both already apologised for that profusely, so I should feel bad about bringing it up again.

But I don't.

Summer winces. "I am *so* sorry for that."

She glares at Lucy, but the look admittedly doesn't have the intimidation factor she's aiming for, either because Summer is a submissive wolf, or she's just too nice to stay mad at anyone.

Lucy just shrugs coldly. "Well, I'm not sorry. It got us what we needed."

Jason shakes his head. "Lucy, you don't have authority to interrogate people."

It sounds like something he's admonished her for in the past. I wonder how many maverick interrogations she's carried out before.

"I do," Lucy lifts her chin defiantly. "I'm acting beta when dad and Anton are away."

"Questionable," Summer snorts.

"Look guys," Tori interjects, raising her head from the image of the map on my phone. She's been staring at it like she can dive in and pull Anton out from the screen or something. "We have more important things to talk about. Like getting this information to your parents so they can find out where Anton is."

"And Cody," Summer reminds her. "We also need to find Cody."

Tori waves one hand dismissively. "Of course. Both of them. I mean, they're probably together, right?"

"I'll give dad a call now." Lucy flicks her long ponytail over her shoulder before pulling out her phone and dialling a number.

"Lucy." Jeb's voice booms out from the phone. "What is it?"

He's obviously a loud phone talker. Typical boomer.

Lucy grimaces and holds the phone away from her ear before turning down the volume.

"Dad, we have some information about where Anton and Cody might have been taken to."

Then Lucy launches into a concise summary of the information she interrogated out of me, conveniently leaving out the part where I was drugged and tied up. Making it sound like I just spontaneously volunteered all this information.

Cue eye roll.

"Wait," Jeb's voice booms out, interrupting Lucy's explanation of the five possible locations to investigate in Montana. "You're telling me that Tobias Finch is on pack lands?"

I can practically feel the growl lacing my name.

Lucy narrows her eyes at the phone. "*That* is what you are taking away from what I've just said? How about sending people to investigate those locations in Montana? Couldn't you send some of the enforcers that are travelling with you? Maybe if we split enforcers into different groups, we could cover more ground and…"

"Get that Finch kid off pack lands. *Now*."

"Dad. You're missing the point…"

"Enough. We've spent all day meeting with the Black Hills pack and nearly started a war over nothing. Everyone is exhausted. We're going to be home tomorrow morning. We are not going to just start sending enforcers all over Montana to go on a wild goose chase and start confronting random packs on kidnapping charges. Alpha has a plan…"

"Oh yah. And what's that?" Lucy snaps. Summer and Jason are both gaping at her, faces pale.

There's a drawn-out sigh on the other end. "I'm not giving you all the details. But just know that the pack is advertising a sizeable reward as a first step…"

"A reward? That's the grand plan?"

"I'm not discussing this with you."

"Dad…"

"Enough. Discussion over. And get that latent miscreant off our territory."

The call ends and Lucy looks up from her phone, a mixture of surprise and horror on her face.

"That went well," I say sardonically.

Lucy just stares at her phone, as if it's going to sprout teeth and attack her.

Beside her, Tori stands abruptly, brushing invisible crumbs from her latest Lululemon ensemble. "No offence, but your dad is an idiot. Your alpha is too."

Lucy glares up at her but Tori doesn't seem to notice.

"I'm sorry, but I'm not just going to sit here and hope someone hands Anton over for a reward. Not when I know he's probably been kidnapped by a murderer and dragged off to some backwater mountain pack in Montana."

"*I'm* not just sitting here," Lucy hisses defensively. "I'm doing everything I can."

Tori gives a dismissive waive as she starts clearing the table. "I know. You got information we needed. That was great." She turns to throw Lucy a patronising smirk over her shoulder.

I raise my hand, like I'm answering a question in class. "I wouldn't really call that whole process great. For the record."

Tori and Lucy both ignore me.

"But now real action is needed," Tori continues primly. "Action that *your* pack clearly isn't willing to take."

She waltzes back to the table to clear the remainder of the dishes, piling them by the sink.

"Okaaay," Lucy drawls, "and what exactly do you want me to do about that?"

She stalks over to the sink, ostensibly to help Tori with the dishes but probably aiming to make her aggressive stance more effective. Tori looks Lucy up and down in overt assessment before giving Lucy her back and turning to the sink.

"Well, nothing." Tori cocks her head to one side as if considering. She washes a plate, then hands it Lucy who dries it just a little too vigorously. "You have to stay here, listen to daddy. But I don't. I'm going to go find my mate."

"Future mate," Summer quips from the table, darting a conspiratory look at Jason.

Jason's lips quirk as he struggles to holds back a laugh.

Tori whirls around, soapy hands flying to her hips. "Glad to see this is all a big joke to you, Summer. Out of everyone, I would have thought *you* would understand what I'm going through. Cody might not be your mate, but everyone knows you guys are close, and Cody has pretty much said he thinks you could be his mate."

I watch as the colour drains from Summer's face and then floods back into it, turning a brilliant shade of red.

"We – we aren't mates," Summer stammers out, sounding like she's saying it to reassure herself rather than convince anyone in the room. "And, of course I'm worried about him. I'm worried about both of them."

"Tori is right." Lucy admits sourly. "We can't just sit back and hope a reward does what is needed. It's too risky." Then her grey eyes flash with mischief as she adds, "There's two weeks left of winter break. What's to stop us from taking a little road trip?"

Jason shakes his head. "Hate to be the deputy downer here, but our parents aren't going to let us drive to Montana to track down some murdering kidnapper."

"I'm eighteen," Tori interjects haughtily. "I don't need anyone's permission to go find my mate." She emphasises the word 'mate' and Jason rolls his eyes.

Lucy throws the dish towel onto the stack of dishes with a flourish. "I've got my car. What's dad going to do? Track me down. If he does, he'll just follow me to Montana, which is where he should be anyway. Looking for Anton."

Summer and Jason both exchange a look. "That'd be a bold move," Jason says cautiously. "Your dad would be pissed. Like, super pissed."

Jason looks at me, then says in a mock whisper, "Lucy's dad is scary."

"Like father, like daughter," I reply dryly.

Summer bites her lip. "If we're going, we should leave tonight. Get a head start and everything."

Lucy nods. "Agreed."

"Wait, what?" Jason gapes at Summer. "You're not actually going along with this crazy idea, are you?"

Summer's lips press together, forming a thin line.

"I think it's a good idea, actually," I say, then feel my cheeks heat as everyone turns to gape at me.

I mean, I guess my opinion doesn't really count here, since I'm not pack and I'm not the one risking parental wrath. Not one to stop while I'm behind, I continue offering my unsolicited advice.

"If you find them, then you can just call your dad and get the enforcers out there to deal to the pack. If it's a dead-end lead, then what, your dad grounds you or something? Takes away your car?"

"Yah, something like that," Lucy says, frowning slightly.

"Seems worth the risk if you ask me."

I've spent the last couple months wondering what would have happened if I'd come out into the kitchen while the killer was there. If I'd ignored my dad's insistence that I hide. Would dad have fought the killer? Avenged mom's death?

If I've learned anything, it's that sometimes parents have to be disobeyed for the greater good.

"Well, I'm in," Summer reiterates.

"What about your mom?" Jason asks Summer, "She's not just going to let you go."

"Oh, she won't even notice I'm gone," Summer says dismissively, "especially if I tell her I'm staying at Lucy's place."

Jason frowns, raking his fingers through his mousy hair as he looks from Lucy to Tori to Summer.

"So you guys are all going?" he asks, not expecting an answer.

He looks over at me, pimples showing starkly against his pale cheeks. There's less of them now then there were before, but the sudden pallor makes them stand out more than usual.

"What about you?" he asks.

My eyes round in surprise. What about me? Do I want to cram into Lucy's car and drive for hours with these wolves?

Spending time with them in close proximity only increases the chances that they'll learn my secret. All it takes is one slipped contact lens, or for me to issue another unintentional alpha command.

And if we find my dad's old pack, what then? As hungry as I am for retribution, I don't think I'm ready to face my mom's killer.

In fact, I know I'm not ready.

Of course, my wolf has different views on this. He's raring to hunt, to fight, to avenge mom and fulfil our promise to Cody. Out of everything, that promise to Cody is driving him the hardest, the need to protect roiling like a small flame in my gut. I strongly suspect that flame has the capacity to turn into a wildfire and eat us both alive.

I swallow, trying to push down the warring thoughts swirling like water and oil in my head. The confusing dance of wolf and man. As seems to be happening more and more, the wolf wins out.

"I - I think I'll come with you," I say, my own surprise at this declaration mirrored on the faces around me.

Lucy scoffs. "What makes you think we'll let you?"

Summer shoots her an incredulous look.

The threat of exclusion is enough to rile my wolf, and I lift my chin, feigning confidence. "Well, for one thing, I know the kidnapper's scent better than all of you," I say. "I've also proven that I've got the best sense of smell – at least in human form."

They might be better at tracking in wolf form, but there are lots of situations where going into wolf form are not possible. Like in cities. Or anywhere where there might be people.

In other words, pretty much everywhere.

"Maybe, but I doubt we can trust you to help us," Lucy says acerbically. "Since you haven't exactly been forthcoming with information."

"That's not fair, Luce," Summer argues. "He's told us lots."

"Under pressure," Lucy counters, then turns to glare at me.

"If you'd said from the start that your dad's pack was from Montana, and that the kidnapper was from that pack, then our whole pack wouldn't currently be in North Dakota. But instead, you made up this elaborate lie about your dad being from Russia, then were super cagey when asked about the kidnapper's scent. And to top it all off you've just been pretending to be a submissive wolf to make the pack more sympathetic towards you." She puts on a mocking pout. "Like oh, poor latent submissive wolf, guess we better look after him. He couldn't possibly harm anyone. He can't even shift."

Stalking towards me, she brings her face close to my own and says, voice soft with anger: "Well guess what, Finch – if that's even your real name, which I sincerely doubt – your game is up. I've got you all figured out."

As she says this, she presses her pointer finger into my chest, partially shifting just enough so that I can feel the threat of her claws through my t-shirt.

I hold her gaze, and give her a slow smile. The sort you'd give a girl if she was leaning into kiss you.

Just because I know that'll piss her off. Throw her off balance.

It's only half faked.

Her violent proximity causes fascination and fear to thrum through my veins in equal parts. I'm pretty sure fascination is winning out here, because when your own life holds little worth, it's difficult for fear to get a foothold.

"Glad to see we're finally getting better acquainted," I wink. "Feel free to figure out more of me, if you're game."

Lucy just wrinkles her nose in disgust and shoves me away.

"I think Tobias should come with us," Tori says.

This earns a look from Lucy that causes both Summer and Jason to cringe, and which Tori dutifully ignores.

"He could be valuable, and I'm not about to turn away any help at getting my mate back."

"Future mate," Lucy retorts snippily.

"Excellent," I say, rubbing my hands together. "I'm all packed and ready to go."

"Your grandparents won't mind?" Jason asks.

"Nah," I say with a shrug. "They'll just think I'm staying here. It's totally fine."

I'm pretty sure grandpa would completely lose it if I told him I was heading out to find dad's old pack, since my being recognised by any of them would result in my being put down.

But there's no point in mentioning that.

"You coming too?" I ask Jason.

Jason furrows his brow pensively. "I could tell my mom that we've gone up to Meadowlark for a few days to do some skiing…"

Summer nods enthusiastically. "That's a great idea. It's forecast to snow, so that's pretty believable. I can tell my parents the same thing."

"I'm not telling my dad anything," Lucy says. "He'll be more pissed later if he finds out I've lied. Better just to go and ask forgiveness later."

Clapping her hands together, Tori tosses her hair over her shoulder and speaks with the authoritative volume she probably uses to teach her yoga classes.

"Now that we've got that all settled, the car will be leaving in thirty minutes. So everyone, pack your bags!"

"Um, by 'the car', do you mean *my* car?" Lucy hisses, "Because I am not an Uber. We'll leave when I'm ready to leave."

Tori just rolls her eyes, not deigning to give Lucy a response, then saunters out of the room. Presumably to pack within the self-declared timeframe.

"Yay, road trip," Summer mock-whispers sarcastically, flashing a surreptitious grin at Jason and me.

Chapter 17

Tobias Finch

It turns out the forecast for snow was no joke. Five hours later, we're forced to pull over in the middle of nowhere, about an hour west of Billings, Montana.

"There's a hotel up ahead," Summer says helpfully, leaning forward in the front passenger seat and squinting through the flurry of snowflakes, her voice barely audible over the howling wind. I can just make out the neon glow of a sign though the blizzard.

Lucy pulls off the road, expertly correcting the vehicle as it fishtails down the off-ramp. When we get close enough to see the hotel, it becomes evident that it is more motel than hotel. One of those old school ones with two levels and the doors outside, built from concrete and cinder blocks.

"I'll go book us a room," Tori says, pulling her tote purse onto her lap and waving one hand magnanimously. "Seeing as I'm the only one over eighteen."

"You're barely eighteen," Lucy reminds her.

"Which means I can also have a credit card." Tori flashes the black card with her manicured fingers, tosses her hair and glides out of the car.

At least, she attempts to glide out, but the force of the wind and snow hits the door hard enough to push her back into the car. She lets an annoyed huff, mutters something about barbaric weather conditions, then scrambles across the parking lot to the motel office.

She comes back several moments later with a room key.

"Room 28," she says through chattering teeth as she climbs into the back seat. "That way."

She points to the far end of the motel, where the building and parking lot remain obscured by the falling snow.

"Wait, you only got one room?" Lucy asks incredulously.

"I'm not made of money," Tori retorts.

"There's five of us," Lucy argues.

Tori just waves one hand. "There's two beds and a pull-out couch. Plenty of room."

Lucy scoffs, shaking her head and grumbling under her breath about cheap Californians as she carefully drives across the parking lot, navigating ice patches and shoulder-high snow drifts.

"Do you have snow tires?" Jason asks, nervously gripping the handle above the backseat window.

Oh yah. I've been in the middle seat this whole time because, as Lucy put it, I'm a latent loner mongrel who is lucky to be allowed in her car at all.

"Of course, I do," Lucy snaps. "It is winter, isn't it?"

I feel Jason flinch beside me.

"Just checking," he whispers, sinking back into his seat.

I have to admit, I share his concern about the ability of Lucy's car to make the journey across Montana if the weather keeps up.

The little five-seater might have four wheels but it's definitely not four-wheel drive. The heater craps out intermittently, the car makes a disconcerting rattling sound if you go over fifty and occasionally there's a strange grinding sound underneath the car. There's also a small crack on the windshield.

It actually was only a chip in the glass when we started our journey, but somewhere between the raging wind and the sub-zero temperatures, that chip has grown to a finger length fissure in the glass.

I give Jason a reassuring smile. "It's supposed to clear up tomorrow afternoon," I tell him, pointing to the weather forecast on my phone. "I'm sure we'll be fine."

He just nods, mouth set in a grim line.

The room is small, musty and looks like it hasn't been redecorated since the place was built in the seventies. We all wrinkle our noses as we step inside, shifter senses balking at the smell of dust, mould, and unsavoury human odours that are probably emanating from the questionable stains on the carpet and quilts.

"Dibs on the pull-out couch," Summer calls out, darting towards the brown couch sagging against one smudged beige wall.

Tori shakes her head. "Nah-uh. You had shotgun in the car the whole way here. I'm getting the couch."

Summer shrugs. "Okay, sure. If it means that much to you."

She waltzes over to one of the double beds, peels back the quilt and throws her bag onto the sheets.

At least the sheets look clean. That's something.

Tori starts unfolding the pull-out couch and Summer shoots me a mischievous grin.

The pull-out creaks and groans before unfurling in a crumpled heap of metal, thin mattress and wrinkled bedding. Tori frowns at the sight, then turns to narrow her eyes at Summer.

Lucy bites back a triumphant smile as she says: "Like you said. Plenty of room, right?"

Jason and I climb into the other double bed, neither of us bothering to change out of our clothes. Jason flicks on the television and everyone winces at the horrifyingly loud volume as *Wonder* by Shawn Mendes blares on MTV.

"Sorry, sorry guys."

He quickly turns the volume down, and I focus on the screen, letting the music drown out Lucy and Tori's bickering. They're still arguing about who should get the pull-out couch when sleep claims me and I drift into darkness peppered with the sound of the television and Lucy's voice.

It's strangely soothing, and for the first time in months, I sleep without nightmares.

…

"You have got to be kidding me. If this is your idea of a joke, I swear to the gods…"

Lucy's voice pierces my sleep, and I blink dazedly against the bright light filtering through the multi-coloured drapes of the motel room.

"Unfortunately, it's no joke," Summer replies tersely, voice higher than usual. Almost panicked sounding. "Go see for yourself."

There's the rustle of sheets, then an icy blast as someone swings open the door to the motel room.

"Close the door," Tori grumbles from across the room. "Its freezing."

I sit up to see Tori huddled under a thin blanket, her feet hanging off the end of the misshapen couch bed. Lucy storms back into the room a moment later, face pale, eyes wild.

"What's going on?" Jason mumbles from beside me, yanking the blankets up over his ears. "It's too early."

Lucy just stands in the doorway, shaking her head.

"My car…" she whimpers. "The windshield…"

She rubs both hands over her face, as if trying to wake herself from a bad dream.

Summer nods solemnly. "I told you. It's completely wrecked."

I rub my head. "Can you guys explain? You're making zero sense right now."

Lucy bares her teeth at me, almost looking relieved to have a target for her anger. "My f-ing windshield collapsed overnight," she hisses. "Like, the whole entire thing has just caved in. My car is full of snow. There's glass everywhere…"

I cut her off, raising one hand in the air. "Hold the phone. Did you just say 'f-ing'? Why not just swear like a normal person?"

"Are you not listening, Finch? Is everything a joke to you?"

Jason sits up next to me, suddenly alert. "Wait, your windshield is broken? Can't we get it fixed or something?"

Lucy shakes her head. "It's Saturday morning and we're in the middle of nowhere. The chances of us finding a mechanic are basically nil. The best I could do is get it towed home but…"

She trails off, not stating the obvious.

If we turn back now, it's game over for the mission to find Cody and Anton.

"Well, I'm not turning back," Tori announces from her crumpled couch-bed on the far side of the room. "I'm going to get my mate. I'm not letting some minor car problems get in my way."

"There's nothing 'minor' about having no windshield, Tori," Lucy growls with exasperation. "It's an essential part of a motor vehicle. Like, you can't drive the car without it."

Tori waves one hand dismissively. "We'll just rent a new car. I can put it on my credit card."

Lucy snorts derisively, then strides over to the window, pulling the curtains back. "Look around. Do you see any car rental places nearby?"

Reflexively, I look out the window too, but all I can see is snow whipping around violently, blocking out everything but the shape of the nearest cars in the motel parking lot.

Tori pulls up her phone, ostensibly to start searching for a car rental place. "I'm sure there's one nearby," she muses, coral nails tapping furiously on the screen.

"I can tell you right now, there won't be," Lucy says.

Summer holds up both hands in a placatory gesture. "I think you both need to calm down…"

Tori and Lucy turn in unison to glare at Summer.

"Don't look at me like that. You've been going at it since yesterday. It's not productive. We need to evaluate our options like sane people and then figure out how to proceed, okay. Option 1," Summer holds up her index finger. "We track down a mechanic and see how long it will take to get the car fixed up. Option 2," Summer holds up a second finger. "Someone catches a bus back to Billings to get a rental car. Option 3," she holds up a third finger. "We call our parents and go home."

Lucy shakes her head at the proposed option 3. "No way. We are not calling my dad."

"Okay then. We look at options one and two." Summer turns to Jason, who is still sitting in bed looking around the room dazedly. "Jason, can you research what mechanic or auto-body shops there are close by and see if any are open?"

Before he can respond she cocks her head, looking at him with confusion. "Did – did you shift in your sleep or something? Your shirt is shredded."

The rest of us look over at Jason and, yep. His shirt looks like it's been ripped at the seams.

"Um," Jason looks down at his shirt, his face turning a vibrant shade of pink. "Yah. Yah, I guess I must have." He looks over at me sheepishly. "Sorry, man."

"It's all good."

It doesn't really bother me if he shifted into his wolf form in his sleep. I sure as heck didn't notice. I mean, there's a bit of wolf hair on the sheets, but that's fine.

That doesn't seem to appease him. He wrings his hands. "I – I haven't done that in years actually. Not since my dad…" he trails off, biting his lip. "Not sure what brought that on."

"Honestly, it's really fine," I say. "Feel free to sleep in your wolf form if you want. Doesn't bother me at all."

Jason nods. "Yah. Okay."

He picks up his phone from the bedside table, presumably to start searching for mechanics, though he seems grateful to have an excuse not to look at anyone for a while.

After several long minutes he breaks the silence. "Hey, I found one." He swipes his screen, reading something, then adds: "It's actually super close to here. We could probably walk, even with the blizzard. I'll call them first, but the website says they're open."

"That's great, Jason. Thanks!" Summer practically beams, then looks smugly at Tori and Lucy, brushing her hands together. "See, ladies. Nothing to get worked up about after all."

Tori huffs and traipses off to the bathroom, pink make-up bag tucked under her arm.

Lucy gives Summer a bored, unimpressed look before flopping down on the bed beside her and flicking on the television.

Summer looks over at me and Jason, eyes twinkling with mischief. "Didn't I tell you guys this road trip was going to be totally awesome?"

SNOW AND ICE buffets us as we stand outside the rusty garage door that purports to be an auto-body and mechanic shop.

Anyone looking at us would think we are out of our minds – five teenage kids huddled beside a closed garage door during a raging blizzard.

That is, if they could see us through the snow.

"There's a side door here," Jason points out, half yelling to be heard over the wind.

Even still, the wind carries away his voice.

"There's a doorbell too."

Jason rings the buzzer.

I strain to hear it, but sound and scents tangle on wind and snowflakes in a confusing cacophony, so who knows if the thing is actually working. For a shifter, the noise of the storm is almost overwhelming on the senses.

The door swings open and we're greeted by a giant of a man with a scarred, craggy face, close cropped brown hair and shoulders so broad he's wider than the door frame.

A gust of wind blows past us, causing a flurry of snowflakes to tumble into the hallway behind him. The man's nostrils flare as if he's scenting the wind and his eyes widen, flashing a preternatural yellow. Thick lips curl up, baring a row of stained teeth and he fixes Jason with a menacing glare.

"Wolf."

He says the word like it's a curse.

I can feel Jason tremble, can practically see his body quiver with the need to shift and run.

Instinctively, I step forward and shove him behind me, tilting my chin up to meet the stranger's eyes with my own.

"We called about a car repair," I say evenly.

I'm close enough now to pick up the stranger's scent, even with the swirling wind at my back. He smells of fresh turned earth, honey and blueberries. And definitely shifter.

He stares down at me, gaze unflinching.

If I'd been raised among shifters, maybe I'd be able to tell what animal he is just by scent or look or some other tell. But given the size of this guy, I think it's fairly safe to guess bear shifter.

I make a point of tilting my head to the hallway behind him. "Is there an office or something so we can come in and chat?"

He looks over the group of us for a long moment, taking in Lucy, Tori and Summer huddled under the awning, their coats clutched around them. Jason standing behind me, probably with his eyes downcast in the picture of lupine submissiveness.

The stranger grunts, then waves us in, muttering something about messy pups and wet dog smell.

The office he leads us to probably better fits the description of man cave, with its dilapidated couch, mini fridge, coffee machine, neon sign that looks like it was stolen from a bar, and small television blaring college basketball.

Once we're crammed inside, he rounds on us. "What's a bunch of pups doing out here, in the middle of a blizzard? This is no place for wolves, not this close to the Bear Tooth mountains."

His green eyes flash yellow again as he takes us all in, wrinkling his nose. "This here is bear territory."

Lucy steps forward, chin held high, bearing almost regal with formality as she holds out her hand in greeting. "I'm Lucy Stone, daughter of the beta of Clear Creek pack."

He takes her hand reluctantly, looking over the group of us warily.

"We were passing through and got caught last night in the blizzard." Lucy nods to the group of bedraggled teens behind her, all dripping melted snow onto the threadbare carpet. "The windshield of my car caved in and we were hoping you could repair it. Then we'll be on our way." She pauses, then adds, "We have no intention of infringing on bear territory."

"Clear Creek, eh. I've heard of your pack. Wyoming, right?" The man's expression softens slightly, but not enough to erase the frown etched on his rugged face.

From the lines around his mouth and eyes, I get the feeling he's the sort of person who would rather smile. Or maybe, he used to smile.

He's certainly not smiling now.

"They'll be no fixing any windshield until early next week, young she-wolf," he grumbles. "Gotta leave time for ordering parts, and what with it being the weekend…" he tapers off, and I can see Lucy's shoulders slump.

Beside me, Tori lets out an exasperated whine. I half expect to see her stamp her foot. "Do you have a car we could borrow while we wait for repairs?" Tori asks, "You know, like a courtesy vehicle or something? We really need to get on the road."

The man lets out a rumbling growl that I think might be laughter. It's hard to tell.

"A courtesy vehicle?" More rumbling laughter. "Lady, that'll be the two posts holding you up. Or four, if you go furry." He shakes his head, chuckling at his own joke.

His brief outburst of mirth is suddenly stifled and he looks over our group with a suspicious frown. "What's a bunch of pups doin' out this way alone anyway? And in a blizzard?" He narrows in on Lucy. "Does your alpha know you're here?"

Lucy doesn't answer and the man's frown deepens. "I'm not going to be helping out a bunch of runaways," he says. "We don't need that kind of trouble with your pack. Us bears, we keep to our own out here."

"I'm not a runaway," Tori says, tossing her hair over her shoulder. "I'm eighteen."

The bear shifter raises one eyebrow, looking pointedly at the rest of us. "Maybe. But I doubt the rest of them are."

His eyes land on me, and the silence stretches on, building to an uncomfortable tension that hums like the sound of the neon sign on the wall.

There's nothing that Summer, Lucy or Jason can say to defend themselves. Because all it would take is one call to their alpha to expose any lie they might tell.

I step forward. "We're tracking two kids – two pups," I correct, using the terminology he used, even if it's hard thinking of Cody and Alton as pups. "They went missing a couple days ago and we're fairly certain the shifter who took them lives up in northern Montana. These guys aren't runaways," I say, pointing to the others, "they're just trying to find their packmates."

I hesitate, wondering how honest to be with this guy. After a lifetime of avoiding shifters, it's not in my nature to be trusting. I know that.

But if we're going to have any chance of getting out of this snow filled hole in the middle of Montana, we're going to need this guy's help.

I look at the bear shifter's face - craggy and scarred, rough stubble over smile lines, kind earthy green eyes that are looking at the group of us with a mixture of protectiveness and concern.

My wolf likes him. Almost wants to trust him.

"I'm not even pack," I admit. "I'm a lone shifter."

The bear shifter's eyes widen at that admission.

Not surprising, it is basically the equivalent of walking into a bear den and saying 'hey, I'm alone in the world, no one will care if I go missing. In fact, the shifter world would probably rejoice'.

I carry on. "My mom was killed by my dad's old packmate. The scent of the wolf that took our friends, it's the same scent as my mom's killer."

A lump forms in my throat at those words. I've said them more in the past couple days than I have since she died. Maybe it will get easier?

"This could be a matter of life and death for our friends. Any help you can give us to get back on the road could make a real difference."

The bear shifter looks at me for a long moment, letting his eyes drift over the others, expression inscrutable.

Finally, he heaves out a sigh, gesturing to the worn couch behind us.

"Sit down," he says. "It sounds like we have a lot to talk about."

AN HOUR later and we are in a bulky nine-seater fitted with snow tires, slowly ambling along the freeway towards Missoula.

The bear shifter, Orrin Brown, sits behind the steering wheel, the gentle cadence of his voice interrupting the country music blaring through the van's blasted-out speakers.

After hearing our story, Orrin had explained that a sixteen-year-old bear shifter had gone missing from bear territory a week ago. The cub was his nephew, and although they had caught the scent of wolves near Orrin's sisters' home, they hadn't been able to track the kidnappers.

Then yesterday, Orrin had caught wind of a bobcat shifter going missing. This time, it was the sixteen-year-old brother of Orrin's apprentice. When Orrin had investigated, the same wolf scent had lingered near the bobcat's home as well.

"I didn't realize cat shifters and bear shifters co-existed in the same territory," Jason muses from the back row of the van.

He clearly feels comfortable that Orrin doesn't pose a threat, because he's been pretty chatty since we piled into the van, peppering the bear shifter with questions, trying to fill in the gaps of his knowledge on other shifter breeds.

"I always thought of bears as solitary animals."

Orrin lets out a short, mirthless laugh. "We are solitary." His eyes flash in the rear-view mirror as he takes us all in. "And I'm no exception. I should be hibernating right now, not playing chauffeur for a bunch of mangey pups."

He takes another bite of the meat stick in his hand. It's his third one since we got in the car ten minutes ago.

"I'm only awake on account of Danny going missing. Couldn't sleep after that. And then Red's little brother…" He lets out a low, rumbling growl. "Let's just say I've been a bit riled up since then."

"Red, he's a bobcat, right?" Jason clarifies. "And he works for you?"

Orrin shrugs. "Yah, well, he don't need to hibernate like I do. Good to have someone around who can keep the business going while I sleep. Watch my back a bit."

"Is that why the bears and cats share territory?" Jason asks, trying to sound casual but unable to mask his interest. "For defensive purposes?"

"You sure ask a lot of questions, pup," Orrin bites out.

Jason flinches at the harsh tone, slumping back into his seat.

Orrin must notice the movement in the rear-view mirror, and shakes his head apologetically.

"Its fine. I get it. You wolves don't get out much, I know how it is. Yes, we co-exist for defensive purposes, but also because we don't have much of a choice. Cats and bears need a lot more space than wolves because of our anti-social natures, so to speak. And we need wild space to hunt and fish. You can't just put a bunch of bears or cats on a ranch and let them run around like you wolves do. What with human development and farming in these parts, those wild spaces have gotten smaller and smaller. We had to learn to live together. Even then, misunderstandings happen."

He gives a wry smile, expression dark. I wonder if it's those misunderstandings that have left him with those scars across his face and forearms.

It takes a lot to leave scars on a shifter.

"How long to Red's place?" Lucy asks from the other side of the van.

Orrin agreed to accompany us, and lend us his giant van, as long as we agreed Red could come with us. Seeing as Red's brother was one of the people who have gone missing, this request seems fair enough. Lucy, however, has been pretty vocal about not wanting any delays.

"Another twenty minutes in these conditions." Orrin tilts his head at the road ahead of us.

It's impossible to see more than twenty feet ahead through the blizzard and, as if on cue, a particularly strong gust of wind buffets the van, causing it to careen partially into the other lane.

"Why, not driving fast enough for you princess?"

Lucy ignores the jab, looking coolly out the passenger window. There can't be much to see, just endless white moving and swirling with dizzying relentlessness.

"Just calculating where we're likely to stop for the night," she says.

Orrin lets out an irritated rumble. "In this weather, might as well ask how long's a piece of string."

"You sure this Red guy is trustworthy?" Lucy asks.

I notice then how stiff her posture is, the way she's pushing at the cuticles on her fingers. Leaning forward, as if she can will the vehicle to go faster. It's so subtle, most people would probably miss it. She's anxious, and I don't think it's about the bobcat.

"Not at all. Wouldn't trust him for all the salmon in the world," Orrin rumbles, and I exchange a worried glance with Summer, who is sitting in the row of seats behind Lucy and I, next to Jason. "But you won't find a better tracker. Not for the type of prey you're following, anyway. And he's got good reasons not to piss me off." Orrin pauses, considering, then adds, "I'll ask him to make the same blood oath I made."

The bear shifter lifts one paw from the steering wheel, showing the freshly healing mark on the palm of his hand.

Lucy had refused to let Orrin join us until he swore a blood oath to do us no harm. He'd then asked us for a similar oath, which we'd grudgingly given. My own palm still stung from the bear shifter's hunting knife. I healed faster than a human, but not as fast as a shifter who could fully tap into their animal abilities.

When I'd naively asked about the risk of blood-borne illnesses, everyone had just laughed at me. Once they realized I wasn't joking, Jason had explained as seriously as he could that shifters don't get diseases like humans do.

"Surely, you've noticed that you've never gotten sick before, right?"

It's becoming glaring obvious that there are some serious knowledge gaps when it comes to understanding my own kind.

I blame dad.

Lucy gives a curt nod in response to Orrin's assurances regarding Red.

"Good," she says, looking back out the window. "That should work."

For several long minutes, the only sound is the howling of the blizzard, the rumbling of the van and the groan of country music over the stereo. To my surprise, it's the somewhat taciturn bear who breaks the silence with a question aimed at Tori.

"You're mated to one of the pups?"

Tori preens, sitting straighter in the front passenger seat, casting a look of superiority around the van. "Yes. Anton Stone, the beta's son, is my pre-destined mate."

"Future mate," Summer clarifies from the back seat. There's a stifled laugh from Jason beside her.

"There's no bond yet then?" Orrin asks, "You haven't – um – finished things."

Tori flushes, though I couldn't tell if it is from embarrassment at Orrin's question, or irritation at Summer. "We're waiting until we finish high school. But it doesn't change anything about how I feel…"

"I'm not asking about your feelings, lady." Orrin lets out a rumbling laugh, as if the very thought of him inquiring about Tori's feelings is laughable. "I was just wondering if you could feel him through your bond. You know, tell if we were getting closer and all that. Assume wolf mate bonds work the same as bear ones in that regard?"

"They do," Jason chirps from the far back seat, sounding like he is answering a teacher's question in class. "From what I've read, wolf mate bonds give the bonded pair the ability to sense each other emotionally and cognitively, unless the physical distance is too great. Of course, this only applies where the mates have accepted one another and left their mating marks…" His voice falters, his expression turning pensive.

I wonder if he's thinking of Ross, the human mate he hasn't been able to claim. The one his pack won't accept.

"And none of you can feel the two pups through your special wolfy pack link?" Orrin asks.

"It doesn't work like that," Lucy says, almost impatiently. "We can only communicate through the link if we're in close proximity. Maybe a couple of miles. Alphas can sense the location of their wolves from a bit farther, apparently. But *that* power doesn't extend to the rest of the pack."

Orrin lets out a disgruntled huff, then turns down a gravel drive. After several minutes, a small cabin comes into view, the wood building half buried by snow drifts. The van horn blares and, moments later, a hooded figure emerges, darting through the driving snow and climbing into the seat next to me in the van.

Actually, to be more specific, he climbs into *my* seat, forcing me to move into the middle, so I'm seated between him and Lucy. And just like that, I have the middle seat again. Typical.

I immediately forget my concerns about the new seating arrangement when the newcomer pulls of the hood of his parka. For several long moments, I just gape. Like, rude, open mouthed gaping. He quirks a brow in response, eyes flashing cat in challenge. I shut my mouth and force my eyes away from the tufted cat ears on his head, dropping my gaze to meet his own.

"They're called ears, wolfy," the feline drawls as he shoves a duffel under his seat and straps on his seatbelt.

Orrin chuckles as he reverses the van out of the driveway and heads back towards the freeway.

"Red here is a little tender about his ears," Orrin explains. "And his tail too for that matter. Though you're not likely to get a glimpse of that unless we need to shift." Another chuckle.

Red lets out a low hiss in response, then turns to glare out the window. If I could see his tail, and if bobcats had tails longer than a little puff of fur, I imagine his would be twitching.

"You're a demi?" Jason asks excitedly from the back corner of the van.

Maybe he's feeling bolder after asking Orrin so many questions without getting his head bitten off. Or maybe he just feels safe because of the seats separating him from the feline.

"I mean, you can fully shift right? But then can't lose all your cat features when you're in human form?"

"Gold star for you, pup," Red sneers at Jason. "You read a few books, did you?"

Jason doesn't answer, but I'm caught on the term. *A demi.*

"What is it when someone can't shift back from their animal form at all?" I ask Jason, thinking of Jamison, stuck in his wolf form.

To my surprise, Tori pivots from her seat at the front to answer me.

"That is called going feral."

There's a sadness to her voice that I haven't heard before as she adds, "Shifters like that have to be put down."

"Put down?" I ask, alarmed. "Why?"

"When a shifter goes feral, their human side takes the backseat and it's the beast who runs the show. Feral shifters are dangerous and unpredictable. They'll attack pack members, even those closest to them…" Tori's voice trembles slightly at this last statement and she turns away.

I stare at the back of her head, mind racing. By the way she's talking, she must have known a wolf that went feral. But this doesn't sound at all like Jamison. I can't imagine him attacking grandpa. Not to mention I was a stranger when he met me, and welcomed me into his den.

"The lady's right," Orrin confirms. "Shifters that go feral have been known to attack their own children, siblings, even mates."

"Are you sure?" I ask. "I mean, are there ever times when they could be stuck in their animal form but just act like a normal shifter?"

Orrin shakes his head. "Not that I've ever heard of."

"As great as this academic chat is," Lucy interrupts, "Kitty Cat here needs to swear that oath we discussed before we go much further."

Red bristles at the nickname, leaning across me to fix Lucy with a cold stare. She just stares back at him, face impassive, though I don't miss the way her fingers tap on the ledge below the window.

I press back in my seat, trying not to feel like I'm right in the middle of some weird stand-off between Lucy and Red, but it doesn't really help.

"And you," Lucy snaps irritably at me. "Do you really need to man-sit with your legs apart like that? You are taking up way too much space here."

She indicates where my thigh barely brushes against her own on the seat.

I just look at her incredulously, trying to work out if she's for real, then down at my legs.

Now that I'm in the middle seat, my leg room is seriously impacted by the crappy design of this archaic mini-van. I'm not exactly short, so it is virtually impossible for me to sit in this seat without widening my knees.

"Yah, um, hate to break it to you, but there is no other way I'm fitting in this clown car," I tell her seriously.

"Clown car? It's a van, Finch. A van."

She pushes her leg against my own, as if she can move it over or something. Of course, my knee is wedged into the back of the driver's seat, so her efforts are completely futile.

"Move. Your. Fat. Self. Over," she hisses, pushing against me with each word.

Yep. I think she's actually lost it.

Also, even though I know it's really not the time, my body gets the wrong idea about her leg pressing up against mine. Like, she's playing footsie with me or something. Not trying to push me away.

My cheeks flush, and I shift awkwardly in my seat, trying to adjust myself so no one sees the increasingly obvious sign of the effect she's having on me.

As if cued by whatever shifter gods delight in making life as embarrassing as possible for me, her eyes drop to my lap and widen. The leg pressed beside mine stills and I hear her breath catch before she quickly turns away to look out the window.

I rub my hand down my face, trying to wipe away the burning red that's probably staining every single one of my features.

Something tells me it's going to be a long, long drive.

Chapter 18

Tobias Finch

"I swear to do Red Irving no harm."

If I thought cutting across the middle of my palm was uncomfortable last time, it's even worse cutting across a half-healed scar when my hands are frozen from standing out in a blizzard.

The worst part is, the whole blood-letting part of this is completely pointless for me, if what grandpa said was true.

Any promises made by a born alpha are binding. Regardless of whether there is a blood oath.

Just like before, I'm the last one to give the oath. My blood drops from my palm into the snow before I wipe the blade and hand it back to Orrin.

This time, I don't point out that failing to sanitise his knife between uses risks transmitting blood born illnesses. I've been laughed at enough about that today.

I frown at the cut on my palm, already starting to knit shut.

“Right, back on the road,” Orrin says.

It’s a pointless request since its colder than a freezer out here and everyone is already piling into the van, seeking out shelter and warmth.

We drive for a long while with only the sound of the blizzard and Orrin’s country music. Summer and Jason have fallen asleep in the far back seat, Lucy is reading some book on her phone and Tori has her headphones on. Probably listening to some audio meditation or that hippie new-age music she tries to subject us to.

Red hasn’t spoken, but just stares at the snow flurries buffeting the window, as if they hold the answer to some long-asked question.

I suddenly feel bad about the way I responded to his ears. For the most part, I can hide the fact that I’m latent. I can blend in to human society. And as long as I wear contact lenses, no one will know I’m a born alpha either. Hopefully. But Red can’t hide his ears. At least, not without wearing a hood or a hat.

“I’m sorry if I was rude about the ears,” I say to Red, keeping my voice low.

Red turns to look at me, his expression a mask of haughty nonchalance. I can feel his hurt though. It practically flows off of him in waves. The feeling is enough to rile my wolf until the animal is clawing at me, angry that I’ve caused this newcomer pain.

Pack, the defective animal growls, *Red is pack.*

I shake my head at that bizarre thought, but logic isn’t enough to stop me from trying to make things right.

“I should have been more understanding,” I explain, leaning forward. “See, I’m actually latent. Like, I can’t even shift at all.”

Okay, why am I telling him this? First the pack. Then Orrin. Now this strange shifter I’ve literally just met. It’s like I’ve developed verbal diarrhoea since leaving New York.

Red's eyes flare wide in surprise, then narrow. He leans forward, sniffing me delicately before he sits back, running a hand through his shaggy auburn hair and pulling one of his distinctive tufted ears in thought.

"You don't smell latent."

"Well, I definitely am. I just turned sixteen and I've never shifted."

Most wolves shift by thirteen, so not shifting by sixteen is pretty much a sure sign that I'm latent, whatever I smell like.

Also, did I mention I had a birthday? No? Well, that's because it was completely a non-event. The 23rd of December came and went without a soul remembering the date was of any particular importance, other than it being the day before Christmas eve.

I give a mirthless laugh. "I probably just smell extra wolfy from hanging out with this bunch."

Red purses his lips, considering. "Nah. You still don't have the scent. I've met latent shifters before. They have a scent. You don't."

A thrill of hope courses through me at his words and I quickly tamp it down.

How many times in the past two years have I tried to convince myself that maybe I really could shift after all? That I was just waiting for the right moment to call my wolf to the surface.

That hope was well and truly shattered the day mom died. Because if the need to defend my own mom wasn't enough to bring on the shift, I don't think anything will be.

I shake my head. "Trust me. I can't shift."

Red shrugs with feline indifference. "If you say so."

"What do you mean, a scent?" Lucy asks, looking up from the book she's reading on her phone.

"All latent shifters I've met have a scent," Red explains, stretching long legs out in front of him till they press against the back of Tori's seat. "My aunt mated a human." Red wrinkles his nose. "They had three kittens, all latent. They all had a scent. Like the animal had been watered down, replaced with that gross, acidic human scent, if you know what I mean."

I nod. I know exactly what he means, though the smell of humans has never bothered me.

"I thought it was just them. You know, maybe a family thing or whatever. And then I met a bear shifter in these parts who is latent. He had that same smell to him." Red fixes me with a curious look. "You, wolfy, you don't have it."

"Maybe I'm defective even for a defective wolf," I offer.

"Maybe," Red drawls, frowning. "Or maybe it's because of your dominance level," he muses.

My back stiffens despite myself. I've known this bobcat shifter all of an hour and can't think of anything I've done to show dominance. Sure, I've stopped exaggerating submissiveness, now that Lucy and the rest know I'm not really a submissive wolf.

"What do you mean?" Lucy asks, leaning forward with interest.

"Dominant shifters are usually late bloomers. I guess because their animal is too powerful to fit into a young kid," Red explains. "My brother is the perfect example. Kitten didn't shift until he was fifteen." Red gives a caustic laugh. "Not that any of us call him Kitten any more. He's only sixteen, but I recon he'd rival Orrin here for strength. At least in animal form. He's still a lanky thing in his human form."

"Questionable whether he'd be as strong as me," Orrin rumbles out from the driver's seat, clearly not liking the insinuation that a sixteen-year-old shifter could take him on.

"He's the brother that went missing?" Lucy asks gently.

"Yah." Red's expression darkens.

"What's his name?"

"Samson."

"Sounds like a fitting name," Lucy says, "since he turned out so strong."

I turn to stare at Lucy, half wondering if some friendly spirit has possessed her body. I swear I've never seen her this conversational and well, *friendly*. She's almost nice sounding.

She pointedly ignores my gaze, keeping her attention on Red.

Red huffs out a breath. "Yah. Guess it is. Your brother went missing too?"

He gives Lucy an appraising look as he asks this and I feel an irrational urge to punch him in the face.

Lucy doesn't seem to notice the way he is looking at her as she replies: "Yep. Anton."

"He a big guy? Powerful shifter?"

"Yah." Lucy cocks her head in question. "Why?"

Red brushes off the question, fixing Lucy with his pale brown eyes. "What about the other guy?"

"Cody? He's the alpha's son. In line to be the next alpha."

Red strokes his face pensively, rough fingertips rasping on dark stubble.

I know from what Orrin said Red is only 19 or 20 years old, but he looks older. Maybe it's the tired look in his eyes, the harsh set to his jaw, or the jaunty angle of his nose.

He looks like he's had to fight for everything the world has given him, and that fight has never been a fair one.

"That seems to be a common thread with these missing shifters," Red finally says. "A few went missing from Utah last month too, and it was the same thing. Teenage boys, all highly dominant with strong animals. You know, future alpha and beta material. No females. No submissive animals. Obviously no defective shifters."

He points at me and himself when he says this last bit.

Lucy pales at this revelation. "Anton is in line to be beta." Her voice trembles and I find myself fighting the urge to close the small space between us and grab her hand, offer her reassurance.

Of course, that would probably result in me getting a punch to the face.

I fold my arms across my chest instead, tucking my hands under my arms.

"Why would someone kidnap a bunch of strong male shifters?" I ask. "Even if they are young, it seems pretty dumb to take off with a shifter that's capable of ripping you to shreds. Wouldn't it be easier to grab submissive or weaker shifters?"

"Oh, it'd be easier alright," Orrin rumbles from the driver's seat, reminding me he's been listening to our whole conversation. "But that wouldn't likely serve their purpose."

"What do you mean?"

"I mean," Orrin lets out a low growl, the sound reverberating in my bones. "I mean, someone is building a shifter army."

My wolf stirs, as if this is a battle cry it wants to answer.

WHEN WE GET to the hotel that evening, the theory about the shifter army is all anyone wants to talk about. That, and the weather.

If the shifter gods were real, they would be laughing at us now. It's taken us all day to travel what would normally take three hours on clear roads.

I almost question whether it's worth it to drive in the storm at all. We could wait until the storm passes and get to Missoula in less than a day.

Then I remember that the kidnapper is a murderer. A murderer who is most likely building an army. And then I can feel my wolf bucking against the bars of his doorless cage, demanding to go. To track. To hunt. Anxious even to be stopping for the night.

On the bright side, the hotel we are staying at is pretty nice. At least, compared to the dump we crammed into last night. This place is a real hotel, not a motel, plus it has a pool and continental breakfast.

We're also all staying together in a three-bedroom suite.

"If you pups think I'm going to leave you unprotected in a strange city, when there's a murdering kidnapper on the loose, then you've got another thing coming," Orrin had said when Jason was looking through hotel room options online. "I might have agreed not to call your alpha, but that doesn't mean that I think it's safe for a bunch of kids to be travelling alone."

Tori pointed out that she was eighteen, and therefore not a pup. I pointed out that if Red's theory was right, no one would bother trying to kidnap any of us. Orrin wasn't swayed.

"We don't need you to protect us," Lucy had argued. "We are able to protect ourselves just fine."

Orrin had glowered at that, his eyes flashing yellow.

"We gave a blood oath."

As if that statement was all that needed to be said. As if the blood oath not to harm was the same as a blood oath to protect.

My wolf agrees with this interpretation.

Pack. Orrin is pack, my wolf whispers. *Red is pack.*

Great. First Cody. Now Red and Orrin.

In its loneliness, my wolf is apparently deluding itself into thinking it has a pack. I'm starting to be concerned that something is seriously wrong with my wolf. Other than the obvious latent issue.

"You going to the pool?" Summer asks, eyeing me as I slink out of the room I'm sharing with Jason.

She's crammed into a room with Lucy and Tori, but is currently sitting on the couch in the shared lounge. No doubt trying to avoid Lucy and Tori's latest argument about who is going to use the shower first.

"Mind if I tag along?"

"Sure, you can come."

I would rather have the time alone, but I don't have the heart to tell her that. Especially when she looks as desperate as I feel to get out of this room. Away from these people.

"Thanks!"

She flashes me a relieved smile before darting into her room to get changed. A few minutes later and we are padding barefoot down the carpeted hallways to the indoor pool.

"Do you think Red is right? That they're building an army?" Summer asks as we slip into the pool.

She keeps her voice low, eyes darting nervously to the couple sitting in the hot tub, in case they overhear.

"I don't know," I reply cautiously. "I hope not."

Red and Orrin's theory seems plausible, but it gives rise to quite a few questions. Like, why would the shifter who murdered my mom build an army in the first place? Who would that army fight against? And why?

I let out an irritated huff and dive under the water, kicking out in long strokes to the other end of the pool, then back again. Swimming until the angry rumbling of my thoughts has mellowed to a low hum. Basking in the solitude of being under water.

That's when it happens. Pain spears through me, like a branding iron under my skin. I freeze mid-stroke, choking on water for several long moments before I'm able to surface and swim to the edge. Then the pain hits me again, hot as electricity coursing through my bones.

I'm vaguely aware of Summer swimming up to me, asking me if I'm okay. But I'm not in the pool anymore. Not really.

The smell of fear, excrement and burnt flesh is thick in the air, filling my nostrils, making my eyes water.

Snowflakes filter in, reflecting against the dim light, shimmering with the metal wire of a cage and the flimsy walls of a dilapidated warehouse.

A cacophony of human cries and animal growls filling the night.

Rows and rows of cages, so many voices full of pain, anger and despair.

In front of me, red paws coated with mud and dried blood claw at the bars of a cage, the strange metal burning with even the slightest contact…

A panicked breath and I'm back in the pool again, nearly stunned by the cleanliness of the tiles, the smell of chlorine and the bright florescent lights. I rest my forehead on the edge of the pool, panting to catch my breath.

"Tobias?" Summer's voice is pitched high with panic.

"Fine," I grit out. "I'm fine."

But I'm not fine. Far from it.

"Do you need me to get someone?"

I shake my head, mind racing with panic. Because I know exactly what this is, what just happened. Even if I don't know how it happened. Or why it's only happening now.

I need to think. Need to get alone to think. Maybe call grandpa.

Summer grips me by the shoulder. "Tobias, you're scaring me. Tell me what is wrong."

There is no way I'm telling her. Out of all of them, she is the very last person I would tell. Because even if she won't admit it, Cody is hers. And what I've done – well, I have no idea exactly what the implications are, but I'm pretty freaking sure it is going to affect Cody in a big way.

"I think I swam too much," I lie. "Probably need to get some food or something."

"Right. Okay," she nods, biting her lower lip, worry etched on her face. "Then let's get you out of the pool so you can eat."

I nod, even as my wolf recoils at the thought of eating right now. All it wants to do is get back on the road and get to Cody.

Because while I'm not exactly sure how it happened, I do know what it was that I saw.

I was seeing through Cody's eyes. Feeling his pain.

Through a newly-forged pack bond.

Chapter 19

Tobias Finch

I wake with a start to the sound of an alarm blaring, followed by a paw whacking me in the face.

"Watch it, Jason."

I lift an arm to fend off the paws franticly clawing at the bedding as Jason flings himself out of bed and scampers towards the window.

He must have shifted into his wolf form overnight.

Again.

I catch his eyes glinting as he watches me warily from behind the curtains and feel a twinge of guilt at my reaction. He's probably feeling super embarrassed right now.

I reach over to silence the alarm, the face of the hotel clock reading six in the morning in neon lights.

"It's okay." I give Jason what I hope is a reassuring smile. "I didn't mean to freak out. I don't care if you shifted into your wolf again."

Jason drops to his belly behind the curtain, letting out a soft whimper. Sliding out of bed, I get down on his level, holding my hand out to him like he's some dog at a park instead of a half-grown wolf shifter.

"It's okay, man. You didn't scratch me or anything. I'm not mad."

Another whimper. I inch forward and he rolls over, baring his throat to me in the ultimate gesture of lupine submission. My wolf lets out a contented rumble, apparently satisfied that someone is recognising his alpha rank, and I freeze.

This is not normal behaviour. Not even for a submissive wolf like Jason. Maybe towards his alpha, and even then, probably only if he was worried he was pissing his alpha off.

"Jason?"

Maybe I should go and get Summer or Lucy. I've only seen Jason's wolf a handful of times, but I'm pretty sure he shouldn't be acting like this. I'm tempted to order him to shift so I can ask him what is going on, but I also don't want to start using my dominance to boss Jason around. It seems a bit rude.

Sighing, I push to my feet and give Jason a quizzical look.

"I'm going to go for a shower," I say, indicating to the bathroom. "Feel free to shift while I'm gone and maybe you can tell me what this is all about."

There. That's not really an order, but hopefully it will have the same effect.

I give myself a smug smile, congratulating myself on my cleverness as I saunter to the bathroom, grabbing my toiletries bag on the way. Once the door is shut, the first thing I do is dig out my contact lens case so I can take out my contacts. I've been sleeping with them in, which ends up making my eyes feel dry and irritated, but there's really no way around it.

I blink, clearing the sleep from my eyes as I look into the mirror.

And my stomach drops.

Suddenly, Jason's behaviour – well, his wolf's behaviour – makes a lot more sense.

One of my contact lenses must have come out in my sleep because staring back at me is one blue eye and one very gold eye.

I'm not talking amber like grandpa's, or yellow like Orrin's when his bear is showing.

Nope, I'm talking gold. Metallic gold. A colour so unusual that all wolf shifters instinctively know what it means.

Alpha.

I bite back the string of curses that threaten to explode out of me, take out the remaining lens and climb into the shower. I turn the water up to scalding, my heart racing as I stand under the stream.

What am I going to say to Jason? For the life of me, I can't think of any lie that would be believable enough to explain the very unusual eye colour.

And it really could be my life on the line, if Jason tells anyone.

He has to keep quiet. I'll have to make him keep quiet. My gut lurches at the thought, but there's really no other way.

Gritting my teeth with determination, I climb out of the shower and throw a towel around myself. I don't bother with the contacts. Jason's seen what I am. No point hiding it.

What matters is that I catch him before he tells anyone else.

Jason is back in human form when I come stalking out of the bathroom, towel wrapped around my waist. He completely freezes when he sees my eyes, both shining unmistakably gold. Like maybe he'd been hoping it was a trick of the light or something his wolf conjured up.

"You're a …"

"Shh," I say, flicking my eyes meaningfully towards the closed door of our room.

Jason's face pales as I stalk over to him. When I release some of my dominance, his hands begin to shake.

"You can't tell anyone," I order, keeping my voice to an almost inaudible whisper while letting the alpha command slip into my words. "My eye colour, what I am, you have to keep it a secret. Understand?"

Jason gives a trembling nod, cowering under the weight of my order.

"Yes, alpha."

I recoil at that response and almost protest him calling me that, even as my wolf preens.

I'm nobody's alpha.

But I guess if I'm using my alpha powers, it only makes sense that this would be Jason's instinctual response.

"Good." I give a forced smile, hoping to put Jason at ease.

I don't like him looking at me like this, like I'm something to be respected or feared. I want him to go back to treating me like Tobias, ordinary wolf shifter who can't shift.

Not sure of what else to say, I head back to the bathroom to put my contacts in and get ready for another day of travelling. With any luck, we could be near Holland Peak and searching for my father's old pack by the end of the day.

The thought fills me with as much dread as hope. Originally, I had only ever planned to help them find where Cody and Anton had been taken to. And to find out where my mother's killer lives, so that I can plan revenge. As in, a revenge at some indeterminable point in the future.

That was before we picked up Orrin and Red. Before I saw, through the bond with Cody, just how very dire things are. Before I saw and heard the despair of all those other shifters, caged and cold and frightened.

Now it's seeming more and more likely that I'll end up facing my mother's killer sooner than planned.

Of course I want vengeance. But I'm just a sixteen-year-old wolf who can't shift. I might be strong by human standards, and at five-foot-ten, I tower over most boys my age and even some grown men.

That doesn't mean I think I stand a chance against a full-grown shifter. Against teeth and claws and preternatural strength.

I'm afraid. Which I guess is a good sign, since it means I have at least enough sense and self-preservation to realize the odds are against me.

Unfortunately, this sense of fear doesn't extend to my wolf.

My thoughts are interrupted by a knock on the door to our room.

"You guys up? We need to get on the road in ten," Lucy calls from the other side of the door. "The blizzard has stopped."

I come out of the bathroom just as Jason calls out: "We'll be ready. Thanks Luce." He gives me a wary look before shuffling past me to the bathroom, taking care to give me a wide berth.

I finish packing my bag, then plop down on the bed and pull out my phone. I'm not ready to face the others. Instead, I send grandpa a text.

Thought I should let you know, I'm with the Clear Creek pack kids and we're in Montana. Heading to some mountains north of Missoula to look for dad's old pack. Trying to find Cody and Anton.

I pause, then add: *Don't call because I'm with the others and, you know, shifter hearing...*

Grandpa's response comes less than a minute later: *Not happy to hear this. Stay safe. Remember your promise.*

My chest constricts. How could I forget? My fingers still over the screen as I wonder how best to word this.

Sooo… remember how Cody gave me his blood that one time. Well, I think I accidentally formed a pack link with Cody when I promised to help him. Would a pack link let me see what Cody is seeing?

Grandpa is really the only person I can ask about this, so hopefully he has some insight on what is going on.

His response is instant: *Yes. An alpha can tap into the link and look through a pack member's eyes.*

My skin tingles as a cold chill sweeps over me and my fingers tremble as I type: *I made myself Cody's alpha?*

This time, his response takes a bit longer to come.

If you are seeing through his eyes, then yes.

This is not good. Not good at all.

"LET me take a look at the map on your phone again," Lucy says from beside me in the van, holding her hand out to me, palm up.

Around us, the landscape flashing past is blanketed in white, all the hard edges smoothed under feet of fresh snow. It glistens harshly against the cold winter sun, reflecting the blue sky like millions of gemstones. Snowploughs must have cleared the roads early this morning, because the freeway is clear and we are nearly at Missoula.

Wordlessly, I drop my phone into her waiting hand, shivering as my fingertips brush against her warm palm.

"You're unusually quiet," she says as she takes the phone.

If this was Summer or Jason or even Tori, I would think that comment indicated concern.

I know better with Lucy.

"I'm not a morning person," I lie.

The truth is, the closer we get to Missoula, the stronger my sense of Cody gets. I've been reaching out through the bond, trying to see if I can pinpoint where he is. Trying to see if we're close enough for me to speak with him through the pack link.

"Sure," Lucy drawls before focusing on the map on my phone.

I close my eyes, trying to sense Cody again. Images flash behind my eyelids.

Rows of cages. The thin walls of the warehouse. The scent of fear and rage.

A male walks past, aggressively pointing and gesturing instructions to the shifters in cages.

Anger that is not my own simmers quietly. I wait patiently, a predator lying in wait. My eyes follow the male warily, knowing either through instinct or experience that this male is unpredictable and dangerous…

"Which lake should we try first?" Lucy asks the group at large.

"I say we start with whichever one is closest," Orrin rumbles from the driver's seat. He's insisted on driving again, even though both Lucy and Tori have offered to take a turn. "No sense in driving back and forth."

"We should stop in Missoula and pick up camping supplies," Red chimes in.

He's seated on the other side of me just like yesterday, head tilted back to rest on the seat, eyes closed. I actually thought he was asleep.

"Camping?" Tori squeaks from the front seat. "Oh no, I don't do camping."

Lucy snorts. "Of course, you don't."

"It's not like it's a lifestyle choice or a hobby or something, you know that right?" Summer snaps from the seat behind me.

Dark circles bruise the skin under her eyes, making me suspect she didn't sleep much last night.

"Like, you do know you're not going to find Anton waiting for you at some five-star resort, don't you?"

I shiver, because Summer has no idea how right she is.

Wherever Cody and Anton are, the conditions are deplorable. It also has to be somewhere pretty remote, since a shed full of caged shifters would probably be super noisy.

"We should definitely get camping supplies," I say, kicking myself for not thinking of this before we left Buffalo. "I think wherever the pack is, it's pretty remote. We might even have to hike in."

"You can handle a bit of hiking, right Tori?" Summer asks irritably from the back seat.

I turn and cock a brow at Jason who is sitting beside her, hoping he can explain what is going on with Summer. She's normally more patient with Tori than this.

Jason just shrugs his shoulders and grimaces.

"I could really use some drive-through right about now," Red muses idly, oblivious to the argument going on around him.

"Drive-through sounds like a great idea," I say, half because I'm starving and half because I want to a distraction from the weird aggression going on between Summer and Tori right now.

Red stiffens in his seat beside me, then lets out a weird cat like hiss. "Did you just read my mind?"

"What?" I shoot him a confused look. The bobcat is making no sense right now.

He narrows his eyes at me. *Don't mess with me Tobias.* This time I'm looking at Red, and it's more than obvious that his lips aren't moving.

What is going on? I direct this silent question back at Red, and his eyes widen.

You tell me, wolfy. His lips curl back in a distrustful snarl, and the bobcat ears on his head flatten back.

I press my lips together and look away.

As if that will somehow stop the telepathic connection that's formed between us. Of course, it won't. If it weren't for the fact that I've been seeing through Cody's eyes since last night, maybe it would have taken me longer to figure it out.

My mind flicks back to the knife we all used to give our oath. Drops of blood in the snow to seal our promises.

With both Orrin and Red, I went last. That means that some of Orrin's blood and some of Red's blood went into me. Just like with Cody's blood donation. And then I promised not to harm Orrin and Red. Just like I promised to help Cody.

That promise, given when receiving blood - that must have been enough to create a pack bond.

To test this theory, I stretch a tendril of awareness towards Orrin. I don't want to startle him, especially since he's driving the van. I just want to see if I can see through his eyes like I can with Cody.

At first, nothing happens. Then I close my eyes and suddenly I'm seeing the road flick past, watching large hands that don't belong to me turn the steering wheel, listening to a voice that isn't my own humming along to the country music on the radio.

I snap my eyes open. This is bad. So bad.

First, I accidentally made myself Cody's alpha. Now I'm alpha for a middle-aged bear and a demi-shifting bobcat. Neither of whom are pack animals. They probably didn't want an alpha. If they did, they sure as heck wouldn't want some latent sixteen-year-old for their alpha.

I look sheepishly over at Red. He's staring at me, cat eyes out, ears back, looking well and truly pissed in only the way a cat can do.

I bet he has really sharp claws.

Um, Red, I say tentatively though the bond.

Because there is definitely a pack bond there. I can feel it now, like a band in my chest going straight to him and Orrin.

The one with Cody feels thinner, weaker. Probably because he is so far away.

Not the ones with Orrin and Red though. Those are solid as can be. Yep. Pretty solid.

I can practically feel the blood draining from my face. Red is looking at me like he'd like to see the blood draining from my jugular.

Red, we need to talk.

He lets out a low rumbling growl that sounds very much like its coming from his cat, not him.

"Everything alright back there, Red?" Orrin asks from the driver's seat.

"Oh yah," Red says caustically. "Just peachy."

Orrin's not buying it. "Your cat getting a bit frazzled being in the car, eh? We'll be in Missoula soon and you can stretch your legs then. Get a bite to eat, pick up some camping gear, okay?"

Red nods, like he's totally fine with that, but then lets out a displeased hiss. Orrin chuckles and Red glares out the window, the tufted ear closest to me twitching.

You going to tell me what's going on? Red asks through the bond.

I rub both palms over my face. How to explain?

Well, you know when we did the blood oath thing? I say silently, toying nervously with the drawstring on my hoodie. *I think we maybe sort of formed a pack bond…*

A pack bond? I can literally feel the anger pulsing off Red with those three words. More than anger. Outrage. He taps his fingers on the seat beside me, like a cat flicking a tail before turning to glare at me with glowing cat's eyes.

What the actual crap, Finch. Do I look like a wolf to you? Do I look like I want to be in a pack? Bobcats are solitary animals. Solitary. Do you know what that means? That means not in a pack.

Each of his words lash across the pack bond with the fury of a whip.

I resist the urge to flinch, and give him what I hope is an apologetic look. *I know, I know. I'm really sorry. It was totally an accident.*

His lip curls into a sneer before he turns to glare back out the window. *Well, undo it.*

About that… I bite my lip, and cast him a sideways look. He's still glaring out the window, ear twitching. *I don't really know how.*

At that admission, Red's eyes snap away from the window to give me a scathing look.

I rush on, words tumbling out frantically across the bond. *Also, I may have made Orrin a part of that pack, but I haven't told him yet. I'm going to tell him first thing once he's not behind the wheel of this van. Because he would probably crash the car if I started randomly projecting thoughts into his head.*

I pause, then add: *Oh, and also, you can't tell anyone about this*. At this last part, I push dominance through the bond, compelling obedience like I did with Jason.

I have to admit, I feel a bit guilty. After years of not using my dominance, after a lifetime of never using my born alpha power to compel obedience, now I've done it twice in one day.

"Orrin, can you stop the car?" Red growls, voice strained, as if the bobcat within him is struggling for dominance.

Orrin's eyes reflect in the rear-view mirror, concern written on his face. "Sure thing. Just hold on a sec."

The instant Orrin pulls over on the shoulder of the freeway, Red slides the van door open, throwing himself from the van before the vehicle slows to a stop.

"Easy there, Red!" Orrin bellows.

Red ignores him, shifting into his bobcat form mid-air and landing in the snowdrift at the verge of the freeway. Powder explodes as he hurtles towards snow covered rocks and pine forests that line the mountain pass.

"Crazy cat," Orrin mutters under his breath, shaking his head. "Lucky there were no humans around."

We all get out of the car to stretch our legs while we wait for Red and Summer looks after him with concern.

"He is coming back, right?" Summer queries.

"Oh yah, he'll be back," Orrin chortles. "Red's just got a temper on him. Cat can't stand to be cooped up. Probably driving the feline crazy being in a car with a bunch of wolves."

The wolves all gather around Lucy to look at the map on my phone and I shuffle over to Orrin.

"Um, Orrin." I scuff my feet in the snow. "Can we talk about something?"

"Sure thing, pup." Orrin bites off a strip of berry fruit leather. "What is it?"

I tilt my chin towards the front of the car, indicating for him to follow until we're out of earshot of the others.

"Must be pretty serious if you don't want your packmates to know," Orrin muses.

"They aren't my packmates," I remind him, then grimace as I say: "Speaking of packmates… remember how we did that whole blood oath thing?"

Orrin chuffs out a laugh. "Seeing as it was only yesterday? Yah, I do."

I pause for a long moment, staring at Orrin as he eats his fruit leather, watching his jaw work. He cocks one scarred brow at me and I rub my hands together, warming them against the cold.

When I finally speak, my admission comes out as a whisper. "Well, I think that whole process made me form a pack bond with you and Red."

"Impossible." Orrin shakes his head, taking another bite of fruit leather.

Unfortunately, not, I tell him though the pack link.

He stills, jaw stopping mid-chew as he locks eyes on me. Eyes flash between his usual green and bear yellow.

I'm suddenly very aware just how big and intimidating the guy is. And how did he get all those scars on his face? Was that from fighting? They look like claw mark scars.

Orrin turns towards the deep track in the snowbank. The track that has been left by Red's bobcat form bounding through the snow.

That's why Red freaked out, Orrin's voice rumbles through the bond.

I nod grimly.

Orrin narrows his eyes at me. *The others don't know what you are, do they?*

What I am? Does he know what I am?

Blinking in surprise, I say out loud: "Not sure what you mean."

A muscle in his jaw ticks and I suppress a shiver.

Oh, I think you do.

The words feel icy as they slither into my mind. Colder than the fresh snow glistening around us.

Bears might not have alphas, because we aren't pack animals. But I've been at the top of the food chain in my territory for the past twenty years. No other animal – bear or wolf or cat – has ever bested me for dominance or taken my bear in a fight.

A low growl escapes his lips, even as the words stream silently into my mind.

So, you tell me, Tobias Finch, how does a latent wolf make himself my alpha?

I swallow, my mouth suddenly dry, my mind empty of what to say. *The truth, my wolf whispers. Tell him the truth. He's pack. You owe him that.*

"Jason knows," I whisper, then switch back to the pack link as I remember that I should probably keep this discussion quiet from the other's, even if they are out of earshot.

Jason saw my eyes this morning. I ordered him to keep it secret. My grandfather knows. And my dad's old pack knows. That's why they killed my mom. They're hunting for me.

Hunting for you? I feel the surge of protective concern washing off the bear, pushing away his anger about being in this messed up pack I've accidentally created.

Um, yah. I frown. *They wanted to kill me when I was born, but my parents took me and disappeared. Guess someone managed to track me down earlier this year.*

He lets out another low growl, but this time it's not aimed at me. *What kind of sick animals would want to kill a pup?*

I shrug. "Wolves," I say out loud.

The fact that anyone would try and kill a new-born pup might be shocking to this bear, but it sure isn't shocking to me. It's the way things are. My kind are not allowed to survive. End of story.

Except I did survive. So did Jamison.

It makes me wonder how many other born alphas are out there.

The sound of conversation draws our attention back to the van. Red is shaking off snow, back in his human form and pulling on a fresh pair of pants.

Even from here I can see Red's scowl. Orrin quirks a smile at the sight. *You've made a pack out of me and Red, huh? Wonder how that's gonna turn out for you.*

A few minutes later, when we're back in the van and trundling up the road, it registers that I've left out a pretty crucial bit of information.

Hey Orrin, I call out over the bond. Both he and Red jump slightly at the abrupt intrusion of my voice in their heads. *I... forgot to mention one more thing. I accidentally made Cody part of our pack too.*

To my surprise, Orrin just chuckles and shakes his head. *Course you did.*

Red's furry shoots down the bond, hot as the cattle prod Lucy threatened me with a few days ago. *Really, Orrin? You think that's funny? Is this just a big joke to you?*

Orrin's stares at Red in the rear-view mirror, long enough that Red stops fidgeting beside me and I start to worry about Orrin's driving.

It's actually incredibly convenient, Orrin muses. *Tobias can use the bond with his friend to help us find everyone else. Including Samson and Danny.*

At the mention of finding his brother, Red's shoulders relax and he takes a centring breath.

"Everyone is really quiet," Summer chirps, breaking the silence. "Is everything okay?"

I wince, realising that Orrin, Red and I have been having this silent conversation since we got in the car.

"Of course everything isn't okay, Summer. My mate is missing," Tori says. This last word comes out on a higher pitch than the rest, making my wolf shudder. "You know. Just in case you were too busy playing road-trip to remember."

"Sheesh, Tori, calm down. You know that isn't fair." Jason says, leaning forward to be heard over the engine.

This has the unfortunate effect of putting his head right behind Red.

Red, who is already pretty wound up about the whole accidental pack thing, turns around to hiss at Jason, canines elongating into sharp feline fangs. Jason's eyes go wide and he sits back so abruptly his head thuds audibly against his headrest.

At that moment, Lucy's phone buzzes. She lifts it up to see who is calling before grumbling something unintelligible and silencing the call. Only to have it ring again. And again.

"Someone really wants to talk to you, huh?" I say, because I really can't resist the urge to needle her.

She bristles. "It's my dad."

I figured as much. He's been calling her every day since he and Cody's dad got back to the ranch.

"You don't think he might have some useful intel for us, do you?" Orrin asks.

Lucy lets out a caustic laugh. "If he did, he wouldn't share it with me."

"Have you messaged him or anything?" Summer asks. "You know, just to let him know you're okay?"

Lucy shrugs. "You've messaged your parents. Jason's messaged his mom. Dad's a moderately smart guy. He'll figure it out."

Chapter 20

Lucy Stone

Something is wrong with almost everyone in this van. I can feel it. Smell it. Taste it. Like bitter oranges on the back of my tongue.

The way Jason slunk out of the room he was sharing with Tobias this morning was enough to get me on edge, all on its own. And that was before I smelt Jason, the scent of secrets and lies coating him like a second skin. When I asked him if everything was okay, he just froze up and darted away.

Then there was that bizarre moment when Red literally jumped out of his skin and ran off into the snow. I know the cat is damaged, but that sort of public shifting is next level. A human could easily have seen him.

When we all got back in the van, I noticed Red's scent had changed and Orrin's too. Thick with lies and secrets. Bitter.

Tobias always smells like lies. There's nothing new there.

Although lately, sitting next to him in the van, all I've been able to notice is the more pleasant smell of pine, sage and chocolate. My wolf wants to curl up beside him, rest her head on his knee, let him sink his fingers into the fur between her ears.

It's distracting. I should be interrogating him. Not wanting to cuddle up next to him.

Actually, I should be interrogating all of them. Except for Summer and Tori, because the two of them are just as annoying transparent as ever.

I watch Tobias out of the corner of my eye. Quietly observing him. His gaze is unfocused and occasionally his mouth quirks into a half smile, like there is some private joke going on in his head.

It reminds me of the look my packmates get when they are talking to someone through the pack link. If I didn't know any better, I'd say that is what's going on now. But he's not part of a pack. Out of all the things he's told me, that at least I know is true.

I need to get to the bottom of what is going on. Because something is going on.

My phone buzzes again. Dad.

Where are you?

I don't answer.

I've turned the tracking off on my phone so he can't use that to find my location. Alpha can probably use his alpha bond to track us down, but that is not an exact science. And I suspect dad won't want to tell the alpha that I've run off. At least not right away. He'll protect me, like he always does. Not because he cares about me. But because he knows without my gift, he's nothing more than a glorified enforcer. Hardly a beta at all.

Missoula meets us before we know it. It's nothing compared to the cities Tori or Tobias have been to, but it's practically a raging metropolis compared to Buffalo.

For once, I'm glad the bear is driving and not me. I might be able to handle icy roads, but city roads are another matter.

In the summer, Missoula is actually quite pretty, with its river winding through trendy brick buildings, the whole place dotted with trees and wooded pathways.

This time of year, it's dreary. Most of the university students are away on holiday, back with their families for Christmas or up at Whitefish skiing. It's not surprising that the outdoor sporting goods shop we wander into is empty.

What is surprising is the smell of shifter as soon as we walk through the doors.

The sales clerk greeting us looks just as surprised to see us. Possibly a little terrified. He freezes behind the cash register, blinking rapidly from behind round glasses that are so thick they have the effect of making his eyes look even bigger and rounder than they are. My wolf wrinkles her nose at the scent of feathers. Some sort of avian shifter.

"Wh-what brings y-you here today?" The sales clerk stutters before using his index finger to push his glasses up his nose.

He makes no move to come and greet us like a human would. Or like he probably would if *we* were humans. Smart animal. There's no mistaking us as anything but predators.

I fix him with a stare that makes him drop his own gaze. It's good to establish hierarchy right away. Better if everyone knows where they stand.

"We need some camping gear," I say simply, listing off the items we've discussed needing to purchase. "Packs, sleeping bags, a couple of tents. Dry food and a camp stove."

Jason and Summer were both worried about how we would pay for everything, but surprisingly Tobias stepped in, offering to pay for any gear people couldn't afford. He said he has money in a checking account from his inheritance that was recently cleared.

Generosity like that makes me suspicious. People don't give away something unless they want something in return. Or unless they feel guilty. I wonder which is the case for him.

"W-we can help you," the avian shifter stutters in reply. "N-not the b-best we-weather for camping though. They say another storm is coming through in the next couple days."

He wrings his hands nervously, and I stare at him until he looks away again, my packmates already rifling through shelves and display cabinets to find what they need. I follow their lead, though I actually came better prepared than the lot of them. I already have all my camping gear, and just need some dry goods and camping fuel.

To be honest, I don't even need those. I'm perfectly capable of hunting in wolf form. I've done it before. It's just a lot easier to add boiled water to a pre-made camping meal.

Orrin is helping Tobias pick out the right type of gear. For a wolf that can't shift, you'd think Tobias would be a little smarter about having things like boots and coats. You know, the things humans typically need when they go out in the cold.

I roll my eyes. The bear shifter is entirely too nice.

When the sales person catches sight of Red's ears, he tenses. "Y-you shouldn't be out in public," he squeaks nervously. "The humans will see you."

Red just lays his ears flat and flicks his hoodie back over his head, looking like a delinquent teenager as he eyes the avian the studied disinterest typical of cats.

"Humans never see anything. Even if it's right in front of them," Red sneers.

The avian opens his mouth like he's going to say something more, but a stern glance from Orrin silences him.

A few minutes later, I hear Jason introducing himself to the avian and trying to start up a conversation. He keeps his expression open and his posture non-threatening – smiling, hands in his pockets, not standing too close.

Jason is good at that sort of thing. I suppose it can be useful for getting information. Like the bird shifter's name. Which, it turns out, is Harrison.

"So what packs are around these areas?" Jason asks. "Any wolf packs in these parts that we should be aware of? You know, so we don't accidentally trespass on anyone's territory."

Harrison flashes a nervous smile. "You-you're really not from around here, are you?"

Jason shakes his head. "Nope."

"Well…" Harrison pushes his glasses up his nose again before glancing around the shop, as if to be sure no one else but us really is in here. "There's a few wolf packs around Missoula. The ones to the south are pretty friendly. Just small-time packs. Not the kind to tear you to pieces if you accidentally trespass on their borders."

As the avian becomes more confident talking to Jason, I watch them from behind a clothes rack, pretending to browse through the women's clothing as I listen intently.

"Of course, you want to be careful about the Blackwater pack," Harrison says, lowering his voice.

"What's so bad about the Blackwater pack?"

"You've never heard of 'em?" Harrison cocks a pale brow.

"Nope." Jason shakes his head, a friendly, non-threatening smile still stretched across his face.

The bird shifter frowns, looking thoughtful, as if he's not quite sure what is safe for him to divulge. "Well," he tenders, finally settling on something, "they have more fighters than any other pack at the pits."

"The pits?" Jason echoes.

"The shifter fight club."

"Wait - there is a shifter fight club here?" I hear the bald curiosity in Jason's voice. It mirrors my own.

"Oh yeah. Surprised you lot haven't heard of it. Good money to be had if you can fight. Your bear friend there would be just the type to get lots of prime bets."

"Someone talking about bears?" Orrin's voice rumbles from the other side of the store, where he is helping Tobias pick out a down jacket.

Harrison flinches at the sound.

"He's alright," Jason reassures him, but the avian doesn't look convinced.

Tobias and Orrin both make their way over to Jason, and Harrison visibly tenses. I frown. It will be a lot harder for Jason to get information from him with those two there. Especially since Tobias is masking his own dominance less and less every day.

Actually, it is becoming clear that, latent though he may be, Tobias' level of dominance would put him on par with most alphas. I don't know if the others have noticed, but I certainly have.

Orrin is just plain scary - until you find out that behind that rugged and scarred exterior is a painfully soft and over-protective male.

"I- I was just telling your friend Jason here about the shifter fight club," Harrison says. "In fact, there is a fight tonight in a warehouse just north of the city. You could get some good coin fighting or betting."

"We're too young to gamble. Except for Orrin, of course," Tobias says naively.

The bird flashes a devilish grin. “That don’t matter. Not at this fighting ring anyway. Once you’re fifteen, you’re of age in our world.”

Tobias looks surprised at that and I wonder if he even knew that he was of age. His parents really didn’t do him any favours trying to raise him as a human, even if he is latent. Even if they didn’t have a pack. Maybe especially because they didn’t have a pack.

Neither Orrin nor Tobias responds to the bird. Instead, they look at each other as if they are having a silent conversation.

As if drawn to their silence, Red saunters over, arms laden with various camping goods. He’s got a pink hat with cat ears pulled over his own tufted ears and I have to fight to suppress a grin. The hat still has its tag attached and it dangling rakishly over one eye, making him look like a bizarre sort of pirate. It’s almost enough to distract me from the way Red is watching Tobias and Orrin. As if he has joined in their silent discussion.

I frown thinking back to the way they were all acting in the van this morning. It really does seem like the three of them are communicating.

Orrin breaks the silence. “We might check out this fight club after all. Can you write down the address for us?”

“No can-do,” Harrison shakes his head. “That is classified. Can’t have the fights getting broken up by law-enforcement or anything like that. They text the location out thirty minutes before doors open.”

Orrin frowns, and the bird quickly adds, “You give me your number, I’ll text you the address.”

The bear’s upper lip curls in a knowing smile that lacks his usual friendliness. “You’re a part of this illegal fighting ring, are you?”

Harrison doesn’t answer, just shifts nervously on his feet. “Do you want to give me your number or not, bear?”

Orrin huffs in annoyance and pulls out his phone, sliding it across the counter to the avian so he can read his number.

I don't like this, I say to Jason over our pack link. *We shouldn't be wasting our time going to some fight. We need to start checking the lakes that Tobias identified in the map.*

Jason doesn't answer. Instead, he just looks away sheepishly, reminding me that he's been hiding something from me all morning.

I don't like it. Not one bit.

I repeat my concerns to the group when we get out of the store. "It's a waste of time to go to this fight," I tell them.

Tobias flashes me his cocky grin before tossing his wavy brown hair out of his eyes. I feel my pulse pick up and then scowl, hating my reaction to him.

It's just a physical reaction, I remind myself. Just senseless biology or chemistry or something. Probably just because he's the only male wolf shifter who isn't pack that I've spent any amount of time with. It doesn't mean anything.

Whatever it is, it unfortunately hasn't been helped by spending all this time in close proximity to him. Breathing in his scent. Sitting beside him in the van and feeling the heat of his thigh pressed against my own. Eating every damn meal together. Seeing him first thing in the morning, shirtless and with sleep tousled hair…

"Are you afraid to go watch a bunch of shirtless men fight?" he asks.

"They're not men," I counter. "They're shifters. And no. I've seen plenty of shirtless males."

Okay, that's not entirely true. I've seen lots of shirtless males. It's just they're either related to me, or they might as well be, seeing as I've grown up with them.

I do my best to look down my nose at Tobias – a difficult task, since he's taller than me – and remind him coolly: "However, I am afraid that something will happen to my brother if he's with a psychopathic murderer for too long."

"That's why we think we should go to this thing," Orrin cuts in, before some other inappropriate garbage can tumble out of Tobias' mouth.

"That bird in there mentioned that a lot of the fighters come from the Blackwater pack north of Missoula. It may be the same pack that we are trying to locate. It wouldn't surprise me if they are having the boys fight as training, if they really are building some shifter army. That would explain why the Blackwater pack have so many males entering to fight at this club."

I frown, hating to concede that they may be right.

"And what? Do you think this pack is just going to share information with you?" I ask Tobias. "Tell you what they are doing and what their location is? Maybe invite us over for a cup of coffee and a tour?"

Tobias just smirks, as if my sarcastic questions amuse him. "More or less," he says vaguely.

Beside him, Red grins darkly, as if whatever thing he's been silently fuming about all morning has taken a back seat. Orrin gives Tobias a concerned frown that Tobias just shrugs off.

I'm left with the incredibly frustrating feeling that I am missing the point of some joke. Or maybe the entire conversation.

TOBIAS FINCH

The parking lot at the warehouse is full of pick-up trucks, motorbikes and cars by the time we arrive.

Our nine-seater van looks out of place, like some soccer mom turned up accidentally to a motorcycle club. And I'm not talking about your grandfather's social motorcycle club, but rather the more illegal kind.

Which is, I guess, to be expected when you show up to an illegal fighting event.

The two shifters manning the door give us sceptical looks when we approach but let us in. The smell of shifter, blood, sweat and some other scent I've never come across before hits me so hard when the doors open that I almost stumble back. The bouncer to my right doesn't miss my reaction and gives a derisive scoff.

"First time is it, pup?"

I don't respond. My instincts tell me this is not a time for sarcastic quips or for downplaying my dominance. I also don't plan on posturing either. The success of our plan - if you can even call this a plan - depends in large part on my blending in enough to be written off as unremarkable.

Given I am pretty unremarkable, that shouldn't be a problem.

The hard part will be staying conscious in the fighting ring long enough to get answers from people. Because I plan to fight. And I am under no illusions when it comes to my abilities.

Oh, I know I can hold my own in a fight against humans. But I won't be fighting humans. I'll be fighting full grown shifters. Ones who can draw on the strength and speed of their animals, even if shifting into animal form in the ring is against the rules.

At least that's what Harrison, the owl shifter we spoke to this afternoon, told us. I certainly hope he was right about that. If not, then I am totally screwed.

My stomach drops when I see the ring itself. What they call the pit.

In the centre of the warehouse, raised up on a makeshift wooden stage is a massive cage. The cage itself is not that different from the cages I've seen in MMA fights on television.

Inside, the two shifters fighting are coated in sweat, their eyes flashing as their animals' surge to the surface, skin rippling as they resist the urge to shift. I can't tell what type of animals they are, but given one of the fighters is a half head taller than Orrin and looks like a bear even in human form, it isn't too hard to guess what he is at least. His opponent is smaller, but moves with an uncanny sort of grace that reminds me of a cat, expertly dodging the large man's blows.

"He doesn't have the reach to get any hits in," I observe, wincing as the larger shifter's fist glances off the side of the other fighter's cheek. It's not enough to knock him out, but throws the smaller fighter off balance.

"You do a lot of fighting, do ya wolfy?" Red asks, stopping beside me to watch the fight.

The crowd around the cage is like a beast in its own right, a teeming mass of shifters howling at their chosen fighters, shoving and fighting amongst each other as they place bets and vie for the best view of the fight.

"Nothing like this," I admit.

I've trained in boxing and combat sports for fun in New York, but it was just that. Fun. A bit of exercise and competition. In a gym. With humans.

The smaller shifter is tiring, either from the hit or maybe he underestimated the larger male's endurance. He tries to get a hit in, but it's sloppy. Desperate.

His opponent takes advantage of the mistake, landing a perfectly aimed hit that drops the smaller shifter to the ground. The crowd erupts, mirroring the violence of the ring.

Red grins. "I'm looking forward to watching you get your tail handed to you."

I contemplate responding by taking a dig at Red's unshiftable taiI, which is presumably currently tucked away in the back of his baggy pants. Instead, I don't respond. Red's still pissed at me, and to be honest, he has every right to be.

Summer wrings her hands. "I don't understand why you guys think you need to fight in this," she says.

What I intend to be a confident smile comes across as an anxious grimace. Summer knows what the plan is, just as well as the rest of us. She just doesn't like it.

Beside Summer, Lucy coldly surveys the chaos, a look of mild disgust on her face but absolutely no fear. Like a predator watching her prey, ascertaining its weaknesses, planning her attack.

I sense rather than see Orrin come up behind us. Maybe it is the new-found pack bond I share with him, but I can practically feel the energy radiating off of him in waves. His usual cheerful calm has been replaced with an alert watchfulness. He wanted to be the only one stepping into the ring tonight, but in the end, he had to recognise that the success of tonight depends on us having as many ears as possible.

"We sign up at the bar," Orrin murmurs, voice barely audible over the din. "Better get over there before all the fights are full."

I nod and make my way over to the bar, Red and Orrin trailing close behind. When I finally manage to catch the bartender's attention, I expect her to look surprised to see someone my age, but she doesn't bat an eye.

"You gonna order, or just stare?" she asks tersely, as she pours another customer's drink.

"We want to sign up for a fight," I say, trying my best to sound like this is something I do all the time. And probably failing.

She doesn't even look at us. "You'll wanna talk to Harrison over there," she drawls, indicating over her shoulder with her chin.

Sure enough, it's the owl shifter from the store, shrouded in shadow, a clipboard in his hands, those big round glasses reflecting eerily in the red lighting.

"Of course," Orrin grumbles, sounding unamused. "Knew that flighty prick was involved in this thing."

Harrison looks up from his clipboard, his eyes darting furtively between me and Red and Orrin. "Glad to see you made it," he grins. "Fighting or betting?"

"Fighting," Orrin says, then nods to me and Red. "Them too."

Harrison just raises his blond eyebrows, but doesn't comment. "Just need the name you want to use, your age and animal," he says.

"Not our weight class?" I ask.

Mainly because that is such a big part of competitive wrestling, that I just assumed it would matter here too.

Actually, come to think of it, I'm pretty sure that is a relevant factor in every type of fighting I've seen on television.

Harrison shakes his head. "Nah, the audience don't care about that. What matters is we make the fight interesting enough to bet on."

I frown, thinking of the unevenly matched fight I just watched. I don't know much about gambling, but I suspect the odds of the smaller shifter winning would be lower. Would that mean that the return would be higher if he did win? Would that tempt the bolder gamblers?

Either way, it doesn't bode well for me. I'm going to be the underdog regardless. I don't need to be facing off against a bear or a puma.

Maybe I could go up against a duck. Or a groundhog…

We give Harrison the details he asks for. I use Jamison's name. I don't know what my dad's old pack knows about me, but on the off-chance someone here knows my name, it seems smart not to advertise it.

"Righty oh," Harrison says, jotting a few things down on his clipboard. "Orrin, you're up in thirty minutes against Aires, a dragon shifter. Red is the fight after, up against Martin, a rogue wolf. And Jamison," Harrison's eyes blink rapidly from behind his glasses as he looks at me. "You're up against Goliath, a kodiak."

I just gape at him, speechless.

Excuse me, what? I'm sorry, did he just say dragon shifter? How is it no one has ever mentioned that shifters turning into mythical creatures is a thing? Is he for real?

If my dad knew this stuff existed and didn't tell me, then he really did let me down.

My mind whirls before catching on what is probably the most relevant piece of information and then my mouth suddenly feels dry, palms sweaty.

"A kodiak?" I croak out. "You mean, like a really big version of Orrin?"

Just to be sure.

Harrison narrows his eyes at me. "You got a problem with that?"

Yes. Yes, I do. I have a lot of problems with that.

"Nope," I lie. "I'm good."

At least, I'm good right now because I'm still alive. That's probably going to change in about an hour. When some giant shifter pummels me into a bloody pulp.

"Do you know what pack he is from?" I ask. "Or any of the others?"

Harrison fiddles with his clipboard, looking at notes he's scrawled in the margins.

"They don't always say, and the rogue wolf 'aint from a pack. Obviously. But in this case both Aires and Goliath are from the Blackwater pack. That's why they hadn't been matched up yet. Crowd don't like it when shifters from the same pack fight each other. Too much risk of rigging the bets, you know?"

"Um, yah," I say lamely. "That makes sense. Cool."

"Changing room's that way," Harrison indicates to a dimly lit hall at the other side of the warehouse. "Don't be late to your matches."

"Thanks. We won't be."

I'm not really sure what I'm thanking him for, because this is probably the stupidest thing I've ever done.

Chapter 21

Lucy Stone

I've participated in enough interrogations that the sight and smell of blood doesn't bother me, so I'm able to watch the first couple rounds of fights with calm impassivity.

What does bother me is the feel of so many male eyes on me. Well, on us. Because they are also looking at Summer and Tori with that same lascivious hunger. It's part of the plan – the part that I thought up, even if Tobias was against it.

It seemed like a good idea at the time. And I may or may not have pushed harder for it once Tobias cautioned against it. Now… well, now let's just say I understand what it feels like to be the prey instead of the predator. And I don't like it.

I'm perched at one of those barstool-type seats at a table between the bar area and the benches that surround the fighting ring. Jason's sitting beside me, while Tori and Summer sit at another table (I suggested we break into pairs to be more approachable). I had initially suggested we all go into the crowd alone, but Jason wasn't having it. "There's no way I'm wandering around in the crowd by myself," he'd said adamantly.

"Hey gorgeous."

The bravest of the group that's been circling our table for the past fifteen minutes approaches, leaning across the table with a proprietary air. Like he owns this table and I should be thankful he's letting me sit here.

"That your boyfriend?" he drawls, nodding towards Jason.

"Cousin," I lie.

The male smirks. He's close enough that I can detect the scent of alcohol on his breath and tobacco on his skin. I'm not sure what type of shifter he is, but he's lean and wiry, with a narrow face, sallow skin and brown hair. Not chocolaty brown like Tobias' hair, but more a dirty flat colour.

"Let me buy you a drink," he says.

I cock my head to one side, pulling my lower lip through my teeth, as if I'm seriously considering his offer. I'm not.

"I don't know," I say, giving him a flirtatious smile. Like the ones I've seen Tori give my brother. I shudder at the memory. So. Gross.

"What pack are you from?"

"Pinewood." He puffs up his chest as he says it, looking at me like I should be impressed. I have heard of it, actually. And not for the right reasons.

"Hmm." I give a thin-lipped smile. "No thanks."

Pinewood pack is a complete dump of a pack in a town called Truth or Consequences, New Mexico. They used to have a reputation as a powerful pack about fifty years ago. Now… not so much.

They're one of those packs that prohibits members from getting a college education. Or using the internet. Honestly, I'm not even sure if they're allowed to read.

It's very unlikely that someone from the Pinewood pack will have any useful information.

"What?" He stands up, a look of confusion on his face. It's quickly replaced with anger as comprehension dawns. "You have a problem with Pinewood pack?"

"I mean, it's okay."

Lie. It is so not okay. The opposite of okay.

I shrug. "It's not Blackwater though. I've heard they're the up-and-coming pack around here."

The male bares his teeth, clearly incensed. I stare up at him blandly. I'm more comfortable facing his outright aggression than I was his attempts at flirtation. He opens his mouth, no doubt to spew out something offensive, but is interrupted by a low growl.

"I don't think the lady's interested, Len. Best you be moving along now."

The male – Len – spins around to face the newcomer. He's tall and broad shouldered – not quite as big as Anton, but not far off.

"No one asked you, Gareth," Len hisses, but I see the way his body tenses. After a couple seconds he lowers his eyes, grumbling as he slinks away from my table and into the shadows.

I watch him go, then let my gaze slide over to Gareth. Dark eyes meet mine with a disconcerting intensity.

"So, you're a fan of Blackwater."

He says it as a statement, not a question.

I don't respond, just watch him warily as he approaches. He slides gracefully onto the seat next to mine, resting heavily tattooed forearms on the table before he dips his head, nostrils flaring to take in my scent.

"Name's Gareth Yates," he says, mouth curving into a faint smile.

I think it's one of those smiles that's intended to be friendly but sends shivers down your spine instead. And not the good kind.

"Now what's a pretty little thing like you doing in a place like this, talking about the Blackwater pack?"

TOBIAS FINCH

Red and Orrin both win their fights, but it's painful to watch.

Literally.

Thanks to the pack bond, I can feel every hit they take. And they take a lot of hits. Especially Red.

By the time my name is called out, I'm feeling raw and a little scared. Maybe a lot scared. This is nothing like high school wrestling matches.

I wipe my sweaty palms on my gym shorts and step into the ring, flinching as the cage door swings shut behind me. Moments later, my opponent enters from the door at the other side and I feel my stomach drop.

Goliath. Yah. That is an apt description.

The male is at least six-foot-six of solid muscle, so broad he has to turn sideways to get through the door of the cage. He's shirtless, so I can see every line of his obscenely muscled chest and arms, like one of those body builders amped up on bull testosterone. Unlike those humans, whose movements are hampered by their muscle mass, this male moves slowly and deliberately, muscles coiling in readiness to strike.

I swallow, my dry throat making an audible gulping sound. The corner of Goliath's lip twitches. I close my eyes, steeling myself. Reminding myself what the aim is here.

I don't need to win. I just need to stay conscious long enough to get information out of this guy.

The umpire rattles off rules and announces us to the crowd, but I barely hear what he is saying over the buzzing in my ears, the thrumming of blood, the pounding of my pulse.

And then the fight has started.

Goliath ambles towards me, patient in his movements. Waiting for me to make the first strike. I let my eyes flick briefly down to his feet. He's surprisingly light on them, balancing on the balls of his feet, leg muscles bulging as he sways like a tree in a gentle breeze. His fighting stance is relaxed. Practiced.

I lift my eyes to his own. *You can see your opponent's moves in their eyes*, I remember one of the coaches at the boxing gym telling me. Maybe that is true for a practiced fighter. It certainly doesn't hold true now.

All I can see in Goliath's eyes is cold calculation and the promise of pain.

"You're from the Blackwater pack," I say lamely, letting my body settle into a fighting stance that was once familiar and now feels like a sad kinetic memory, tethering me back to New York boxing gyms, training and goofing around with friends. A time when my parents were still alive.

Goliath's eyes flash yellow as his animal stirs beneath the surface. "What business is it of yours?" he asks.

I shrug, bouncing slightly on the balls of my feet, fists raised. "Heard things about you guys, that's all."

The first hit comes without warning, and I barely manage to duck out of its way. Its followed by a kick to the side that meets my ribs so hard, I'm pretty sure I feel bone cracking.

"What kind of things?" he asks, before throwing another jab towards my face. This one glances off my cheekbone.

My brain temporarily freezes, caught between trying to figure out what to say and trying not to get my face bashed in. I opt for staying alive, instinctively going into wrestling mode since that is what I've been doing the past couple months.

Dropping down so that my shoulders are at Goliath's waist level, I dart forward, wrapping my arms around his waist then sliding behind him.

It's more or less a classic slide-by move, pretty basic in terms of wrestling, but seeing as the fear centre of my brain is firing at full power, basic seems like a safe option.

The ultimate aim, of course, is to drop my opponent to the ground by leveraging from behind him where his stance is weaker. In theory, this works really well with larger opponents. Apparently, it does not work so well with giant kodiak shifters. Goliath is as unmovable as a tree trunk. Or maybe a boulder.

He spins expertly around in my hold until he's facing me, and I realize the extent of my mistake.

This is not wrestling and the same rules do not apply.

Goliath grabs me by the shoulders and delivers a brutal knee to the chest. I'm knocked windless, and it feels like my whole rib cage is caving in.

Goliath just shoves me back, chuckling as he waits for me to make the next move. Like he's deliberately drawing this out. Toying with me. In the back of my mind I know I'm supposed to be asking him questions, finding out about the Blackwater pack. But I can barely breathe, let alone speak right now.

His eyes flash and I realize he's about to get another hit in. My survival instincts kick in and I drop low, going for a double leg take-down, like I'm Jordan Burroughs ready to take home the gold in the 2012 Olympics.

This time Goliath drops like a tree being felled. He lets out a low "oomph" sound, the ground reverberating with the impact. I'm dimly aware of the crowd roaring in the background, so I couldn't say whether they're cheering for me or disappointed. It doesn't matter either way. I know Goliath won't be down for long.

"I hear you guys are looking for recruits," I say, assuming that's probably close to the truth, if they are kidnapping shifters to build an army. I'm straining to keep Goliath pinned down, using his own weight against him. As soon as he gets his legs free, I'll need to move fast. "I'm looking for a new pack to join."

Goliath laughs darkly as he kicks his legs free of my grasp. I spring to my feet, darting back into a defensive position, just as he lumbers up to tower over me.

"You think you'd make the cut, do you?"

He lunges forward with a nasty right hook that I barely manage to block. It's followed by another swift upper cut to my solar plexus, then a sweeping kick that knocks my legs out from under me.

I hit the ground with a thud and quickly scramble to my feet again, before Goliath can make a grab for me. He takes a lazy swing at me instead, like a cat toying with its prey. Darting behind him, I try for another take down, this time using one of my legs to wrap around his, taking him down.

"If you're any indication, I'd say they'd be begging to have me," I say, my elbows pressing into his spine.

I know its posturing, but honestly that's all I've got at this stage. Probably not my smartest move.

Goliath lets out a very pissed sounding rumble before rolling us over, flipping us until he's on top, pinning me to the ground with his considerable weight. I think he's going to start laying into me now, but he surprises me by snapping to his feet with more agility than should be possible for someone his size. Maybe he's going to keep messing around after all, maybe this won't be as bad as I thought.

"You have no idea what I'm capable of, wolf," he hisses menacingly as I rise to my feet. Then he cracks his neck to one side, baring his teeth, and the onslaught begins.

Punches come in quick succession. Whatever power he was holding back before, whether to entertain the crowd or to listen to my lippy comments, that's over now. I do my best to dodge and block. I even manage to get a few hits in, though with his superior arm reach, there's no way for my hits to have much effect without stepping into the ambit of his relentless pummelling.

And it is relentless.

Going by the level of pain my face is experiencing, Goliath's berserker punching phase goes on forever. In reality, it's probably less than thirty seconds. Maybe closer to fifteen. And then my vision fills with black spots, the roaring in my ears sounding like an ocean as the floor rises up to meet me, like its ready to swallow me whole.

I must black out for a moment, because when I flicker back to consciousness, the crowd is cheering and the world is tilted sideways, my cheek pressed against blood-stained wood. I'm vaguely aware of Goliath kneeling down beside me, the scent of his sweat and slightly sour breath near my ear.

"If you still think you've got what it takes, you can come with us pup," the giant whispers. "Let's see how long you last up at Salmon Lake."

My mind wraps around the word, holding it close like some treasure found in the turmoil of barrelling waves and sand at shore break. *Salmon Lake, Salmon Lake*, I repeat to myself.

I'm so relieved to get this information that some part of my brain mistakenly gets the idea that I'm safe. Cued by this false sense of security, the pain receptor valve in my nervous system that was blocked by adrenaline suddenly unblocks. The pain of all the hits I've taken comes flooding my system like an unwelcome house guest, taking up residence.

I take a deep breath that probably sounds more like a whimper before the roaring in my ears becomes a depthless ocean, swallowing up all conscious thought, leaving only darkness.

Chapter 22

Lucy Stone

I haven't been paying attention to the fights, so I'm taken off guard when the name Jamison is called and Tobias Finch steps into the ring. His chest is bare above his gym shorts, the flat muscled planes of his torso looking almost tan under the red lights.

It's not the first time I've seen him shirtless, but it is the first time I've seen him like this.

Expression resolute, shoulders back, jaw set as he's taking in an opponent. There's nothing soft or sarcastic about him now. He practically radiates power and grim determination - even in the face of an opponent who looks to be twice his size.

I shudder, taking in the hulking form of the kodiak shifter stepping into the ring with him.

"You know the pup?" the male beside me asks.

I start. I'd almost forgotten the newcomer was there. Gareth Yates.

Jason answers for me with a terse: "Yah."

Jason is not looking at either me nor Gareth Yates though. His eyes are fixed on Tobias with a combination of awe and fear. I wonder if it has to do with the sight of a shirtless Tobias which, I will admit, is certainly something to look at. Just because I don't trust the guy doesn't mean I'm blind.

Or maybe it has something to do with whatever Jason is hiding from me.

As if feeling the question in my stare, Jason turns towards me.

"What?" Jason asks.

I just raise a brow and flick my head towards the ring.

Jason blushes, a deep red that hides the brush of pimples on his cheeks. Shaking his head, he whispers: "It's not like that. I've got a mate, remember."

Truth. I can taste its sweet, clean flavour on my tongue.

"Then why the embarrassment?" I tease.

I know it's wrong of me to use Jason's discomfort like this. Shifter culture might be accepting of same-sex couples, trusting fate to match you with the best person, but human society is not always that understanding. Especially in the part of the country where we have grown up.

As expected, Jason gets defensive. He throws his arms up saying: "It's something else, okay. I can't really talk about it. Let's just say that 'Jamison' is a lot more powerful than he's been letting on."

Jason reddens, looking away, as if even that was divulging too much information.

I glance back at Tobias, my curiosity piqued.

Information about Tobias and his opponent, aptly named Goliath, is announced over a loudspeaker – just boring stats - and then I recall the shifter on my other side. He's looking between the ring and me with bald curiosity, and I realize he would have heard what

Jason said about Tobias being powerful. I want to slap myself for being so stupid. If the kidnapper is targeting powerful male shifters, then we have basically just painted a target on Tobias' back.

As if reading my mind, Gareth asks in a low voice: "Why are you talking about my pack?"

I feel my spine stiffen, blood going cold. We really have put Tobias at risk.

I stretch my senses out to get a read on Gareth.

The original plan was to flirt information out of the patrons here. Find some guy from Blackwater and get him to spill the pack's location. Maybe with a promise to come visit or something. That might have worked with guys like the creeper Gareth chased away. I get the feeling it won't work with Gareth.

There's a coldness emanating from him, like the blade of a knife left out in the snow. He's also thick with deception, smelling of as many lies as Tobias. Unlike with Tobias, there isn't the undercurrent of attraction to soften the scent of lies.

I shrug. "I've heard interesting things about it."

I flare my nostrils, taking in more of his scent. It's not the same as whatever wolf we scented outside Anton and Cody's windows. He's not the kidnapper. This male smells of sandstone, juniper berries and wild oregano. I'm not even sure if he's wolf, or something else.

Gareth scoffs. "It's interesting alright." He tilts his head to the ring. "That kodiak is one of our enforcers. He's just toying with your boyfriend, by the way."

"He's not my boyfriend," I snap defensively, but as I look toward the ring, I can't help the sinking feeling in the pit of my stomach.

The crowd jeers as Tobias scrambles to his feet after being thrown across the ring. I want to scream at each and every one of them.

Gareth just smirks. The look is replaced by a grudging nod of respect when Tobias tackles Goliath at his legs, bringing the larger male to the ground.

"Not bad," Gareth muses, "though I can't say I'd be trying to attract Goliath's notice."

"What do you mean?" I ask.

"First you tell me what you've heard about our pack."

I bite my lip, briefly deliberating on what to say. Given the strong scent of deception surrounding this guy was there the instant he sat down, there's a good chance whatever lies he spinning have nothing to do with me. That doesn't mean I can trust him. But it might mean he's a traitor to his pack. I've smelt enough traitors to recognise the scent.

"I've heard not everyone in your pack wants to be there," I whisper, "and that you're growing your numbers."

His eyes widen in momentary surprise. Like he wasn't expecting so much honesty. Then he says: "Be careful who you say that to."

I nod, then stiffen as he leans towards me, nostrils flaring to take in my scent. The flash of a knowing smile brightens his eyes.

"I thought so," he murmurs, almost to himself.

"Thought what?" I ask, edging away from him.

On my other side, Jason sits up taller, turning his attention away from the fight, taking a protective position behind me. The very thought of Jason trying to protect me from anything sends a pang to my chest.

"You're Anton's sister."

I gape in shock, momentarily speechless until rage fills my system. There is only one way this male knows my brother, and that's if the Blackwater pack really does have him. I want to grab this guy by the front of his worn-out band tee and pull answers from him. Or teeth. Or fingernails. I'm not picky.

"Where is my brother?" I hiss.

"I think you know the answer to that question," he replies.

"And can you tell me where your pack lands are?" I ask.

Gareth gives me a pitying look and opens his mouth to say something, but just then the crowd erupts into cheers and yelps and howls.

The fight is over. Tobias' body is sprawled lifelessly on the ground. Summer and Tori are trying to push their way through the crowd to get to him, their progress hampered by the mass of people. The kodiak shifter is looming over Tobias, saying something to his prone figure before standing to receive the crowd's praise, both fists raised over head.

The male standing in the ring looks absolutely terrifying.

I don't like seeing Tobias like that. He looks so much smaller without the smirk and swagger. For once, he looks his age. I can imagine him as a child, loved by his parents, playing at some park in New York. Living as a human, mostly ignorant of the darkness of the shifter world. Innocent in a way I was never allowed to be. My wolf wants to protect him.

"Don't come looking for our pack lands, Lucy Stone," Gareth says.

I spin to face him, almost baring my teeth at the sound of my name on his lips. I never told him it. Never introduced myself.

He gives a sad half-smile at my reaction.

"Your brother told me your name. Said his biggest fear was that you would try to find him."

My heart sinks at hearing that. There are few things Anton fears.

"Why?" I whisper.

Gareth leans forward, keeping his voice so low that even with shifter hearing, it would be impossible for anyone but me to hear him over the roaring din of the crowd. "People tell a lot of secrets when they're being tortured. I think you'd know that as well as anyone."

My blood runs cold, both at the thought of Anton being tortured, as well as at what Gareth is implying. Anton has told my secret.

I want to be sick. Only the worst torture could have forced that secret from his lips.

"Just be thankful I found you, and not one of the others." He tilts his chin towards the fighting ring, where Goliath is lifting an unconscious Tobias from the ground. "I might have been forced to take the blood oath, but I'm not going to be their pawn." This last part is said with a snarl as he pushes up from the table, looking down at me. "Take your friends and get out of here. Before anyone else figures out who you guys are."

And then he's gone. Disappearing into the crowd.

I want to chase after him. Demand answers. Demand he tell me where their pack is.

Because to hell with Anton's misplaced protectiveness. I'm finding out where they are and I'm getting my brother back. Hearing how dangerous they are, hearing that Anton's been tortured – that only makes me more determined than ever.

I'm standing up, ready to push my way through the crowd, when someone grabs my elbow. I jolt, reflexively readying myself to strike out, but it's just Tori.

"Tobias is gone," she says, her face pale, eyes wide with panic.

I just stare at her with momentary confusion. What is she talking about? Tobias was just in the ring. I saw him. Summer and Tori were getting him.

That's when I see Summer heading over to us, face contorted in an expression of frenzied helplessness.

"What do you mean, he's gone?" I ask.

"I – I don't know." Tori's lower lip is trembling, tears threatening to spill from her big eyes.

Its times like these I'm inclined to doubt that fate is really as wise as we all pretend. Or maybe fate just has a twisted sense of humour. Why else would my brother be fated to mate with someone as air headed and weak as this female? There's no way she can be expected to be beta female of a pack.

"I think the other fighter took him," Summer says as she joins us, practically panting with the effort of running through the crowd. "That big guy."

"Goliath?" I ask.

Dread twists like a serpent in my chest, and I share a look with Jason.

Jason gives a grim nod.

"He - that shifter, the kodiak – he's from the Blackwater pack," I croak out.

Summer's lips part, but she doesn't say anything. She doesn't need to. We all look at each other, quiet and horrified for a long, painful moment. Tori, with tears spilling silently down her cheeks, leaving mascara tracks in their wake. Jason, biting the back of his hand between his teeth – a nervous habit of his I had almost forgotten about. And Summer, jaw clenched as she tries to keep her composure, not out of any misplaced stoicism, but because she doesn't want to make the situation worse by adding drama.

I take a deep breath, drawing myself up tall. Letting the turmoil of fear solidify, forming a core of solid steel. Letting the raging tempest of emotions turn to ice.

"We need to find the others," I finally say, meaning Orrin and Red.

Orrin and Red will help us. Any scepticism I initially had about joining forces with a bear and a bobcat shifter is long gone. They might not be pack, but they've sworn a blood oath.

More importantly, they share our enemies. And Gareth Yates reminded me of one important thing tonight: nothing creates allies like a common enemy.

Chapter 23

Tobias Finch

A few summers ago, my parents and I went up to Cape Cod for a holiday. We rented a sail boat. Nothing big, just a little boat that two people could easily sail. It had cushioned seats by the tiller where you could sit in the sun, and a small bunk bed you could lay down on inside the boat if you climbed through the hatch.

The waves were like a lullaby, rocking the boat relentlessly until I fell asleep. Like a child in its mother's arms. I ended up sleeping on the floor down in the hull of the boat, because I wanted to be out of the sun, but even at thirteen, the little bunk bed was too small to be comfortable.

With my ear pressed to the floor, I could hear every wave that brushed against the hull. I could hear the wind billowing in the sails. I could hear my parents' laughter. I swear, I could even hear the distant sounds of wales and dolphins - though that was probably just my imagination.

This is the antithesis of that moment.

The side of my face is pressed against a hard, rumbling surface. My ears are filled with the roar of a motor, wheels spinning over gravel and a harsh, one-sided conversation as someone barks orders into a phone. All I can smell is engine oil, stale fast-food, and the lingering scent of strange shifters.

I squeeze my eyes together, trying to make sense of where I am. The last thing I remember is standing across from that kodiak shifter in the ring. What was his name? I can picture his face – broad and meaty, one of those square, chinless faces that houses dark eyes with more cunning than intelligence.

Goliath.

I had asked him where the Blackwater pack was. Did he tell me? I feel like he did.

The surface beneath me gives a particularly violent bump, causing the side of my face to lift and then slam back down. Pain radiates through my cheekbone, into my skull, in my teeth. I'm suddenly aware of everything else that hurts. My ribs and sternum, every time I take a breath. My shoulders and wrists.

Come to think of it, I can't actually move my arms…

Everything comes rushing back to me then, like water when a dam breaks. My eyes shoot open and I feel my lips curl back into a snarl as my wolf protests. I'm on the floor of some work van, my arms bound behind my back, my body bruised from a very public beat-down.

My ears focus on the loud voice coming from the front seat. From this angle, all I can see is the partition that separates me from the driver, nothing else.

I recognise his voice though. Goliath, the kodiak from the fight. There's only one place he'd be taking me.

Why though? To be an unwilling recruit for their shifter army? I almost laugh at how preposterous that idea is - and then my blood runs cold. What will they do with me when they find out I can't shift? Or worse, when they find out who and what I really am?

My head thuds against the floor of the van, sending jolts of pain down my spine. It wakes me up enough that I remember. Salmon Lake. That's where Goliath said their pack lands were.

Desperately, I reach out through my new-found pack bond. Two lines are thinning, stretching. Presumably those go to Orrin and Red, getting weaker as I move farther away from them. The one that was only a faint shimmer – no more than gossamer thread, really – is growing bolder. Humming with life and pain.

I reach out along the two thinning lines, casting my thoughts towards Orrin and Red. *Salmon Lake*, I shout down the bond. *Salmon Lake. Salmon Lake.*

It feels like one of those old-fashioned games of telephone, where you try and use a tin can to communicate. I strain, listening for a response. For even the feeling that they've heard me.

Another thought rushes through me, one I send unintentionally down the line. *I need to let grandpa know. I promised him I would.*

The van makes a sharp turn, causing me to be thrown face-first into the wall of the vehicle. There's a flash of pain, the metallic scent of blood filling my nose and throat, and then I'm falling back into that roaring ocean, the sea around me swallowing me up.

Lucy Stone

"We shouldn't have let him fight," Orrin growls from the driver's seat for the tenth time. He hasn't calmed down since we left the warehouse, our nine-seater barrelling down the highway.

No one replies. There's nothing left to say. We've re-hashed everything. Gone over every shred of information we all picked up this evening.

None of us feel that the operation was worth it. Especially since we aren't any closer to discovering where the Blackwater pack territory is located. And now we're a man down.

I'm acutely aware of the empty seat next to me where Tobias would normally sit. It's a tangible reminder of his absence. Of the very real peril that Anton and Cody face.

Red lets out a low hiss, body stiffening as if he's readying for some attack. At the same time, Orrin lets out a rumbling growl. I can see his hands tightening on the steering wheel, knuckles turning white.

"What is it?" I ask.

They're quiet for so long, I don't think anyone's going to answer me. And then Red asks: "Does anyone have Tobias' grandpa's phone number?"

I blink, surprised. What a bizarre question.

"I do," Summer chirps from the back. Like she's super excited to finally have something to contribute in this disaster. "Well, actually, it's the landline for his grandparent's house. Do you want it?"

"Yah. That's be great." Red's voice sounds strained.

Summer reads it out to him, and then Red's holding his phone to his ear.

"Won't it be too late?" Summer asks anxiously, "It's almost midnight."

Her face is streaked with tears. I guess she's been silently crying in the back seat since we found out Tobias was missing.

Like a typical feline, Red ignores Summer's questions. I can hear the phone ringing and then, finally, a male voice answers.

"Sir," Red drawls, like this is some social call and not a rude midnight wake-up. "Your grandson has been taken by the Blackwater pack. We're heading to Salmon Lake now. He wanted us to let you know. Said something about a promise."

A series of expletives come through the phone, so loud that I'm pretty sure everyone in the van can hear them. Red holds the phone out, grimacing and glaring as if it has personally offended him. Then he turns the volume down low enough that it's impossible to hear the voice on the other end.

"No offence, but we are fully aware of how dangerous Blackwater is," Red replies snippily, reaching up to tug at one of his tufted ears in annoyance.

Tobias' grandfather says something on the other line that causes Red to snarl.

"Calm down," Orrin warns, "The old man doesn't know you. Of course, he's not going to trust you."

I furrow my brow in confusion, looking between Orrin and Red. If I couldn't hear what's being said on the other end of the phone, then there is no way Orrin can. Unless…

"We'll keep you updated on our movements," Red snaps into the phone, "Assume you've got a mobile or something?" He pauses, types something into his phone and then repeats a number back.

When Red ends the call, I pivot in my seat to face him. "How do you know he's at Salmon Lake?"

Earlier, we had gone over all the information we collected, which wasn't much. There was no mention of Salmon Lake.

Red looks sheepish, then pretends to be reading something interesting on his phone.

"Red?"

He doesn't answer, and I look at Orrin. "What is it you guys aren't telling me?"

The smell of lies and secrets is so thick, it's almost stifling in this van. I'm tempted to crack my window, even though its well below freezing tonight.

"I don't think we can," Orrin says reluctantly, flashing me a weak, apologetic smile in the rear-view mirror. "It's not our secret to tell. You're just going to have to trust us on this one."

"Trust you?" I scoff. I look back at Summer and Jason. "You guys hearing this? First, no one knows where the pack-lands are. Now, suddenly, out of nowhere, Orrin and Red are sure it's at Salmon Lake. Am I the only one who isn't okay with just trusting them on this?"

Summer wrings her hands. "Well, they gave a blood oath..."

I just gape at her, then turn to Jason. He shrugs, refusing to meet my eyes. "I trust them," he says weakly.

Tori pipes up from the front seat, probably annoyed that I haven't asked for her opinion. "I don't see what's wrong with going to Salmon Lake first. Unless you have any better ideas."

It's not our secret to tell, Orrin had said. There is a secret then. I don't like it. In my experience, untold secrets are dangerous.

And what about your secret, a little voice in my head chides. I ignore it. That secret is different. Keeping it keeps me safe. Keeps my pack safe. Because if word of my gift gets out, other packs would fight to have me. To steal me away, by force or trickery. Like had happened to my mother.

"Fine," I bite out. "Let's go to Salmon Lake." Pulling out my phone, I ask: "Do we know for sure that's the right place? Like, should I call dad and tell him to get a team of enforcers to meet us there?"

Because as much as I want to rush in and pull Anton out of Blackwater territory, I remember what that shifter Gareth had said at the bar. It was dangerous. Worse, it was an unknown danger.

I shiver, thinking of Tobias on the road ahead of us, maybe only several miles ahead of us, careening to that destination. Towards those unknown dangers.

"You should call your dad," Orrin finally says, after a long moment of deliberation. "By the time he gets close enough to be of any assistance, we'll have more information."

I nod, steeling myself for a conversation I have been dreading. After screening my dad's calls for days and ignoring his texts, there is no way this conversation is going to go well.

"I've looked up this Salmon Lake place," Jason pipes up from the backseat, face lit in blue tones from the glow of his phone in the darkness. "There's a state park and campground along the east side of it. That's where the road runs. The west side of the lake is only accessible by foot though. Or boat, I guess."

He pauses, then adds: "The west side of the lake is all national forest as well."

"Blackwater is probably on the west side then," Orrin muses. "They wouldn't have their pack territory close to humans."

"That's what I was thinking," Jason agrees. "We'll need to turn off a bit before the lake if we want to hike in to the west side. Tori, I'll send you the directions so you can help Orrin navigate, okay?"

"I'm calling my dad now," I announce to the car.

"Good luck," Summer offers weakly.

"Is he that scary?" Red asks.

"You have no idea," I murmur, before hitting his number.

Despite the late hour, he picks up on the first ring.

"Lucy."

How is it that just one word can have such an impact? Convey so many things? It's like all his anger, disappointment, and possessiveness is compacted into the four letters that make up my name.

"Dad."

I try to keep my voice steady, but even to my ears it seems to waver. He's just a male. Just an ordinary male, I remind myself. But even if our parents cease being gods by the time we're out of childhood, that power over us still lingers, doesn't it?

"Where are you?"

The question snaps out like a whip, sharp and angry.

"We're just outside of Missoula."

I can hear a low rumbling growl through the phone, can imagine his eyes flashing as his wolf tries to surge to the surface, barely restrained with his temper.

I swallow. "We found out where Anton has been taken."

I recall my conversation with the shifter at the warehouse then. Gareth had seen my brother. So I know my brother is alive, and that the Blackwater pack have him. Probably Cody and the others too. A sliver of satisfied pride glimmers low in my stomach. Our visit to the fight club wasn't a complete waste of time after all, was it?

"I met someone from the Blackwater pack," I say, lifting my chin. "He told me they have Anton."

There's a long pause on the other line, before dad lets out his breath in a low whoosh. "I've heard of them."

"You have?"

"Unfortunately," he says. "Not good things. A couple years back there was some sort of exodus. A lot of wolves left that pack, chose to become rogues instead."

I frown. It must have been more than a couple years ago, or surely I would have heard about it. But a couple years for dad and a couple of years for me mean entirely different things.

"Do you know why?" I ask, wondering if it has something to do with why Tobias' father left the pack. Or why the shifter I met earlier in the evening thought they were so dangerous.

"Not exactly," dad replies, "One of the rogues I questioned had mentioned a cruel alpha. Some really abhorrent things, if the male was to be believed. He was pretty far gone, though – close to going feral. He'd lost his mate and pup, if I remember correctly…"

He trails off, leaving the worst part unsaid, and I shiver. When we were young, dad had been a council enforcer, responding to calls in our region when there were rogue shifters causing problems, that sort of thing. He didn't talk about it much. There was little satisfaction in punishing desperate rogues. Even less in putting down those who had gone feral from loss.

"The shifter I met, he tried to warn me away from going to Blackwater. Implied it would be dangerous," I say, then add. "Especially for me. He said they'd questioned Anton…"

I put emphasis on the word 'questioned', hoping dad will get what I'm trying to tell him. What I can't say with others in the car with me. The Blackwater pack might know what I am. And more likely than not they tortured Anton to get that knowledge.

Dad lets out a low growl, letting me know he definitely understands what I'm saying. "You absolutely shouldn't be going to Blackwater," he says with the finality of parent used to being obeyed.

"Aww, we thought a hike into their pack territory would make a nice day-trip," I say, forcing sarcasm into my voice, hoping it hides that this is actually the very thing we are planning to do.

"You are not to go near their territory," he snaps, then pauses, listening. "Are you in a car right now?" He must be able to hear the rumbling of the engine, the sound of the van flying down the freeway. "Please tell me you're not driving there right now. Lucy…" My name comes out with a growl so ferocious, I slink down into my seat without realising it.

"Maybe…" I say reluctantly.

"Do. Not. Go there," he orders.

But that's the great thing about phones. As much as I can hear his anger and dominance, I can't actually feel it. And even if I could, dad isn't my alpha. I'm not sure he realizes it, but my dominance levels probably rank close to his own. He can't actually compel me to do anything.

I press my lips together, not wanting to argue with him, but refusing to lie to him either.

"Lucy…"

"It's at Salmon Lake," I say, before he can make any more demands that I have zero intention of complying with. "Probably on the west side of the lake. Oh, and they took Tobias too."

Dad snorts at that. "Why on earth would they take a submissive, latent wolf with no pack?"

I bristle, suddenly feeling defensive of the boy who has travelled with us these past couple days. The boy who laughed off my attempts to interrogate him. Who put himself at the mercy of a kodiak shifter in an effort to get information that would help Anton and Cody – wolves that aren't even his packmates.

"There's more to him than meets the eye." The words tumble out, and I blink in surprise at them.

"Is that so?" he asks icily.

I roll my eyes, reminded of his extremely misplaced reaction to my bringing up Quentin Slade a few weeks ago. Instead of responding to his question, or attempting to defend myself, I just say: "Blackwater has taken other shifters too. Not just wolves. All young males with some level of ability or dominance."

My eyes shift to Red. I don't want to tell dad about Orrin and Red. It will just give him one more thing to worry about. One more thing to lecture me about. 'Don't mix with other shifters,' he always told me. Just like he always warned me away from lone wolves. Not that I ever had much chance of associating with shifters from either category. At least, not until now.

"There's a theory that Blackwater is building a shifter army."

"A shifter army?" There's no mistaking the steely menace in his voice.

"Yah." I pull my knees up to my chest and rub my face with one hand, feeling more tired after a couple minutes of talking to my dad than I've felt this whole trip.

"Are you sure?"

I grit my teeth. Obviously, I'm not sure. But I'm planning to find out. I don't say this though, since he's already made it pretty clear he's against us going to Blackwater. Instead, I say: "I guess you'll find out when you get there."

"When *I* get there?"

"You, the alpha, the enforcers," I clarify.

"Ah…"

There's a long, uncomfortable silence before dad says: "We can't just invade another pack's territory, you know. Not without proof of wrongdoing. If we do, well – that's enough to start a war. Especially if you're mistaken."

"I'm not mistaken," I retort hotly.

"I'm not putting the safety of our pack at risk based on a hunch," he hisses. "We have to follow protocol. Reach out to the other pack…"

I can hear him talking, but the words themselves are swallowed up by the ringing that starts in my ears. I don't need to hear the words to know it's a string of inane excuses. Maybe he doesn't care that Anton has been taken. Maybe this is his idea of revenge for my disobeying him. I do know that he's never cared about protocol in the past. I've attended enough of the interrogations he's run to know that much.

Betrayal burns in my chest like a brand, hot pain coiling into smoky anger.

"I'm going."

I sling the truth out like a dagger. There's no point in hiding the truth from him, not when I'm heading towards far greater dangers than parental anger. To my surprise, my voice is calm and even.

"We're driving to Salmon Lake now, and we'll probably hike in first thing tomorrow. I don't know if I'll have cell service there. We'll try to confirm whether Cody or Anton are there, and if we can, we'll call you and let you know. But just to be clear, I'm not going to sit around and wait for you to make phone calls. I'll be doing what I can to get them out."

And then, without waiting for a response, I hang up the phone.

My hands are trembling so hard I almost drop my phone. My heart is racing. Pounding. With their shifter hearing, everyone in this van must hear it.

And yet I feel freer than I ever have before. It's better than running in my wolf form. Better than skinny dipping under the full moon. Even better than when I drove my own car for the first time.

"Wow," Summer says, letting out a low whistle.

"I know." The word catches in my throat.

I've never openly defied my father before. Heck, I've never really disobeyed him. Not even on little things. Not even surreptitiously. If he told me not to wear a dress, I didn't wear it. If he asked me to make lasagne for a pack meet, I did it. When he told me to keep my gift a secret, I did it. Even if it meant seeing and hearing things no child should ever have to see, and having no one to confide in about it.

My phone rings, dad's picture flashing on the screen. It's the one of him and me when I was nine. Before mom left. He's smiling, his arm around me as I hold out a trout we caught together. He looks like a different male with that smile. I don't think he's smiled since mom left. At least, not like that.

I press ignore, silencing the call.

He's going to be so angry.

When mom left, he destroyed the house. Shifted into wolf form and spent the night tearing everything apart. Mom had loved that house. It was like her third child.

I guess I should be grateful he didn't destroy me and Anton too.

Anton had snuck into my bedroom that night as I lay with my head under the covers, trembling at the terrifying sounds of howling and crashing.

"Do you want to go to the waterfall?" he had whispered, lifting me from my bed, helping me into my coat and shoes. "It's a full moon. We can see if those mer-wolves want to come out."

"There's no such thing as mer-wolves," I said sulkily. The skin on my face had felt stretched from dry tears and snot. I had wanted to go with mom. Had wanted it so bad. And she'd left without so much as a goodbye.

"How do you know?" he teased. "Maybe the only come out at night. You'll never find out if you're too chicken to go look."

"I'm not chicken," I snapped back, swinging sleep-mussed pigtails over my shoulders.

"Prove it," he smirked. "Race me there."

And so we ran. Both in human form, because I was only ten and he was twelve and neither of us had shifted yet. But I was still aware of the wolf in me, joyful of the freedom of sprinting up the rocky landscape under the luminescent glow of the full moon. *This is right*, she had whispered to me then, like an invisible guardian spirit. *Run. Run and be free. Be safe.*

There were no mer-wolves, though we watched for them until I fell asleep under the willow tree, cradled in my brother's arms.

It was Cooper Winslow who found us both the next morning, like two pups piled on each other in sleep. He brought us back to the main lodge to stay with him, Cindy and Cody. The alpha pair had said dad was sick, and we could go home when he got better.

Several weeks passed before dad came to bring us home. When he did, everything in my room had changed – the colour of the walls, the patchwork quilt grandma had made, the wooden frame of my little bed dad had carved with little wolves and fawns. Even my books and toys were gone, a few sparse and unfamiliar items in their place.

"I felt like re-decorating," he had explained dryly. He had looked so menacing when I'd pushed him about where my toys had gone that I dropped it.

It was years before I truly understood what had happened. What my brother had saved us from. Dad had gone feral. Or at least, as close to it as someone can go and still come back.

Would he have torn me apart with as little thought as he ripped my childhood quilt? I hope not. Whenever I think of that night – which is as infrequently as possible – I like to think his parental instincts would have prevented him from harming me.

Now that hope is a fragile, brittle thing. Like the thin sheets of ice coating the asphalt on this dark freeway.

In its place is something I've never felt before, rough and gritty as bare earth under snow. It feels a bit like – confidence? Or maybe the beginnings of an acknowledgement of myself? And under it all is resolution, humming with strength.

I am going to find Anton. And I am getting him back.

Chapter 24

Tobias Finch

"Tobes? Is that you?"

The voice piercing the haze of sleep is rough but familiar. I blink, fragments of now and memory and dreams spinning together like the broken pieces in a kaleidoscope.

"Oh man," another voice whispers. "That's definitely him. What happened to his face?"

I swallow, trying to wet my lips with a too-dry tongue. This movement is met with the metallic taste of fresh blood from what must be a split lip, but I barely register the pain. It's a drop in the bucket. And my body is just one big bucket of pain right now.

"What do you think happened to his face, you idiot?" an unfamiliar voice snipes. "You saw who brought him here."

"Keep it down," another voice hisses. "They'll hear you."

The voices fall silent at this warning, and for several minutes there's only the sound of different people breathing, the creaking of metal and the faint thud of distant footsteps.

I use the silence to piece myself back together and take the world in through the one eye that isn't swollen shut. What I can see… well, let's just say it makes that first motel we all crowded into look pretty five-star.

I'm in a cage – yes, an actual cage – in some sort of draughty warehouse or barn. I can feel the icy night air moving across my skin. Other cages are scattered haphazardly around the warehouse.

Wolves and other animals stare at me from out of the majority of the cages, their eyes glinting intelligently in the dim artificial light. In other cages, boys sit with their knees pulled to their chests or lay curled on their sides, all wearing clothing that appears to be in various states of decomposition.

The whole place smells of piss, fear and desperation.

I would know where I am from that smell alone, even if I didn't see a familiar head of dark curls and pair of blue eyes. I've smelt this place when I've stretched into Cody's mind.

"Nice place you got here," I say. Or at least, that's what I try to say. My lips feel numb, and I'm not sure I can actually move my jaw.

I think Cody understands me though because he shakes his head in disbelief. "It really is you."

None other, I reply though the bond. Because at least telepathic communication doesn't require me to move my face.

I feel a shock of disbelief shoot through the pack bond I share with him. He's silent for a long moment before I hear his voice stretching though the bond back to me.

Did my dad let you join our pack?

Oh yah… Well, this is a face-palm moment. Or it would be, if my hands weren't still tied behind my back and if my face didn't feel like a slab of meat.

The thing is, I'm not really sure when my bond with Cody clicked into place. With Orrin and Red, it was pretty obvious. I took their blood, I made them a promise and not long after, the bond had formed.

With Cody, nothing happened after he gave me his blood. And nothing happened after that promise I made him. What had I said? *If you ever need anything – if they make you leave the pack or whatever – let me know and I'll do what I can to help you. I've got your back.*

Maybe the bond only formed when I started acting on my promise? When I made the decision to try and find Cody and Anton with the rest of our crew? That makes the most sense, since I didn't feel the bond until we were travelling through Montana.

No, I tell him through the pack link. *I didn't join your pack. You – um – you sort of joined mine, Accidentally.*

I force myself to look at him through my one good eye. His face is a mask of calm, but I can feel his panic and rage pulsing, dark and furious.

"How?" he says out loud, as if the very idea of using the pack link he shares with me is offensive. "How did this happen?"

I let out a long sigh through my nose. Even the air moving through my sinuses hurts. I'm pretty sure my nose must be broken. Squeezing my good eye shut, I mumble through swollen lips: "It's a long story."

And then, silently, through the pack link, I tell him everything. Because I owe him that. By being an aberrant freak of nature, I've cut him out of his family's pack. I've potentially taken away his role as future alpha of the Clear Creek pack. Maybe I can undo it. But maybe I can't. I honestly don't know, and it's not like there's a handbook on how to be a born alpha. We aren't supposed to exist.

When I explain that I'm a born alpha, the rage radiating down the bond I share with him is almost palatable, and several minutes pass before he speaks again.

"Anton and I both stopped feeling our link to the pack when we were several hours out of Buffalo," Cody muses out loud. "But we were still able to communicate with each other until a few days ago. I just figured it had something to do with being so far apart from our alpha, you know?"

Yah, I reply through the bond. *I'm sorry. I really am. Once we get out of this, I can try to fix it.*

When I tell him about mom's murder, and the connection to the shifter who kidnapped him and Anton, I feel his anger take on a different edge. Sharper, more acute, and almost vengeful.

Can you describe the scent? he asks through the bond. *Or better yet, share your memory of it through the bond?*

I can do that? I ask.

I can practically feel him roll his eyes. *Yah. That's like, pretty basic stuff, man.*

I was never part of a pack before, okay? Cut me some slack, I reply defensively.

Slack? The word cracks down the bond like a bullwhip. *You made yourself my alpha. Slack is the last thing you're going to get from me.*

I shudder at those words. Not because I'm afraid of Cody. I'm not. At least, not much. I just wasn't expecting this level of animosity from him. I don't blame him for being angry and guilt at what I've done leaves its bitter taste on the back of my tongue.

But this isn't the time to deal with his anger or my guilt. We're in cages on what is almost definitely Blackwater territory. I'm in the hands of shifters who wanted me dead as a new born pup. Who were willing to hunt my parents down to try and find me.

The only reason I'm still alive is my captors haven't discovered what a prize they have.

I draw up the memory of the first time I smelled that scent. Charcoal and pine mingled with the metallic smell of blood on the kitchen floor. The sound of my father's keening wails…

I take that memory, full of scent and sound and pain, and send it down the bond to Cody. His eyes widen in shock, though I don't know if it's in recognition of the scent, or at the violence of the memory.

"Shit," he mutters, shaking his head. "I'm sorry, Tobes. Really sorry."

Is the scent familiar? I ask tersely through the bond, ignoring his sympathy. What is there to say? Mom is dead. The only thing that I can do now is find her killer.

I stare up at the bars of my cage. I'm not exactly doing great at enacting vengeance. If I'm lucky, I'll make it a day or two before they figure out who and what I am. Once they do, I'm basically defenceless.

"It is familiar." Cody's voice is a low whisper. "It's the alpha. Huxley Black." The calm mask he's been wearing twists into an expression of disgust as he says the male's name. Then he adds: "He's the one who took us."

Huxley Black. I hold the name in my mind like a poison tipped arrow.

"You'll probably meet him in the morning," Cody adds softly.

I shiver. Does he know what I look like? Will he recognise me? If he does, it's unlikely I'll see the end of tomorrow.

Not wanting to think about that, I ask: "What's the deal with the cages?" Unlike my conversation with Cody, I speak these words out loud, using the pain in my jaw to bring me back into my body. Into the now.

To my surprise, it's not Cody who answers me, it's someone else.

"Oh, don't think of them as cages," a voice says dryly.

I think it's one of the voices I heard speaking earlier. I can't see him from the angle I'm laying at, but his voice is at once deep and scathing. Like gravel mixed with broken glass.

"Think of this as your daily reminder that everyone can be free, and that our captivity is just an illusion of our own making."

I wrinkle my brow, trying to make sense of what he is saying.

"Morrigan's tits, Danny," someone drawls, "Tobes here is going to think you've lost it."

"Maybe he has," another voice snipes.

As much as I hate the nickname Cody has coined for me, I don't correct them. Going by Tobias right now would be pretty stupid if Huxley Black knows my name. While the others are speaking, I use the pack link to ask Cody to keep my name under wraps for now. I'll need to ask Anton the same thing.

Speaking of which…

Cody, I say through the bond, *where is Anton?*

I feel a sick feeling of dread and fear pulse through the bond in response, and I almost regret asking. Before Cody can reply though, the second person who spoke speaks out again.

"What Danny is – rather cryptically – trying to say here, is that they're holding us in these modern yet minimalist living arrangements until we agree to join their pack. New conscripts get more – let's say – roomier accommodations." He chuckles, the sound like a smooth purr.

Someone – I think Danny? – lets out a low growl in response.

"And you guys… you don't want to join their pack?" I ask.

"Obviously," the male sneers. "Though if you would like to, I'm sure old Hux will be more than happy to have another grunt swear fealty to him."

I snort then. Actually snort. The movement causes my nose to throb.

"Is something funny?" the male asks darkly.

"Oh, lay off, Samson," Cody snaps defensively. "He's literally just woken up and…"

My mind catches on the name 'Samson' and I stop listening to whatever Cody is saying.

Samson was Red's little brother. And what was Orrin's nephew's name – wasn't it Danny?

"Samson," I grit out, interrupting what was probably the start of an argument between Samson and Cody. "You're Red's little brother, right?"

There's a surprised intake of breath from Samson's direction, and everyone falls silent for a long moment. Finally, Samson asks tentatively, "How do you know Red?"

I don't answer. Partially because it hurts too much to speak, but also because I don't know how much I can say in this warehouse. I don't know who could be listening in the dark. If Orrin, Red and the rest are coming for us, I don't want to give away their element of surprise.

Instead, I ask Danny: "And you're Orrin's nephew?"

"Yah…" I hear the distrust in Danny's voice, but there is not much I can do to dispel that. Not without giving away more information than may be safe.

"You gonna tell us what this is about, wolf?" Samson's hisses, sounding very like his older brother.

I smile into the darkness, thinking of Red's ever-present cat ears and that stupid pink cat ear hat he bought at the camping goods shop in Missoula. My lip cracks with the movement and I can taste fresh blood on my tongue.

"I don't know how much I can say," I whisper. I want to tell them that Orrin and Red are probably on their way here – at least, I hope they are. I want to tell them that Orrin and Red are part of my accidental pack, along with Cody.

Neither Samson nor Danny push for any more information, so they must understand, at least partly. They know better than I do what dangers lurk in the dark corners of this warehouse. Who might be listening. Who can and cannot be trusted.

"Can you tell me what to expect tomorrow?" I ask. "Like, when do we get let out of these cages?"

Samson huffs in irritation, and for a long moment I don't think he's going to answer. When he finally does, he keeps his voice low enough that it won't carry beyond our cluster of cages.

"Hux and his enforcers bring us breakfast," he says bitterly, "but only those who are ready to take the blood oath can eat it. Those who refuse get a different start to their day. Hosed down with cold water, taken out and beaten by the new conscripts, used as target practice…" I hear the bars of his cage rattle as he shudders. "It's a good thing shifters are hard to kill, or we'd all be dead already."

"How long?" I ask, bile rising, "How long have you been here?" I seem to recall Samson and Danny were picked up a while ago.

It's Danny who answers. "Long enough to wish for death."

The creaking of metal hinges, a gust of icy wind and booted footsteps alerts us to someone entering the warehouse. My nostrils flare, trying to catch the newcomer's scent, but my nose is clogged with dried blood, and the scent of urine and dirt is too overpowering. The warehouse falls completely silent, as if everyone is holding their breath. A pair of boots appear in my line of vision and I feel my pulse spike, adrenaline shooting through my blood like a hit of some performance drug. I struggle to slow my heart-rate, calm my breathing.

"I thought I heard talking," the owner of the boots growls out from above me, his face obscured by the awkward angle I'm lying. "Alpha Black must be letting you get too much sleep if you are awake in the middle of the night chatting away like a bunch of girls at a sleepover. Maybe it's time we start visiting you lot overnight."

There's a faint whimper in the darkness – one of the wolves, I think. The male standing over us chuckles darkly before stalking away.

None of us dare to speak after that. I'm not sure if anyone manages to go back to sleep either.

I lay awake, waiting for my injuries to heal, wishing I could shift to speed up the healing process. The warehouse slowly grows lighter as dawn light filters through a few grimy windows, sunlight highlighting the cracks in the walls. I know there's only minutes before I come face to face with mom's killer. This could be the last dawn I see.

I close my eyes against the light. I don't want the last things I see to be cage bars, filth, blood and desperation.

Instead, I picture Lucy. Her grey eyes full of fire. The way her long legs looked under that white sundress, when I followed her across the ripe grass of the ranch towards the bull pen. The way her white teeth flashed in the sun as she lured me after her with false smiles. Then the basement, how fearless she looked when she threatened to torture me for information.

I imagine her scent – lavender and fresh rain on grass – until it erases the scent of blood and urine and fear. I recall the feel of her skin as her arm brushed against mine when we sat side by side in the van, and the way electricity always seemed to jump between us at each fleeting contact.

Finally, I recall the feel of her eyes when I fought Goliath in the fighting ring. The look of fear and fury when I took that final hit, as if she wanted to jump into the ring and fight beside me. Maybe I only imagined it, but I want to see what it would take to make her look at me like that again.

And now Lucy is on her way here, along with all the others.

I don't know how strong the Blackwater pack is, but there is no way Lucy and the others can take on a homicidal alpha and bunch of enforcers – especially when one of those enforcers is Goliath.

I lick my lips. My split lip has healed shut and I can see through both eyes now, but my face throbs. It's probably swollen and covered in bruises. For once, this might be a good thing.

An idea surfaces – one I didn't dare contemplate as a possibility when faced with last night's icy darkness. Now, with the fresh ugly dawn painting my surroundings in horrifying technicolour, there is no ignoring the reality of my situation.

I have to get out of here quickly, or I'm dead. Eventually, my disposable contact lenses will give out, exposing me as a born alpha. Or someone will order me to shift and figure out I'm latent. Either way, I can't imagine they will just let me go on my merry way once they realize I'm not fit to be a conscript for their shifter army.

I reach out through the bond, whispering against Cody's sleepy consciousness.

Cody? You awake? I think I have a plan.

Lucy Stone

"Wh-who in their r-right mind would live in this godforsaken place?" Tori's teeth chatter as we huddle in sleeping bags inside the tent. She's pressed against my side, and as much as I hate being close to her, I know we all need the body warmth.

"Well," Summer drawls from my other side, "I don't think anyone is arguing that the Blackwater pack shifters are in their right mind. You know, since they like kidnapping, killing and starting up armies." Compared to Tori, she seems relatively unaffected by the cold. Like me, she's endured similar conditions in Wyoming.

"You can always shift into your wolf form," I suggest. In fact, it would be great if Tori shifted, because then she'd have to stop talking and I might finally get some sleep.

“I d-don’t want to g-get out of the sleeping bag,” she says, drawing the down sleeping bag tight under her chin.

“You can always take a turn on night watch,” Red suggests dryly, his voice carrying effortlessly from outside the tent. Where he is currently on night watch. Orrin and Jason both snicker from the tent all the guys are sharing.

“N-no w-way,” Tori shivers.

I roll my eyes in the darkness. No surprise there.

To say Tori is out of her depth camping would be an understatement. Not that hiking in the snow at night and pitching a tent in the dark is a typical camping experience, but still.

“I’ll take a turn,” I huff, watching my breath cloud above my head. There’s no chance of sleeping anyway, and I’ll be warmer walking around.

I duck out of the tent and am greeted by a clear sky full of crystalline stars peeking through the tops of pine trees. Under the trees, deep snow glistens, reflecting the light of the stars and waning moon, muffling the ambient forest sounds.

Red grins when he sees me. “I’ve only been on watch for a few hours. I can keep you company if you want.”

“Sure,” I shrug. Still, I’m grateful for his offer. I don’t want to be alone.

“I was just going to do a walk of the perimeter,” he suggests, nodding towards the dark line of trees, “You want to come along?”

I nod, then follow him in silence to the area we marked out earlier in the night. We listen for the sounds of any intruders, check the snow for footprints. There is nothing - beside those marks we’ve made ourselves.

“How far do you think it is?” I ask, my eyes fixed northwards in the darkness.

With every mile we've walked, I've been hoping to feel Anton through our pack bond, but there's only been silence. Not even the whisper of the thread that would normally connect us.

As if reading my mind, Red asks: "Any sense of Anton through your pack bond?"

"No." The answer comes out sharper than I intend.

Red frowns. "That could mean anything, right? I mean, it doesn't mean…" He trails off, but I know what he was going to say.

"Doesn't mean he's dead? No."

I shiver, recalling Gareth alluding to Anton having been tortured. "It could mean we're not close enough, or that we're heading in the complete wrong direction. It could mean Blackwater isn't at Salmon Lake, and we've got the location wrong."

Red pulls his pink hat over his head, its fluffy cat ears reminiscent of the real cat ears tucked beneath. He rubs the back of his neck contemplatively. "It could mean something has broken the bond."

I narrow my eyes at him. "Like what?"

"Another bond." He gives me a wary look, like he knows I'm not going to like what he has to say. "If they're building an army, they'll be asking the shifters they recruit to swear some sort of a blood oath, right? Form a new pack, or whatever it is you pack shifters do. If he's joined their pack, wouldn't that break his old pack bond?"

I stare at him, feeling the blood drain from my face as a mixture of dread and relief courses through me. That would be a reasonable explanation as to why I haven't felt him through the pack link. And yet…

"Anton would never agree to join their pack," I say vehemently.

I can't imagine Anton forsaking the Clear Creek pack. He's too loyal. At the same time, that would be infinitely preferable to the alternative.

"He might not have had much of a choice," Red grimaces.

"You mean…" I press my lips into a thin line, not wanting to say it.

"Yah." Red frowns, his own eyes turned northwards. "I mean, how else are they going to convince people to fight for them? They're not exactly winning hospitality awards if they're kidnapping shifters and dragging them up to this hellhole." He waives one hand at the frozen landscape around us. I have to concede he has a point.

We walk the rest of the perimeter in silence until we're back at the campsite. Steady breathing and faint snores come from both tents. At least some people are getting sleep.

"I can take over now," I say. Red might as well get some sleep. And I want to be alone with my thoughts.

Red nods his thanks, silently climbing into the tent he shares with Orrin and Jason.

I turn my gaze up to the stars, though I'm hardly seeing them as I think about what Red said.

What will it mean if Anton has joined the Blackwater pack? Will he be blood sworn to fight against the Clear Creek pack when they arrive? And will the Clear Creek pack even come? Or will it just be us – a little band of teenage shifters plus one full-grown bear who runs a mechanic shop – on a desperate mission to get back our friends?

Chapter 25

Tobias Finch

I manage to whisper the bones of my plan to Danny and Samson before the guards come. To my surprise, once Cody assures them that I can be trusted, the pair agree to go along with it.

"At this point, what do we have to lose?" Danny says dryly.

Not the greatest vote of confidence I've ever had, but I'll take it.

"Great," I say, plastering on a smile. My jaw throbs in response.

Samson just fixes me with that penetrating feline stare which is so much like his brother's. I can tell he's nervous about our plan, and I can't blame him. For all he knows, I'm using this opportunity to betray them all to the alpha in some sort of bid to win favour.

Of course, if Samson knew what I really was, he wouldn't be worried at all.

Everyone falls silent when the mouth-watering scent of bacon, hash browns, toast, smoked salmon and coffee waft into the warehouse. I hear a few whimpers from those in their animal forms as enforcers saunter in, carrying platters of steaming food.

"I didn't know you were running a bed and breakfast," I say when boots stop outside my cage, and the familiar scent of Goliath makes its way past my swollen nostrils. "Though I have to say, I don't think I'll be leaving a five-star review. Bondage theme really isn't my jam." I wiggle my bound wrists for emphasis.

Goliath lowers himself to my level.

"You think you're funny, do you, Jamison?" he growls, eyes glowing yellow.

I just grin in response, glad he's using the name I gave at the fight last night. I would wink, but even though my eye is no longer swollen shut, the muscles on my face aren't quite up to that level of aerobic activity.

"Who wants breakfast?" another voice booms out. "Fresh cooked eggs, buttered toast, hot bacon… All you have to do is swear the blood oath and you'll go to sleep on a bed with a full belly every night."

The male speaking sounds like one of those infomercials. You know, the ones promising white teeth overnight at one fifth the usual price if you order now.

"If you don't swear the blood oath – well, you know the drill. I hear our new conscripts are working on their target practice this afternoon…"

I let out a snort. Goliath kicks my cage in warning.

"Sign me up," I say caustically, "I mean, I'm a big fan of eating food and shooting things, so I'm sure I'll fit right in to your pack."

The infomercial guy saunters over to my cage. "Excellent! 'Bout time we had a reasonable one come through." He bends down to look at me, a smug look of triumph on his face.

I raise an eyebrow and feel my lips twitch with suppressed laughter. This guy actually thinks I'm serious. These idiots just threw me in the back of a van and left me in a cage all night with my hands tied behind my back. Do they seriously think I'm going to join their pack just because they're offering me breakfast?

Yes. Yes, they do.

And given the plan we have just made, that's a good thing.

"What's your name?" infomercial guy asks.

"Jamison."

"And you're prepared to join the Blackwater pack as a new conscript? Partake in the trials to determine your rank? Swear fealty to alpha Huxley Black?"

"It's my life's one ambition," I deadpan.

He grins, showing several missing teeth which probably correlate to the millions of brain cells missing from in his skull. "Hear that, boys?" he announces to the warehouse as he unlocks my cage. "That's the attitude we're looking for. Jamison here has just arrived, and already he's taking the initiative to make something of himself."

The door of my cage creaks as it swings open, and there's a long pause before infomercial guy realizes that I can't actually climb out, since I'm lying face down with my hands tied behind my back. Someone roughly hauls me out, putting me on my feet and deftly slicing away my bindings. I nearly gasp at the pain as blood rushes into my joints. Its strangely reminiscent of when Lucy and Tori tied me up for questioning in the basement. Except this is much worse, since I'm pretty sure my ribs and nose are broken.

"Thanks," I say, doing my best to straighten my spine out while looking at each of the enforcers. There's five of them. Goliath, Infomercial Guy, and three others who look like the hired thugs in some mafia series. In other words, exactly the kind of upstanding characters one would expect from an establishment like this.

"Is there somewhere I can go to take a piss?" I ask irreverently.

Goliath narrows his beady eyes at me and opens his mouth to say something that I probably won't like, when Cody interrupts him.

"I'll come too." Cody's voice is hoarse, as if just saying those words costs him. "I'll take the blood oath."

Goliath's eyes widen in surprise and Infomercial Guy beams.

"Me too," Danny grinds out.

"And me," Samson raises his hand, like he's ordering a drink instead of offering to sign his freedom over to a psychopathic alpha. "One blood oath for me."

Infomercial Guy rubs his hands together, grinning manically. "Excellent! Alpha Huxley is going to be pleased. You're all making the right choice for your futures."

He starts to drone on about the benefits of serving the Blackwater pack while the other enforcers unlock Cody, Danny and Samson's cages. I barely hear what he says – some propaganda about how powerful the pack will become, and all the glory we'll get. I'm too busy watching the way Cody hobbles to his feet, as if it's too painful to stand. I fight the urge to stand beside him and offer my support. It would make him look weak, and he wouldn't thank me for it.

Danny and Samson don't look to be in much better shape. Danny is cradling one arm and Samson looks thin and shaky, like a strong wind would knock him down. I hate to think how long they've gone without proper food and what sort of treatment they've been subjected to.

"I'll – I'll take the blood oath too," a voice calls out from behind me. I turn, arching a brow in surprise at the cage where a grey wolf had been. In its place is a boy about my age with hair and eyebrows so blond, they're practically white. His clothes are torn, as if he's shifted while wearing them, but he's managed to haul the scraps of his boxer shorts on, at least.

"Me too. I'll do it too," a dark-skinned boy says, his voice soft but his eyes hard. His gaze meets mine and he lifts his chin slightly. I wonder if he overheard our plan, or if he's just being guided by animal instinct.

Meanwhile, Infomercial Guy looks like he's just won the lottery. He can't believe his luck. They've been trying to break some of these shifters for weeks and now, suddenly, they're all happily falling into line, agreeing to swear the blood oath.

I suppress a grin and force myself to tamp down the gloating feeling of triumph rising in my chest. Now is not the time to celebrate. Not when there are still so many things that can go wrong.

FOR ALL THE hype and fear-mongering, Huxley Black is a surprisingly unexceptional looking male. He's probably only a little taller than me – maybe five-foot-eleven – with a wiry build, auburn hair, dark eyes that are a little too close together, a jawline that's a little too heavy and a thin long nose that looks like it should be holding up wire rim glasses.

That's not to say he's not intimidating. He reminds me of those old school gangsters from that show Peaky Blinders. Like, he's the kind of guy who would slice you up with razor blades just for looking at him wrong.

Or the sort of guy who would murder your mom.

My blood boils looking at him, and it takes every bit of self-control I have not to lunge for him. My wolf is frantic, desperate to break free of the cage of my human form so he can tear this alpha to pieces with tooth and claw.

I take a deep breath, forcing my heart-rate to calm, relaxing the muscles on my face.

You okay, man? Cody asks through the bond. I wonder if he can feel my distress, or if he just knows how hard this moment must be for me.

No, I reply honestly. *But I'll manage.*

I have to manage. Our plan depends on it.

My focus is so fixed on Huxley that it takes me a while to appreciate the bizarre room we have been brought to. It's large and empty with a raised platform at one end. Huxley is seated on a wooden carved chair atop the platform.

Actually, the monstrosity is probably better termed a throne – if a throne was sculpted from pine with a chainsaw. It's like one of those kitschy bear or wolf sculptures that litter every tourist stop in this part of the world. Several of those very sculptures surround him on the platform, presumably to represent the various types of shifters that make up his pack: wolf, bear, some sort of cat and a bird of prey.

I press my lips together to bite back what would be a very inappropriate and ill-timed laugh.

Huxley looks us all over, his upper lip curling slightly as if the sight of us disgusts him. To be fair, the six of us don't exactly look like soldier material. From the glimpse I got of my face in the bathroom mirror on the way here, it looks like someone put my face through a meat grinder. Which (pain aside) is actually great, since it means there's little chance of Huxley recognising me.

The other guys look like a cross between prisoners of war and dishevelled street urchins, half-starved and injured with clothes in various states of filthy decomposition. Even Danny, who is the biggest of us, looks like a dirty child compared to the clean and composed alpha.

"Kneel," Huxley orders, like he's some king receiving court.

Through the bond, I feel Cody balk at the order. *It's okay*, I reassure him. *It doesn't mean anything.*

Reluctantly, he sinks to one knee, the rest of us following suit.

"So," Huxley drawls, standing from his hideous throne as he saunters down the steps of his platform. "You think you have what it takes to be part of the Blackwater pack?"

He strides slowly between us, and I make sure to keep my chin up even as my eyes are fixed to the ground. It's a fine line between showing appropriate submission to an alpha without actually coming across as submissive. The Blackwater pack doesn't want submissive shifters. They want fighters – but fighters that can be controlled. I pretend that is what I am, hoping to be sufficiently boring so I can escape his notice.

"Answer," he snaps, brushing close enough past me that his scent nearly overwhelms me. That scent that has haunted my nightmares for months. Paired with blood and screams and…

I'm snapped out of my dangerous reverie by Cody's foot sharply connecting with my leg, and I realize Huxley is waiting for me to answer.

"Yes, sir," I say flatly, keeping my eyes fixed to the floor, ignoring my wolf as he snaps and snarls within me. If I could shift, I don't know if I'd be able to hold him back from taking control right now.

Huxley grunts in what I'm hoping is satisfaction as he strides past me, ascending the dais and sprawling lazily in his wooden throne.

"Then approach, and swear the oath," he says, holding out his hand.

One of the enforcers approaches him, drawing a hunting knife and slashing it across Huxley's palm. Blood wells in the cut, dripping onto the floor and the wooden throne. Another enforcer hauls up the first of us – the blond boy whose name I've since learned is Christopher Bell – and draws the same blade across the boy's palm. Then Huxley reaches out, clasping Christopher's bloody hand in his own.

"Repeat after me," the first enforcer orders. "I freely offer my fealty to the alpha of the Blackwater pack. I swear to protect the Blackwater pack with my life."

Christopher repeats this, and I wait for Huxley to make some similar oath of protection. I've never seen a blood oath formed (at least, not a normal intentional one) but I recall grandpa explaining that an alpha would normally swear to protect the new member. Huxley makes no such oath, just gives a nod before pulling his hand away and dismissing Christopher.

The same process is followed for the dark-skinned shifter (whose name I learn is Tyrone Jefferson), then Cody, Samson and Danny. I've intentionally placed myself at the back of the group, and I'm the last to ascend the dais.

I barely feel the blade as it cuts into my palm, either because my system is already overloaded with endorphins from my existing injuries, or because I'm about to join myself in blood to mom's killer. I lift my chin, meeting his eyes with my own, hoping he can't see the hate boiling beneath the surface.

Doubt sinks like a stone in my gut as I approach him, hand outstretched. What if I'm wrong and this doesn't work? Or what if it does work? I think about the five guys behind me, the risk they've all taken. The trust they've placed in me.

It's too late to turn back. Quick as an adder, Huxley takes my hand in his, pressing his bloody palm against the open wound in my own.

Time seems to slow down and for a long moment all I can see are his dark, cold eyes boring into my own. I can feel the beating of his heart, and beyond it, the beating of other hearts. I can feel the threads connecting to them, like loose strings resting in the palm of my hand. All I have to do is close my fist around them. Take them as my own. Cut the other tendrils free.

For the first time since I've been in Huxley's presence, my wolf stills, like a predator watching its prey, hungry for the power it can practically taste.

And then I speak the words. "I freely offer my fealty to the Blackwater pack. I swear to protect the Blackwater pack with my life."

Huxley gives a slow smile, the expression incongruous with his cold expression, and I feel an icy jolt of recognition.

I’ve seen that smile a hundred times before on my father’s face.

Chapter 26

Tobias Finch

"Right, Jamison."

There is no mistaking the rage on Samson's face as he cages me against the wall of the barracks, one forearm pressed against my windpipe.

"You going to tell us what's going on? Because I'm pretty sure we've just joined this messed-up pack and you've given us no explanation on how that is supposed to help us get out of here."

I hold my hands up apologetically, even as I fight the urge to roll my eyes. This is literally the first moment we've had away from the watchful presence of the enforcers, who have just deposited us in the barracks with instructions to shower and change into our uniforms.

There hasn't exactly been ample opportunity to talk escape strategy.

Especially when my mind has been distracted with wondering who exactly is Huxley Black, and whether he is related to me. There is no doubt in my mind that he was the male from my parents' wedding photos, even if he no longer looks like the cheerful youth he appeared to be in those photos.

I'm momentarily distracted from answering Samson when Christopher pulls out one of the garish-looking uniforms we are meant to be wearing and grimaces.

If a prep-school procreated with a cowboy-themed Vegas hotel, these uniforms would be their hell-spawn. Red flannel button-downs embossed with the Blackwater pack's name and logo (a crest featuring a wolf, cat, bear and eagle) to be delightfully paired with beige cargo pants. And not the trendy type of cargo pants, but the ones your fifty-year old uncle stopped wearing ten years ago when he realized they weren't cool. This ensemble is apparently incomplete without steel-toed cowboy boots, an embossed leather belt and silver belt buckle (also featuring the Blackwater crest).

I cringe, before turning my attention back to Samson.

First, we shouldn't be talking about this out loud, I suggest through the pack bond, speaking to Samson as well as Danny, Cody, Tyrone and Christopher.

"Fine," Samson hisses, stepping back to fold his arms across his chest.

Second, there's a few things you should know.

I pause, swallowing nervously as my heart batters violently against my ribcage. I look into the faces of the five guys staring at me.

Samson's lean muscles bunch with tension as he waits for my explanation. Danny's impassive face and stormy brown eyes promise a slower but more violent fury. Tyrone's lips are curved into a frown that is more thoughtful than angry. Christopher's white blond eyebrows are raised almost to his hairline.

When my eyes meet Cody's, he just gives a little smirk, like he knows what I'm going to say and is waiting to see how this all plays out.

Fan-freaking-tastic.

I sigh, then whisper through the bond: *My name is Tobias Finch, not Jamison. And I'm a born alpha.*

A barrage of different emotions pours into me down the bonds I share with these guys: shock, fear, confusion and – from Cody – amusement laced with anger.

I thought born alphas were a myth, Christopher muses.

Nope, not a myth, I assure him. *It's just that most of us are killed at birth.* I give a mirthless smile.

I was born into this pack, and they would have killed me when I was born, but my parents escaped. They never spoke about it, and I didn't even know this was their old pack until Cody and Anton were kidnapped.

I look at Cody, the unspoken question about what has happened to Anton flitting between us. Neither of us have seen him or heard about him during our brief tour of the compound after swearing the blood oath. It's an unsettling mystery, but one that has to be addressed later.

Huxley Black killed my mom several months ago, I explain hurriedly though the bond, hating discussing this part of my past.

But there is no way around it. Not if they are going to trust me. Not if we are going to succeed.

I recognised his scent after he kidnapped Cody and Anton, and we managed to figure out they had been taken here.

"We?" Danny asks out loud, cocking his head to one side.

Some of Cody's pack mates, I say vaguely, feeling suddenly protective of my friends. *And also, Orrin, your uncle, and Red, Samson's brother.*

A mixture of disbelief and hope flashes across Samson's face.

They should be on their way here. Or at least, getting help from Cody and Anton's pack.

Samson takes a step back, sitting heavily on one of the low beds that line the walls of the open plan warehouse that makes up the sleeping quarters of the barracks. He leans forward, resting his elbows on his knees, his lanky limbs looking comically large as he perches on the tiny bed.

My brother is on his way here?

Um, yah, I reply, hoping that it's the truth. *Probably…*

Quickly, I feel for the thread connecting Red and Orrin to me. It's harder to do with these other threads now, and theirs is thinner. But I can feel them, stronger than before, feelings of determination pulsing along the fine cords.

I offer up what I hope is a contrite smile as I continue my explanation through our pack link. *Also, I've accidentally made them part of my pack before I took the blood oath, so I think that means they're part of our pack now too.*

Samson narrows his eyes at me. *Wait – what exactly do you mean by 'our pack'?*

It's Cody that answers, amusement and rage coating his silent words: *Because, cat, if what I know about alpha-lore is correct, Huxley Black no longer has a pack. Tobias is a born alpha. It's impossible for a born alpha to join any pack, other than as an alpha. When he and Huxley exchanged blood, it didn't make Tobias part of Huxley's pack. It made Huxley part of Tobias' pack – and with him, all of you. Since your blood was on the same knife.*

Samson stares at Cody, mouth open in disbelief. Beside him, Tyrone throws back his head and laughs. A maniacal laugh that sounds startlingly loud in the silent bunkhouse. He presses his hand to his mouth, abruptly cutting off the sound, but his dark eyes dance as he looks between me and Cody.

"Amazing," Christopher says with a snort, shaking his head as he buttons up the flannel shirt of our uniform. "Absolutely amazing."

Danny frowns, rubbing the (rather impressive) stubble of his jaw with one hand. *How is it that Huxley hasn't noticed he doesn't have a pack anymore?* he queries.

Not a clue, I reply with a shrug, even as panic spikes through me at the mere thought of detection. This is something I've been worrying about as well.

My guess is he'll figure out something is wrong eventually, I suggest, hoping that 'eventually' means significantly later. Hopefully not today. I know that's probably asking for too much though. He'll most likely notice something is wrong the moment he tries to use his alpha dominance to compel someone.

"And what about the rest of the pack?" Christopher asks out loud.

I frown, thinking of the feeling of those hundreds of threads being cut loose when my hand grasped Huxley's. "I guess they're free agents now?" I shoot Cody an inquiring look.

"Gods," Samson mutters, "you really have no idea what you're doing, do you?"

"No idea at all," I reply honestly. "I hadn't really thought beyond the whole blood oath part."

Samson shakes his head, looking unimpressed.

Cody's voice pulses silently in our heads. *I think Tobias is right, and the rest of the pack will have been disbanded when Huxley and Tobias exchanged blood. But I don't think that means we can just walk out of here. There are bound to be shifters loyal to Huxley, blood oath or not. Like those enforcers. And I doubt Huxley is just going to roll over and let you take his wolves.*

"Not just wolves," Samson interjects, pointing to himself and Danny. I look at Tyrone, wondering what type of animal he is, with his dark skin and vivid green eyes.

Whatever, Cody retorts silently with a shrug. *The point is we're going to have to figure out who will be loyal to Tobias – or at least, what shifters just wants to leave this place. And who remains loyal to Huxley.*

Okay, I agree, because that sounds like a sensible plan and it's a relief to defer to Cody.

He's the real leader here. The one who has actually been training since birth to be an alpha. I feel like I really don't have anything else to offer here, besides breaking the pack bond everyone had with Huxley. Which I've already done, so mission accomplished, right?

And then what? Samson asks.

A slow grin spreads across Cody's face. Not his usual sunny smile, but a cold expression that is more bared teeth than anything else. *Then we fight.*

Lucy Stone

"Any word from your dad?" Summer asks as we plod through the snow.

I grunt as a patch of snow that looked deceptively firm gives way under my boot, plunging me down until I'm thigh deep in a snow drift. Despite the cold, I'm burning from exertion under the midday sun, rivulets of sweat snaking down my back and dampening my forehead.

"Nothing," I sigh, wiping my face with the back of my hand before pulling my phone out of my pocket to check. I frown at the screen. "There's no cell service." I glare at the snow in front of me. It glistens and sparkles happily like a tween girl's unicorn notebook. "You know, this would be a million times easier if we shifted," I point out.

"Agreed," Jason huffs from behind me, "Except then we'd have to leave behind all our gear."

"You know," Summer chimes in, "when we were at the camping goods store in Missoula, I saw these little packs that dogs could wear. We should have picked some of those up. You could totally rock one of those in wolf form."

I stare at her blandly, trying to work out if she's being serious. I'm guessing not, but you never do know with Summer.

Tori shakes her head. "No way that would work." She starts listing off reasons on her fingers. "First, they wouldn't be big enough to fit all our gear. Second, we are all waaay bigger in wolf form than your average German Shepherd. I doubt they make packs that would fit us. Third…"

Summer lets out a snort, pressing one hand to her mouth to suppress the laughter bubbling up. Tori glares at her, then tosses her ponytail over her shoulder disdainfully. I shake my head, exchanging a look with Jason.

Summer and Tori have been at each other's throats the past couple days in the most awkwardly passive-aggressive way, and I couldn't really tell you what has caused it. I mean, Tori gets under my skin, but then so do most people if I'm being honest. Summer is usually the one who gets on with everyone.

Maybe she's just worried about Cody and doesn't know how to express it. I mean, it's not like they're mates or anything. I don't even think they're dating. But you'd also have to be blind to think they were just platonic friends.

"Everything is just one big joke to you, isn't it?" Tori snaps. "My *mate* has been taken away. I have no way of knowing if he's okay. I mean, he could be being tortured, killed, anything."

I shoot her a glare, hoping she shuts up. The last thing I want to hear right now is her fearful ramblings about what could be happening to my brother, especially when I can't feel him through our pack link.

Tori continues on, completely oblivious. "I guess I shouldn't expect you to understand what it's like. I mean, Cody and Anton are just packmates to you, aren't they?"

"That's hardly fair," Jason chastises just as Summer says: "Anton's just your future mate, remember."

Tori lets out a low growl that is more wolf than human, her green eyes flashing bright as the wolf pushes close to the surface.

"Why don't you just do some yogic breathing and calm down?" Summer retorts, as she plods through the snow, hands tucked under the straps of her backpack to give some relief to the pressure on her shoulders.

She doesn't seem to notice how close to the surface Tori's wolf is right now.

"What did you say the other day? That's right." Summer adopts a nasally valley-girl sort of inflection. "*Just breath in all the good energy that the universe provides, and breath out all the anger and tension from your…*"

Summer's mocking advice on mindful breathing is abruptly cut short as Tori abandons her human form – and her pacifism – to fling herself at Summer's back. Summer catapults face first into the snow and is promptly obscured by a snarling tan wolf and the shreds of what was once Tori's expensive active-wear ensemble.

Jason leaps away from the fray, stumbling back until he's sitting waist deep in the snow. Orrin and Red call out from behind us. I'm vaguely aware of them running up to join us as Tori tears into Summer's pack, bits of tent and sleeping bag joining the shreds of Tori's clothing in the snow.

Then Summer shifts. Hazel fur explodes through her down coat, causing feathers to fly everywhere. It's like one of those pillow fight scenes, only without the pillows and girls in their PJs jumping on beds. Instead, it's a snarling mass of brown and tan fur, snapping teeth, flashing eyes.

"Knock it off," Orrin bellows, stupidly attempting to get in between the two girls, like he honestly thinks he can just grab them by the scruffs of their necks and pull them apart as if they're fighting chihuahuas. They both pause their fighting long enough to snap at him, resuming their battle when he backs off, hands raised, shaking his head in disbelief.

"This about the bed? The front seat?" Red asks, his head cocked to one side as he observes the fight. He looks like he should be holding a bag of popcorn and binge-watching a series on Netflix, not watching a wolf fight in the middle of enemy territory. "Or the diet coke?"

"The – what?" I ask, as Tori's tan wolf slams Summer back into the snow, making the most of her notable size advantage. Summer's wolf is small and sleek. A fast runner. Not really much of a fighter, if I'm being honest.

So I don't expect to see the dark brown wolf wriggle out from under the tan wolf's paws, snapping and clawing. Red continues his impassive explanation. "You know when we stopped at the gas station, and Tori was giving Summer a hard time about getting a diet coke. Going on and on about how it has aspartame in it, how Summer was going to get cancer."

I frown. Definitely did not hear that conversation.

"Then Summer 'accidentally' spilled her coke all over Tori's bag," Red continues, as Summer darts behind Tori, snapping at her tail. "I don't think Tori was very impressed."

I press my lips together, trying to suppress a grin. Tori has this Alexander McQueen tote that she loves like it's her first-born child or something. Refuses to put it on the ground, freaks out if it gets a speck of dirt on it.

"Cut it out," Orrin shouts, throwing handfuls of snow at the two females. I think he mutters something about idiot wolf pups, but it's hard to hear over the snarling and yipping.

Jason grabs my arm so hard I flinch. There's panic in his face, but he's not looking at Tori and Summer. He's looking across the snowy clearing where the largest wolf I've ever seen steps out of the treeline. The wolf's black fur contrasts starkly against the white snow as he lifts his nose to the air, taking in our scent. A grey-haired male appears beside him, too far for me to make out his face.

Orrin notices the newcomers at the same moment, his large frame moving with surprising speed until he's standing between us and them. My inner wolf nods her head in approval at the protective gesture. Apparently unconcerned by the aggressive move, the large black wolf just cocks his head to one side and pads slowly but deliberately towards our group.

I can see Orrin's muscles tensing beneath his sweater as he fights the urge to shift into his bear form.

"State your business," he growls.

The wolf, unsurprisingly, doesn't answer. The male keeping pace beside the wolf calls out, "You state yours first, bear." The male's eyes turn to me, and he's close enough now that I can see the wrinkles etched on his face. "What are you doing with pups from the Clear Creek pack?"

I gape. How does this stranger know what pack we're from? Summer's wolf presses against my right side, flanking me in silent support just as Jason leans in on my left. My wolf rises, seeking control, wanting to protect my weaker packmates. I shove her down. I need human intelligence right now, not a wolf's aggressive instincts.

"Who is asking?" I call out. This could be an ally of our pack, someone alpha Winslow sent to help Cody and Anton. Though that still wouldn't explain how they have recognised us.

The wolf is close enough now that I can make out his eyes. They're a gold colour I've never seen before. Not amber or yellow but true gold. The colour of legends I believed were as fabricated as the myths of the shifter gods the elders still worship. Jason must notice his eyes at the same time, judging by the shocked intake of breath.

"Tobias…" Jason whispers, before clutching his throat and giving a sputtering cough. "I can't…" he wheezes to himself, "Promised." He gives another cough.

The old man nods, as if he understands whatever it is that Jason is trying to say. "Yes. I'm Tobias' grandfather. John Vance." He tilts his head to the wolf. "And this is his great-uncle, Jamison." At the sound of his name, the giant wolf lets out a rumbling growl of approval.

Red lets out a mirthless laugh. "Of course, you are." He points an accusatory finger at the massive wolf. "That's where Tobias gets it from."

I shoot Red a questioning glance. "Gets what from?" I ask.

Red doesn't answer, and I narrow my eyes at the old man. "I thought Tobias' grandparents were human."

In fact, I had been in their house less than a week ago, and the only shifter scent I'd picked up was from Tobias. I hadn't met his grandfather, but the grandmother had definitely been human.

The old man's upper lip twitches. "You thought wrong."

I grind my teeth. One more lie from Tobias Finch. I shouldn't be surprised. But I can't stop the surge of disappointment.

I look back at Jamison, at those eyes swirling like molten gold, and decide to address the proverbial mammoth in the forest. "You're a born alpha."

The black wolf nods, his giant head as big as a horse's, and I feel it then. As if he's just uncorked a bottle, waves of alpha power roll over us, suffocating and comforting all at once. Beside me, Summer's wolf drops to its belly in the snow, whimpering and thumping its tail submissively. I can feel my own wolf doing a similar thing within me.

"That's enough, Jamison," John says, idly stroking the wolf between his ears.

It's a familiar gesture, even between packmates. The sort of thing reserved for family or the closest of friends. A pang of longing mixed with fear spikes through me. It's the sort of thing Anton would have done if I was in wolf form.

The black wolf lets out a disappointed huff and as quickly as it came, the alpha power dissipates, leaving a light emptiness in its wake. Orrin shakes his head and I hear Red give out a low, pining growl.

"Don't worry about Jamison here," John continues. "What he is or isn't doesn't concern any of you." He tilts his chin towards the trees at the north end of the clearing. The direction we had been heading before Summer and Tori's fight. "What matters is finding the Blackwater pack, and getting my grandson back." He gives Tori and Summer hard look, adding, "And preferably not drawing the attention of the Blackwater pack before we get there."

I open my mouth to argue. The fact that this Jamison guy is a born alpha does concern us. It concerns every wolf shifter in the country. Maybe the world.

"Agreed," Orrin says, shooting me a silencing look. "We all have people to get back from the Blackwater pack. That's our first priority."

I glare at his back but keep my arguments to myself. For now. Because the need to get Anton back has become a panicked, living thing, that's only grown since I haven't been able to feel him through the pack link.

Later, we can talk about what it means that a living, breathing, legend is standing just feet away from me. In the meantime, it can't hurt to have two more shifters on our side.

Chapter 27

Tobias Finch

"I feel ridiculous," Christopher mutters under his breath, shifting uncomfortably in the beige cargo pants and tugging at the collar of his flannel button down.

We're heading towards the open field the enforcers pointed out to us. Presumably to be issued our guns and do some ultra-macho target practice stuff.

"You look ridiculous," Tyrone quips.

Christopher glares at him. "You're wearing the same uniform."

Tyrone lifts one shoulder, never breaking his languid, confident stride. "I can make anything look good."

"They're not that bad," Danny argues, looking down at the uniform stretched across his broad form. "Shirt could be a bit bigger though."

Samson chuckles. "Don't think they make them in bear size. And I get the feeling Blackwater pack is too cheap for custom made."

"I'm not that big," Danny argues and I'm forced to bite back a smile. The guy is at least six-foot-six and built like a line-backer.

Cody is quiet as he surveys the various outbuildings, absorbing the faces and uniforms of the shifters we pass on the way. His nostrils flare as he takes in each new scent.

Are you looking for Anton? I ask through the bond.

Cody nods imperceptibly.

We'll find him, I say reassuringly, even as a growing sense of unease settles like lead in my stomach.

Cody responds with a grunt before flicking the dark mass of curls off his forehead.

The other guys continue on, commenting on the uniforms and buildings, oblivious to the quiet tension.

"These are pretty impractical for shifting," Samson complains, pointing to the buttons on his shirt.

Christopher nods vigorously in agreement. "And also, guns? That's cowardly as all get up. We're shifters. We should be – you know – shifting." He gives a derisive scoff. "In my pack guns were only used for executions. You know, silver bullets. Out of mercy."

"Nah, I think it makes sense," Samson drawls. "What if the shifters you're fighting against use guns? You can't expect everyone to be all honourable and shit. Its war."

"We shouldn't even be going into war," Danny argues, sounding almost petulant. "I mean, we're kids."

Cody and I exchange a look behind Danny's six-plus-feet and very non-childlike looking frame.

"Well, we won't be going to war, will we?" Tyrone's voice is low enough that I doubt anyone outside our group can hear him, but I tense nonetheless. "At least I don't plan to. Apart from fighting whatever suicidal shifters plan to stand between me and the road out of this dump, I have no plans to go to war."

"Where are you from again?" Christopher asks.

Tyrone snorts. "Wouldn't you like to know. Bet you want to see my animal too."

"You'll have to shift eventually," Christopher argues. "Don't know why you're being so cagey about it. You a duck or something? Mouse? Wombat?" He flashes me and Cody a mischievous grin. "Maybe our new alpha here will order you to shift, and then we'll all see."

It takes me at least thirty seconds to realize that by 'new alpha' he means me and I jerk my head up in surprise.

"I'm not ordering anyone to shift," I say quickly, throwing my hands up in front of me. "Actually, I'm not ordering any of you to do anything." I look at my new packmates, hoping they see how serious I am. "And don't call me alpha. It's weird." I wrinkle my nose. "I am *not* anyone's alpha."

Christopher furrows his white-blond brow as he looks at me in confusion. "Umm, hate to break it to you Tobias. But yah. You are."

I frown, but am spared the futility of arguing my point when we reach the shooting range.

'Shooting range' is probably a generous description.

It's more of an open field at the southern-most end of the buildings with makeshift targets littered haphazardly around. The only thing identifying it as our intended destination are the copious amount of bullet shells in the dirt, and the two enforcers leaning against a wooden fence with a bunch of old-looking rifles propped beside them. Beyond them are about twenty other shifters I've never seen before, all wearing the same standard-issue nightmare that our group is wearing, and all appearing to be between the age of fifteen and twenty.

"Pick up your guns, boys," the first enforcer orders.

I recognise him as the overly-excited enforcer with missing teeth who pulled us from our cages early this morning, and resist the urge to smirk. This guy doesn't seem like much of a threat, even with a loaded gun in his hands. He's got that easily-outsmarted-villain look about him, somewhat reminiscent of the bad guys in those old-timey *Home Alone* movies that always air around Christmas.

If all the other conscripts or recruits (or whatever they are called) hate being in the Blackwater pack as much as we do, this could be a good time to fight our way out.

One look at the stony, determined, expression on Cody's face tells me he's thinking the same thing.

We pick up our guns and sidle up to the other shifters, all of whom are already holding guns and staring at the two enforcers with that bored, detached look reserved for the most unimpressive of teachers.

Missing-teeth guy doesn't seem to notice. The enforcer beside him – a squat, burly guy with chest hair pouring over his collar – is glaring back at us, much more aware than his companion of the collective apathy directed at him.

Missing-teeth guy cracks a grin, and I notice for the first time that both he and the other enforcer have name badges sewn onto the front of their uniforms. His just reads 'Ed' while the shorter guy's says 'Jonas'.

"Today Jonas and I will be teaching you lot how to load a gun and shoot a moving target," Ed beams, holding his rifle in his arms like it's his first-born pup. "Since this is just practice, we'll be using regular bullets." He lifts one hand, a copper-coloured bullet pressed between his thumb and forefinger. "In a battle, you'll be using silver." Beside him, Jonas extends one gloved hand, unfurling his fingers to expose a gleaming silver bullet.

There's a collective shiver at the sight of that deadly metal, glinting like moonlight in the sun. I don't think it escapes anyone's notice that Jonas is wearing gloves to avoid touching what is essentially a highly toxic allergen. A violent smile cracks the short enforcer's lips.

Ed starts giving a detailed explanation of firearm anatomy, narrating his show-and-tell with as much enthusiasm as David Attenborough discussing Emperor Penguins. While he addresses his audience, the five of us whisper through the pack link.

In the end, it's Christopher who comes up with the plan.

I'll distract the enforcers to give you guys a chance to talk to the other guys, Christopher says through the bond. *See if you can figure out if whose side they're on. If they seem cool, maybe let them know that the bond with Huxley Black has been broken?*

There's a hum of agreement along our pack link.

We should also offer for them to join Tobias' pack, Danny suggests. *That way we can all communicate with each other. Also to make sure no one turns on us.*

I cringe at the suggestion of adding shifters to this sham pack, even as I have to agree with Danny's reasoning.

Ed has finally finished his gun anatomy lesson, and has moved on to showing us how to load a rifle. There's a few muffled groans from the group of boys, followed by the faint sound of metal clinking as bullets slide into chambers.

How exactly are you going to distract the enforcers? I ask.

In response, Christopher just flashes a mischievous grin, even as the colour drains from his already pale face. Then there's the abrupt sound of a gun firing, the sickening, meaty sound of a bullet sinking into flesh and bone, and a keening wail. Christopher crumples to the ground, his gun falling at his side.

"My foot! Oh, gods, my foot!" Christopher yells, before letting out a lengthy – and rather creative - stream of expletives.

Blood pools beneath him, vibrant against the grey hard-packed snow. Then he's cut off from view as the two enforcers bend over him. Ed shouting questions about what went wrong, and Jonas growling about the idiocy of trying to teach pups to be soldiers.

I'm so stunned by the scene in front of me, that a full thirty seconds passes before I remember that this must be the distraction Christopher promised us. When I turn to the pack of boys, I see Cody already huddled amongst them, speaking in hurried, hushed tones.

"Heck yah, I'll join your pack," one of the guys whisper shouts, flashing me a wild grin. He's tall and lanky, pale skin peppered with oversized freckles and red hair styled into a rough faux-hawk. Colourful tattoos peek out at the wrists and neck of his flannel shirt.

The sight of the tattoos is surprising, because shifter healing abilities make it virtually impossible for tattoos to work. The only way I've heard of is for small amounts of silver to be mixed in with the ink, the constant burn of poison slowing the healing process long enough for the ink to stick.

I've also heard that it takes months for the silver to leave the body, and that it's so painful that shifters have been known to go feral during the tattooing process.

That this guy has what appear to be full-length sleeves on both arms tells me one thing: he's absolutely crazy.

"Um, okay… Great." I say.

I'm trying to smile, but honestly, I feel a bit queasy, either from the sight of Christopher's blood, or the idea of taking on more pack-mates. Maybe both. All the while, I can feel my wolf strutting. Like the delusional animal really thinks he is some proud alpha watching over his pack.

Before I can react, there's the flash of a knife and the bite of pain as the tattooed shifter grabs my hand, slicing across the palm and pressing his own bloody palm against my own.

"I, Hamish Clarke, swear fealty to you and all that crap," he says irreverently, clapping me roughly on the shoulder. Instantly, I feel the bond tethering me to him. I feel his unique presence at the end of it, like storm tossed wind against sandstone cliffs.

He unceremoniously drops my bleeding hand, turning to the crowd behind him. Metal flashes as he draws the knife from his pocket, flicking the blade out and pointing it at the watching crowd. "Now, do you want me to cut you, or would you rather cut yourselves?" he asks sardonically. "Because either way, you're going to bleed for Tobias here. It's just a matter of how much."

Hamish must enjoy a certain level of respect – or fear – from the conscripts, because every single one of them presses a bloody palm to my own, swearing themselves into my pack within the space of a couple minutes.

My pack. The thought is absolutely ludicrous. I'm not supposed to exist, let alone lead a pack.

The background noise of Christopher's whimpers have faded away and when I turn to look at him and the two enforcers, I can see that he's shifted, the bullet working its way out of the grey wolf's flesh. There's a dull *thunk* as it finally slides free and hits the ground.

"'Bout time," Jonas growls. "Shift back, pup."

The enforcer nudges Christopher with the toe of one booted foot. Christopher obeys, though the shift and the quick healing look to have cost him. His pale face is coated in a sheen of sweat, even as he gives me a knowing look.

Did it work? he asks through the bond, and I can feel his fatigue and lingering pain with the question. *Did they join our pack?*

I nod, throat constricting as I watch him rise to his feet and gingerly pull on his uniform. I've just met this guy this morning, and he's taken a bullet for me. A literal bullet. Shot himself in the foot so that we can have a better chance of getting out of here alive.

I don't deserve him. I don't deserve any of them.

But they have me. I'm their alpha. Even if it's just temporary. Even if there's a way to break the bonds and dissolve this pack once everything is over. For now, I'm it.

"Well, if you useless animals are done shooting yourselves," Jonas drawls, "it's time to bring out the targets."

He points to the field stretching out in front of us, the snowy landscape moulted grey and brown where it's been trampled underfoot.

At the edge of the clearing, about a hundred and fifty yards away, a cluster of figures is moving towards us. Ten of them appear to be tied together with some sort of rope as they walk in that awkward way that makes me think they've been injured somehow. Or maybe hobbled? Another four figures – enforcers, based on the black of their uniforms – flank them.

"Once the targets are cut loose, they'll likely run," Jonas explains, waving one hand dismissively at the bedraggled figures. "But before we start, let me make sure you all know the rules." He flashes the first smile I've seen from him. The expression is disturbing on him, to say the least.

"These targets are all dissidents. Traitors and rebels. Shifters who refused to swear fealty to your alpha. Or worse, who swore fealty and then betrayed our pack." Jonas twists his head left and right, cracking his thick neck. "They deserve what you're going to give them and worse."

The ten figures hobble closer and I squint, trying to make out their faces. Even with my shifter vision, it's still too far to make out their features clearly, but I can see the pained way their bodies move. The tallest of them has a discernible limp.

"Your orders are to shoot each and every one of these targets. Those targets that are hit and survive will have the opportunity to seek forgiveness from Alpha Black, and swear fealty if they have not already done so." Jonas sneers. "It's a greater generosity than they deserve."

I watch the shifters approach, a sick feeling of dread creeping along my skin as their faces come into view.

"Failure to hit a target will result in that target being re-captured and publicly executed. So, before you get any misplaced ideas about showing mercy," Jonas glares at us, "remember that mercy will only result in these miscreants' death."

I shudder at his cold, gleeful tone but don't take my eyes off the approaching shifters and the enforcers leading them. I recognise Goliath first, his size and build making him unmistakable even with the distance.

"Guns loaded," Ed orders, his voice rising in pitch with eagerness. "Take your positions but don't fire until our guys are well clear."

I almost snort at that instruction. Like, he actually thinks we are stupid enough to just start shooting. Though if I knew how to shoot, I'd probably be tempted to take a shot or two at Goliath. Maybe just his kneecaps?

The enforcers cut the hobbled shifters out of their bonds, moving them forward with what look like cattle prods, driving them into a run toward us.

And that's when I recognise him. Face contorted with pain and rage and bruises until his features are almost unrecognisable. Hand clutching his side, as if he's trying to hold broken ribs in place. Limping heavily.

Anton. Freaking Anton is a target.

I can tell Cody recognises him the same moment I do by the spike of adrenaline that courses from him to me through the pack bond.

In the distance, the enforcers have shifted into their animal form, peeling away from the ten shifters hobbling and running towards us. Leaving our targets clear to shoot at without risk of friendly fire.

"All right boys." Ed rubs his hands together gleefully. "Ready, aim…"

Don't shoot. I send the silent order through our link, unconsciously packing enough alpha command into it that some of the boys around me actually drop their guns into to the snow.

My heart is racing, thudding as loudly as the hooves of that bull that chased me down. I have absolutely no idea what I'm doing, but I know without a doubt I can't let them shoot Anton. I've heard the way Lucy talks about him, like he's the one person in the world she loves.

Mine, my wolf growls, his possessive instincts flaring to life as the injured shifters make their way to us across the snow. *My pack. My shifters. Mine to protect.*

All the while, I can feel the strength of my new packmates feeding into me like electricity. Twenty-eight different threads connecting twenty-eight different souls to my own. I want to cower under the power, to disconnect the threads, something. Anything to make it stop.

But my wolf feeds on it, and I'm not sure if the next order I give comes from me or him.

Protect the targets.

Around me, some of the meeker of my new packmates spontaneously shift into their animal form as this second alpha command rolls off me. Ed and Jonas' eyes widen in shock as they look at me, no doubt feeling the power, even if they haven't heard my silent order.

"What the…" Ed murmurs, shaking his head, just as Jonas growls, "What in the devil is going on?"

And then all hell breaks loose.

In a flash, several of the guys turn on Ed and Jonas, taking them to the snow in a matter of seconds, disarming and incapacitating them.

At least I hope they're just incapacitating them. It's hard to say for sure.

Another group sprints towards the guys hobbling towards us, shouting words of encouragement as they go. Assuring them that we won't shoot them. That we're on their side.

I stand, momentarily frozen with uncertainty over which of the two groups I should help. Then I notice the three enforcers – the ones that brought the 'targets' to the clearing. They have turned around, making their way back from the distant edge of the clearing to reclaim their now-freed captives.

Horrified, I watch as a very familiar kodiak – now in bear form - sprints towards Anton and some of the other slower, more seriously injured boys, with a speed that should be impossible for a creature that size. Even if I stood a chance of taking on Goliath in his animal form, there is no way I could reach him in time to stop him. There is no way any of us can reach him.

Anton seems to realize his predicament, because his eyes widen and he tries to run. He doesn't shift though. None of them do, even though shifting would heal their wounds and give them strength and speed to run away.

No doubt they've been given something to stop them from shifting. To make them easier targets.

I swallow back the bile that rises, my hands trembling with panic. That's when I notice the fully loaded rifle clutched to my chest.

Goliath is still far enough away that I could fire at him without accidentally hitting Anton and the others. I've never shot a gun before. But I've played my fair share of 'Call of Duty' and arcade games. I've watched movies. It can't be that hard.

Taking a deep breath, I lift the gun to my shoulder. Holding it how Ed showed us before. Lining the sight up with Goliath's giant form. At least he's a pretty big target. That should make things easier.

Before I can second guess the wisdom of my decision, I pull the trigger. The gun recoils with more power than I expected, slamming into my shoulder, causing me to momentarily lose sight of the bear.

My eyes flick up when I hear a pained, angry roar and, for a brief moment, I feel a surge of elation. *I've hit him. I've hit Goliath. I actually did it.* A grin cracks across my face, painfully pulling at the still-healing cut on my lip, awakening the bruises across my jaw.

Until the bear rolls to his feet, shaking his head dazedly for a brief moment before turning yellow glinting eyes towards me. Blood trickles from his right flank, turning the tawny fur a deep brown, but he seems otherwise unaffected. I'm momentarily confused, but then I remember.

These are just ordinary bullets. Aimed to injure, not to actually take down a shifter. Definitely not enough to take down a kodiak shifter.

Goliath lets out an angry roar and the grin falls from my face. There is no doubt in my mind that his animal recognises me. My wolf certainly recognises him. *Fight*, my wolf urges me, hackles rising, remembering the encounter with the bear in the fighting ring. *Bad idea*, I tell him, but the dumb animal is too drunk on power to listen.

The kodiak turns towards me, leaving Anton and the others, like a bear distracted from his hunt by the annoyance of a bee's nest. He knows I'm not a threat to him, but I've pissed him off.

In my peripheral vision, I can see Cody, Danny and Samson leading the charge, closing in on the nearest of the injured shifters. At least I've had the effect of drawing Goliath off Anton and the others. Silver linings, right?

Goliath is so close now, I can see the steam rising from his nostrils, can make out the long claws on his front paws with each galloping stride before his paws sink into the deep snow. I let the gun slip through my fingers as I prepare to run, to get as far away from the kodiak as I can.

Only, my feet won't move.

Fight, my wolf urges again, *Fight. Protect your pack.*

I feel it then. My wolf's instinct pressing in on me, stronger than it's ever been, bolstered by the power of my pack. Binding me to my unspoken and unbreakable alpha promise to protect.

I'm not an alpha, not really, I want to argue. I'm barely sixteen and I can't shift. There is literally no way I can face this kodiak in my human skin and make it out alive.

My wolf ignores me, standing firm and I'm forced to brace myself for impact. It's like standing on the tracks, watching a train approach. The seconds slow down. I can see each of the kodiak's hairs, the texture of the rough wet skin on his nose, the yellow plaque on his long canines. I stop breathing and the cold panic that has been coating my skin changes, blooming into something so hot it's like fire in my bones.

I'm going to die. Right here. Today.

In the moments before your death, they say you see your life flash before your eyes. But no images of my parents present themselves to me. No visions of my happy childhood to carry me across the bridge between life and death.

Instead, my reality is suddenly fractured into twenty-eight different perspectives, like a multi-player video game with too many players on one screen. One where I can also feel what each character is feeling.

I feel Cody's rage as if it's my own. His wolf fights with an enforcer, aware of Anton weak and helpless in his human form at his back.

I can see a black paw reaching out in front of me as Tyrone leaps towards a group of armed enforcers, snarling at the burn of a bullet ripping through his flank.

I feel the freedom of air beneath wings as Hamish dives, screaming wildly with talons outstretched, heedless of the gunfire tearing up the air around him.

I feel Red's astonishment at the unexpected mayhem as he approaches the clearing, followed by the rush of protectiveness when he sees his younger brother, shifted into his bobcat form and locked into a deadly battle with a mountain lion.

And then I'm jolted back into my body as Goliath collides into me, tumbling and rolling in a mass of snarling teeth and fur and claws and snow. The heat in my bones rages, cracking and snapping like a wild fire, burning through every cell in my body with excruciating force. I bare my teeth in protest, biting and clawing at the pain. Blood fills my mouth, but it's not my own. Screams fill my ears, but my own voice is silent, except for the low growl ripping viciously from my chest.

Fight. Fight. Protect my pack, the beast inside of me orders.

Only it's no longer coming from inside of me. I'm the one trapped inside, looking out through eyes much more capable than my own of taking in every little detail.

Through the scent of blood – Goliath's blood, I realize – I can smell pine and snow and the scent of every single one of my packmates, like signatures written on the parchment of my soul. Further on, there is the familiar scent of lavender and fresh rain on grass. The scent that tortured me for hours on end in the confines of Orrin's van. And then the pungent scent of grandpa's tobacco.

It's almost enough to distract me from the kodiak snarling beneath me, but the realisation that Lucy and grandpa are close by only fuels my wolf's aggression. The need to protect overrides every other consideration. *Goliath is a threat. All the other enforcers are a threat. A threat to our pack. To our family. To our mate.*

Our mate. The truth of that thought sends a jolt of surprise through me. My wolf just snorts. He knew. He always knew and I was just too dumb to listen.

My teeth release the bear's flank before locking down on his neck. I can feel Goliath's pulse thundering between my jaws. *One bite,* my wolf assures me. *All it will take is one bite and our mate will be safe. Our grandpa will be safe. Our pack will be safe.*

The need to sink my teeth into the bear's flesh is visceral, even as the human side of me – the very trapped human side of me – is disgusted by the thought of ending a life.

Painstakingly, I manage to wrestle just enough control from my wolf to stay the bite. Silently, my teeth clamped on his pulse, I will the kodiak to submit. To go limp beneath my grasp. To show his throat in a sign of submission.

Instead, Goliath lets out a rumbling growl, long yellow claws tearing at my belly as he thrashes and fights against my grip. Refusing to give in.

I can't. I can't do this, I silently plead with my wolf. *I don't want to be a killer. A monster. I just want to be Tobias Finch. I just want to go to school and hang out with my friends and maybe date Lucy if she'll ever stop hating me.*

My wolf ignores me, wrestling back control. Moments later, the kodiak lays still beneath me. I leap back, tongue lolling from my mouth, the taste of blood in my throat. I stare in horrified silence as Goliath's lifeless form turns the snow red.

We were born for this, my wolf reminds me. He lifts our head towards the fray, eyes narrowing in on the newly arrives enforcers attacking our pack. Attacking the weak and injured shifters we had decided to protect.

I don't want to fight, I argue weakly. *We shouldn't have to fight. We're just kids.*

My wolf ignores me, paws thudding against the snow as we sprint to join the fight. Revelling at the feeling of power, at the freedom of four legs finally able to run, at the beauty of the battle.

We were born for this, my wolf reminds me again. And then I'm shoved to the back, forced to watch as we let the noise and smell of the fight envelop us.

Chapter 28

Lucy Stone

Tobias Finch's wolf is the most beautiful and terrifying thing I have ever seen. A sleek gold coat, tawny and metallic against the shimmering snow. Golden eyes, like Jamison's, only full of fire.

And he's big. Bigger than Jamison. Bigger than any wolf I've ever seen.

Watching him fight, it's hard to believe this really is Tobias Finch. I might not believe it, if I hadn't watched him shift. If that pine, sage and chocolate scent floating across on the breeze wasn't so familiar to me.

Only it's different now. Darker. More powerful. And lacking the usual bitter tang of lies.

"There's Anton." Jason's voice cuts through my thoughts, forcing me to pull my eyes away from the golden wolf.

My heart sinks at the sight.

My brother, battered and broken. In so much pain he can barely stay upright, let alone walk. His back is to us, and I can see the horde of unknown shifters hurtling toward him, Cody amongst them. I want to call out to him, and feel his name catch in my throat. I stumble and Summer grips my elbow to steady me.

"It's okay," Orrin rumbles, offering his reassurance. "That group there are pack." He nods a chin in the direction of Cody and the unfamiliar shifters. "They're coming to help Anton and the others."

It's then I notice Anton is not the only injured shifter. At least ten figures hobble across the snow, aiming towards the sombre settlement at the far end of the clearing.

"Those ones in black aren't pack," Red growls, narrowing cat's eyes at the figures emerging from the tree-line to the left. A few pause to shift, becoming a large pack of dangerous looking wolves, but the rest remain in human form, the glint of metal from their rifles reflecting in the sun.

"They're carrying guns." Disbelief coats my voice.

"Cowards," Red snarls.

Jamison rumbles his agreement from behind us. I flinch inwardly at the sight of the massive wolf as he prowls past, paws silent and head lowered as he stalks his prey.

"They could have silver bullets," Tobias' grandfather warns from the back of our group, but Jamison ignores him, heading straight towards the armed shifters.

"I'm going with him," Tori proclaims, already stripping off her pack and coat as she prepares to shift.

Summer's instantly at her side, expression stormy. "That's a bad idea. You're not a fighter. Anton wouldn't want you to get shot for him…"

Tori rounds on Summer, eyes blazing.

"Anton is injured. I can't just stand here and watch them shoot my mate."

She looks back to the group of enforcers. A few have lifted their guns to their shoulders, taking aim at the group of injured shifters and the 'pack' that has come to help them. Her hands give an involuntary tremor but she shucks off the rest of her clothes, shifting fluidly into a sleek, tan wolf.

"Of all the stupid, idiotic things," Summer hisses at Tori's retreating form as she starts throwing off her own pack and clothes.

"What are you doing?" Jason asks warily.

Summer just gives him a look. Jason pales.

"Let her go," I say.

Summer and Tori might not be trained to fight, but I've seen how vicious their wolves can be. More than that, I know what it's like to be held back. To be told it's not my place to fight because I'm a female.

Wordlessly, I start undressing, getting ready to shift. Orrin and Red have already shifted, and are sprinting across the snowy expanse towards the armed shifters at the far end of the clearing.

"I promised Jamison I wouldn't fight." Tobias' grandfather wrings his hands, looking at me and Jason apologetically. "That was the bargain we struck," he explains. "I bring him along but I don't fight."

"Elders shouldn't have to fight," I say hurriedly, repeating words I've heard my own father say countless times.

Elders are the keepers of our knowledge, of shifter lore. If we send them to the slaughter like common soldiers, we lose the heart of what we are fighting for.

I flinch as the sound of gunfire echoes across the clearing. It's followed by a screech and the flurry of feathers as some avian shifter plummets to the snow. Once on the ground, he shifts into his human form, the screeches replaced with human sounding cries of pain.

As if the sound is a call to my wolf, I'm suddenly on all four paws, racing across the snow. Vaguely, I'm aware of Jason cursing at my back, but the sound is drowned out by the roaring in my ears, by the cacophony of animal and human sounds, blaringly loud as I adjust to my wolf hearing.

Anton, I cry through the pack link. *I'm coming Anton. I've got you.*

My heart sinks when I'm met by silence. But I can see him. He's here. He's alive, hobbling in amongst the mass of injured shifters and the shifters who have come to help them.

In a matter of moments, I'm at Anton's side, pressing against him, demanding that he lean on me. My wolf whimpers as he drapes one arm over me, overwhelmed by the familiar scent of home and safety mixed with blood and pain.

"It's okay, Luce," he rasps out. "We're going to be okay." But I can feel his body tremble beside mine.

What did they do to you? I ask through the pack link, whimpering again when the question is met with silence. Around us, the sounds of snarling and fighting grow stronger.

Anton runs his fingers through my fur reassuringly. "They forced me to join pack Blackwater," he explains, as if reading my thoughts. "I – I didn't want to do it. Tried to stop it but…"

His voice trails off, and my stomach sours as I recall what Gareth Yates implied when I spoke with him at the bar outside Missoula. Torture. My brother. My protector. Tortured.

"It doesn't matter now." His steps falter and he tightens his grip. "The pack bond is broken. I'm not sure exactly how it happened, but I felt it snap a few hours ago. We all did."

Ahead of us, two grey and white wolves slam into a panther, toppling the feline into the snow. Anton tenses beside me, pulling us to a stop.

"Those wolves are enforcers," he croaks out. "Blackwater enforcers."

I nod, recognising the wolves as the shifters who had accompanied the gunmen. The panther springs up, snarling and hissing as he strikes out at the pair of wolves. Expertly, the wolves dance out of his way, flashing lupine smiles as they start to circle and bait the cat. It's a classic hunting move when wolves faced against larger predators. One I've seen our own enforcers use dozens of times.

The cat lunges forward, claws outstretched towards the first of the wolves, oblivious to the second wolf readying an attack from behind. Instinctively, I snarl in warning and the panther turns just in time to throw the second wolf over his back with a disgruntled hiss.

I realize my mistake when two pairs of intelligent wolf eyes turn my way, gleaming angrily in the afternoon sun. Beside me, Anton trembles.

"I can't shift," he warns, voice full of desperation. "I can't shift and fight."

I draw myself up to my full height, feeling the prickle of hackles rising on my back, the rumbling growl tear from my throat.

"You can't fight them," Anton cautions.

But it isn't his choice. It isn't mine either. The fight is here, staring me down. I step forward, putting my brother behind me as I bare my teeth.

The wolves charge, kicking up snow as they barrel towards me. I stand my ground, locking eyes with the closest of the two wolves – the one who was baiting the panther. Hopefully that panther takes the second wolf. If he doesn't… Well, there's no point in thinking about that.

The first wolf slams into me, teeth locking onto my shoulder, claws raking my back. I roll, snapping and clawing as I try to shake him free. He's almost twice my size – a full-grown male wolf, trained to fight. An enforcer.

Females aren't meant to fight, my father's voice rings in my head, memories battering my senses just as much as the snow and teeth and claws. *Stubbornness isn't a replacement for strength, Lucy. Stop trying to change the natural order.*

What about Morrigan? I had argued. *And Leto?* Pointing out that our history is peppered with stories of wolf goddess warriors – some so well known that even humans remember them as myths.

Dad had scoffed derisively, thick lips peeling back in a snarl. *You sound like your mother*, he'd said. The woman who had left him. Who had left us without so much as a goodbye. Without a letter to let us know where she was, that she was okay.

Maybe I am like my mother. I don't know. I was so young when she left, my memories are tinged with the haze of childhood and then tainted by my father's stories.

Teeth and claws tear into my skin, ripping past the pale fur of my coat, so deep into my flesh I can feel the scrape of tooth on bone. A lupine scream sounds from my throat and I'm aware of someone calling my name, over and over.

Abruptly, the wolf is gone. Thrown off me with enough force that I stagger in confusion at the sudden absence of my attacker. I shake my head, letting the snow and blood fly from my fur, eyes searching frantically for my opponent and the source of my unexpected relief.

Air catches in my lungs when I see him. The golden wolf. Tobias' wolf. Like beast made fire, tearing into the grey and white wolf with feral abandon. He lacks the finesse of a trained fighter, moving instead with the wild grace of a true animal. In a matter of moments, the grey and white wolf is a lifeless heap in the snow.

Tobias turns to me, liquid gold eyes burning, nothing of the boy present in them. I fight to suppress a shudder, grateful for the steadying feel of my brother's arm wrapping across my shoulders.

"Who the heck is that?" Anton asks, voice full of trepidation and awe.

I don't answer. It's impossible in my wolf form, without the pack link, and I'm too tired to shift.

Nearby, the panther has finished his fight, letting out a triumphant growl as the second grey and white wolf slumps to the snow. The golden wolf huffs approvingly in the cat's direction before turning his eyes back to me. My own wolf demands I lower my eyes, show submission. I ignore her, keeping my head up, my eyes locked on his.

It's just Tobias, I tell my wolf. *He won't hurt us*. The sentiment feels true, but if life has taught me anything, it's that anyone can hurt you. Even the people you trust the most. Especially them.

Good thing I've never trusted Tobias Finch.

I feel Anton's grip on my shoulder tighten as the golden wolf moves towards us, head lowered, nostrils flaring until he's close enough that I can feel the heat of the wolf's breath, his pine, sage and chocolate smell enveloping me like a blanket.

"Gods." Anton sniffs the air, then lets out a hysterical sounding laugh. "Is that… no way that can be…Tobias?"

Tobias chuffs his assent but doesn't take his eyes off me. I tense as he brings his muzzle to my neck, then let out a surprised whimper at the feel of his tongue. He's cleaning my wounds, I realize, too stunned to move. It's not the first time a wolf has done this, but usually it's a packmate, a family member, a close friend. Tobias is not pack. A few days ago, I wouldn't have even said he was my friend.

"She'll be fine," Anton bites out defensively, trying to shove Tobias away from me. Tobias merely lets out a low growl before turning back to my injuries.

To be fair, it really does help, even if it is awkward. Or at least, it's awkward to my human side. But after the adrenaline of fighting, my wolf is firmly in the driver's seat. And she thinks this is just fine. I nudge Anton, trying to tell him it's fine, that I don't mind.

I tell myself it's just because shifter saliva apparently has all these healing properties, as well as pain relief. And the stronger the wolf, the stronger the magic. It has nothing to with this being Tobias. Nothing to do with the feelings his presence elicits in me.

When Tobias tries to roll me onto my back to heal the bites on my belly, it proves to be too much for Anton.

"Nope. Nope, nope, nope," Anton says, hobbling between Tobias and me, completely unintimidated by the terrifying size of Tobias' wolf. "Look, I get that you're wolfing out right now, but this is my sister. And what she needs – what all of us need actually – is to get inside and find somewhere safe."

Anton's words seem to reach Tobias, because the golden wolf away backs with a reluctant huff, giving my neck one last lick before trotting off towards the horde of shifters making their way across the meadow.

I'm vaguely aware that the sound of gunfire and fighting has stopped, that more and more voices are replacing animal sounds as people shift back into their human forms, most likely to speed up the healing process. Some of them pass by us, chatting animatedly as they make their way towards the sombre looking buildings.

The fighting must be over.

Still in my wolf form, it's hard for me to catch the meaning of their words, the direction of their conversation. But I can hear the mixture of excitement and relief in their voices. I can tell they are young – my age or a few years older. And when I catch their scents, there are so many different types of shifters its almost heady. But amongst it all, on every single one of them – the scent of truth.

TOBIAS FINCH

The battle is a blur in my memory, a confused jumble of movement and sound punctuated by moments of clarity. Goliath's lifeless body. The crunch of metal between my teeth as I ripped the rifles from the gunmen's hands. Jamison's howl as silver bullets tore through his flank. The taste of his blood on my tongue as I licked his wounds to heal him. The burning pain of the pack bonds breaking when I lost two of my shifters – a fox and an owl.

I never even got to know them. I didn't even know their names. And still their loss was more painful than any injury I've ever sustained. Even now, the taste of my failure lingers in my mouth, mixing with the metallic tinge of blood on my tongue.

So much blood. So. Much. Blood.

"You were epic out there."

Hamish's voice punctuates my thoughts, sharp as the call of his red-tailed hawk, bringing me back to the brightly lit room of the pack-house.

"Never seen anything like it. Between you and that black wolf, they didn't stand a chance." His dark chuckle skitters across my bones. "You tore them to pieces."

I did. Unfortunately, that is the one thing I can remember with painstaking clarity. Each kill. Every single one. So many. So, so many.

All those years wishing I could shift, wishing I wasn't latent, only to find out that my wolf is a blood-thirsty monster.

"Any sign of Huxley Black?" I ask, wanting to change the subject.

Hamish shakes his head. "I didn't see him." He turns to the other two following close behind. "Cody? Tyrone? Did either of you guys see ole' Hux?"

It's no surprise to me when they both confirm in the negative. Because I can feel Huxley. Can feel the thread that links me to him getting thinner and thinner as he moves away. Running like the coward he is.

It's unnerving, not knowing where he is. Like being able to hear a wasp in the room without seeing it. Even more unnerving is the fact that I'm Huxley Black's alpha. How messed up is that? Though I guess I should have foreseen that would be the unintended consequence of breaking his bond with the whole pack.

"I think everyone is here," Cody says, scanning the room with the sharp awareness of someone born and trained to lead.

I can tell he's taking in each face, remembering each name. He probably remembers what animal they are too, what role they played in the fight.

He nods in my direction. "You should make a start."

I sigh, running my hand over my face. My skin is slick with dirt and sweat. I'm wearing borrowed sweatpants, my standard-issue uniform laying in shreds somewhere in the meadow. Probably between corpses.

As if sensing my discomfort, Christopher places one hand reassuringly on my shoulder. "You got this, buddy."

Buddy. This guy has barely known me twenty-four hours, and he thinks he's my friend.

I resist the urge to snort out a laugh. Instead, I glare at the raised dais, the garish wooden throne and animal carvings. There is no way I'm getting near that thing.

I move to the wall opposite the stage, pressing my back against it, as if I can draw support from the timbre frame. Or maybe just sink into it. That would be nice, if I could disappear.

The room falls silent, conversations faltering as scores of eyes turn towards me expectantly.

Grandpa with Jamison at his side, the large wolf looking almost comical with bandages wrapped across his torso.

Red has one arm slung around Samson's shoulder.

Orrin stands beside Danny, a look of surprised relief on his face.

Anton sits slumped into a chair, looking like death warmed up as Lucy, shifted back into her human form, stands behind him like a sentry. Her grey eyes meet my own, expression unreadable.

Our mate, my wolf whispers, rumbling at the recollection of that wolf attacking her.

I blink, nowhere near ready to process what that means.

I mean, of course I like her. I really like her. When I first met her, I thought maybe I'd be able to convince her to go to a school dance with me or something. Maybe go to the movies, hold her hand, kiss her. I may have even dreamt about more than that. Like what it would feel like to have her pressed close to me, how soft her skin would be under my fingertips…

That was before she tried to have me gored by a bull, then ignored me, then threatened to torture me for information.

Now I'm just hoping for cordial conversation. Yep, that seems like a reasonable goal.

Mating? A bond more permanent than marriage? I let out a low breath, letting it hiss between my teeth as I shake my head. Can't really see that one happening.

Cody gives me an encouraging nod, even as his mouth is set in a thin line, eyes cold.

I swallow, feeling my heart race behind my ribcage. Of course, my wolf is preening. Basking in the attention, in the power, like the megalomaniac that he is. Unfortunately, he's completely useless at doing anything but tearing things apart. Not particularly helpful on the public speaking front.

Good thing I've perfected the art of affected nonchalance.

Shoving my hands into the pockets of my borrowed sweatpants, I lean against the wall, pretending like I don't care that my wolf is a psychopathic killer. Like I don't care that I'm standing shirtless in a room full of shifters. Like I definitely don't care that the girl I have a crush on – and who's apparently my mate - can barely stand to talk to me.

"Well ladies and gents," I drawl, "we did it." I force myself to smile. "We took down the Blackwater pack."

The room erupts in raucous cheers. I want to cringe in embarrassment at the sound, even as I'm grateful not to have to speak.

I don't fault them their happiness though. Not when we managed to take down about thirty-five full-grown enforcers. Not when all our lives and freedom was on the line.

Five of the enforcers have been taken prisoner, cuffed and locked away in the same holding pens that not so long ago held Anton and the other shifters destined for target practice. One turned against his own on the battlefield - a coyote shifter named Gareth Yates that Lucy said she recognised from the fight club. He agreed to join my pack, as a show of good faith or whatever.

So now I have twenty-six shifters in my pack. Twenty-seven if you count Huxley Black. Which I don't.

Having a pack – that is a problem. A real problem.

I lift one hand and the cheering subsides to a calm hum.

"Most of you here are sort-of in my pack now." I give what I hope is an apologetic grin. "I just want to make it clear that – well, I know you all have homes to go back to. Families, packs, prides, flocks, whatever you want to call them." I waive one hand dismissively. "I'm not asking any of you to stay with me or be a part of this pack. I mean, this was really just a temporary thing."

The room goes quiet. An awkward, heavy sort of silence that has me shuffling my feet and wishing I could disappear.

"Hold on." Hamish breaks the silence, lifting one finger and fixing me with a stony look. "You're not talking about disbanding our pack now, are you?"

I nod emphatically, grateful for the red-head's bluntness. "Yep. Yes. That's exactly what I'm saying."

"I'm not okay with that." He folds both tattooed arms across his chest, pale freckled cheeks reddening with anger.

"Um…" I gape at him, then look around the room. Similar expressions of disbelief and anger stare back at me.

Not at all what I was expecting here. I flick my eyes towards Cody, to my grandpa, hoping for one of them to step in. Cody's expression is unreadable. Grandpa looks almost sympathetic, but it's hard to tell.

When no one says anything, I say: "Won't your old packs want you back?"

"Mine wont," Christopher scoffs derisively, his face is paler than usual. I wonder if it's from shooting himself in the foot, from the battle, or the mention of his old pack. "I might not have wanted to join the Blackwater pack, but that doesn't mean I wanted to stay at my old pack."

He toes the wood floor with one bare foot, not offering up any further explanation. There's a story there, I realize. No one our age would want to leave their pack without good reason, but it's clearly one he's not willing to share. Not yet anyway.

"I'm not too keen to go back to my pride either," Tyrone says, his lips pulled into a frown. "I'd rather stay with you. Make our own rules, you know. Down with the system and all that."

I shake my head, at a loss of what to say, then look at Orrin and Red. They unwittingly got thrown into this farce of a pack. Surely, out of anyone here, they'd want out of it.

Red shrugs. "I wasn't part of a pack before. My kin, we don't really do packs or prides." His lips curl into a snarl, cat ears twitching as he speaks. "But seeing as Samson and Orrin are in this thing, it means I can do that whole mind-talking thing with them. It's actually kind of useful." He fixes me with a hard look. "But don't go expecting me to follow you around, or be in some shifter army, or any of that crap." He gives an irritated roll of his shoulders. "I'm a cat. We don't really do orders."

I try - and fail - to suppress a grin at Red's self-professed distaste for authority, even as my heart races nervously in my chest.

Orrin shrugs. "I'm going home to hibernate after this." He gives a dramatic yawn, then adds, "It don't matter to me whether I'm in a pack or not, as long as it don't affect my getting' some sleep and running my shop when I wake up in the summer. Like Red said, the mind-talking is pretty handy."

Danny rolls his eyes. "Telepathy, old man. It's called telepathy."

Orrin gives his nephew an indulgent smile and ruffles his hair. Danny grimaces at the show of affection, but I notice the faint smile that plays across his lips.

"Okay…" I wrinkle my nose. "Just so I'm clear – you guys all *want* to keep the pack bond?"

My question is met with nods and shouts of 'yes'. There are even a few 'yes, alpha's' which totally make me cringe. I quirk a brow at Cody and to my surprise, he gives a sharp nod, although his lips remain pressed into a frown.

I suspect there's still a lot we need to talk about. Later. We'll talk later.

"All right then," I say tentatively, "I guess if you don't want to break the bond..."

"Hate to break it to you, alpha," Gareth Yates, the ex-Blackwater enforcer, calls from the far end of the room, "but I don't think you could break the pack bond even if you wanted to. It doesn't work like that, at least as far as I know." He nods in grandpa's direction. "I'm sure your elder here will tell you the same thing."

Grandpa purses his lips, his fingers absently weaving through Jamison's coat as his forehead wrinkles in thought.

"I've never heard of an alpha breaking a pack bond," he says finally. "Not without another alpha coming in and defeating him, or putting a new bond in place, like in the case of a transfer."

He gives me a wry smile.

"Or like I understand happened with this pack's old alpha," he says, gesturing with one withered hand around the wood-panelled room of the pack-house, eyes glinting in amusement as they land on the wooden monstrosity of a throne at one end.

"Since you're a born alpha, I'm not sure it would be possible for the pack bond to be broken," Grandpa continues with a shrug. "At least, that's what the legends say. That a bond with a born alpha is unbreakable."

You have got to be kidding me. Talk about a life sentence. I've created a pack, made myself an alpha, and now it looks like there's no escaping this. I'm barely sixteen and I literally shifted for the first time a few hours ago. I'm about as far from ready to lead a pack as anyone could possibly be.

I let out a defeated sigh as the weight of what I've done presses down on me. And this, my friends, is probably why my kind are killed off at birth.

Hamish gives a smug, satisfied smile, like the fact that it's impossible to break the pack bond is the best news he's ever heard. I narrow my eyes at him, but he looks completely unapologetic.

"You going to claim this territory then?" Hamish asks eagerly, with about as much subtlety as a sledgehammer. "Take over the Blackwater pack lands?"

"Umm…"

I hadn't planned on having a pack, let alone thought about taking over any territory. My eyes rove around the wood-panelled meeting room, snagging on the hideous wooden throne, then to the small windows exposing the wintery mountain landscape outside.

I'm almost certain this is my birthplace. The place my father came from, even if he never spoke to me about it. I should want to stay here, shouldn't I? Aren't we supposed to long for home, to be drawn to it like the needle of a compass, always seeking our true north?

In a world where I was born normal, I would have grown up here, would have played in these forests, learned to hunt beside my father. This would have been my home.

There is nothing homelike about it now. If anything, the very smell of this place repulses me. It smells of pain and sorrow and longing. Like it's absorbed all the pain of the boys standing before me.

Outside, the afternoon sun has painted the snow pink. It should be beautiful. Instead, it just reminds me of all the blood we spilled, the way it marred the trampled snow.

My eyes land on Lucy, and all my uncertainty evaporates.

"I'm going back to Buffalo." The words escape my lips before I can even think them through, before I've even really decided. "I have to finish school."

It's a weak excuse. I could finish school anywhere, could get a GED or whatever. Honestly, I doubt a high school education will do much to prepare me for being the alpha of a pack.

Lucy's eyes narrow with suspicion, and I wonder if she knows.

Cody looks at me like I've lost my mind, shaking his head and making his dark curls fall across his forehead.

"Tobes, you can't bring twenty-something shifters to live at your grandparents' house. You know that right?"

I run both hands over my face. Of course, I know that. It's a two-bedroom house and grandma doesn't even know that shifters exist. So yah, I know I can't bring more than twenty guys - who turn into a menagerie of animals – to stay at my house. I also know I can't stay here. Away from Lucy.

Grandpa clears his throat.

"There's Jamison's land," he says hoarsely. "I've got one-hundred acres of forestry in those foothills. It's close enough to Buffalo that you could finish off your schooling." He gives Cody a knowing look before adding, "And far enough away from the Clear Creek pack territory that it shouldn't create tension."

I blink. "Jamison's land?"

That was Jamison's sanctuary, made to keep him safe from shifters, from a world that demands born alphas be destroyed as soon as they draw their first breath.

I look at Jamison. "Are you okay with that?"

Jamison gives one long blink in affirmation just as grandpa says: "He is. He suggested it."

I raise my eyebrows, completely taken aback even as gratitude swells in my chest.

And that's when I hear it. The steady thrum of helicopter blades cutting through the air overhead, growing louder and louder until it's like a hungry beast raging outside the doors.

I practically sprint outside, my wolf's protective instincts driving me to act before I can think, to move towards the perceived threat and eradicate it.

Three helicopters land, kicking up mud and snow, spattering the walls of the nearby cabins. I feel more than see my pack come into formation around me - Cody on my right, Hamish on my left, Tyrone and Christopher behind me, Red lurking farther back, blending into the building's shadows.

My muscles ripple and tighten with the need to shift, but I hold it back, terrified of what will happen if my wolf gets control again.

So much blood. There was so much blood.

The door of the closest helicopter swings open and a familiar figure climbs out, ducking his head under the spinning blades, black eyes full of fire as they scan the crowd that's come to meet him. I feel a jolt of surprise and recognition through the bond I share with Cody as we both realize who has arrived.

Cooper Winslow, alpha of the Clear Creek pack, dressed head-to-toe in black tactical gear, looking ready for a fight. A look of horror slides across his face when his eyes land on me, taking in the golden gleam of my eyes, no longer masked behind contact lenses. At the pack poised defensively behind me. At his own son standing at my side.

Jeb Stone leaps out after the alpha, landing with a lightness that should be impossible for a person his size.

"Dad."

Lucy's quavering gasp of surprise is almost a whisper.

Unlike Cooper, Jeb looks straight past me, as if me and the pack around me don't exist. His thick lips are curled back in a snarl, expression hard and focus entirely on Lucy.

"Dad."

I hear Lucy say again, louder this time, as if she is forcing her voice to sound strong.

I turn to look at her, taking in her pale face, eyes so wide the whites are visible. Her lips give an almost imperceptible tremble. Anton stands beside her, looking like a broken soldier fresh off hell's own battlefield. The muscle in his jaw ticks as he narrows the one eye that isn't swollen shut to glare at his father.

"Lucy. Anton."

Jeb's voice is cold, sounding for all the world like his children have betrayed him. Not at all how a father rescuing his children from a psychopathic alpha kidnapper should sound.

He tilts his stubble-covered chin towards the helicopter.

"Get in. Now. You're going home."

Epilogue

Cody Winslow

I used to love coming to dad's office.

As a child, I thought he looked like the president at his huge mahogany desk.

I never felt more privileged than the few times he would let me climb onto one of the leather couches to read or do my homework while he worked. Listening to his confident voice boom out while he took calls from leaders of other packs or managed our family's investments, all while I was cocooned in the scent of leather and books and dad – that was heaven. That was safety. That was the promise of my future.

Some people might have balked at having their future mapped out for them. Might have rebelled against their parents. Might have wanted to pave their own path.

I never did. What I wanted and what they wanted was perfectly aligned.

Maybe it's because it is the future I was created for. Born for.

Nature destined me to be an alpha. Strong. Honourable. Likeable. The gods, in their wisdom, had placed me into my family to inherit this pack. And I didn't doubt that fate would select Summer as my mate.

Sweet, submissive, intelligent Summer. The ideal female to help me run this pack, when the time came.

Everything was perfect.

Until Tobias Finch.

Today, when the heavy wooden doors to dad's office swing shut behind me, I am filled with a mixture of shame and dread.

As soon as we are alone, dad turns to face me, the mask of the concerned and loving father sliding away, replaced by the cold, hard visage of the alpha.

"Cody Winslow," Dad asks, his voice coated with lethal quiet, "what have you done?"

I lift my chin.

"I did what I had to do," I answer. "I did the right thing. You know it was the right thing. There was no way I could have known he was a born alpha."

I've thought about this a lot in the past twelve hours since dad and Jeb had us airlifted from Blackwater pack territory. I lay awake thinking about it, running everything over and over in my head.

Tobias Finch became my alpha because I gave him my blood to save his life. If I was faced with the same decision, I would probably make the same mistake.

There is no way I'd let a guy bleed out. It goes against every instinct. Against my very nature.

"It was the wrong decision," dad hisses through clenched teeth. "I told you at the time not to do it, and you didn't listen. You disobeyed me, and now look where we are."

He crosses his office in three long strides, turning his back to me as he reaches into the cabinet, pulling out a decanter filled with amber liquid and pouring himself a glass. He tips the glass back, empties its contents, and then pours himself another. When he finally turns his gaze back to me, his black eyes are blazing silver with his wolf.

"You aren't even pack anymore," he says.

"I'm still family," I retort, squaring my shoulders. "I'm still your son."

"You're not pack. So you're not my heir," he says.

As if all that matters is whether I can wear the crown when he is done with it.

"I could see if there's a way to break the bond," I offer. "Tobias won't mind. He won't keep any of us in the pack against our will. He's said as much."

Dad gives a curt shake of his head. "You know that's not possible."

"It might be," I argue, panic rising in my chest. "We could try."

I hold out my hand, palm facing up.

"Get a knife. I'll swear fealty to the Clear Creek pack right now, right here, and we can see if it will break the bond with Tobias."

Dad's lip curls into a disdainful sneer.

"Put your hand away, son. It's not possible to break a bond with a born alpha. You know it. I know it. Every elder in this pack knows it. It's why the freaks are killed off at birth."

It's true. Of course, I know it's true.

My shoulders slump, like the knowledge of this truth is a burden that I can't shake off.

"You'll have to leave the pack lands," dad continues, but I cut him off.

"Whoa, wait, what? You're kicking me out?" I ask, my voice rising in pitch. "You're kicking me out of the house? Where am I supposed to live?"

Dad shrugs. "With your alpha. Wherever you want. I really don't care where you live."

He narrows his eyes at me.

"But let's make one thing clear. After today, you don't step foot on Clear Creek land. Ever."

My eyes widen, but dad just stares back at me impassively as he continues: "You don't contact my wolves. You don't try and recruit them to your new joke of a pack."

He fixes me with a knowing look.

"And that includes Summer."

I open my mouth to reply. To say something. Anything. But my voice catches in my throat.

Summer.

Not see Summer.

Dad gives a dark, secretive smile and then says: "There's only one way to break the bond, and you know it. You want your position back, you want to come home - you take care of the pack bond first. You take care of the problem that is Tobias Finch."

To be continued in
Accidental Alpha

Accidental Alpha - Book Two

Chapter 1

Tobias Finch

"Where should we park this one, alpha?"

Christopher's voice rings out from the open window of a pick-up truck, an almost obscenely happy grin spread across his face.

Behind him, an RV teeters precariously on the steep gravel road. A road that would certainly not be to code, if it were anywhere else but on private property in the middle of nowhere in Wyoming.

I rub both hands over my face, feeling the grit of sweat and dust coating my skin. It's warm for late April, the midday sun feeling particularly relentless.

"Just park it by the other ones," I reply tiredly. "But maybe by the edge of the clearing, closer to the trees. It's for Arlo and Theo."

"Ahh, right. Good plan, boss."

Christopher gives me a knowing smile before shifting the truck back into drive and continuing the slow ascent.

Arlo and Theo are two of the original twenty-four shifters who came back with me from Blackwater territory. Being owls, they don't particularly like being woken up during the day. They also have mouths that match their tempers.

Let's just say it's better for everyone if they aren't in the thick of things.

Cody sidles up beside me, attention fixed on the tablet in his hands, probably checking one of the many spreadsheets he's using to keep track of deliveries and contractors.

"That's the tenth RV," he announces. "So just three to go now."

Yep. I know all this. I also know how much each of those RVs cost and how much we spent on groceries last week feeding twenty-four shifters.

Hint. It's a lot.

Most sixteen-year-olds have ordinary jobs. Like working at a grocery store, mowing lawns or flipping burgers.

If only I could be so lucky.

When I'm not at school, I'm here, trying to make this isolated plot of land in the foothills of the Little Bighorn mountains comfortable enough to be considered habitable. So far, the best I've managed to come up with is RVs, tents and the blueprints for something permanent.

At least we've been able to afford RVs, thanks to the money we got selling the Blackwater territory. It turns out that by defeating Huxley Black and taking over his territory, under shifter law, I owned the land. Which meant I was able to sell it to a neighbouring wolf pack who had been wanting to expand their territory, and who also didn't want the risk of another pack moving in if I left it vacant.

"The builders can start in two weeks, if the weather holds," Cody continues, fingers tapping on the screen. "They'll start with the central lodge, but they want to do the foundations for all the buildings at the same time. More efficient that way."

"Sure. Okay," I reply, trying really hard to sound interested and engaged.

I must fail abysmally, because Cody gives me a sharp look.

"Then there's the matter of picking a beta. And enforcers. Setting out everyone in the pack's ranks…"

I let out a frustrated sigh.

It's been three long months since the fight at the Blackwater territory. The Blackwater Fight. That's what the guys are all calling it, anyway. Or Blackwater for short.

I think of it more as a massacre.

My wolf killed fifteen shifters that day. Tore them to shreds as if they were little more than a flock of lambs. Revelled in the bloodshed. The power.

I feel sick just thinking about it.

"Are you listening to me, Tobes?"

I blink rapidly, trying to recall what Cody had been saying.

"Um... the pack ranking system?" I say lamely.

He shakes his head, drawing the tablet to his chest as he frowns at me.

"The pack run, Tobes. I was talking about the pack run. It's a full moon this weekend, and your pack is going to want to run. Fly. Whatever."

I fight to supress a smile. Cody still struggles to remember that most of the shifters in this pack aren't actually wolves.

"Yah. Okay," I say. "If some of the guys want to do a run, that's fine by me."

He lifts an eyebrow. "You need to join them."

I wrinkle my nose. The last thing I want to do is let my murderous megalomaniac wolf loose on the world.

"You're their alpha. *Alpha.* They're going to start asking questions if you don't start joining them for pack runs," Cody lectures.

"Uh-huh, yah, so…" I scrub my hand through my hair, then wince as my fingers snag in the tangles. "I don't really feel like shifting…"

Cody looks horrified, visibly paling as he gapes at me.

"Please tell me you haven't gone without shifting this whole time. It's been three months. That is seriously unhealthy."

I bite the inside of my cheek, then look up towards the clearing where the RVs are parked, hoping that the gravel road will bring a distraction from this conversation with Cody. Unfortunately, it doesn't.

"Hey, so back to selecting enforcers," I say, trying to deflect the conversation away from the topic of my shifting.

Not that I particularly want to talk about selecting enforcers either.

"I was thinking everyone currently living at our territory could be an enforcer. If they want."

Which means we would have twenty-four enforcers, since that's how many of us are living in RVs and tents on Jamison's territory. Red and Orrin stayed back in Montana, but they've been threatening to come visit once the weather warms up and Orrin comes out of hibernation. So, I guess then we'd have twenty-six. No, twenty-eight when you count Gareth and Hamish, who also aren't here…

Maybe that *is* too many enforcers.

"You're kidding me." Cody says incredulously, eyebrows disappearing under the dark curls that have fallen across his forehead. "No pack has that many enforcers."

"So what? It's our pack," I say with a shrug. "We can do whatever we want, right?"

Cody taps his fingers on the back of his tablet, jaw ticking in irritation. It's not the first time we've had this conversation.

"There needs to be structure. Pack rankings. A hierarchy."

I shake my head.

"I disagree," I say, willing my voice to stay calm despite the building irritation.

Cody and I don't usually go head-to-head.

In fact, I've been pretty happy to let Cody run things. He's organised the architects and contractors for the buildings, made all the design decisions, chosen which pack members should room with each other, and created working rosters for the many, many boring tasks that need to be done.

But this is the one thing I feel strongly about. I didn't want to be alpha, and I sure don't want to be at the top of some pyramid scheme.

"I want everyone in this pack to be equal," I say firmly. "I'm not going to have crappy power dynamics. I don't want anyone having more say than anyone else. If I have to be alpha of this pack, fine. Whatever. It doesn't have to be…"

I don't get the chance to finish my rant because searing pain tears through the right side of my chest, hitting me with enough force to cause me to stumble backwards. A second later, the cracking of thunder rips through the clearing, a sound totally incongruous with the clear blue skies.

Pressing my fingertips to my chest, I'm momentarily confused by the warm dampness I find there. Until I lift my hand and see blood.

So. Much. Blood.

I drop to my knees as a second crack echoes and this time I hear the hiss of a bullet singing its deadly song mere inches above my head.

Vaguely, I'm aware of Cody shouting for help, of Tyrone's voice calling out to us from the cluster of pine trees that line the gravel road.

Within me, my wolf is raging. Clawing at the cage I've built in my mind to confine him. Maybe he only stayed in it to humour me. Or maybe the pain is like fuel to him. Either way, in a matter of moments he's tearing the mental cage I've created apart, as if it's made of tissue paper.

My bones crack, skin and flesh rippling, and for a brief moment, the pain of shifting overpowers the burning pain of the gunshot wound. Then the pain of shifting subsides, leaving power and anger in its wake.

I take a deep breath, drinking in the familiar smell of the forest and the scent of my pack, all magnified a hundredfold in this lupine form.

Amongst the familiar is the distinctive scent of an unknown shifter, mingled with the acrid smell of silver and gunpowder. My hackles rise, and I let out a low growl, ready to chase. To hunt. To attack.

"Alpha, stop."

Samson's voice rings out from across the clearing.

"Let Tyrone and Danny deal with him. You're injured."

He's by my side in a matter of moments, long limbs moving with feline grace as he sprints towards me. He lets out a low hiss between clenched teeth when he gets close enough to see my injuries.

"They weren't messing around, that's for certain. Not every day you see silver bullets."

I rise to my feet, ignoring Samson's insistence that I stay put. Ignoring the pain radiating from my right side. A pain that hasn't lessened at all by shifting into wolf form.

Probably because of the chunk of silver still imbedded in my body.

I pause the clumsy attempts to move my four legs when I notice Tyrone and Danny have already tackled the strange shifter to the ground, Cody sprinting over to assist them. The assailant writhes and struggles, but Tyrone and Danny easily overpower him.

By the time I hobble over to them with Samson at my side, the shifter is lying motionless, Tyrone's half-shifted claws pressed to his throat.

"Move and you're dead," Tyrone hisses, lips close to the stranger's ear.

The stranger trembles beneath him, eyes glowing with fury as he takes short, panting breaths between gritted teeth.

Cody bends down, bringing himself eye level to the male.

"You better start talking," Cody growls, neck muscles bunching with tension. "Who sent you? What pack are you with?"

"I - I'm not with a pack," the shifter stammers out. "It was just a job."

"A job?" Tyrone's lip curls in disgust. "What, are you a rogue for hire?"

When the shifter doesn't answer, Tyrone tightens his grip, letting the tips of his claws pierce skin.

"Answer me, you sack of shifter trash," Tyrone hisses.

"Yah," the stranger grinds out, glare flicking between Cody, Tyrone, Danny and Samson.

When he finally looks over at me, some of the fire leaves his eyes.

"So, it's true then." His gaze rakes over my golden fur, now stained with blood, then travels up to my gold eyes. "The only born alpha to rule in over two-hundred years. I didn't believe it."

He gives a mirthless laugh and shoots me an accusatory glare, tilting his chin in the direction of the bullet wound in my shoulder.

"How are you even still standing?"

I open my mouth to reply, then realise I'm still in my wolf form.

I try to push for supremacy, to shift back to human form, but my psychopathic wolf won't budge. He's been caged for too long and is now apparently relishing the power of being in control.

Instead of responding to the shifter's question, I bare my teeth and growl in reply. As if that conveys all the information anyone could possibly require.

The shifter's body trembles at the sound, and I notice for the first time how ragged looking he is. His clothes hang off his overly-thin frame, his straw-coloured hair lays flat and greasy on his scalp. Dirt coats his skin, darkening the fine wrinkles of his face, the creases of his neck.

"It was a job," he repeats, and then the words come tumbling out of him. "I needed the money. It was nothing personal, okay? I wouldn't have taken it if I'd known the rumours were true. I'm not an idiot, you know."

The human side of me believes him. He looks hungry. Desperate, even. I could almost pity him, if there wasn't a silver bullet currently imbedded in my flesh.

Unfortunately, my wolf does not share these feelings of sympathy. Especially when the pain from the silver is only getting stronger, as if the toxic metal is leeching into my blood, counteracting my body's ability to heal itself.

My wolf's murderous intentions must show in my eyes, because the shifter blanches and looks away, expression almost pleading as he looks between my pack mates.

I doubt he'll find any sympathy from them either.

"Who hired you?" Cody snaps, blue eyes like the depths of a glacier as he stares down at the shifter.

The stranger gives a defeated sigh.

"I don't know who the client is. I work through a broker. We aren't told the names of our clients. And would it matter if I did tell you? I know how this works. You aren't going to let me walk, whatever I say."

Cody grunts his agreement, and my wolf huffs approvingly.

"That might be true, shifter," Tyrone growls out, voice cold and lethal, green eyes flashing dangerously. "But we can make sure your last moments are painful enough that you'll wish for a quick ending."

Tyrone flashes a toothy smile, the whites of his partially elongated canines stark against his dark skin.

It's strange to see this cold, aggressive side of Tyrone. Out of all of my pack, he's the most laid-back. The sort of guy who drapes himself over furniture rather than sitting in it. Who listens to others' conversations with a bored, sardonic smile.

With the exception of that horrible day at Blackwater and today, I don't think I've even seen him exert himself with so much as a slow jog.

The rogue gives an involuntary shiver.

"Look, all I know is, whoever put out the hit, he was willing to pay a lot to make sure your alpha here was dead," the stranger says, nostrils flaring. "Offered ten thousand dollars to any shifter that could take him down. I doubt I'll be the only one coming this way to cash in."

"They gave you our location though," Cody muses, drawing to his full height as he casts me a worried glance.

As far as I know, there aren't many out there who know of our location. Jamison's land – now our land – was kept off the radar for years. My pack mates have been in touch with their families, so their previous packs might know where we are. The Clear Creek pack would certainly have an idea, since we haven't exactly kept it a secret from the Clear Creek kids at school.

But other than the Clear Creek pack, I don't think anyone knows about us.

Gareth and Hamish might have told some shifters about us, Samson reminds our little group, speaking telepathically through the pack bond. *There's no saying who they could have met in their search for Hux.*

Samson is right. Gareth and Hamish have been away for the past couple months, trying to track down Hux and the Blackwater enforcers who absconded with him. So far, they haven't had any luck, but the last time we spoke they alluded to doing some 'light recruitment' on the side. Gods only know what that means.

"Oh, the boss knows your location, all right," the rogue sneers, glaring at Tyrone, who still has his claws pressed to the rogue's throat. "So don't go thinking killin' me off is going to solve your problem. It 'aint. The bounty is out there. And last I checked, born alphas weren't invincible. It's only a matter of time before someone gets you, Tobias Finch."

My wolf bristles, unimpressed by the male's threats. The human (and more logical) side of me reluctantly acknowledges the rogue has a point. I might be hard to kill, but I can be killed. At least, I think I can. In any event, I don't like the idea of being shot at by silver bullets again.

Tyrone fixes the rogue with a look of unmasked disgust.

"For someone with nothing to say, you sure talk a lot," Tyrone complains.

Turning to Cody, he says: "I'm tired of listening to this guy. And Finch is bleeding all over the place. Let's get alpha up to the lodge and see if Theo is awake so he can get him stitched up. Or whatever it is Theo does."

"Good call," Cody agrees, jaw ticking as he eyes the rogue. "You take Tobias. Danny and Samson can help me put this guy in the shed."

In my periphery, I'm aware of Jamison lurking where the trees are thickest, his dark coat blending effortlessly in the shadows. Even with no pack link between us, his wary dislike of having this rogue in our territory is palpable. He follows Danny, Samson and Cody as they haul the rogue to the shed. No doubt planning to keep a close eye on the rogue himself.

Cody reaches back to give the black wolf an affectionate scratch between the ears, a gesture which Jamison returns with a playful nip. Even with the pain clouding my thoughts, I can't help but shake my head in wonderment at the friendship that has formed between Jamison and some of the pack.

Especially with Cody.

I lift my head at the sound of a truck rumbling over gravel, and even that small movement sends a jolt of pain down my foreleg. I catch a glimpse of Christopher leaning out the window of the driver's seat, blond hair dishevelled, smooth cheeks flushed before my vision blurs.

"Let's get you fixed up, hey buddy," Christopher says, swinging down from the cab to help Tyrone.

"You don't want to shift back to human form and make our life easier?" Tyrone asks as he and Christopher struggle to haul my wolf form into the back of the truck.

Fair request. My wolf form is considerably heavier than my human form.

Unfortunately, my wolf is a selfish jerk who isn't ready to give up power.

It's my turn, the wolf rumbles within me.

I can practically feel the creature's smug satisfaction at being in control again. It's as if the pain doesn't even bother him.

Well, the pain certainly bothers me. Pain that is made considerably worse by Christopher and Tyrone pushing and pulling at my awkwardly large form.

"Yah, Tyrone has a point," Christopher concedes, grunting with effort. "This would be way easier if you were about a hundred pounds lighter. Not to mention, I'm pretty sure all the fur is going to make it hard for Theo to get the bullet out."

My wolf huffs in annoyance. I would roll my eyes at the dumb animal. If I had control of my body, that is. Which, I don't.

I'll give you control again on the full moon, I reluctantly promise the animal. *That's like, a few days away. Okay? Deal?*

I can feel my wolf's resolve wavering, but the animal is still not convinced.

Lucy, my wolf whispers. *We need to see Lucy. Our mate.*

We see her at school every day, I remind my wolf. *Literally five days a week. How is that not enough for you?*

But I know that isn't what my wolf means.

Every night, the animal pushes me to venture over to Clear Creek territory. To check on her. Make sure she is safe. Happy.

It's a stupid idea. A suicidal idea, really. After I accidentally stole Cody, who was next in line to be alpha of the Clear Creek pack, they have made no secret out of their dislike for me.

I could just go over there, my wolf threatens smugly. *I could keep control and go there tonight, once we are healed.*

And this is why I haven't shifted since Blackwater. My wolf has some serious issues.

Fine, I tell my wolf snappishly. *Just give me my body back now.*

The pain in my right shoulder is spreading, radiating through my spine, down my right foreleg. I just want to get back to my pack's overcrowded makeshift lodge and have Theo dig this bullet out already.

My wolf relinquishes control, giving me back the reins as magnanimously as an emperor throwing copper coins to its subjects. I shift back to human form before the psychopathic animal can change its mind.

"What in the actual…" I hiss out, groaning around the pain of bones and muscle shifting into place around the silver bullet still lodged in my chest. I look down, a wave of nausea hitting me when I see my right side coated in blood and dirt.

"Oh good. You're back," Tyrone says dryly, positioning himself under my left side as he helps me into the back of the truck. "Now try not to bleed to death back there."

I snort out a breath through my nose. It's supposed to be a laugh, but it sounds more like a whimper.

Being shot totally sucks.

Chapter 2

Lucy Stone

Anton's exuberant shouting cracks through my dreams, jolting me awake.

I frown in frustration, reaching out to try and grasp the memory of my night-time wanderings, but it slips through my fingers like sand. I close my eyes against the morning light, hoping that will bring the images back.

No such luck.

"I got it! I got it!" Anton's voice booms out, close enough that I know he must be standing above me.

I groan, glaring at my brother through sleep crusted eyes.

"What is wrong with you?"

It's Saturday morning. No one should be waking me up right now.

My bed dips as Anton sits on the edge of my bed, roughly shaking me by the shoulder.

"Are you not listening? I got the scholarship, Luce. I'm going to play football for USC."

I blink rapidly, trying to process what he's saying.

"USC?" I ask blearily. "You – you're going to USC?"

A grin spreads across his face, bright enough to rival the obnoxious morning sun as he says: "Yep. I sure am. On scholarship."

My heart sinks, dropping like a lead weight to the pit of my stomach. The feeling of disappointment is quickly followed by guilt.

I shouldn't begrudge my brother's happiness. Not after everything he went through. Not after all he's done for me.

But the thought of him moving to California. Leaving me with the Clear Creek pack. Leaving me with dad…

I feel sick just imagining it.

"That's awesome," I say, forcing a smile. "They would have been crazy not to pick you."

Anton beams.

"I'm going to call Tori. But I wanted to let you know first."

I sit up in bed, brushing a tangled mass of blond hair from my face.

"Does dad know?" I ask, giving Anton a serious look.

After everything that happened with the Blackwater pack, dad has been less than supportive about Anton going away.

Anton's brow dips at my question, his lips pressing into a hard line.

"No."

I bite my lip, hating to point out the obvious.

"He's not going to like it," I say.

"I know." He spits those two words out like the seeds of some bitter fruit, then stands abruptly from his seat on my bed. "But I'm done trying to make him happy. That's all mom ever tried to do, and look where that got her."

I tilt my head, staring at him with a mixture of shock and confusion.

"What do you mean?" I ask warily.

This is the first time I've heard Anton talk about whatever happened between mom and dad. Actually, I don't think Anton has spoken about mom since she left all those years ago.

Not that I talk about mom much either. Not when it's a sure-fire way to get dad to fly into one of his rages. Something he's been doing enough of lately as it is.

Anton's expression shutters at my question.

"Nothing," he says, turning to leave the room. "Forget I said anything."

He's out the door before I can protest, but I know better than to chase him down and demand information. He's never been the sort to talk freely about much of anything, except maybe football. And I know from experience that when it comes to anything important, the more you push, the more he clams up.

Which makes me wonder what exactly they did to him at the Blackwater pack to get him to tell my secret.

I shudder just thinking about it. Remembering how broken he looked on that snow covered field.

It was only a few months ago, but now, with the sun streaming in through my window and the foothills cloaked in fresh spring green, it seems like a lifetime away. Like someone else's memory.

I flop back on my mattress, closing my eyes against the morning light, trying to shake the heaviness that has settled in my chest with Anton's news.

Maybe I can go back to sleep. At least if I'm asleep, I don't have to think about being left behind.

UNFORTUNATELY, I don't get much time to escape back into sleep before dad is pounding on my door.

"Get up," he orders gruffly. "Alpha needs us in the bunker. We've had a rogue trespassing on our territory this morning."

I press my face into my pillow, grinding my teeth at dad's use of 'us'. He and I both know that I am the only one needed for interrogating trespassers.

"Now, Lucy."

Rolling my eyes, I throw aside my blankets and quickly pull on jeans, a hoodie and tennis shoes, shoving a cloth face mask into my pocket at the last minute. It's one of the many left over from when we had to wear them to school, this one black with the grinning teeth of a skeleton printed across it. Now useful in masking my identity from whatever poor soul we are questioning.

The room dad calls a bunker is really just a basement underneath the utility shed. I suppress a smile when we reach the building, remembering how Tori and I brought Tobias here.

I hadn't understood then how Tobias could be so irreverent and fearless. At the time, it had annoyed me. Now that I know what he really is, it makes a lot more sense. Actually, everything about him makes a lot more sense.

I descend the dark stairwell, blinking to let my eyes adjust to the dim light, wrinkling my nose at the ever-lingering scent of fear and pain, strong even under the cloth face mask I'm wearing.

All feelings of amusement slip away when my eyes land on the female tied in the corner.

One side of her face is swollen with fresh bruises. Her dark eyes are rimmed with red, and while her face is dry, mascara tracks mar her cheeks. Her wrists and ankles are bound, arms stretched up above her to one of the hooks bolted into the ceiling. Even in the dim light, I can see the way her body trembles, either from fear or fatigue and being forced to hold such an uncomfortable position.

She looks young. Maybe early twenties, possibly younger. She's pretty too, beneath the grime and bruises. I frown, looking between dad and alpha Winslow.

What happened to her? I ask our alpha through the pack link. *Why is she so beat up? And why is she tied up like that?*

Alpha Winslow shrugs.

"She was already injured when we found her," he replies out-loud. "When she put up a fight, we had no choice but to restrain her."

I narrow my eyes, tasting the lie in his words. Why would he lie to me? He knows my gift.

No more questions, truth seeker.

The alpha's order snaps through the pack link, his words weighted with enough dominance that I have no choice to obey.

Like every member of his pack, I am physically bound to follow his orders. Even if I don't agree with them.

I grind my teeth and turn my gaze back to the young female. Her eyes are wide, fearful as an animal caught in a trap. When they land on me, on the black hoodie pulled over my head, the grinning skeleton face mask hiding my features, her lips tremble.

"I'm Cooper Winslow, alpha of the Clear Creek pack," Cooper begins, his tone steady and non-threatening.

It's a ruse. One I've seen him use too many times to count. Pretend to be this kind, welcoming, protective wolf. Get them to open up. To think it's all just one big misunderstanding.

Until he rips the truth from them, using me as the scalpel.

"This is my beta," he says, nodding towards dad. He doesn't bother to introduce me. I don't expect him to.

"You're being held because you were trespassing on Clear Creek territory. We don't want to hurt you, but I also have to keep my wolves safe, understand?" Cooper pauses, giving a reassuring smile. "So we're going to ask you a few questions, and if everything checks out, we'll be able to let you continue on your way, okay?"

The female nods, worrying her lower lip.

"Okay," she agrees, voice surprisingly steady.

"Good."

Cooper grins, a sharkish look that doesn't spread to his eyes. He pulls a metal folding chair towards himself, sitting on it backwards with his legs spread wide and arms resting over the backrest.

It's an intentional move, designed to make him look relaxed. Casual. Approachable.

"Let's start with your name, shall we?" he says.

"Tania Goode," the female replies quickly, wetting her lips nervously.

Truth, I say over the pack link.

"Tania. That's a nice name," Cooper drawls. "And what brings you to this part of the world Miss Goode?"

The female's eyes flick to mine, brow furrowing. No doubt wondering who the silent, faceless figure in black is, and what my role is in all this.

"Answer me," Cooper says.

The female squeezes her eyes shut, as if trying to block out the reality she finds herself in.

"We just want to help you, Tania," Cooper says reassuringly, but I can smell the lies on his words, thick and acrid.

"I ran away from my pack," the female finally says, the words coming out in a broken whisper. "It wasn't safe for me anymore. I was seeking refuge. Trying to find another pack."

Truth, I say through the pack link, even as my chest squeezes with pity.

Cooper's eye's glint with barely contained avarice.

Packs are always trying to grow their membership, and ours is no exception. Plus, it's no secret that our pack is short on females.

"You were looking for the Clear Creek pack?" he asks.

Tania shakes her head.

"No. Not the Clear Creek pack."

Cooper's expression darkens at this response.

"What pack then?" he asks.

"The Liberty pack," she replies, dark eyes blinking candidly.

Truth, I assure alpha Winslow.

I haven't heard of the Liberty pack though, and by the frown on Cooper's face, I don't think he has either.

"Tell me about this Liberty pack?" Cooper asks. "What makes you think it's a good place to seek refuge?"

I bite the inside of my cheek. I am more interested in finding out what Tania is running from. In learning what could have possibly happened to make a young female shifter take on the risk of going rogue, completely by herself.

"You haven't heard of them?" Tania asks with a frown. "I was told they were in Buffalo, Wyoming. In the foothills of the Little Bighorns. That's around here, right?"

Cooper's expression remains a stony mask, but I can feel his anger pulsing through the pack link.

At Cooper's expectant look, Tania continues: "I- I was told they have a strong alpha. And lots of enforcers, so they can keep refugees safe."

She gives a watery smile before glancing up at her hands, hooked to the ceiling and bound above her head.

"I've heard they treat all their members equally, even the submissive ones. They're supposed to be progressive." She wrinkles her nose thoughtfully. "Whatever that means. But it's got to be better than things with Drake and Hux."

My blood runs cold at that name. *Hux.*

I'm pretty sure I heard Huxley Black called Hux, that day at Blackwater.

I feel Cooper telepathically prodding me for my truth reading, jolting me from my thoughts.

True, I say through the bond. Then I add: *I think Hux might be Huxley Black, the alpha who tortured Anton.*

Beside me, dad's jaw ticks, the only sign that he's heard what I've told him and Cooper.

"Who is the alpha of this so-called Liberty pack?" Cooper asks.

I frown behind the fabric of my mask.

Not important, I want to say. What is important is finding out whether Hux is Huxley Black and if so, where he is so we can hunt him down.

"Umm, I'm not really sure," Tania admits. "The shifters I spoke with wouldn't tell me the alpha's name. They only said that he was really, really powerful. And that the pack would keep me safe."

Truth, I whisper through the pack link.

Cooper's nostrils flare, the only outward sign of his irritation. I want to roll my eyes because I'd say at this stage, it's pretty obvious that she's talking about Tobias Finch's pack. There are no other packs in the Buffalo area and, whether Cooper likes it or not, Tobias would certainly fit the description of being a powerful alpha.

In fact, he might be the most powerful alpha there is.

"Well, Miss Tania Goode," Cooper drawls, "I'm going to be completely frank with you. I can't in good conscience let you go to this Liberty pack."

Tania's brow shoots up in surprise.

"Wh-why not?"

"The truth is, they're not a good pack. We've had dealings with them before, heard complaints about how they lure in female shifters and then mistreat them." Cooper shakes his head, a bland smile playing across his lips. "It's not the place for a nice young lady like yourself to go."

I wrinkle my nose behind my mask, the smell of lies pungent. Not that I would need my gift to know that Cooper is lying.

I know Tobias Finch. And I know Cody. Neither of them would ever harm a female.

Tania glances up at her bound hands again, no doubt wondering when this alpha, who is apparently so concerned for her wellbeing, is going to untie her.

"I- I can't go back," she finally says, squeezing her eyes shut to hold back tears. "There's no way I'm going back."

"Of course not," Cooper says soothingly, rising in one fluid motion from his chair before stalking over to her. "We wouldn't ask that of you."

Gently, he reaches up to brush a stray lock of hair out of her face, his fingers lingering on the fresh bruise marring her left cheekbone.

When he pulls a knife out from the holster on his belt, Tania flinches.

"Shh," he says, as he slices through the rope in one fluid motion. "I'm not going to hurt you."

Tania's arms drop to her sides and she gives a gasp, stumbling as she wraps her arms around herself, rubbing at her shoulders for a long moment before bending to untie the ropes at her ankles.

"Thanks," she says half-heartedly, eyes darting nervously between Cooper and dad. "So, umm, what… I can go now?"

"Oh, no," Cooper shakes his head. "I can't let you do that. It wouldn't be safe. Not for someone like you, not with the Liberty pack so close by."

His lips tilt into a smirk as he closes the space between them, grasping her bare shoulders in his large hands and guiding her towards the stairs. His eyes trace the length of her body, glinting lasciviously at the generous curves and smooth honey coloured skin visible beneath the dirt, blood and tattered clothing.

"No, Miss Tania Goode. You'll be staying with us for the foreseeable future. But don't you worry. We'll take good care of you."

I can taste the lie on those words too.

Chapter 3

Tobias Finch

The night air is filled with a cacophony of animal sounds, punctuated by the rhythmic beating of bass from Arlo's speakers. Apparently, owls have a particular idea of what celebrating the full moon should involve, and it sure isn't running through the forest and howling at the moon.

Unsurprisingly, the cats also weren't on board with a traditional pack run.

"I'm more of a sprinter," Tyrone had said. A statement to which Samson and the other cats had vigorously agreed.

And so here we are, sitting in our various animal forms under the light of the full moon, listening to Arlo's questionable selection of drum and bass music.

Also, the full moon is barely visible, since Theo procured a laser projector from gods only know where and has managed to rig it up to the same gas generator that powers the massive speakers.

Blue, yellow and red lights flash incessantly in time with the beat of the music, casting coloured shadows across the pines that encircle the clearing we've made for the RVs. Jamison and grandpa sit at the edge of the clearing, eyeing the spectacle warily.

Despite the noise and light, my wolf is in heaven.

Surrounded by its pack, power practically bleeds into my wolf, thrumming as steadily as the electronic beat. My wolf drinks it in, hungrily.

When *Freedom* by Sub Focus & Wilkinson comes on, my wolf rises to its feet. The injury from the silver bullet is well and truly healed now.

And the rogue who caused that injury? Well, let's just say Jamison's wolfish nature got the better of him.

My wolf eyes the other born alpha with respect and Jamison returns the gesture, golden eyes that mirror my own flashing in the neon lights.

I feel Cody slink up beside me. His massive red wolf only comes up to my shoulder, despite towering over the other three wolves in our strange menagerie of a pack.

Run, alpha? he asks through the pack link.

Restlessness coats his words, and I can practically feel his hunger for movement and speed as if it's my own.

Yah, I say. *Yah, let's run.*

In response, the other wolves stand to join us. Christopher, lean and grey with sky-blue eyes. The two brothers, Noah and Ollie, one nut-brown and the other a sandy beige. All of them eager to run, brimming with energy.

Cody bounds over towards Jamison and grandpa, crouching down in front of the massive black wolf and yipping playfully. Jamison huffs, gold eyes glinting with amusement as he bats the younger wolf away. Still, when I look to Jamison and grandpa, extending the invitation their way, Jamison shakes his head.

"Another day," grandpa says, waving one wrinkled hand dismissively. "We'd just slow you down."

There is no mistaking the wistful look in Jamison's eyes though and, for the hundredth time, I wish I could speak to the wolf mind to mind.

When Noah gives Ollie a playful nudge, which Ollie returns with an annoyed nip, I know it's time to move. My wolf lopes ahead, certain the other males will be following close behind as I take the narrow dirt path weaving its way through the forest to the rocky ridge-line above.

Enjoy the run, you masochists, I hear Tyrone call through the pack link, his voice laced with amusement. There's a rumble of agreement from the cats and bears of our pack.

Stop being so lazy, Christopher snaps back, but I feel the affection in his words. Like all of us, the grey wolf loves our odd pack. Even the cats and bears, who would rather lounge and eat than run and hunt.

It's a feeling my wolf shares, although his affection is doused with possessiveness.

My pack, he whispers, pulling at each of the threads that connect us to our pack. Drawing power from each connection.

We run for hours, until the sound of the drum and bass are far behind. Until it's just the music of paws on earth and stone, of huffed breaths alongside the rustle of spring grass and leafless shrubs.

It's not until we're running high above the lip of Crazy Woman Canyon that I realise where my wolf is taking us.

Alpha, Cody cautions, coming up beside me.

When I don't slow my pace, Cody presses his body into mine, as if he can turn me around, herd me back to our territory.

My wolf gives an annoyed growl.

Alpha, we really should turn back now.

I know, I want to say. *Completely agree with you.*

Instead, I just power on, paws moving relentlessly forward. Because, unfortunately, my wolf has put himself in the driver's seat again and the animal has a one-track mind.

Lucy. Lucy. Lucy.

Her name beats a wild staccato in my mind. A rhythm to match the thudding of my paws and the frantic pulsing of my heart.

This is a terrible idea, I tell my wolf. *In fact, it's a little stalkerish. Lucy made it pretty clear earlier this year she doesn't really like me. You know, the whole bull incident. Nothing says dislike better than attempted murder-by-goring.*

My wolf rolls one shoulder, as if he's shrugging off my concerns, then continues on without breaking his stride.

Why don't I just ask her to the school dance, I suggest reasonably. *Or I could ask her on a date. To the movies or something.*

Both of those options would be a lot more normal than skulking around her pack's property in the middle of the night with my little band of wolves. Both would be a lot less likely to start a pack war.

My wolf huffs, as if the thought of a pack war amuses him.

Before I know it, we're in the foothills overlooking the Clear Creek territory. I can hear wolves howling in the distance. Probably the Clear Creek wolves on their own full-moon run in the mountains.

Cody presses against me again, more forcefully this time.

What are you doing, Tobias? he asks, the silent words laced with worry. *You know we can't go there.*

Why not? my wolf responds, a low warning growl accompanying the telepathic words. *I am the alpha here, not you.*

Cody flinches, backing away, head lowered.

Sheesh, Tobes, he says, no doubt realising it's the wolf that has control now, not me. *You've got to get your wolf under control, man.*

My wolf just casts him a disdainful look before bounding down the steep incline that leads straight into Clear Creek territory.

Straight towards Lucy Stone's house.

Lucy Stone

The alpha house is eerily quiet as I tiptoe down the empty hallway.

Cooper and Cindy will be somewhere in the mountains overlooking the ranch, leading the pack run. I would normally be with them, running alongside dad and Anton near the head of the pack, bathing in the light of the full moon, enjoying the freedom of movement and being in my wolf form.

Not tonight.

My nostrils flare as I pass by the doors of the guest rooms, taking in the scents lingering in the hallway. Cooper and Cindy's scents are there, alongside the scent of some of the enforcers and lower wolves who clean for the alpha couple, but that isn't what I am looking for.

I lick my lips nervously, considering shifting into my wolf form, when I hear the faint sound of muffled sobs coming from behind one of the closed doors. I press my ear to the door and take a deep breath, sighing in relief as I detect the faintest scent of rose and cinnamon.

She is here.

Carefully, I try the door knob. I'm not surprised when it doesn't budge. On the other side of the door, the sound of crying stops, replaced by the patter of footsteps as someone approaches the door.

"W-who is it," Tania's voice trembles, close enough that I know she must be right on the other side.

"Can you open the door," I whisper. "Or is it locked?"

"It's locked," she whimpers, voice heavy with defeat.

I bite my lip. I expected as much.

My pulse thrums like a war-drum in my ears as I pull the screwdriver from the pocket of my hoodie. I weigh the tool in one trembling hand.

This is going to get me into so much trouble. There's no way I won't get caught. Even with the sage I've rubbed all over my body, there's still the risk my scent will be everywhere. That somehow, they'll know it was me.

On the scale of bad life choices, this ranks right alongside driving up to Montana to rescue my brother. That stunt got me grounded for a month and lost me my car. This stunt – well, I don't really know what they'll do to me. I do know that it won't just be dad punishing me.

I shudder, recalling the way the alpha's eyes raked over the young female's body, lascivious and proprietary. The way he touched her cheek.

I recall the sweet scent of her honesty and the bitter taste of his lies.

Worse than that is this sense of *knowing*. Stronger than instinct, and not unlike my ability to detect lies. A sense that has been growing, as much as I try to ignore it.

Ever since the whole Blackwater incident, I've been getting these little flickers of truth, like frames slotted surreptitiously into an old movie reel. Random flashes of past, present, future, all tasting of truth.

Most of the time, it's impossible to make out what they are – or *when* they are, for that matter. But the image I had after Tania's joke of an interrogation was clear enough. She is in imminent danger.

And now here she is, locked in the heart of the alpha house.

He hasn't told any of the pack about her, and he's prohibited me and dad from mentioning her. Which means whatever he has planned for her, it can't be good.

I swipe a sweaty palm over my face and stare at the doorknob, as if it holds the answer to what I should do.

But there was never any question, was there? Because if I don't help her, I'll be complicit in whatever it is the alpha has planned.

I clench my teeth, steeling myself. Then I jam the screwdriver into the lock, pulling the handle several times, until there is a distinctive, satisfying cracking sound.

You always hear about people picking locks with hairpins. I'm sure that's great if you want to be discreet, leave the lock intact or whatever. But it's a million times easier to just break the lock mechanism and open the door.

Which is exactly what I do.

"W-who are you?" Tania asks, repeating her earlier question as she stares at me, her brow furrowed in bewilderment.

I shake my head. I'm taking enough risk as it is. There is no way she is getting my name.

"My name isn't important," I tell her, grabbing her arm to pull her down the hallway.

For a moment, she doesn't budge. I turn to glare at her, and she cringes under my stare.

"We don't have a lot of time," I snap impatiently. "Unless you want to stay locked up here, we need to leave now. Everyone's out on the pack run, but they'll be back soon."

She blinks, realisation dawning. "You - you're breaking me out of here?"

I look pointedly at the now very destroyed lock, the screwdriver still dangling out of the broken mechanism.

"Obviously," I say dryly.

Tania heaves in a trembling breath, shooting me a look of confused gratitude before saying: "Okay. Wow. Okay. Yah, let's get out of here."

Good choice, lady, I think to myself. Now let's see if we can get you off pack territory without getting caught.

I freeze when we get outside the alpha compound, surprised to find we made it out without being noticed. But there really is no one around.

Maybe the gods really are with me for once.

Tania pauses on the grass outside the backdoor, tilting her head up to stare at the cloudless night sky, moonlight blotting out all but the brightest stars. She takes a deep, tremulous breath, then looks at me, eyes wary.

"Where am I supposed to go?" she muses, more to herself than to me.

"You'll go to the Liberty pack," I tell her firmly.

Her eyebrows shoot up in surprise, disappearing behind thick dark bangs that are no longer coated in dirt and blood. She obviously managed to have a shower while locked away in the alpha house. I can only hope she ate something, because I suspect she has a long journey ahead of her tonight.

"Your alpha said that they aren't safe," Tania says with a frown, rubbing absently at the bruises on the side of her face.

"He lied," I say shortly. When she doesn't look convinced, I roll my eyes. "He also locked you up against your will," I point out, "so is it really that surprising that he lied to you?"

She bites her lower lip contemplatively.

"No, I guess not," she says, voice low, almost musical. Then she gives me a hard look, full of more wary intelligence that I had supposed her capable of. "But how do I know I can trust you?"

"You don't," I acknowledge reluctantly. "But if you want a chance to escape, this is it."

I cast a nervous glance towards the mountains, eyes tracing the ridge-line to the left of the wide valley of our pack's ranch. The howls of my pack mates echo in the distance.

"We don't have much time," I tell her. "Can you shift?"

To my dismay, she shakes her head. "No," she says apologetically, "I can't. Your alpha gave me something after dinner. Some sort of drug…" she trails off, rubbing one bare arm nervously. "It made me groggy for a while. I'm still a little out of it, to be honest. I definitely can't shift yet."

My stomach clenches at her admission. Not just because this is going to make the journey slower, but at the unspoken implications.

"Did he…" I look at her sidelong, cheeks heating. "Did anything happen?"

She shrugs noncommittally, and a pained silence follows. I clear my throat.

"If you're wanting to leave, we better start moving," I say, nodding towards the foothills to the right of the valley, just beyond my home. "I can take you part of the way. At least until you're off our pack's territory."

I pause, looking her over, taking in her bare feet, thin tank top and sweat pants. At the end of April, it might technically be spring, but it's cold enough I can see my breath. With the clear night skies, the temperatures are likely to drop to below freezing. Not to mention, seasons mean very little when it comes to the Wyoming mountains. You can easily get trapped in two feet of snow in the middle of July. This time of year, any type of weather is fair game.

"We'll stop by my place on the way out and I'll get you some clothes," I suggest. "Maybe some shoes too, if I've got any that will fit you."

"Okay. Thanks." She casts me a weary smile, dark eyes glistening with teary gratitude.

It makes me uncomfortable and I turn away, stalking along the trail that leads to my house with a terse, "Come on."

Tania follows wordlessly, her bare feet soundlessly picking up the path in the dark and I'm forced to acknowledge that she certainly moves with an enviable level of stealth and grace.

"What type of animal are you?" I ask, finally giving into my curiosity. We're almost at my house, the lights shining from the windows like hopeful beacons.

"Umm, do I have to tell you?" Tania asks nervously, coming up to walk beside me.

She's my height, I notice, but the way she moves and holds herself, you'd think she was much smaller.

"Is it a condition of you helping me?" she asks.

I shoot her an incredulous look.

"No. Of course not."

She blinks up at me, as if she wasn't quite expecting me to say that.

"Oh… okay." A tentative smile. "I'd rather not say then. If it's okay with you."

"Sure. Whatever you want," I shrug.

Of course, now I'm even more curious. I give a light sniff, trying to take in her scent without being obvious, as if I might be able to guess from that alone. Rose, cinnamon and… something else. Something different. Not cat. Probably not bear. Definitely not wolf.

How mysterious.

When I open my front door, Tania visibly flinches at the sound and the sudden rush of light. She falls back, practically pressing herself into the side of the house as she leans into the shadows.

"I take it you'd rather wait outside?" I ask dryly.

She gives a barely perceptible nod.

"Okay then," I say. "Wait here and I'll be right back. Don't go anywhere though, okay?"

Another nod.

I sigh, then rush inside, squinting as my eyes adjust to the glaring brightness. I move quickly, grabbing clothes and shoes before filling an old backpack with food and a bottle of water. It's not enough to last more than a day, but it should be enough to get her to Tobias' side of the mountains. Or at least last her until she can shift again.

I'm relieved to see she's still waiting in the shadows when I come back outside.

"This should fit you," I say, heaving a sweater and down-filled coat into her arms. "See if these shoes fit too."

Her eyes widen, mouth forming a little 'o' of surprise as she takes in the pile of clothes, the backpack laden with provisions.

"I- I can't accept this," she argues, attempting to push the things back. "There's no way I can repay you…"

"Seriously?" I snap, unable to keep the irritation from my voice.

Because giving up some old clothes and a bag of food is really the thing I am least concerned about here. What is much more concerning is what will happen to me if I get caught helping this rogue escape our territory.

"Just take the clothes, okay." I give her a hard look, and she winces.

I feel a momentary twinge of guilt, but its swept aside when she starts putting on the layers of old clothes, the shoes and the pack. I give a satisfied nod once she's dressed, the pack slung over her shoulders. Maybe I am being a bit harsh. Still, hurt feelings are better than freezing or starving to death.

"Right," I say. "Let's go."

She follows obediently, slipping into the same graceful silence she used on our way to my house as we make our way up the rocky incline of the foothills.

I do my best to take the path that keeps us hidden in the shadows of boulders and leafless trees, conscious of the bright moonlight. This way takes longer, and the footing is more difficult, but I'm not running the risk of being seen. Not when I am so close to getting her out of Clear Creek territory.

My heart races anew at the thought of being caught. At the questions Cooper will ask when he notices Tania is missing. At how my dad – already volatile and on edge since Anton's capture – will react. I shudder, increasing my pace, even as I hear Tania starting to pant with exhaustion behind me.

And that's when I hear it.

The distinctive rustling and thud of a pack of wolves running in the underbrush.

My blood turns to ice in my veins and I freeze, resting my palm on the cold granite boulder next to me in an effort to steady myself. Behind me, there is the sharp intake of breath followed by a whimper, letting me know Tania has heard them too.

Silently, I curse myself. Did part of my pack decide to run on this side of our territory, and I just didn't notice? Or had I gauged the distance and location wrong in the first place?

The noise grows louder and I crouch down, hoping to go unnoticed. I know Tania will be doing the same.

On the trail ahead of us, the bushes part with an explosion of twigs and rocks. Icy fear is replaced by confusion and shaky relief when a huge, golden wolf comes to a skidding stop ahead of us. Molten gold eyes lock with my own, gleaming with a hungry, possessiveness that causes me to blink in confusion.

"Tobias?" I ask, brushing myself off as I stand to face him.

As if it would be possible to mistake him for anyone else. I might have only seen his wolf once, during that horrible fight at the Blackwater territory, but I doubt there is any other wolf that would match him for size or share his unique, other-worldly colouring. Not to mention the distinctive eyes of a born alpha.

Eyes that I had thought were only myth, no more real than Leti, Morrigan or any of the other shifter deities.

The golden wolf nods, just as a familiar red wolf comes up beside him, giving me a huff of recognition.

"Oh, hey Cody," I smile, relief surging through me at the sight of the wolf I've known my whole life. Regardless of how much he might have annoyed me when he was alpha-to-be, I trust him. Know him.

Without thinking, I reach out to pat my old pack mate. Before I can sink my fingers into the soft red fur between Cody's ears, Tobias gives a low growl, snapping at Cody and pushing him away. I pull my hand back in shock.

"Really, Finch?" I narrow my eyes at the gold wolf.

The animal just huffs, then presses his own giant snout under my hand. In an instinctive reaction, I stroke the wolf's head before I can stop myself, watching as he closes his eyes in obvious pleasure at my touch.

"You are such a weirdo," I mutter, rolling my eyes.

Logically, I know I should be intimidated by this wolf. At the very least, I should feel the confused irritation that Tobias usually provokes in me. But I don't. There is something strangely endearing about the wolf version of Tobias Finch.

I know I shouldn't pet the animal. It's only encouraging bad behaviour. But even as I think this, I can't help but enjoy the feeling of silky fur under my fingers.

It's also impossible not to revel in his scent, that chocolate and sage scent so full of warmth and magnetic power. It sends a jolt of electricity straight to my core, like jumping off a cliff or plunging into icy water. It's terrifying and exhilarating at the same time.

There's the sound of cracking and snapping, and then Cody is standing before me, an angry flush colouring his features.

He's completely naked, but we've grown up together, shifted together, so his nudity doesn't bother me. What does bother me are the dark circles under his eyes and the way his high cheekbones protrude more than they should.

"Stop patting him, Luce," Cody hisses. "He's being a pain and you're only encouraging him."

I press my lips together to keep from laughing, but drop my hand away. Partially because obeying Cody is still second nature, but also because I know he's right.

Tobias gives a whimper at the loss of contact, the sound so incongruous with the giant animal before me that I really do laugh, the sound abrupt in the still night air.

Cody shakes his head. "You've got to tell him to shift back," he says, jaw ticking with annoyance. "His wolf has completely taken over and he won't listen to anything we say."

There's an edge of panic in Cody's voice that I haven't heard before and I stare at him for a long moment before it dawns on me. I'd been so immersed in my own fear about being caught, that I'd completely forgotten. Cody is forbidden from coming onto Clear Creek territory. His being here could start a pack war.

Actually, Tobias being here could start a pack war.

At that thought, all amusement falls away from my features and I shoot the golden wolf an incredulous look.

"What were you thinking, Finch?" I ask, my lips pressing into a frown.

I'm suddenly acutely aware of Tania behind me, crouching down in the shadows and doing her best to hide from this pack of wolves.

Here I was, trying to convince her that the Liberty pack is trustworthy, and they're invading Clear Creek land like it's no big deal. Acting like unruly pups instead of an established pack.

I put my hands on my hips, doing my best to look intimidating and stare Tobias down. While awkwardly looking up at him.

"You need to shift back so I can talk to you," I say. "Right now."

The golden wolf just cocks his head, mouth opening in a panting lupine grin as his eyes glint mischievously.

"I'm serious, Finch."

The wolf ignores me and tries to press his nose under my hand again. I give Cody an exasperated look.

Cody cocks his head, expression going distant. It's an expression of his I know well, and can only mean he's having a silent conversation through his pack link. When Cody's eyes re-focus, he gives a faint grimace before shooting me an apologetic look.

"Umm, Luce?" Cody says, nervously rubbing the back of his neck with one hand. "Tobes says he'll shift back if you agree to go to the dance with him. And by Tobes, I mean his wolf, obviously. Tobes is… kind of in the backseat right now…"

Anger rises in me, hot and furious as I narrow my eyes at said wolf. I take it back. The wolf version of Tobias Finch is not endearing. Not. At. All.

"Really?" I say, lifting one eyebrow. "You invade Clear Creek territory in the middle of the night to what - ask me out on a date?"

I gesture angrily at the rogue shifter crouched behind me.

"I'm literally risking everything right now to help this shifter escape so she can seek sanctuary in your stupid pack, and you just thought just you'd prance your wolfy self over here to blackmail me into going out with you?"

Behind me, Tania lets out a low whimper and I realise I'm probably frightening her with my aggressive reaction. Not to mention, every minute we spend here is only increasing the chance of us getting caught.

I take a deep breath, attempting to calm myself, only to get a lung full of Tobias' mouth-watering scent. Big mistake.

My pulse picks up, blood heating in my veins, as my body completely ignores the very justifiable anger I'm trying to sustain. My wolf lunges for the surface, wanting to press her face into the golden wolf's neck, to take in more of the delicious scent. The she-wolf scowls at me as I push her back down, huffing her displeasure.

As if scenting his effect on my body, the golden wolf steps closer, nostrils flaring.

I put out one hand to stop his approach.

"Nope," I say, popping the 'p' at the end of the word. "Not going to happen, Finch." I toss my ponytail over my shoulder. "You want to ask me out, you ask me with words. In human form. Without leverage."

The wolf huffs, as if it finds my anger amusing.

"I mean it," I say. "You shift back now or I will never, ever, even *consider* going on a date with you."

Wait, does that mean I am considering going on a date with him?

Golden eyes stare at me for one long moment, as if trying to work out whether I'm being serious or not. And then there is the cracking and popping of bones and tendons as golden fur disappears, leaving a very embarrassed and very naked Tobias Finch standing in front of me.

I tilt my head to the side and give him what I hope is a scathing look.

"Hello, Finch. Good of you to finally join us."

Even in the moonlit night, I can see the twin spots of red flaring on his cheeks. He fidgets uncomfortably, angling himself and using his hands to try and cover himself as he struggles to meet my eyes.

I really must be a horrible person, because I feel the shadow of a smirk ghosting across my lips as I fight the temptation to let my eyes travel down for just one quick glance.

Out of general curiosity, of course. Nothing more.

"Shoot. Oh man. Lucy," Tobias groans, drawing one hand across his face, as if he can wipe away the embarrassment glowing there.

"Can we just say, for the record, that my wolf is a complete psychopath? Like, the animal has no moral compass. I'm also pretty sure he hates me. I had absolutely no part in the decision to come over here. We were on our pack run, and my stupid wolf just took over."

Tobias grimaces, then adds: "Look, what I'm trying to say is, I'm really sorry about all this…"

I cut him off with a wave of my hand, because as entertaining as it is to watch Tobias squirm, there are bigger things at stake here.

"Whatever. I get it," I say. "We can talk about it later. At school or something. But you guys have to get off pack territory now. And you need to take Tania with you."

I step aside, gesturing to the female crouched behind me and watch as Tobias and Cody's eyes widen in surprise. It's as if they really hadn't noticed her hiding there.

"Umm, take her with us?" Tobias gives me a questioning look. "Why? Who is she?"

I glance nervously over my shoulder, eyes and ears reaching out to where I last sensed my pack on the ridge at the far side of our territory.

The howls are louder now, and I swear I can see the flicker of movement at the point where the valley basin reaches up to the mountains, indicating they're making their way back from the run.

"She's a refugee from some other pack," I explain quickly, realising I don't actually know what pack she is from or even what state. "She was caught trespassing on our land, looking for your pack and Cooper locked her up. I'm pretty sure he was going to hurt her."

I shoot Cody a hard look, half expecting him to defend his dad. His expression shutters, but he remains silent so I continue.

"She mentioned escaping someone named Hux," I add, biting my lip as I recall the female's response in the basement, and how Cooper refused to question her further about it. I turn to look at Tania and tentatively ask: "What is Hux's full name?"

Tania swallows audibly, eyes flicking over the group of strange male shifters, three of whom remain in wolf form, and then back to me.

"H-huxley Black."

At the sound of that name, Cody gives a sharp intake of breath and several of the wolves growl. Tania flinches, pressing closer to my side.

Instinctively, I flare my nostrils, scenting the truth in her statement. Cold anger flares, furious as a snowstorm and I clench my hands into fists at my sides, feeling the prick of claws pressing into my palms as I fight the urge to shift.

Huxley Black. The male who tortured Anton. Huxley Black. The male who knows my secret.

The name repeats in my head like a dark promise.

Tobias remains silent for a long moment, golden eyes locked on Tania, his usual expression of casual nonchalance replaced by a dangerous brittleness. As if at any moment, he might shatter into a million razor-edged shards. When he finally speaks, his voice is low, rich with the power of his wolf.

"I offer you the protection of our pack," he says formally, before holding one hand out to Cody, palm up.

Wordlessly, Cody takes one partially shifted claw and draws it across Tobias' palm, leaving fresh blood to well up in its wake. When Tobias extends his bleeding hand to Tania, her eyes widen and she gives a small gasp.

"W-what, just like that?" she squeaks out. "You're offering me a place in your pack, just like that? No testing? I don't have to fight anyone for position?"

Tobias snorts, formality dissipating as the corner of his full lips quirk up into a grin.

"Nah. We don't do that sort of thing. You want a place, you have one."

He drops his bleeding hand to his side, then shrugs.

"Or if you just want to stay with us for a while, that's fine too. You don't have to join."

Tania stares at him for a long moment, mouth open, then turns to me.

"Do you trust this male?" she asks in a low whisper, eyes searching mine.

I blink, weighing her question.

If someone had asked me this four months ago, I would have said no. Categorically, no. Now…

I look at Tobias, my eyes absently tracing over his broad shoulders, defined pectoral muscles, the hard planes of his stomach tapering into a distinct V and feel my mouth go dry. Now that he's no longer pretending to be a submissive wolf, now that he's accepted his role as an alpha, he practically exudes quiet power and understated strength.

My wolf pants longingly him and I silently curse the animal. His looks, his strength, that is not what is important here.

What is important is that the acrid smell of lies is gone, his sage and chocolate scent are warm with truth.

I also know from the few hints Cody has dropped that Tobias didn't want to be alpha. He just took on a pack to break everyone free at the Blackwater compound. He probably would have preferred to remain hidden. To keep the secret of what he was.

No doubt he has put a target on his back by admitting he's a born alpha. It was a brave decision. An honourable move that my wolf respects.

So do I, if I'm being honest.

I lift my eyes to meet his own, feeling my cheeks heat at what probably looks like a blatant perusal of his body. I expect to see those gold orbs glinting with amusement. Instead, he's watching me with quiet vulnerability. And something more. Something pained and hungry.

I wet my lips and turn to Tania.

"Yes," I say with firm conviction, even as my own thoughts swirl with confusion. "Yes, I trust him."

Tania nods once, then squares her shoulders and holds out her hand to Tobias.

"Okay," she says shakily, looking between Tobias and Cody. "Okay. I want to join your pack."

Chapter 4

Tobias Finch

An additional pack member is pretty much the last thing I could have possibly wanted.

I have no idea what we are going to do with this female who insists on hiking the full fifteen miles back to our territory in her human form. Who flinches every time me or the other four wolves look her way. Who, judging by the bruised state of her face and the scent of fear wafting off her, has clearly experienced some serious trauma.

My wolf preens protectively, flexing his alpha muscles at the thought of playing the white knight to some damsel in distress.

I want to smack the dumb animal upside his wolfish head. He's not the one tasked with the impossible job of helping this female adjust to life in what is currently an all-male pack.

I mean, we live in a glorified trailer park. We eat barbecued steak or hamburgers for dinner most nights. And I strongly suspect some of the guys haven't done laundry in at least a month.

As we pick our way across the ridge-line above Crazy Woman Canyon, the sharp stones bruise my bare feet and an icy wind gusts past, smelling of spring snow and making me wish for clothes. The rest of the guys are walking back in wolf form, but I opted to stay in my vastly inferior human form.

There is no way I'm giving my wolf control again anytime soon. Not after that stunt he pulled with Lucy.

If Tania is bothered by my nakedness, she doesn't show it. If anything, she seems more fearful of the four wolves walking behind us.

I plaster on what I hope is a congenial smile, the expression stiff with my frozen cheeks.

"How did you find out about our pack?" I ask.

Tania shoulders her backpack, eyeing me with guarded wariness. "I-I met some of your pack mates." Her voice is so breathy it's almost carried away on the wind. "After I ran away from my old… pack."

There's something in the way she says 'pack' that snags my attention. Like maybe she meant to say something else.

"Which of my pack mates did you meet?" I ask, though I suspect I already know.

"I don't actually remember their names," she admits. "But I do remember one of them had lots of tattoos. Like, all over his body. Even his neck."

I nod. Yep. That would be Hamish and Gareth. I feel my lips curving into a wry grin. Gods only knows what stories they told in an attempt to sell our pack to this poor female.

"How far is it to Liberty pack territory again?" she asks.

I cringe inwardly at the name.

Cody has been pushing me to name our pack for months now, and I've refused. Naming a pack – it just makes it all feel too real. Like maybe if we don't have a name or structure, we can just be a bunch of guys that hang out together.

Now I'm stuck with the name that Hamish and Gareth have coined: the Liberty pack.

Great.

"Probably another seven miles," I answer, though it's difficult to gauge.

I don't remember all of the run to Clear Creek territory, since my wolf was in control and only giving me snippets of awareness when he felt like it.

"We should be there before dawn," I add hopefully.

She gives a noncommittal sound that could mean 'okay great'. Or it could mean 'I hate hiking this really sucks'.

We walk in silence for several long minutes, the only sound the howling of the wind in the canyon below and the scratching of wolf claws on rocks. Finally, I ask the question that's been weighing on my mind since Lucy dropped the bomb of Huxley Black's name.

"What is this about you escaping from Huxley Black?"

Tania visibly flinches before giving me a furtive, side-long look.

"I- I escaped him." Her voice, now a low whisper, catches in her throat. "Him and Drake."

There's a long expectant silence as I wait for her to continue.

"It's hard for me to talk about it," she admits, pressing one hand to her sternum, as if to ease the ache forming there. "You're my alpha now. I know you can just order me to tell you. But I… I'd rather not talk about it just yet. If that's okay."

She casts me a pleading look, brown eyes glinting with unshed tears in the moonlight and I feel a pang of guilt for having asked her about it.

"You don't have to tell me," I assure her, stomach churning at the thought of using alpha compulsion on any of my pack-mates. "And just to be clear, I'll never force you or any of my pack to do or say anything. You're free, okay? Free to tell me no. Free to disagree with me. Whatever."

Tania gapes at me in surprise, nearly stumbling as she comes to an abrupt halt. "Disagree with you?" she squeaks. "I could never!"

I scoff. "Trust me. You can." I nod my head towards the four wolves trailing behind me. "Those jerks do it all the time."

Christopher lets out an amused chuff and Cody turns to nip at him.

Tania eyes them warily.

"And what about the hierarchy? My - my animal is submissive. So won't I have to listen to the other pack members?"

"No way." I smirk as a thought occurs to me. "Actually, they'll probably be jumping up to follow your orders."

She shoots me a confused look.

"Our pack is all-male." I explain. "The only female that comes onto our territory is my grandma. Trust me, these guys are going to be bending over backwards to try and impress you."

"All-male?"

Even in the moonlight, I can see the colour drain from her cheeks.

"I- I'm the only female?"

"Um. Yah." I grimace. "Sorry."

She looks completely horrified, but I don't really know what I can say to reassure her. Some of the guys are pretty rough. At least once a week, there's a brawl between a couple of them to settle some petty dispute. Only a few days ago, Theo Brightwell gave Ken Bwy a black eye because Ken's alarm went off at six in the morning, and he didn't turn it off fast enough.

To be fair, Ken's alarm had been blaring for at least ten minutes.

"Look," I say, steering the conversation back to what I really want to talk about. "You don't have to tell me what happened, but do you happen to know where Huxley Black is now? Or where he was last?"

Tania swallows audibly. "He – he's in Southern Utah," she replies. "At least, he was. In a desert south of Escalante."

I furrow my brow. "What is he doing there?"

Tania shrugs. "I don't know. He's formed some sort of alliance with Drake and his lair, I guess."

I blink, my mind catching on the word lair, then lick my lips. "Um... by lair, do you mean..."

Tania nods solemnly. "Dragon shifters? Yep."

I stare unseeingly into the dark depths of the canyon below us, mulling over what that means.

I still find the concept of there being dragon shifters somewhat unbelievable. I mean, I know most humans would find what I am unbelievable, but still. Dragons?

Also, how is it that Gareth and Hamish didn't pick up this crucial piece of information when they sent Tania our way?

A chill of unease slides up my spine and I glance surreptitiously at Tania from the corner of my eyes. She seems non-threatening enough. But I know well enough how that can be faked.

We still don't know who ordered the hit on me, but someone clearly wants me dead. What if it is Huxley Black? What if he's figured out where I am, and Tania is just one more assassin sent in retaliation for my taking over Huxley's pack?

It is possible that Huxley at least knows who I am by now. That I am the wolf he was searching for when he murdered my mother and was chased away by my father. That I'm the wolf that should have been killed at birth.

My mind flicks back to mom and dad's wedding photos, the image of Huxley Black standing beside dad with a broad smile on what was then a youthful face. A smile that was so like my dad's.

I shiver not even wanting to think about the possible implications of that. Because even if, by some unkind twist of the threads in fate's tapestry, he is family by blood, he stopped being family the moment he left my mom dying on our kitchen floor.

"You said two of my pack mates sent you towards our pack," I ask, trying to keep my tone casual. "Did they ask you about Drake and Huxley?"

I wait with bated breath for her to respond, even though I know she can't have told them anything. For months now, they've been searching for clues as to where Huxley Black has ended up. If they'd had any leads, they would have called me.

Tania bites her lip, rubbing her bare hands together to ward off the cold night air. "No," she says simply. "They never asked. I just said I was running away from a – a dangerous situation and they told me about the Liberty pack."

I purse my lips, contemplating what she's told me. It seems legit. I'd hate to second-guess her if she's telling the truth. Still, I'll have to give Hamish and Gareth a call as soon as we get back to our territory.

"Can I ask…" Tania starts tentatively. "You and Lucy both sounded like you knew Huxley Black. How do you know him?"

I give her a long look, doing my best to push away the lump of disappointed dread burrowing itself in my chest. I might not want a new pack member, but I want a traitor even less.

I really hope she's not a traitor.

Finally, I say: "That's a long story. And it's not just mine to tell."

"THIS IS LIBERTY PACK TERRITORY?" Tania asks.

She furrows her brow in mild disbelief, surveying the cluster of RVs that make up our living quarters and the partially constructed circular log house that we call the lodge.

'Lodge' is a generous description of the small, temporary structure we've built for eating, hanging out in and playing video games.

Outside the lodge, smoke rises from several barbecues and gas camping stoves as the guys tasked with breakfast duty work to fry up pancakes, eggs, bacon and steak.

Farther along the clearing, sheds sit haphazardly, housing washing machines, power tools, and construction materials.

It's all a bit, well… unfinished looking. Maybe a little muddy, with trampled grass in between the RVs and wheel ruts where the trucks have driven off the gravel road. But the morning light casts everything in a warm golden glow, and the smell of breakfast cooking is welcoming enough.

"This is it," Christopher says, clamouring down the steps of a nearby RV, a grin spread across his face.

As we'd gotten close to home, he and the other wolves had sprinted ahead, presumably to alert the rest of the pack that we had a newcomer. Judging by Christopher's wet hair and freshly shaven face, he also had time to have a shower and shave. I give him a glare, more aware than ever of the fact that I'm stark naked and probably suffering minor frostbite.

Christopher just laughs at my expression, tossing me a pair of pants and sweatshirt before turning back to Tania.

"We recently got running water and electricity, so that's been pretty sweet," Christopher explains mildly as he sidles up to Tania, tucking his hands into his pockets.

Now that he's not in his wolf form, some of her wariness of him has gone, but her stance remains tense and guarded as she takes in her surroundings.

"We still use generators to power some things though. And we don't really have a kitchen yet, just fridges in the lodge there." Christopher points to our very homemade looking log roundhouse. "And then the stoves and barbecues are outside." He gives a shrug. "Whatever. It works. It's all just temporary, though. Isn't that right, alpha?"

"Uh-huh."

My voice is muffled in the sweatshirt I'm still pulling over my head. Once it's on, I tuck my hands under my arms in an effort to warm them, hoping to bring some feeling back to my numb fingers.

"We're putting a few buildings up," I agree, then pause to scowl at the at the so-called lodge.

It seemed like a good idea at the time to build something ourselves using YouTube tutorials. It turns out, making buildings that are structurally sound and aesthetically pleasing requires some skill. Which, apparently, none of us have.

"Real buildings," I clarify. "Built by actual builders. That thing over there doesn't count."

In fact, I'm looking forward to taking it down. Demolition looks way more fun than construction.

"Tobias is downplaying," Christopher chuckles, shaking his head. "We're putting up more than a few buildings. It's basically going to look like a five-star resort once its finished. They'll be an awesome communal building with hotel-suite type rooms, then a bunch of little cabins for those that want more privacy. Or families or whatever." Christopher wrinkles his nose. "It's kind of hard to imagine any of us having families though."

I give a wry smile. "That was Cody's doing," I explain. "He said he was future proofing things."

"It sounds like it will be really nice," Tania says wistfully. She hauls the backpack from her back, lowering it to the ground, then rubs her shoulders. "So, um, where should I stay? Will I be in one of these RVs?"

Christopher and I exchange a look. Everyone is crammed two or three to each RV as it is. The lodge is definitely not suitable for sleeping in. It's barely suitable for sitting in.

I don't know what this female has been through, but I highly doubt she's going to want to share an RV with a couple of strange male shifters.

I open my mouth to respond, but am interrupted by the very unexpected sight of Tyrone jogging across the clearing, right towards us.

My whole body tenses, instantly on edge. Tyrone never jogs. None of the cats do. They lounge. Or they attack. There is no in-between.

He stops abruptly in front of us, eyes fixed solely on Tania. His shoulders are tense, muscles bunching as if readying for a fight. His green eyes are flashing cat, pupils lengthening, their pale green colour a stark contrast to his rich dark skin.

"Tyrone," I say warningly, infusing enough alpha command into my voice that Tania trembles beside me.

It looks like his animal is having some sort of reaction to there being a newcomer on our territory, and while I know that can happen, the last thing I want is Tyrone frightening her.

"Mine," Tyrone growls out, eyes flicking menacingly towards me.

My wolf bristles at the challenge, but I shove my animal back down. Only a couple of hours ago, my wolf was attempting to blackmail Lucy into going on a date with me. He doesn't get a say anymore.

"Tyrone, get your cat under control, okay?"

Tyrone responds with a low growl, white teeth flashing. His canines are longer than they should be, and sharper, as if he's partially shifted.

I sigh. Of course, it falls on me to keep Tyrone from making an idiot of himself.

Being an alpha is the worst.

"This is Tania," I say, trying to keep my tone as neutral as possible. Like I'm making a normal introduction and Tyrone isn't half gone to his animal. "She was seeking refuge so we've let her join our pack. We'll introduce her to everyone at breakfast, but we've just hiked all night so she's probably going to want to have a rest first…"

"Mine."

The one word comes out in a purring rumble as Tyrone completely ignores what I'm saying, fixing his eyes on Tania before stalking purposefully toward her, nostrils flaring. Each movement is full of predatory grace. I instinctively step in front of her protectively.

My protective movement seems to tip Tyrone over the edge. His gaze snaps to me as he hisses, deep and guttural, before crouching down as if preparing to attack.

My wolf presses impatiently at me, the animal hungry to take charge and deal with this insubordination.

With tooth and claw, my wolf urges me. *Show him who the alpha is.*

I ignore the deranged canine, opting instead to stare Tyrone down in my human form and brace for impact.

Tyrone leaps - only to be swept up in a flash of spotted fur and hurled to the ground. It takes my brain a couple seconds to realise what has just happened, and by the time I do, Tyrone is shoving to his feet, blinking rapidly at the bobcat in stunned bewilderment.

Not just any bobcat. Samson. Tyrone's closest friend.

For a moment, I think maybe Tyrone is going to snap out of it. Like maybe getting knocked to the ground was enough for him to regain control of his animal.

No such luck.

Tyrone shifts, clothes exploding and ripping, giving way to sleek black fur and at least two-hundred pounds of muscle. Samson might be big, but Tyrone is bigger. Alpha material in his own right.

In fact, Tyrone was in line to be alpha at his old pride before he was abducted by Huxley Black last winter. Which is why he wanted to stay with my pack. Just like me, Tyrone had no interest in being alpha.

Unlike me, Tyrone had a choice in the matter.

I watch with horrified awe as the two cats fight, teeth and claws ripping into fur and flesh in wild fury. I'm vaguely aware of Tania pressing against my side, trembling at the violence.

Cody barrels down the steps of the RV he shares with me, his shouted questions and reprimands joined by the shouts of the guys cooking breakfast. In moments the whole pack is gathered around, circling the fighting shifters like kids watching a fight on the playground.

Only no one is egging them on. We know better than that. A fight like this - with our animals at the helm - it can turn deadly.

When Tyrone pins Samson to the muddy earth, baring his teeth to his best friend's exposed throat, I realise it's time to step in.

"Stop," I order, letting the alpha command roll off me, filling the air with the weight of its dominance. "Shift back and knock it off."

Unlike the time I ordered grandpa to shift, the order flows effortlessly. Instantly, the two cats are peeling away from each other, hissing and snarling as the shift is forced upon them, until two naked males are standing, chests heaving as they glare at each other.

They both look terrible, coated in mud and blood and lacerations.

"What in Morrigan's name is going on?" Cody bellows, looking between Tyrone and Samson.

Tyrone is the first to speak, the words erupting from his lips in a deep rumble as he points one trembling hand in Tania's direction.

"She's. My. Mate."

Samson bares his teeth at these words, looking for all the world like he wants to lunge forward and attack Tyrone all over again.

"That's impossible." Samson bites out. "You're a liar."

"Don't call me a liar. You think I'd lie about something like that?"

"I don't know," Samson retorts petulantly, folding his arms across his bare chest. "Maybe you would. I've only known you for a couple of months. Who knows what you would do? But either way, you can't be her mate. Because I am."

Apparently incapable of articulating a response, Tyrone lunges for Samson - only to be held back by my lingering alpha command, as if it's some invisible chain weighing him to the muddy earth. He settles for glaring at Samson instead, teeth bared in silent threat.

I blink at the pair of them, then turn to Tania. Her dark eyes are fixed on the males, wide and unblinking. A deep flush has spread across her face, visible even amongst the fading bruises and dirt.

Cody steps up beside her, head tilted as he examines her critically.

"Is this true? Are they both your mates?"

Tania nods, licking her dry lips and taking several steps back from Tyrone and Samson.

"I'm sorry," she says hoarsely, casting furtive glances between me and Cody, as if she isn't sure who she should be apologising to. "I should have warned you… I didn't know…"

"Wait." I hold one hand out to silence the stilted apology. "Warned us about what? It's not like you could have known these guys would be your mates."

Tania gives me a look that is half plea, half apology.

"No. No, of course I didn't know. But I knew I might have more than one." She pauses, toying nervously with the zipper of her coat.

"My mother had three mates. My sister had five." She gives a little shrug. "It's just our species, I guess."

Beside me, Christopher lets out a low whistle. "Three or five mates." He shakes his head in disbelief. "I've never heard of that before."

Cody rounds on her, eyes narrowed. "Wait. What type of animal are you anyway?"

Tania bites her lip and looks at me. I just shrug and give her an apologetic smile. I mean, I might have told her I wouldn't force her to tell us what her animal was, but I sure didn't promise that I'd keep anyone else from asking her.

"I'm a fox shifter," she admits with a defeated sigh. "An arctic fox. I didn't want to say anything because you guys are obviously all big, scary, predator animals, and my fox is really shy."

"We won't let anyone hurt you," Samson promises gallantly.

Tyrone glares at him, like he can't stand the thought of his friend so much as speaking to his mate. Still, he nods his agreement, eyes softening when he looks at Tania.

"Yah. You're safe with us."

"So what, arctic foxes aren't monogamous like the rest of us? That's a bit gross, don't you think," Cody comments, upper lip curling in disgust.

My wolf bristles defensively, angry that Cody would dare to insult our newest pack member. I'm sure dad said something about monogamy. I just wish I could remember what it was, then I could leap to Tania's defence with some educated-sounding arguments. Or that Summer was here. She would know what to say.

Samson and Tyrone beat me to it. Well, not with educated arguments. With the defence part.

Both males lunge for Cody, yelling obscenities, ready to defend the honour of their new-found mate. In an effort to stop an all-out brawl, Christopher tackles Tyrone to the ground, and I grab hold of Samson, though not before he lands a blow to Cody's face.

Samson struggles for a moment under my hold, stilling once he realises it's me restraining him.

My wolf puffs out its chest, smug in the knowledge that one of our most powerful pack members respects our role as alpha, even when the feline is lost in rage.

"Okay," I say on an exhale, releasing Samson's arms once I'm confident he won't try and attack Cody again. "You two need to go put some clothes on." I point one finger at Tyrone and Samson, making a circle in the general direction of their very exposed junk. "I get that you two are all worked up about Tania being your mate, but she probably doesn't want to see all of that right now."

I ignore their grumbles of protest and turn to Christopher. Tania is standing close behind him, like she has decided he is the safest person out of us.

It's a good call. He's probably one of the nicest guys in the pack, and well-liked enough that none of the other guys ever mess with him.

"Can you take Tania to your RV? We'll work out where she's going to stay after breakfast, but she probably needs some peace and quiet for a moment, okay."

"Sure thing, alpha," Christopher agrees.

Tania shoots me a look of gratitude. My wolf lets out a smug chuff.

I turn to face Cody. He meets my stare, blue eyes glinting with self-righteous indignation. Like maybe he expected me to take his side, to reprimand Samson for hitting him.

The look infuriates my wolf. *This is our pack*, my wolf growls. *We are the alpha.*

Deliberately, I step closer to him, until we are nose-to-nose, our chests practically touching. He doesn't lower his eyes, but I notice the flicker of doubt in them.

It isn't enough to appease my wolf. The animal wants submission. Obedience. Respect.

"Tania is our pack mate," I say.

Pack. Pack. Pack, my wolf pants.

I try to keep my voice even, but with my wolf pressing so close to the surface, the words come out as a low rumble.

"You will respect her. Protect her. Just like you would any of our pack. And if I ever hear you attack her like that again…"

Anger rises at the memory of his words, at how he thoughtlessly attacked our newest member when she should have been made to feel welcome.

I shake my head, trying to break loose of my wolf's hold on me.

Only after several deep, centring breaths am I able to speak again, though this time the words come from my wolf. Like the animal has temporarily accepted it might not have control of my body, but it sure as heck will get its two cents in this conversation.

"When you attack any member of this pack, you attack me," I say, the words of my wolf rumbling strangely over my human lips. "This time, I'll let it slide. Next time, I'll take it as the challenge it is."

Cody's eyes widen, and he takes a step back, dropping his gaze in submission even as his cheeks colour in anger, blending with the red swelling starting up under his left eye.

"I'm sorry, alpha," he says, teeth clenching over the words. "It won't happen again."

I nod. My wolf is satisfied with his retreat, with his apology. But as I watch Cody stomping off towards the RV we share, I can't ignore the sick feeling of dread rising in my stomach.

This isn't over.

I've been more or less happy to let Cody run this pack. After all, he's the one who has been trained to be an alpha. He's older. He knows how to lead. How to make everything work.

I'm just a sixteen-year-old who barely got his driver's licence and who can't even control his wolf.

But we have different ideas about what a pack should look like. I want a pack where everyone is equal. Where we look out for each other, like a family. Where being with a human or having multiple mates is no big deal. Where even a born alpha freak of nature like me can be accepted.

I think Cody wants something that looks like the Clear Creek pack, with all its old prejudices.

But he isn't alpha. I am.

Even if I wish I wasn't.

Chapter 5

Lucy Stone

I sprint down the hill towards our house, effortlessly picking my way through the rocks and low-lying bushes that pepper the moonlit landscape. My mind is racing faster than my feet, stumbling over the magnitude of what I have just done.

I have betrayed my pack.

And yet it doesn't feel like a betrayal. Sure, I'm terrified of getting caught. But there is no guilt. No sudden Macbeth moment where I'm lamenting getting my hands dirty.

No. I'd do it again.

And that thought terrifies me.

I have always been the good girl. Worried about what dad would think, about what the alpha would think. Loyal to the pack.

I didn't want to be like mom. Selfish. The sort of person who would sacrifice her own children at the altar of her personal happiness.

And then Blackwater happened, and it wasn't a matter of choosing my own wants over protecting the pack. It was a choice between protecting Anton or making dad happy.

I chose Anton.

Tonight, I chose Tania.

I'm inside my house before I know it, scarcely aware of the path I've taken. Thankfully, the house is still empty, its hallways dark and silent. Dad and Anton will still be running with the pack, though no doubt they're making their way back home by now.

I throw my clothes into the washing machine in an effort to get rid of any lingering scents that might betray me, then climb into the shower. The hot water burns my hands and face, skin still sensitive from icy wind.

In hindsight, it was really lucky Tobias and Cody were there. Even if it was dangerous for them to be on pack territory. It meant I didn't have to go all the way to the top of the ridge, and it saved Tania from having to make the journey to Tobias' pack by herself.

The Liberty pack, I remind myself with a smile. What a name. Somehow, I doubt Tobias picked that one.

I tip my head back under the shower spray, then slather on enough shampoo to fill the bathroom with lavender steam, hoping it is enough to wash away Tania's scent, or the scent of Tobias and his wolves.

Tobias.

My cheeks heat at the thought of his chocolate, sage and pine scent. At the way his perfectly sculpted muscles glowed in the moonlight after he shifted into human form. At those eyes, like molten gold, fixed on me with unabashed longing.

So much longing, that his wolf was prepared to blackmail me into going on a date with him.

It should annoy me. If it were anyone else, it would annoy me. Piss me off, actually.

Instead, my wolf is preening. Totally smug in the knowledge that such a powerful wolf wants her.

I roll my eyes at the animal, even as I stupidly wonder whether Tobias will muster up the courage to ask me out on Monday.

My heart races at the thought, that traitorous organ sending butterflies careening in frenzied flight around my stomach.

I should turn him down. Dad wouldn't approve of me going to the dance with him. Neither would alpha. They might even forbid it.

Let them try, my wolf snarls. *They don't own us.*

I'm inclined to agree with her.

I'm sick of being dad and alpha Winslow's pawn, their secret weapon. I want a voice. I want recognition for my role in this pack.

I turn off the shower, inhaling deeply as I step into the thick steam, hoping the lavender will calm the rebellious rage rising like a hurricane in my chest. It doesn't. Maybe it's the full moon, or because I missed the pack run, but my wolf pushes hot and angry under my skin. Like my human form is caging her in, restricting her.

A knock on the door causes me to start, the hairbrush in my hand clattering to the tiled floor.

"Lucy, is that you?" Anton asks. "Are you done yet? What are you even doing in the shower at this time of night?"

My nostrils flare in agitation, and I will my heart to stop racing. It's just Anton. He probably wants to shower after his run with the pack.

Wrapping a towel around myself, I crack the door open and glare up at my older brother.

"Can you wait?" I snap.

"I did wait," he retorts. "It was freezing out there. I need to warm up."

"You'll survive," I say primly. I give him a smile, the kind that bares all my teeth, then slam the door shut in his face.

And that's when the images hit me, so strong that the warm lavender mist of the bathroom fades into the distance. It's like watching disjointed clips a of movie, only with *feel* and *smell* and *taste*.

Alpha Winslow is standing in the hallway of the alpha house, face contorted with rage as he stares at the broken lock of Tania's door…

Wolves are circling our house, their noses to the ground, tails raised high as they follow some scent, pausing when they reach the dark alcove outside our front door. A large brown wolf – my father, I realise with a jolt of recognition - lifts his head and howls, the sound full of fury and betrayal…

Dad is hauling me from my bedroom, callused hands vice-like as they grip my upper arms. I can hear the panic in my voice as I demand an explanation. He merely clenches his jaw, refusing to meet my eyes with his own…

I blink, and the images fade, ephemeral as mist.

I'm back in the bathroom, back pressed against the door, hands trembling as I clutch the towel to my chest.

What in the name of Morrigan was that?

The truth, my wolf whispers, her voice solemn. *Could you not smell the truth?*

I shake my head. Maybe the heat of the shower is making me hallucinate. Or maybe I'm having some sort of adrenaline crash. After everything I did tonight, that would not surprise me.

Hurriedly, I pull on my pyjamas, towel dry my hair, then slip silently out of the bathroom.

"Bathroom is free," I call as I pass Anton's room.

He grumbles some response that I don't quite hear. Something about girls taking forever in the shower.

"You better get used to it," I retort. "Tori isn't exactly low-maintenance, you know."

"Hmm," he replies, pushing past me, although his lips curl into a small smile at the mention of his mate.

I feel an inexplicable pang of jealousy at the way his expression softens. What would it be like to be loved like that? To have someone smile at my faults? To have someone want me just for me?

I turn away, not wanting to see his happiness and head towards my darkened room at the end of the hall.

When I was little, I thought my parents loved me like that. Then mom left. And dad… I shudder, recalling dad's destructive rage after mom's departure, and the coldness that followed.

Now, dad's affection - icy as it is - is always contingent on something. On my playing the role as obedient daughter. On my being truth-teller for the pack. On my wearing the right clothes or cooking the right dinner.

I flop down onto my bed, not bothering to turn on the lights. There is calm in the darkness, and with my preternatural vision, I can see every item in my spartan room clearly. Midnight has long past, and I should be going to sleep, but I feel wide awake.

I pull on my headphones, scrolling through my old iPod for music to listen to, irritation rising anew as I hold the archaic device. Dad confiscated my phone months ago, and it still hasn't been returned to me. This ancient thing plays music, but nothing else.

I close my eyes, listening as *Destroyer* by Of Monsters and Men plays. The music only seems to fuel my anger, stoking the fire until it's a burning rage. It's an anger my wolf seems to share. Only, while I am able to keep my face expressionless and my eyes dry, my wolf is snarling, clawing, howling.

She's always been a bit of a drama queen.

The creaking of hinges causes my eyes to fly open, and I sit up, quickly tugging the headphones off.

Dad looms in my doorway, a dark silhouette, backlit from the light in the hallway. Even with his face in shadow, there is no mistaking the harsh set of his mouth, the glower in his half-narrowed eyes.

"What is it?" I ask, blinking rapidly, as if I've just been startled from innocent sleep instead of dark brooding. I rub my eyes, give a dramatic yawn then ask: "How was the pack run?"

He doesn't answer, just stalks silently into my room until he's standing over my bed.

"Where were you this evening?" he asks.

"Here," I say with a frown. "Why?"

"Did you hear anything unusual? See anything?"

I wrinkle my nose, cocking my head in a show of confusion. "Like what?" I ask.

"Anything," he snaps. "Footsteps. Rustling. Animal sounds."

"No," I say, shaking my head, then give a little shrug. "I had my headphones on for most of the evening though." I give my iPod a pointed look, then ask: "By the way, when are you giving me my phone back?"

"When I've decided you've been adequately punished for your disobedience." He waves one massive hand dismissively. "And that isn't up for discussion right now. You're answering *my* questions. We had a security breach this evening. That is more important than your selfish demands."

The anger I've been holding back rushes to the surface and I'm speaking before I can rein it in.

"My selfish demands?" I hiss. "It's my phone. I bought it. And I'm sixteen."

A year past fifteen, the age of adulthood in shifter culture. A fact dad is well aware of.

"Plus, I'll be seventeen soon."

Okay, in a few months, but still. The point is, I'm not a child. With my role in the pack, I haven't been a child for a long, long time.

"You're still my daughter," he growls. "And I'm still your beta. You live under my roof. You live in my pack. So you'll follow my rules and take whatever punishment I see fitting until you're mated."

"Mated?" I force out a derisive scoff, but it sounds too breathy.

"Yes, mated." He leans forward, close enough that I can see his eyes flash as his wolf presses to the surface. "The alpha and I have discussed it. You'll be joined with a male of our choosing, one who is willing to join this pack. We can't risk losing your gift to some other pack."

My eyes widen, and I swallow down the squeak of surprise that threatens to burst out of me at his proclamation.

"Um, what?"

The question wooshes out with a shocked exhale. It's all I can get out, even as my mind races.

An arranged mating? What about my fated mate? What about love? More importantly, what about my gods-damned free will?

Dad nods, but there is no missing the vindictive glint in his eyes, as if he is relishing this show of power.

"Alpha Winslow is in talks with several packs to discuss possible pairings and alliances. It should all be arranged by this summer."

"This summer?" I squeak, climbing out of bed. The iPod and headphones thud to the ground but I don't care. I gape at dad for a long moment, and then the words rush out of me.

"I'm only sixteen. I can't get mated. What about high school? What about university?" I shake my head, a crazed sounding laugh bursting from my lips. "No way. Absolutely no freaking way. An arranged mating? You must be out of your gods-damned mind if you think I'm getting mated to some stranger. This isn't the dark ages. Or some weird religious cult."

I step forward, my eyes locked on his in a direct challenge. It's a move I've never made before. I've always showed dad the respect appropriate for his rank in the pack, even the few times I've subversively disobeyed him.

But now, my wolf is taking control. She has long ago stopped viewing this male as above her in the pack, even if he is my father. He might be physically stronger, but in her eyes, he is weak.

Protect yourself, my wolf demands.

"I won't do it," I say, meeting his eyes with my own.

"You'll do as you're told," he growls, teeth bared as he presses his face close to my own.

"No, I won't," I reply steadily. I don't lower my eyes. I'm not backing down from this.

His body trembles with barely restrained rage. With the way he's looking at me, I know I should be afraid, but I'm not. Maybe part of me still believes that this male would never harm me. He's my father. My beta. It's his job to protect me.

Which is why I don't even flinch when he raises his arm. It's not until I'm careening across my room, colliding with my dresser that I realise my mistake.

I let out a surprised grunt, blinking at dad confusedly as I push unsteadily to my feet. I lift my fingers to my throbbing face, wincing at the sharp ache in my ribs.

He hit me.

Dad hit me.

Tears well in my eyes, unbidden proof of my shock. As real as the physical pain is, it's secondary. The real pain is internal, invisible, stemming from an injury that I know instinctively will be irreparable.

Broken trust, my wolf whispers, giving a name to my injury. She isn't surprised at dad's betrayal, but there is no gloating from her. Instead, she merely bares her teeth at the male while telling me: *Open yourself to the truth.*

Whatever that means. Infuriatingly cryptic animal.

I blink away the tears, and my room fades away with it. Suddenly, I'm in my parent's bedroom. Only, it's how it was before mom left. Before dad raged and destroyed every item inside, down to the forget-me-not wallpaper.

Mom is crying, cowering against the wall, arms raised defensively as dad pins her to the wall. There is no mistaking the red swelling on mom's cheek and the fist-sized hole in the drywall behind her head.

"He – he's my mate, Jeb," mom whimpers. "It's fate. Fate. What do you want me to do about it?"

Dad growls, moving to press his arm against her windpipe.

"If you leave, you'll never see the kids again."

Fresh tears pour down mom's cheeks. "If I stay, you'll kill me," she whispers, the sound half choked from her sobs and the pressure of dad's arm on her throat.

Truth. I can taste the truth in her words.

Dad shakes his head, as if denying the accusation. "If you go, I'll kill you both," he hisses. "You and that rogue bastard."

There is truth in his words too, the kind that sends a chill to the marrow of my bones.

Mom whimpers out a plea, the words inarticulate. When dad finally lifts his arm from her throat, she takes in large gulping breaths.

"I'll stay," she wheezes, "I'll stay. I'm sorry Jeb. I'm sorry."

Triumph flits across dad's face. The self-satisfied look so similar to the look he gave me moments before.

But I can taste the lie on her words, acidic and harsh.

I blink, and I'm back in my room, dad's face wavering in front of my own as my vision blurs with tears.

"You hit me," I say stupidly.

My mind is racing at what I just saw, what I felt. I want to blame it on dizziness, on fatigue. Just like with the visions in the bathroom earlier this evening, I don't want this to be real.

Truth, my wolf assures me.

Dad's jaw ticks, but he doesn't respond to my accusation.

"You're grounded." His words are heavy with finality. "You're to stay on pack territory until further notice. I'll contact your school on Monday to inform them of your absence."

"For how long?" My voice is hoarse, an echo of my mother's choked whisper in my vision.

He doesn't answer. Then he's out of my room, slamming the door behind him, leaving me alone in the darkness.

Chapter 6

Tobias Finch

When Monday morning comes, I'm so nervous I think I might be sick.

The rest of Sunday was full of pack business, like moving Samson and Tyrone into a tent so that Tania could have their RV, and calling Gareth and Hamish to update them on Huxley Black's possible whereabouts. Not to mention all the annoyingly mundane alpha stuff, like organising building timetables and pack chore charts.

None of it was enough to wipe my discussion with Lucy from my head.

You want to ask me out, you ask me with words. In human form. Without leverage, she had said.

I'm pretty sure that means she wants me to ask her out. I mean, if she was going to say no, she would have turned me down then and there, right?

I find myself looking at the door each time a student files into Mrs Spring's English class, my wolf practically leaping up each time, frantic with the expectation of seeing Lucy. When class begins and she hasn't arrived, the animal begins to sulk, laying his ears back dejectedly as he rests his chin on his paws.

My wolf's disappointment turns to worry when Lucy isn't at lunch. The dumb animal is pacing, wanting to ditch school and run to the Clear Creek pack territory to check on Lucy.

Lucy. Keep Lucy safe, my wolf demands.

Inwardly, I sigh at the animal. *It's that sort of attitude that got us into trouble on Saturday night*, I remind him. Of course, he doesn't listen.

"Lucy isn't coming to school today," Jason informs me when he sees me staring at the vacant seat at our lunch table. The seat Lucy would normally be sitting at. "Neither is Anton. Their dad called in and said Lucy has glandular fever."

"Um, isn't that serious?" I ask, trying to keep the worry from my voice.

See, my wolf says, sounding like an annoying know-it-all. *She needs us. Our mate needs us.*

"It would be," Summer says, sliding into the seat beside Cody, "if Lucy actually had glandular fever. Which she doesn't."

Jason shoots her a warning look, which Summer pointedly ignores.

"What?" Summer snaps at Jason. "I'm not going to sit here and pretend that Lucy is sick when she's not. I mean, these guys aren't idiots." She points one finger at me and Cody. "They know just as well as any of us that Lucy can't actually get glandular fever, or any other human disease for that matter."

I frown, suddenly feeling like an idiot because, yah, of course that should have been obvious.

"So then why is her dad saying that she's sick?" I ask, looking between Summer and Jason.

Jason's cheeks redden, and he stares at his lunch tray. At the strange mix of beans, chicken and corn chips that I think are supposed to be nachos.

"That, my friend, is the million-dollar question," Summer says, popping a ranch covered cherry tomato into her mouth, completely oblivious to the way Cody is staring at her as she eats.

"Have you asked her what's going on?" Cody asks. "You know, through the pack link."

"Of course." Summer rolls her eyes. "But you know Lucy. That girl is about as sharing with her feelings as you were with your action-hero toys back when we were kids."

Summer gives a half smile at the memory before her expression turns serious.

"I can tell you what I think though. I think her dad is pulling her out of school. I mean, glandular fever is one of those diseases that puts humans out for like months, right?" She turns to Jason, cocking her head to one side as she asks: "Didn't Ross Slade get that back in Freshman year and it put him out of school for about a month."

Jason gives a slow nod. "Yah, that's right. He said it was the sickest he's ever been."

"Well, there you go," Summer shrugs, her lips pressed into a thin line. "The last day of school is just three weeks away. I think it's safe to say Jeb has some reason for wanting her out of school for the rest of the school year."

"But why?" I ask, brow furrowed in confusion. "Why wouldn't he want her at school?"

Summer gives me an exasperated look. "Because her dad is a controlling asshole. Because ever since Blackwater, he's been like a million times worse than before. Honestly, who knows why he does what he does."

"It could be because of Tobias," Jason offers, shooting me an apologetic grimace. "I mean, it's no secret that the beta doesn't like Tobias. Neither does the alpha, actually." Jason's ears burn red as he looks nervously at Cody, then back down at his lunch.

Cody grunts his acknowledgment, avoiding my gaze.

I know his dad banned him from Clear Creek territory, but we haven't really talked about it. It's just another one of those awkward truths that hovers between us every time we argue about pack structure or how many enforcers to have. One more thing for me to feel guilty about.

I would hate to think that I'm the reason Lucy is being pulled out of school.

Summer shakes her head vehemently. "It's not because of Tobias. If that was the case, Jeb would have pulled Lucy out of school months ago. No, it has to be something else."

My wolf is beginning to pace, his anxiety turning into something more insistent under my skin. It's a feeling I'm starting to share. After all, Lucy helped Tania escape from her pack's territory last night. What if she got caught? What if she really is in trouble?

"Can you find out?" I ask, rubbing at my temple in an effort to alleviate the pressure building there. Pressure from the unanswered need to shift, to give my wolf control.

No way am I giving that insane animal control again. Nope. Not a chance.

Summer gives me a pitying look. "I'll try. Not making any promises though."

"Thanks."

The need to check on Lucy has become almost unbearable. Like a meteorite caught up in the earth's gravitational pull, I'm ready to become a burning mass of rock if that's what it takes to get closer to her.

Don't even think about going onto Clear Creek territory again, Cody warns silently through our pack link, as if reading my mind.

I shoot him a surreptitious glare, my wolf bristling at the command. *We're the alpha*, my wolf reminds me.

Yah, thanks megalomaniac wolf, I'm aware of that little factoid.

I'm not going to.

My reply sounds petulant, even through the bond.

Cody just lifts one eyebrow in disbelief before turning away. I let out a sharp exhale and bite the inside of my cheek. I know this is another conversation Cody and I will be having later.

"WHAT HAVE you done with my shoes?"

"Oh, you mean the shoes you left inside the tent again. The ones that smelled like rotten cheese?"

"Please. You were probably just smelling your own meat farts. Where are they?"

I blink dazedly, staring at the ceiling of my RV as the sound of Samson and Tyrone arguing draws me from my sleep.

A sleep in which I had been having a very realistic and very enjoyable dream about Lucy Stone.

It's been more than three weeks since I've seen her. Three weeks since that moonlit night when my idiot wolf took charge and ran all the way to Clear Creek territory. Three weeks that she's been holed up at Half Moon ranch.

Our mate, my wolf rumbles, pacing and snarling with discontent. *We need to see our mate.*

I take a deep breath, rubbing my face with the palms of both hands. The imagined scent of her still lingers in my nostrils, warming my body. I swear I can taste the trace of her lips on my own. Unconsciously, I let out a low groan, closing my eyes as I let one hand dip below the sheets.

"Are these your shoes?" I hear Ollie call from somewhere else outside, his voice jarring me back to reality.

The very unfortunate reality in which I'm the alpha of a pack of over twenty guys living in RVs and tents with paper thin walls.

"Yah. Those are them."

There's the sound of feet thudding as Samson runs over to wherever Ollie is to retrieve his shoes, and then a string of colourful curses when he discovers that they are completely soaked.

"You left them outside in the rain? Really?"

From where I am inside the RV, I can't make out Tyrone's reply, though there is no mistaking the cold amusement in his tone.

Whatever he says, it's enough to send Samson into a rage. When the arguing turns to snarls, I know that both males have shifted. Again. I let out an exasperated sigh before reluctantly rolling out of bed.

By the time I'm climbing down the steps of the RV that I share with Cody, the panther and bobcat are engaged in some sort of feline stare-off, their sides heaving from the exertion of their fight. They're both covered in superficial scratches, but neither of them appears to have any serious injuries.

Instead, it looks like the biggest casualty in their latest tiff is the tent they have been sharing.

"Really guys."

I rub my eyes, regarding the tent mournfully.

I just bought that thing three weeks ago and now it is completely shredded, strips of orange and grey fabric fluttering in the warm spring breeze.

Guess I'll be taking a trip into town to buy a new tent from the sporting goods store. So much for a relaxing Saturday morning.

"What was it this time?" Noah asks, head cocked to one side as he eyes the wreckage. "Was Samson snoring again?"

"Honestly," I grumble, "who even knows."

Before Tania arrived, Samson and Tyrone were good friends. Well as much as two cat shifters possibly could be. Okay, so they spent time in close proximity to each other while ignoring the other's existence. As far as cats go, that is basically like declaring each other besties forever.

Now they've become obnoxiously and aggressively territorial, spending hours each day doing that weird cat stare-off thing and fighting over the smallest provocation.

Tania choses this moment to emerge from her RV, stretching sleepily as she surveys the damage with confusion. She gives a delicate sniff, then wrinkles her nose.

"Why does it smell like cat urine?" She gives another sniff, then asks: "Did somebody pee on my RV?"

"Breakfast is ready," Christopher calls out, coffee mug clutched in his hands as he makes his way over towards us from the lodge. When he reaches Tania's RV, he stops in his tracks, face contorting in revulsion before making a choking sound, spitting out a mouthful of coffee.

"Good gods," he gags, eyes watering, "that is disgusting."

He looks at the two cats, pointing one finger accusingly.

"That is seriously messed up you guys. There is a 'no scent-marking' rule for a reason. Super gross. Also, I think it's pretty safe to say that is not the way to win points with Tania. There is literally no one who would be impressed by that."

He shakes his head then extends one arm to the female in question, beckoning for her to follow.

"Come on," he says, "leave those two idiots to stare it out and come have some breakfast."

Tyrone and Samson both give low rumbling growls in Christopher's direction, either at his words or at the fact that he's talking to their mate. Tania shakes her head in disbelief before following Christopher to the lodge.

"Right guys," I say, drawing one hand across my face, "you need to shift back and get this mess cleaned up. And wash down the RV too, okay? I'm going to head into town and get a new tent. I'll try and get something bigger this time. Unless… maybe you guys don't want to share anymore?"

No, we'll share, Samson rumbles through the pack link.

After the first fight Samson and Tyrone had over Tania, they had both apologised profusely to her, promising they'd never do it again, vowing they'd be able to get along if she accepted them as her mates.

She wisely didn't believe them.

They've been sharing a tent for weeks now, trying unsuccessfully to prove to her that they're capable of getting along, while she's been staying alone in what used to be their RV, mainly hanging out with Christopher.

The two cats have even accused Christopher of trying to 'steal their mate'. Christopher thinks this is hilarious, and makes a big show of putting his arm around Tania's shoulders whenever they're around.

"You should really tell them that you're into guys," I had advised him after Tyrone 'accidentally' body-slammed him a couple weeks ago.

Christopher had just chuckled, then pointed to the shirt he was wearing. The one with a rainbow flag and the words 'sounds gay, I'm in' printed across the front.

"Nah, I want to make them sweat it a bit longer. Serves them right for being such imperceptive idiots."

He had a point.

So here I am, on the first weekend of summer break, refereeing yet another cat-fight instead of sleeping in.

The panther crouching on the other side of the wrecked tent huffs grudgingly in agreement with Samson's assurance that they can share, even as he continues glaring at his adversary. Tent shreds are swirling around in the wind. I can tell by the way Tyrone's tail is twitching, the panther is barely resisting the urge to bat at the fluttering pieces of fabric.

"Okay. Great." I say, brushing non-existent dirt off my hands and giving a tight smile. "Glad that's settled."

Then I head towards the lodge for breakfast and coffee. I can't take any more of this alpha business without caffeine in my system.

I'VE BARELY LIFTED my coffee to my lips, about to take that first delicious sip when Cody asks: "Any updates from Hamish and Gareth?"

I glare at him over my mug before taking a long swig.

"Nope."

"We should give them a call this morning," he says authoritatively. My wolf bares a tooth in a silent snarl, not liking Cody's tone.

"Agreed," I say tersely.

"Then we should have another pack meeting to discuss the building plans," he continues, eyes fixed on the tablet in front of him. "The contractor mentioned we can cut down on costs and get the central lodge built faster if some of the guys pitch in."

Cody is always doing this. Listing off what needs to be done, like I don't already know. Carrying around his stupid tablet and reading things off it like he's the gods-damned overseer on a factory floor or something.

My nostril flare in agitation.

"Yah. I know. We've got a meeting planned for this afternoon."

Then, before Cody can say something else to piss me off, I pull out my phone and dial Hamish, putting it on speaker so everyone can hear. I take a long, satisfying drink of my coffee as I wait for him to pick up.

"Alpha."

Hamish's voice comes across the line, steely and laced with sarcasm. He knows I hate being called alpha. Pretty sure that's why he keeps doing it.

"Any update on Huxley Black's location?" I ask.

"Straight to it, eh? Don't even want to know how we're doing or anything." Hamish chuckles. "We're fine, by the way. Great weather down here in Southern Utah, though some of the locals are a bit strange. One of the leads we followed sent us to a commune near Moab. We thought maybe it was Drake's lair, since humans often mistake shifter groups as human communes."

Hamish pauses, his voice going muffled as he pulls away from the phone to say something to Gareth. Presumably telling him to join the call, because moments later Gareth's clipped, "morning boss" comes across the line.

"Anyway," Hamish continues. "It was just a bunch of weird humans, not shifters. And when I say weird, I mean weird. These guys were wearing old-timey clothes, like it was the 1800's or something. And I'm pretty sure they were all related."

"How's that shifter we sent your way doing?" Gareth asks, cutting off Hamish's rant.

Tania beams, leaning across the table to get closer to my phone.

"Hi Gareth. Hi Hamish. I'm good. Thanks to you guys."

The bruises on her face and body have long since faded, the dark circles under her eyes are gone. More often than not, she's smiling at the bizarre antics of her two would-be-mates, or laughing with Christopher.

Occasionally, her eyes get the haunted look of someone who has seen things they would rather forget, but I get that. My past is full of ghosts who whisper their dark remembering's to me each day.

Still, she seems happy.

My chest clenches at the thought, a strange welling of gratitude and affection rising up, warm and glowing. I think it's coming from my wolf, because he gives a contented murmur, basking in the satisfaction of keeping our pack safe.

"There might be a couple more shifters heading your way," Gareth announces. "Two females and one male. Rogues looking for a safe haven."

My wolf puffs out his chest, smug in his ability to provide that safe haven.

I frown. We're already doubled up in RVs and sleeping in tents. Orrin and Red will be here soon too, so there'll be two more bodies to house. Two more mouths to feed. All the while, the construction bills keep coming in.

On top of that, it hasn't exactly been easy explaining to my human grandma why I need to live in the forest with a bunch of guys. I've kept most of the pack hidden, only introducing her to a handful of the guys. I've told her I'm working with them to build an exclusive mountain resort, using the money I inherited from my parents.

She thinks the guys are co-investors, interested in sustainability and Wyoming's beautiful landscape.

It probably helps that she thinks the Winslow's are involved in the project, since Cody is always hanging around when I go to visit her and grandpa.

"I knew spending time with the Winslow family would be good for you," she said to me on one of my visits. "Now look at you. A young entrepreneur. Your mom would be so proud."

I hated the way she beamed at me, so full of blind pride. Like I'd done something important, instead of just stealing a pack and getting funds from a territory I didn't want. A territory that didn't belong to me.

Guilt had sat heavy with Sunday dinner's beef stew.

I doubt she would be proud of me if she knew the truth of what I am. Alpha of a pack by accident, with an unapologetic psychopath of a wolf living inside of me.

"Not sure if we've got room for more members," Cody says, responding to Gareth's announcement, his words mirroring my own thoughts. "At least, not until we get the main lodge built. Not to mention, we don't really need more mouths to feed."

Somehow, hearing my own concerns on Cody's lips makes me realise how stupid they are. If these rogues are anything like Tania, they're running for their lives. Desperate for safety.

We might not have amazing housing. Or any housing, really. Unless you count tents. But we can give them safety.

As much as I hate to admit it, my pack is basically a standing shifter army, exactly what Huxley Black intended to create. The difference is, these guys are willing to be here. And they're loyal to me.

The look on Tania's face cracks me open. The way her warm smile slides away, dark eyes swimming with embarrassment as she regards the breakfast Christopher made her. Like she's seeing the cost of each piece of toast, each bite of scrambled eggs.

Anger rises quick and hot, tempered by shame at my own thoughts.

"We've always got room," I snap. "We'll just put up more tents if we need to. There's always money for food. And the lodge should be built in a couple months anyway."

I give Cody a hard look, my wolf pushing me to put the other male in his place. Remind him who is alpha.

He holds my gaze for a long moment, colour rising to his cheeks, then looks away.

On the other end of the phone, Hamish clears his throat. I grimace. In my anger at Cody, I had momentarily forgotten we had Hamish and Gareth on speaker.

"We're heading over to Canyonlands National Park today," Hamish informs us. "One of the rogues we sent your way said he'd heard about a dragon lair in that area. It might not be Drake's, but we figured we should scope it out. Seeing as it's close by."

"Yah. Okay," I say, rubbing the back of my neck with one hand. "Sounds good to me."

Still, I can't stop the sinking feeling of disappointment. With each passing month, the chance of finding Huxley Black feels increasingly impossible. Especially after the information from Tania only led us to more rumours and empty leads.

As if reading my thoughts, Hamish says: "We'll find Huxley Black, don't you worry about that, Alpha." He gives a low chuckle, the sound skittering across my bones, dark and mirthless. "If he's truly hiding out with Drake, it's only a matter of time. You can't keep a lair that size hidden forever."

I stare at the phone for a long time after the call ends, hoping that Hamish is right.

Chapter 7

Tobias Finch

"Are you sure that's the only tent you have left?" I ask, grimacing at the pink and purple monstrosity on display at the local hunting and fishing store.

The woman nods, her mousy brown ponytail bobbing with the movement.

"That's all we have left from last summer's stock," she explains. "It'll be a couple weeks before we get the new season stock in."

She cocks her head to one side, eyes traveling down to my denim jacket and Air Jordan's, then back up to my shaggy brown hair. It could probably do with a trim. Her lips purse into a frown.

"You're not from around here, are you?" she asks. "You from California?"

I open my mouth to answer, but she cuts me off with a wave of her hand.

"Look kid. It's really too early in the year to be going camping in these parts," she explains. "Every year, some tourist comes along from California or Arizona, thinking they'll go on some adventure in the great outdoors. And then a snow storm comes. Or they try and take a selfie with a bison. Or they wander off into some thermal pools." She gives a derisive snort. "Then our state's resources are taken up with having to evacuate these idiots." She fixes me with a hard look. "Do you even know about bear safety?"

I press my lips together, fighting the urge to laugh. I wonder what she would say if she knew a bunch of teens had been basically camping out in the Little Bighorn mountains all winter.

Of course, we aren't ordinary teens. As shifters, we can handle the cold. And there is no way a bear or any other natural predator would try and attack me or one of my pack. I doubt they'd even wander on to pack territory. Natural animals are wary of shifters, and with good reason.

"Yes, ma'am," I say, trying to emulate the tone I've heard Cody use with adults so many times. "I can assure you, I'll be taking every safety precaution."

She frowns, disbelief written on her features. Maybe I should have sent Cody in to town after all.

"Look, can I just buy the tent?"

I MANAGE to leave the store fifteen minutes later, armed with bear spray, hiking boots, a new coat and the tent. By the time I'm turning off main street and onto the freeway, the sun has crept to the middle of the sky, announcing that nearly a whole morning has passed.

I slow involuntarily as I drive past the turnoff that leads to the Half Moon ranch. To the Clear Creek pack territory and Lucy. Not seeing her this past month has been torture, but short of trespassing onto their territory, I don't know what to do about it. I can't call her. I have no way of contacting her. The best I've been able to do is text Jason and Summer to make sure she's okay.

It's not enough for my wolf. Not enough for me, if I'm being honest. I need to see her with my own eyes. Just to make sure she's alright, I tell myself. It has nothing to do with the more primal need to be close to her. To breath in her sweet lavender scent. To feel my heart race with anticipation, wondering if those grey eyes will ever be full of longing instead of disdain.

Okay, it has everything to do with that.

She's our mate, my wolf reminds me. Once again, stating the obvious. Like this is a fact I'm liable to forget.

I turn the volume up on my stereo, *Run* by OneRepublic blaring through blown-out speakers as I grit my teeth against the need to turn this car around and drive straight to Half Moon ranch, regardless of the risks.

It would be a bad idea. A terrible idea. Like, the kind of life choice that could start a shifter war in the middle of Buffalo, Wyoming.

I'm so focused on resisting the urge to drive to Lucy that I don't notice the massive truck veering across the center line of the freeway until the explosive sound of metal crunching fills my ears. Then the world is spinning upside-down, like some sort of messed up roller coaster ride, turning over and over in slow motion until everything comes to a screeching, jolting stop.

I must black out for a moment, because the next thing I know, I'm staring through a shattered windscreen, pinned upside-down in my seat by the airbag and seatbelt. The unfamiliar sound of voices reaches my ears, and I let out a sigh of relief, thinking it must be someone coming to help me out of the tangle of metal and plastic that used to be my car.

Until the scent of shifter hits me. Two males, and not from my pack.

"Hurry up," one of them hisses from the other side of the crumpled car door. "We don't have much time before the human authorities get called."

"I'm trying," the other voice retorts, pitched high with panic. There's the sound of claws on metal as he tries to pry open my door, the whole vehicle rocking with the effort.

I blink rapidly, trying to clear my brain, trying to think. *Think, think, think.*

Panic rises, the old fear of strange shifters pulsing with all the weight of my parents' warnings as I feel my breaths come in quick pants.

I'm trapped, helplessly suspended, like an insect in a spider's web.

Shift, my wolf urges me. *Shift and let me fight.*

I shake my head, recalling the damage my animal left in his wake on that snowy field at Blackwater. Maybe if we were in the forest, away from civilization. Maybe if my wolf could be trusted not to become a psychopathic killer. But there is no way I'm giving the animal control on the outskirts of Buffalo, on a freeway where any human driving past could see.

"Got it," the second shifter calls out triumphantly.

The crumpled door flies open to reveal an unremarkable looking male with thinning brown hair and slightly crooked teeth. When my eyes meet his own, his smile falters.

"He's awake," he says, stepping back in an effort to put distance between us.

"So what?" the shifter behind him calls, voice laced with impatience.

"So, he's a born alpha," the male closest to me retorts as he reaches into his pocket, silver flashing in the sun as he pulls something out. A blade, I realise.

"He's a teenage kid. A pup," the other male snorts derisively. "Should be the easiest job we've taken all year."

Job. My mind catches on that word, recalling the unforgettable pain of that bullet over a month ago. That's what the rogue had said then too. I was a job.

I lick my lips, eyeing the knife with a sinking dread.

"Who sent you?"

My voice is raspy, catching in my throat.

There's a flicker of pity in the male's eyes as he leans closer to me, even as he lifts the knife.

Shift, my wolf urges again, beating against the cage of my mind, *shift, shift*.

I ignore the animal, lifting my arms, ready to shield myself from the blade, doing my best to ignore the sickening twinge in my shoulder. I'm pretty sure something is broken. Or maybe dislocated. It doesn't feel right, doesn't move right.

The male lunges, and I press my eyes shut, prepared to feel the sting of metal. Instead, there's a roaring sound, followed by the cracking of bones and tearing of clothes as someone shifts.

When my eyes fly open, the knife-wielding shifter is gone. I can barely make out glimpses of fur and teeth, the sounds of snarling and snapping filling the air. Then silence, and nothing but empty asphalt.

"Hello?" I squirm, pulling at my seatbelt, trying to unbuckle it so I can climb out. "Who's out there?" I crane my neck, trying to look out the back of the car, hoping to see what's become of my attackers.

There's a huff of hot air on my face and I whip around, coming face to face with a bear. A very familiar bear.

"Orrin."

I practically slump into the airbag with relief at the sight of his scarred face and yellow teeth.

The bear huffs again. I feel the echoes of relief, lingering anger and building amusement filter across the pack bond. Orrin lifts one paw, expertly slicing the nylon seatbelt with one claw.

Should have shifted. Cut yourself free, Orrin chides through the pack bond.

I come free of the seatbelt, collapsing like a rag doll onto the broken glass and gravel that coats what used to be the roof of my car.

My face heats as I scramble out, cradling my sore arm against my body. Orrin's yellow eyes miss nothing, and the bear shakes his shaggy head.

Shift. Heal.

"Yah, I know," I say defensively, limping over towards what I assume to be Orrin's truck. Red is standing beside it, quickly pulling on shorts and a hoodie.

"Well, if it isn't our favourite wunderkind," Red drawls, flicking his hood up to cover the tufted ears. "Still making friends, I see."

"Where did they go?" I ask, scanning the freeway for the two shifters.

Red shrugs. "Gone. Took off almost as soon as we shifted." He nods towards the pair of black tire marks on the worn asphalt. "It's lucky we showed up when we did."

Behind me, there's the sound of Orrin shifting, followed by the rustling of clothes.

"How did you guys know I was here?" I ask, looking between the two of them as I climb into the backseat of the truck.

It takes a while. The truck is high, the kind you need to pull yourself up into. I wince at the movement, using my one good arm to haul myself up into the back seat, the other arm hanging limp at my side.

"We didn't," Orrin grunts, swinging himself up into the driver's seat and starting the engine. "We were on our way to pack territory, and just happened to be driving past."

I stare at him in confusion for a long moment before the memory returns, flitting through my consciousness like a lost butterfly.

I let out a groan, leaning forward until my head thumps on the back of Red's headrest.

Orrin and Red told me about a week ago that they would be coming out to pack territory as soon as school finished, and I had totally forgotten. Now we're not only a tent short because of Samson and Tyrone's little cat fight this morning, we've also got two extra shifters to house.

"We need to buy more tents," I mumble.

"Really?" Red chuckles. "You just got attacked and you're worried about tents? Did you hit your head or something?"

"We've got tents," Orrin rumbles, lifting one giant hand from the steering wheel to give a dismissive wave. "What we need to know is who those two shifters were, and how they knew where you'd be."

"Your guess is as good as mine," I say with a shrug. "They said it was a job. So assume they've been hired by the same person who hired that rogue last month."

Orrin frowns at me in the rear-view mirror. "Maybe. But I don't think we should be assuming anything. Especially since those two shifters didn't attack you on your pack territory. They attacked you on the road. Which means they knew where you'd be, and when you'd be there."

My blood chills.

How did they know that I'd be driving back from town? Did they have someone following me? Or some sort of tracking technology? Like, something on my phone or on my car?

With a sense of dread, I pull my phone from my pocket. The screen – which got cracked last year when Lucy set me up to get gored by a bull – is now completely shattered.

"You should probably ditch that, just in case," Orrin says.

I nod, mentally adding 'buy new phone' to the growing list of things to do.

"But you should also think about whether you trust everyone in your pack. I doubt anyone would be working with Huxley Black, but someone could be working with their old pack, sending information out or something."

I frown, not liking where this is going. Sure, I've only known the guys for a couple of months. But they are my guys. My pack. After months working together to carve out a place for ourselves, they feel like my family.

Pack. My wolf insists. *Pack, pack, pack.*

"Just think about it," Orrin says gently, turning the truck up the gravel mountain road that leads to our territory. "I'm sure they're all loyal to you, but they could still be conflicted, have old loyalties they feel bound to. And let's face it. There's a lot of shifters out there who won't like the idea of there being a living born alpha, let alone one with a pack that is more or less a standing army."

I guess he has a point. If I was worried about being a target before, that is nothing to what I am now. A born alpha with a pack.

Good, my wolf rumbles contentedly. *Let them fear us. They should fear us.*

"Okay," I concede reluctantly, "I'll think about it."

Except the truth is, with the exception of Cody and the Clear Creek pack, I know very little about the packs, prides and flocks the guys all came from. From what I do know, most of them have no reason to be loyal to their old homes. Which is why they opted to stay with me in the first place.

Not that it would have been possible for them to leave. Not when the blood bond with a born alpha is one that cannot be broken.

As the truck makes its way up the mountain road, I run through what I know of my pack mates' histories in my head.

Tyrone had been next in line to lead his pride, even after making it clear to his parents that he had no desire to lead. Apparently, cat prides can be volatile. Brutal, even. He would have faced challenges for his position nearly every month. Despite his strength, he doesn't actually enjoy fighting.

"I'm a lover, not a fighter," is what he has said to me on numerous occasions.

Even though he's currently disproving that mantra, at least where Samson is concerned.

Samson has no old pack loyalties. He's what would usually be a solitary animal, just like Red, Orrin, and Danny. Same as Rob Ratel, who is about as anti-social in his human form as in his vicious honey badger form.

Then there's Christopher. The grey wolf was from some neo-traditionalist pack in Michigan. One that didn't let their pups off pack territory for school and didn't have access to the internet. Despite knowing he has no interest in girls, Christopher's pack also wanted him to enter into an arranged mating with a female. For the purposes of bloodlines, apparently.

Christopher wasn't having any of that.

"What about Cody?" Red asks, speaking loudly to be heard over the rumbling of the engine. "I mean, it's no secret the Clear Creek pack don't like you. They're also the only pack that we know for sure knows of your location. And wasn't Cody in line to be alpha?"

I open my mouth to argue with Red, to tell him that I trust Cody. But then I remember the way Cody looked at me at breakfast, full of challenge and barely masked distaste. The many things he's challenged me on over the past month. How he just can't seem to let the outdated values of the Clear Creek pack go.

In the evenings, when it's just the two of us in the RV we share, he's quiet and broody. I can't even recall the last time I saw him smile.

I put his unhappiness down to the fact that he couldn't see Summer outside of school. But what if it is something more?

A dull ache forms in my chest at the thought of Cody betraying me. Betraying our pack. It hurts almost as much as whatever injury I did to my shoulder in the crash, joining with the pounding behind my eyes from hitting my head.

"Let's just focus on finding Huxley Black," I say, rubbing my face with the one arm capable of movement.

It's possible Huxley Black knows where I am. It's possible he's the one behind the attacks.

Because there is no doubt in my mind that Huxley Black wants me dead. He's wanted me dead since the day I was born. And that was before I destroyed his pack, stole his army and irrevocably bound him to me with a blood bond, essentially preventing him from leading a pack of his own.

My wolf lets out a smug huff at the thought, even as the deranged animal paces restlessly to track our adversary down.

Find him, my wolf rumbles impatiently. *Find the killer.*

Because my wolf is not concerned about the threat Huxley Black poses. He doesn't care if Huxley knows where my pack is, or if he's the one behind the attacks.

No, my wolf is pretty single-minded when it comes to Huxley Black. The animal wants revenge.

And so do I.

Chapter 8

Lucy Stone

June has always been my favourite month. It's the month the wildflowers make their appearance. Delicate and ephemeral, born of melted snow, they seem to laugh at their harsh mountain surrounds, daring each winter frost to try and destroy them. As if they know the snows that invariably kill them each winter will only feed their beauty the next summer.

June is also the month I turn seventeen.

I wanted to have a picnic to celebrate. Somewhere off pack territory so that Cody and Tobias could come. Maybe the alpine meadow overlooking Lake De Smet that is famous for its wildflowers.

We would lay our picnic blankets on the large, flat rocks and eat sandwiches and cake. Just me, Summer, Jason, Cody and Tobias. We would laugh and talk, our voices blending with the trill of the meadowlark and robins.

Maybe Tobias would ask me on that date.

Maybe I would say yes.

The twenty-fifth of June comes and goes. No different from every day since that night I helped Tania escape. Except for the handful of times alpha Winslow has needed me to assist with interrogations, I haven't left our house.

Dad would probably have confined me to my bedroom, except he still needs me to cook dinners for him and Anton.

I haven't felt the sun on my skin or seen this summer's wildflowers. I haven't let my wolf out to run and bathe in the moonlight.

The animal inside me is going mad.

"We're needed in the bunker after dinner," dad announces abruptly, almost causing me to drop the pizza I'm making for dinner, shocking me out of my self-pitying reverie.

"The enforcers picked up another rogue today," he continues, not waiting for my response. "A male making his way to the Liberty pack territory."

"Okay."

I keep my face expressionless as cold fingers of dread snake their way up my arms, tightening across my chest.

I remember what happened to the last rogue headed for Liberty pack.

I set the table, serving dad and Anton before sitting down to my own plate of pizza and salad. For a long moment, there's only the sound of chewing, ice clinking in water glasses and the hum of the overly bright kitchen lights. I take a deep breath, steeling myself to ask the question I haven't dared ask for weeks now.

"Dad, how much longer am I going to be grounded for?"

Dad freezes, jaw clenching over his mouthful of pizza as he lifts his eyes from his plate.

I give him what I hope is a conciliatory smile in return. Trying to show him I've learned my lesson. Silently reminding him that all these long weeks, I've been the good daughter. I've done my duty to our family. To the pack.

"Just because, I was thinking maybe I could organise something this weekend for my birthday. Like a picnic or something," I say hurriedly, wanting to make my case before I lose the nerve.

And yes, I'm also subtly reminding him that it was my birthday yesterday. Since he forgot.

"A picnic?" he asks, expression unreadable as he clenches one large hand around his water glass.

I look at his face, trying not to think about what those hands are capable of.

"Yah, a picnic. Just something casual. It doesn't even have to be off pack territory."

I mean, obviously I would love to get away from pack territory, but at this point I'll take what I can get. Outside the house seems like a good place to start.

"No."

I blink in surprise at his answer, waiting stupidly for him to give some explanation. When none comes, I ask: "Um, what do you mean? Like, no for this weekend? Maybe next weekend."

"I mean, no. No, you're not leaving this house until I say so."

He gives me one hard stare before turning back to his food, taking a bite of pizza in a clear signal that he has nothing further to say on the matter.

There's a strange, inexplicable pain in my chest at this cold dismissal. I feel my mouth go dry, stomach tightening until the food on my plate looks like an unsurmountable task instead of a meal. My wolf, who has been in a manic frenzy for days now, stills, her attention fixed on the male that sired her.

"I can't just stay in here forever," I protest, voice rising in pitch despite my best efforts to stay calm. "I need to get out. My wolf needs to get out."

"This isn't up for discussion."

I look to Anton beseechingly, silently begging him to step in. To reason with our dad.

Anton just shakes his head, the movement barely perceptible, as if he's afraid of catching dad's notice.

Just be patient, Anton suggests weakly through the pack bond. *Dad will come around.*

I don't bother to respond. Of course, Anton won't step in. The last time he said anything, dad threatened to get alpha Winslow to withdraw permission for Anton to attend USC.

As if reading my thoughts, Anton's mind brushes against my own apologetically. *You know I can't jeopardize my ability to go to USC. Tori needs me.*

I just stare at him. *I need you,* the selfish part of me wants to say.

But then I remember how hollow Anton was for weeks after coming back from Blackwater. How I still hear him calling out with nightmares at night.

Maybe getting away from Buffalo and being near his mate will be the best thing for him. After all he's suffered, he deserves that bit of happiness.

I won't ask him to give it up.

"Right, let's go," dad says, standing abruptly from the table, tilting his chin at me in an unspoken order to follow. "I don't want to be up all night."

Then he stalks out of the room, leaving me staring at my full plate.

"I'M TELLING YOU, I don't have any information about the Liberty pack, other than what I already told you."

The male's voice has reached a pleading pitch, and I can tell by the way his skin is quivering, he's fighting the urge to shift. Fighting his animal's instinct to run.

Prey, my wolf muses.

The way alpha Winslow has him tied up, he won't be shifting or running any time soon.

Truth, I tell dad and Cooper through the bond, even as I want to roll my eyes with exasperation.

It's obvious this rogue – a middle-aged male named Ben Holden - doesn't have any useful information. He's just another unfortunate stray who inadvertently wandered across our territory trying to find Tobias Finch's pack.

Dad knows it. Our alpha knows it. I'm not really sure why they insist on wasting everyone's time questioning this guy.

When alpha Winslow delivers another warning blow, I have to look away. For once, I'm thankful for the hood pulled up over my head and the mask covering my face as I lean into the shadows.

If dad sees me cringing he'll chastise me for my weakness, like he's done before.

It's disloyal to the pack. It shows you don't agree with the alpha's judgements.

Maybe I am not as loyal as I thought. Because I know what alpha Winslow is doing is wrong. Just like what he did to Tania was wrong.

"Well, Ben Holden," alpha Winslow drawls, apparently finished using the male as a punching bag, "let's see if you have anything further to say to us tomorrow morning."

Dad and Cooper turn to head up the stairs, content to leave the rogue tied up and shuddering under the pain of his injuries.

I know I should follow them up the stairs. I shouldn't look. I should harden my heart to whatever pity I feel for this guy. I mean, this isn't the first rogue I've seen in similar circumstances. It won't be the last.

Except he's innocent, my wolf reminds me. *You could smell the truth in his every word.*

I swallow hard, squeezing my eyes shut against the urge to turn back. To offer him some words of conciliation and apology.

Protect him, my wolf whispers. *You can protect him.*

I shake my head, forcing my feet to ascend the stairs, even as it feels like I'm climbing a mountain.

I barely got away with helping Tania escape. Even then, I'm sure dad and alpha Winslow both suspect my involvement in that. There is no way I could get away with it a second time.

That's when the vision hits me, images of truth so violent and ugly that I'm forced to brace myself against the cold cement wall beside the stairs. The sound of my own breathing mingles with the rogue's screams in my vision, cries so pained and pitiful that I feel tears pricking behind my own eyes, hot and angry.

When the vision finally fades, I'm left panting and trembling on the stairs, looking up at dad and Cooper's backlit silhouettes as they wait for me in the doorway.

They're going to kill him.

I can feel the blood drain from my face with the truth of that thought.

Protect him, my wolf pleads. *You're the only one who can.*

This time, I don't argue with her.

"WH-WHO IS THERE?"

Ben Holden's voice sounds faint and muffled in the darkness. From my position at the top of the stairs, I can see his eyes glinting reflectively, pupils dilated as he strains to see in the dark.

I don't answer, not wanting to risk my voice being heard by one of the enforcers on patrol. Instead, I pocket the screwdriver I used to break the lock on the door to the bunker before slinking noiselessly down the stairs.

"What do you want with me?" he whimpers, flinching as I come into view.

It's barely a hoarse whisper this time, as if his throat is dry from calling out. Or maybe he's just thirsty.

I lift one finger to my lips, willing him to stay silent. Only when I'm standing beside him, close enough that the scent of stale blood is filling my nostrils, do I dare to whisper my reply.

"I'm getting you out of here."

He cowers when I pull the utility knife from my pocket, causing me to still my hand at the ropes binding his hands.

"I'm not going to hurt you," I assure him. "I'm just going to cut these ropes, okay?"

His nostrils flare as he gives a curt nod, but he holds still.

"We don't have much time," I whisper. "Can you walk?"

For some reason, the sound of my serrated knife sawing through the thick rope seems amplified, as loud as a chainsaw.

Ben nods, licking split lips as he watches me warily.

"Yah, I can walk," he says, shaking his arms when I finally get the ropes free, flexing and curling his fingers in an effort to get the blood flowing back to them. "I can't shift though."

That doesn't surprise me. Shifters are usually injected with a light sedative when they're being detained, partially to keep them from shifting and partially to make them more manageable. Still, it's not ideal.

"The enforcers on patrol check the bunker every fifteen minutes," I say, bending to saw through the last ropes on his ankles. "That doesn't give you much time to make a run for it. I've got a bag for you with supplies. Water, food, clothes, that sort of thing."

I stole the clothes from Anton's room. They might be too big on this male, but it's better than nothing.

Even in summer, the nights are cold. Especially in the foothills.

"You'll need to head due east," I continue, handing him the pack and shepherding him towards the stairs. "Head to up the foothills until you reach the top of Crazy Woman Canyon and follow the ridge-line. That should take you straight to Liberty pack."

I pause, because I haven't actually been to Tobias Finch's territory. I just know roughly where it is from what he and Cody told me.

"If you get lost, there's a shifter who lives on the outskirts of town. John Vance. He lives at the end of Cottonwood Avenue in a little white house. He can point you in the right direction."

I give the rogue a hard look, seriously hoping that I'm doing the right thing in giving him Tobias' grandparents' address.

Ben Holden nods, wincing as he shoulders the pack. We've reached the top of the stairs now, and I can smell the sweet scent of grass and sage blowing in through the open door on the night air.

"Thank you," he croaks, taking my hands in his own. I'm surprised by the touch, but don't move to pull away. "Morrigan bless the winds you travel on."

"Be fast," I reply. "Don't get caught."

And with that, he is gone, darting soundlessly towards the foothills. For a moment, I watch him go, admiring the way he slinks into the shadows, managing to stay hidden even with the light of the waxing moon.

Then I remember the enforcers. My heart races, adrenaline pumping at the thought of running into one of them as I trot towards my house.

Shift and run, my wolf urges. *Leave. Leave. Leave.*

With the sweet night air in my lungs and the moonlight on my skin, it certainly is tempting. Especially when it's been ages since my wolf has run. When there is no end in sight for my home detention. When dad is threatening me with an arranged mating to some unknown male of his and alpha Winslow's choosing.

But where would I go?

I'm not foolish enough to think I could go to the Liberty pack. Even if I could get past the awkwardness of asking Tobias for a place with his pack, the reality is that dad and alpha Winslow will never let me go. I'm too valuable a commodity.

My leaving would only start a pack war. One in which those I care about would be bound to get hurt.

This doesn't stop the sight of my house from filling me with a claustrophobic sense of dread. The dark windows like soulless watchful eyes, glossy with reflected moonlight.

Run, my wolf urges again. *Run. Run. Run.*

I ignore her, taking one last deep breath of night air, steeling myself to return to the prison of my home.

As tempting as it is to run, there has to be a better way. Dad and alpha Winslow need me. The pack needs me. Surely that must be enough. Surely, I can leverage my position, convince them to give me back my freedom. I just have to stay strong and keep proving my loyalty to the pack.

I can do that.

"Lucy Stone."

I freeze at the familiar cold sound of alpha Winslow's voice, those two words at once a question and an admonition. My heart ratchets up until I'm sure it will burst from my chest.

Run, my wolf begs. *Run. Run.*

But I'm no coward. I turn around to face him, squaring my shoulders and lifting my eyes to meet his own.

"Strange time of night to be outside," Cooper drawls.

The corners of his lips tilt up, dark eyes crinkling at the edges, but there is no kindness in the expression.

He steps forward until he's nearly a foot away from me, nostrils flaring. Without warning, one hand snakes out, grabbing my wrist before I can pull it away. Keeping his eyes on my face, he lifts my hand, turning it palm up before giving a sharp inhale.

"You smell like the rogue," he says, fingertips pressing into my wrist so hard I know they'll leave bruises.

My pulse beats its war drum in my ears, demanding that I run, that I fight. I force myself to hold his gaze, will my voice to remain steady as I blink at him with mild confusion.

"The rogue?" I ask. "Do you mean the rogue we interrogated this afternoon?"

"Obviously." Cooper narrows his eyes at me, jaw ticking. "Why do you smell like him?"

"I'm not sure," I say, pressing my lips together thoughtfully. "Maybe from doing dad's washing this evening? I certainly didn't get close enough to touch him while you and dad were questioning him, so it must have been dad's clothes."

This must be a convincing enough proposition, because Cooper's expression relaxes imperceptibly.

I'm holding back the sigh of relief that has risen in my chest, starting to pull my hands away from Cooper's grasp when Cooper stills, eyes going glassy in that way that tells me someone is speaking to him through the pack bond. A moment later, his eyes sharpen, boring into me with unmasked fury as he tightens his grip on my wrists.

"The rogue is missing," he hisses, baring white teeth with the words. "According to my enforcers, someone broke the lock and cut his ropes."

"Oh." I try to sound surprised, but my lips struggle to form even that one syllable.

The alpha hauls me forward, big hands cuffing my wrists as he heads towards our house. He must telepath my dad, because dad is holding the front door open for us before we reach the awning, expression stony as he ushers us inside.

"What's going on?" Dad grips me roughly by the shoulders as he lowers his face in front of my own. His eyes are wild, flashing erratically as his wolf battles for supremacy. "What are you doing out of the house? And what's all this about the rogue escaping? Did you do this?"

Fear closes like a vice around my vocal cords, and I just stare at him, unable to answer.

"According my enforcers, the lock was broken in the same way as the lock on the other rogue's door. The female rogue," Cooper informs my dad, looking over my head as if I'm not even there.

Tania. Her name is Tania, I want to say. But I keep my lips pressed together.

I might have been stupid enough to help two rogues escape. That doesn't mean I'm about to admit anything.

"It's likely that whoever helped that rogue escape was also responsible for this more recent incident," Cooper continues.

His voice is a cool, icy tone that would lead those unfamiliar with him to think he was indifferent to tonight's happenings.

I know better.

Dad narrows his eyes at me. "Tell me you didn't have anything to do with this."

I grit my teeth, refusing to answer, even as I try to tamp down the rising panic.

"The scent of the male rogue is on her, Jeb," Cooper says.

I feel dad's fingers press into my shoulder at this revelation.

"By the gods, Lucy..." Dad shakes his head, as if trying to regain control, then says: "Is this you retaliating for being grounded? Is that what this is? One little bit of merited punishment and you turn traitor? Turn against your own pack? Against your family?"

Traitor.

That word. So jarring. Harsh. It's not a word I imagined would ever be applied to myself. But I suppose it's true, isn't it?

Technically, I am a traitor.

"Her reasons don't matter," Cooper says simply. "The fact is, she can no longer be trusted. Which means she's staying in the ranch house with me and Cindy until we decide what to do with her."

In other words, he's putting me in one of those secure hotel-like rooms they have at the ranch house. Something that locks from the outside. Something the enforcers can guard.

My nostrils flare with indignation, but I stay silent. Silence is the best weapon I have. Maybe the only weapon I have, actually. If you can even call it a weapon. Okay, maybe it's more of a defence. Or security blanket.

I am so screwed.

Chapter 9

Tobias Finch

"With respect, Alpha, we shouldn't be training females to fight." Cody crosses his arms over his chest. "It goes against tradition, against the natural instinct of wolves to protect their females and young, against…"

"I don't care."

The words snap out with more volume than I intend. I force myself to stop. Take a deep breath. Rein in the very wolfish desire to bite Cody's head off.

Gods, I wish Summer was here. She'd know what to say to Cody. Have some well-reasoned arguments backed by statistics or something.

Me? Well, I'm just going by my gut.

I rub one hand over my face, then continue: "Our pack has one female – who isn't a wolf, by the way, so I'm not even sure how wolf instincts are relevant. The pack voted that everyone would have enforcer duties. Tania is part of the pack. Therefore, she needs to be trained to be an enforcer like everyone else."

"And if there's a war?" Cody demands. "What then? Do you think Samson and Tyrone will be happy when you send their mate to the front lines? You think they'll let her go?"

Behind me, I'm aware of Red giving a little chuckle and muttering something that sounds like 'Samson will do whatever Tania tells him to do'.

"If there's a war – and hopefully, there never will be – then she'll at least have the skills to fight and defend herself if she needs to." I let out an exasperated sigh. "I'm not Huxley Black. I'm not trying to build some army and I will never ask anyone to fight if they don't want to. All I'm trying to do here is let Orrin train her to do some basic fighting, along with everyone else."

Beside me, Tania toes the dirt nervously with one worn sneaker, clearly uncomfortable with being the focus of another argument between me and Cody.

I want to tell her it's not her fault. If she wasn't here, no doubt Cody would find something else to complain about.

Cody shrugs. "Well, when there's a fight and you have dissension in your ranks because Tania is on the front lines, don't say I didn't warn you."

"Fine." I bite out. "Consider me warned."

I turn to Orrin, giving Cody my back, clearly signalling that this conversation is over.

"Is this space okay for training everyone?"

I wave one hand, indicating the grassy meadow around us. It's separated from the main lodge area - which has now become a muddy building site full of heavy machinery and construction workers - by a dense copse of trees.

"Yep, this will be fine," Orrin rumbles. "We won't be shifting, so even if your human workers do see us, it shouldn't raise too many questions."

I nod, then line up beside my pack mates to face Orrin, like he's an instructor in some outdoor gym class or something.

Orrin's brow drops, his scarred face wrinkling with the movement.

"What are you doing?"

"I'm joining your class," I answer, pulling my sweatshirt off and throwing it in the damp grass beside my feet.

In typical Wyoming fashion, the morning started off with a frost and has now turned into a raging furnace. Like the weather here can't just pick one theme for the day and stick with it.

Orrin shakes his head, rubbing his mouth with the back of one large hand, as if he can wipe the bemused smile off his face.

"Look, kid," he chuckles, "we were all at Blackwater, okay. Well, except for Tania here." He shoots Tania a friendly smile. "We saw what your wolf can do. I've never seen anyone fight like your wolf can. I'm not sure what you think I can teach you."

I squeeze my eyes shut against the barrage of images that assault my mind at the mention of Blackwater.

Blood on the snow. Red like mom's blood on the kitchen floor. Charcoal and pine and wolf filling my nostrils, the scent thick with fear and hate.

I push the images back. Away, away, away.

"My wolf isn't going to help if I'm fighting in human form," I argue, then give a wry smile. It feels forced. "And let's face it, I could probably do with a bit of help in that department. You saw how quickly Goliath knocked me out in that fighting ring."

Sure, my wolf can fight. It's probably the only thing the psychopathic animal is good for. It's getting him to stop that is the challenge.

"You have a point," Orrin nods with a solemnity that doesn't match the smile lines creasing the corners of his eyes. "Goliath was twice your size though."

I give a dry laugh, because, yah, it's true. I might be a born alpha. My wolf might be a giant beast who is great at killing things. But I am still just a sixteen-year-old boy. Maybe I've grown an inch or two since the winter, but it's not enough.

The truth is, I'm not sure I *want* to fight in my wolf form again. I'm not even sure I want to shift again. The last time I gave my wolf control, he ran over to the Clear Creek pack territory and tried to blackmail Lucy into going on a date with him. The animal is clearly deranged.

"Right, kids," Orrin says, his lips tilting into a half-smile as he surveys the group of shifters in front of him. "Let's get started."

With a few notable exceptions, we probably look like a bunch of dishevelled high-school kids at a summer camp, wearing wrinkled and unwashed gym clothes and muddy tennis shoes.

Only, unlike kids at summer camp, no one is looking at Orrin with a look of bored disinterest. Some of the guys even bounce up and down on the balls of their feet with eager anticipation.

Everyone heard about Orrin's fight in the pits. We all watched him fight that day at Blackwater. And then there are his scars, the marks of hard lessons learned etched across his bare arms and face.

Not to mention, we've been cooped up together all winter, fighting and bickering over petty stuff like wet laundry and cooking duty. We all need an outlet. Some of us more than others.

From my position at the back of the class, I can see Tyrone and Samson eyeing each other, shoulder muscles bunching. They're so caught up in thinking about sparring with one another that neither of them notices the way Christopher is watching them, a look of gleeful mischief on his face.

I rub my hands together, shifting my weight from one foot to the other, warming up my muscles.

This is going to be fun.

"YOU DIDN'T HAVE to punch me that hard," Tyrone complains, glaring at Christopher through the one eye that isn't swollen shut. "We were just sparring. Orrin said not to use our full strength."

Christopher rolls one shoulder lazily in a shrug.

"Be glad I didn't use my full strength then," he says, lips quirking with the hint of a smirk.

Samson laughs, the sound abruptly cut off when Red cuffs him behind the head.

"Don't think the rest of us didn't see Christopher take you to the ground in less than five seconds," Red chastises, rubbing one hand over his ever-present cat ears in open frustration. "It's like everything I taught you just fell out of your brain or something. Since when does a bobcat get bested by a wolf?"

"Hey, it's not like we were in animal form," Samson argues, throwing up his hands. "And Christopher is not normal. He's like the terminator." Samson shakes his head, then points one accusatory finger at Christopher. "Where did you learn to fight like that, anyway?"

Christopher grins.

"Training," he says simply, then turns to wink at Tania. "Guess you know who to come to if you want any pointers. I can teach you how to keep these guys in line."

Tania laughs, the sound sweet and melodic. She's been laughing more and more since she arrived, real happiness replacing the fear and sorrow that was etched onto her features.

"Puh-lease," Samson snorts, but Tyrone elbows him, giving him a silencing look before flashing a hopeful smile at Tania.

"You can keep us in line anytime you want," Tyrone tells Tania, blinking with mock innocence. A move that is completely ruined by his rakish smile and swollen eye.

"Oh yah," Samson agrees, slowly catching on. "Definitely. No force required."

"You guys are the worst," she says, shaking her head.

But there is no mistaking the faint blush that rises to her cheeks as she presses her lips together in an effort to suppress a smile.

Tyrone opens his mouth to reply – no doubt to spout out some other awkwardly flirtatious comment – when I catch a flicker of movement in the trees to the west. Christopher must notice it the same time that I do, because we both move instinctively, putting Tania, Tyrone and Samson behind us protectively as we turn to face the unknown threat.

A middle-aged male emerges from between two pines, face pale and hands raised, palms facing outwards. His clothes are worn, stained with dirt and days of travel. His features look drawn, the beak-like nose and large dark eyes over high cheekbones that are almost too prominent, as if he hasn't had a regular meal in weeks.

"I mean no harm," he calls out, voice surprisingly strong. "I come seeking refuge."

I let out a relieved breath, forcing my body language to relax, even as I continue to watch the newcomer with wary carefulness. After two attempts on my life in the past couple months – both of which resulted in quite a lot of pain – I'm understandably a little on edge.

Not my wolf though. The animal seems to completely lack any healthy fear. He wants to trot over to the newcomer, tail up, and welcome him into our pack, no questions asked.

Again, not the smartest animal.

Christopher and I stand, waiting, letting the male approach. I'm vaguely aware of Tyrone and Samson taking Tania away, no doubt moving her to safety, just as the sound of heavy footsteps behind me indicate another pack member has come to join us.

"Hey guys," Danny says, huffing out a breath. "Samson said you might need back-up."

"We're okay," I assure Danny. But I don't take my eyes off the newcomer as I say: "I'm Tobias Finch. Welcome to our territory."

The male gives a watery smile, darting a nervous look at Christopher and Danny.

"I know who you are, alpha. Would have known *what* you are even without seeing your eyes."

"Oh, okay…."

I wonder momentarily what he means by that, then realise how intimidating we probably look, all three of us, staring him down. I give what I hope is a reassuring smile and wave one hand towards my pack mates by way of introduction.

"This is Christopher and Danny."

Pack. Pack. Pack, my wolf pants gleefully.

"Nice to meet you."

The stranger casts each of them a quick look, then turns back to me, eyes flicking up to mine momentarily before settling on the ground in front of him.

"I'm Ben Holden. Two of your pack – Gareth and Hamish – sent me your way and said you could give me refuge."

Yah, I figured this was one of the rogues they had mentioned.

"I would say come over to the main lodge, but it's currently surrounded by construction," I say with a grimace. "We've got some tents set up over this way though. You can meet some of the others and then we'll figure out where to put you."

I sweep one arm out awkwardly towards the thick cluster of trees that screen off several marque-style tents. Our makeshift space for pack meals and meetings during the day while construction workers are here.

As we head towards the meeting tent, Christopher sidles up to Ben.

"Where did you come from?"

His tone is friendly, body language open, but I know the wolf is carefully assessing the stranger, looking for any movement that could indicate a threat.

"Northern Arizona," Ben replies, a little breathless as he trots to keep pace. "I ran into your other pack mates when I was crossing through the desert in Southern Utah. I hitch-hiked through Utah and part of Wyoming, but had to hike from Sheridan over to Buffalo. Got a bit caught up in Clear Creek territory."

My heart jolts at the mention of Clear Creek territory, my mind instantly going to Lucy.

"What happened at the Clear Creek territory?" Christopher asks smoothly.

To an outside observer, Christopher looks calm. Mildly interested. Like he's asking Ben what he did over the weekend.

But I'm aware of the way Christopher's jaw ticks, of the anger humming through the pack bond, hot as the midday sun. No doubt he's remembering how we found Tania. The way she looked when we took her from Clear Creek territory, trembling and bruised and frightened.

In the weeks since she has been here, Christopher has become her closest friend. The one she has trusted to confide in. And while he hasn't repeated anything she's said to him, I know from what little he has said that she had some pretty horrible things happen to her.

First at the hands of Huxley Black and Drake. Then at the hands of alpha Winslow.

If he was a true alpha, he would have helped her. Like we did, my wolf points out with painful smugness.

"They held me for questioning," Ben explains with a shrug. "Roughed me up a bit. Don't think they would have let me go, but a little she-wolf broke me out of there."

"Who?" I snap, tone harsher than I intend. "What she-wolf?"

Although I'm pretty sure I already know the answer.

"I – I don't know her name."

I can smell the fear licking off him, like maybe he thinks I'm going to attack him for his failure to answer. I want to kick myself for reacting so strongly.

This guy doesn't need some alpha he's just met growling at him. Even if the thought of Lucy putting herself at risk sends hot panic racing through my blood.

"She had blond hair, grey eyes. Was probably about your age, but it's hard to tell. It was dark."

Lucy. It was definitely Lucy.

"Did she get caught?" I ask. "Was she okay?"

I have to press my lips together to bite back the other questions I want to ask. Questions this guy definitely won't have the answers to. Like, did she look happy? When will they let her off pack territory? How can I get in contact with her?

Since school ended, neither Summer nor Jason have been answering text messages. Not from Cody and not from me. Meaning they are probably all on a ban from communicating with our pack.

Ben gives a pained grimace. "I have no idea. There was only a small window of time for me to escape. I don't know what happened to her."

She's fine, I tell myself. *She'll be fine. She's done this before and got away with it.*

Still, an inexplicable feeling of dread rises up, clawing at my chest. Urging me to shift and run to the Clear Creek territory. To check on Lucy.

Lucy, my wolf whimpers. *Lucy. We need Lucy.*

I shake my head in an attempt to clear my thoughts, forcing my eyes to focus on Ben. On the situation before me.

Ben is more than just travel-worn. He's injured. Exhausted to the point of barely being able to stand. Emaciated, going by the look of his gaunt features and the ragged clothes hanging off him.

There is more at stake than my own wants. Right now, this shifter needs me. He needs an alpha who will protect him. Who will provide him with safety.

My wolf growls in protest, driven by the primal need to see his mate. But even the psychopathic animal acknowledges our obligation to protect this newest member of our pack.

Pack. The wolf lets out a disgruntled grumble. *Pack is everything.*

I take a deep breath.

I might not have wanted to be alpha of a pack, but I am. And, like it or not, it's long past time for me to step up.

Lucy Stone

Two days.

I've been trapped in this room for just two days, and already I'm losing my mind.

The first couple hours, I was sure alpha Winslow would come in and deliver some sort of punishment. But he never came. Instead, the only contact I've had with the world outside these four walls has been the enforcers who deliver my meals three times a day.

I've reached out to Anton over the pack bond, only to be met with stony silence. Either he's intentionally ignoring me, because I'm a traitor to the pack. Or he's under orders not to communicate with me.

Either way, it hurts.

There's also no television in this room. Probably because alpha Winslow is a sadistic asshole. Which means I've had a lot of time to think.

Well, think and have pointless visions. Because the little glimpses of past, present and future have started coming with alarming regularity. There is no denying that my gift has changed, grown from truth-telling to something more.

Seer, my wolf whispers. *You're a truth-seer. Morrigan's gift.*

Unfortunately, not a single one of these unwelcome visions has given me any insight into what is going to happen to me, or how I'm supposed to get out of this mess. I mean, why would they? This supposed gift has never been anything but a curse to me. Why would that change now?

All the while, guilt, anger and regret wrap me up in their smothering embrace, winding their arms around and around me until each breath comes shallower than the last.

Not regret at helping Tania and Ben escape, at betraying my pack, being disloyal. No, it's worse than that. I regret being so stupidly, blindly loyal in the first place.

It shouldn't have taken a vision to make me see that my dad had been abusive to mom. That mom had been fleeing for her life, not abandoning us. All the signs were there. Or at least, they would have been if I had just opened my eyes and looked past the blinding haze of misplaced loyalty.

I mean, how many times had mom brushed off questions from me and Anton about some bruise on her face or arm? How many times had dad silenced mom with a stern look across the dinner table?

And then when she left, the way he raged and destroyed the house. Completely unapologetic. Like it was her fault that he'd lost control, not his.

It certainly shouldn't have taken being locked up in this room to see that alpha Winslow is a cold, calculating monster who will stop at nothing to further his own agenda. That should have been obvious the first time he had me attend an interrogation, when I was just a child who's only experience with spilt blood was skinned knees on the playground.

Bile rises in my stomach as I consider how many rogues have entered our territory and never left. How many shifters met their end at alpha Winslow's hands. At the part my simple truth-telling might have played in their punishment or demise.

And then, there was the way I treated Tobias.

I feel the blood drain from my face as I recall leading him into the bull pen. Even now, the image of him in those moments before the bull charged him down is burned into my memory. His expression had been so open and trusting, almost childlike, with the late afternoon sun turning his brown waves into a golden halo.

I watched him bleed and didn't feel an ounce of guilt.

I was a blind, blind fool.

Not anymore.

Now it's like someone has wrenched my eyes open, shoved my face in front of a mirror and forced me to look at myself for the very first time.

I rub my face between the palms of my hands and stare at the crisp white walls of the immaculately modern room I'm locked up in, as if my eyes can bore holes through the walls with the fire burning inside me.

Unfortunately, they can't.

I could rage. I could let my wolf loose and tear apart this room I'm locked in. Shred the bedding and the curtains. Mar the perfectly white walls.

I cock my head to one side, studying the space in front of me like it's a blank canvass prepared for the art of my destruction. It's certainly a tempting proposition. My wolf likes the idea.

Only, that would make me just like *him*, wouldn't it?

Lucy?

Summer's voice comes through the pack bond, clear and jarring as a church bell. My eyes fly open, fingers gripping the covers of the bed I'm seated on.

Lucy, what's going on? Are you okay?

Two days ago, I would have told her that I was fine and to mind her own business. Two days ago, complaining would have felt like weakness at best and a betrayal to my dad at worst.

But I'm not the same person I was two days ago. That person was a blind fool who deserved to be locked up.

Summer, I answer cautiously, that one word sounding fragile even over the bond.

I feel her relief at my response flood over me, warm as her namesake, and I can't help the faint smile that ghosts across my lips. Even that small expression feels stiff and awkward, as if the muscles on my face have forgotten the movement.

No, I'm not okay.

Admitting this feels like peeling off armour, like standing naked and vulnerable. At the same time, a weight lifts at the small admission.

Actually, I'm about as far from okay as possible.

And then I tell Summer everything. Everything. How I'm locked up, how I betrayed the pack, about my role as a truth-teller. I even tell her about the visions.

I cut away my ugly truths and lay them at her feet, like the discarded skin of a reptile.

Maybe I'll regret it. Maybe she'll be as disgusted with me as I am. But at this stage, what do I have to lose?

Chapter 10

Lucy Stone

That's it. I'm breaking you out of there.

Summer makes this announcement with unmovable finality.

I can feel her anger pulsing across the bond with the words, a sort of electric energy that shoots through my system like caffeine, pulling me from the sludge of self-pity.

I don't think that's a good idea.

But my heart races at the prospect of escape.

If you get caught, there's no saying what alpha Winslow will do to you.

Summer scoffs and I imagine her wrinkling her nose in disdain.

I won't get caught.

She must feel my uncertainty, that pang of doubt mixed with bitter hope, because her tone softens as she adds: *There's no point in arguing with me. I'm doing this. It's not even about you. Not really. I mean, obviously I wouldn't want to you leave you locked up, even if you have been pretty awful.*

There's the hint of laughter in her tone at this last bit, but her words ring heavy with truth. I have been awful.

No, this is about them, she continues. *About the way this pack is run. I know you all laugh at me when I talk about the patriarchy and about the culture of toxic masculinity in this pack. And that's fine.*

There's an edge to those words that clearly says it's not fine, but I don't interrupt her.

The truth is, I've had enough. I've had enough of being told I can't apply to Mills – or any other college - because the boys are already going to USC and UW. I've had enough of knowing my voice will never matter in this pack, simply because I'm a submissive wolf who happens to have a vagina.

I let out a choked cough, the sound abrupt against the plain white walls. She carries on.

I mean, they've made it pretty freaking clear that my only value is my ability to mate and have pups.

She sniffs disdainfully.

Well, I'm not going to be someone's little helpmeet, making casserole for pack events and raising a litter of pups, just for them to be brainwashed into thinking that only those with a Y chromosome have any worth.

Summer falls silent, leaving me gaping at the empty bedroom as I try to digest the word vomit that she just spewed into my head. I mean, of course I agree things are unfair but…

I don't see how breaking me out of here changes anything, I reply reasonably. *Packs have always been a male-dominated culture. My leaving isn't going to change that.*

An exasperated sigh comes across the bond.

I'm not talking about changing them, Summer snorts. *I'm sorry, but males like your dad and alpha Winslow, they are never going to change. I'm talking about standing up to them. I'm talking about showing them that they don't get to write all the rules. I'm talking about living my own life…*

My eyes widen in awe as the realisation hits me.

You're talking about leaving. You – you're going to go rogue.

Her answering silence says everything.

That's a bad idea. A really bad idea, Summer.

I'm not debating this, she retorts, tone clipped, sharp with irritation. *Just be ready to leave after midnight tonight, okay?*

AFTER BREAKING two shifters out of similar confinement, it's strange to be on the receiving end of a jailbreak mission. And, going by the horribly loud clanging and scraping sounds outside my door, Summer is equally unfamiliar with this activity.

"You're making a lot of noise out there," I whisper-shout, wringing my hands as I wait helplessly on the other side of the door. "Someone is going to hear you."

Honestly, I don't know why the enforcers haven't come running already. She's making enough noise to be heard throughout the whole alpha compound.

Summer lets out a breathy chuckle, the sound closely followed by what can only be described as a jack-hammer ripping metal.

Gods, I am so screwed.

"Summer…" I hiss, not even trying to mask the terror in my voice. "What are you doing?"

"Shh. Stop distracting me," she chides, the faintest hint of amusement coating her words.

The sound of power-tools whirring resumes, followed by the sound of metal thudding on the carpet of the hall outside my room. I look down, blinking in surprise at the gaping hole that used to be a doorknob with a complex locking system.

The door swings open unsteadily, dust and metal shavings falling like snow in its wake, revealing a beaming Summer, who drops the drill kit she was holding, then brushes her hands together in smug satisfaction.

I dart forward, looking frantically down the hall, completely expecting to see enforcers thundering towards us. But there is nothing.

I turn back to face Summer, brow furrowed in confusion. How did she manage to make that much noise in the middle of the alpha house and not draw any attention?

"Come on," Summer laughs. "Let's get out of here."

She wraps an arm around my shoulder, leaning to rub her cheek against my own. My wolf bristles at the contact, but allows it, acknowledging the need of her wolf to be close to its pack mate.

As soon as we step out into the warm night air, I pause, momentarily overwhelmed by the sensation of being outside for the first time in days. I inhale deeply, ready to drink in the scents of summer grass, sage and wildflowers - only to be hit with the acrid stench of smoke.

And not barbecue smoke or even the sweet smoke of a bonfire. No, this is the eye-watering scent that only grass, pine-needles and living wood make when they burn.

The smell of a wildfire.

That's when I see the orange glow cresting the western foothills, flickering brightly against a smoke-filled sky.

I look at Summer, eyes wide.

"A wildfire?"

Summer smirks.

"I told you I wouldn't get caught, didn't I?"

I shake my head, at a complete loss for what to say. My first instinct is to tell her how stupid starting a fire is. Everyone knows how fast a wildfire can move, how it can destroy miles and miles of forest and wildlife in a matter of days. Not to mention homes and human – or shifter – life.

But then, if she hadn't started the fire, she would have almost certainly been caught. And while alpha Winslow might be content to lock me up for betraying the pack, if only because he needs my gift, I doubt he'd extend that same courtesy to Summer.

I stare at the blaze for a long moment, a mixture of awe and fear at the glowing tendrils snaking long fingers towards the sky, then let my gaze track back to Summer.

Her brown eyes glow like embers, as if they are reflecting the distant fire. A hard jaw has replaced the usual soft, conciliatory smile. Her soft, curvy frame radiates power and steely determination. Maybe it's the way she is standing, shoulders squared and chin tilted up. Maybe it's the knowledge that this submissive she-wolf just started a fire and broke me out of the alpha house. Whatever it is, I feel like I'm seeing her, this girl I've known since childhood, for the very first time.

"Oh, don't worry," Summer says dismissively, giving me a gentle shove. A silent reminder to keep moving. "Jason helped me extend the firebreak, so the fire is actually pretty enclosed. They'll have it out in no time."

Her words are followed by the distant whirring of helicopters as our pack's enforcers rush to put out the fire, buckets full of water swaying beneath the choppers. I know others will be following overground, ready with shovels to dig out firebreaks.

I trail Summer wordlessly, letting her lead me to her car, a little red Honda that she worked all year to pay for. It's not new, but it looks roadworthy enough. And it's got a full tank of gas.

I roll down the window as she drives, closing my eyes in ecstasy at the feel of the wind on my face, at the rumbling movement of the car. At the ever-growing distance between me and the Clear Creek territory. My wolf gives a wavering sigh of relief, too overwhelmed with the joy of freedom to do anything but breath in the smoky night air.

Free, my wolf sings, tilting her head to the smoke-filled sky. *Free, free, free!*

Summer hooks her phone up to the stereo, *Tiny Riot* by Sam Ryder crackling through blown-out speakers.

As she sings along, belting out the chorus and tapping her fingers on the steering wheel in time to the beat, I resist the urge to roll my eyes even as a smile stretches painfully across my face. Of course, Summer would have a theme song ready to play for our escape.

TOBIAS FINCH

I'm watching a concrete truck pour the foundations for our main lodge when my phone rings, the sound jarring and abrasive.

For a moment, I contemplate not answering. It's probably grandma calling to see if Cody and I are going to come over for dinner that evening. She's been hounding us for days to visit.

I feel guilty about blowing her off, but now that there have been two attempts on my life, it seems irresponsible to lead potential killers to my grandparents' house. Especially when my grandma is just a human.

When the phone keeps ringing, I slip it from my pocket to silence it, only to start when I see Hamish's name flashing across the screen.

"Hey." I lift the phone to my ear as I trot away from the construction noise, heading towards the sheltering pines at the edge of the clearing. "What's up?"

"We've found Hux," Hamish says, not bothering with pleasantries.

I blink.

"You've found Huxley Black?" I repeat stupidly, as if the confusing thrum of excitement, rage and fear at Hamish's words have momentarily blocked crucial synapses in my brain.

Hamish scoffs. "That's what I said, alpha. Pay attention."

I can hear Gareth chastising him in the background, but Hamish's rudeness doesn't surprise me. Actually, there's a certain honesty in it that I like. Hamish might be terrifying and slightly-unhinged, but at least I know he wouldn't lie out of some misplaced goal of making me happy.

That's something, right?

"Now, I know you're probably going to get all vengeful and want to come in with your big, golden wolf, like you're karma incarnate or some crap," Hamish says, very concisely paraphrasing the trajectory my wolf's thoughts had started to take.

"But before you load up a bus and bring the whole pack down here, there's a few things you need to know."

There's the sound of footsteps in the background, measured and unhurried, as if Hamish is pacing back and forth in the room of whatever motel he and Gareth are staying at.

"First, Hux is with Drake, just like the little fox said. He's staying in Drake's lair – presumably as a guest, but who really knows what's going on with that, since we know that, when it comes to power, Hux is about as sharing as Gareth is with the keys of his new Mustang."

I hear Gareth say something in protest, the words faint and muffled in the background.

"The point is, Drake's lair is big. Maybe the same size as our pack. And easily defensible. I'm talking big sandstone cliffs overlooking flat desert. The only cover you'd have would be a couple of rocks, some skinny cacti and malnourished juniper bushes. If you try to get in there, you'll be charcoal briquettes in a dragon barbecue."

Dragons.

I draw my hand across my face, still unable to comprehend the fact that there are shifters who turn into dragons. I'm not sure why this is so surprising to me, considering I turn into a giant golden wolf. Maybe because I only found out about dragon shifters a few months ago.

Which is why I lamely ask: "So they really breath fire, then?"

Hamish gives an exasperated growl, and then Gareth takes over the call.

"Hey Tobias. Yah, they really breath fire." Gareth gives a low chuckle. "Look. What Hamish is trying and failing to say is there is no way we can get Hux while he's holed up with Drake. At least, not in a direct attack. Not even if we had the whole pack here."

"Okay."

I appreciate the logic in what they are saying, that we can't attack Huxley Black head on. My wolf is less understanding. The animal wants to unleash his pack, unleash the monster on Huxley Black and any shifter who dares to shelter him.

Kill the killer, my wolf urges. *Protect your pack.*

But my wolf isn't the one in control here. At least, he won't be if I have any say in it.

Vengeance, my wolf rumbles.

"Still, there's a chance we might be able to draw Huxley Black out. Hamish has an idea of how we could do this."

Gareth pauses, and there's the sound of muffled arguing, Hamish's voice raises an octave as he speaks. Then Gareth gives a resigned sigh, saying: "Hamish is right. We shouldn't speak too openly about our plans on the phone, just in case. We can go over things in person when you get down here."

"Oh. Okay." I blink in surprise. "You guys think I should come down there?"

"Yah." There's the hint of a smile in Gareth's voice. "Don't let your wolf get too excited though. And bring some back-up. Not too many. Nothing that will draw attention. Maybe three of the guys."

I nod, then remember he can't see me.

"Yah. Okay."

Already my mind is whirring as I try and think who would be best to bring with me. Not Tyrone and Samson. They won't want to leave their mate. Christopher might not want to leave Tania either, come to think of it.

"I'll text you the coordinates," Gareth says, interrupting my thoughts. "Be safe, alpha."

The call ends, leaving me alone under the pine trees, the distant sound of construction mingling with the sweeter sound of water trickling in the moss-covered stream nestled between boulders in the forest.

Through it all, I can hear the sound of my own heart, beating frantically against my ribcage.

Huxley Black, it seems to chant. *Huxley Black. Huxley Black.*

The male has been the centre of my vengeful thoughts and blood-soaked dreams for so many months now that he has become more monster than man. More myth than memory. Finding out where he is – it's at once surreal and anticlimactic.

"Everything okay?"

Cody's voice startles me and I spin to face him.

He must have come from the training grounds at the other side of the forest, traveling on footsteps so light that even my shifter hearing hadn't picked up the crackling of dry pine needles underfoot.

"Oh, hey Cody."

I force a congenial smile.

After all the arguments we've been having, I've been trying really hard to be friendly. Show him that I do appreciate all the hard work he's put in.

It's hard. I'm not sure I'm that good at being friendly.

Cody looks me over, expression searching, eyes landing on the phone still clutched in my hand.

"Who were you talking to?"

"Hamish and Gareth," I respond without hesitation. I'll need to brief the whole pack soon anyway, so no point in holding things back from Cody. Even if I don't fully trust him. "They found Huxley Black and want me and a few others to come down there."

I pocket my phone, then tilt my chin towards the training grounds. It's the only place we can meet during the day where we won't be overheard by the human construction workers.

"I'll call a meeting and we can go over everything then," I tell him.

Cody nods, eyes narrowing slightly as his lips press into a thin line. I wonder briefly if he's annoyed at having to wait for information, or if it's something else, but my concern is about as fleeting as the sunlight flickering between the shadowy trees.

I don't have time to worry about Cody's feelings. There is a killer to find.

"YOU DON'T HAVE to stay here just because of me," Tania says, toying nervously with the zipper of her oversized hoodie, dark eyes darting between Tyrone, Samson and Christopher.

As expected, all three of them made it pretty clear they didn't want to leave her unprotected. Well, her would-be-mates didn't want to leave her unprotected. Christopher didn't want to leave her at the mercy of Samson and Tyrone's awkward attempts to win her over.

"If I go, who is going to keep these two from pissing all over her RV again?" Christopher had very reasonably pointed out.

"Honestly, it's fine," I say, flashing Tania what I hope is a reassuring smile. "I don't need them to go. It can be anyone. From what Gareth and Hamish said, I just need a couple of guys to travel down with. Those two have some plan to draw Huxley Black out, but we won't be fighting Drake's lair or anything."

"Not that Samson or Tyrone would be much use to you if there was a fight," Christopher quips, waggling his pale eyebrows in the two cat's direction. "Given how weak their most recent performance was."

Samson returns this jibe with a glower, but Tyrone just laughs, a deep, breathy sound that huffs through his nostrils.

"That was in human form," Tyrone drawls.

He's looking more relaxed than I've seen him in weeks, long legs stretched out in front of him, arms draped across the back of one of the camp chairs set up under the large marquee style tent.

I wonder if his improved mood has something to do with the fact that Tania is letting him sit closer to her than usual. Or maybe he's finally figured out that Christopher isn't the potential rival for his mate's attentions he thought he was.

"You know, it would be a different story if we were in animal form," Tyrone continues, white teeth flashing in a smile that is equal parts warning and friendly banter. "You've seen my cat fight."

Christopher smiles, dipping his head in silent acknowledgement. We all know what a strong fighter Tyrone's panther is.

I also know how much both Tyrone and his cat hate to fight. Which is another reason I wouldn't ask him to come with me, even if he wasn't so driven to stay and protect Tania from all the unseen and unlikely threats.

I mean, I highly doubt anyone would launch an attack on our territory. No one is stupid enough to want a war. Which is why, so far, every attack has been aimed at me and me alone.

"I was thinking I'd bring Cody with me," I say tentatively, interrupting Christopher and Tyrone's verbal sparring.

After what Red and Orrin suggested, I've been watching Cody closely. I don't think he's feeding information to the Clear Creek pack. I mean, that just doesn't seem like something he'd do. From the very beginning, he's been the one organising things, dealing with construction schedules and all those mundane – but admittedly, very important – details.

Why would he put in all that effort just to sell-out the pack? I don't buy it.

That doesn't mean I trust him enough to leave him unsupervised at Liberty pack territory though.

To my surprise, Cody actually looks pleased.

"I'd be happy to come along," Cody says, squaring his shoulders, cheeks flushing slightly with pride at being chosen. "I can be ready to leave as soon as you need."

I give him a grateful smile, then look at Orrin and Red. I know they only just arrived in Buffalo, but I trust them.

They're also older. Well, Orrin is ancient. Probably like fifty or something. Red is in his early twenties but looks old. Cody and I will get a lot less attention traveling down to Southern Utah if we have people who look like adults with us.

Also, Orrin has years of experience defending his own territory up in the Beartooth Mountains. Something tells me that might be useful, even if we aren't going there to fight.

As if reading my mind, Orrin takes a bite of the beef jerky stick he's holding before giving me a wry grin, the motion stretching the scars that run like silver along his cheeks.

"I can drive you down to Southern Utah," Orrin drawls, eyes flashing with amusement. "And Red here will come too. Won't you, Red?"

Red doesn't look pleased, but gives a curt nod, cat ears twitching.

"I'll come along, but I'm not fighting in any battles. And don't be giving me any orders either. I already told you, I might be in this pack…" Red lifts his fingers, making quotation marks in the air as he says the word 'pack'. "But I'm a solitary animal."

"Don't be so dramatic." Orrin huffs, jaw working over the beef jerky. "You listen to instructions in the shop well enough, and it hasn't killed you yet."

Red opens his mouth to snap out some retort when the crunching and thudding of footsteps running over underbrush causes the whole tent to fall silent.

Having the humans nearby has made us all on edge when it comes to discussing anything during the day. We're all aware of the consequences if some unsuspecting construction worker stumbles across someone shifting, or overhears some conversation that can't quite be explained away. Or sees Red's ears.

As if thinking the same thing, Red quickly pulls his hoodie up, glowering as he covers the unshift-able ears.

Only, it isn't a human. Instead, it's someone I never expected to see in the heart of Liberty pack territory, flanked by a scowling grandpa and bristling Jamison.

I'm leaping to my feet before I know it, chair toppling backwards as I practically jog across the meadow to meet him.

"Jason! What are you doing here?"

Chapter 11

Lucy Stone

"I think you took a wrong turn," I say, squinting at the map on Summer's phone. "I'm pretty sure you weren't supposed to get off the I-70."

In the interest of putting as much space between us and the Clear Creek pack, Summer and I have driven through the night, only stopping for gas, energy drinks and taking turns driving when one of us gets tired.

Our general plan, which we formulated while careening down the highway last night, is to drive to Southern California, where Tori's pack is. I doubt they will take us in. They won't want to spark a conflict with the Clear Creek pack. But they might be able to help us find somewhere safe to go. Or at least offer us some protection while we get our selves set up.

I rub my eyes with the back of my hand, blinking away the lingering grit of sleep, then look at the map on Summer's phone again. Of course, because Summer has driven us into the middle of freaking nowhere, there is no cell service, so it's hard to say where we actually are in relation to the map.

"This is the I-70," Summer insists. "I swear there was no sign that said 'exit' or anything like that. The road is just small looking because we're in the desert."

I look at the road ahead of us, a single lane going each direction, asphalt pock-marked with holes the size of craters, interspersed with lumps where some road crew tried making repairs about fifty years ago.

On either side of the road, the red and dun coloured landscape stretches across to the horizon, barren desert peppered with scrubby plants.

The only breaks in the emptiness are the occasional rock formations, jutting like monoliths from the earth. I want to call them mesas, but I don't think that is quite right, since they aren't flat on top. Instead, they look like the creations of some surrealist painting, melting and looming forms that could almost be mistaken as the deteriorating statues from a long-forgotten era.

There is no glimmer of a building or town. No road sign to give a clue as to what road we are on. No billboards telling us that the next town is the last place to get ice-cream for a hundred miles.

Yah, this is definitely not an interstate.

We drive in tense silence for another twenty minutes before Summer's car lets out a little 'ping', the sound surprisingly loud in the confines of the Honda. I watch as Summer's eyes flick to the dashboard, then widen in alarm, colour draining from her face.

"Oh shit. Oh shit, shit, shit."

"Summer…"

Summer doesn't answer, just shakes her head, fingers gripping tightly around the steering wheel as she glares at the dashboard like it's just told her women lost the right to vote.

I crane my neck to see what she is looking at and… yah. It's bad.

"You let the car run out of gas?" I say incredulously. "How did that even happen?"

"Oh, don't blame me," Summer snaps. "You've been driving this car too."

"Well, first of all," I say, lifting one finger in the air, "I filled up the car right before you took your turn driving again. Secondly…" I lift a second finger in the air. "I was asleep until about twenty minutes ago. So yes, I think it's fair to say that *you* let the car run out of gas."

To my horror, Summer takes a deep breath before leaning over her steering wheel and breaking into shuddering, heaving sobs.

Instantly, I wish I could take my words back. Shove each insensitive syllable back into my mouth.

Summer has risked everything to help me escape. What does it matter if she let the car run out of gas? What does it matter where the blame lays? We're in this together. Equally doomed by each other's stupid life choices.

"I'm sorry," I say, reaching over to pat her shoulder.

I don't think it's anything I've ever done before, and the gesture feels awkward, even to my wolf. Like it's something I know I should do, simply because I've seen other people do it.

"I didn't mean it, okay?"

I give her arm a few more light pats, hoping I've delivered the comforting touch correctly.

Summer turns to me, disbelief mingling with the tears streaking her face.

"Are you… are you apologising?" she asks, the words half choked between sobs.

She shakes her head, giving a little snort before turning back to look at the road, then adds, her voice steadier: "I don't think I've ever heard you apologise before."

I frown. Surely that can't be right. We've known each other since we were babies. I must have said sorry about something at some point.

"Maybe we'll make it to a town before the gas completely runs out," I lie hopefully.

Desert stretches as far as the eye can see with no sign of an upcoming town in sight. We both know nothing short of a miracle will enable this car to make it to the next gas station.

Another long silence ensues. Summer has stopped ugly-crying, but every so often she gives a little hiccup, the sound a prelude to the next wave of silent tears ready to stream down her cheeks.

Finally, the engine sputters, its death throes lasting just long enough for Summer to pull the car to the side of the road.

"Well," I say tentatively, eyeing the empty desert warily, "what do you think we should do?"

Judging by the sun, it's late afternoon now. We're both exhausted from driving. I'm a little hungry.

I look around the car, taking stock of what resources we have. I frown at the two nearly empty water bottles, half-eaten bag of cashews, and now empty candy wrappers. Not a lot to work with.

In answer, Summer flops her head forward dramatically until it's resting on the steering wheel.

"We can try and hike out," I suggest sensibly. "If we follow the road, we're bound to end up in civilization at some point."

Beside me, Summer gives a little sniff.

"Or we wait here and try and wave down the next car that drives past," I continue.

I look at the road ahead of us, then turn around and look back. There are no other cars as far as the eye can see. And we're shifters, so we can see pretty far.

I haven't seen another vehicle since waking up, actually. Which means option two is not really on the table.

"We should walk," I conclude, swinging the car door open with a sigh.

Even though midday has passed, the world outside the air-conditioned car is hot and dry. The sort of heat that radiates through the soles of your shoes and crisps your hair with the efficiency of a hair blow dryer.

I lick my lips, feeling suddenly thirsty just thinking about the small amount of water we have to last us for our hike through the desert.

It's okay, I assure myself as I start to heft essentials into a small backpack. *We're shifters. We're resilient.*

My wolf puffs out her chest a little, bolstered by my pep talk.

Summer follows my example, wordlessly climbing out and packing her own bag. I give her what I hope is a reassuring smile.

"It's okay," I say with false cheerfulness. "We'll stick to the road and maybe someone will drive past and pick us up."

FOUR HOURS later and the sun rests low on the horizon, painting the landscape in fiery oranges and reds.

It would be beautiful, if my mouth wasn't as parched as the rocky soil crunching beneath my sneakers. If my stomach wasn't as empty as the tank in Summer's car.

A car which is now far, far behind us.

Three vehicles have driven past since we've started walking. Two cars and one pick-up truck, to be precise. Of those, not a single one has stopped.

This completely baffles me.

I mean, as a girl you constantly get told how you shouldn't hitch-hike because you'll invariably end up kidnapped and murdered. However, I can now say this is statistically incorrect. Going by the three cars that have flown past us, it's more likely that you won't get picked up at all.

Either these people are heeding the warnings about the dangers of picking up hitchhikers, or they just can't be bothered helping people in need.

The sun finally disappears below the horizon, the last display of bright colours replaced by grey shadow, like a fire giving way to ash when it's extinguished. Almost instantly, the suffocating heat fades, drifting away on an idle, dusty breeze. By the time the grey sky turns black enough to showcase a brilliant display of stars, Summer and I are both shivering.

"M-maybe we s-should find a place to camp for the night," Summer suggests through chattering teeth. "We'd be a lot warmer if we shifted."

I frown, considering.

The temperature seems to be dropping quickly, and neither of us are equipped for the cold. At least, not in human form.

Still, we are shifters. We can take pretty low temperatures, even if we don't shift. We might be uncomfortable, but we won't die.

We do, however, need water. And quickly. The need for water is only going to be worse when the sun rises again.

I shake my head, rubbing my bare arms with my hands to try and warm them.

"We should keep walking," I say. "We're less likely to get dehydrated walking at night than during the day. It makes sense to try and cover as much ground as we can before the sun comes up."

Summer wrinkles her nose in distaste at this suggestion before letting out a defeated sigh.

"Okay. Fine."

Walking doesn't stop Summer from pulling her phone from her pocket every couple minutes, checking for a signal and holding it up in the air, as if giving it a couple extra feet elevation will somehow improve the cell phone coverage. Unsurprisingly, it doesn't.

When she does this for about the twentieth time I finally snap.

"You're going to run out of battery if you keep doing that. Then we won't be able to call anyone once you finally do have reception."

"I told Jason I'd message him when we stopped for the night," Summer explains defensively, pocketing her phone. "He's going to be worried when he doesn't hear from me."

"So what? You can just message him in the morning or whenever we have reception."

We're walking through an unknown desert at night with no water. Jason's feelings are the least of my concerns right now.

"That's true…" Summer muses, frowning.

In the distance, a coyote's yipping howl pierces the icy night air. My wolf lifts her head haughtily, pretending like she doesn't want to let her own voice join with this lesser canine.

She totally does.

"Do you think that's a real coyote," Summer asks, "or a shifter."

"No idea," I admit, cocking my head to one side as I strain to listen to the answering yips echoing the first call. Now that I think about it, there is something in the way the animals are communicating with one another that seems intentional. Intelligent.

The only coyote shifter I've met – at least knowingly – was that coyote shifter from the Blackwater pack who defected and joined Tobias' pack. And I was around him for all of five minutes in human form.

"More likely than not it's a natural animal," I say, voice ringing with more conviction than I feel.

"Hope so," Summer says, her voice lower now, as if she's afraid the coyotes will hear us. "I wouldn't want to accidentally run into a strange pack of shifters in the middle of the night."

No. Neither would I.

I suppress a shudder, thinking of the uncertain fates of all the shifters who were caught trespassing on our territory. Would Summer and I be treated like those shifters were? Like we are nothing less than common criminals, just because we have gone rogue?

This morbid train of thought is interrupted when a pair of headlights suddenly come into view, bright enough that I have to shade my eyes with my hand. As the vehicle approaches, Summer and I scramble to the road, arms waving as we attempt to get the driver's attention.

I send a silent plea up to the shifter gods. *Please stop, please stop, please stop. And please don't be a serial killer.*

After the three earlier rejections, I'm not actually expecting this person to stop. Honestly, I'm not even sure if they'll be able to see us, given how dark it is on this unlit road.

Which means when the car does pull over, I'm so taken aback I just stand awkwardly, staring at the idling car like it's one of those UFO's this part of the country is famous for, instead of an ordinary station wagon.

"You girls need a lift?" a man asks, rolling down the window.

With the glare of the headlights and the surrounding darkness, it's impossible to make out his face. But his voice sounds friendly enough.

"Our car ran out of gas," Summer explains, stepping tentatively towards the man's car.

I can tell she's being careful not to get to close, trying to ascertain the trustworthiness of this man before putting herself in arm's reach.

I move to stand beside her, squinting into the darkened windows of the car. I feel a surge of relief when I see the front passenger and backseat look empty. Trustworthy or not, it would be pretty impossible for one human to overpower two shifters. Even if he had a weapon.

"Any chance you would be able to give us a ride to the closest town so we can buy some gas?" Summer asks.

The man chuckles. "I can do you one better. I've got a spare canister of gas in the back of my car. Always smart to carry extra in these parts. You tell me what direction your car is in and we can get you girls back on the road in no time."

Summer's relief surges through the pack bond, mirroring my own feelings.

"Wow, thank you so much," Summer exclaims, practically lunging for the car door handle.

Despite her haste to get out of the cold, she wisely goes for the back door, not the front passenger door. I nod in silent approval. It will be a lot harder for him to pull anything if we're sitting behind him while he's driving. Still, I follow close behind her, not wanting to risk us getting separated.

The first thing I notice when I get in the car is the overpowering smell of air freshener and leather seats. It's so pungent that, with my wolf sense of smell, I nearly gag the moment I put my head in the car. Which is why I don't notice the other scents until I've pulled the door shut.

Shifter.

And below that, the astringent smell of lies.

TOBIAS FINCH

Despite it being hot enough that Jason's mousy hair is plastered to his forehead, his face is pale, lips pressed together until they are almost white.

I trot over to him, giving grandpa and Jamison a hard look, hoping they aren't the reason Jason is practically trembling with anxiety.

Grandpa just raises one bushy eyebrow, the shadow of a sardonic grin quirking the corner of his lips. I wish I knew what that expression meant. Wish I could communicate with him and Jamison on the pack link. But they are on their own. Outliers, even though we treat them as part of this pack. Their own little pack of two.

"Hey Tobes," Jason says, lowering his eyes when I get close.

I grit my teeth at this behaviour. Ever since that day in the hotel room, when my contact lens came out revealing the golden eye of a born alpha, Jason has treated me with wary respect and deference.

I liked it better when Jason thought I was just an ordinary shifter. A submissive wolf. Someone like him.

"Is everything okay?" I ask.

I'm aware of Cody joining us, taking his usual place at my right-hand side. For the first time in a while, I'm thankful for Cody's presence, if only because it might help Jason feel welcome. Safer.

Jason shakes his head. "No. No, it's not okay."

He looks up at Cody and the barest flicker of relief passes behind Jason's eyes before it's quickly replaced with a look quiet desperation.

"Summer and Lucy are missing."

Those five words detonate like a bomb, destroying the façade of welcoming calm I'd been wearing with the aim of soothing Jason's nervousness.

Missing. Missing. Lucy is missing.

My wolf is howling, raging, clawing to get free. To track down our mate. Find her. Protect her.

"What do you mean?" I ask, aware of my hands trembling at my sides as I struggle to contain my wolf.

Now is not the time to tantrum-shift and give control over to some stupid animal. No, I need to talk. To listen. To plan. To not be a raging fur-beast.

Jason licks his lips but when he opens his mouth to speak, all that comes out is a sort of pained choking sound. His eyes water, and he blinks his eyes furiously to stem the tears before they can fall. Then he looks at Cody, sorrow and panic glinting in his hazel eyes.

"There's an alpha command on you, isn't there?" Cody asks, expression hardening, nostrils flaring in evident distaste. "Dad put some sort of restriction on your talking about something?"

Jason just nods, looking miserable.

"Oh, okay." I frown, looking between Cody and Jason. "Well, is there any way around it? So that you can tell us what's going on?"

"You could order him to tell you," Danny suggests, coming up on my left. "You know, use your born alpha power."

My wolf nods approvingly at the bear, pleased with his suggestion. The wolf also approves of the giant's calming presence. At the way he's always placing himself at our side when the thinks trouble might arise. Never aggressive, but always ready to defend.

Grandpa shakes his head. "That wouldn't work." He gives Jason a pitying look. "Or at least, not in the way you'd want it too. It would override Cooper Winslow's orders, but it wouldn't replace them. So you'd just make Jason here suffocate to death."

Jason shudders, looking at me beseechingly as he says: "Um, yah. Let's not do that, okay?"

My wolf cocks his head, ruthlessly considering whether it would be worth it. Whether Jason would be capable of providing us with some information that would enable us to track down Lucy, or whether he would simply suffocate before he could speak.

"Got it," I say, lifting my hands and forcing a friendly smile. At least, I hope it's friendly-looking. It feels more like a grimace. "No alpha commands from me."

"You could get him to change to your pack though," grandpa suggests. Casually. As if he's talking about trading baseball cards, and not stealing a rival pack's shifter. "That would make any previous alpha commands null and void."

I blink, trying to work out if grandpa is serious. I mean, he doesn't usually joke around. He's not really the joking sort of guy. Now that I think about it, I don't think I've heard him make so much as a pun.

"I don't think that's a good idea," I say carefully, when it dawns on me that grandpa is being serious. "I mean, Jason's family is in the Clear Creek pack. And also, I'm pretty sure that would be a good way to start a pack war."

Jason runs one hand through his hair, biting the inside of his cheek as he keeps his eyes fixed on the ground.

"I – I was actually going to ask if I could join your pack," he murmurs, face flushing red.

My eyebrows shoot up.

"You were?"

He nods, lifting his gaze briefly to meet my own, hazel eyes brimming with a mix of too many emotions to name. I feel an unexpected pang in my chest, the need to protect Jason rising up like tidal waters greeting the full moon.

Pack, my wolf rumbles. *Jason is pack.*

Yah, okay, crazy animal, I silently retort. *You say that about everyone.*

And then I mentally shoulder-check my wolf, shoving him back into the cage I've constructed for him. I imagine it looking somewhat like a dog kennel because after the little stunt he pulled with Lucy, it's safe to say my wolf is going to be in the proverbial dog house for some time.

"Why?" I ask, studying Jason. "Why would you want to join my pack?"

Jason shuffles nervously.

"A lot of reasons," he admits, looking up again to give me a pleading look. "Most of which I can't actually explain given the whole… you know…" he waves one hand, indicating to his throat, presumably referring to whatever gag order alpha Winslow has in place.

I nod.

"Yah. Okay. We'll make you part of the Liberty pack."

Liberty pack.

It's strange hearing the name Gareth and Hamish coined for our pack, especially from my own lips. Still, I can admit there is something nice about the name. Not catchy. Probably not even cool. But comfortable, like an old hoodie you'd never wear to school but love putting on the second you get home.

"You shouldn't do that, alpha," Cody warns, stepping closer from his position at my right. "Your instinct on this was right – it could start a pack war."

I give Cody an exasperated look. It's honestly like the guy is trying to challenge me at every possible opportunity. I don't get it.

"I'm not turning Jason away," I explain, forcing at least the semblance of patience into my tone.

Not an easy feat when my wolf is seething, baring his teeth and demanding to put my pack member in place. My wolf only sees the challenge. I see that too, but I can also see that Cody means well. Of course he wouldn't want a war between his old pack – the pack his family is in – and our pack.

No one wants that.

"If Jason wants to join this pack, he's welcome to. I wouldn't turn anyone away."

I give Cody a pointed look, silently reminding him of my view on this when he protested taking in rogues.

"I especially wouldn't turn away Jason," I add. "He's my friend."

Cody's nostrils flare in clear agitation, but he doesn't argue further.

Danny comes up on my left, pulling a utility knife from his pocket. I feel the ghost of a smile tug the corners of my lips because I can see why some of the other guys teasingly refer to Danny as 'Boy Scout'.

At first, I thought they were saying he was straight-laced and uptight, which just didn't make sense to me, because he's not. Now I'm starting to realise it's because the guy is always prepared. Like, who carries a utility knife? What else does he have in his pockets? Snacks? A first-aid kit? Rope for tying up intruders?

I flick the blade open, quickly running the tip along the inside of my palm, then pass the knife to Jason, handle first. He mirrors my action and I hold out my hand.

"I swear to protect you as a member of my pack," I say simply.

Since accidentally creating this pack, Cody has reminded me on numerous occasions that making an oath to a new alpha is a solemn occasion, usually accompanied by fancy speeches and elaborate promises.

I really don't see the point in all that. Since I'm a born alpha, the pack bond can be created just by exchanging blood and me making a promise to protect. I don't need anyone to promise to obey me.

I can make them obey.

Not that I would.

Jason stares up at me, eyes wide as he takes my hand in his own.

"I swear fealty to you, Tobias Finch, and I swear to protect this pack with my life."

It's more than I would have asked for. My wolf lets out a contented rumble, the beast just as satisfied with the awed expression on Jason's face as the words themselves. Warmth spreads in my chest as the additional thread connecting me to Jason weaves itself into place. I do my best to ignore the surge of power that comes with it, dropping Jason's hand and wiping my bloodied palm on the leg of my worn denim jeans.

I tilt my chin towards the large tent, where nearly all my pack sit at an array of beanbag chairs, tables and folding camp chairs, watching us with unabashed curiosity.

"Come meet the rest of the pack," I say. "And tell me what happened with Lucy and Summer."

Chapter 12

Lucy Stone

The first thing I do is try to open the door and jump out of the back seat of the car, but the door won't open. Neither will the window.

By the time I fully appreciate that Summer and I are locked in the back seat, the car has already taken off down the road, jolting wildly as it careens over potholes.

With escape an impossibility, I follow the only natural course of action available to me. Like any trapped animal, I fight.

"Stop the gods-damned car," I yell, lunging forward in an attempt to reach between the two front seats and grab the driver.

Anticipating my attack, the driver jerks the steering wheel, causing the car to swerve. With my seatbelt off, I'm thrown across the back seat, colliding with Summer before the pair of us crumple against the door, momentarily dazed.

By the time I right myself, readying to try and reach forward again, there is the unmistakable sound of a gun cocking and bullets sliding into a chamber. My blood runs cold and I still, heart thundering as my mind claws wildly for the best course of action.

Fight. Shift. Shift and fight, my wolf demands, her words hammering in time with my heartbeat.

"Sit down and put your seatbelts on," the man orders.

There's enough alpha command in his voice that Summer whimpers, but in the absence of a pack bond, his orders aren't compelling. He might be an alpha, or at least a dominant shifter, but he's not my alpha. Nor is he a born alpha. Not like Tobias.

When neither of us move to obey him, he turns around, looking away from the road to glare at the pair of us, the metal barrel of a gun glinting menacingly in our direction.

"Seatbelts," he says again.

Summer swallows audibly before reaching over with a trembling hand to buckle her seatbelt into place.

While I might concede that he currently has the upper hand, I'm not going to put my seatbelt on just because he says so. Especially when he clearly does not care about safety, given how crazily he was driving, and the minor matter of him not watching the road while waving a gun around. I glare back at him, arms crossed over my chest, contenting myself with this small act of defiance.

He shakes his head, but turns back to the road, holding the wheel with one hand and the handgun with the other.

"Where are you taking us?" I demand.

Silence.

"Who are you?"

More silence.

Summer gives me a beseeching look. One that probably means 'please stop antagonising our kidnapper' but I ignore it. If this guy wants to lock me in a car and threaten me with a gun, I'm going to make it my life's mission to annoy him. At the very least.

I kick the back of his seat.

The stranger chuckles. Actually chuckles. A low rumbling sound that sends a chill down my spine.

"Look, little she-wolf," he says, dark amusement lacing his words, "have a tantrum all you like, it's not going to change a thing. If anything, you should be happy I picked you up. Grateful. I probably saved your lives."

I give a disbelieving snort.

"I'm serious," he says. "There's been some unsavoury characters in these parts. Dangerous rogues. Shifters who would as soon tear you to pieces as look at you. Or worse."

His eyes flick up to meet mine in the rear-view mirror, an unsettling yellowish-green that seem to glow with fanatical fire.

"At least with us, you know you'll be safe," he continues.

The words themselves are laced with enough truth that I know he at least believes what he is saying is true. That, in itself, is unsettling. Almost as unsettling as the fact that this shifter is wearing what looks to be a very expensive suit in the middle of a desert, as if he's stepped out of some mafia film set.

"Really?" I say, raising my eyebrows in challenge. "Is that what the other people you kidnapped at gunpoint told you? That you made them feel safe?"

Summer nudges me in the ribs but I ignore her.

I know it's stupid to antagonise this man. He's armed, at the steering wheel and clearly has a nebulous grasp on reality. Yet for some reason, I can't stop myself.

Maybe it's my wolf. The normally taciturn creature is now a full-blown rage beast from being locked up for months. It's as if all the anger I've been harbouring towards dad, alpha Winslow, even Anton – all of it has chosen this very moment to test the dam I'd so carefully built. I'm barely holding it back.

I'm surprised when the male just tilts his head back and laughs. A rich, throaty laugh that would be disarming if he wasn't using the handgun to tap on the steering wheel at the same time.

"You know, I think I like you," he finally says, laugh tapering off, leaving a coldness in its wake. "What's your name, she-wolf?"

In what might be the only smart thing I've done in months, I press my lips together, refusing to answer.

"Not going to tell me, eh?"

He doesn't sound at all surprised by this obstinance. Instead, he tilts his head, catching Summer's eyes in the rear-view mirror.

"What about you?" he asks Summer. "Do you have a name?"

Summer licks her lips, rubbing her sternum with the palm of her hand, as if she can push back the anxiety rising there.

"Summer," she says, voice catching in her throat. "Summer Green."

The stranger dips his head in acknowledgement, then looks back at the road. Free from the scrutiny of his watchful gaze, I take the opportunity to study him.

Despite the fine wrinkles at the corners of his eyes and the peppering of grey along his temples, he could be described as handsome. His suit is immaculate, hair perfectly styled and a close-trimmed beard highlights his jaw-line. If I could see them, I bet his shoes would be freshly polished. And I doubt they would have been polished by him.

My eyes flick around the dark interior of the car, taking in the leather seats, the high-tech looking screen on the dashboard, the shiny wooden inlay on the inside of the doors. I tilt my head, catching the silver glint of a Mercedes logo on the middle of the steering wheel and resist the urge to roll my eyes. Of course, this guy would drive a Mercedes.

The corner of his lips quirk up in a smug grin, as if he can feel me looking at him and he's confident that I will approve of whatever I see.

"I'm Drake," he says. "Drake Zmey."

I frown. *Drake.* I've heard that name before. Where have I heard that name before?

"I'm the prime of the Monument Lair."

The prime. Lair.

My eyes widen, lips parting in surprise as it dawns on me where I've heard his name before. I'm pretty sure Drake was the shifter who, along with Huxley Black, Tania had said she'd been running from.

Drake notices my surprise and smirks.

"I take it you've heard of us. Now you see why I said you girls were lucky to be picked up by me?" he says. "These are troubling times for shifters. Troubling times. And we're the biggest lair in the country. Who better to keep you two safe?"

Safe.

I wrinkle my nose at that word and glance accusingly at the car door. At the child-lock that is keeping me trapped inside. I've been free for less than twenty-four hours and here I am, being held prisoner by another alpha. Prime. Whatever.

Only now, I have no idea what Drake's agenda is, what he plans to do with us. And it's not just me at risk, it's Summer too.

TOBIAS FINCH

"Wait. So you're telling us you haven't heard anything from Summer or Lucy since noon yesterday?" Cody asks, leaning forward on his camping chair until his elbows rest on his knees.

"Um. Yah, that's pretty much it," Jason replies with a grimace.

He's perched awkwardly on a beanbag chair, eyes darting nervously between me and Cody. As an omega, no doubt he can sense the unspoken tension running between the pair of us.

While I don't like the fact that no one has heard from Summer or Lucy since yesterday, I'm still stuck on the fact that Lucy was basically kept prisoner by her dad and then alpha Winslow. My wolf is raging, frantic at the thought that Lucy was being mistreated, that she was unhappy, and we did nothing about it.

"Where were they when you last heard from them?"

"Grand Junction," Jason says. Then, no doubt sensing my confusion, adds, "Colorado." He rubs the back of his neck with one hand. "They were on their way to Southern California. I think the plan was to meet up with Tori's pack or something. I'm not really sure."

"Then they could be anywhere," I point out. "They could already be in California."

Jason shakes his head. "No. Summer promised she'd check in at least three times a day. She was supposed to message me when they stopped for the night."

I pull out my phone, frowning at the screen as I pull up Grand Junction on the map, then try to work out what road they would take from there to get to California.

"They would have taken the I-70?" I ask, squinting at the screen. "And then the I-15 through Vegas?"

"Yah," Jason nods. "Probably. That's the most direct route."

I look at the two roads snaking across the lower half of Utah and my frown deepens.

If what Jason is saying is right, then Lucy and Summer have gone missing somewhere in Southern Utah.

Huxley Black is in Southern Utah. Near a tiny town called Hanksville, according to the text Hamish sent me about an hour ago with their location.

While I know it's a massive part of the country, I can't stand the thought of Lucy being within a hundred-mile radius of Huxley Black.

Actually, I don't want her in the same state as Huxley Black.

"And you didn't want to report this to my dad?" Cody asks, glowering at Jason. "They've been missing since yesterday and you didn't let anyone from their pack know?"

Jason gapes at him, mouth opening and closing like a fish as he visibly pales. I round on Cody, barely able to clamp down on the anger flaring in my chest, hot as wildfire on dry grass.

"You're kidding me, right?" I snap, rising to my feet. I'm aware of the plastic chair tumbling back behind me, of the sound of voices murmuring at my sudden outburst. "Jeb and your dad kept Lucy locked up and put a gag order on Jason and Summer so no one would know what was happening. Then Summer literally broke Lucy out, like a shifter-version of Shawshank Redemption. In what world do you think it would make sense for Jason to report anything to your dad?"

Cody crosses his arms, tilting his chin up at me defiantly.

"Dad is Jason's alpha. He's all of their alpha. He has a right to know. Not to mention, Clear Creek pack have the resources to search for them."

I feel my upper lip curling, exposing my teeth, the expression more wolf than man.

"The only right your dad has as alpha is to protect his pack. Which he clearly sucks at doing, at least where Lucy is concerned."

My voice has dropped in pitch, becoming a low rumble that belongs as much to my wolf as me and I can feel my wolf pushing for supremacy. The need to shift and challenge Cody right now, in the middle of my pack, in the middle of this tent, it's almost unbearable.

And completely impossible, given the group of human construction workers on the other side of the strand of trees.

I take a deep breath, willing myself to calm, demanding my wolf stay contained. The last thing I need right now is my psychopathic animal running the show.

"This isn't just about Lucy," Cody argues, his voice raising in pitch. "Summer is missing too and dad could help find her."

Jason shakes his head, making a few stuttered sounds before finding his voice.

"I-I'm sorry Cody, but that's the last thing Summer would want. Your dad is really pissed at her right now. At both of them." Jason swallows audibly, then adds: "He's probably pissed at me too, if he's figured out I was involved. Which he probably has by now, since I've left the pack."

Jason gives a faint shudder, then continues with a tremulous sigh.

"If alpha Winslow tracked them down, it would only be to punish them. Summer and Lucy both. So yah, giving your dad information just wasn't an option. That's why I came here."

Orrin comes up behind Jason, resting one giant hand on Jason's shoulder as he fixes Cody with a hard look.

"You did the right thing, kid. Don't let Cody get to you. I'm sure he's just upset to hear the girls have gone missing, so he isn't thinking straight."

Cody's nostrils flare imperceptibly, but he doesn't say anything.

Red saunters over, leaning against one of the plastic folding tables, surveying our small group with an exaggerated yawn. Most of the pack have wandered back to the main lodge to grab lunch or to see if the construction crew needs help.

"We should just hit the road already," Red suggests, table creaking under his weight. "The sooner we get to Rockville or Huntsville, or whatever the backwater town is we're meeting Hamish and Gareth at, the better."

"Hanksville," Cody snaps irritably.

"What?" Red looks at him quizzically.

"Hanksville. The name of the town is Hanksville."

"Oh. Right." Red shrugs, lips quirking upwards. "Whatever it's called, we should stop wasting time nattering like a bunch of old women…"

"Nattering?" Samson snickers from behind him. "What are you, like eighty?"

Red narrows his eyes, but doesn't deign to respond.

"We need to meet up with Hamish and Gareth to figure out the plan for dealing with Huxley Black," Red says, fixing his eyes on me, completely ignoring his younger brother. "I know you guys are worried about Summer and Lucy, but we aren't going to help them by sitting here talking about things."

I clench my jaw. As far as I'm concerned, the fact that Lucy and Summer are missing is just as big a problem as Huxley Black. Bigger, if I'm being honest.

Red must see my annoyance because his expression softens. I remember then that he knows Lucy and Summer too. He spent days traveling with them, camping with them. He fought alongside them.

"Look, I want to find them too," Red says, looking almost uncomfortable at the admission. As if being caught caring about someone else's wellbeing is a fatal character flaw. "But if they did go missing in Southern Utah, then we have a better chance of finding out what happened to them if we are down there too. We aren't going to be much use to them here in Buffalo."

"Yah, okay," I say tersely, forced to acknowledge the logic in what he's saying. Even if it feels wrong to keep pursuing the plan to get Huxley Black when Lucy is missing.

Our mate, my wolf reminds me. *She's our mate.*

Cody gives an annoyed huff and rises from his seat.

"Guess I better go pack. Wouldn't want to slow us down or anything."

There's no missing the sardonic edge to his voice and I stare at his back for a long moment, watching him stalk through the long grass of the meadow before he disappears into the trees. Then I look over at Jason.

He's sunk into the beanbag chair, knees drawn up to his chest, looking as if he's hoping he can disappear into its pillowy depths. I get that now familiar pang just above my sternum. The ache to protect, to do everything I can to make the members of my pack happy.

"You can come with us if you want," I tell Jason, hating the thought of leaving him alone with a bunch of strangers.

I mean, I know they're his new pack now, technically. But the truth is, he doesn't really know any of them.

"We could use your help with whatever the plan is for Huxley Black," I continue. "And if you're with us, we have a better chance of finding out what happened with Lucy and Summer."

Especially since I'm still hoping that Summer just lost her phone or something. Maybe there is some mundane reason why Summer hasn't been in touch with Jason.

Maybe we'll go to Southern Utah and get a call from her while we're looking for Huxley Black.

"Um," Jason blinks up at me in surprise, then gives a weak smile. "Sure. Yah. That'd be great."

Chapter 13

Cody Winslow

Unbelievable. Un-freaking-believable.

Summer and Lucy are missing and all Tobias cares about is getting revenge on Huxley Black.

My stomach twists at the thought. Summer. My Summer. Missing somewhere in the vast space between here and California.

I know this must be Lucy's fault. Summer would never have abandoned the Clear Creek pack on her own.

Abandoned me.

I'm so caught up in my anger that several minutes pass before I realize I've walked past the RV I share with Tobias, my feet carrying me into the dense pine forest to the west of what will one day be the main residential centre of the Liberty pack.

I look back at the scene. RVs are scattered around the large clearing. Bikes, cars and trucks parked randomly between them. Beyond the RVs is the construction site, with freshly-laid foundation and framing clearly marking where the massive lodge will stand.

I feel a surge of pride looking at it, the bones of a structure that, until now, has only existed on paper. I've poured nearly every waking moment of the past few months into bringing this project into fruition. Worked with architects and draftsmen, organised contractors and sub-contractors. Looked over building schedules and regulations on my tablet until my vision blurred. Picked out tile and paint colours and doorhandles.

I've done everything that Tobias couldn't be bothered doing.

And still, he won't name me as his beta. Insists on having this egalitarian system where some rogue who joined a few days ago is on the same level as me, regardless of my contribution.

I should have been alpha. Would have been, if not for Tobias.

Instead, I am here, being dragged along on a hunt for Huxley Black when I should be looking for Summer. Tobias knows what she means to me. Who she is to me. But I guess hard work and loyalty don't mean anything in this pack.

Above me, storm clouds gather, quickly blotting out the sun and thickening the air with ether and charged humidity. Moments later, thunder rumbles, an echo of my own discontent.

In this part of Wyoming, summer storms can roll in with as little ceremony as a neighbour making a house call. Still, my mind instantly goes to the job site, worrying that rain could cause delays in the finely crafted building schedule.

I shouldn't worry about it. It should be Tobias' problem. This is his pack, after all.

But I can't. My instinct, my education, every lesson I absorbed ensconced in the leather couches of my dad's office – everything I am demands that I care. That I take charge. That I do what is required to protect the pack.

Even if it's not my pack. Not really.

My wolf whimpers at the thought, ears drooping, tail hanging low.

Just then, my phone rings, cutting through the dark train of thought, jolting me back to the lonely pines and the smell of distant rain on the foothills.

I pull my phone from my pocket, then stare at the number on the screen.

Dad.

Several long moments pass before my brain is able to tell my trembling hands to answer the call. When I do, my voice catches in my throat.

"Hello?"

"Cody." Dad's voice is clipped, and I can practically see him pacing his office. "We need to talk."

I wait in expectant silence, knowing better than to push him to speak, but practically vibrating with the need to hear his voice. Hear the news he has of Summer. Because this has to be about Summer. What else could it be?

"We've got a situation," he says. "Some of our pack members have gone missing."

My nostrils flare, furious at the matter-of-fact way he is speaking about this. He knows what Summer is to me. He knows.

"Now, I don't doubt you've got a good idea about where they have gone. So I'm only going to tell you this once." His tone hardens, the rumble of his wolf coming through his voice as anger gets the better of him. "We will not hesitate to strike out at your pack for stealing our females. Think of this as a courtesy call. Me giving you a chance to have them returned to us."

I blink in confusion, thinking for a long moment that he's referring to Tania, the only female member of our pack. And then it dawns on me.

He thinks we have Summer and Lucy.

I take a deep breath, running my hand over my face in frustration. Now, not only are Summer and Lucy missing, but we could be on the brink of a pack war. A completely pointless pack war. And of course, like everything else, it falls to me to do something about it.

"We don't have them," I say. "I just found out a couple hours ago that they are missing, but I swear we don't have them. I don't even know where they are."

There is a long, heavy silence on the line, and I can practically hear the violent machinations of dad's thoughts as he tries to discern whether what I am saying is true or not.

"Is that so?" he asks. There is so much bitter disbelief in those three words that I almost flinch, as if he's struck me.

"I swear it."

Surely he knows me well enough to know I would never lie to him.

There is a disgruntled rumble on the other end. It sounds like a reluctant acknowledgement before he says: "Tell me what you know."

So I do. I tell him everything.

I tell him about Jason showing up and swearing over to our pack. I tell him about Summer and Lucy's plan to go to California and how they went missing sometime after Colorado. How we suspect they could be somewhere in Southern Utah - which is not exactly useful intel, but at least it's something.

I know it might be wrong, but I tell him about Huxley Black and the plan to go to some remote area near Hanksville and draw him out. I tell him about my anger at the alpha's decision, how I think we should be working to track down Summer and Lucy instead.

As the words tumble out, they don't feel like a betrayal. They feel like me asking my dad for help. Seeking out the guidance I should have had as I became alpha of my own pack. Because he's the only one who really knows what I feel for Summer.

I've never felt more alone than I do now, in the midst of this pack of lost boys, under the rule of an alpha who doesn't want to lead. Rejected by my old pack, pushed away by my own family.

I haven't clicked with any of the pack. Sure, they respect me. But I miss having friendship. Real friends, who my wolf can lean against and play with and run with.

Strange as it is, the wolf that I'm probably closest to is Jamison. Maybe because he also knows what it is like to be born to lead, but have no pack. To be part of a pack, but on the outside. To give everything you have, and get nothing in return.

More than anything, I want my dad to help me make sense of everything.

"I'm sorry to hear that," dad says when I finish. His voice is unusually soft, almost sympathetic sounding. "It's an unfair position for Tobias to put you in." He gives a long sigh, then adds: "It just goes to show the danger of having a born alpha rule. Like I've always said, it isn't birth that makes someone able to lead. They need training in order to make the right judgement calls."

I can't remember dad ever saying this, actually. But I'm not about to argue this now. Not when he's finally speaking to me like I'm his son, not the enemy.

"I want to help you," he continues. "I know what Summer means to you. Not to mention, she's a valued member of our pack."

I frown, unable to ignore the scepticism rising at this claim as I recall Jason's concerns.

"You wouldn't want to punish her for running away? For helping Lucy escape?" I ask.

Dad gives another long sigh, then says: "We both know Summer is a submissive wolf. No doubt Lucy bullied the poor girl into helping her escape. I doubt she would have come up with such an elaborate plan on her own. Who knows what Lucy said or threatened?"

Dad's words echo my own suspicions and I grit my teeth at the thought of Summer being threatened. Coerced. Forced away from the safety of her pack.

"What should I do?" I ask, the question falling effortlessly from my lips.

It feels so natural to ask dad for advice, as comfortable as running beside him under the full moon or slipping into his office after school. Just hearing his voice, knowing he wants to help me – it's like the sweetest balm on the ache I've been harbouring for months.

"Well..."

I can hear dad's footsteps in the responding silence. The tapping of his boots on the wooden floor of his office. I can tell from that sound alone that he's pacing. Thinking.

"You should go with your alpha to Hanksville," he finally says. "Help him draw out Huxley Black. After what Huxley did to you and Anton, it's only sensible to neutralise that particular threat to shifter society."

"Okay..."

I can't help but be disappointed at this. It might be wrong, especially given what Huxley did to Anton, but I could care less about getting revenge. Not when every molecule of my being is aching to track down Summer. To keep her safe. To have her close to me.

Dad must sense this, because there is the edge of a smile in his voice as he says: "Now hear me out. I know you want to get to Summer as soon as possible, but you also don't know where she is, except that she might be in Southern Utah somewhere. If you go with Tobias to Hanksville, you'll only be closer to where you need to be to start looking for her."

I nod, conceding the logic in this. It's basically what Orrin and Red said. Still, my wolf growls that this is an unnecessary delay.

"Then, once you've taken care of Huxley Black, we can send a contingent to come and meet you."

"You'll help me find Summer?" I ask, eyes flying wide in surprise at this unexpected offer.

Dad doesn't answer, instead says: "Son. You remember our last conversation? You remember what I said to you the last time you were home?"

My blood chills, stomach churning as I recall that horrible day. When dad banished me from Clear Creek territory. When dad banned me from talking to Summer outside of school.

"Of course I remember," I say, the ice in my voice matching the cold that suddenly seeps down my arms, to my fingertips.

"Do you remember what I asked of you? What I asked you to do?"

I swallow.

"You know he's a danger to our whole society," dad continues. "You know what needs to be done before you can be with Summer again."

I close my eyes, leaning against one of the gnarled pines chilling this part of the forest, relishing the rough feel of the bark on my skin. If only because it brings me back to now. To here.

I don't want to think of what dad asked of me all those months ago. I've ignored it. Pushed it away. But now…

"What you're asking… that's a coward's way," I argue, the words stilted as I try to articulate the wrongness of his demand. "I'm not a murderer. Not some assassin."

"No. Of course you aren't."

I can't tell if these words are meant to be placatory or taunting.

"I'm not asking you to murder him in his sleep," dad continues. "I'm just asking you to help us help you. Let us know where you plan to intercept Huxley Black, then we can come and meet you.

We can take care of Tobias. With him distracted and out in the open, it will be best opportunity we have to get to him."

I press my hand to my stomach, suddenly feeling sick.

"I don't like it."

"Of course you don't," dad snaps. "But sometimes being an alpha means doing things you don't like. Or have you forgotten that while you've been off gallivanting with that joke of a pack?"

I bristle at the unfairness of this. All I've done the past few months is work tirelessly for this pack. I've given up everything for it. Given up the position I was born to. Given up Summer.

"You don't have to lift a finger. Don't even have to be there if you don't want to," dad continues. "All I'm asking is for information. Coordinates."

"What about the other guys?" I ask. "I don't want anyone to get hurt."

Dad gives an irritated huff. "Listen to yourself, Cody. Are you a dog, eager to please your master? Or are you a wolf?"

My wolf whimpers, ears lying flat against his skull. *Wolf*, the animal whispers. *Always a wolf. Always his son.*

When I don't answer, his voice softens and he says: "I just want to help you, son. I just want to see you home again. You deserve to have your birth-right. You deserve to have Summer by your side. You want that, don't you?"

A lump rises in my throat, choking off the possibility of any response. Dad continues.

"Your mom misses you, you know. She hasn't been the same since you left. You have no idea what it's like for her. You're all that she has."

Heat burns behind my eyes at those words. At the unspoken reminder of the brothers and sisters I should have had, if fate had been kinder. At the pups taken from this world before they could draw their first breath, some before I was born and some after.

"Just let us help you come home. Give us the information we need to take care of Tobias Finch for you, and then we'll help you get Summer back. You can both come home. Who knows, maybe you'll even be mated when she finishes High School next year."

There's no ignoring the hot tears that track down my cheeks now, betraying me with longing for the picture he's painting.

And then he says the words that seal my fate. For better or worse.

"I love you, son."

A sob rips from my chest, and suddenly, I'm a little boy again. A child held in the strong arms of the man I've idolised, back when he was more god to me than father.

How many times have I sought those words since I was old enough to understand them? How many times has he given me silence instead?

"Okay," I croak out, barely intelligible. "Okay. I'll do it."

Chapter 14

Tobias Finch

I don't think I've ever been anywhere as hot as this place. And that's saying a lot, because New York summers are notorious.

Also, this little town in the middle of nowhere in Utah makes Buffalo look like a thriving metropolis. As far as I can tell, the only purpose of this place is to serve as a base for people to visit Capitol Reef, one of the least visited National Parks in the country.

Hidden gem. That is what they are calling it.

Well, it's hidden alright.

As I survey the landscape surrounding Hanksville, I can easily imagine dragons living here. Or at least, dragon shifters.

"Roll the window back up," Red complains from the front passenger seat. "It's hot as balls out there."

Orrin gives an answering chuckle from the driver's seat before taking a bite of one of the venison meat-sticks he insisted on carting with him from Wyoming.

Reluctantly, I roll up the window, letting the stifling air from the truck's air-conditioning unit cool the cramped space. I wrinkle my nose at the stale scent of shifter-sweat, meat-sticks, fast-food containers and soda. Beside me, Jason squirms in the middle seat. His obvious discomfort yet again reminding me to feel guilty about having a window seat.

I had offered to trade with him, but he refused, looking meaningfully at Cody. Cody, who is currently staring out the other window, maintaining his sulky silence. Cody, who has barely spoken two words to me since we left pack territory.

I guess Jason feels like he needs to be physical a barrier between us.

It's easy enough to find the motel, since it's one of a handful of little buildings scattered like blocks in the endless dusty terrain.

"Doesn't look like much," Cody comments as he climbs out of the truck, frowning dubiously at the motel before pausing to stretch. He pulls out his phone, tapping out a quick text, then slips it back into his pocket.

"Everything okay with the site?" I ask, assuming he's messaging one of the contractors.

I might have been a bit slack on the whole getting our pack buildings built thing, but I want to make up for it now. Make sure he knows that he doesn't have to do everything on his own.

He looks at me blankly for a moment before giving me a curt nod, then turns his back to me.

I sigh as Jason looks anxiously between me and Cody.

At least I tried, right?

"Let's get our bags inside," Orrin suggests. "Shouldn't linger out in the open too long. Never know who could drive past."

I look at the road outside the motel and the near empty parking lot, then quirk a brow at him. Still, I do as he suggests because I can feel the heat radiating up from the asphalt, as if it's trying to cook me alive through my shoes.

I raise my fist to knock on the door of room nine, only to have Hamish fling it open, his eyes squinting against the afternoon sun as he looks us over and ushers us in.

"Took you long enough," Hamish says, crossing his tattooed arms over his chest as he leans against the TV stand in the corner of the room. Gareth tilts his chin at us as we enter, though he looks half-asleep seated on the room's only chair, one booted foot resting across his knee.

When Jason comes in, both Gareth and Hamish tense, a sharpness that wasn't there before entering their features. Hamish lifts the corner of his upper lip in what could just as easily be called a snarl as a grin. Gareth merely opens his eyes, looking suddenly alert.

"What is he doing here?" Hamish asks, pointing one accusatory finger at Jason.

The movement only serves to draw attention to the intimidating swirl of colours trailing up Hamish's arms from his fingertips to his neck, reaching all the way to his jawline. Jason's eyes flare wide at the sight of Hamish's tattoos, and I can't say I blame him.

With our preternatural healing abilities, ordinary tattoos don't last on shifters. Silver is required to slow the healing process long enough for the ink to stain the skin. Unsurprisingly, this process is painful enough that very few shifters opt to get tattoos, or if they do, they only get small ones.

After being hit by one solitary silver bullet not too long ago, I have a whole new appreciation for the unfathomable pain Hamish would have subjected himself to in order to get his ink.

"He's part of our pack now." I give them both a hard look as I toss my duffel bag down on garishly patterned carpet. "So save the posturing, okay. We don't have time for it."

The words burst forth, laced with more alpha command than I have a right to use towards my pack members, and I feel instantly guilty.

I guess after being stuck in that truck for hours, marinating in the wordless tension that has escalated between Cody and me, I have completely lost the ability to be patient or tactful. Or maybe it is the constant humming fear over what has happened to Lucy and Summer.

Hamish lifts one brow, but weirdly seems more impressed than offended by my outburst.

"Glad to see being alpha hasn't gone to your head or anything," Gareth drawls, pressing his lips together in an attempt to suppress a smile.

"Sorry," I sigh, running one hand through my tangled mass of hair. "We've driven through the night to get here and I've been stuck in the car with these jerks. Not to mention, a lot has happened since our call yesterday, okay."

"What happened?" Hamish asks, muscles rippling under his t-shirt as he straightens, eyes flashing with savage alertness.

"Summer and Lucy have gone missing," Cody blurts out. "They went missing a few days ago, and might be in Southern Utah somewhere."

There is no mistaking the edge of panic in Cody's voice. It mirrors my own growing sense of unease, adding fuel to it like kindling in a fire. I do my best to tamp it down, to ignore the mournful howling of my wolf as the beast claws at the cage I've built around him.

Lucy. We need to find Lucy, the animal pleads.

"We need to look for them. Organise a search party or something," Cody continues, voice rising in pitch.

It's the most he's spoken since we've left Buffalo, and in the periphery, I'm aware of Orrin and Red unloading their bags and shifting awkwardly, clearly uncomfortable by Cody's sudden effusiveness.

Gareth cocks one head to the side, surveying Cody with mild curiosity.

"Aren't Summer and Lucy from the Clear Creek pack?"

Cody levels a glare at his pack mate but gives a curt nod.

"So shouldn't the Clear Creek Pack be looking for them?" Gareth asks. "I mean, it sucks they have gone missing. But I don't really see how it's our problem, you know."

My wolf snarls at Gareth's callus dismissal and I open my mouth, prepared to spout out some reprimand, then pause. I haven't told anyone about what Lucy is to me. Sure, they know I like her. It wasn't exactly a secret that my wolf ran all the way to Clear Creek territory and tried to blackmail her into going out with me.

But no one knows that she is my mate. Not even her.

If I'm being honest, I don't think it's a fact I've been ready to address.

My wolf might be ready to claim her, mark her as our own and drag her back to the Liberty pack territory where he can put her in his den and keep her safe forever and ever, whether she likes it or not. But we've already established that my wolf has serious issues when it comes to judgment and appropriate social boundaries. I mean, the animal is also perfectly fine with collecting pack members like they're baseball cards.

Or going on killing sprees.

I shudder, squeezing my eyes shut in an effort to block out the unwanted images of the blood-stained snow at Blackwater.

To my surprise, it's Jason that responds, silencing Cody with one trembling hand as he steps to the center of the room.

"With respect," Jason says, raising his eyes to meet Gareth's own in an uncharacteristically assertive move, "it's more complicated than that."

As Jason explains the events leading up to Lucy and Summer's escape from Clear Creek territory, I watch Hamish and Gareth's expressions change from surprise, to respect, to simmering anger.

Hamish looks practically gleeful when Jason describes how he and Summer set a contained wildfire above the Clear Creek ranch to create a diversion for Summer and Lucy's escape.

"That was a good move," Hamish says, tilting his head towards Jason with respect. "Wish I could have seen their faces when they realised Summer and Lucy were missing."

"It was a dangerous move," Cody snaps. "Could have burnt the whole damned forest down."

Jason winces, but Hamish waves one hand dismissively. "Nah, not with the fire barriers and the choppers. It sounds like Jason here knew what he was doing."

"It was stupid and reckless," Cody counters petulantly.

From his seat across the room, Gareth narrows his eyes at Cody, studying him with an unreadable expression on his face.

"They didn't have much of an alternative," Gareth says finally, rubbing the light stubble on his jaw contemplatively. "Who knows what they would have done to Lucy if Summer hadn't helped her escape."

"Summer shouldn't have been helping Lucy escape in the first place," Cody snaps, nostrils flaring. He turns an accusatory glare on Jason. "You should have stopped her. Should have left Lucy for my dad to handle. She betrayed the pack and now Summer is out there somewhere…" Cody waves one hand wildly towards the curtained window of the cramped motel room. "Now who knows what has happened to her. All because of Lucy."

This time, the fury erupts from me before I can tamp it down.

"Don't blame Lucy!" I growl, striding forward until I'm facing Cody. Without thinking, I shove at his chest, causing him to topple onto the bed behind him.

He's momentarily swallowed up in the layers of patchwork quilts and lacy pillows, staring up at me with his face contorted in rage. I move forward, fists raised, ready to defend the attack I know is coming - only to feel strong arms banding around my torso, the scent of berries and venison meat sticks filling my nostrils as Orrin hauls me back.

Gareth and Hamish are on Cody in the same moment, creating a barrier between the pair of us.

"Can you two just settle down already?" Jason pleads. He's taken up a position away from the fray, back pressed against the door, eyes wild as he looks between me and Cody. "You guys have been fighting since we left and it's not helping anyone."

"Agreed," Red says, shoving past everyone to get to the coffee maker at the far end of the room. "You dogs are reminding me every day why I don't really do packs."

He turns his back to us dismissively, attention ostensibly fixed on finding the coffee filters and starting the coffee machine. The distracting move has the immediate effect of draining the tension from the room and, as I watch his tufted cat-ears flick irritably in our direction, I can't help but wonder if that was his intention.

"Jason is right," Orrin rumbles from behind me, his arms like bands of steel around my shoulders. "Fighting isn't going to help anyone find Summer or Lucy. You pups need to calm down. They'll be plenty of chance to let your aggression out in the coming days."

I nod, and feel Orrin's grip on me loosen.

"Yah. Fine," Cody bites out, then shoulders past Gareth and Hamish, striding angrily to the small bathroom and shutting himself inside.

When he's gone, Gareth and Hamish exchange a look and I can feel various levels of wary discontent flooding across the pack bond from both of them. As I stare at the bathroom door, I can't help but wonder if Red and Orrin were right and maybe Cody is giving information to the Clear Creek Pack after all.

"We need to talk about the plan," Gareth says, sitting back in the armchair.

The rest of us follow his lead – Jason and I perching on the edge of one of the two beds, Orrin sitting heavily on the other, Red leaning beside the coffee maker and Hamish sitting against the TV stand.

When we are all comfortable, Gareth gives a wolfish grin and asks: "You boys ever trapped rats before?"

Chapter 15

Lucy Stone

"What do you think are the chances of someone coming to rescue us?"

Summer is laying face up on the bed we've been sharing for the past two days, one arm draped across her eyes to block out the glaring morning sun. I shoot her a pitying smile.

"Do you want the real answer, or the one that will make you feel better about things?" I ask, throwing the covers off and climbing out of bed. This earns a disgruntled grumble from Summer, who rolls over to one side, giving me her back.

As I sit on the edge of the bed, I slowly take in my surroundings.

The cramped room with roughcast walls that look like whitewashed stucco, rounded in the corners to give the room an almost cave-like feel. One small window which must be pointed directly east, given the way the morning sun shines through it like a high beam. A very small connected bathroom. An empty closet. And this bed.

Oh. And of course, a door that appears to be reinforced with steel, which we do not have the key to.

No television. Definitely no internet. Not even a used paperback to help pass the time.

"I think the better question is what are their plans for us?" I say when Summer doesn't reply. "Besides joining their lair and assimilating. Whatever that means."

I give a derisive snort at that because, yah. No way in Leto's underworld am I joining this lair. I barely got away from the Clear Creek pack.

I close my eyes, wishing for one of my visions to come and give me some indication of what is going to happen. What I need to do.

But there is nothing. The newest manifestation of my gift has been oddly silent since our escape. Not even a whisper of the past, present or future.

No doubt this is contributing to Summer's low mood. Ever since I told her about the visions, she's been asking me almost daily if I've seen anything for our future. The fact that I haven't – the fact that my gift has been silent when we need it the most – I think it has disappointed her.

A knock on the door startles me from my reverie, but I quickly relax when the rattling of keys and clinking of plates on the opposite side tells me it's just the elderly shifter tasked with delivering us our meals.

Sure enough, the old male hobbles in, bending awkwardly under the weight of a large tray laden with plates of eggs on toast, bacon, sausages and – thank the gods – coffee. I give him a tight smile, nodding to the small bedside table.

Not like there is any other available surface to put the tray on.

His answering smile is broad, showcasing a couple of missing teeth. I'm aware of Summer sitting up beside me, the bed shifting as she turns to face our daily visitor.

"Good morning, Karen," she says cheerily, tossing the messy length of brown hair over one shoulder.

The male's smile falters. "Name's not Karen," he replies, sliding the tray onto the table.

Summer just beams at him, giving him that intentionally annoying smile I've seen her use on my dad and alpha Winslow so many times before.

"Well, feel free to tell us your real name," she says, leaning across the bed to grab a cup of coffee from the tray. "Or why we are being kept here. Or anything really."

She takes a long sip from her mug, giving an exaggerated groan of pleasure at what we both know is probably cheap instant coffee.

"Delicious as always," she says, tone full of simpering sarcasm as she bats her eyelashes up at him. "And such great service."

The elderly male presses his lips together in an attempt at looking disapproving, but I can tell he's trying to suppress a smile. I'm just relieved to see Summer coming back to life, resorting to cheerful antagonistic quips instead of silently crying.

"Look, you know I can't tell you girls anything," the male says, glancing nervously over his shoulder to the open door behind him. "Under strict instructions, you know."

"Oh, come on," Summer retorts. "What are we going to do? We're locked in here, you know."

He responds with a dejected sigh, then shuffles towards us, giving one lingering glance to the door behind him. Dropping his voice to a low whisper, he says conspiratorially: "If I tell you something, you can't let on you heard anything from me, okay?"

Summer nods emphatically.

“You can count on our silence,” I assure him solemnly.

His answering smile is watery, even as his eyes flicker nervously towards the door.

“You girls don’t have anything to worry about,” he whispers. “No one is going to hurt you. Not at this lair. We’re just short females here, and Drake hasn’t been able to recruit any new ones. You’ll be presented to his top fighters as potential mates.”

He says this last bit as if he’s just announced that we’re being given cake for breakfast.

At Summer’s horrified squeak, he steps forward. “They’re all eligible bachelors,” he rushes on, palms up and eyes wide. “And I can assure you, after the challenges take place, you’ll be paired with the best.”

“A mate?” Summer sputters, nearly dropping her coffee. “These males… they’re going to challenge each other to take us as… mates? What in the actual…”

“Shh.” He hushes her, waving one hand in a frantic plea for her to be silent.

Summer complies, not wanting to get the male in trouble. Instead, she contents herself with glaring up at him and mouthing a very clear “no”.

I must look equally unimpressed because he glances between us before shrugging apologetically, even as he furrows his brow in confusion.

“Just the messenger,” he mutters, backing warily out of the room as he adds, “Thought you girls would be pleased.”

“Pleased?” Summer practically squawks after the door shuts behind him.

The sound of her voice drowns out the ominous snicking of what I’m sure must be an industrial strength lock. Something tells me my paltry lock-picking skills wouldn’t work here, even if I had the tools.

"Why on earth would we be pleased about being auctioned off to be mates to some dragon brutes?"

"They might not be dragons," I point out sagely, thinking of the Blackwater pack with its motley mix of shifter species. "And it doesn't sound like we're being auctioned off. I think we're prizes or something."

"And that is better how, exactly?" Summer cries.

I sigh.

It's not better. Maybe it's worse, actually. Because whatever males have the privilege of picking us are bound to be the most powerful of what is likely to be a dangerous group of shifters.

"I'll tell you what it is," Summer continues, brown eyes blazing with untamed fire. "It's the product of centuries of misogynistic practices in the shifter world. Like, I can't even say I'm surprised, really. Pissed, sure. But not surprised. It's only a step away from what the Clear Creek pack does. Telling Jason he can't mate with a human. Trying to get Cody to transfer to some South Dakota pack to strengthen bloodlines."

I open my mouth to object, the need to protect the Clear Creek pack still my first instinct, then fall silent. Summer gives me a knowing look.

"You know I'm right," she says, voice softening with unspoken sympathy. "Your dad literally locked you up so he could arrange some mating with a complete stranger. That is pretty much the same as what is happening here. As in, it's absolutely barbaric. Like, dark ages barbaric."

She pauses, cocking her head thoughtfully, then adds: "No, actually that was worse, because he's your dad. He's supposed to protect you, have your back. At least this Drake guy is a complete stranger. So there's that."

I feel unwelcome sting of tears pricking behind my eyes and look away, not wanting her to see the impact of her words as the reality of dad's betrayal washes over me.

Not just dad, but Anton.

My breath hitches at this jarring realisation. Anton betrayed me. Anton, who knew what was happening every step of the way. Anton, who expected me to sacrifice my own happiness so he could move to be closer to his true mate and follow his dreams of playing college football.

My wolf whimpers, laying her ears flat and resting her chin on her paws.

"Sorry," Summer whispers, reaching across the bed to pat my shoulder.

The touch is tentative, as if she isn't sure whether I'll turn and snap at her for the gesture. I'm not angry at her though. I know Summer didn't mean to be hurtful. She's just being Summer, speaking every thought that crosses her mind without any filter.

"It's fine," I lie, resisting the urge to shrug off her touch.

The last thing I want to do is make Summer cry. I've seen enough of her crying the past couple days to last me a lifetime.

Instead, I give her a tight smile, swallowing down the roiling anger. Anger that tastes more and more like sorrow.

This isn't the time for weakness.

"We'll figure out a way to get out of here," I assure her, placing my own hand over her own, voice steady with a confidence I don't feel. "At least now we know what to expect."

THE NEXT COUPLE hours pass with predictable boredom. After forcing ourselves to eat breakfast – no easy feat after hearing we're supposed to be trophy mates in this backwater lair's archaic competition – we descend into a tense silence.

Normally, I enjoy silence. And solitude. Despite being part of a pack my whole life, I'm not particularly social and neither is my wolf.

This silence is different though. It hums noisily like an old theatre reel, each of my past actions and mis-steps played back to me over and over again until I'm not sure what is reality and what is the exaggerated fabrications of my imagination.

Finally, to break the relentless silence, I turn to Summer and ask a question I've always sort of wondered about.

"Do you think you and Cody are mates?"

Summer gives a snort of surprise from her recumbent position on the bed beside me.

"What?" She sits up abruptly, giving a fervent shake of the head. "No. Absolutely not."

I lift a brow, admittedly surprised by her response.

Cody has made it no secret that he thinks he and Summer might be mates. And I know from overhearing dad and alpha Winslow talk that Cody was banned from contacting Summer as a punishment for defecting to Tobias' pack.

Summer must read the scepticism on my face because she cringes, brown eyes flicking away guiltily.

"Look…" She toys with one lock of hair before glancing back to me, expression pleading. "I know there was a time that Cody thought we might have been mates, but I've told him that we aren't. At least, I'm pretty sure we aren't. I know we won't know for sure until we're a little older or the mating urge kicks in or whatever." She gives a dismissive wave of her hand.

"Why did he think you're mates then?" I ask, genuinely curious.

As far as I've heard, there's no halfway house where the mating urge is concerned. You either feel it or you don't. Sometimes it will be directed at the person you least expect. Or a person you don't even like.

Summer blushes. Not the pretty, sweet kind of blush that people try to emulate with cosmetics, but a blazing red flush that extends to the top of her forehead and down her neck.

"I don't know what I was thinking." Her blush deepens with each word. "It was close to my heat, so I could blame it on that."

She rubs her cheeks with her palms, as if trying to erase the embarrassment written there.

"We hooked up, okay. It was a one-time thing but Cody somehow got the idea that it meant something more. Like we were meant to be mates or something."

She sighs, staring down at her lap.

"It was both our first times, and Cody figured I wouldn't have – you know – unless my wolf knew at some instinctual level that we were predestined mates. He said something about female virtue, females saving themselves for their mates and all that crap."

Summer shakes her head, wrinkling her nose at the memory.

"I told him that was just a bunch of sexist propaganda, that female virginity was a social construct created by the patriarchy to control and devalue women. But you know Cody. He never listens to anything. He's just like 'okay, Summer, you're so cute with your little opinions' and then goes on thinking whatever crap his head is filled up with."

When Summer looks up at me, the blush has finally faded from her face, though her eyes still glint with a guilty sort of desperation.

"I just wanted to experience it. And I wanted it to be with someone I liked and trusted. Someone I felt comfortable with. Cody is one of my best friends – we've been friends our whole lives. I wanted to share that experience with him. It didn't mean I wanted to spend the rest of my life with him."

The mixture of emotions I feel at Summer's declaration is strange, difficult to place.

My first reaction is mild disgust. Like maybe I should think less of her for doing that with Cody. After all, from the moment I learned what sex was, the importance of waiting for your mate has been drilled into me. Dad even went so far as making me promise him that I wouldn't 'engage in any illicit dalliances' before being formally mated.

Of course, when I had given him my promise, I had assumed whoever I mated with would be my true mate. My soul's own match. What better thing to wait for? What could be more wonderful, more romantic, than to share that experience for the first time with the being who would cherish me above all others?

I now see that is not what Dad had in mind at all. The realisation makes bile curl in my stomach.

Summer must see at least some of this on my face, because she tenses, wrapping her arms around her chest defensively.

"Don't look at me like that."

There is no anger in her voice, only a soft sort of patience. As if she's tutoring a younger student who has fallen behind in their classes.

"It's my body. I'm not saying sex isn't a big deal. Just that it's different for different people, and for me – well, it was something I wanted to experience on my own terms, you know? It doesn't have anything to do with who I am as a person. I'm still the same. Still me."

Yah. Okay. Maybe Summer is right. I guess in the big scheme of things, it's not a big deal. I mean, it certainly can't be worse than injecting someone with horse tranquilizer and tying them up to interrogate them. Glass houses and all that, right?

Looking at Summer's drawn features, the way sorrow and guilt are etched in circles under her eyes, it's impossible not to feel sorry for her. My wolf wants to protect her, to attack the threat she is facing, however intangible it may be.

This doesn't surprise me though. No matter how much Summer annoys me, my wolf has always been protective of her.

What does surprise me is the strange twinge of jealousy snaking its way through my chest. Not like I'm jealous about Cody, or jealous that Summer experienced something that I haven't even come close to. No, it's more that I'm jealous of her bravery. Of the undeniable moxie she has to go after what she wants, no matter how crazy.

Just like the night that she started a wildfire and broke me out of the alpha compound, I feel like I'm seeing Summer for the first time. How strong she is. Confident. Fearless, even - despite being a submissive wolf.

This gives way to a more uncomfortable realisation, as if Summer is a mirror in which I can finally see myself. All this time, I prided myself on being strong. Stoic. A dominant wolf. Loyal to my pack.

Really, I've just been weak. As eager to please as an omega.

I swallow, looking away as the shame of this realisation hits me.

"I'm sorry you had to go through that with Cody," I say lamely, at a loss of what else to say. "That must have been really…"

My voice trails off because I don't know what it would have been like for her.

"That's okay. It's past now. I'm pretty sure Cody knows that we aren't pre-destined mates or anything. Besides," Summer gives a wry grin, though it doesn't meet her eyes. "We've got bigger problems to worry about than my love life. Like, you know, this whole thing."

She makes a circle with her pointer finger in the air, indicating to the room around us, then starts listing off our problems on her fingers as if it's a shopping list.

"Being kidnapped in the middle of a desert. Being locked in a room with no entertainment whatsoever. Being trophy mates…"

"Good point," I say with a dry laugh. "Who cares about you and Cody? We're totally screwed."

"I know, right?" Summer chortles. "So screwed."

Maybe it's the stress of the past couple of days, but I can't help but laugh at her response. A deep, belly laugh that is totally inappropriate given our current circumstances. Summer's eyes widen momentarily in surprise at the sound of my laughter before she breaks into hysterical giggles.

Suddenly, it's like we are tween girls at a sleepover, laughing manically about absolutely nothing, completely caught up in the insanity of the situation. Tears are streaming down my cheeks, the laughter almost as cathartic as crying. Summer is clutching a pillow to her stomach, doubling over with giggles, struggling to breath.

It's at that very moment that the door to our room swings open.

We both startle, laughter wilting and humour clattering like glassware on the bare floor as we turn to face the newcomer.

It's not the elderly shifter bringing our lunch.

Instead, it's a younger male, maybe nineteen or twenty, dressed in an immaculate three-piece suit, black tie loose and draping around the open collar of a crisp white shirt. The whole ensemble is completely out of place here, in this spartan room overlooking arid desert, and yet it looks natural on him, as if he's dressed this way every day of his life. Who knows, maybe he has. With his clear skin, rich brown hair and strange green eyes, he would probably look like a Versace model or something - if his face wasn't contorted into an arrogant sneer.

When those eyes land on Summer, his breath hitches, expression morphing from one of disgust to shocked disbelief. He nearly stumbles, bracing himself against the doorframe as if it's the only thing keeping him upright. Or maybe, given the hungry expression kindling in his gaze like a newly-started fire, as if it's the only thing keeping him from lunging forward.

Instinctively, I step forward, putting myself between Summer and this potential threat to my pack mate. Behind me, I hear Summer whimper as she rises to her feet, the sound of short, panting breaths telling me she is just as affected by the entrance of this male.

"You," he says, the word half animalistic growl, as if whatever beast living inside of him is straining for the surface. He drags one hand over his face, ruffling the perfectly styled hair until it falls over his forehead.

"You," he says again, stepping forward.

"Stop!"

I pull my shoulders back, drawing myself up to my full height, letting him hear the dominance in my tone. Letting my wolf push close enough to the surface till I know my eyes will be flashing quicksilver.

Whoever he is, I want him to see that he won't be getting near my friend without getting through me first.

He blinks rapidly, green eyes focusing on me dazedly, as if he's only just noticed that I'm in the room. His expression hardens, jaw ticking.

"Move."

I shake my head, suddenly conscious of the male's larger size. He must be at least six foot two, the fabric of his suit jacket stretching over muscles that seem to be expanding before my eyes. Green eyes flash, pupils extending to long reptilian slits and I swear I can see the faintest rippling of green scales across his temple.

I swallow, mouth suddenly dry. My wolf snarls within me, wanting to turn and run before what she instinctively knows to be an apex predator.

Dragon, my gift warns me, the image of fire fanned by batting wings flashing through my mind. If I wasn't so frightened, I would roll my eyes at it. At this useless, temperamental gift that has been silent for days, only to give me obvious and inconsequential information.

"Move," he says again, lips curling back to expose elongating canines, neck muscles cording.

I very much want to obey him. Only, I can hear Summer panting behind me, can practically feel her trembling.

He steps forward, closing the distance between us, shouldering past me as if I'm no more than a leaf floating on the wind. I stumble, spinning in an attempt to keep Summer in my sights.

By the time I right myself, the dragon shifter is standing before Summer, large hands gently grasping her narrow shoulders as his whole body practically vibrates with wild need. The way he's looking at her, it's as if she's his whole world. As if she's the most precious and valuable treasure he's ever encountered. As if he wants to consume her.

Summer stares back up at him, eyes wide, full lips parted, cheeks pink. Her hands tremble as she reaches up to rest them lightly on the lapels of his suit jacket, wonder and fear written in equal measure on her face.

I shiver, steps faltering as I realise with a confusing mixture of exhilaration and dread what I'm seeing.

"Mate," the dragon shifter rumbles, bending down to press his forehead to Summer's own.

The word becomes a rumbling purr, the sort of sound that vibrates to your very bones. He takes a deep breath, closing his eyes as his nostrils flare. Summer shivers, eye lids fluttering as his breath skitters over her skin.

"My mate," he says again.

Chapter 16

Tobias Finch

"You do realize that this is probably the stupidest idea you've ever had, right?"

Red points an accusatory finger at Gareth, upper lip curled in a sneer. One of his cat ears twitches in an unconscious display of irritation.

"If we're lucky, you'll end up dead," Red continues. "If we're unlucky, the rest of us will end up dead with you. You really think Hux is just going to walk out to the desert, unarmed and by himself, right into your little so-called-trap? We're talking about a guy who was the alpha of a pack, who managed to carry out a nationwide kidnapping scheme to build a shifter army. He's not an idiot."

Gareth just gives a slow, languid sort of grin as he leans back in his chair, eyeing Red with knowing amusement.

"You think it's funny, do you?" Red hisses, shoving off his perch and causing the coffee-maker to rattle. "Well, you won't think it's funny when Hux arrives at your so-called trap with full back-up."

Red crosses the distance between him and Gareth in two long strides, stopping in front of Gareth's chair so that he's looming over him.

"And you won't think it's funny when you call for back-up and I don't come," Red continues. "Because unlike you, I actually like being alive."

At the other side of the room, Hamish looks furious on behalf of his friend, his brow contracted into a hawk-like furrow. Gareth just gives a low chuckle, lifting one booted foot to rest on his knee, looking for all the world like Red's aggressive behaviour isn't riling him.

Sensing Hamish's tension, Orrin steps forward, pulling Red back by his elbow.

"Stop being so dramatic, cat," Orrin grumbles, giving his shaggy head a disbelieving shake. "I'm sure these guys have more to their plan than sending Gareth out into the desert as bait for Huxley Black."

Cody choses this moment to step out of the bathroom, dark curls dripping and plastered to his forehead as if he's just been for a shower, cell phone clutched tightly in his fist. His eyes flick over the scene in front of him, simmering rage momentarily replaced by bemused interest.

"What did I miss?"

"Oh nothing," Red quips. "Just an expose of the wily coyote's genius."

This does elicit a growl from Gareth.

"Red," Orrin warns, hauling his friend back to the other end of the room. A room that suddenly feels much too small.

I sigh, exhausted by the relentless displays and posturing.

I just want to end the threat that is Huxley Black and be done with it. I try to tell myself the driving need to find Lucy has nothing to do with my impatience.

But it does. It totally does.

"What's the rest of your plan?" I ask, leaning back to rest on my elbows until I'm practically sinking into the worn mattress and patchwork quilt of the motel bed.

It's clear that Gareth and Hamish have more to their plan than sending Gareth out into the desert as bait. They're just drawing things out. Making sure everyone is interested in hearing whatever brilliant plan they've concocted.

Hamish grins, flashing sharp white teeth before turning to Gareth.

"You going to tell them?"

"We've got a guy inside Drake's lair," Gareth admits, lips curling into a smug smile.

"An informant?"

I frown, thinking for some reason of all the warnings Orrin and Red gave me about trusting Cody.

Gareth nods.

"We managed to reach out to him after we located Huxley Black. By accident really. Do you remember Aires?"

I shake my head.

"I remember him," Orrin says, giving a dark chuckle as he releases his grip on Red. "Dragon shifter had a mean left hook and even meaner temper. Wasn't too happy when he didn't win in the ring." The bear shifter cocks his head thoughtfully. "He was from Blackwater pack, wasn't he? I don't remember seeing him at pack territory."

I shudder, not wanting to recall the bloodbath at Blackwater territory.

"That's the one," Gareth agrees. "He was an enforcer for Huxley Black. And no, he wasn't at the Blackwater Fight. He helped Huxley escape. Flew him right out of the territory."

"In dragon form?" I ask, incredulous. Pretty sure someone would have noticed if a dragon was flying around Blackwater territory.

Gareth chuckles. "No, though I wouldn't put it past him. Aires is not the most cautious of shifters. A bit impulsive, isn't he Hamish?"

Hamish shrugs. "You worked with him, not me. I was just a lowly recruit. You were an enforcer."

"Hmm. Good point. Anyway, no. He didn't fly out in dragon form. The pack had a chopper hidden a couple miles away from headquarters and Aires used that to fly Huxley out of danger."

"Such a coward," Hamish growls and I wonder whether he's talking about Huxley or Aires.

"But you trust him?" I ask. "You trust this Aires guy?"

"Not a bit," Gareth admits. "But he has his reasons for wanting to get rid of Huxley, and he's given us a blood oath not to sell us out."

Red scoffs derisively. "So what? He's just going to deliver Hux into our waiting hands?"

"More or less," Gareth shrugs. "He'll let Huxley know he has intel on my whereabouts." He flashes me an amused smile. "You know Hux has been gunning for me since I left his pack and joined up with you, right?"

"No," I admit, though I figured as much. If Huxley holds a grudge against me for accidentally stealing his pack, no doubt he's angry at Gareth for abandoning him.

"Well, he does. Though he probably hates you more."

"Do you think it was Huxley Black who ordered the hit on Tobias then?" Cody asks. He's leaning against the open bathroom door, towelling his wet hair.

"We're not sure," Hamish admits. "From what we know, Huxley still hasn't located the Liberty pack."

I shudder, recalling the searing pain of the silver bullet, the dislocated shoulder.

"Aires has been able to give us that much info at least," Gareth agrees. "Huxley doesn't know where our pack is."

Gareth grimaces, then adds: "Of course, we've been sending more and more rogues to our pack, so it's only a matter of time before news gets out that there's a born alpha with a pack in Wyoming."

My mind races at this information. I know we didn't know who was behind the attacks, but I had assumed that it was Huxley Black. Maybe because he already haunts my nightmares. Maybe because I know for a fact he wants me dead.

Knowing that it wasn't him should be a relief, but instead it sends a chill snaking down my spine. I have an enemy. Someone who has already tried twice to get to me. And I have no idea who it is.

How can you defend against that?

"Okay, so let me get this straight," Red says, folding his arms across his chest. "You're going to wander out into the middle of the desert and pretend to be injured. As bait, or whatever. Then you're going to rely on this dragon shifter to send Huxley Black your way. The same dragon shifter who Orrin beat to a pulp. The same one who flew Hux away from Blackwater. Am I missing anything?"

"Nope. That pretty much sums it up," Gareth says.

"Great," Red deadpans. "What could possibly go wrong?"

Lucy Stone

I stare disbelieving at the scene unfolding in front of me. At this stranger holding Summer in his arms, as if she's his most precious treasure. Summer, with her head tilted back, eyes closed, completely giving herself over to the fevered bliss of the mating urge.

When his hands start trailing down her sides and she tilts her head up to meet his searching mouth, it becomes clear that someone needs to step in.

I clear my throat.

"Um, excuse me," I say, trying to ignore the prickling feeling of colour rising to my cheeks. "Can you two stop for a moment? We need to talk about what is going on."

The only response is the smacking sound of their lips meeting and the rustling of hands sliding over clothes. Gods, I feel like old Mrs. Levinson when they used to let her chaperone the school dances. Like, maybe I should get out my ruler and wedge it in between their writhing bodies.

"That is enough," I say again, going for a bit more volume.

When that doesn't work, I march over to the door – which is currently sitting unguarded, and which Summer's new friend left wide open – and give it a dramatic swing, turning the door knob noisily.

"Don't mind me. I'm just going to escape now," I announce loudly.

When even that doesn't get the male's attention, I give an exasperated sigh, and slam the door shut. If I didn't care about Summer so much, this would be the perfect opportunity to make an escape. The dragon is clearly distracted.

But I can't leave her. Not after she risked everything to get me free.

I march over to the small bathroom, fill a cup with water and stride purposefully back to the oblivious couple. Then I fling the full cup of water right at their blissfully unaware and conjoined faces.

It works a treat.

The dragon's furious eyes land on me while Summer practically stumbles back, dazedly wiping wet hair from her face.

"Excellent," I drawl, doing my best to ignore the dragon's rumbling growls. "Glad that I finally have your attention."

Summer blinks rapidly, still rubbing at her face, as if to clear away the haze of the mating frenzy as well as the water. It must work, or at least provide her with some amount of self-awareness, because her eyes round and she turns a horrified stare at the stranger.

"Good gods." She presses one palm to the side of her face. "What on earth just happened?"

"I think we all know what happened," I say, before the dragon can open his mouth and get all 'mate, mate, mate' on her again. "This jerk – who obviously works for the lair that kidnapped us, might I add – came by. Probably to tell us about how we're going to be the bride-prizes for his lair's little antiquated mating competition. Then, voila, the mating urge hits and suddenly your body is no longer controlled by your brain, it's controlled by your..."

"Okay, okay!" Summer's horrified expression deepens as colour drains from her cheeks. "I get the point."

The dragon looks stunned, eyes flicking between me and Summer with confusion.

"I am your mate," he tells Summer, stepping towards her, arms outstretched as if he's going to pull her back in for an embrace and pick up where they left off.

Summer steps back, holding her arms out in front of her, palms facing outwards.

"No. Nope, nope, nope." She gives her head a vehement shake.

His brow furrows, handsome features contorting with what can only be described as pure misery.

"I am," he argues. "You know it. You felt it."

Summer shakes her head, lips trembling as they're pressed together in a thin line. She casts me a pleading look, and I think I know what she's asking.

She's too close to the edge, too full of instinct and feeling to make any rational arguments right now.

I level him with a cold stare.

"You might be her mate. But can you honestly say you didn't come in here planning to give us to whichever shifter won your lair's competition? That you didn't plan to give your own mate away?"

I wave one hand meaningfully at the door. The door that he unlocked only minutes ago. Where he stood sneering at us, at least until he recognised Summer for what she was.

"Can you honestly say you aren't involved in holding us prisoner? In keeping your own mate locked up against her will?"

As I speak, anger rises in my chest, hot and choking. My wolf surges close to the surface, full of wild rage at being cooped up for so long. It's impossible to keep from baring my teeth and I have to clench my teeth against the urge to yell. To scream. To rail against this perfect stranger as if he is solely responsible for everything that has happened to me in the past couple months.

Now is not the time to lose my temper, I remind myself. Not when, for the first time in two days, we have an opportunity to escape. I just have to play our cards right.

Be smart, Lucy. Be smart.

The dragon bares his own teeth at me, but all aggression falls away when he looks at Summer. She's staring up at him, eyes moist, lips trembling, as if silently begging him to deny my accusations. To assure her of his innocence, so that she can fall into his arms again.

The dragon's face pales and he stumbles back, looking as if Summer has just slapped him in the face.

"I…I was… I didn't…" he stammers, his eyes riveted on Summer.

Summer blinks, hot tears welling up, making silent tracks down her cheeks. For the first time in days, I'm not angry at her for crying.

Right now, her tears are a weapon that only she has the power to wield.

"You were," I say accusingly, lifting my chin haughtily. "And you don't deserve her."

The stranger lets out a strange choking sound, one hand rushing to his throat. He shakes his head, as if denying my words. But I can tell by the tortured expression on his face that they have found their mark.

Good.

"Then prove it," I say softly. "Find a way to get Summer and I out of here."

His eyes widen at the sound of Summer's name, and he looks at her with pained adoration.

"Summer," he murmurs, taking a cautious step towards her. "Is that your name?"

Summer nods, too overcome with emotion to speak.

"Beautiful," he says wistfully. "Perfect."

When she remains silent, he continues.

"I'm Aries. Aries Zmey."

He extends one hand towards her in greeting.

Summer stares at the proffered hand for a long moment before compulsive politeness gets the better of her and she takes it. I watch as she shudders at the light touch, then quickly drops her hand to her side.

"Great," I say, putting my hands on my hips. "Now that we're all introduced, let's talk about how you're going to get us out of here, Aries."

Chapter 17

Tobias Finch

It turns out I am not a hot weather person. Or a hiking and camping person. Or a desert person.

Self-discovery is a good thing, right?

"How many more miles is it?" I ask again, blinking against the blinding sun as I wipe sweat from my eyes with the back of my hand. "Twenty? Thirty?"

"Just another fifteen," Gareth chuckles. "Then we'll stop and make camp for the night. It'll only be a couple hours' hike to our location after that."

I nod, then pause to adjust the heavy pack I'm carrying.

We're hauling in six days' worth of rations, even though it's only a day and a half hike to our destination. At first, I thought that was a bit overkill. Like, I get wanting to be prepared and all that, but did we really need to carry in about a million gallons of water?

Looking at the landscape unfurling before us, I'm starting to question whether we brought enough.

White sandstone stretches in seemingly endless undulations, marked only by the occasional stunted juniper bush and other equally scraggly-looking plants. I think I've seen one lizard, panting and emaciated as it crouched in the shade of a rock. Maybe a few black beetles. And definitely no water.

The sun beats down on our backs, already relentless at eight o'clock in the morning. I swear I can feel just as much heat radiating up from the earth beneath my feet, as if the sandstone stored yesterday's sun like bricks in a pizza oven. Sweat drips down my back, trickling down my spine beneath my thin t-shirt.

And we've only been hiking for an hour.

I briefly contemplate shifting and hiking in wolf form, until I realise that there would be no way to carry this massive pack as a wolf.

My wolf gives a smug little rumble as I reach this conclusion, content to rest lazily in the background. He licks one furry paw and looks meaningfully at his thick golden coat, as if to remind me that he's not exactly equipped for this sort of climate either.

And so here I am, hiking along a rarely-travelled trail called Sheets Gulch in the Capitol Reef National Park.

Also, I use the term 'trail' loosely, since there is actually no way to differentiate our path from the surrounding landscape.

The plan is to follow this trail for several miles until we reach a point where Gareth and Hamish have decided we can safely camp for the night, then continue on away from the trail toward a remote location in the middle of nowhere, where they have decided we can safely lure Hux into what will undoubtably be a perfectly laid trap. Then, once we've dealt with him, we hike back out and drive happily home to Buffalo.

What could possibly go wrong?

"We're coming up to the no cell-phone coverage zone," Gareth announces from his position at the head of our group. "This is the time to send any last-messages. We won't have service again until we hike back out."

I grimace, then pull my phone from my pocket.

We alerted the pack to our plans last night, so there is a back-up crew ready to come look for us if they don't hear from us in six days' time. Still, I should let grandma and grandpa know where I am and when I'll be back.

Hey gramps, I tap out, conscious of the need to keep my message as vague as possible, in case grandma reads it. *I'm heading with some of the guys into a remote part of Capitol Reef. Won't have cell phone service and will message in six days. The guys at the build site can update you with more info.*

He'll know that 'build site' really means 'pack'.

He also already knows that we're down in Southern Utah and that we were meeting with Gareth and Hamish with a plan to track down Huxley Black, so this information won't come as a surprise.

Still, I know he'll worry.

I lift my phone, quickly bring up the camera, flash what I hope is a convincing smile, and take a selfie. Cody is in the background, looking at his own phone.

Perfect. Grandma loves Cody. Probably more than me, if we're being honest. *I'm so glad you've made friends with the Winslow boy*, she always says.

I send the photo to grandpa, knowing he'll share it with grandma as well.

Grandpa's message comes back almost instantly.

Thanks, stay safe. Will check in at the build site today.

There is a pause, then one more message pings on my phone.

And we're coming down there if we don't hear from you in six days.

I roll my eyes, but don't bother trying to argue with the old man.

Grandpa and Jamison have made it clear that they'll do whatever they want. Not like I could tell them what to do, in any event. They're in their own little pack, just like they have been since the day Jamison was born.

"Right, let's keep moving," Hamish orders from his spot at the rear of our group. "This sun isn't getting any colder."

I groan and slip my phone back into my pocket. I know he is right, but it felt really good to stop and rest for a moment.

Also, I'm already starting to feel a little hungry. I look back over my shoulder, watching enviously as Orrin pulls a venison stick out of his pocket and tears off a bite.

No doubt sensing the direction of my thoughts, Orrin narrows his eyes at me, tightening one dinner-plate sized hand possessively around his snack.

"Don't even think about it, pup," he rumbles. "Eat your own food."

I sigh, thinking regretfully of the trail mix packed in my own bag. I hate trail mix. Why had I thought that would be a good thing to pack?

IT TURNS out I didn't need to be that worried about overheating. A couple miles into our hike, the trail leads into a narrow gulch. The unforgiving sandstone walls reach up at least a hundred feet on either side, barely leaving enough room for us to walk single-file.

Some of us – namely, Orrin – have to literally squeeze between the rock walls at several points. Watching him reminds me vaguely of an octopus contorting its body to fit through a crevasse. A very large and inflexible octopus. With a beard.

The bright side of hiking at the bottom of this gulch is that the sun's light never reaches us. In fact, it's decidedly cool nestled between the cliffs. Like a cave. Or Jamison's den.

"How much more of this is there going to be?" I hear Red ask from his position several people behind me.

"Why, you getting tired, cat?" Gareth drawls from the front.

Despite the fact that we're all spread out single file, our shifter hearing combined with the unique acoustics of the gulch means that we're able to hear each other as if we were all sitting around the table together.

The thought of a table instantly makes me think of food, and I press my hand to my stomach, trying to calm the incessant hunger.

"Red here gets a little claustrophobic, don't ya, Red?" Orrin replies amicably, his words punctuated by the sound of chewing.

I have no idea what he is eating, but it's starting to feel deliberate now. Like he's rubbing in the fact that he brought all these delicious looking snacks, while the rest of us have nuts and dehydrated trail rations.

"I don't like tight spaces," Red retorts, and I can hear the scowl in his voice. "Or deserts. Or poorly laid plans."

Hamish laughs, evidently amused by Red's discomfort. I can't help but shudder because Hamish laughing is always a creepy sound. Like dry bones clattering in the wind. Or the edge of a knife running against the whetstone.

"We'll see how funny you think it is when your buddy gets taken by Huxley Black," Red retorts.

"Not this again," Gareth groans from the front of our line, palming his face in frustration. "I thought we went over this back at the motel. Yes, it's not a completely water-tight plan, but it's as good as we're going to get. If you don't like it, stay behind."

"Um, more importantly, how are we getting over that?" Jason interrupts from his post behind Gareth, coming to a halt and pointing to the mass of rocks ahead of us.

I crane my neck to see around him, and instantly see why he is concerned.

The winding sandstone slot opens up in front of us to showcase a murky looking pool of water, before it narrows again, closing over a boulder about as wide as a truck and tall as my grandparents' house. The only way to get past it, as far as I can tell, is to wade or swim through the water, climb up the sheer face of the boulder and then scale down the other side.

Not impossible, I guess. If you were an experienced rock-climber. Which I'm not.

"That water looks disgusting," Red points out as he sidles up behind me. "Definitely going to get an infection if you go in that."

"We're shifters," I point out sagely, "we don't get infections."

"Yah, I don't know," Red shakes his head, eyeing the pool warily. "I think that water might be an exception to the general rule."

"Ah, you wouldn't like it even if it were a hot spring," Orrin counters. "Typical cat."

"Who cares about the water?" Jason says. "What about that massive boulder?"

"We climb it," Gareth says nonchalantly.

"Without ropes?"

"Yes." Gareth grins. "It's not like the fall would kill one of us. Worst case scenario you get a couple bruises, especially with the water at the bottom."

"And this is the only way?" Jason queries.

Gareth waves one arm at the sandstone walls on either side of us. "You see any other route, wolf?"

"I'll go first," Cody offers, shouldering past from the back of the group. "I'm crap at climbing, so if I can make it, all of you can."

He flashes Jason a reassuring smile as he moves to the front and I feel a pang of guilt marring the gratitude that goes out to him. He really does care about his pack. About his friends.

Even when I first came to Buffalo, Cody had been welcoming. Protective. Somehow, I've forgotten that. Let my irritation at him overtake my ability to see his good qualities.

Cody shrugs out of his pack, then takes off his hiking boots, tying them to the straps of his backpack.

When he pulls a short piece of rope and a carabiner out of the top of his bag, Hamish lets out a derisive snort.

"Of course." Hamish says mockingly. "What else do you have in there? A first aid kit? Swiss army knife?"

Cody ignores him, passing his pack to Gareth.

"Hand this up to me once I'm at the top, okay?"

We all watch in silent fascination as Cody wades through the murky water – which turns out to only be about knee-deep – before wedging himself between the wall of the slot and the boulder. Slowly, painstakingly, he shimmies up the crevasse, his back pressed against the wall of the slot, his knees pressed into the boulder.

At about halfway up the boulder, the space opens up, and Cody is forced to press belly-first onto the boulder, hands and feet scrambling as he searches for holds. For a moment, I think he's not going to find any. That the slick surface of the sandstone boulder will send him sliding back down into the shallow pool.

When he manages to heave himself up to the top of the boulder, there is a collective sigh of relief. Not because falling would have been that disastrous. We're shifters. We're pretty resilient, and we heal fast.

More because watching him make it to the top assures all of us that we can do this too.

From the top of the boulder, Cody lowers the rope down to Gareth, carabiner end dangling like a fishhook. Gareth strides out through the murky water, hooks the bag to the carabiner, and we all watch as Cody heaves it up, his shifter strength making the feat look effortless.

"Show off," Jason mutters.

Cody grins, a full grin that shows all his perfect white teeth and dimples, transforming him for a moment into the boy I first met at school. The self-assured jock, loyally protective of his friends. Of me.

When his eyes meet mine, the grin falters, his expression shuttering into a cold mask that reminds me eerily of alpha Winslow. I hold his gaze, my wolf pressing me to maintain dominance, even when my gut is churning with a confusing cacophony of emotion.

When I first came to Buffalo, I didn't want Cody as a friend. As a protector. But now the warmth between us has morphed into an impassable chasm, a gap as unbridgeable as the sandstone slot looming above our heads, and I don't know how to fix it.

His jaw ticks and he looks away, calling down to Gareth to hook on the next backpack.

I feel Jason press up beside me, silently offering his support in a very wolf-like gesture. As the new omega of our pack, he's no doubt feeling the unspoken tension between me and Cody through the pack bond.

"I'm good," I lie.

He gives a low scoff, not buying it for an instant.

"He's just worried about Summer," I offer by way of excuse. "He'll be fine once we get Summer and Lucy back."

If we get them back, the doubtful part of me whispers. I shudder, not wanting to think of that. I can't think of that. Not now. Not here.

Lucy, my wolf growls. *Find Lucy.*

Jason just looks at me, but doesn't answer. I don't know what else to say, because the truth is, the tension between Cody and I has been slowly brewing and escalating for months now. Maybe since Blackwater.

"Next bag," Cody calls out.

I blink, realising it's my turn to hand my backpack and hiking boots over. Gareth takes it from my fumbling hands, hooking it expertly and I watch it swinging as Cody hauls it up, muscles of his forearms bunching with each effortless movement.

From his point on top of the boulder, the sun that has been absent from the base of the gulch pours over him like a spotlight. His golden skin glistens with sweat, the black curls falling over his forehead are highlighted with sunlight. With his perfectly sculpted features, he's like the renaissance portrait of the angel-warrior we studied in art class.

From his place at the head of our group, brimming with confidence as he perches atop the boulder, he looks every bit the alpha. And despite the irritated insistence of my wolf to the contrary, I suddenly feel inadequate. Like an imposter.

He should be the alpha. Not me. I might have been born for it, but he was raised for it.

"Your turn, Finch," Hamish calls out from behind me.

I look up, realising that Gareth has already followed Cody up and over the boulder, and that it's my turn to climb. Taking a steeling breath, I slosh through the water and wedge myself between the rocks, starting the arduous task of climbing over the chokestone, praying to all the shifter gods – real or imagined – that I don't fall.

Chapter 18

Lucy Stone

Summer has been unusually quiet.

To be fair, she has been quieter than usual since we were kidnapped by Drake and hauled off to his lair. Locked in what appears to be a network of buildings contained in the hollowed-out sandstone cliffs in the middle of the desert. At least, that is what it looks like from the one small window in our room-turned-prison.

Since Aires left, her silence has taken a sombre, pensive tone. She hasn't resumed crying, but the dark circles under her eyes are etched with sorrow.

"What are you thinking?" I ask, turning away from the window. The landscape beyond has darkened, the sun finally slipping below the horizon. "Are you worried about tonight?"

Tonight, when we are going to escape. Tonight, when we put our faith completely in a strange dragon shifter and hope for the best.

Summer shakes her head. "No. Not really." She gives a small shrug. "I mean, I'm a little worried we might get caught, but Aires seems pretty confident that he can get us out of here, so I trust him."

Well, that makes one of us.

"You do?"

I walk across the room, sitting down carefully on the bed next to her.

Aires has been annoyingly vague about how he plans to get us out of here. He's told us that we'll be taking a helicopter – which, apparently, he can fly, though I have my doubts – and then hiking to a meet-up point. But he has stubbornly refused to tell us who we are meeting.

This seems like a pretty crucial detail to omit. I mean, even if we can trust him – which, again, I'm not convinced - how do we know we can trust these strangers?

"Yes. I do," Summer says simply, as if trusting a complete stranger who was previously helping to hold you captive is the most natural and logical thing in the world.

She sits up from the reclining position she's adopted most of the afternoon and evening, her shoulder pushing against mine.

"Besides, I really don't see what choice we have but to trust him. I mean, it's not like we have other options for getting out of here."

She has a point.

Suddenly, she stiffens, turning to give me a curious look before leaning down to sniff me, then wrinkling her nose. My wolf balks at the gesture, disliking being appraised like this from a submissive wolf.

I frown, more concerned that I've got bad B.O. than about wolfish pecking order and pack dynamics.

"You smell."

"Gee, thanks," I reply dryly.

Despite my best efforts to stay clean using the little bathroom, they haven't exactly gifted us with deodorant or soap or anything. Which, considering they plan to pair us off as mates to the winning warriors, seems a bit short-sighted.

"No, not like that," Summer says, shaking her head. "I mean, you've got a kinda sweet, musky smell." She pauses, giving my shoulder another delicate sniff, then nods solemnly. "Yep, that's what I thought."

"What?" I ask, even as realisation coils with icy dread in my stomach when I calculate the date. How many months have passed since my last one.

"I think you're going into heat."

Crap.

I rub my face roughly between the palms of both hands, then clutch my hands to my stomach, as if I can somehow press pause on my shifter biology.

Crap, crap, crap.

"It's okay."

She pats my shoulder reassuringly, and I fight the urge to duck away from her touch.

"Sorry." She grimaces, quickly withdrawing her hand. "I hate being touched when it's that time too."

I just grit my teeth, suddenly aware of the way my skin feels extra-sensitive. Of the way every little thing seems to irritate me. I probably would have noticed it sooner, were it not for my legitimate anger at the general crappiness of our situation.

"Look, I'm sure we'll be out of here before the peak of it hits," she offers hopefully. "And at least you know Aires won't be that affected, because of the mating urge and all that."

Summer frowns when she mentions Aires, even as a faint blush rises on her cheeks.

"Yah, that's true," I say, suddenly relieved beyond measure that we are escaping tonight.

If I went into heat here, gods only knows what would happen. Especially given their plans for us.

I could create a frenzy. Like, real fighting instead of just some stupid competition. Worse, I could be convinced to do something I would seriously regret later.

I shudder.

Most female shifters only go into heat for a couple days, and thankfully it only happens every six months. Back at home, I would have just stayed in my room for a day or so, until the worst of it passed. The walls of our house - and the presence of dad and Anton - were enough to keep away any males stupid enough to be drawn by my scent. And I could take care of my own discomfort in the privacy of my room.

"What about the strangers?" I ask, clutching my stomach tighter. "You know, those shifters that Aires said are meeting us in the desert somewhere?"

"Yah. Good point," Summer muses, her brows pulling together in evident concern. "I guess we'll just have to tell Aires, make sure we camp with you far enough away…"

Her voice trails off, because what is there to say? I'm going into heat, whether I like it or not.

I feel like I'm on a high-speed train with no brakes, heading straight for a cliff. All I can do is hold on and hope I come out the other side.

WHEN SUMMER TELLS Aires about our little predicament – namely, my body's sabotage plans – he just shrugs, completely non-plussed.

"I know," he says, brushing invisible lint from the shoulder of his suit-jacket with one hand. "I could smell it when I came in earlier today."

"Really?" Summer asks, eyebrows shooting up in surprise.

"Of course. Dragon shifters have a superior sense of smell." He gives me a self-satisfied smirk before adding: "We also aren't slaves to our baser impulses. Unlike you wolves."

He reaches over to sling one arm around Summer's shoulders, but she shrugs out of his grasp, glaring up at him. When he makes a grab for her a second time, she pushes the palm of her hand against his chest, shaking her head in exasperation.

"What is this?" he asks, staring down at the small hand pressed against the white of his dress shirt, then blinking confusedly at Summer. "I'm not allowed to touch my mate?"

"Let's just focus on getting out of here, okay?" she says sternly. But her hand trembles faintly against his shirt. "And can we put the whole 'mate' thing on hold for a bit? We only just met, and I don't know anything about you."

The line between his brows deepens.

"I am your mate," he counters, reaching up to cover her hand with his own, pressing it against his heart. "Just like you are mine. It isn't something we can put on hold."

Summer's cheeks heat furiously, but she doesn't look away.

"That doesn't mean I'm going to accept you," she retorts. "Not without knowing a lot more about you than I do. And let's face it. What I do know so far is not particularly appealing."

Aires frowns, as if surprised by her words, then brightens.

"Ask anything you like, and I'll answer," he says, leaning forward in a further effort to close the distance between them.

I wave both hands and shake my head.

"Nope. No, you won't. Not until we are out of this compound and somewhere safe." I glance meaningfully at the door, then back at the couple. Aires is standing right in front of Summer now, the top of her head almost tucked under his chin, his nostrils flaring as he takes in her scent.

"Not controlled by your baser impulses?" I ask flatly, putting my hands to my hips. "Really?"

Aires shrugs and gives a self-deprecating grin.

"You've discovered my weakness," he deadpans unapologetically, not taking his eyes from Summer.

"Lucy is right," Summer says shakily. "We have to get out of here. Every minute we delay puts all of us in danger."

When Aires doesn't move, Summer gives him a little shove and says: "Aren't you supposed to be protecting me from danger? Like, isn't that what you alpha-male types do? Protect your mate from danger, keep the weaker females safe from harm?"

I suppress a smile at the biting sarcasm in her voice.

"You are always safe with me, mate," Aires responds solemnly, either completely missing her sarcasm, or intentionally ignoring it. "I would destroy anyone who tried to harm you."

Summer snorts derisively.

"Great," I say. "Then get us out of here, okay? Less talk, more action." I clap my hands together for emphasis and jerk my chin at the door.

"Fine," Aires sighs defeatedly, withdrawing from Summer with the same reluctance as a child stepping back from his birthday cake. "Let's go."

When he unceremoniously opens the door and beckons for us to follow, I freeze.

The space beyond is silent and dark as a cavern. Anything – anyone – could be waiting there.

Tentatively, I step forward, putting Summer behind me. If there are any dangers lurking, it should be me that meets them, not her.

Slowly, my eyes adjust to the dark just enough for me to make out the rough stone walls of a hallway. The hewn uneven texture makes me wonder if it was carved out by hand, with some sort of pick-axe.

"This way," Aires whispers from behind me, before shoving past me so he can lead the way into the darkness. Summer's hand is clasped tightly in his own, and she trails after him.

Blindly, we follow Aires through tunnel after dark tunnel, our bare feet whispering over cold sandstone. Even Aires, wearing hard-soled dress shoes, manages to keep his footsteps silent. I want to ask where everyone is, and how he knows which way to go, but bite my tongue. There will be time for questions later, when we get out of here.

If we get out of here.

After several sets of stairs, the tunnel finally opens up and we are greeted by the beautiful scent of fresh night air, rich with sage and juniper.

Freedom, my wolf sings, tilting her head up to the moonless sky.

But I know we aren't free yet. Not this close to the lair, where enforcers or guards will surely be lurking.

Only, there is nothing. No one. No bulky figures cloaked in shadow. No rustling of movement or crunching footfall.

As we follow Aires away from the cliff-face and towards a cluster of juniper trees, I can feel the tension draining from my shoulders, leaving the tremors of spent adrenaline in its wake.

When I see the silhouette of a helicopter behind the trees, my relief is so strong, it's practically intoxicating. Summer lets out a shaky exhale, as if she has been holding her breath.

"Your ride, ladies."

Aires throws open the helicopter door, motioning us forward with the same nonchalance as someone opening the door of a pick-up truck. Instead of what is probably a million-dollar helicopter.

Summer hauls herself up, letting out a low whistle of appreciate as she settles into the seat and starts to strap herself in.

It's not the first time either of us has been in a helicopter. Our pack has a few of them that they use for ranching, dealing with fires, that sort of thing. In fact, after the fight at Blackwater, we flew home in helicopters, since dad and alpha Winslow insisted that we weren't allowed out of their sight.

Aires nods approvingly as he watches us adjust the shoulder harnesses to fit our smaller frames. Still, he checks us both over, quickly but expertly adjusting straps and making sure the communication units on the headsets are turned on. Only when he is satisfied does he strap himself in, put on his own headset, and start the engine.

I tense anew at the hum of the blades. While they are muted under the earmuffs, I know it will be a piercing roar outside, advertising to anyone within earshot that the helicopter is about to take flight. I half expect to see the door we exited from fly open, to see enforcers armed with guns and teeth and claw chase us down with predatory efficiency.

But there is nothing. No one. Not even the reflective glint of eyes in the darkness to hint at the presence of anyone but ourselves.

And then we are airborne. Lifting gracefully into the night. My heart jumps into my throat with the sudden movement, and the feeling is exhilarating. Like when Summer broke me out of the alpha house - what now seems like a lifetime ago. Like running in wolf form through the forest. Like skinny-dipping at the waterfall in the foothills above my house.

I'm free. I'm really free. And this time, I'll die before I let anyone lock me up again.

Chapter 19

Tobias Finch

"Rise and shine."

Hamish's voice pierces the pre-dawn darkness outside my tent. It's clear from the sharp amusement in his tone that he's getting way too much enjoyment from waking us up.

I groan before rolling in my sleeping bag, pulling my coat-turned-pillow over my head. I'm aware of Jason moving in his own sleeping bag beside mine, and more distantly aware of the shuffling sounds of the others waking in their own tents.

When someone comes and gives the outside of our tent a vigorous shake, I'm forced to admit defeat. If I don't get up now, chances are someone will collapse my tent over top of me. Or worse, eat all the breakfast rations.

"I hate camping," Jason admits, grimacing as he sits up, his features shadowed by the headlamp dangling from the roof of our tent. "I never understood why people do this for fun."

I chuckle. After last night, I'm inclined to agree with him.

"I swear to Morrigan I was sleeping on at least ten rocks," he continues, shivering as he pulls on his jeans inside his sleeping bag. "And what happened to the heat? It was at least a hundred degrees all day yesterday, and then as soon as the sun set, poof!" He snaps his fingers for emphasis. "It was freezing."

"Tell me about it," I grumble, unzipping my sleeping bag and climbing out.

Unlike Jason, I slept in my clothes last night. I look down at my crinkled t-shirt and shorts with smug satisfaction, congratulating myself on my camping efficiency.

We manage to break down our tents and pack up our gear in about fifteen minutes while Orrin and Gareth hover over compact cooking stoves, boiling water for instant coffee and packets of oatmeal.

The coffee is bitter, but caffeinated. The oatmeal a tasteless sugary sludge that I struggle to swallow down, but at least it mostly fills my stomach. Still, I can't help eyeing Orrin's stash of venison sticks enviously as I watch him organise his pack. I might even drool a little.

The sun is still below the horizon when we break camp, casting hues of orange and red into a purple sky, the vibrant colours promising warmth even as we shiver against the cold desert air. My breath puffs in thick clouds with each exhale, and the whisper of a frost glistens white against red sandstone.

I trudge behind Gareth, adjusting my pack and watching the landscape change with the approaching dawn. At some point during our hike yesterday, the sandstone morphed from white to a rich, reddish orange, making the world around us appear even more otherworldly than before.

"Not much farther now," Gareth assures us, glancing between the terrain map in one hand and the old-fashioned compass in the other.

He gives a satisfied nod before tucking the items back into the brain of his pack, then points at an outcrop of red rocks ahead of us. The rocks rise from the otherwise flat desert like worn-out statues, round and misshapen like weathered garden gnomes.

"Just past those rocks."

I should be nervous. I should be thrumming with anxious energy, eager to take down Huxley Black. Eager to end the threat to my pack. To finally have vengeance on my mother's killer. Maybe even to find out who Huxley Black is. Why he wanted me killed when I was a new-born pup. Why he stood beside my father in my parents' old wedding photos, his wide smile a twin to my father's own.

Instead, I feel hollow. Disconnected from my body. The only thoughts that seem tethered to this world are Lucy-thoughts.

And maybe, if I'm being honest with myself, I'm not really ready to think about Huxley Black, and what I'll have to do next.

I thought I was. I thought I wanted revenge. But somehow my thirst for it has faded, leaving the need to find Lucy in its wake.

The rock-goblins are farther away than they seem and by the time we reach their looming shadows, the sun has peaked over the horizon, glaring with the promise of unrelenting heat. I cast my eyes around their odd shapes, wondering vaguely how they were formed and what the world would have looked like here before time and water and wind carved the rock away.

Behind me, I'm aware of Hamish and Gareth having an animated discussion about using the terrain to our advantage, using the rocks to create an ambush, that sort of thing.

I know I should be listening and joining in. That is what an alpha would do, after all. Heck, a real alpha would probably be planning the ambush. But I don't know anything about setting a trap. And when I think about letting my wolf out and fighting, all I can think about is what the red sandstone would look like covered in blood.

Then I remember the red-stained snow at Blackwater, and the image makes me feel sick.

"Tobias? Tobias Finch, is that you?"

At the sound of her voice, the dark memories dissipate like mist, replaced by the glaring light of the dawn. I look around, frantically searching for its source, for her. I almost think it is a mirage conjured by my own desperate imagination.

But then I hear her again.

"Jason? Cody?"

My wolf whimpers, a broken, choked sort of cry that very nearly escapes my own lips as my eyes land on her. On them.

Lucy and Summer, flanked by a male I've never seen before. I have no idea who he is and honestly, I don't care. To be honest, I barely even notice Summer.

All I notice is Lucy. Lucy, Lucy, Lucy.

With the light of the rising sun at her back, she looks almost other-worldly. Like some ancient goddess rising from the desert, offering death or salvation.

"Lucy," I croak out, staring stupidly at the group as they approach, my eyes wide in surprise, my mouth hanging open.

Run to her, you idiot, my wolf urges me. *That is your mate you are staring at. Tell her what she is to you. Mark her. Make her yours forever. Yours.*

I grit my teeth, silently willing my wolf to kindly shut up and get back in his cage. He's already proven himself to be woefully inept on the romance front. I don't need him shoving in and messing everything up. Again.

To my surprise, Lucy smiles at me. A small, tentative smile that doesn't show her teeth and barely crinkles the edges of her eyes.

I swear my heart almost stops at the sight of that smile.

"What are you guys doing here?" Jason cries out, pushing past me as he drops his pack, sprinting to close the distance between us and them, arms outstretched as if he's ready to sweep Summer up in a hug.

I'm pretty sure that is what he intends to do, until the stranger walking with them steps into his path, blocking Summer from view.

Jason freezes, tension rippling over his limbs as he stares up at the newcomer. I tense too, really noticing the stranger for the first time. He's tall and powerfully built, his classically handsome features twisted into a menacing scowl. With his black Henley and tactical pants, he looks more like a special-forces operative than a hiker out enjoying the natural splendour of this gods-forsaken desert.

My wolf bristles, instantly seeing a potential threat, eager to attack the newcomer first and ask questions never. Given how close the male is to Lucy, I'm almost inclined to go with my animal's instincts - until I see Summer reach out and gently move the male aside, giving him a reassuring pat to the shoulder. As if he is an overprotective Labrador, not a seriously scary looking shifter.

"What are we doing here?" Summer asks, flashing Jason a smile as she effortlessly sidesteps the male blocking her path. "What are *you* doing here?"

Before Jason can respond, Summer turns to glare up at the male by her side.

"Why didn't you tell us these were the people we were meeting? We know these guys."

"I gave a blood oath," he explains with a shrug, looking down to give Summer a smile that is half apology, half adoration. "I couldn't have told you anything. Even if I had known you already knew these guys." He cocks a brow, eyeing her quizzically. "How do you know the Liberty pack, anyway."

"He's not from the Liberty pack," Summer retorts, pointing at Jason.

"Uh, actually, I am in Liberty Pack now," Jason admits, raising one hand like he's answering a teacher in class. He looks sheepishly back at me, then adds: "Tobes here added me to his pack a few days ago. After I came to warn him that you guys were missing."

"Did you come here to look for us?" Lucy asks, grey eyes fixed hopefully on me.

Guilt shreds through my chest at that question, and I turn away, unable to hold her gaze as shame spreads across my cheeks like a banner. I don't want to see her smile fall when she realises that I put capturing Huxley Black over finding her and Summer.

"Well," Jason starts, wringing his hands nervously. "We didn't actually know… see, we were already coming this way because…"

"Summer! Lucy!"

I'm momentarily grateful when Cody's voice booms out from behind us, the thudding of his booted footsteps cutting off Jason's fumbling explanation.

As Cody approaches, the male who is apparently Summer's self-appointed bodyguard resumes his place in front of her, ignoring her irritated huff.

"Get out of my way," Cody snaps impatiently when he comes face-to-face with the newcomer.

"No."

The male's answer is clipped, unyielding, and I watch as Cody's demeanour morphs from impatience to barely restrained rage.

"She's my girlfriend," Cody retorts, lunging forward.

I'm not sure if he means to attack the male, or just move him aside. Either way, it's enough that the newcomer snaps.

I watch in horror as the male's skin shimmers, metallic scales rippling across his exposed forearms, reflecting glaringly in the bright sun. Green eyes morph, pupils elongating into slits as his lips peel back to expose gleaming fangs.

"Aires, calm down," Summer cries, eyes wide in horror as she bands an arm around his waist in an effort to hold him back. "He's not my boyfriend, okay." She peers around the male – Aires – to frown at Cody. "Seriously, Cody. What the crap? I'm not your girlfriend."

Cody jolts, like Summer has dealt him a physical blow. Beside him, Jason winces and flushes red, as if feeling the sting of Summer's rejection himself.

Given the pack link, he probably is.

"What – what are you talking about?" Cody asks, rubbing his chest with one hand. Like he means to ease the burn there as if it's a physical wound. "We were together. We – we've *been* together."

Summer colours slightly but doesn't release her hold on Aires as the signs of his partial shift start to slowly recede under her touch.

"We weren't dating," she argues. "We were never officially dating. You know that. I've told you that."

"No." Cody shakes his head stubbornly. "You slept with me. It meant something."

"Oh dear gods," Summer murmurs, pressing the palm of her free hand to her face. "Can you not?"

"You." Aires lets out a threatening rumble, looking for all the world like he's going to shift into whatever reptilian creature lives under his skin. "You slept with my mate?"

"Your – your mate?" Cody chokes out, hand rising to his throat. He stumbles back and Jason grips him by the elbow to steady him. "No. No. She can't be."

"It's true, Cody." Summer's voice waivers slightly, even as she lifts her chin. "It's the truth, okay. Technically."

She looks pleadingly up at Aires, trying to draw his attention down to her. "Look at me. Look at me, Aires. I need you to calm down, okay?"

To my surprise, Aires obeys, the quivering rage subsiding incrementally as he locks eyes on her. He turns to stare at Summer as if there is nothing else in the world, running his arms up and down her bare arms.

I shake my head, looking over at Lucy to give her an "is this for real" look. She just folds her arms across her chest, giving her head a small shake, jaw ticking.

"Well, shit." Gareth's irreverent chuckle cuts through the tense silence. "I thought for sure we were finally going to see your dragon form."

"Go to hell, dog," Aires responds lightly, ducking his head to bury his face in the space between Summer's neck and shoulder.

"Been there," Gareth retorts. "And I left. You should have done the same."

"Here now, aren't I?"

"Yah, but where's Huxley?" Hamish asks.

The question seems to snap Aires out of his Summer-induced trance.

"I remember you," he says, turning to point an accusatory finger at the hawk shifter. "You were one of the recruits."

The word 'recruit' is accompanied by the hint of a sneer. Like maybe Aires wants to remind Hamish of his place in some historical pecking order.

Hamish just grins, teeth flashing menacingly in a way that's strangely reminiscent of skulls and graveyards. The cords of his neck bunch under the vibrant colours tattooed across his flesh.

"And now I'm one of Tobias' main guys," Hamish says gloatingly. "Part of the Liberty pack. Tell me, dragon. You ever seen a born alpha before? You see what they can do on the battlefield?"

I resist the urge to cringe in embarrassment at Hamish's praise as Aires looks me over warily.

"You're Tobias Finch?" he asks.

I just stare back at him, because it's kind of a stupid question. Not sure how many other shifters there are with gold eyes. Not to mention both Lucy and Jason called me Tobias less than five minutes ago.

Aires gives a dry chuckle at my non-response, then turns to Gareth.

"I couldn't bring Huxley Black. I know I said I would. But things came up. Plans changed…"

He trails off, turning to look at Summer again like she's the true north to his internal compass, and his expression softens.

"My dad picked Summer and Lucy up on the desert road a few nights ago," Aires explains, absently reaching up to tug at a lock of Summer's hair.

Summer frowns at the gesture, looking ready to swat his hand away.

"Wait," Lucy interjects, blond brows drawing together. "That was your dad? Drake is your dad?"

"Unfortunately."

The word is bitter, full of unspoken disappointment. Aires looks down at Summer again, as if seeking solace by keeping her in his sights.

"It was either help these two escape, or bring you Huxley Black." He shrugs. "Summer is my mate. There wasn't really a choice to make."

Hamish lets out a disappointed huff and I shoot him a silencing glare. Because I'm grateful.

I might not know this Aires guy. Actually, going by first impressions, he seems like a bit of an arrogant jerk.

But he saved Lucy and Summer.

"You made the right choice," I say, half-startled by the volume of my own voice. It must be the effect of the sandstone structures surrounding us. Like maybe they create some sort of natural amphitheatre.

"Thanks for bringing Lucy and Summer to us," I continue formally, conscious of everyone's eyes on me. I can feel Hamish's stunned disbelief and Cody's simmering rage coursing through the pack bond.

"We owe you a debt."

Aires cocks his head to the side, lips curving in a cold smile.

"Oh, I didn't bring them to you, wolf," he says. "Summer is mine."

Cody gives a warning rumble, but it's Summer who responds.

"Nope." Summer shakes her head, shrugging free of Aires' relentless grasp. "I'm not yours, actually." She waves one finger at him as she steps out of his reach. "You saved us, and that's great and all, but let's not forget that you would have probably left us to rot if I wasn't your true mate. And also, I really don't know what to do with the whole mate thing yet."

Aires opens his mouth to protest, but Summer silences him.

"No. Nope. Not going to hear it right now. You can give me your excuses later."

Summer drapes an arm around Lucy in an almost protective gesture. I suppress a grin as Lucy winces, like the affectionate touch offends her.

"Right now, Lucy and I are going with these guys." Summer points meaningfully at our little group. "Because I trust them. And because I am still very much processing all of this."

She circles one hand in Aires direction, clearly referring to him as the thing that requires processing, then pauses, cocking her head to examine Gareth and Hamish.

"Actually, I don't really know those guys." She tilts her chin towards Gareth and Hamish. "But I trust the rest of them." She smiles as she looks over me, Jason, Orrin and Red. The smile falters a little when her eyes land on Cody and she adds: "Mostly."

Aires blinks at her in surprise. Only proving how little he actually knows his mate, because even I could have predicted that response to his possessive statement.

"So, what then? You're going with them? Just like that? Are you joining the Liberty pack?"

"Maybe." Summer says haughtily, flicking the mass of hair off her shoulders. "I haven't decided yet."

Aires' nostrils flare.

"Summer..." Jason chides, shaking his head and pressing the back of his hand to his face to hide his smile.

Summer winks at him, but the playful gesture is hollow, only serving to showcase the dark circles under her eyes.

I wonder if she regrets helping Lucy escape, running away from the safety of the Clear Creek pack.

"You can stay with us either way," I assure her, tucking my hands into my pockets. "Join the pack, don't join the pack. It's up to you."

Aires narrows his eyes at me, like he's trying to see if I have some ulterior motive. Some interest in his mate, maybe? I give him a bored stare in return, keeping my shoulders relaxed, stance wide. Adopting the usual pose of affected nonchalance that seems to be my go-to when I'm faced with potential conflict.

Until I glance at Lucy and notice the look of wary gratitude ghosting her pale features. Those grey eyes, fixed on me, as if I'm the only person here worthy of her notice.

That's probably just wishful thinking. Or maybe my wolf's delusions seeping through.

Still, my whole body tenses under weight of that stare, until the muscles that ache from hiking and camping are practically humming with renewed energy.

"You too, Lucy," I say, flushing at the way my voice deepens huskily when I say her name.

It takes conscious effort not to look away, drop my eyes. But that would be the wrong move to make around a bunch of shifters, when embarrassment can so easily be misread as submission. As weakness.

If anyone knows about the impact of body language, it's me. I spent the first fifteen years of my life perfecting the art of blending in, appearing non-threatening.

"You're welcome to stay with us too," I say again, silently congratulating myself on how even my voice sounds this time.

"Thanks."

Lucy shrugs out of Summer's grasp as she walks towards our group, pausing only to give Aires a pointedly disapproving look. Summer follows close behind her, the pair of them heading straight towards Jason, like he's the safest one out of all of us.

Inexplicable jealousy rises in my gut at that thought, but I quickly tamp it down. Everyone likes Jason. Not to mention, only a few days ago, Jason helped set the fire to cover Summer and Lucy's escape. They've been a team, a pack, real friends for their whole lives.

I've known them all for less than a year. And most of that time, I've been an outsider.

Still, I want to be Lucy's rock. I want to be the one she comes to. The one that makes her feel safe and protected.

She moves past me, her arm barely brushing against my own, sending sparks skittering over my skin. Heat coils in my core, tingling at the base of my spine and my nostrils flare as I take in her scent.

And good shifter gods, her scent.

I've never smelt anything like it. It's like every wonderful thing about her has been magnified by a factor of a million and it's literally all I can do not to fall on my knees before her right now, in front of everyone, and beg her to touch me.

I freeze, terrified that if I move, I'll do just that.

My eyes widen as a choked groan escapes my lips. She looks up at me, blinking in surprise, her grey eyes so close to my own that I can see the deep blue encircling the irises.

I watch in silent, petrified fascination as she leans towards me, her own nostrils flaring almost imperceptibly, delicately taking in my scent. Then the colour drains from her face, lips parting as she gives a little gasp of surprise.

My gaze dips to her mouth, fascinated. I wonder what it tastes like. What it feels like.

"You," she whispers, her voice so low that I doubt the others can hear her, despite their shifter hearing.

I tear my eyes away from her lips and back up to her eyes, but I'm practically trembling now. My wolf is panting like a dog, too overcome to even articulate any of the stupid thoughts he usually bombards me with.

There is accusation in her stare. Accusation and wonder, mixed with a strange sort of heat that seems to change the storm grey of her eyes to a molten silver.

I realize then what has put the look of stunned bewilderment on her face. She feels it. The surging tug, the invisible tether pulling behind the ribcage. That knowing sense of rightness that laughs in the face of logic or reality.

I know because I felt it several months ago, on the bloodied snow at Blackwater. I know, and I still have no idea what I'm supposed to do about it.

"Yah," I whisper, clenching my jaw as I give her a slow nod.

She blinks at my admission, then takes a deep, steadying breath before turning and walking away. I'm only half aware of the stilted sound of her laugh as she greets Jason, of the more formal tone as she acknowledges Red and Orrin. It's mostly drowned out by the thrumming of my own pulse, the overwhelming sense of need and the sobering weight of my own doubt.

Doubt because she knows. She knows. And she's going to reject me.

Chapter 20

Cody Winslow

I glare at the broad back of the stupid dragon shifter for hours, tensing every time I see him reach out to touch Summer. The only thing that keeps me from completely losing my shit – and probably becoming a heap of charred wolf - is the fact that Summer keeps pushing him away, politely but firmly refusing his advances.

I'm not your girlfriend.

Those cruel words play in my head on repeat. A fitting soundtrack to this hike from hell.

I have no idea why Tobias agreed to let Aires come with us. He's a complete stranger.

No, he's worse than a stranger. He's a member of an enemy pack. Lair. Whatever.

He's the one who helped Huxley Black escape. Huxley-freaking-Black. The shifter who killed Tobias' own mother. The shifter who tortured Anton, who kidnapped me and pretty much all of the Liberty pack.

And Tobias is welcoming Huxley Black's accomplice into the Liberty pack, offering him a place there. Like he's Oprah Winfrey handing out free cars.

"You should really run this past the rest of the pack," I had suggested sagely, before we started our hike back. "I doubt they are going to want him to join, after everything that he's done."

Tobias had just given me an annoyingly bland look. The kind that says he's not going to fight with me about this. Not going to rise to the challenge.

I wish he would though. Because part of me wants to fight him, even if I know he would win.

"They accepted Gareth," Tobias had reasoned, "and he had been an enforcer with the Blackwater pack too. Plus, let's face it. If Summer joins, Aires will probably eventually join anyway."

"Only if Summer accepts him," I had reminded him.

Tobias had just cocked an eyebrow, giving me a look like I was short a few brain cells, then scampered off to talk with Red and Orrin.

So here I am, hiking at the back of the group. Keeping as far as possible from everyone. All while watching Summer like I'm some creepy stalker.

When I think about what I was a few months ago - what I had a few months ago - my current position is almost laughable.

When we stop for lunch, I watch as Summer leans and whispers into Aires' ear, those full lips just inches from him. Whatever she says makes him tense, jaw ticking in agitation, but he gives a curt nod, like he'd do whatever she asked, even if he hated it.

When Summer starts making her way over to me, I almost drop my bowl of rehydrated spaghetti Bolognese.

"Hey Cody," she says, toeing the red earth with one sneakered foot.

Unbidden, my eyes track along the lines of her body, hungrily taking in her full, old-Hollywood curves, her sun-browned arms left bare by the black tank top, the long legs that end in delicate ankles.

Is it weird to notice someone's ankles? I don't think I've ever noticed a girl's ankles before, but there is something about Summer that makes me take in every single detail.

She's just so gods-damned perfect.

"Hey," I say.

I want to smile at her. I want to see her smile back at me, like she used to, riding beside me in my pick-up truck. But the skin on my face feels too tight. Like, if I smile, it might crack.

"About earlier," she begins, then stops, taking a deep breath and rubbing her hands over her arms. "I'm really sorry. I know everything I said, well, it all probably came out a bit harsh…"

She trails off, looking up at me, soft brown eyes full of apology, then adds: "I want us to still be friends, okay. You've always been my friend. One of my best friends. I don't want to lose you."

A bitter laugh escapes my lips, the sound ricocheting like gunshot off the sandstone walls of the slot we've been hiking in for the past half hour.

"I mean it," she insists, lips pulling into a frown. "I want us to be friends. I care about you."

"You care about me?" I say caustically, shoving the plastic spork I've been struggling with for the past ten minutes into the disgusting mush purporting to be spaghetti. I set the bowl aside, not caring if any of it spills.

Summer flushes, an angry sort of colour that goes to the tips of her ears, as she narrows her eyes.

"You going to accept him?" I ask, tilting my chin in the general direction of the reptilian idiot.

"I don't know."

Summer throws up her hands as she says this, the irritation quickly replaced by a desperate sort of uncertainty.

That's one thing I've always liked about Summer. How expressive she is, how open she is. She could never hide anything from me.

"I haven't decided what to do," she admits. "It's all so… unexpected."

I nod. At least that is one point we agree on. Because I always expected she would be my mate. I was sure she was my mate.

Knowing that she's not, that there is someone else who shares that bond with her… I press my fist to my chest, pushing against the knot of rage churning there, eating away where I think my heart used to be.

"You could reject him."

The words crackle from my lips, a dry whisper that catches on the hot air gusting from above the rim of the gully.

"You could come home to the Clear Creek pack. Come home with me."

"But you're not at the Clear Creek pack," she says, brow dipping in confusion. "You're at Liberty pack."

I lift one shoulder in a non-committal shrug.

She's right, of course. She just doesn't know that is all about to change. That by the end of tomorrow, if all goes well, the Liberty pack will be disbanded. I'll be free to come home. And so will she.

My gut twists at the thought, cold guilt snaking up my insides for the hundredth time since my call with dad.

"You could choose me," I whisper, hoping the distance and the shape of the gully keeps most of my words from travelling to the others.

Not because I'm worried about offending Aires. No, I would like to give him a reason to fight with me. A good brawl, a good fist-fight. That would relieve some of the tension pushing out from behind my ribcage.

But I do have enough pride that I don't want everyone hearing me beg. And what I'm doing right now – that feels a lot like begging.

"It's not going to happen," Summer says, expression hardening. Like she's steeling herself to deliver news she knows I'm not going to like. "You and I – we're not happening. We're not going to be a couple. Even if I hadn't met Aires, you and I still wouldn't be getting together."

"You can't know that."

"Um, yah, I can."

She wrinkles her nose when she says this. It takes everything I have to resist the urge to reach out and run my finger down the bridge of her nose, smooth the lines there.

A few months ago, I would have. She would have let me. Welcomed my touch, even. How did we go from that – from sharing the most intimate moments – to this?

"So, what? It just meant nothing?" I ask hoarsely.

She gives me a sympathetic look. And that – that hurts almost as much as not being able to touch her.

"Not nothing," she sighs, cheeks flushing. "But I told you at the time it didn't mean we were serious. I told you…"

She trails off, looking away. Looking back towards Aires, as if the pull of the mating bond is so strong, she can't bear to have him out of her line of sight.

"I thought you meant you just wanted to wait until the mating urge kicked in," I say. "I thought you didn't want to announce anything to our pack until we knew for sure. But I didn't think that changed what things were between us."

Summer makes a frustrated sound at the back of her throat before rising to her feet.

"Wait," I say, frantic to bring her attention back to me.

I sound like a grovelling pup, like a whimpering omega, pawing at her feet. I should care about that a lot more than I do. Maybe later, I will. But right now I just need her to look at me. Not him.

"Summer, please."

She pauses, giving me an unreadable look over her shoulder.

I stand, pulling myself to my full height. Reminding her of who I am. What I am. That she wanted me. Enough, at one point at least, to give herself to me.

"If you had never met Aires," I say, then cross my arms over my chest protectively, tucking my hands to hide the way they are trembling with barely restrained emotion. "If you had never met him, would you have chosen me? Eventually?"

"I don't know." Summer sighs, running one delicate hand through her hair. "I just don't know, okay."

Then she is stalking off, heading back towards where Lucy and Jason sit. Where Aires hovers, watching for Summer with eyes that flicker unnervingly between human and reptilian.

I slump back down, digging my fingers into the cool sandstone beneath me, welcoming the bite of pain when I press a little too hard, and I think about her words.

That she might have chosen me, if it hadn't been for Aires.

I look over at Tobias then. He's sitting beside Red, Orrin, Gareth and Hamish while they talk about gods know what. He's pretending to listen, but I can see the way his eyes flick over to Lucy every couple seconds. Like he's more interested in watching the she-wolf than doing his job as an alpha.

I know why of course, even if no one has said anything. We can all smell her.

I would probably be more affected by it, if it weren't for the other she-wolf crushing my heart between her delicate hands. Hands that are currently as animated as birds in flight as she laughingly relays some anecdote to Jason and Lucy.

I guess that is why Summer and Jason are keeping Lucy company away from everyone else. Smart. I just hope it doesn't stir up trouble. Lucy has caused enough trouble already.

I narrow my eyes, watching the pale-eyed female with wary irritation. In a way, it is her fault that Summer met Aires in the first place. Her fault and Tobias' fault.

If Lucy hadn't defied my dad and gotten herself locked up, Summer wouldn't have felt the need to run away with her. And if Tobias had chosen to track down Summer and Lucy instead of going after Huxley Black, we could have found them before Drake did. Before Aires had a chance to meet her. Before she ever felt the pull of the mating bond.

I clench my jaw, feeling a strange sense of relief for the first time in days as some of the guilt I've been harbouring trickles away, my resolve strengthening.

Working with dad, it is the right thing to do. I'm sure of it now.

It might not be Tobias' fault that he's a born alpha, but he is. He should never have been born and now it's up to me to put things right.

With Tobias out of the picture, I'll be free to join the Clear Creek pack again. I'll have my rank back. And maybe then, Summer will look at me like she used to. With respect and longing.

Maybe we can get rid of Aires too. Sure, Summer might be upset for a while, but she barely knows him. She'll get over him eventually. And I'll be there, helping her recover from her grief. As familiar and safe as home.

Because she'll be coming home. With me.

Chapter 21

Lucy Stone

I can't believe it. Just can't believe it.

My mind was still reeling from the surprise of seeing Tobias and Jason and the rest of the pack here, in the middle of the desert, when I caught his scent. Felt that tug.

I didn't think it would be so strong. It's like the very marrow of my bones are connected to him, pulling me towards him. It's uncomfortable and strange. I've never felt so out of control, and I don't like it.

Also, going by the flicker of surprised recognition I saw on his face, I'm pretty sure he already knew.

For some reason, that thought sends the rage simmering in my chest to a full-on boil.

How long did he know? And why in the gods' names didn't he tell me? Why didn't he check on me while I was locked away at the Clear Creek territory? That's something a mate would have done, right? Checked that I was okay?

Unless he doesn't want to claim me.

I worry my lower lip, barely watching where I'm placing my steps as I trudge behind Jason, following the never-ending path snaking along the bottom of this ravine. Gully, slot, whatever it is that they call it.

I pause to look up at the sheer sandstone walls reaching up on either side of me. It's at least a hundred feet to the top, where a red sky announces that the sun has started to set. If I were to stretch my arms out, my fingertips would brush the smooth, cold walls.

I'm not normally claustrophobic, but the closeness of the stone, the absence of the wide expanse of sky – it's starting to grate on me. After months of being cooped up, trapped and imprisoned, my wolf sees these walls as just another cage.

"You doing okay?" Summer asks, coming up behind me.

"Yah, I'm fine," I lie.

"Why'd you stop?" she asks.

I pull my eyes away from the distant red sky and look down at my feet. She's right. I have stopped.

"Do you know when we're stopping to set up camp?" I ask.

I seriously hope we aren't sleeping in the bottom of this pit. Flash flood safety risk aside, the thought of spending a whole night camped down here makes me want to scream.

"No idea," Summer replies casually, before giving me a light shove forward. "But I'm sure we'll be stopping soon. How's the heat going?"

I grit my teeth, then continue forward at a faster pace than before. Partially because I really want to get out of this gully before we set up camp, but also to escape Summer's question.

The heat is not going well. Not at all.

I press my hand to my stomach, wishing there was a way to put an end to the ever-growing feeling of need blooming there.

I mean, there is a way to put an end to it, at least temporarily. But that is obviously not an option right now.

I look up to glare at the back of Tobias' distant form, as if he is personally responsible for the hell my body has decided to unleash on me right now. Honestly, it kind of feels like he is.

Tobias is near the front, right behind Gareth – the only one who actually knows where we are going. With the snaking turns of the sandstone walls, this has meant that Tobias has blessedly been out of my line of sight for most of the afternoon.

Of course, that hasn't stopped his delicious chocolate and pine scent from wafting temptingly back to me.

A barely restrained sigh catches in my throat as Tobias stops to heft off his pack, his black long-sleeved t-shirt riding up, exposing rippling back muscles and smooth unblemished skin. When he pulls the shirt down again, my wolf lets out a low, needy whimper before rolling onto her back, squirming uncomfortably.

It's only when I see Gareth, Red and Orrin taking off their packs that I realise we seem to be stopping.

"We're going to camp here for the night," Gareth announces. Since he seems to be our hike-leader or whatever.

I frown, eyeing the sparse, uneven ground nestled between the towering cliffs doubtfully.

"Wouldn't it be better to keep going?" I ask, not hesitating to voice my disagreement with what appears to be some very idiotic decision-making.

I point to the high walls of the sandstone slot penning us in.

"I mean, everyone knows you aren't supposed to linger in gullies like this, because of flash flood risks. Isn't it better to keep going and camp once we're out of the gully?"

At Clear Creek pack, I probably wouldn't have spoken out like this. I mean, I'm not exactly the type to sit at the back of the class and keep my mouth shut, but at Clear Creek pack, speaking out like this would have been seen as a challenge. Dad would have hauled me out back and given me a piece of his mind, for sure.

I shudder, thinking of the last time dad yelled at me. The first time he hit me. And that vision I had, that knowing, whatever you want to call it. About mom.

I push those thoughts aside and stare at Gareth unblinkingly, not caring if it's seen as a challenge.

This isn't my pack. Tobias isn't my alpha. I don't even know if Gareth is his beta, or just this little group's camp leader.

I've had enough of following orders and being caged in to last me a lifetime.

Gareth chuckles, running one hand through dirty blond hair. The movement makes the muscles of his forearms bunch appealingly.

At least, it would be appealing if this was a normal heat, and not a heat where every single ounce of desire coiling in my belly was directed like a flashing neon sign towards Tobias Finch.

"We could keep hiking," Gareth admits, lips curving lazily into a sardonic smile as he bends to open his pack. "But this gully goes on for several more miles. We're about a mile from the chokestone, and it would be a real struggle to get past that in the dark."

He points to the strip of sky above our heads, and I look up, surprised at how quickly it has changed from red to dusky purple. In only a matter of minutes, stars will be glimmering there, cold diamonds suspended in the black.

"This is the widest point before the gully ends," Gareth continues, not even looking at me as he pulls out a camp stove and starts setting it up. "So, it's the best place to camp."

Then he starts pouring water into a pot, lighting the fire on the small gas stove beneath it, before pulling out various food ingredients.

So, that's it. Conversation over.

I give Summer an incredulous look, hoping she at least will back me up here. She just shrugs unhelpfully, then plops down in an exhausted heap beside her own pack.

Instantly, Aires is there, kneeling beside her, helping her unpack, pulling out her jacket and sleeping bag. Fussing over her like he's the white knight in their love story, and not the villain we all know he is.

I haul my own pack from my shoulders with a little more force than necessary, letting it thud to the ground. I'm busy recklessly tugging the contents free, trying not to be impressed at all the useful gear Aires packed for me, when I feel a tap on my shoulder.

I look up, butterflies rising nauseatingly from the pit of my stomach to my throat, until I realise its Jason and not Tobias standing over me.

"Want any help?" Jason asks, a hopeful grin stretching across his boyish face.

"No," I snap, turning back to tug at a corner of fabric that I'm pretty sure is a sleeping bag.

The offending item flies out, fluttering to the ground a few feet away from me like a falling leaf and I realise it's a compact puffer jacket. An expensive looking one, going by the logo, designed specifically to be as lightweight as possible for backpacking. Jason helpfully picks it up, handing it over to me.

"Thanks," I say, snatching the jacket from his hands and putting it on over my white tank top.

The sun seems to have dragged all its warmth with it, and the air in the gully has taken on a decidedly chilly feel. I try not to be too grateful to the dragon shifter, but it's impossible not to soften towards him just a little bit when I slip the coat on.

"I have extra food rations if you need anything," Jason continues, peering with unabashed curiosity into my pack. "You know, just in case Aires forgot anything."

I snort. Based on what I've pulled out so far, that seems unlikely. I give a little smirk, thinking gleefully of Aires rushing around to pack for me, despite what a hard time I've given him. All because he wants to impress Summer.

Jason shakes his head at me, as if he can guess the train of my thought and disapproves.

"You should really let Summer decide what to do about Aires on her own," he murmurs. "I know from experience that it's not very nice when people put pressure on you not to accept your true mate."

I blink up at him, my momentary confusion quickly replaced by a nagging sense of shame. I had completely forgotten that Jason had a mate. Has a mate. That human boy at school. What was his name again?

"That's not the same," I argue, pointing one finger up at him. "Your mate…" I pause, flushing when it becomes apparent that I really have forgotten his name. "Your mate wasn't an accomplice kidnapper."

"Ross," Jason says tiredly, like having to remind people of his mate's name is not an uncommon occurrence. "His name is Ross Slade."

"Yah, that's right," I say, recalling the boy's laughing face. "I think I had advanced calculus with him last year. He's really smart."

"Ross is super smart," Jason agrees, beaming slightly at the praise of his mate's intellectual prowess. "And nice. Really popular. Everyone at school likes him."

"Which is exactly opposite to the situation here," I say, tilting my chin towards Aires. "Nobody likes him."

"It is the same."

My eyebrows lift in surprise because I can't actually remember the last time Jason argued with me about anything. Sure, he'll tease me about things all the time. But he doesn't usually hold his ground like this.

"The Clear Creek pack didn't want me with Ross because he's a human. You don't think Summer should be with Aires because he's an entitled jerk or whatever."

Jason makes a circular motion with one hand in Aires general direction, and I'm vaguely aware of the dragon's eyes lifting to us, surveying us with a muted sort of curiosity.

I ignore him. I don't care if he knows we're talking about him. It's not like I've made it a secret what I think of him.

"That is not the same," I insist, frowning up at him from my seat on the cold, uneven sandstone. "The Clear Creek pack doesn't approve of Ross because of stupid prejudices. I don't approve of Aires because of facts. Like the fact that he was one of the shifters keeping Summer and me locked up. Like the fact that he's Drake's son. There's a difference."

Jason shifts uncomfortably on his feet, clearly torn between wanting to say more in defence of his argument, and wanting to follow his usual non-confrontational omega instincts. Instinct must win out, because Jason changes the subject.

"What is going on with you and Tobes?" he asks, pursing his lips together in a teasing grin.

"Nothing," I say, probably a little too quickly as I pretend to be fascinated by the ingredients list on the back of the packet of dehydrated rice and beans.

"Uh-huh," Jason scoffs, lowering himself to my level and taking the packet out of my hands. "I'm not blind, you know. Plus, Summer told me all about how Tobias came to pack lands in his wolf form a few months ago."

I make an irritated sound in the back of my throat. Typical Summer.

"That gossiping little ..." I start, but Jason cuts me off with a wave of his hand.

"Please," he says dismissively. "You know I can get that girl to tell me anything. And you know she's incapable of keeping secrets. So, what's going on with you two?"

"It's nothing."

The lie tastes bitter on my tongue.

Jason cocks a brow in disbelief, but doesn't argue. He might not have my gift, but he's a good reader of people. Like most omegas, he's highly empathetic, reading emotions on peoples' faces just as easily as he feels them across the pack bond. We might not share a pack link anymore, but no doubt he can see the flicker of guilt that accompanies my lie.

It doesn't matter. I'm not telling him anything. Not yet, anyway. Not while Tobias is hardly speaking to me. Not when he's known for months that we are mates and hasn't done anything about it.

I can't really blame Tobias for that though, can I? I've been absolutely horrible to him from the start. I mean, I got him gored by a bull. Drugged him and interrogated him. If he isn't sure about acknowledging me as his mate, I only have myself to blame.

Still, the thought of him not accepting me fills me with a raging sense of betrayal.

Which is about as confusing as the unequivocal sense of possessiveness aimed at him.

I don't even know him. Last year, I didn't even like him. And now, here I am, ready to throw myself at him.

I could blame it on hormones. But the truth is, I'd been warming up to him since our trip through Montana.

I remember the way his leg pressed against mine in the back seat of the van and flush at the sudden surge of heat pulsing through my body, tingling across my skin like electricity.

Beside me, Jason gives a low chuckle, before rising to his feet. I narrow my eyes at him, daring him to say anything, but he just smirks, annoyingly wagging his eyebrows at me before walking away.

When I look at Tobias again, it's to see him staring right at me, expression an unreadable mask. Somehow, even though he's at least twenty feet away, the feel of his eyes on me is like gasoline on a bonfire, igniting the strange, unwelcome fire in my core.

I quickly look away, pressing my hand to my stomach again, as if I can stifle the longing rising there.

It's going to be a long, long night.

Chapter 22

Tobias Finch

The scent of Lucy Stone mingles with the faint notes of sandstone and juniper, warming my blood against the cold night air. I take a deep breath, relishing the delicious torture. Grateful for the darkness hiding the hungry flush burning across my cheeks.

There's been an anxious energy thrumming below my skin all day. Not just because she knows. But also because my wolf's instincts are being driven nearly to a fever pitch.

I think I knew at a basic level what that change in her scent was. Or at least, my body knew. But when Red said something about it – let's just say I very nearly lost my shit.

Now all my wolf wants to do is claim her. Sink his teeth into her and mark her. Make her ours. Irrevocably ours. So that every other male here knows who Lucy Stone belongs to.

Which is completely inappropriate.

I drag one shaky hand over my face, rubbing at the light scruff ghosting my jaw. At some point in the past six months, I went from hardly having to shave to needing to shave every morning. Sure, I'm not about to grow a full beard like Orrin. But the days of peach fuzz – as Summer calls it – are gone.

I take another deep breath and push the desires of my wolf down. He might be ready to claim Lucy, but I'm not. And I'm pretty certain Lucy isn't ready for that either.

Sure, I want her. I've wanted her since the first day I saw her in the hall outside English class, scowling and glorious as a Valkyrie as she told me to leave. Those feelings haven't faded.

But I also want her to like me. To trust me. To want to be around me.

I think about my parents. The way dad would buy mom flowers on his way home from work. The sappy grin on his face announcing what he had done well before he'd handed her whatever cheap bouquet he'd picked up on his professor's salary. How mom would look at dad while he rambled on about feminist theory or whatever crap he was writing an article about. Like every word out of his mouth was actually interesting.

That's love right there, isn't it? Adoring even the most awkwardly unlovable aspects of someone?

I don't know if I'll ever have that with Lucy.

I shove the thoughts of my parents down, letting my longing for them join with the other tumultuous desires in the walled-off recesses of my mind. It hurts too much to think about them. Especially when we were so close to catching Huxley Black. When I was so close to having revenge. To having some sort of closure.

I look at the sleeping figures of my pack mates and friends, sprawled out head to toe and shoulder to shoulder in sleeping bags along the bare floor of the gully. Nothing above them but the looming sandstone walls and, above that, the sliver of a cloudless night sky.

I think some of them were surprised when I offered to take first watch, but nobody complained. Now the gully is filled with the lull of sleeping breaths and quiet snores. Or, in the case of Orrin, not-so-quiet snores. Hardly surprising after two days of hiking and the anxious anticipation of a fight which never eventuated.

I knew I wouldn't be able to sleep though. Not with Lucy so close. Not with my wolf's wild possessiveness thrumming through my veins, demanding I keep watch over my mate. Protect her.

That's something I've failed at these past couple of months. Just like I've failed at being an alpha to my pack.

Well, I'm stepping up now. Or at least, I'm going to try.

I look away from the sleeping forms, casting my attention to the depthless dark of the sandstone slot. It's unlikely anyone would attack us here, but not impossible. I think back to the hit and run in Buffalo. How someone had known where I would be and when.

Soundlessly, I pad toward the darkness, relying on my shifter vision as I make my way over the rocky uneven ground. I figure I'll walk a few minutes in this direction, scope it out, then head back and do the same on the other side of our camp. It might even make sense to wake one of the others – Red maybe, or Hamish – so that we have someone guarding each end of the gully while everyone sleeps.

I'm just about to turn and make my way back to the encampment when I hear the faintest scuffling, like bare feet over rocks. I spin, muscles tensing, nostrils flaring, ready to take on my attacker, when the distinctive scent of lavender and cut-grass, rich with a heady floral sweetness, nearly brings me to my knees.

"Lucy?" I choke out, staring into the darkness. I can just make out the silhouette of her form as she moves towards me, graceful as a shadow. "What are you doing awake?"

"Hey," she replies, the word a whispered breath falling from her lips, filling the space between us.

She's close enough now that I can see starlight reflected in her eyes, can make out the thin silver rim of her irises around dilated pupils.

Close enough that if I lifted my hand, I could trail my fingers through the silky ends of her blond ponytail.

"I couldn't sleep," she tells me, inching closer.

I can feel the warmth of her body now, heating the mere inches between us. I wonder if she can hear the wild hammering of my heart.

"Oh," I say stupidly, taking a stumbling step back and blushing as that one syllable ends on a squeak. She moves forward, following my retreat with the insistence of a magnet.

"You're my mate," she says accusingly, eyes narrowed.

I jolt with surprise as my back hits the cold sandstone wall. She closes the space between us, balling her fists into the fabric of my long-sleeved t-shirt.

"Um, yah. I guess I am," I admit, willing my voice to stay steady as I reach back, clawing my fingers into the cold sandstone, resisting the urge to wrap my arms around her, pull her close to me.

Ours, my wolf rumbles. *Ours*.

"I should have known," she murmurs, leaning forward to trace the column of my throat with her lips, drinking in my scent.

The feel of her breath on my skin as she exhales sets my whole body alight, nerve endings coming alive and heart pounding until I can hear it echoing in my ears like a war drum.

"Your scent," she whispers, lips tracing up towards my ear. "It was always different. Put me on edge. Now I know why."

Her hands release their hold on my shirt, and for a moment I think she's going to step back. But then she's trailing her fingertips across my chest, down my stomach, along my sides.

"Lucy," I groan, pressing back into the rock. Like that's going to do any good. "Lucy, you have to stop."

"Why?"

Her fingers dip under my shirt, sliding up the bare expanse of my chest. I nearly whimper at the feel of it, at the way each light caress leaves a trail of fire in its wake.

"This isn't what you want," I say, lifting my chin when her lips come precariously close to my own. "You don't even like me. It's just the – um – you know..."

Gods, I'm such an idiot. Like, I can't even say the word. *Heat. Heat.* Even thinking the word makes my whole face burn with embarrassment.

"Please," Lucy whimpers, lifting her hands from under my shirt to run her fingers through my hair, pulling my head down towards her own.

Her lips crash against my own with a desperate sort of force, tasting like strawberries and rain. For a moment, I freeze, hands pressed into the wall behind me.

And then my resolve collapses, like a dam under a flash flood or a house beneath a wrecking ball, and suddenly, I'm kissing her back. Meeting her tongue with my own, wrapping my arms around her, pulling her close, drinking her in. Like she's air and I'm fire and I don't even care if we burn up together and all that is left is a pile of cold ash on the sandstone floor.

She presses her body against my own, deepening the kiss until I no longer feel the ruthless stone wall at my back. All I'm aware of is Lucy. The soft warmth of her curves, the velvety skin beneath my fingertips, the taste of her mouth.

Lucy. My mate. The other half of my soul.

Claim her, my wolf insists. *Mark her. Make her yours.*

I drag her closer, fingers gripping the soft flesh of her hips. The feeling of her pressed against me like this... it's torture. Exquisite torture. I never want it to end. And yet I need more. I need everything.

"Tobias."

Hearing my name on her lips, breathless and hungry like that. Gods. It's the sweetest sound. I tip my head back, staring up at the stars as I try to catch my breath, panting as I feel her lips brushing along my neck again. Kissing. Tasting.

The soft kisses become more insistent, as frenzied as her roving hands, as panicked as my own breath. And then there is the sharp sting of teeth grazing the tender skin at the crook of my neck. Nibbling, testing…

My eyes fly open, blood running cold. No. Nope. Nah-uh.

"Stop."

The word erupts from my lips as I grab Lucy's shoulders, pushing her away. It's surprisingly difficult, despite my larger size and even with my shifter strength.

"You have to stop. You don't know what you're doing."

She stares up at me, eyes wide and glazed with lust as she presses towards me, her hands grasping at my wrists in an effort to free herself. But I know if I let her go, she'll be up against me again. Touching me, claiming me, marking me as hers forever. And I don't know if I would stop her.

Actually, I'm pretty sure I would mark her right back.

Shit. This is bad. Really bad.

"Please," she whimpers, fingertips trailing along my arms. "Please, Tobias."

Gods, I want to. Every part of me wants to. But I can't. I won't. It wouldn't be right. Not when she's like this. Out of control.

We have to talk first. I need to make sure she knows what she's doing. That this is what she really wants. Because once she marks me, once I mark her, that's it. It's not like a drunken Vegas wedding that can be annulled a few days later.

It's forever.

"No," I tell her firmly, clenching my teeth around the wrongness of that word. "No."

She blinks up at me, some of the haze clearing from her eyes. "You – you don't want me?"

"No," I say, shaking my head for emphasis. "I do. I do want you. Just not like this. Not right here, okay?"

The colour drains from her face, hands dropping to her sides. She's trembling like an autumn leaf, either from the cold or adrenaline. I want to wrap my arms around her. Draw her to me. Warm her with my own body. But I don't trust myself. Not right now. Not when the memory of the shape of her is practically tattooed across my skin.

"Let's get back to camp, okay?"

The words catch in my throat and I ball my fists at my sides to keep from touching her.

She gives a curt nod, refusing to meet my eyes with her own. Then she's turning away, practically sprinting into the darkness, back towards the encampment without a word.

Chapter 23

Lucy Stone

"You okay, Lucy?"

It's at least the tenth time this morning that Jason has asked me this.

"I'm fine," I grit out. I try not to wrinkle my nose at the bitter taste of my own lie.

I wish it was cold enough for me to wear a hoodie, just so I could pull the hood up over my head and hide from the world.

I've never been more embarrassed in my entire life.

I basically threw myself at Tobias, like I was some sort of sex-crazed deviant. Pressed him up against the wall and thrust my tongue down his throat. He had to literally pry me off his body, like I was some alien creature trying to glom onto his face.

Which is more or less what I had done.

Heat pricks my cheeks at the memory, and I rub my face with the palms of my hands.

I'm pretty sure I was going to mark him. Sink my teeth into his neck right there, without even asking permission. That's basically the shifter equivalent of dragging someone to the alter and shoving a wedding ring on their finger. Sure, it wouldn't have been binding, unless he bit me back. But it's not exactly the done thing either.

"You're not okay," Jason argues, pressing his shoulder against mine as we walk through what I sincerely hope is the end of this gods-forsaken sandstone slot.

It's the same sort of move he would do if he was in wolf form, a physical manifestation of his support. It's sweet. And annoying.

"I can practically feel your embarrassment," Jason continues, his tone hushed. "You know embarrassment is my least favourite emotion, right? You're literally torturing me right now."

"Then go walk with someone else," I snap.

"Just tell me what's going on," he whines. "Maybe I can help you."

I just scoff because, yah, that's doubtful. Unless Jason has a time machine so I can go back and punch myself in the face before making a complete fool of myself.

Jason leans towards me, giving a surreptitious sniff in my direction.

"Can you not?" I say, shrugging away from him.

But Jason seems completely unperturbed. That's the downside of submissive wolves. Especially omegas. The second their wolf classes you as 'protector', they're in your space, full of boisterous and interfering energy, wanting to help you in any way they can. Whether you want it or not.

"You smell less, um, fruity," he announces cheerily. "That's good, right? I mean, you always get a bit grumpy when you're all…" He trails off, waving one hand emphatically in my direction.

"Really?" I say, tilting my head back in exasperation, looking up at the thin slit of pale blue sky peeking through the shadowed expanse of sandstone caging us in.

Still, it's hard to be mad at Jason. Especially when most of my anger is currently directed at myself. And Tobias. Because I'd be lying if I said I wasn't a little angry at Tobias too.

To distract myself, I glance back at Summer. She's walking beside Aires and speaking in hushed tones, a frown etched on her face. Cody follows far behind them, scowling. I know I should be worried about the three of them, but honestly, I don't have the emotional capacity to worry about their little love triangle.

I turn to survey the group walking in front of me. Red and Orrin trudging in silence, Orrin gnawing some weird homemade meat stick thing. In front of them, Gareth, Hamish and Tobias speak animatedly. Well, actually, Gareth and Hamish are speaking. Tobias just seems to be listening.

As if he feels me staring at him, he glances back over his shoulder, gold eyes meeting mine with the accuracy of a heat seeking missile. His words from last night ring in my head.

I do want you. Just not like this.

Gods, what is wrong with me? How is it he was able to have so much self-restraint, while I had basically turned into some 'wanton hussy' – as my dad would have called it - throwing myself into his arms.

But then I remember the feel of his lips on my own, the bite of his fingertips as they'd pressed into my hips. And I know he felt something. He wasn't completely unaffected.

That has to mean something, right?

"It's probably another thirty minutes until we reach the chokestone," I hear Gareth say, pulling Tobias' attention back to himself. "If we don't break for lunch, we'll be out of the slot in a few hours, and then back at the car by early afternoon."

"You guys that worried about someone coming after us?" Tobias asks.

I shiver at the sound of his voice.

Gareth shrugs noncommittally but Hamish gives a curt nod, tattooed muscles of his neck bunching as he clenches his jaw.

"As far as Drake and Huxley Black are concerned, you just stole two females and Drake's son away from their lair," Hamish explains. "Of course, they're going to come after you."

Tobias frowns, but Gareth gives a dry laugh.

"You overestimate Hux's abilities, hawk," Gareth says, shaking his head. "Sure, they'll be pissed. But there's no way he's going to know that we took them, or even where we are. Aires flew out of there, remember. Even if they do find the chopper, it'll take them ages to track us."

"Not if Drake shifts into his dragon form," Hamish counters. "Not if they have any avians in their lair. If I was tracking by wing, I'd find us within hours."

"We had a crow," Aires announces from behind me, making me start. I guess I shouldn't be surprised he's been eavesdropping like myself. "He left our lair several weeks ago though. Didn't like how things were being run."

"Seems to be a common theme." I wrinkle my nose, thinking of Tania. Of the way Summer and I were treated. "Maybe your daddy needs to re-think his PR campaign."

Aires narrows his eyes at me but I hear a few chuckles of agreement from the front of our group and shoot him a smirk.

"Can't imagine Hux is helping in that department," Red observes dryly.

"Drake isn't going to shift into his dragon form," Aires says, pointedly ignoring both my and Red's remarks. "So there won't be anyone tracking us by wing."

"How do you know that, dragon?" Hamish asks, throwing Aires a sceptical look over one shoulder. "He might think it's worth the risk of being seen."

"It's not about being seen," Aires explains, a strange sort of expression ghosting across his face. It passes too quickly for me to pinpoint. "He's got a… problem. With his dragon form."

"Really?" Hamish turns to face Aires fully, white teeth flashing gleefully as he walks backwards, rubbing his palms together and giving the dragon his undivided attention. "What sort of a problem?"

Aires' lips tighten, nostrils flaring, and I think for a moment he's not going to answer. But then he looks down at Summer, expression softening, and lets out a breath.

"His dragon is small," Aires admits, eyes flickering with guilt. Like even now he still can't stand the thought of betraying his own father.

For some reason, it makes me think of my own dad. After everything he's done to me, would I still feel guilty at spilling his secrets?

"His dragon is much smaller than it should be," Aires continues. "And his wings won't hold him."

"How on earth has he managed to keep a lair for this long?" Orrin asks, itching at the scruff on his neck.

Aires shrugs, then says: "He's always had me. Well, except for when I left to join up with Huxley's pack for a while. But then I came back, so…"

He trails off, his cryptic response raising more than a few eyebrows. But when it becomes clear he's not going to divulge any more information, Hamish shrugs, turning back to Gareth and Tobias to discuss the risks of being attacked.

And that's when it hits me. Hot and fast as a midday wind rushing across the desert. Blinding me, swallowing me up in the copper smell of blood and gunpowder and bitter lies.

The gully around me shifts and changes, narrowing to close around a towering boulder. I can hear voices echoing down from the rim of the slot, familiar as my own. Familiar, but unwelcome.

The voices of Dad and Anton, alpha Winslow and some of the enforcers.

"We've got him," I hear dad call out, his baritone echoing down the hundred or so feet to where I stand on the gully floor. "He's down."

Dad's face appears then, contorted with battle lust and excitement as he peers over the rim, one finger pointing down towards the boulder at the end of the slot. My eyes track his movement, landing at a strange heap nestled at the base of the rocks, about twenty feet ahead of me.

There is no mistaking the familiar head of brown hair, the unmoving torso, the muscled arm, laying at an unnatural angle. The golden eyes open and unseeing.

My heart sinks, turning to lead at the base of my stomach as a scream rises in my throat, tearing out of me with a force to echo the searing pain behind my ribs.

Another gunshot joins my scream, the sound ricocheting off the sandstone walls, followed by a heavy thud. I spin in time to watch Aires drop to his knees, hands half-shifted into claws, clutching at the front of his shirt, as if he can hold in the lifeblood pouring out of him.

Summer's screams join with my own, followed by the indiscernible cries of Tobias' pack mates - some already shifted into their animal forms – echoed by the hungry shouts of the males at the top of the gully rim.

As if pulled by some magnetic force, my eyes land on Cody, standing at the back of our group, unmovable as an island in a swirling sea. His jaw is clenched in a hard line, arms pulled tight across his chest.

Despite the twenty or so feet between us, despite the scent of blood and dirt and gunpowder, despite the painful ripping in my chest, I can smell him. The acrid scent of dishonesty and betrayal, razor sharp. Icy blue eyes meet my own and he lifts his chin defiantly, as if challenging me to accuse him.

It's then I remember he doesn't know. He doesn't know about my gift. None of them do, except Summer. And the two males standing on the gully rim, looking down at us, guns loaded and ready.

I point one accusing finger at Cody, baring my teeth as my face contorts with rage and pain.

"You."

Chapter 24

Tobias Finch

I watch in horror as Lucy gives a pained cry, eyes rolling back while her knees give out from under her. Instinctively, I lurch forward, as if there is some way to close the impossible distance between us before she hits the ground.

Jason breaks her fall, catching her up in his arms, teetering briefly under the sudden dead weight and the weight of both their packs. Aires is beside Jason moments later, helping him lower Lucy to the ground with surprising gentleness.

"What's happening?" I ask, looking frantically between Jason, Summer and Cody.

"I – I don't know," Summer whimpers, wringing her hands. "I've never seen her do this before."

"Me neither," Jason says, his hands still cradling Lucy's head, as if he can't bear the thought of letting it rest on the rough stone.

Something about that sends an irrational rush of jealousy shooting through me and suddenly I can't stand the thought of anyone holding Lucy but me. I kneel beside him, ignoring his protests as I gently shove him away and pull Lucy's head onto my lap.

Her brow is furrowed as if in pain, teeth bared, eyes open and rolled back so that only the whites show. Gently, I run my fingertips along her forehead, as if I can smooth away the lines with my touch. Her skin feels clammy, cold. Like my own feels after a nightmare.

"Lucy, baby," I whisper, leaning close enough to brush my lips against her hair.

I can feel everyone staring at me, can sense the murmurs of confusion pulsing down the bond from my pack mates, but I don't care. I just need to be close to her. I just need Lucy to be okay.

I can feel her short, panting breaths on my cheek, smell the faint whisper of lavender and fresh grass on her skin. But this time, instead of sending heat rushing to my core, her scent cuts into my chest, causing a strange sort of warmth to expand behind my ribcage. For once, my wolf is silent. Like even the dumb animal knows that now is not the time for his possessive rhetoric.

"I've got you," I murmur, brushing the pale strands from her forehead. "I've got you."

Her eyelids flutter at the touch, blinking dazedly before storm-grey eyes land on me.

"You're okay," I say, though I'm pretty sure the words are more to assure myself than her. "You're going to be okay."

She lets out a low whimper, eyes widening and pupils constricting almost to pin points as she struggles to sit up. I help her rise to a seated position, barely resisting the urge to pull her onto my lap and wrap my arms around her. I settle for keeping one hand on her back. For support, obviously.

"Easy does it," Orrin says from above us, the rumbling cadence of his voice somehow comforting. "Don't sit up too fast."

She twists to look at me, her eyes roving up and down my body, almost as if she's surprised to see me there. Or as if she's checking me over for injuries, when really it should be the other way around.

"Thank the gods," she murmurs, almost to herself, before squeezing her eyes shut. "Thank the gods."

"What happened, Lucy?" Summer asks, kneeling to thrust a water bottle into Lucy's hands. "Did you get dehydrated or something?"

Lucy shakes her head, but takes the water from Summer, tilting her head back to take a long drink.

"Not dehydration," Lucy says breathlessly before swiping her mouth with the back of her hand. "A vision."

Summer nods, a look of dawning comprehension lighting her features. She's the only one who appears to have any idea about what Lucy is talking about, and I can feel mixed emotions of confusion and disbelief filtering across the pack bond from.

"A vision?" Jason queries, wrinkling his nose, lips tilting down into a sceptical frown. "You never mentioned you have visions before."

Lucy rolls her eyes. "Yah, for a number of reasons. Which I'm not going to elaborate on right now, okay? We don't have much time. At least, I don't think we do…"

She purses her lips, then looks over at Gareth.

"How far is it until that chockstone thing you were talking about?" she asks him.

Gareth purses his lips in thought. "Maybe twenty minutes. Half an hour. Why?"

"Because they're coming for us," Lucy says, the words tumbling out in breathless pants. "The Clear Creek pack. They're going to attack from up above when we get to the chokestone. With guns."

She points one trembling hand to the sliver of sky looming above us at the top of the sandstone slot.

"Alpha Winslow, my dad, Anton, a couple of enforcers. They're going to shoot at us when we get to the chokestone."

She turns, fixing Cody with a look that can only be described as feral rage.

Like, I've seen Lucy pissed off before. In fact, last year I would have said seethingly angry was her default setting.

But this is different. There's a wildness to her anger. Like she wants to shift into her wolf form and tear the flesh off Cody's bones.

"He knows," Lucy says, pointing one accusatory finger at Cody. "He sold you out. Betrayed you."

"Please," Cody snorts derisively, lips curling back into a sneer. "Listen to yourself. What are you now, a fortune-teller?" He looks at the rest of us. "You guys aren't buying this crap, are you? Visions? Really."

"It's the truth," Lucy retorts.

Her voice is even, but from my position next to her, I can see her jaw tick, can see her fists clenching in her lap. She stares up at me, grey eyes burning hot as molten silver.

"They shot you," she says, and I don't miss the way her voice quavers when she adds: "In my vision, they shot you. I – I'm pretty sure they killed you."

She squeezes her eyes shut, then looks up at Summer. "They shot Aires too. Right in the chest."

Summer gives a gasp of surprise, eyebrows shooting up to her hairline.

"What a bunch of crap," Cody scoffs, glaring at Lucy with unmasked disgust. "No wonder dad locked you up. You're absolutely bat-shit crazy."

"That's enough!"

The words snap out of me like a whip and, without realising it, I'm springing to my feet, stopping when my face is only inches from Cody's. The desire to strike out at him, attack him for insulting Lucy – it's visceral.

But then I remember Quentin Blake. The bloodied ice of the school parking lot. I remember Blackwater. The snow painted red.

I take a deep breath, pushing the anger down into the ever-filling well as I content myself with saying: "You have no right to talk to her like that. None at all. Be sceptical if you want, but be respectful."

"Respectful." Cody's upper lip twitches. "She hasn't earned my respect."

Hamish pushes between us, thrusting one tattooed hand against Cody's chest, causing him to stumble back.

"That's enough, wolf. Your alpha gave you an order."

All traces of mocking laughter have faded from Hamish's face, leaving only lines as harsh and jarring as his red faux-hawk. I'm suddenly reminded of the first time I met Hamish. When he swore fealty to me without so much as a second thought, then turned his knife on the others, bullying them into joining my pack as well.

"It's easy enough to figure out if the Clear Creek pack are up there," Hamish continues, tilting his head to the slit of sky above us. "I'll just shift into my hawk form and have a look."

"Won't they notice you?" Lucy asks.

At some point she must have risen too, because she's standing beside me, close enough that her lavender scent washes over me, at once soothing and stirring me to action.

"I mean, I'm guessing you're bigger than a normal hawk, right?" she continues. "Which means they'll know you're a shifter."

"They might, if they see me," Hamish drawls. "But they won't. I know how to fly without being seen."

"I think it's a good idea," I say, nodding my approval, grateful for a solution. For a way to find out the truth.

Not that I think Lucy is lying. Maybe it's just because she's my mate, or maybe it's that I could practically feel the frantic terror coming off of her in waves when she first came to, but I completely believe Lucy. Logically, I know I shouldn't. After all, I've never heard of anyone having visions of the future.

But then, dad more or less raised me to be a human. This could just be one of the many things I wasn't educated about. Like the fact that I didn't know I can't really get sick. Or the fact that dragon shifters are a thing.

In a matter of moments, Hamish has stripped down to his tattoo-covered skin, completely uncaring of his audience. Actually, it's almost like he wants everyone to see him. To notice the way his tattoos coat not just his arms and neck, but his whole torso and legs. An artistic advertisement of just how insane this male is. Of the pain he's able to endure.

He flashes Cody one last challenging smirk before leaping into the air, feathers taking the place of inked skin as a giant red-tailed hawk lifts effortlessly towards the blue slit of sky.

"We should get ready for an attack," Orrin suggests when Hamish disappears past the lip of the sandstone slot. "Just in case someone spots him. Get into defensive positions."

I frown at the sandstone walls caging us in, then up at the strip of blue above us. The gully narrows slightly at the base, its smooth walls offering no protection. We're completely vulnerable here.

"What do you suggest?" I ask, the question directed at Orrin. Because he's the oldest. Because he's fought before, and has the scars to prove it.

"I could shield everyone," Aires suggests, stepping away from Summer's side and shrugging off his backpack. He eyes the gully critically, as if mentally calculating its shape and size. "If I shift into my dragon form, I can wedge myself up in the wider part of the gully and act as a shield."

I peer up at the sandstone walls, trying to envision a giant dragon wedged up above us. A laugh bubbles up my throat at the ridiculousness of it, but luckily I manage to stifle it, so it just comes out as a strange choking sound.

"No way," Summer argues, shaking her head adamantly. "Then you'd just get shot."

Aires practically beams at this declaration.

"You're worried about me," he says, reaching across to toy with a lock of Summer's hair, chuckling as she steps back to avoid his touch, her cheeks colouring.

"Of course. I'm not a complete monster."

"There's nothing to worry about, beautiful. Bullets won't do much against dragon hide. Sure, my wings might get a bit torn up. But nothing that won't heal. Trust me, I'll be completely fine."

"He's right," Lucy says, her eyes going momentarily glassy, voice taking on a hollow sound. Then she blinks, eyes re-focusing as she gives her head a little shake, adding: "Dad and the alpha won't see Hamish. But Aires is right about the dragon form. The bullets won't harm him."

Aires starts to undress, about as self-conscious as Hamish was earlier. Only he's standing right in front of Summer, staring right at her.

"Whoa, whoa, whoa," Summer cries.

Her hands fly up to cover her eyes, doing nothing to hide the fact that her face has turned a vibrant shade of red. She's dropping her hands a moment later though, staring in awe as Aires grows and transforms before her eyes.

Where Hamish shifted in less than a second, Aires' shift is slow, almost arduous. His body expands, skin becoming green metallic scales, hands and feet becoming claws. When wings sprout and unfurl from a scaled, muscled back, it reminds me of a time lapse I saw of a butterfly emerging from a chrysalis.

Honestly, it looks a little painful.

As he shifts, he climbs, claws digging into the slick sandstone with the efficiency of ice picks, manoeuvring up the sandstone slot until he's essentially a dragon canopy, casting us in shadow.

"Holy crap," Summer says, blinking up at him in amazement, one hand pressed to her chest. "Holy freaking crap."

The dragon lets out a purring rumble in response, like the animal is pleased by its mate's awe of him.

"Now what?" Red asks, eyeing the dragon's belly warily as he slides to a seated position, his back resting against the sandstone wall. "We just sit and wait?"

"Guess so. Unless you have a deck of cards or something," Gareth deadpans, slumping down beside him.

Orrin snorts, lips curling in mild amusement as he shakes his head, pulls out another one of his homemade venison meat sticks and starts to unwrap it. I stare at it, probably a little too long because Orrin looks at me, eyes narrowed.

"Not a chance, pup."

"Only you," Gareth says, pointing a finger in Orrin's direction. "Only you would have the balls to call our alpha a pup."

Orrin shrugs. "Balls have nothing to do with it. I've defended my own territory for longer than you've been alive. To me, you're all pups." He looks up at Aires, a thoughtful frown tipping the corner of his mouth. "Well, except maybe that one."

"Um, guys…" Jason says, his voice pitched with anxiety.

I turn to face him, frowning when I notice he's at the far end of the gully, no longer under Aires' cover.

"Get back over here, Jason," Summer calls.

"Not so loud," Lucy hisses, pressing one finger to her lips. "We don't know how the sound will carry."

Jason trots back towards us, face pale and expression drawn.

"Guys," he says, dropping his voice to a whisper, light brown eyes so wide, the whites are fully visible. He points one shaking hand toward the gully, in the direction of the chokestone. The direction we had been heading, until a few minutes ago. And then he says the three words that nearly cause me to sink to my knees.

"Cody is missing."

Chapter 25

Tobias Finch

"I knew it," Red grumbles, running his hand over one tufted cat ear. "Knew that bastard couldn't be trusted."

Orrin nods, then gives me a pitying look. "We did tell you, pup," he says, reaching up to scratch one bearded, scarred cheek. "After the hit and run, remember."

I close my eyes, reaching down the pack link towards Cody. I can feel him running, can feel the wild beat of his heart as his paws pound the sandstone path towards the chokestone. I can feel the distance growing between us with each bounding stride he takes, the pack bond holding him to me stretching thinner and thinner.

I wonder how long it will take before it goes silent. Before I can no longer speak to him, mind to mind.

Whatever our disagreements, he's still my pack mate. He belongs to me. With me. With my pack.

My wolf lets out a disapproving rumble, demanding that I order him to return. Command him to heel.

I want more than that. I want to understand why he betrayed me. I want things to be right again between us. Maybe not like they were before I became alpha. Maybe they can never be like that again. Still, there has to be a way to fix this.

Cody, I say, pushing the words across the thinning link towards him. Holding them out, like an offering. *Cody, you don't have to run. We can work this out. Whatever it is, we can work this out.*

My words are met with silence, though the answering pulse of disbelief and anger tells me he has heard every word.

"You could just order him to return," Gareth suggests out loud, mirroring my wolf's desires. "I mean, you're his alpha. You're a born alpha. He'd have to listen."

I shake my head, frowning down the meandering hallway of the sandstone slot, as if I can somehow see along its bending length to wherever Cody is running now.

I won't use my alpha command. Not on Cody. Not like that. If I did, I'd be no better than Huxley Black, creating a pack by force, demanding their obedience without free-will. Without real loyalty.

"No," Lucy says, her voice unusually soft as she sidles up to me. "Tobias is right. We should let him go."

I know there are a million other things I should be worrying about right now. Cody. The Clear Creek pack. Hamish soaring overhead. The dragon clawing for purchase above our heads. Huxley Black and Drake, mere miles away from us in this gods-forsaken place.

But for some reason, my mind catches on her use of the word "we". The sound of that word on her lips causing an unexpected warmth to rise in my chest, unfurling like the petals of some wildflower in the desert, rebellious and vibrant against cold stone. I turn to offer her a tentative smile.

"What?" she asks, frowning in confusion. "What's so funny."

"Nothing," I say, shaking my head, but I can't wipe the smile from my lips. "Nothing's funny."

"Then why are you smiling like an idiot?" she snaps. But the insult lacks its usual bite, and I feel my smile growing.

"You said 'we'," I say, pressing my lips together in an attempt to hide my amusement. "And you agreed with me."

"I didn't agree with you," Lucy counters, flicking the end of her ponytail over one shoulder. "I just said you were right. There's a difference."

I raise one brow, doing my best to bite back the smirk tugging at the corners of my lips.

"I'm sorry, but why aren't you ordering Cody to return?" Gareth interrupts, drawing my attention away from Lucy. "You know he's just going straight to daddy, right? Back to the Clear Creek pack? You should order him back. Punish him."

My wolf bristles, lips curling at Gareth's tone. At the use of that word "should".

I take a steadying inhale, pushing my wolf's agitation down. Gareth isn't Cody. He's not challenging me. Not really. He's just trying to help.

Before I can articulate my response, Lucy is there, practically leaping towards Gareth's face, hands balled into fists at her sides.

"He's letting him go because, unlike you, he's actually using the grey matter taking up residence in his skull."

Gareth narrows his eyes at her, losing his usual nonchalant demeanour. Lucy just glares back at him, completely unfazed.

"What do you think would happen if Cody came back?"

When Gareth doesn't answer, Lucy sighs resignedly. Like maybe she's trying to explain algebra to a five-year-old, and has just accepted that the kid is not going to understand it.

"There's really only two ways this could go." She holds up one finger for emphasis. "First, Cody would continue to sell us out to the Clear Creek pack, feed information to his dad, whatever." She holds up a second finger for emphasis. "Or, you guys lock him up or kill him. Whatever it is your pack does to traitors. And then the Clear Creek pack would have grounds to openly retaliate. They could drag all their allies in to the battle too – and you know, they have a lot of allies, right? And then poof." She waves her hand, fingers perilously close to Gareth's reddening face. "That would probably be the end of the Liberty pack."

I stare at Lucy, impressed. And slightly embarrassed. I hadn't actually thought about any of those things. I just didn't want to order Cody around.

"Lucy has a point, scavenger," Red drawls, surveying the pair from his seat on the gully floor. He's leaning against the sandstone wall, arms outstretched and resting on his knees, head tilted to rest on the stone behind him. "Don't be sore just because the little she-wolf has better tactical skills than you do. I mean, you're not really that surprised, are you? Your most recent demonstration of genius was to have yourself be bait in a trap."

Gareth turns to glare at the cat. Red just smiles in reply, showing all of his teeth.

"Speaking of great ideas," Jason interjects, guiding Summer towards us. "I think Summer and Lucy should join our pack."

"Um, no." Lucy gives an almost violent shake of her head. "No way."

"Jason is right, Luce. Think about it," Summer pleads. "What do you think alpha Winslow is going to do the moment we're in reach of the pack bond? Do you think he's going to just let us go? Even if they lose the element of surprise, they can still order us to go with them."

Summer wrings her hands, face paling as she adds: "I am not going back to that pack. It was bad before, but now…"

Her voice trails off as she looks up meaningfully at the scaled mass perched above us. Red notices and gives a dry chuckle.

"Now you're a rebel who set fire to their forest, broke Lucy out of jail and broke their golden boy's heart by finding your true mate?" Red suggests caustically. Apparently, watching Lucy berate Gareth has cheered him into becoming talkative. "Yah, I'd say that's a good enough reason not to want to go back to the Clear Creek pack."

"Please, Lucy," Jason begs, ignoring Red's commentary. "It's a good pack."

Lucy's shoulders slump, breath coming out in a whoosh. "I don't know," she starts, looking between Jason and Summer, lips pressing together in a thin line. "I wasn't planning on joining any pack..."

She looks at me, grey eyes shining with vulnerability. It reminds me of the way she looked at me last night, when her usual coldness had been replaced with heat. A heat that had stoked the fire in my blood, had me answering her kisses with my own.

I stare back at her, rubbing the back of my neck with one hand, unsure of what to say.

Lucy is pack, my wolf inserts, tipping his head up to sniff longingly in Lucy's direction. *Lucy is ours.*

I frown, not quite agreeing with the animal. I mean, I know Lucy is my mate. Maybe I've known it, at some instinctual level, from the moment I caught her lavender and fresh grass scent in English class. Then, her scent had filled me with a fluttering anticipation that had bordered on dread. Even the wolf in me had wanted to run from it. Run from her.

Now, even with the aching pull behind my chest drawing me closer and closer to her, even with the hunger thrumming through my veins, I'm still a little afraid of her. The thought of having her in my pack, seeing her everyday – it's terrifying.

Lucy is pack, my wolf insists, his rumble rising to a growl. *Belongs at our side. Keep her safe.*

Safe. Yah, the animal might have a point there.

"It – it would be great if you joined our pack," I offer lamely.

Lucy nods stiffly, eyes flicking away from my own.

"Yah," she finally says, the word coming out on an exhale. "Yah, okay."

Lucy Stone

Gareth's knife is out, ready to make the first binding cut across Summer's palm, when the fluttering of feathered wings catches our notice.

I look up, squinting to try and see beyond the giant mass of dragon still wedged in the rock above us. It's impossible to see anything except scales, and by the time the red-tailed hawk comes in sight, he's gliding to the ground, feathers shifting effortlessly into tattooed flesh.

"Growing your pack again, hey alpha?" Hamish asks dryly as he yanks on his pants, sharp eyes taking in Tobias and Summer's outstretched hands and the knife at the ready.

When no one answers, Hamish looks up at the dragon perched above us and flashes a smile that is about as warm as a grave, as friendly as the bared teeth of a skeleton.

"Nice roof," Hamish deadpans. "Glad to see the dragon found a way to be useful. You going to make him part of the pack too?"

He says this last part with a smirk aimed in Gareth's direction. No doubt recalling Gareth's earlier adamant objections to having Aires be part of the Liberty pack.

"We've already talked about the dragon," Gareth snaps, tapping the flat of his blade against the palm of his hand in annoyance. "Are the Clear Creek pack up there or not?"

"Oh, they're up there alright," Hamish drawls, sparing me a wary glance before turning to face Gareth and Tobias. "Exactly as the little seer said, from what I could tell. Five males, all of them armed. I couldn't get close enough to tell what type of bullets they had. Assuming they're silver though. Otherwise, what's the point?"

Seer. The word conjures up images of old women in gypsy caravans, of tarot cards and crystals. Is that what my gift has become? An unpleasant shudder courses through me at the thought.

"I'm not a seer," I argue lamely. But the words leave a bitter taste in my mouth, taunting me with their untruthfulness.

"Uh-huh. Whatever you say." Hamish shrugs. "Either way, we need to finish up here. I spotted Cody's wolf running like his fur was on fire. It won't be long before he reaches his buddies. Heck, he might be there now."

"Yah. Okay." Tobias holds his hand out to take the blade from Gareth, making a long cut along the palm of his hand. "Let's do this thing."

I blink at him, practically gaping as he takes Summer's hand in his own, quickly giving an oath to protect, not demanding any oath from Summer in exchange.

"Right, your turn," he tells me, holding the bloodied knife out to me, hilt first.

I wrinkle my nose. Not because of the blood, but because I've never heard of a pack bond being formed like this, without an oath from the person joining the pack. Not to mention the complete absence of ceremony and solemnity.

It's nothing like what I've seen at the Clear Creek pack.

"Hurry," Hamish urges, glancing worriedly upwards. As if he's expecting to see alpha Winslow peering down at us at any moment.

"Fine," I hiss, snapping the blade from Tobias' outstretched hand.

I grit my teeth through the bite of pain as the blade cuts the tender flesh of my palm, then hold my hand out to Tobias.

I don't remember joining the Clear Creek pack. I would have been a child when the ceremony took place. Old enough to speak, to recite whatever words alpha Winslow instructed me to say. Young enough to probably have blubbered at the binding cut. At least I would have had my mom's arms to comfort me.

I'm not sure what I expect – maybe pain at the breaking of my bond with the Clear Creek pack. Maybe a pull similar to the incessant thrum behind my ribs, pulling me like the needle of a compass towards the boy in front of me.

Instead, a warmth rushes up my arm, soothing as a caress, settling like liquid honey in my chest.

It's like taking that first sip of hot chocolate after playing all day in the snow. It's like seeing a friend after a long absence and folding them into a hug. It's like spring sunshine on your face after a long winter.

My breath hitches in surprise as I close my eyes, savouring the feel of it, never wanting it to end.

It's like coming home.

Chapter 26

Lucy Stone

"Any bright ideas on how we're going to get out of here?" Red asks, brushing sand from his pants as he rises to his feet. "Because I don't know about you, but I don't particularly like the idea of sitting here, waiting for silver bullets to rain down on us."

He pauses, tilting his head up at Aires. The dragon is as immovable looking as a boulder, casting us in shadow and hiding us from view.

"And we can't hide under your dragon friend forever."

"He's not my friend," I remind him, absently rubbing the cut on my palm with the thumb of my other hand. It's already knitting closed. With my shifter healing, it should be no more than a fading scar by the afternoon.

"I think we should try and hike out," Summer suggests. "They know we're here, so there is no point in trying to back-track."

"No way," Jason shakes his head. "If we do that, they'll just fire at us."

"They'll do that anyway," Summer points out. "You think they're just going to wait for us to come to them? No way. As soon as Cody gets to them, they're going to be heading our way."

"Yah, I don't think running is the answer," Gareth agrees, rubbing one stubbled cheek thoughtfully.

For once, his usual sleepy, sarcastically unconcerned look is gone, eyes glinting with razor focus, lips curling into a cunning smile. I can see the coyote in him now, that predatory mischievousness that delights in unsolvable problems.

"Especially when there are more of us than them," he continues. "We should have the advantage."

"But they have guns," Jason reminds him sagely. "Silver bullets. Not to mention, we're down in this gully."

Gareth waves one hand dismissively, but I can't help but gape at Jason.

In the Clear Creek pack, he would never have spoken up about strategy. I don't think I've ever heard him give his opinion about anything. Even when alpha Winslow forbade him from pursuing his mate, Jason kept quiet, keeping his discontent to himself.

"Sure, we don't have the best position…" Gareth begins.

Red cuts him off with a scoff. "That's the understatement of the year. Cody has basically served us up to them on a silver platter. And there is literally no way the terrain could be less in our favour."

"We have a dragon," Hamish interjects, pointing to the mass of scales perched silently above us. "That negates the minor terrain issue."

"Minor terrain issue?" Red throws up his hands, then points accusingly between Gareth and Hamish. "I said following you two out here would be a death trap, didn't I? This is why I don't do packs."

"Oh, calm down," Orrin rumbles, rising to his feet. "You're getting all worked up for nothing again."

"Nothing!" Red's eyes flash warningly, cat ears flattening against his skull. "This is hardly nothing, bear."

Tobias stands back, watching, listening as everyone argues about what the best course of action is. No one actually coming up with a real plan, but everyone quick to shut the other's ideas down.

My head takes that moment to throb violently, the sounds of my new pack mates' raised voices echoing painfully in my skull. Squeezing my eyes shut, I press my hands to my temple, trying to shut them out.

And then I see it. The vision whispers across my mind, like images painted on silk, blotting out the now with the ripples of an uncertain future.

A choice. A possibility.

My eyes flutter open to nine inquisitive stares and I lick my lips, tasting dust and grit on my tongue.

For the briefest of moments, stupid as it is, I consider keeping what I saw a secret. The compulsion to hide my gift, drilled into me by years of training and threats, it's almost strong enough to override reason.

I square my shoulders, shrugging off the mantle of secrecy, the chains of conditioning. The time for hiding my gift is over. I left secrecy lying in the dust when I told them about my vision of the attack. There is no sense in holding back now.

"I know what we need to do," I say firmly, looking straight into the golden pools of Tobias' unwavering stare. "I know how we can get out of this."

Chapter 27

Tobias Finch

"No." The word escapes my lips before I can hold it back. "Absolutely not."

I know I should probably be a little more tactful, but Lucy's proposal is probably the worst idea I've ever heard. My wolf growls his agreement. Good. Even the dumb animal knows this is a terrible idea.

Lucy's expression darkens, and she narrows her eyes. The look is so reminiscent of how she looked the first day I met her, I almost smile.

Almost.

"No way," I say again, shaking my head adamantly. "I can't let you and Summer do that."

"Wait, so you'd let me go?" Jason asks, half teasing. Like maybe he's trying to lighten the tension building between us, filling the cramped space of the narrow sandstone gully like static electricity.

I shake my head. "No. No one should go. If anyone is going to go, it should be me."

Lucy scoffs.

"Do you have a death wish, wolfy?" Red snaps, pushing away from the sandstone wall. "Or are you just dumb? Those assholes have come here to shoot you. You. No one else."

"I'm not letting any of you guys put yourselves at risk for me," I argue stubbornly. "I'm your alpha."

"So, what?" Lucy crosses her arms over her chest. "You've been my alpha for all of five minutes, and now you're going to order me around?"

The move highlights the swell of her curves under her tank top. My mind wanders unhelpfully back to last night, recalling the way she felt pressed up against me. Warm and soft and *mine*.

I grit my teeth, drawing one hand over my face.

Not the time. Now is not the time.

"No. That's not what I'm saying," I say, waving my hands in front of me, like maybe I can clear her accusations from the air like a visible fog. "I'm saying it's my job as the alpha to protect my pack. Letting you guys go out there as bait – that is the exact opposite of protecting my pack."

"Beg to differ, alpha," Hamish drawls. A dark grin spreads across his face as he emphasises the last word. Because he knows how much I hate it.

"Really?" I say caustically. "What a surprise.

Hamish just chuckles, running one tattooed hand through his red faux-hawk.

"If you're dead, you can't protect your pack. You head out there alone, and they shoot you." He makes a gun with one hand, pointing it at me. "Bang. Dead. Bye-bye alpha."

I give him a bland look, hoping he can see how unimpressed I am. He returns it with a smirk.

"Once you're dead, they'll pick the rest of us off, or assimilate us into their pack. Whatever suits their agenda. Not just us, but all the guys back at pack territory too." His smirk fades, eyes hardening. "So, if you think running ahead and using yourself as bait is going to protect anyone, you're a gods damned idiot, alpha."

My wolf rumbles his irritation at the male, wanting to snap his teeth and force compliance. Force respect. Completely unconcerned with what Hamish is actually saying, or whether the arguments are logical.

And that, right there, is what is wrong with my wolf. Because I have to concede that Hamish is right. No matter how much I hate it.

"Fine," I sigh. "But that doesn't mean Lucy, Summer and Jason should be sacrificing themselves either."

"It's not a sacrifice if it works," Hamish points out.

"It will work," Lucy says adamantly, and there is so much confidence in her tone that I want to believe her. "I've seen it."

I stare at her for a long moment, meeting her grey eyes with my own. The way she's standing there, stance wide, arms crossed, eyes shimmering with silver fire - I can tell she's practically vibrating with the need to protect her new pack, and it reminds me of how she looked when she announced she was rescuing Anton.

I admired that loyal protectiveness then. Now… now I could practically fall to my knees before her. I'm completely awed that she would give that loyalty to my pack. To me.

I don't deserve it. Maybe I'll never be able to deserve it. But gods, I'm going to try.

It's also a huge freaking pain. Because I want to wrap her up in my arms, drag her away from this place and keep her safe from every possible danger. Preferably somewhere alone. Maybe without clothes.

"You need to let us do this," Jason murmurs from beside me, resting one hand on my shoulder as he looks between me and Lucy, understanding flickering in his intelligent eyes. "We're wolves. And we're part of this pack. If we're going to get out of this together, you need to let us do this. You need to let us fight for the pack."

My wolf flicks his ears, lifting his nose in reluctant acknowledgement of what our omega is saying. As much as I hate the thought of any of them – especially Lucy - going into danger, the animal recognises the primal need to fight. To protect the pack. The instinctive knowing that we can only survive together. That an alpha is only as strong as his pack.

"If you want me to stay behind, you'll have to make me," Lucy says challengingly, before flicking her blond ponytail over one shoulder. "Because I'm going, Tobias Finch. Whether you like it or not."

"Is that right?" I say, raising one eyebrow, the shadow of a grin ghosting my lips, even as anxiety knots in my stomach.

She tilts her chin defiantly in response and my wolf lets out an amused huff. Yet another reminder of why the dumb animal is in a cage.

When anyone else challenges my authority, the megalomaniac animal wants to attack them and cause grievous bodily harm. When Lucy does it, he thinks it's cute.

"Fine," I say, gritting my teeth. "We'll do it your way. But I still don't like it."

Chapter 28

Lucy Stone

I'm running, paws thundering wildly over the dry, cool sand, my heart thumping frantically against my ribs, it's beat a rhythmic staccato that demands to be answered by wolf song. I tilt my head, giving the nut brown she-wolf beside me a lupine smile before letting out a howl. Her eyes widen in surprise just as the pale brown wolf trailing behind us gives his answering yip.

What are you doing, Summer asks through the bond.

A new bond. A new pack link. A new pack.

As reluctant as I was to join Tobias' pack, I'm almost giddy with the thought of it now.

Or maybe that's just the adrenaline of finally letting my wolf run after so many months of captivity.

Running, I reply slyly. *I'm running.*

Well, obviously. I can practically hear the smile in her voice. *But why are you making so much noise?*

Because it feels good to sing? Because even my wolf wants the world to know she'll never be silent again? I don't answer her, letting another howl slip through my lips.

This time, she joins in with her own, our voices echoing down the length of the sandstone gully.

"That's Summer and Jason," I hear a familiar male voice call out, the sound muted even to my wolf ears as it travels down from the rim above us.

Cody.

"And that's Lucy," another voice replies.

I pull to a stop, ears twitching, turning to take more of that voice in. Anton. My brother.

I freeze at the sinister clicking of someone cocking a gun, of a bullet sliding into the chamber. The sound skitters across the sandstone walls, turning my blood to ice, making my hackles rise along my spine.

"State your business," alpha Winslow calls down to us, voice ringing with authority, weighted with alpha command.

I feel the order slide off my fur, harmless as water.

Well, now I know what I always suspected, but could never test while I was subject to his authority. I am stronger than him.

Beside me, Summer shifts, rising gracefully to stand in one smooth movement. This close to her, I can see the way she's shivering, either from the coolness of the shaded gully, or from fear. Maybe both. I press against her, leaning my flank against her thigh in a silent offering of support.

"We – we managed to escape," she warbles, the tremor to her voice lending credibility to her lie. "We just want to come home now. Can – can you get us out of here."

They don't answer, but the murmur of hushed voices trickles down to us. I can make out every other word, can discern the tones of doubt, the lyrical rising and falling of disagreement.

I wait, muscles tensing under my white fur, certain that a denial will come. Doubt wars with the trust I should have in my own visions. Surely Cody will know that neither I nor Jason would want to return to the Clear Creek pack? Surely dad and alpha Winslow must know that I would never return, not after how they've treated me?

A clattering sound pulls me from my thoughts, making me flinch and bare my teeth, until I realise it's just the sound of a rope snaking down towards us.

"We'll have to haul you up one at time," Anton calls down.

I stare up at his face, at least a hundred feet above me, drinking in the familiar features I know as well as my own. For the first time since leaving Clear Creek territory, I feel a twinge of guilt. I left him behind, without so much as a goodbye.

And now I'm going to trick him. The twinge blooms, growing to the weight of a lead ball in my stomach.

"You need to tie it around yourself," Cody says, when the rope finally hits the ground.

"I-I'm scared of heights," Summer admits, clutching the rope to her chest like it's a lifeline, but making no move to secure herself to it.

"We've got it tied off up here," Cody assures, a gentleness to his tone that I haven't heard in months.

It reminds me of the old Cody. The Cody I grew up with. The Cody who I teased. The Cody who was going to be my alpha one day.

"Anton, Jeb and I will pull you up. We won't drop you. I promise," he says, and even from this distance, I swear I can see the dimples pulling at the corners of his cheeks as he smiles.

"I don't know," Summer says warily.

"Send Lucy or Jason up first then," alpha Winslow's voice booms out, sharp with urgency. "We don't have all day."

"Be patient with her, dad." I hear Cody pleading with him. "She's just scared, okay."

"She can be scared later."

"I'll climb up," Jason calls out, voice steady.

I glance over at him, my ears flicking in surprise. He'd shifted so quietly, I hadn't even noticed.

Are you sure? Summer asks through the bond.

Positive, he replies, giving her a wan smile. *It has to be me. You know they're only bringing us up because Cody wants you*. He pauses, frowning at me thoughtfully. *And maybe because they want Lucy's gift.* He gives a little shrug. *I'm just collateral. Baggage. The side dish to the main event.*

I snort at that, though it's a strange wheezing sort of sound since I'm in wolf form.

You aren't, Summer silently argues, but she steps back to let Jason loop the rope around his waist and legs, tying it off when it vaguely resembles a climbing harness.

Wish me luck, he says through our pack link. *Hopefully I don't get killed before the rest of the guys get there.*

He says it jokingly. To lighten the tension he can no doubt sense coursing through both me and Summer. Still, I give a low growl of disapproval.

No one is going to die, I remind myself. *No one is going to die.*

At least, not if my gift can be trusted.

TOBIAS FINCH

For some reason, I thought it would be flat up on top of the ridge. I guess because, when you look up at the rim from the base of the gully, it's just one consistent line. Sure, it rises and falls a little bit as you go along, the wall higher in some spots and lower in others. But nothing to indicate that there is essentially a deadly rock obstacle course looming above you.

I can now see why my original suggestion that we all just climb out of the gully and hike out from up here was laughed at so heartily by Hamish.

Hamish gives a knowing smirk when he sees me surveying the landscape with a frown.

"See what I mean, alpha? We'd never be able to hike out this way. Pity you wolves aren't blessed with wings like me and Aires here."

Aires lifts his bat-like wings, not fully extending them, but just letting them give a little flutter. It seems like a smug flutter.

"No use having wings that can't be used ninety-nine percent of the time," Gareth grumbles, glaring at the dragon in question. "The second you get off the ground, people will be taking photos. At least no one is going to notice a coyote. Or a hawk."

Red grapples his way over the ledge, scrambling to his feet before pausing to bend at the waist, resting his elbows on his knees as he wheezes to catch his breath.

"True," Red says between breaths as he unties the rope from around his hips.

I'm momentarily surprised to hear him agreeing with Gareth for once. Until he says: "But people like to shoot coyotes. They don't usually shoot bobcats. We're a more likeable animal."

"That's not true and you know it," Orrin growls, an edge to his voice I've never heard before. "Humans will shoot anything that moves. Give them a gun and they think they're gods. The top of the food chain. The ultimate predator."

"Aren't they?" I ask.

Maybe it's naïve. Or maybe it's just because I've basically been raised a human. But I had always thought that humans were at the top of the food chain. Well, humans and shifters. And Bengal tigers.

Orrin shoots me an incredulous look, then waves one meaty hand at the landscape around us. The landscape that looks like it's just been pulled from a science fiction film showcasing an inhospitable planet.

Red and white sandstone rocks rise and fall at odd angles, jagged as sharks' teeth, occasionally giving way to person-sized crevasses and pits, with drops of at least a hundred feet. Even worse than the jagged boulders are the smooth patches of what Gareth has informed me are called 'slick-rock' – massive sheets of stone as easy to walk across as an ice-skating rink. Most of those also drop off unexpectedly to stony pits that wait like the open maws of beasts.

"Look around you, pup," Orrin says, indicating to the hellscape surrounding us. "Do you think a human could survive in this place for more than twenty-four hours with nothing but what the gods gave them? With their thin skin and their fragile bodies? No. Of course not. Nature is the ultimate predator." Orrin's eyes narrow as he presses one thumb against his broad chest. "We are the ultimate predators."

"Okay, old man," Red says, thumping Orrin on the back. "You can get off the soapbox now."

Orrin shrugs away from Red's touch, grumbling about disrespectful felines as he ambles with surprising grace across the rocky landscape.

We follow after him, heading slightly south of where Hamish said the Clear Creek pack was. The general plan is to sneak up on them from behind while Lucy, Summer and Jason distract them.

Though even if they do manage to spot us, at least we'll be out of the gully. So we won't be completely at the mercy of their guns.

Looking across the barren wasteland in front of us, I'm not so sure this idea is going to be very easy to execute. First of all, it's going to take us much longer to traverse the boulders and death pits up here than it takes to run along the flat of the gully. Second, while the boulders do provide some coverage, it seems a bit like playing laser tag. Or paint ball. Like, sure, there's all these things you can use for cover, but at some crucial point you're going to be exposed.

Only this isn't paintball. And I know from experience that bullets – especially silver ones – really, really hurt.

"You're going to have to shift back to your human form," Hamish tells Aires. "There is no way we are going to be able to sneak up on them if you're ambling along the size of a house."

The dragon tilts his head at Hamish, one slitted eye blinking eerily as a giant nostril flares, letting out a hot gust of air.

"Guess that's a no then," Hamish chuckles, shaking his head. "Fine. But you give us away, and it's your mate's life you're risking, lizard."

A low rumbling growl is the only response before the dragon is slinking after Orrin, his scaled belly scraping over jagged stone, clawed feet pulling him forward.

It's not long before I'm trailing at the end of the group, close behind Red, carefully picking my way over boulders and crevasses. I stretch my mind out to Lucy, Summer and Jason, feeling the threads of the link I share with them. I can feel Cody too, my link with him growing stronger as we get nearer.

Which probably means they are all together. Or at least, close enough.

Tentatively, I reach down the link I share with Lucy, vibrant and thrumming with her unique energy.

Lucy? I say down the bond, hoping that we're close enough for her to hear me.

What is it?

Her words brush across my mind, sensuous as a caress, making goosebumps rise on my arms despite the scorching midday sun. Gods. Hearing her in my mind, sharing a pack bond with her and not touching her – it's almost too much to endure.

You guys doing okay? I ask, hoping she can't hear the tense longing in my words.

Fine.

The words come out haltingly, as if she isn't quite sure that she is fine, and then she's silent for a long moment. Not like she's ignoring me, but more like she's put me on hold while she talks to someone else.

They're hauling us up to the rim, she finally explains. *Jason is going up first. He's climbing as slowly as possible. Summer and I will do the same. We'll take as long as we can, give you guys time to get here.*

Okay, I respond, then pause, realising I don't actually know how long it will take to reach them. *We're moving as fast as we can.*

I know.

I swear I can hear the faintest of smiles on those two words, warm and delicate as a Wyoming wildflower.

Even when I let the connection drop, and silence fills the space her words had occupied, I can still feel the thrum of the bond between us.

Pack, my wolf reminds me eagerly. *Lucy is pack.*

For once, I can't even deride my wolf's smug satisfaction.

Chapter 29

Lucy Stone

There's something surreal about being hoisted over the rim of the gully, leaving the claustrophobic space I've been forced to share with nine other beings for the past twenty-four-hours, and coming face-to-face with my dad.

It's only been a handful of days since I left the Clear Creek pack territory, roaring into the night with Summer, leaving a wildfire in our wake. Only a handful of days, and yet, as I take in dad's familiar features, something seems different.

The heavy jaw, thick brow drawing together over dark brown eyes, the hard line of his mouth – those are all the same. Only now, there's a flatness in the way he looks at me, almost like he doesn't see me at all. Deep lines crease his forehead, finer lines marring his cheeks, as if years rather than days have passed. And while he's still a giant of a man, towering over me with his six and a half feet, wider than even Anton or alpha Winslow, I no longer feel like he wields the power of a god.

Maybe this is how he's always looked, and I've just never noticed. Maybe I'm seeing him for the first time with the veil of childhood lifted. Maybe I'm finally seeing the man.

Jeb Stone.

"Hi dad."

I look down, scuffing my bare feet against sandstone, plastering on what I hope is a contrite looking smile. I try to recall how I would have acted towards him in the past – respectful, obedient, loyal – and do my best to channel that.

Meanwhile, my wolf is snarling, hackles rising along her spine, demanding that I challenge this male, let him see who and what I really am. I'm fresh from a run in my wolf form, with the vision of my mate's death seared across my mind and the energy of a new pack bond humming behind my ribs. The animal is strong, close to the surface. It's harder than usual not to let her emotions bleed through.

"Put on some clothes," he grunts, thrusting a pair of shorts and t-shirt into my hands.

They are several sizes too big – Anton's, by the look of if – but I pull them on, grateful to have an extra barrier between me and the Clear Creek wolves.

Only once I'm dressed does dad speak to me again, his gaze flat, expression inscrutable.

"You ran away."

I blink at him, letting my lips pull down into a confused frown.

"Yah, we managed to get away from the Liberty pack," I say innocently. "We followed Cody. That's why you guys are here, isn't it? To rescue us?"

Someone gives a derisive snort – probably the squat-faced enforcer currently helping Cody and Anton haul Summer up from the gully – and dad's face contorts into a scowl.

"No. You ran away from home. You, Summer and Jason left pack territory."

I bite the inside of my cheek, mind racing to figure out what to say about that particular part of the story. I recall the wildfire, the tools Summer left in the carpeted hallway of the alpha house, and realise there is no point in trying to evade the truth.

"You locked me up. What was I supposed to do? Just sit there?"

"Don't be so dramatic." Dad waves one meaty hand dismissively. "You make it sound like we put you in jail or something. You were grounded. Kids get grounded all the time. That doesn't give them the right to run away from home. To disrespect their parents."

He shakes his head, making a frustrated sound in the back of his throat.

"You know, it's hard being a single parent. I'm just trying to do what is best for you. Keep you safe. Make sure Anton can have a good education. Ensure you both have a future in the pack. But ever since the Blackwater incident, you've been so gods-damned wilful. Disrespectful. Ungrateful. It's like that Tobias Finch pup you've been hanging out with at school has been a bad influence on you."

Dad takes that moment to lean forward, nostrils flaring as he takes in my scent. He wrinkles his nose, baring slightly yellowing teeth in the process.

"You even smell like him. I can smell the loner's stink all over you. Disgusting. Morrigan's tits, don't tell me you've been sullying yourself with that sorry excuse for a half-breed shifter…"

I close my eyes, drawing in deep steadying breaths behind clenched teeth as my emotions war with each other, struggling under the barrage of his words.

I try to focus on the sounds of the others heaving Summer up from the gully. On Summer's protests and overly dramatized exclamations of fear. On Jason's fast-paced ramblings as he tells alpha Winslow some made-up tale about how we were coerced into joining the Liberty pack and our subsequent escape.

They're doing their part to distract the Clear Creek wolves. To protect our new pack in the only way we can.

But the wolf in me is angry. Violently angry. Calling for blood. Demanding that I rise up, protect my mate, protect my pack with tooth and claw. Protect myself.

Meanwhile, the child in me is cowering, drowning beneath the onslaught of guilt and shame, practically gasping for his approval as if it's the air I need to breath. Because even after everything – after being locked up, after him hitting me, after knowing what he did to mom – I still want his love.

When I open my eyes, I realise he's finally fallen silent, dark eyes fixed on me with an almost maniacal intensity. I'm so caught up in wondering how he's gone from his earlier, almost apathetic, dismissal of me to this that I completely miss his question.

"Answer me," he grinds out.

I stare up at him, frowning, and this time, I don't have to fake my confusion.

"I'm sorry, what did you say?"

"I. Said." He steps forward, so close that his bared teeth are only inches away from my upturned forehead, violently enunciating each word. "Did. He. Touch. You?"

Instantly my mind races back to last night. To the way I practically threw myself at Tobias, pleading with him, running my hands all over him. As if I owned him, body and soul. The way our lips felt crashing together when he finally kissed me back. The warmth of his strong arms wrapping around me, the gentleness of his hands on my waist, of his callused fingertips brushing my ribs.

Warmth pools low in my belly at the memory, heat rising to my cheeks. The pressure behind my ribs tightens, constricting almost painfully in protest of the physical distance between me and Tobias.

A distance that I can feel lessening with each passing minute.

I shouldn't be able to feel it. As far as I know, only the alpha of a pack can use the pack bond to gauge the location and distance of his pack members. I certainly never felt it with alpha Winslow, when he was my alpha.

I give dad a saccharine smile.

"What do you mean, touch me?" I ask, widening my eyes with mock innocence. "Oh, do you mean did he hurt me? Like hit me or something?"

Dad narrows his eyes, red darkening his features. Like my alluding to his striking me is a personal affront.

Meanwhile, I'm aware of Summer gasping loudly as she's lifted over the rim of the gully before collapsing in a boneless heap. Of Jason's incessant ramblings as he divulges false information about the Liberty pack to alpha Winslow. Information which Cody will no doubt later correct. But for now, it's clearly holding the alpha's attention.

Dad reaches out, clutching the front of my t-shirt in one hand, bringing his face close to my own.

"I meant, did he touch you inappropriately."

I can feel Tobias getting closer, the pack link I share with him humming gleefully in my chest.

We're almost there, he says through the pack bond, his voice full of anxious anticipation as it carries across to me. *Thirty seconds*.

I blink up at dad, forcing my expression to remain as bland as possible, even as I want to wince at his closeness, at the sour warmth of his breath on my face.

"I'd say hitting is pretty inappropriate, wouldn't you?" I deadpan, then cock my head, as if considering something. "Although, locking people up against their will is also pretty inappropriate. So is lying to them about why their mother left."

Dad's fist tightens in my shirt until he's practically lifting me from the ground, the vein on his temple pulsing, his thick neck cording, lips pulling into a snarl. All the brown fades from his eyes, until they are shimmering black pools, depthless as the moonless light. Like there is some demon rather than a wolf lurking beneath his skin.

I shiver, true fear running like ice in my veins.

The only other time I've seen him look like this was the night mom left. The night he tore our house to pieces.

I'm suddenly very aware of the gaping cliff at my back, of the claws extending from dad's fingers as he partially shifts, of the silver bullets laying chambered in the rifle at his feet.

The words erupt from him in a growl, as much wolf as man.

"You little ungrateful slut. You think you can talk to me like that? I'm your gods-damned father!"

Panic rises, momentarily debilitating as he drags me towards the rim. I can feel cool air swirling from gully behind me, like the open mouth of some monster.

"Stop!"

Tobias' voice calls out from across the rocky landscape, so full of alpha power that I almost whimper in response. I watch in surprise as dad jolts, like he's been struck with an electrical current, dark eyes widening in shock.

"Do not harm her," Tobias orders, the alpha command rolling across like a tidal wave, heavy and raw and suffocating. "Don't harm my mate."

TOBIAS FINCH

I thought I was well acquainted with fear. With horror and loss. I thought nothing could be worse than seeing my mother's broken body on the kitchen floor. Than loosing my dad days later. Than watching helplessly as my wolf destroyed shifter after shifter on that snowy battlefield at Blackwater.

It turns out there are worse things.

Watching Lucy Stone dangle precariously above the cliff that drops into the gully is one of them.

In the space of an instant, the potential of a life with Lucy flashes across my mind, giving me a glimpse of what a future with my soul-twined mate could be like. I see her at my side when I wake in the morning, her hair mussed with sleep, a softness in her expression that is all the more precious because it is only reserved for me. I see us growing up together, making each other stronger, happier, filling each other's broken pieces with the shards of our own loss.

I see flashes of a future I haven't even begun to imagine yet, one that is full of home and life and insignificant moments that somehow expand to become the whole world.

I'm filled with a yearning like I've never known, deep and clawing, gripping the very fabric of my being. In that moment, I know watching that future get ripped away from me would destroy me. And I suddenly understand why my dad succumbed to the breaking of the mate bond.

Vaguely, I'm aware of the alpha command slipping from my lips, of shouting some order at Jeb Stone as I sprint towards my mate. My Lucy.

Distantly, I'm aware of my feet moving effortlessly over the rugged terrain, like water flowing over stones in a stream. Moments earlier, I would have been stumbling, grappling, heaving under the scorching sun. Now I am wind and air and movement. Now I am as much wolf as man.

The beast is free, but so am I, and – in this moment at least – we move together in perfect synchronicity.

In seconds I'm wrapping Lucy in my arms, pressing her body close to mine, relishing in the fact that she is here. She is alive. She is with me.

"Tobias."

The word is murmured against my neck, warm with the sweetness of her breath.

I close my eyes, momentarily forgetting the enemies that surround us.

Only for a short moment.

"Tobias, the gun," Lucy says, pulling back, eyes wide with fear.

That's when I'm aware of shuffling nearby, the scraping of metal on rock as someone lifts one of the discarded rifles.

"Drop the gun," I say, the alpha command rolling off my tongue. I can feel the order pushing out like a tidal wave around me, as natural as breathing. "You will not harm me or my pack."

The answering growls and the clattering of weapons dropping tells me this order has been felt. These sounds are shortly followed by the thudding of feet – and the scraping of dragon claws – as the rest of my pack reaches us.

Reluctantly, I tear my eyes away from Lucy, surveying my approaching companions. I still can't bring myself to release her from my hold. I settle on holding her close to my chest, her head tucked under my chin.

"Well, that's one way to resolve things," Red says dryly, eyeing the Clear Creek wolves with wry amusement. "Guess that's why no one likes born alphas, eh?"

"Let go of my daughter," Jeb growls out, his face red, eyes bulging as they dart between me and the rest of my pack with unmasked fury. "You have no right to touch her."

He makes no move to approach me, bound by my order to do my pack no harm.

"Stooping to using your born alpha power," alpha Winslow drawls, his voice like ice as he ignores the furious demands of his beta. "Are you so afraid of fighting us, pup?"

"Says the alpha who's using guns like a human," Orrin rumbles, kicking one of the offending weapons with a booted foot. It careens over the rim of the gully, the sounds of gunshot and exploding metal echoing up to us moments later. "Whatever happened to fighting with tooth and claw? Like a real shifter."

Alpha Winslow turns his cold eyes on Orrin, lips curling up to expose sharkish teeth.

"I doubt you would be so bold if it weren't for this pup's orders keeping us at bay," alpha Winslow observes.

"Are you calling me a coward?" Orrin retorts, fists balling at his sides, shoulders bunching.

"Enough."

This time, I keep the alpha command from my voice, even as I give Orrin a meaningful look. Right now isn't the time for exchanging words with the Clear Creek pack. Maybe there will never be a time for it.

I mean, they tried to shoot me, so what is there to say? They want me dead. I don't want to be dead. Seems like we're at a bit of an impasse where differences of opinions are concerned.

I let out an exhale, and take in the scene around me.

Summer has moved from her position at the cliff's edge to stand beside Aires, who is currently shielding her with his huge dragon form, as if still not convinced that the Clear Creek pack won't harm us.

At some point Jason pulled on someone's shorts, and he's standing at my side with his arms crossed over his bare chest, staring down Jeb Stone in an uncharacteristically aggressive manner. Orrin and alpha Winslow are engaged in a similar stare-off while the other guys are slowly circling in, silently picking up the Clear Creek pack's discarded firearms. Expertly disabling them.

"I don't want to fight with you, Cooper," I tell the alpha, suddenly feeling drained. "We don't want a war. We just want to go home. I'm sure you want that too."

One of my guys gives a derisive snort – probably Hamish – but I ignore him. Instead, I look at Cody, unable to ignore the heavy sense of disappointment pulling at my limbs and tightening in my throat.

"You can go with them," I say, tilting my chin at the Clear Creek wolves.

Cody's expression hardens, jaw ticking as he glares his silent response. My arms are still wrapped around Lucy, and I find myself holding her tighter, trying to ground myself in her warmth.

"I never would have forced you to stay with us, you know."

My brow furrows as I try to work out what made him betray us to his dad's pack in the first place. He'd given so much to the pack, seemed so dedicated.

No, he was dedicated. I know he was. That kind of work – it wasn't an act.

"All you had to do was say and you could have left," I tell him. "I'm sure we could have figured out a way to break the pack link."

Actually, I'm not sure. From what grandpa has told me, it's impossible to break the pack bond with a born alpha. Still, I would have tried. For Cody – for any of my pack – I will always try.

"It wasn't about that," Cody retorts bitterly.

"Well, what was it then?" I ask, hating how my voice rises in pitch at the question. "Why did you do it?"

The sense of betrayal and loss rises up, quickening like the tide towards the full moon and some of the confidence drains from me. I suddenly feel more like the sixteen-year-old that I am, and less like an alpha.

Cody's frown only deepens, his eyes flicking momentarily over to where the massive dragon is barring Summer from view, then back to me.

"It was for Summer," Lucy says from beside me, voice distant as she answers my question. "He did it to get Summer back."

"No," Cody shakes his head, baring his teeth. "That isn't why."

Lucy's nostrils flare as she delicately sniffs the air, then turns to look up at me. *It's a lie,* she tells me through the pack link, and I shiver at the feel of her mind brushing up against my own. *I can tell. It's part of my gift. And it's a lie.*

I stare at her, unsure of what to say to this. Obviously, there is a lot I didn't know about Lucy. A lot.

It doesn't matter though. I mean, it doesn't change how I feel about her. Who she is. What she is.

Mine, my wolf whispers. *Mine.*

I give her a tentative smile, hoping she can read the thanks there, even if it's mingled with the sting of Cody's betrayal. And then I turn to face Cooper.

"Go back home," I tell him, pushing the alpha command into my voice again, trying not to balk at the answering pulse of power that rises up each time I tap into that ability.

Like the power wants to be used. Like each time I use it, my wolf is growing. Expanding.

"Leave us alone and take your pack home."

Chapter 30

Lucy Stone

It's surreal seeing them all turn and leave without so much as a backwards glance. Without demanding that we come with them. Without trying to negotiate to have me, Summer and Jason returned to the Clear Creek pack. One moment, they're surrounding us, glaring at us and the next moment they're retreating.

Even Anton. He leaves without a goodbye – without even meeting my eyes, actually - following after dad, a duffel slung over his shoulders like a backpack.

I stare after them until their figures disappear amongst the rugged maze of sandstone boulders.

Hamish shifts, handing his pack to Gareth before taking to the air. No doubt to follow the Clear Creek pack and make sure of their retreat. The rest of us prepare to drop back down into the gully, since Gareth assures us it remains the fastest way to the vehicles they all left parked alongside the desert road.

"How did you do that?" I ask, tilting my head to stare at Tobias in wonder.

I have only ever heard about the power of born alphas in legends. Seeing it in real life, well… it's unnerving to say the least.

Tobias still hasn't relinquished his hold on me and I'm surprised at how right it feels to be close to him like this. He looks down, golden eyes meeting my own, giving me a look that sends my heartbeat fluttering to an almost dizzying pace.

"I'm not really sure," he says finally, and I shiver as the rough pads of his fingers idly trace my bare arm. "It used to be hard to do. Before I had the pack, when it was just me, it took a lot of work…" he trails off, a strange expression crossing his face. "When I ordered grandpa to shift for the first time – back when he had Alzheimer's and needed help shifting – it took several tries before I got it right. Even then, I don't think it was as strong as it is now."

"Is that why you didn't use it at Blackwater?" I ask, recalling the way his golden wolf moved with pure animalistic grace across the snow, tearing down the enemies in its path. "When we were all attacked, you shifted and fought instead of using your alpha command."

Tobias' expression darkens and he purses his lips, considering. When he speaks again, his voice is so low, it's almost carried off on the sun-baked wind.

"I didn't think to try it then. Honestly, I'm not even sure it would have worked. Not for so many shifters. I think my wolf gets stronger the bigger the pack gets," he muses. "And the alpha command gets stronger too. Or easier to use, maybe?"

"That would make sense," Jason says excitedly, his abrupt interjection making me start.

Somehow, I had forgotten he was there, helpfully lurking an arm's length away from us.

"I mean, that is what all the stories say, isn't it?" Jason continues, rocking forward on the balls of his feet. "That born alphas would get stronger and stronger the bigger their pack was? That is one of the reasons there was a move to do away with them – they would get into these bloody fights over numbers and territories. Of course, I think the alpha command had something to do with it, since it made it virtually impossible for anyone who wasn't a born alpha to lead…"

Jason trails off, cheeks reddening when he realises everyone is staring at him. I'm pretty sure my mouth is hanging open.

"How do you even know all this stuff?" I ask, not really expecting him to answer.

Jason turns a deeper shade of red – a feat I would have thought impossible, considering he's currently the shade of a ripe tomato.

"I – well, you know," he stammers, rubbing his bare arms nervously with his hands, "I might have read a few things… talked to some of the elders… especially after I found out Tobias was a born alpha…"

"You mean you intensively questioned every single elder you could find," Summer says accusingly, brown eyes glinting with mischief. "So you could fan-boy over Tobias from afar."

"I was not fan-boying," Jason retorts.

"Uh-huh. Sure."

"Either way, it's interesting," Orrin muses, pausing in his work of tying off one of the ropes that I think we're meant to use to belay down into the gully. The bear eyes Jason appraisingly. "It begs the question of how many other born alphas are out there, hiding like Tobias and Jamison. And what is going to happen if they take power like Tobias did."

"Agreed," Gareth calls out over his shoulder. He's using a rope to lower one of the packs down to the gully floor. "It could be dangerous if there are more born alphas out there. We should be prepared. Build up our defences. Train the pack…"

"No."

I look up at Tobias, surprised.

"No," he says again, giving a sharp shake of his head.

"What do you mean, *no*?" Gareth asks, rubbing a stubble-covered jaw. "We should be defending ourselves."

"Not against born alphas," Tobias says. "That sort of fear – that's what got my parents killed. That's what sent grandpa into hiding with Jamison. I'm not going to be a part of that. If anything, we should be reaching out to born alphas, offering them a place with us."

He gives a shrug, affecting nonchalance, but pressed up against his side like I am, I can feel his body tensing, muscles rippling. He cares about this.

"I mean, obviously they can't join the pack officially," he continues. "But they could still be a part of things, just like Jamison is. They shouldn't have to be in hiding, alone, just because the shifter world is afraid of power."

"I don't know," Orrin says slowly, lips drawing into a frown. "That would just be asking for trouble. What if another born alpha tried to take your pack?"

"How would you even reach out to them?" I ask.

Before Tobias can answer, the flutter of wings overhead draws our attention to the sky, everyone tensing until the familiar shape of Hamish's red-tailed hawk comes into view.

"We should get going," Red suggests, ears flattening against his head as the avian lets out a high-pitched call before circling down to the ground. "Before Hamish draws the attention of every shifter in the area. Just because the Clear Creek thugs have left doesn't mean Huxley Black isn't going to track us down."

Hamish shifts mid-landing, crouching as his bare feet thud against the uneven rocks. In typical helpful omega fashion, Jason is at his side in an instant, handing him clothes he's procured from who knows where.

"Relax, kitty-cat," Hamish drawls, pulling on a pair of shorts. "I did a quick fly-by and no one is trailing us. We'll be fine."

Red narrows his eyes, looking unconvinced.

"Red is right," Gareth tells Tobias, earning a surprised blink from Red and a frown from Hamish. "We need to move if we're going to get to our vehicles before sundown. All of this stuff, we can talk about it when we get back to pack territory."

"Yah, okay." Tobias traces his fingertips along my arm before releasing his hold on me. Even with the sun beating down on me, the air feels cold in his absence. "Let's go."

TOBIAS FINCH

We arrive back in Buffalo around noon the next day, dirty from days of camping in the desert, and tired from driving through the night.

At one point on our drive, someone had suggested getting a motel and stopping to rest. But then we remembered the Clear Creek pack. And Huxley Black.

It just made more sense to get to pack territory as quickly as possible.

Still, the drive wasn't that bad. Even when I was pressed in between Lucy and Jason in the back seat of Orrin's truck, the trip was actually… pleasant. The fact that Lucy's thigh had been pressed up against my own for most of the journey might have had something to do with it. It certainly didn't hurt that, at one point, she had rested her head on my shoulder and slept.

"How do you know he's going to be loyal to us?"

My eyes fly open at Samson's abrupt question and I blink, willing my exhausted brain to wake up, to recall what my pack has been arguing about for the past few minutes.

We're gathered in the large meeting tent, dirty coffee cups littered on every surface. Nearly everyone is here, so folding seats and beanbag chairs spill out the open sides of the temporary structure. In the distance, the faint hum of construction serves as a reminder that the humans building our lodge are close by.

"I don't think we can trust him," Tyrone agrees, fingers tapping the plastic arm of the foldable camp chair he's sprawled into. "I mean, he didn't leave Huxley Black back when he had the chance at Blackwater. Why trust him now?"

I lean forward, pinching the bridge of my nose. So, we're still talking about Aires then. Good. Great. Glad to see we haven't moved on from that little topic in the past twenty minutes.

Don't get me wrong. I'm all for having these little meetings and giving everyone a chance to have their opinions be heard. It would just be nice to have a shower first. Maybe another cup of coffee. Or some sleep.

"He is sitting right here," Summer says primly, colour rising to her cheeks as she reaches out to pat the leg of the dragon shifter in question then pauses, leaving her hand hovering mid-air. "So stop talking about him like he's not in the room."

"Tent," Christopher counters, blond brows flicking upwards as a mischievous grin flits across his face.

"Room, tent, whatever." Summer waives one hand dismissively. "Just get him to swear an oath or something. Because if you don't let him join the pack, he's probably just going to lurk on the outskirts of pack territory like a stalker."

She says this part with an exasperated look at Aires.

"True," Aires shrugs, unashamed.

"Ridiculous," Samson sneers before looking at me. "Alpha, are you going to let this happen? Let him blackmail his way into our pack? We shouldn't stand for it."

"Agreed," Tyrone nods, lips pursing into a frown.

I almost want to smile because I'm pretty sure this is the first time Samson and Tyrone have agreed about anything since Tania's arrival.

From her seat between the two males, Tania is smiling. Beaming, actually. As if her two mates' suddenly amicable attitudes towards each other is for her benefit.

"You guys are such hypocrites," Danny points out, wagging one meaty finger in their direction.

Of course, neither of the cats bristles at the insult, because Danny always manages to make insults sound like endearments.

Or maybe it's just that the young bear shifter towers over everyone. Including Orrin.

"I mean, you have both acted like complete idiots over Tania," Danny continues, chuckling to himself. "I'm pretty sure you would lurk outside whatever territory she was staying at, whether you were welcome there or not. So I don't think it's blackmail. I think it's just fact."

"Also, shouldn't the fact that Aires is Summer's mate count for something?" Jason asks, voice tremulous as he tries to ignore the dozens of eyes on him. "We shouldn't be keeping mates apart, right?"

Jason's cheeks redden, and I suspect he's thinking about his own mate, Ross Slade. The human who has no idea about what he is to the wolf sitting beside me, let alone anything about our world.

"But Summer hasn't claimed him yet," Samson argues.

"Terrible argument, buddy," Christopher murmurs, shaking his head with mock disappointment before smiling knowingly in Tania's direction.

Tania doesn't smile back though and she looks away, dark eyes shuttering. A protective anger wells inside of me.

She shouldn't be pressured into deciding anything, into making some life-long commitment, even if Tyrone and Samson are her true mates.

We're just kids.

Okay, not kids exactly. We're all adults by shifter standards, since the age of majority is fifteen. Some of us – like Tyrone and Tania - are even adults by human standards. That doesn't mean they're ready to take the irreversible step of claiming their mate, of entering into a bond breakable only by death.

A bond that could kill them if broken.

Unconsciously, my eyes land on Lucy. She's leaning against one of the metal tent poles, surveying the pack with tired watchfulness. I get the feeling she's memorising more than people's faces. The way she watches, it's like she's taking a measure of their souls.

She must feel me staring at her because she turns her head, grey eyes meeting my own as her lips curve into a faint smile. Lips that I now know the taste of.

I'd like to think that, one day, I'll claim her as my mate and she'll claim me. I mean, she clearly doesn't hate me anymore. I'm pretty sure she likes me.

That doesn't mean either of us are ready to enter into an unbreakable, soul-deep bond.

And Tania shouldn't feel rushed into this either.

Reluctantly, I pull my eyes away from Lucy and look back at the guys sitting at the table across from me, then at the others sprawled around the periphery.

There's no order to seating. No ranking.

Summer and Tania both sit at the plastic table across from me, simply because their respective mates more or less shoved everyone else aside to give them places closest to the now-empty bowls of chips and dip. Tyrone, Samson and Aires all perch close to the two females. Christopher leans close to Tania, though whether it's to annoy Samson and Tyrone or to offer Tania support, I really don't know. Danny is at my left because ever since I was shot, he's acted like my unofficial bodyguard and shadow. And Jason is at my right.

Where Cody would have been.

Gareth is half-asleep lounging in a beanbag chair, head tilted back, eyes nearly closed. Hamish leans against one of the tent poles with almost menacing alertness, idly sharpening his favourite knife. Arlo and Theo, the two owl shifters, both look exhausted and annoyed as they squint against the sun while Noah and Ollie, the wolf brothers, frown at each other from across the tent.

"It doesn't matter that Summer hasn't claimed Aires," I say, inwardly cringing as every set of eyes turns to me, bodies straightening in seats. Even Gareth sits up, wiping what appears to be drool from one corner of his mouth.

Maybe one day, I'll get used to this. To being called alpha. To watching my words settle with undeserved weight over a room, just because of my rank. Still, I'm not sure I'll ever like it.

"If he wants a place in this pack, he can have one, if that is what Summer wants. It should be up to her. I mean, she's his mate, so she's going to be more affected than any of us by his being part of the pack. Or not being part of the pack."

I pause, giving Summer a reassuring smile before looking over the rest of the group.

"I'm not going to deny someone a place just because they might betray me," I continue, instantly thinking of Cody, of the way he'd looked at me before he left with the Clear Creek pack, face contorted with hatred. "I don't want us to be a pack ruled by fear."

I rub the back of my neck, wishing for the hundredth time that I was one of those people gifted with the ability to make persuasive speeches. But I'm not. I'm just Tobias Finch, accidental alpha to this group of shifters who deserve a better leader than I could ever be.

Pack, my wolf reminds me, his wolfish heart filling with an animalistic pride. *This is our pack.*

"So if Aires wants to be a part of the pack, and if Summer is okay with it, then he's welcome to join," I say tiredly.

Aires inclines his head in my direction, surprise and gratitude lighting up his features. The tent erupts in chatter, everyone talking at once. Samson and Tyrone don't look particularly upset by my decision and even Gareth and Hamish – who vociferously opposed Aires joining the pack a few days ago – seem unconcerned by my announcement.

Good. Hopefully that means this meeting will be over soon and I can go back to my RV and take a shower. Grandma invited me over for dinner tonight, and I'm wanting to grab some sleep before I head over there.

I look over at Lucy again. Maybe I can convince her to come with me to my grandparents' house tonight so they can get to know her. And so I don't have to let her out of my sight.

"Are you going to do the pack bond now, alpha?" Danny asks, pulling my attention back to the whole Aires issue.

I shrug, looking pointedly at Summer. "Is that what you want?" I ask her.

Summer pales, but gives a silent nod.

"Okay, cool," I say. "We can do it now."

"Guess you'll be wanting this."

Hamish saunters towards us with his freshly sharpened knife. I resist the urge to smile, recalling how he held that same knife at Blackwater and basically threatened everyone to join my pack.

This time, I see the knife for what it is. A reluctant peace offering to Aires. A show of his acceptance of my leadership, of the decision to let Aires join.

“Thanks, man,” I say, reaching out to take it.

Crack.

The shot of a gun causes me to freeze, hand hovering mid-air above the knife as my whole body stills, blood turning to ice in my veins.

Crack, crack, crack.

Three more shots follow the first, and this time I know without out a doubt they are too loud. Too close.

Definitely on pack territory.

My wolf surges to the surface, hackles rising, teeth bared, incensed at the thought of anyone threatening its territory. Its pack. Its mate.

I don’t shift, but there is no suppressing the wolf either. Just like when I saw Lucy teetering over the gully rim, the world falls away, the barrier between me and my wolf falls away, and I’m moving. Running. Flying over grass and between trees, the shouts of my pack behind me as I race towards danger.

Chapter 31

Cody Winslow

From the passenger seat in dad's pick-up truck, I watch the wooden fence posts rush past. I should be taking in the scenery, rejoicing at the familiar mountains, relishing the crisp air flowing in through the open window.

Instead, the thought of returning to the Clear Creek territory fills me with sickening dread.

Home. This is home, I remind myself.

But when the ranch house comes into view, its black modern façade and large windows gleaming in the midday sun, I have to accept the harsh truth.

This is not my home. Not really. Not anymore.

I cast a surreptitious glance in dad's direction. His large hands grip the leather-wrapped steering wheel of the truck, jaw clenching as he stares at the road ahead. He's been silent most of the long drive to Buffalo, refusing to answer any of my questions once it became clear I wouldn't divulge any information about the Liberty pack.

I can't. I won't. Not when I know Summer is there. Not after she and Lucy and Jason tricked dad and Jeb.

Because I know my dad. I've spent my life watching him broker deals with other packs. I've listened to his meetings and seen how justice is dealt out. He doesn't forgive. And his punishments are deadly.

The sound of a phone ringing jolts me from my thoughts. Dad casts me one coldly disappointed look before fishing the phone from the pocket of his jeans. Like always, he's wearing a fresh button-up and crisp denim, looking for all the world like a wealthy rancher.

"Yes."

Dad's voice is smooth. Polished as the wood veneer of the truck's dashboard. That one word packed with effortless authority.

He pauses. Listening. The only sign of his emotion the tapping of one finger on the steering wheel. The rest of him is calm, his face unreadable as a mask.

"You sure it was him?"

Another pause, and then a frown cuts across dad's mask, dark brow dipping menacingly over his eyes.

"You'll get your money once I have my proof," dad snaps, a low growl rumbling form his chest before he abruptly ends the call.

I wait, curiosity piqued and wanting to ask him what that was all about. But I know it's pointless. He'll either tell me, or he won't.

At this point, I'm betting on won't.

To my surprise, he pulls the car over, putting it in park at the side of the gravel road before killing the engine. We're only minutes away from home, parked alongside the grassy flatlands that lead up to the foothills, where the ranch house glints like a black beacon.

My confusion quickly morphs into a burst of panic when dad pulls a small knife from his breast pocket and, for a brief moment, I think dad might be going to attack me or something.

"Really?" dad says, upper lip curling in disgust at my momentary show of fear.

I cringe at my own idiocy, embarrassment stinging my cheeks.

Of course, dad isn't going to kill me. And if he did want to kill me, I doubt he'd try doing it with a small knife in his truck. I'd heal from the wound, and it would just end up getting blood all over his upholstery.

"Give me your hand," dad orders.

Tentatively, I obey, offering him my hand palm-up as realisation slowly dawns.

"Hold still."

And that's the only warning I get before he's unceremoniously drawing the blade across my palm. I flinch, the small movement earning a look of ire from him before he runs the blade across his own palm.

"Don't let the blood fall on my seats," he warns before he grabs my hand in his own. "Now give the oath."

I blink, mind racing at the implications of those words. *Give the oath. The pack oath.*

Dad knows as well as I do that I can't swear fealty to him while Tobias Finch lives. The only way dad would ask this of me is if Tobias Finch was gone.

My mouth is dry, throat hoarse as I form out the words.

"I, Cody Winslow, swear fealty to Cooper Winslow and the Clear Creek pack."

Nothing.

Dad's hand tightens around my own, the calluses of his palm pressing painfully into the fresh cut welling beneath his grip, as if he can force the pack link by the strength of his will alone.

Still, nothing.

Not even the whisper of a bond, no feelings of warmth or connection. No familiar sound of my dad's voice through the pack link.

Nothing.

I should feel disappointed. I mean, it's what I wanted, right? To return to the Clear Creek pack? To have things return to the way they used to be.

Instead, a wave of relief surges through me, offering a momentary respite from the guilt that's been sitting like a stone in my chest ever since I agreed to sell out Tobias.

"Gods," dad rumbles, dropping my hand in disgust, before wiping the blood from the palm of his hand with a cloth handkerchief. He doesn't offer me anything to clean up with, and I'm forced to cradle my bleeding hand, angling the palm up to keep the blood from dripping onto his seats.

"I knew that guy couldn't be trusted," dad continues, grumbling to himself as he starts the truck engine. "Hiring rogues. Morrigan only knows who they shot. Obviously wasn't your gods-damned alpha."

He spits out 'alpha' like it's a bad word, lips curling into a sneer. The wolf in me riles, instinctively wanting to defend the male that I'm still bound to.

Alpha, my wolf reminds me petulantly. *Tobias is our alpha.*

I wince and push my wolf aside, ignoring the animal's distress. I don't need it feeding my own guilt.

Dad picks up his phone, dialling a number with one hand as he drives the truck towards the ranch gate.

"Yah. It's me," he says into the phone, tone curt. "You won't be getting your money. Your guy got it wrong. I don't care if he says the wolf he killed had gold eyes, I'm telling you, he got it wrong."

There's a long silence and dad frowns, finger tapping irritably on the steering wheel. Then he turns to me.

"What colour is Tobias' wolf?" dad asks.

For a moment, I contemplate refusing to answer, just like I've refused to answer all his other questions. But then, Anton has seen Tobias shift and fight, so no doubt dad will just ask him if I don't tell him.

"Gold," I mutter, slumping down into the oversized leather seat of dad's truck. It makes me feel small, vulnerable. Like I'm still a pup instead of a full-grown male shifter.

Or maybe it's just being around dad that does that.

"You hear that?" dad snaps into the phone. "Gold. Not black. Now get your operation under control or I'll hire someone else next time, got it?"

He ends the call without waiting for a reply, dropping the phone on the centre console before giving me a sideways glance.

"It looks like your alpha is still alive," dad rumbles. "Just like I thought." He shakes his head, frown deepening. "Not sure what we're going to do with you in the meantime. Can't just let you wander around, not with the pack bond in place. I guess we'll have to…"

I stop hearing what he's saying. Don't even notice as we drive through the ranch gate and park outside the ranch house. My home. I don't notice my dad getting out of the car or hear my mother's voice as she calls out to me from the front door.

Black. Black. The wolf they shot was black.

My blood turns to ice, lungs compressing until it's impossible to draw breath. I'm drowning. Drowning under the weight of my wrongdoing. I look down at my hands, almost expecting to see them coated in blood. Innocent, innocent blood.

Instead, it's just my own.

My wolf howls, his mournful call joining the roaring in my ears.

There is only one wolf it can be. One wolf with gold eyes and black fur.

You should have protected him, my wolf whimpers. *He was an elder. An elder. He was your friend.*

I lean forward, pressing the heels of my hands against my eye sockets, not caring about the blood smearing on my own face as my breath comes in short pants.

You betrayed your pack, my wolf continues, sorrowful cries becoming angry growls.

I can feel the animal's ire directed at me, can taste his bitter disgust. This time, I don't even try to silence my wolf, because he's right.

He's right, and now Jamison is dead.

To be continued in
Wolves of War

Wolves of War - Book Three

Chapter 1

Tobias Finch

"Shift."

The alpha command pours from me, full of power, like water breaking out of a dam. It's so easy. It shouldn't be so easy.

But nothing happens.

"Shift."

My hands sink into Jamison's fur, feeling for the bullet wounds. Feeling for his heartbeat. The rise and fall of his breathing. I have to make him shift.

"Shift."

There's another scent present, faint amongst the smell of blood and silver and gunpowder and death and damp earth. It rises and swirls with memories of charcoal and pine. With blood on the kitchen floor.

"Shift."

The word cracks out like thunder, like it could sunder the earth in two. Jamison's fur is wet beneath my fingers. Wet and so still. So, so still.

Rage is dark and blinding. Or maybe that is just my tears, catching in my throat and burning my eyes.

I'm not crying though. I'm not. I'm an alpha. I'm supposed to lead this pack.

"He's gone. Tobias. Tobias. You need to stop. You need to stop, okay. He's gone."

Distantly, I'm aware of someone shaking my shoulders. Trying to pull me back. Danny, maybe? Beyond him, the whimpering of wolves, the low growl of the cats, the fluttering of wings.

"Are you sure?" someone murmurs from behind me.

"I'm sure. There's nothing we can do. It's too late. Hit him right in the heart."

A wolf presses beside me, warm brown fur leaning against my side. A pair of strong arms wrap around me, tugging me up to my feet, rumbling at my back as I struggle. I need to touch Jamison. I need to make him shift.

"He's gone, Tobias."

The arms around me tighten, lifting me, enveloping me in the scent of honey and blueberries. I could fight it. Maybe I should.

My wolf lets out a plaintive whimper.

"Grandpa," I choke out. "I have to tell grandpa."

Even as I say it, I know that I can't. I can't. I can't tell grandpa that his baby brother is gone. The brother he raised. The brother he gave up everything to protect.

The feared born alpha.

Reduced to lifelong exile.

Reduced to silence and memories with a handful of silver bullets.

Lucy presses up beside me, her warm hand grasping my own as Orrin steps away, leaving me to stand on my own feet.

"He's already on his way," Lucy says.

I force myself to look away from Jamison and look at Lucy instead. She meets my eyes with her own, expression unreadable as she reaches up to swipe away the wetness staining my cheeks.

Not tears though. I'm not crying.

"You saw?"

She gives a reluctant nod.

"But you didn't see this?"

The words tumble out before I can stop them, bitter and sharp. Full of accusation.

The mask slips then, grey eyes widening with hurt. Her hand drops from my own, leaving coldness in its wake.

"That's not how it works," she retorts, wrapping her arms around herself, blinking rapidly. Her eyes are dry though. Not like mine. But I'm not crying. "I can't control what I see. When I see it."

I open my mouth to reply but am interrupted by the sound of footsteps thudding, the crunching of sticks and leaves. I turn to watch grandpa running, his feet moving, carrying him faster than someone his age has a right to move.

He falls to his knees, hands hovering over Jamison's lifeless form.

"Jamison."

Something in that one word, in the frantic desperation, it cracks me open. My vision blurs, greens and blacks and browns swirling as my wolf surges forward, rippling and straining under my skin, demanding to break free. Beside me a wolf lets out a low keening howl, his voice tremulous, until it is joined with another and another.

My muscles tense, shuddering under the desire to shift.

"Who did this?" grandpa asks, his question directed to the un-answering trees. "Who would do this?"

The sound of bones and tendons snapping and popping fills the forest until I know the whole pack is here in feather and fur, surrounding us. I can feel the anger and sorrow of my pack mates thrumming across the bond, echoing with my own.

I can hear all their voices across the pack link too, a veritable cacophony that reverberates relentlessly in my skull.

It had to be the Clear Creek pack.

Cody. Cody betrayed us.

They were after Tobias. It's probably the same guns for hire as before.

It could be Huxley Black and Drake. They're getting us back for taking Lucy and Summer.

No, they don't know where we are, remember.

Clear Creek. It had to be Clear Creek.

I shake my head, wishing I could silence the chatter.

Grandpa turns to face me, his wrinkled face streaked with tears.

"I knew as soon as it happened," he explains. "I felt it. Felt him go… And then the silence."

His throat works as he swallows, jaw clenching, eyes squeezing shut.

I know what that feels like, the sudden silence of the pack link. I felt it when dad died. It was like being cut adrift in a storm. Like losing your anchor.

"You can join our pack," I offer lamely, because I don't know what else to say.

Grandpa nods.

"I think it was the Clear Creek pack," I say when grandpa doesn't answer.

Another nod.

I draw one shaky hand across my face. Around us, my pack circles restlessly, surrounding me and grandpa. Surrounding Jamison's fallen form. Waiting.

We should run, Gareth urges across the pack bond, the tan ears of his coyote lying flat against his skull. *Run and sing.*

Hamish cocks his head to one side, surveying the pack with cunning, unblinking eyes from his perch above us. *We should fight*, he suggests. *Make them pay.*

No. No, we need proof, Jason argues, tail drooping as he lowers himself to the earth, ears back, resting his chin on his paws.

Lucy is silent, the white wolf like a statue of ice at the edge of the clearing, pressed close to Summer's nut-brown wolf. Beside them, Aires stands in his human form. The only one besides me and grandpa who hasn't shifted.

"We should bury him," grandpa says, turning back to look at Jamison. "And sing his soul home."

Chapter 2

Lucy Stone

I've attended my fair share of funerals. Said that last farewell to beloved pack elders. Stood silently as their loved ones gave tearful speeches or shared false, tremulous smiles over ham sandwiches and blueberry muffins.

I've never seen anything like this.

"It's what he would have wanted," Mr Vance, Tobias' grandpa, explains, his voice hoarse and throaty as if he's been crying.

His eyes are dry though. Dry as the parched summer earth that Jamison is lowered into. Dry as the pine needles that line his earthen resting place.

"He loved this land. He wouldn't have wanted to leave it."

"He shouldn't have had to leave it," Tobias retorts, voice tinged with bitter anger.

Mr Vance leans wearily on his shovel before casting his grandson a long, pitying look. Tobias ignores it, throwing one more shovel-full of earth onto the mound.

"That's enough," Mr Vance says, gently pulling the shovel from Tobias' grasp. "It's done."

Tobias blinks rapidly, looking away in an attempt to hide his tears. It's a futile effort, when the scent of his sorrow is as thick as the pine and earth scent of the forest. Especially when we are all in feather and fur.

This is our show of solidarity and respect to the shifter who couldn't shift. The born alpha trapped in his wolf form for so many years. Until the very end.

"I'll join your pack," Mr Vance says abruptly, drawing Tobias away from Jamison's final resting place and towards the edge of the clearing. Towards his patiently waiting pack. "Jamison would have wanted that."

Tobias wipes reddened eyes with the back of his hand, dirt streaking with the tears.

"Yah. Okay."

Mr Vance holds out his hand and Tobias blinks in confusion.

"Oh. What, now?"

"Now."

"But, Jamison…"

"You've done everything you could for Jamison. He's safe. It's done. Now I want to run with my grandson and his pack. I want our song to guide his spirit home."

THE STARLIGHT IS cold and brilliant against the nearly moonless sky, the milky way cresting in an arch above the purple silhouette of the Little Bighorns.

The night run and wolf song to guide the spirits of the newly-buried home to the gods, that is a tradition I am familiar with. What is less familiar is the cacophony of other animal sounds joining what would normally be an eerie lupine symphony.

The coyote's yip. The bears' low rumbles. The cats' mournful purrs. The piercing cries of the avian shifters. It should sound strange, but it doesn't.

It sounds right.

Another thing that is completely new is that I can feel the pack. I can feel the hum of sorrow and anger thrumming across the bond, so much stronger in my wolf form. I can feel the desire to retaliate. The thirst for vengeance. The worried pity. The fear of danger. The adoration of the run and wind and freedom.

It's almost overwhelming, all these conflicting emotions and I wonder idly if this is how Jason feels all the time.

I don't like it. It's distracting. And uncomfortable.

Which is why I don't notice when we leave the Liberty pack territory.

Where are we going?

Jason's worried voice broadcasts across the pack bond, waking me from my trance. I blink, cocking my head to the side as I take in my surroundings, looking at where my paws have carried me.

We're running along the ridge above Crazy Woman Canyon. Far away from the sheltering pines of the Liberty pack territory. Towards the Clear Creek territory.

Justice, Tobias answers, and the one word is so thick with *alpha* and *wolf* and *anger* it makes my stomach clench. There is almost nothing of Tobias in it.

Um, what? Jason asks, his panic palpable.

We're going to get justice, Tobias answers. *For Jamison.*

Maybe it's the confusion of all the different emotions on the pack bond. Maybe it's the fatigue from all the events leading up to tonight

– from running away, being kidnapped, escaping Drake's lair, finding out Tobias is my true mate, joining the Liberty pack. Either way, it takes me several long moments to understand the meaning of Tobias' words.

Wait, what? I ask, steps faltering over the loose granite stones as I pull to a halt. *You can't possibly mean…*

They killed Jamison, Tobias retorts, his own stride never slowing. *They tried to kill me and they killed him. I'm going to get revenge.*

There is an eruption of thoughts and words and feelings across the pack link then, though the cries for *war* and *attack* and *revenge* are louder than the whispered concerns of the more submissive pack members. Even Mr Vance – normally calm and collected – seems caught up in the collective bloodlust.

Panic rises in my chest, my own emotions fighting against the tug of my pack, of my alpha. *Run. Run and fight*, they all seem to say. I sprint after them, paws thudding against stone as I surge to catch up to Tobias. But he's fast. So fast, and so many of our pack members block the narrow path between me and him.

Stop, Jason urges over the pack link. *Tobias, you have to stop.*

He doesn't stop. Doesn't even glance back as he races towards Clear Creek territory.

It's not until we reach the foothills overlooking the Half Moon Ranch that Tobias slows, allowing me and Jason to catch up.

To my surprise and horror, Jason throws himself in Tobias' path, baring his teeth to the larger wolf, ears pinned back against his skull in obvious fear.

In human form, Tobias is probably only a couple inches taller than Jason. In wolf form, Tobias is nearly twice the size of Jason's sleek brown wolf.

Tobias lets out a warning growl, gold eyes flashing dangerously.

Any other time, Jason would whimper. Roll over. Show his throat in submission.

Move, omega, Tobias orders, the words full of dominance but stopping just short of an alpha command. Still, even my wolf shudders at the order.

The omega holds his ground, giving a tremulous snarl in reply.

No.

I feel Tobias' surprise, then anger. A red, deep anger that is pure wolf.

Move.

I whimper, knowing instinctively that this is the final warning. That if Jason doesn't move, Tobias will attack. And the attack of an alpha putting one of his wolves in their place, it can be brutal. Deadly, even.

Jason lifts his chin, trembling as he meets the alpha's eyes with his own.

There is a flicker of hesitation in the golden wolf's eyes. A brief moment where the look is more Tobias than wolf. Then it's gone, and the golden wolf is lunging forward, teeth bared, claws extended.

In a matter of moments, Jason is on his back, whimpering as Tobias pins him to the ground, jaws around his throat.

Tobias, please, Jason cries out through the pack bond, his words rushed and frantic. The brown wolf's eyes are wide, practically rolling back with fear. *My mom is down there. My grandparents. Please.*

The golden wolf's answering growl is merciless. I'm not even sure if the animal can understand what Jason is saying. Maybe the creature is beyond speech.

Around us, the pack waits watchfully, muscles coiled like collective springs. No one dares to move. They all know as well as I do that to interfere with an alpha disciplining a pack member – that would be akin to a challenge.

My stomach twists as I think of dad. Of the way he lost control of his wolf. Nearly going feral as he tore our house to shreds. As I think of alpha Winslow, practically drunk on power and control.

I had thought Tobias was different.

My wolf's ears flatten, but the bitterness of disappointment is quickly overpowered by a surge of protective anger.

Jason is *mine.*

My friend. My pack mate. My wolf. Mine to protect.

Before I can stop myself, I'm rushing forward, teeth bared, ears back, slamming into Tobias' side with as much force as I can muster. I'm barely half his size, even smaller than Jason actually, but my wolf is fierce. And pissed.

I might as well have run into a brick wall at full speed. Pain radiates through my shoulder, the bone-deep sort of pain that leaves the taste of metal in your mouth.

I stumble back, whimpering. I'm pretty sure I've broken something. Broken or dislocated. It feels wrong.

The golden wolf lets out a grunt, turning his head to stare at me in shocked dismay, releasing Jason's throat in the process. Without hesitating, Jason rolls out from under Tobias' grasp, scrambling frantically to my side. He leans against me, just enough so that he's bearing some of the weight from my injured side, and I can feel him trembling.

The feel of that trembling – of Jason's fear – it's like gasoline to the fire of my anger.

I meet the golden wolf's stare with my own.

Turn back, I tell him.

I let every ounce of dominance, every ounce of anger pour into those words. I want him to feel it. I want them all to feel it. I let the challenge show in my posture, my rumbling growl, the flash of my eyes. I want him to know that I'll fight for this. I'll stop him or die trying.

Mate, the golden wolf rumbles, the word whispered across the pack bond. I know instinctively that it's said only for me.

His nostrils flare, tale lifting as he steps closer to me, golden eyes glinting with indulgent amusement. The look only serves to rile my wolf.

You think to challenge me? he asks.

There is no aggression in the words. Not even the hint of irritation. No, it's like the wolf is laughing.

My wolf bares a tooth, narrowing her eyes at the male.

Jason is right, I tell him, planting my paws firmly on the ground in front of him. *We can't attack the Clear Creek pack. It's wrong.*

Because it's not just his family there. It's my family. It's Anton. It's every wolf I've grown up with. The elders and the pups. The families, asleep and unsuspecting in their dens.

The golden wolf tilts his head to one side, studying me.

Wrong?

The word comes across as a question. Like the animal has never even considered morality before. Like the word isn't part of the beast's vocabulary.

Yah, wrong. You can't attack innocent people in their sleep.

The wolf chuffs, stepping forward until he's practically towering over me, enveloping me in that delicious sage, pine and chocolate scent that is uniquely Tobias Finch. My idiot wolf softens, her anger fading as she takes in that familiar scent, a warm longing building in its place.

Would it make you happy? the insane animal asks. *If I do as you say?*

I blink at him, confused. It's not about making me happy. It's about not being a complete psychopath.

Um, yah, I tell him.

Okay, he replies.

He trails his nose along my neck, rumbling as he presses his neck against my own. I want to snap at him. But my wolf leans in, closing her eyes in pleasure at his warmth.

Traitor, I hiss at her.

She ignores me.

I'm suddenly reminded of when Tobias came to the Clear Creek territory a couple months ago, trying to blackmail me into going to the school dance with him. His wolf had been in control then. Just like now.

Afterwards, it had almost seemed funny.

Now?

Now the stakes are higher. The wolf isn't here to ask me out. He's here to deal out death. My wolf might be willing to overlook that, but I'm not.

Okay? I ask, trying to make sense of his reply.

In answer, the golden wolf tilts his head at me, then turns, silently ordering the pack to return home.

Chapter 3

Tobias Finch

Two full days pass before my wolf gives up control. Two sleepless days and nights of tirelessly prowling our territory. Watching the borders. Checking for intruders.

Keep our mate safe, my wolf reminds me. *Protect the pack.*

Occasionally, I see grandpa in the woods too, eyes closed, chin resting on his paws as he lays beside the freshly-turned mound of earth near Jamison's den. I would worry about him, but I know he goes home to grandma each evening, so at least he's warm and fed.

You need to shift back.

Orrin's voice comes across the pack bond on the dawn of the third day. I can feel the weight of his concern pressing against me with the words, relentless as the morning sun.

Keep watch, my wolf tells him. *Danger. Protect pack.*

More and more I'm thinking in *image* and *scent* and *feel* instead of words. It's becoming increasingly difficult to form sentences.

Your pack needs you, Orrin insists. *They need you. Tobias. Not the wolf.*

But Tobias didn't keep Jamison safe. Tobias didn't protect the borders. Tobias let danger come with silver bullets and death.

The wolf can keep them safe though. With tooth and claw and power.

This isn't going to bring him back. And he wouldn't have wanted this for you.

I can smell the bear now, the earthy scent of honey and berries. I curl my lips in a snarl. My wolf doesn't want company.

The bear huffs, shaking his shaggy head as he digs at the ground, presumably to unearth whatever grubs or roots he's found there.

I could order him to leave. Order him to give me my space, to stop pestering me. And he'd obey. He'd have to obey.

You're going to lose her, Orrin warns, voice rumbling low and gentle across the pack bond. *If you don't shift back and fix things, you're going to lose her.*

Even in my wolf-driven state, I know who he means.

Lucy.

The image and scent of the she-wolf momentarily fills my mind, pushing out the Jamison thoughts of *grief* and *anger* and *hate* and *guilt.*

In its place is the lilting sound of Lucy's voice as she spoke to Tania and Summer in their trailer last night. The feel of her soft skin beneath my fingertips as she pressed against me in that sandstone gully back in Southern Utah. The taste of her lips on my own. The feel of her power and bravery as she faced me down and defended Jason.

Shame seeps in at that recollection, darkening the light-filled remembrances.

I should never have attacked Jason like that. Loyal, brave Jason, who left his pack to save Summer and Lucy.

He disobeyed us, my wolf argues.

But I feel the way the wolf's muscles tense with discomfort and note the way his claws dig into the earth. Even the psychopathic animal knows what he did was wrong. He just doesn't want to admit it.

Good. He should feel guilty.

Give me back control, I tell the wolf.

The animal resists, tightening his iron-clad grip on my mind. Caging me in.

After days trapped in this form, I know there is no point in trying to fight him. The wolf is stronger than I am. Much stronger. If he wants to take control, he will.

Reasoning also doesn't seem to work.

So, I change tack. I imagine Lucy. Recall what it feels like to hold her close to me. The warmth of her body pressed against mine, her soft curves moulding to my hard planes. I imagine what it would be like to lay with her for hours, to talk to her and listen to her and explore her. I imagine the sorts of things we would say to each other. I imagine how her laughter would sound with her lips brushing against my neck, the way her fingertips would feel trailing across my skin.

I imagine all the things that require a human form. I let my longing for them fill every part of my body, until my hunger becomes the wolf's hunger.

Let me shift back, I urge the wolf, when the hunger becomes a dizzying fever-pitch. *Let me shift back and I'll go to Lucy.*

Even as I think the words, my stomach lurches with anxiety at the thought of ever speaking to Lucy again. Quickly, I tamp those thoughts down. I don't want the wolf to sense a trap. To sense that I'm tricking him.

Eventually. I'll speak to Lucy eventually. It's not a lie.

There is a long pause, and finally I feel the wolf release his hold on me. The relief is instant and palpable, if a little painful. Like unhooking the animal's claws from my skin.

"Welcome back to the land of the living," Orrin says, shifting into his human form, a smile creasing his cheeks.

His eyes look sad though. Sad, and tired. I frown up at him.

"Hey."

The word catches in my throat, raw from so many days of disuse.

"Come on, pup. Let's get you fed and rested. Things always look better with a full belly and twelve hours of sleep."

I give a disbelieving huff, but follow him anyway. Eating and sleeping won't keep my pack safe. It sure as shit won't bring Jamison back.

"I can see you don't believe me, but trust me on this." Orrin forces a smile. "Once we get a full-cooked breakfast in you, it'll be a lot easier to handle."

Bitterness churns at those words, twisting and cutting. It's almost been a full year since my mother's death at the hands of Huxley Black and I still wake up thinking she's still alive and I'm back with my parents in New York, only to have the memory of that loss crash down on me when sleep lifts.

No, I don't think any amount of eggs and bacon will make Jamison's death easier to handle.

Enough of my feelings must come through the pack bond, or else Orrin is just good at reading expressions, because he lets out a sigh, drawing one rough hand over his bearded face.

"I'm not downplaying your loss here, okay. I'm not saying it's going to be easy. Because it won't be. All I'm saying is you got to keep moving forward through the pain. And you need food and sleep to do that."

"What would you know?" The words grate along my vocal cords and I pause, rubbing at my throat. "You're just an old mechanic who hibernates at least four months each year. What do you know about anything?"

Orrin's expression hardens, eyes flashing yellow as his scars go vivid, stark reminders of battles fought and won. A low rumble reverberates in his chest as he turns to face me, his movements slow but with a grace that belies his size.

"What do I know?" he asks. "Pup, are you really so ignorant as to think that I've never known loss in my fifty years on this earth? Do you think someone like me lives alone by choice? That in all these years, I've never had a mate? Never had a cub? Never been more than the male you see before you?"

He throws his arms wide as he says this, the gesture somewhat disconcerting given he's completely naked. I can't even think about that though, because my mind is lingering on his words. On the unspoken truths.

A mate. A cub.

Where are they now? I want to ask, but even I'm not that insensitive. My mind flits back to that moment above the gulch, with the Clear Creek pack and their guns. The way Orrin had reacted, that had been more than just a normal shifter abhorrence for firearms. It had spoken of deep-seated anger. The kind of anger that comes with loss.

I swallow hard, squeezing my eyes shut. I want to shove the words back in my mouth. I want to tell him I'm sorry, even if I don't know what I'm sorry for, exactly.

"Look, I'm not going to pretend I've got all the answers," he says. "All I'm saying is that you have to keep going. Day by day. Because you're here. You're alive. Right now, that might seem like a curse. It might seem like a curse for a long time to come. But I can promise you, eventually you'll wake up and see that life has its blessings too."

I grit my teeth, feeling the unwelcome burn of tears pricking behind my eyes. Because it's not just Jamison's loss that I feel. It's the loss of everything else. Mom, dad, my old life in New York. Like losing Jamison has brought all that old pain back to the forefront, just when I thought I was doing okay.

Orrin grasps me by the shoulders, grip firm as he lowers his forehead to my own.

"You're going to hurt. Sometimes, you're going to cry. That doesn't make you less of a man. Less of an alpha. You got that?"

I nod, squeezing my eyes shut.

"And you're not alone in this, okay? You've got a pack now. You've got me. You've got all of us."

I nod again, and Orrin pulls away.

"Good. Now let's get you something to eat."

Lucy Stone

"Tobias has shifted back."

Summer announces this with complete nonchalance, like she doesn't know what Tobias is to me. Like she hasn't been avidly watching our every interaction – or lack thereof – since we got back from Southern Utah.

Honestly, I'm surprised she hasn't busted out the popcorn already.

"So what?" I shrug, standing up from my little bed in the main living room of the RV I share with Tania and Summer. So that I can transform it into the bench seat for our dining table.

Summer eyes the sad little bench pityingly.

"You know, you could sleep in the room with us. The bed is massive. There's plenty of space."

I scrunch my nose, giving her a look of unmasked disgust.

"No thanks."

Sure, I like Summer. She's probably my best friend. And Tania is about as unobtrusive as someone can possibly be. Still, being crammed in an RV with them is a little much. Sharing a bed with them? Yah. Not going to happen.

"Anyway, Tobias is having breakfast in that horrible monstrosity they call the lodge," Summer continues. "With a bunch of the guys. He looks like crap. Like he hasn't eaten or slept in days. Honestly, I don't think he has. I guess he's going to sleep and then we're going to have some sort of a meeting tomorrow."

"What about?" I ask, like that's all I care about. Like my heart doesn't ache at the thought of Tobias going without food or sleep for days.

I shouldn't care. I mean, it was his own choice.

"No idea." She shrugs. "I think it's about lots of things. Pack structure. The construction. Security."

I nod. Standard pack stuff then.

"Cool."

"Uh-huh."

Summer raises a brow knowingly, a mischievous smile playing across her lips.

"Stop it," I hiss.

She just laughs.

"Have you decided what to do about Aires?" I ask her smugly. Because I know she hasn't, and it's a sore point for her.

She waives one hand dismissively, then turns to start the coffee maker, leaning one hip against the kitchen counter.

"I'm not doing anything about Aires. If he wants to be my creepy stalker, that's his choice. Once Tobias gets himself together, no doubt he'll make Aires a member of the pack, and then he'll just be Aires my pack mate, nothing more."

"Uh-huh," I say, mirroring the tone she used with me moments before.

She narrows her eyes and points a finger at me.

"I know what you're doing. And it's not going to work, okay. We all heard Tobias call you his mate. We were there, you know. He wasn't exactly subtle about it."

I shrug.

"And you guys were all touchy-feely the whole way back from Southern Utah. Like, you couldn't keep your hands off of each other. It was kinda gross, actually. Well, in an awkwardly cute sort of way."

Summer smiles at me expectantly, but I feel my expression shutter. Those hours tucked next to him in the car feel like they were a lifetime away. Like they belong to some other girl. Someone filled with warmth and excitement and hope for a new life.

Now they just remind me of the hollow feeling in my chest.

"Summer, she doesn't want to talk about it," Tania chides, her voice gentle as she pads soundlessly from the bedroom.

She's wearing an oversized t-shirt which I strongly suspect belongs to Samson, since it falls to her knees and smells vaguely of cat. The sleeves go to her elbows, giving her an almost child-like pixie sort of look, though she is starting to look less emaciated than she did when I first saw her a few months ago. Her curves are more pronounced, her face fuller.

"Yah, well maybe it's good to talk about things, you know," Summer retorts. "It's not healthy to bottle things up."

Tania flinches. I give Summer a pointed look and shake my head.

To talk to Tania, you'd think she's always lived with the Liberty pack, that is how little she mentions her past. Even to me, who has seen her covered in bruises and helped her escape.

Summer blushes, grimacing apologetically.

"She'll talk about things when she's ready," Tania replies steadily, her voice low and musical as she fills two mugs with some of the freshly brewed coffee, then pours herself a bowl of cereal. She keeps her eyes fixed on her breakfast, even when she slides into the seat across from me and passes me the second cup of coffee.

"And if that is never, that's okay too."

I sigh, then take a long drink of coffee. I don't know much about what happened to Tania, but I'm pretty sure my situation is nothing like hers.

"Guys, it's not that big of a deal. Tobias is my mate. I just found out a few days ago. We got a little bit excited about things at the start, and now we're just giving each other some space."

"You mean Tobias wolfed out for a few days," Summer says with a knowing nod. "Yah, I can see how that would be annoying."

"I'm not annoyed."

And it's the truth. I wasn't expecting to be the centre of Tobias' attention when his uncle had just been shot. That isn't what bothers me.

It's the harsh words Tobias spoke. The way he implied I should have foreseen the attack. Like I had failed somehow. Like I was only as good as my gift, and he had found me wanting. And then his uncontrolled rage, the way he attacked Jason, his own friend. The omega.

All of it reminds me so much of dad that I feel sick.

"I don't want to talk about it."

Chapter 4

Tobias Finch

It's dark when I finally wake, blinking dazedly into the dim interior of my RV. Danny's incessant snores drone like a saw, the noise occasionally punctuated by whimpering and scratching as Jason's wolf hunts phantom prey in his sleep.

Soundlessly, I slide out from under my covers, letting my bare feet rest on the cold floor as I get my bearings.

I'm back at Liberty pack. Free from my wolf form. Jamison is dead. I'm the alpha. I have to be okay. Lucy is here.

Lucy.

I blink into the darkness, letting the blankets slip to the floor as I rise to my feet. In the light of day, the thought of facing Lucy was terrifying. Now, ensconced in darkness, the need to check on her thrusts itself forward.

I'll just go past her RV, make sure she's okay. Like I've done at least twice every night in my wolf form since we got back to Liberty pack territory. She won't even know I'm there.

Crisp night air greets me when I step outside, filling my nostrils with the welcome scents of *pine* and *earth* and *pack*. I pause for a long moment, drinking it in. Feeling the threads connecting me to my pack, relishing the knowledge that they are all close.

Well, all except Cody. And Huxley Black. Though I don't think of Huxley as pack, even if the bond runs between us, weak though it is.

In the distance, two owls call to each other as they hunt above the pines. I know from the sound of their cries that it's Arlo and Theo, out murdering the helpless wildlife. Mainly mice and rats. Which, if you think about it too much, is kind of gross.

An errant breeze flicks my hair in front of my eyes, momentarily obscuring my vision and carrying with it what is undeniably the sweetest smell. *Lavender* and *fresh grass* and *Lucy*.

My eyes fly open and I breath deeper, feeling along the pack link for her. It's easy enough to find her, to locate the thread that connects me to her.

Find her, my wolf urges. *Track. Find Lucy*.

I want to tell the animal to be quiet. He's had his time. Now he can accept his place in the backseat. Except I am completely in agreement with him on this, even if it's for different reasons.

The wolf wants to claim her. To take what he thinks is his. To mark her as his mate.

I just want to apologize. To do whatever it takes to get her to forgive me. To assure her that I'm going to do better. Be better.

At least, I'm going to try.

IT TAKES LONGER than expected to find Lucy. I'd almost think she was avoiding me, or covering her scent somehow with how difficult it is to track her down.

At first, I'd thought she was close by. Somewhere in the trees at the edge of what has become affectionally known as the trailer park. But when I got there, there was only silence and the whispers of her scent swirling on the wind.

It probably doesn't help that I'm not really a tracker. No doubt someone like Jason would have been able to identify the echoes of Lucy's footsteps on the dry, pine-needle covered earth. Not me. No, I'm just going by scent. And by the tug of the pack bond.

It's only when I've hiked to the northern edge of Liberty pack territory, where the foothills become shorn in by granite cliffs, that I find her. She's resting with her back against a pine tree, head tilted back to stare up at the cloudless sky.

"Hey," she says, not turning away from the stars. That one word floats across on an errant breeze, so faint that if it weren't for my shifter hearing, I'd probably think that I'd imagined it.

"Hey," I reply, slowing my steps as I approach. Like she's a wild animal who might be startled if I move too fast. "What are you doing out here?"

She turns to look at me, eyes reflecting silver starlight.

"I could ask you the same question."

"Fair point."

I pause a few feet from her, the space between us feeling charged and unbreachable. Those few feet, they might as well be a canyon.

I heave a sigh and rub the back of my neck.

"I'm really sorry."

She lifts one pale eyebrow.

"Oh."

"Um, yah. Really sorry." I give a nod for emphasis, then nod again, probably looking like one of those bobble-head toys people put in their cars. "Look, I know you're mad at me…"

"Mad at you?"

She says those words so softly, they're practically whisked away on the wind, yet somehow they manage to feel as sharp as a steel blade, cutting through the space between us.

I freeze, because clearly I've said something wrong. But I'm not sure what the right thing is either.

Maybe there isn't a right thing.

She shakes her head, curling her lip in disgust.

"No, Finch, I'm not mad at you. The only person I'm mad at right now is myself. I should have known better. I mean, you're the alpha. You've got the power, right? So why would you be any different?"

"I – I don't..."

She holds up one hand, cutting me off.

"You basically told me that it was my fault Jamison was shot. That I should have been able to see it with my gift. And I can see how you might think that, but that isn't how my gift works. And surely if you know anything about me, you would know that I would have told you if I had foreseen that. Also, I'm not just my gift, by the way. I'm a person. With feelings. Just because I don't cry, just because I don't make a fuss, it doesn't mean that I don't feel things."

She pauses, pressing one hand to her chest, glaring at me with so much fire that her eyes are practically quicksilver.

"I do. I do feel things," she whispers. "And your words, they cut me deep."

I feel the blood drain from my face, my stomach sickening with icy dread. Honestly, I hadn't thought about what I had said to her in those moments after I came across Jamison's fallen form in the woods.

It's all a haze. A rage-filled, horrible haze.

"I'm sorry," I repeat, but the words sound hollow even to my ears.

The thing is, I've never been good with words. I don't know the right thing to say here, or even if there is a right thing.

She gives a curt nod, looking unconvinced.

"And then you wanted to attack my pack. My *family*."

It doesn't escape my notice that she still refers to the Clear Creek pack as her pack, and my wolf lets out a discontented growl, the sound escaping unbidden from my own lips. Because Lucy is ours. Lucy belongs to our pack. And it belongs to her.

Lucy narrows her eyes at the sound, her own teeth baring unconsciously in challenge.

"Don't get all possessive on me, Finch. Not now. You know what I mean. This might be my pack now, but they are still my family. They're the people I grew up with. And Jason. And Summer. And sure, Cooper might be a controlling, murderous, psychopath. Especially if he is the one behind the hits or whatever. And I guess he might be. It honestly wouldn't surprise me. But Jason's mom? All the elders? The pups? The ordinary wolves just living and working on the ranch, wanting the best lives for their families? *They* are completely blameless."

She pauses, catching her breath.

Without realising it, my eyes trail down the pale skin of her throat, noticing the rapid fluttering of her pulse. If I listen closely, I can hear the staccato beat of her heart, as fast as if she's been running.

"You would have attacked them all," she says finally, voice breathy. She shakes her head, sorrow taking over her expression, dulling the silver fire of her eyes. "If Jason hadn't stepped in - if I hadn't stepped in - you might have killed them."

I swallow back the bile at that. Because it's not a 'might'. I would have killed them. The beast under my skin was ready to end every last Clear Creek wolf in retaliation for attacking our territory. For taking Jamison.

Thank the gods Lucy stopped him.

"I know," I croak out, drawing one hand across my face. "I know."

"Why?" she asks, eyes rounding. Almost like she expected me to argue with her, to try and refute her accusations.

I drop my gaze, forgetting that I'm supposed to be the dominant wolf. The alpha. Instead, I stare at my bare feet, focusing on the dry pine needles and dirt beneath them.

"I can't control my wolf," I whisper, shame burning my cheeks at the admission. "I'm not strong enough to control him."

And that's the truth.

Lucy's eyes widen, lips parting in surprise.

"Yah," I say with a grimace. "That's pretty bad, isn't it?"

I might not have been raised wolf. I might have been raised in New York city with only my soft-spoken father as pack. But even I know that when a wolf takes control, it usually means the shifter is going feral. Feral wolves are a danger to everyone around them – humans, their pack, even those they love.

How Jamison managed to stay in his wolf form for all those years without becoming feral is something I've never understood.

"It's not good," Lucy agrees, worrying her lower lip with her teeth.

She pauses to rub her arms with her hands, and I notice the goose-bumps pebbling on her skin.

"Are you cold?" I ask. But I'm already shrugging off my hoodie and thrusting it awkwardly into her arms before she can answer.

At first, I think she might refuse. Instead, she just nods wordlessly, eyes trailing over my bare chest briefly before flicking away. Even in the starlit darkness of the forest, there is no missing the faint blush that rises to her cheeks. Something in my chest expands at the sight of it, feeling a lot like hope and longing.

"So, your wolf," she says, pulling the hoodie over her head.

It falls to mid-thigh on her and for some reason, seeing her in it fills me with a strange sense of satisfaction. Like, I'm providing for her. Taking care of her. Keeping her warm.

"What have you done to try and get it under control?"

"Um…"

What have I done? I've tried constructing a mental cage. Tried forcing my own will on the animal. Tried bargaining with him. Tricking him.

"Trickery seems to be the only thing that works," I admit.

She smiles at that.

"Oh yah?"

"Uh, yah."

My cheeks redden as I recall the most recent manifestation of that trickery. Actually, come to think of it, Lucy seems to be the only bait the psychopathic animal will fall for.

"He seems to really like you," I say stupidly, face burning. "He'll shift if he thinks it will help things with you. You know, uh, get me closer to you."

Gods. I want to die. Can I just die now?

Lucy presses her lips together as she bites back a laugh.

"Of course he likes me. I'm awesome."

I can tell she's trying to lighten the situation, bring humour in to diffuse the tension that's been stretching between us since I arrived, but I'm grateful. Suddenly, it feels easier to breathe, like a vice has been loosened from around my chest.

"You were able to get my wolf to stop," I say. "That time I invaded Clear Creek territory a few months ago. And then when I was attacking Jason. You were able to make him stop."

"True," she muses.

"No one else can do that," I say seriously. "Not even me."

Lucy frowns at that.

"I'm not going to be the one to fix you and your wolf. You can't put that on me."

"I know," I say, like I know what she means. But I really don't.

She just narrows her eyes at me. I think she knows I'm just saying whatever I think she wants to hear.

"I'm going to get my wolf under control," I assure her, and when I say it, I almost believe that it's true. Almost. "I'm going to figure it out."

She raises a brow.

"You know, I think I told you but, part of my gift is that I can smell lies."

I feel the blood drain from my face as I mentally calculate all the times I've said something that wasn't true. Gods. When I first arrived in Buffalo, I was one big walking talking lie. Always pretending to be something that I wasn't. Covering up each lie with another lie just so that I could keep my secret.

"Yep," she says. "That's part of the reason I didn't like you when we first met."

You smell of lies. Hadn't she said that to me? Was that the same night she injected me with horse tranquilizer?

"Wow. Um, that's pretty…"

Terrifying? Embarrassing? One more reason why it's looking increasingly unlikely that I'm going to win Lucy over?

"Awesome?" she suggests, a half-smile playing across her lips.

"Yah. Awesome." I lie, then cringe.

That makes her laugh. An open-mouthed laugh that echoes around the forest. My chest expands a little more at the sound, and I can feel hope burrowing deep there, insidious as a parasite. Finding the cracks in my defences.

"You know," she says, wiping her eyes with the back of her hand, "I think you're the first person I've told about my gift who hasn't thought it was this wonderful thing." The smile fades and her expression turns serious again. "Alpha Winslow – I mean, Cooper – he and my dad have been using my gift since I was twelve. They had me help with interrogations. Had me tell them whether the people they were questioning were being honest or not."

I gape at her, stomach churning at the thought of twelve-year-old Lucy being used like that. Being exposed to gods knows what. "When you were twelve?" No wonder she had seemed so comfortable tying me up and interrogating me.

"Unfortunately, yes."

She presses back against the tree, pulling the hood of my sweatshirt around her neck like a scarf, then rubbing her hands together. Since we've been out here, the temperature has dropped. I look up at the sky, noticing the dark clouds suddenly obscuring the starlight.

"The point is, I'm not going to be used like that again. I'm not saying I won't help the pack, or use my gift. But it's mine. It doesn't belong to anyone else. That's why I can't be the one to fix your wolf. Because if I do – if I'm all that keeps your wolf from going feral – then suddenly it becomes about what I am, not who I am. I don't want my only value to be my gift or that I'm your mate or whatever. I don't want my only value to be that I keep you sane."

She takes a deep breath, nostrils flaring as she tilts her head back against the tree and closes her eyes.

"I'm probably saying everything wrong. You know, I had a whole speech planned out in my head about what I wanted. How I needed you to prove that you would do better with actions and not words. And now..." she looks back at me, shaking her head with a faint, self-deprecating smile. "Now I just want things to be right between us again. It's like you're some sort of drug, dulling all my anger when I'm around you. Even when I try to hang on to it."

I give a sheepish, hopeful grin and take a tentative step towards her.

"I want things to be right between us too."

She points a finger at me. "That doesn't mean that I'm not upset anymore."

I nod emphatically, but don't slow my approach. The need to be near her, to close the distance between us, it's been pulling at me, prickling under my skin since I caught her scent. Before that, even.

"You're still upset with me," I agree. "Got it."

I brace my arms on the tree behind her, caging her in. This close to her, the sweet lavender scent of her is almost overwhelming and it sends a dizzying heat surging down to the base of my spine. I press my nose against her neck, shamelessly taking a deep inhale.

"I'm serious, Finch."

Her voice is breathy though, and she's trailing her fingertips up my bare arms, leaving goosebumps in their wake.

"I know."

I take another deep breath, drinking in the scent of her, then pull back. I want to look in her eyes. I want to see her face. I want her to see the truth in what I'm going to say to her, regardless of her gift.

"I'm not going to make any promises. I'm just figuring this out. You know, figuring out how to be an alpha. How to be your um... mate."

I grimace, because the sound of that word spoken out loud still seems strange. *Mate. I have a mate. Lucy is my mate.* I shake my head.

"Look, I don't even know how to be a boyfriend. So I'm going to mess this up. A lot, probably. And that's not even including the issues with my wolf. Or all the other shifters out there who want to kill me for being a born alpha."

I clench my teeth, realising suddenly how much danger Lucy is in just by virtue of being in this pack. By being close to me. I press my body closer to hers, as if that will shield her from every unknown danger. Like most of my wolf's instincts, it's completely illogical.

"All I can promise is that I'm going to do my best. For you. For the whole pack."

I press my forehead against hers, feeling the faint whisper of her breath on my own lips. It smells sweet and sad, like strawberries and rain.

"You say you don't want to fix my wolf, but it's too late for that," I breathe, brushing my thumb across her cheek, tunnelling my fingers through her hair. "You make me want to take all my broken pieces and turn them into something beautiful. Just to make you smile. And I'm not ashamed of it. I'll never be ashamed of it."

Lucy lets out a breathy, nervous laugh that whispers against my own lips and skitters across my bones.

"That almost sounded eloquent, Finch."

I start to wonder if she's mocking me, until she tucks her face into the crook of my neck, letting me feel the shape of her smile against my skin.

"You forgot one thing though," she murmurs, reaching up to wrap her hands behind my neck, fingertips toying with the hair at my nape.

"Oh. And what's that."

I try to keep my voice casual, but honestly, with the way she's touching me, it's impossible and the words come out with a barely suppressed groan.

"I'm not your girlfriend."

I furrow my brow, pulling back from her embrace to stare at her in confusion.

"No?"

For a horrible moment, I think maybe she's still mad at me, that she's been toying with me this whole time in retaliation. That thought dissipates when I see her face, the playful smirk tugging at the corners of her lips.

"You haven't asked me out yet," she says.

I grin as heat rises to my cheeks, the discomfort of embarrassment drowned out by the much stronger heat burning – in a completely different way – in the rest of my body.

"You haven't asked me out either," I tease. "You know I'm all for equal opportunity."

I'm only half joking. I might be new to dating. My experience so far might be limited to a couple of middle-school crushes. A few stollen kisses in the hallway between classes and some painfully awkward moments on the dance floor of a school gymnasium. But even I know that a girl can ask a boy out.

"Yah," she breathes, her gaze becoming heavy-lidded as she blinks up at me. "Yah, I guess I haven't."

Clouds rumble in the dark sky above us, thick with the scent of rain and ether, promising summer storms. I feel one teasing drop land on my cheek, another on my shoulder. One glistens on the bridge of Lucy's nose. When a raindrop lands on my lip, Lucy reaches up to swipe it away with her thumb.

"I guess you could be my boyfriend."

I catch her hand with my own, twining my fingers with hers. Partially because I want to. But mostly because every time she touches me, the pounding in my ears gets louder and louder, making it impossible to breathe, to think, to form cohesive sentences.

"Only if you ask nicely," I groan, tugging her against my chest.

She grins up at me, even as the rain starts to pelt down on us, smattering her upturned face until rivulets are tracing the shape of her smile.

"But I'm not nice."

The words are barely audible against the din of the rain on the pines.

"You are," I argue.

"No, I'm not." The smile falls from her lips as she blinks away the rain. "Summer is nice. Tania is nice. Jason is nice. Me? I am not nice."

I frown, racking my brain for an example that I can use to refute her argument, and come up short. Especially when I recall the way she lured me to the bull's pen, or the way she stabbed that needle full of horse tranquilizer into my leg.

"Fine," I concede, wiping the water from my forehead. My hair is soaked now, dripping into my eyes and trickling down the back of my neck. "You're not nice. But you're ferociously loyal. Kind of terrifying. And really, really hot, okay?"

I flash her a smile and lick the rain from my lips. It tastes like Lucy and sorrow and new beginnings.

"So, will you be my girlfriend?"

Her answering rain-soaked smile is the most beautiful thing I've seen.

Chapter 5

Lucy Stone

It turns out I have absolutely no backbone when it comes to staying mad at Tobias Finch. I blame my wolf. Every time I'm around him, the little hussy just wants to melt at his feet.

Which is why I'm grinning stupidly when I finally get back to my trailer, wearing Tobias' oversized hoodie, my lips swollen, my hair and clothes dripping enough water to leave puddles on the linoleum floor.

"Lovely morning for a run," Summer teases, eyes crinkling as she emerges from the little bathroom off the hall, tossing a dry towel in my direction. "And nice hoodie. But you should really get out of those clothes before you turn this place into a swimming pool."

"Thanks," I huff, before hurriedly stripping and drying myself off.

Despite the nearly deafening sound of the rain pelting the metal roof of the RV, I can hear the tell-tale signs of Tania waking up. The faintest morning light is starting to filter through the small windows.

Somehow, I managed to stay out with Tobias in that forest until dawn.

"I take it things are all good between you then?" Summer asks, giving me an annoyingly smug smile before heading to turn on the coffee machine. "You guys kissed and made up. Or was that kissed and made out?"

"Really?" I say, wrapping the towel around myself before sitting down at the table. "What are you, like twelve?"

"At heart, maybe." She shrugs. "Seriously though, I'm glad. You're terrible to be around when you're in a mood."

"I wasn't in a mood," I argue.

Summer just gives me a look, raising one sceptical brow. "Uh-huh."

"You were definitely in a mood," Tania says as she staggers out of the bedroom, her dark, heavy-lidded eyes sparkling briefly with mischief. Then she tenses, her eyes widening fearfully as she drops her gaze submissively. "Sorry, alpha. That was rude of me."

I lift both hands in protest, nearly dropping my towel in the process. "Please. Please don't call me that." I flash her what I hope is a reassuring smile. "And it wasn't rude," I lie. "Remember, I told you, just treat me as an equal."

I swear to Morrigan I must have this same conversation with the fox every second day. No matter how many times I try to explain to her that I'm not the alpha's mate. That I'm not the co-alpha of this pack. That the golden wolf might listen to me, but it doesn't mean I'm in charge of anything. She just doesn't seem to get it. And it's not like she's dense or anything. She's actually super smart. And four years older than me. So there is really no excuse.

"Yes alph – Lucy," Tania nods.

Then she's hurriedly making me a cup of coffee, sliding it across the table like she's a waitress at a restaurant and not my pack mate who

I cohabitate with. I take the coffee with a grateful smile, doing my best not to grimace at her behaviour.

I know why she's doing it. It's her animal's instinct driving her, pushing her to become indispensable to me so that she can feel safe in the pack. I would tell her to stop doing it, if I knew it wouldn't just make things worse.

"Yah, we worked things out," I sigh, answering Summer's earlier question.

I take a long drink of my coffee in an attempt to hide the whisper of a smile threatening to expose itself as I think about exactly how we worked things out.

"I bet you did," Summer says, waggling her eyebrows as she slides into the seat next to me.

"Summer," I hiss.

"I'm happy for you," Tania says, her voice low and sweet as she pulls up the chair across from us. "And for him. He's a good alpha."

"Yah," I admit reluctantly. "I guess he is."

Tania gives me a hard look, her eyes levelling my own. It's the closest thing to a challenge I've seen from her and unconsciously my spine stiffens, my wolf bristling at the unexpected behaviour.

"He *is* a good alpha," Tania insists. "The best I've ever come across. And I've lived in five different packs. Tobias is like no alpha I've ever seen before. Maybe you don't think anything of it, because you're a dominant wolf. You grew up with your dad as the beta. You've always been at the top. You know, a position of privilege." The way she says privilege, it's like a bad word. "But for the rest of us – the submissive animals, the prey animals, and the omegas – packs can be brutal. Alphas even more so."

She pauses, dropping her eyes to stare down at her coffee mug. It's then I notice that her hands are curled around it, clutching it like claws. And she's trembling, the scent of real fear wafting off of her.

I sigh.

"Don't ever be afraid of speaking up around me, okay," I tell her reassuringly. "We're pack. And you're my friend. I like that you speak up."

She lifts her head, giving me a weak smile.

"Thanks."

"And you're right," I concede. "He is a good alpha."

I pause, recalling the vulnerability in Tobias' words as he spoke to me in the darkness of the pre-dawn forest. As he promised to do better. To be better. I might not be able to fix him, but surely being a better alpha is something the entire pack can help him with, right?

"Even more important, he wants to do what is right," I start tentatively, tracing one finger along the handle of my mug. "And he's willing to listen, so that he can do the right thing…"

A knock on the door of our trailer interrupts me, the sound quickly followed by the snigging of the latch and a cheerful "good morning" as Jason lets himself in. He lifts a brow when his eyes land on me, barely suppressed grin tipping up the corners of his lips as he waltzes over to our coffee machine, pouring himself a cup. Making himself at home in our trailer. Like usual.

"You look like you got caught in the rain, Luce," he says, giving me a pointed look. "Funny. Tobias came in soaking wet as well. You guys must have been out at the same time."

"Shut it, Jason," I snap, heat rising to my cheeks.

He just laughs.

"I just came to say the pack meeting is in an hour," he announces.

"You came to drink our coffee. And eat our food." Summer lifts one finger accusingly. "You know, you could have breakfast in your own trailer."

Jason shrugs. "I could. But it smells in there."

"Smells?" Tania asks.

Jason gives her a pointed look. "Uh, yah. What do you think a trailer with three guys living in it smells like? Roses? Especially when one of them comes in at dawn smelling like wet dog, tracking mud everywhere. And when the other one is a bear shifter who thinks it's normal to cure salmon on the kitchen counter." He wrinkles his nose. "It's seriously gross."

My eyes flick around our own RV. My wet clothes lay heaped on the bathroom floor, muddy footprints dotting the faded linoleum. Through the open door at the end of the hall, pillows and blankets and clothes are heaped across the unmade bed.

I seriously doubt our RV is that much better.

"Your RV is much cleaner," Jason assures me, catching my gaze and no doubt guessing my train of thought. "You guys at least do the dishes."

I wince inwardly at the sight of our gleaming countertop, which is entirely owing to Tania's work.

"What is this meeting about anyway?" I ask, hoping to change the subject.

Jason perks up, shoulders straightening and face lighting up at my question. Typical omega. Always eager to be helpful.

"It's about pack structure. Enforcers. Strategy to protect our boundary," he explains, listing each item off on his fingers. "Oh, and also an update on the construction of the lodge."

I nod. So basically, ordinary pack business.

"And you and Tobias – you guys are all good?" I ask. Since the last time I saw Jason and Tobias together, Tobias had just had his teeth around Jason's throat.

"Oh yah, we're good." Jason waves one hand dismissively. "He didn't hurt me and he's apologised." He pauses, a faint blush creeping up his cheeks before he adds: "And he gave me permission to invite Ross onto pack territory."

"Really?" Summer practically squeaks, bouncing excitedly on the bench seat beside me. The movement causes some of my coffee to slosh out of my mug, and I shoot her a glare. Which she completely ignores.

"Yep," Jason smiles. And it's one of those wide smiles that crinkles the corners of his eyes and makes you want to grin in return. "But don't get too excited, okay. Ross and me – we're just friends. And I don't even know if his dad will let him come over."

Summer nods sagely. "If he does come over, I'll be totally cool. Promise."

…

Thankfully the rain has stopped by the time everyone makes their way to the soaked marquee in the clearing. It's early enough that most people are carrying their breakfasts with them, nodding in greeting to each other through bleary eyes. The cat shifters look positively miserable, scowling at the damp, knee-high grass as if it has personally offended them.

Despite the early hour, there's a strange, nervous energy moving through the pack. Even though I've been a member of this pack for less than a week, I get the sense that something is changing. Something big. I wonder idly if it's the fact that there are so many new members – myself included. Or if it's because Cody is gone, leaving some sort of a vacuum in his wake.

"Hey."

Tobias' voice pulls me from my reverie, drawing my attention right to where he's sitting, arms resting across the plastic table. There's a glow behind his golden gaze that wasn't there before and I can practically feel the heat in it when he looks at me.

"Hey," I say, feeling my cheeks warm as I look around the tent, at the camp chairs and damp bean bag chairs littered everywhere, wondering where I should sit.

Tobias nods to the seat beside him, then looks up at me hopefully.

Behind me, Summer gives me a little shove, but I shake my head. As much as I want to be close to him, I'm new to this pack. I don't want to be putting myself out as the co-alpha. Acting like I'm here to lead this pack.

I'm not.

Instead, I lean against one of the metal posts holding up the marquee, then watch in silence as the rest of the pack files in, shoving and jostling for comfortable places to sit.

A thrumming sense of rightness settles in when everyone arrives, humming behind my ribcage. Just like the night of the pack run, I swear I can almost feel them all. Only this time, it's quiet anticipation, hints of nervousness, and mild sorrow. None of the raging blood lust.

Still, it makes my wolf uncomfortable.

"Hey everyone," Tobias says, his voice steady as he addresses the group.

He's leaning back in his chair, eyes half-lidded, looking completely relaxed and still there is a quiet sort of authority in just those two words. It's nothing like the loud, commanding authority of alpha Winslow. It's subtler. It makes you want to lean in and pay attention.

"Thanks for waiting for me while I wolfed out these past couple days," he continues, and this time his gaze flicks to me, meeting and holding my own. "But I'm back now. And we have a lot to talk about."

Chapter 6

Tobias Finch

"No kidding," Hamish smirks, his feet stretched out in front of him as he reclines in one of the damp bean bag chairs. "We gonna talk about what to do with the Clear Creek pack? Because I still think they deserved the hell you were going to rain down on them the other night."

I don't miss the dark look Hamish shoots at Lucy. Or the way her eyes narrow at him in return.

I draw one hand across my face and bite back the irritated growl that rumbles at the back of my throat. My wolf hates being contained in this human form.

"No, they don't deserve it," I say firmly. "And yah, we're going to talk about them. Eventually. But we're going to talk about some other things first."

I give him a hard look. My wolf huffs in smug satisfaction when the hawk shifter clamps his mouth shut, giving me an apologetic nod.

"Right," I continue, letting my eyes settle on the each of the faces watching me. Letting my connection to each of them through the pack bond steady me. Strengthen me. "I've given it some thought over the past couple days and we need to be doing more to protect our borders. To keep our pack safe."

Truth be told, I've thought of pretty much nothing else the past three days as I circled my territory, my four paws practically wearing a path along the perimeter. *Protect the pack*, my wolf had chanted with each step.

And Lucy. I'd thought about Lucy.

"I know I said before we shouldn't have a structure. No hierarchy. And while I still think that is right, I also know we need to be better organised if we're going to defend ourselves. And we are – we are going to have to defend ourselves."

I pause, gritting my teeth around the truth in that statement. Despite the hours of training everyone had been doing with Orrin, despite getting shot a few months ago, the human part of me could never imagine anyone actually attacking us. I mean, we're just a bunch of kids living in RVs and tents in the woods in the middle of nowhere in Wyoming. Who could possibly care enough to come out here, let alone attack us?

Until Jamison.

"We need to do more than train with Orrin. We need to have organised patrols. Maybe even someone to take charge of everyone who wants to be an enforcer. Oh, and some sort of system to let us know if anyone encroaches on our territory. Like, there's got to be some sort of technology available to help us with that, right?"

I look around the group, hoping someone will have a suggestion. I'm not exactly illiterate when it comes to technology, but my experience is basically limited to looking stuff up on my phone.

A bunch of blank faces stare back at me.

Except for Jason. He's leaning forward on his plastic chair so much it looks like it's about to topple over, a huge smile plastered on his face as he raises his hand excitedly. Like this is class or something.

"Actually, this is something I've been thinking about the past couple days, and there is some pretty cool tech out there that we could use," he says excitedly. "At first, I thought you'd have to do something like fence the territory off, and of course that would take forever since this territory is massive. But there's lots of options. Like you can create an invisible fence by using a mix of motion sensors and underground sensors. We would just have to work out how best to calibrate everything, so that you only pick up humans. Or shifters. But I think it's definitely possible."

As I listen to Jason ramble on about the different brands of sensors and their various specifications, I feel a weight lift from my chest. For the first time in what feels like forever, protecting my pack is starting to feel like a possibility.

It also solidifies what I've been thinking. What I had started to accept as I made my nightly perimeter patrols in wolf form day after day. I can't do everything by myself.

"Perfect," I say, interrupting Jason halfway through his explanation of how drone detection could be used to monitor for intruding avian shifters. "That's settled then. You can be in charge of perimeter defence for the pack."

Jason's mouth drops open, all colour draining from his face as he shakes his head vehemently.

"Perimeter defence?"

"Yah. I mean, we can give it a different title. I don't think that really matters. But since you are probably the only one here who has a clue about this sort of thing, I think you should be in charge." I shrug. "I mean, feel free to get any of the others to help you. But honestly, I only understood about fifty percent of what you were saying."

"Tobes, that's… I'm grateful, but…" Jason shakes his head, "I'm an *omega*. I can't be a leader of anything. No one would listen to me."

I scoff.

"I would listen to you."

"Really?" Jason quirks a brow, no doubt thinking of the last time when I definitely didn't listen to him. When I had my teeth around his throat.

I rub the back of my neck and flash him an apologetic smile.

"We'll listen to you," Danny assures him. "This isn't a wolf pack. We're not wolves. Not most of us anyway. And even those of us who are would be smart enough to know that you're the best one to take the lead on this." Danny pauses, cocking his head to the side, a mischievous grin playing at the corners of his lips. "Plus, if alpha doesn't listen, you can just sic Lucy on him. That seemed to work last time."

I groan, palming my face with my hands and ignoring the answering chuckles from my pack mates.

Seriously. I have the worst friends.

"And you said I can get anyone to help me?" Jason asks.

Since my face is buried in my hands, it takes me a moment to realise he's talking to me, not Danny. I look up, careful to avoid looking at Lucy, even though I can feel her stare pressing in on me.

"Um, yah, sure." I shrug. "I trust your judgement."

Jason flushes at the praise, a small smile playing across his face.

"Okay," he says. "Yah. I'll do it."

"Good," I say.

And I mean it. Because I wasn't really planning on letting him back out of this.

"Then the next thing we need is someone to take charge of enforcers. Training, scheduling patrols. That sort of thing."

"Obviously that should be Orrin," Christopher volunteers.

There are several answering nods and mumbles of agreement, even as Orrin glowers menacingly.

"I agreed to train you pups," Orrin rumbles. "I didn't agree to try and organise a bunch of teenage shifters." He pauses, pointing an accusing finger at Tyrone and Samson. "Especially ones who can barely get up in the morning for endurance training."

Samson lifts a shoulder, giving a very feline sniff. "Running is for masochists."

Tyrone nods in agreement. "Exactly. We're *cats*. We sprint. We sleep. We don't jog."

Orrin ignores them, rounding to glower in my direction instead. "It's almost autumn. I need to be getting my den ready for hibernation."

Beside me, Danny lets out a derisive snort. "Please, old man. Spare us the 'winter is coming' speech will you. You know you don't actually need to hibernate, right? Like, we have heating to keep us warm now. And you can get food at the supermarket year-round."

"I *like* hibernating," Orrin retorts, sounding almost petulant.

"And I like being alone," Red counters. "But you decided to drag me all the way out here. To what is essentially a trailer park in the middle of nowhere." Red shudders, tugging at his tufted cat ears irritably before narrowing his eyes at Orrin. "I think it's only fair that you suffer too."

"What about my mechanic shop? I can't just leave all my customers."

"Really?" Red cocks a brow. "You're going to use that sorry excuse for a business as a reason to go back to the Bear Tooth Mountains?

You know I work for you, right? You've been running in the red for the past three years."

Orrin shrugs. "It's an investment. Sometimes you have to put money in to…"

"It's a bottomless pit of debt and rusting car parts. You know it. I know it. Everyone in that town knows it."

Orrin lets out a threatening rumble as his eyes flash menacingly, yellow bleeding in as his bear pushes for supremacy.

Red's ears flatten against his skull in response as the taciturn feline lifts his lip in a lazy snarl, baring one tooth. A tooth that is a little too sharp to be human.

"And… I was thinking I should appoint a beta," I announce abruptly. As anticipated, this has the desired effect of drawing Orrin and Red's attention away from their own dispute, and they both turn to face me with looks of unmasked confusion.

It's a look that is shared by everyone in my pack. Which, considering how opposed I was to having a beta before, is hardly surprising.

What is surprising is how quickly the looks of confusion and surprise morph into relief.

"Thank the gods," Theo mutters under his breath, exchanging a knowing glance with Arlo. "He's finally seeing reason."

"It was only a matter of time," Arlo agrees, nodding sagely.

I just gape at them.

"Hold on." I lift one finger in the air. "You all *wanted* me to appoint a beta? Why didn't you say anything before?"

Arlo gives me one of those looks that says: "Isn't it obvious?"

I frown.

"Please don't tell me you guys were afraid to speak up?"

It's Tyrone who finally answers.

"We weren't afraid, exactly," Tyrone drawls, one finger absently toying with the ends of Tania's ponytail. She edges away from him, putting enough space between them that his hand is forced to drop back by his side. "Just following our strong self-preservation instincts. You know, after you practically jumped down Cody's throat for suggesting we have a ranking system and all."

I wave one hand dismissively. "That was just healthy debate."

"Uh-huh. If you say so, alpha."

He emphasises the word 'alpha', then gives an infuriating smirk. I shake my head.

"Okay, so a beta. Does everyone think we should have one?"

The answering murmur of affirmations and nods tell me everything. I have been a terrible alpha.

"You know I'm all for getting rid of pointless traditions," Christopher says. "But a beta is pretty essential. Especially for you, and especially in a pack this big. Because, no offence, but you're more of a big picture sort of person."

He's right of course. Cody was the one who paid attention to all the details.

Only, now Cody is gone.

My chest constricts at the memory of Cody's betrayal. At the feel of the pack link connecting him to me, stretched by distance.

"If you don't have a beta, we'll probably all go hungry and end up living in these gods-forsaken RVs forever. Because you'll forget to buy groceries and forget to pay the contractors on time," Christopher explains.

"Fair call," I acknowledge with a grimace. I'm pretty sure one of our bills is already overdue, and I can't even remember which one. "So, who wants to be my beta?"

Silence.

Complete and utter silence.

I look around, trying to catch people's eyes, and feel like a teacher who has just asked the class a question. You know, when they threaten to start calling on random students to answer, so everyone tries to make themselves as small as possible.

"Really?" I say dryly.

I thought shifters were supposed to be power hungry. I thought if we had a ranking system, everyone would be vying for position, challenging each other to be beta.

I hadn't considered the alternative. That literally no one wants any of the responsibility that comes along with leadership.

Of course, I should have considered that. I mean, I don't particularly want the responsibility that comes with being an alpha. If I could sit back and let someone else take the lead, I totally would.

"We could have a vote," Jason suggests. "Everyone write down who they think should be beta, and then we count up who gets the most nominations."

Of course, he's the only one brave enough to speak out, since he knows I wouldn't make him my beta. Not if he's going to be in charge of perimeter defence.

Still, it's a good idea. So good that it's only met with a small amount of grumbling.

After several minutes of scrambling around for paper and pens, Danny, Jason and Summer are helping me to count out nominations. The rest of the pack are looking bored and restless, and I don't blame them. This is the last place any of us wants to be on a Saturday morning.

"Um, who nominated me?" Summer squeaks, lifting her head from the pile of paper. "Is this some kind of a joke."

"Here's another one with your name on it," Danny informs her, making a note on his phone.

"You're kidding me." Summer mutters, shaking her head. "I've been with this pack for three days… Ah-hah!" She casts Danny a smug grin. "Here is one with your name on it."

Danny stares at the scrap of paper with his name scrawled across it, as if it's a deadly snake, poised to strike.

"Nope. No way. I am not going to be beta."

"Not really your choice," Red comments, leaning over the table in an attempt to see whose names have been written down. "We agreed to vote. Apparently."

By the time the names are tallied up, it's pretty clear there are only two contenders. Summer. And Orrin's nephew, Danny.

Both of whom are glaring at their pack mates like they've just been made the subject of some cruel prank.

"It's a tie," Jason tells me, rubbing his hands together. "They've both got the same number of nominations. You'll have to choose one."

And just like that, Summer and Danny turn their glares on me.

"I swear to Morrigan, if you make me be your beta, I'll figure out a way to make you pay," Summer threatens through clenched teeth.

"We're friends, right?" Danny cajoles. "Friends don't make friends be their betas."

I shoot them both an apologetic smile, but it feels more like a grimace. Still, there's a certain rightness in the thought of either of them being my beta.

Both, my wolf argues. *Make them both be our betas.*

Of course, my wolf would say that. Because my wolf is greedy. Hungry. Wanting more of everything, no matter what I give him. More pack. More power. More Lucy.

And apparently, more betas.

For once, I'm inclined to agree with him on this. Not because I think I should have two betas. But because if I choose them both, neither of them can get too mad at me. Also, it would make their work easier.

"You can both be my betas," I suggest, with as much false cheerfulness as I can muster.

They both stare at me, twin looks of disapproval on their faces.

"So… maybe you can take charge of planning a pack run for the full moon next week?" I ask them hopefully.

Because, regardless of whether I want to run as a wolf or not, that is part of being an alpha. Organising events to bring everyone together. Keeping everyone fed. Building housing that isn't a complete embarrassment. Putting in systems to keep everyone safe.

So that what happened to Jamison doesn't happen to anyone else.

Because I promised Lucy I would do better. Be better.

And I can't do it on my own.

With the matter of betas resolved, I turn to Aires, my head cocked in silent question. He casts a hopeful look at Summer, who studiously ignores him, then gives me a curt nod, holding out his hand.

There is no missing Gareth's frown and Red's disapproving scoff, but I ignore them. We already decided days ago that Aires was going to be made pack.

Hamish slides his knife across the table to me - a switch-blade that I'm pretty certain is illegal in a number of states, and which he sharpens regularly. He gives Aires a hard look.

"Betray him and I'll end you, dragon," Hamish says.

Aires curls his lip disdainfully, not bothering to reply.

I clear my throat, meeting Aires' eyes with my own.

"Right," I say, "let's do this."

Chapter 7

Cody Winslow

Coming home to Half Moon Ranch was never supposed to be like this.

I was supposed to come home victorious. Free. With Summer by my side and my future ahead of me.

The truth couldn't be farther from that unrealistic fantasy.

When we arrived home a week ago, dad didn't even park the truck outside our house. Instead, he drove past it, following the winding gravel road to the far end of the Clear Creek pack territory. To a small cabin, half fallen into disuse, as far from the main lodge as possible.

"What is this place?" I had asked when I first surveyed the rugged interior of the one-room structure. It looked like it had been built of logs and cobwebs about a hundred years ago, and smelt of dust and cattle and rats.

"Just one of the cabins our ranchers use if they're out on the range overnight," dad had explained with a shrug. "And your new home."

My new home.

Home.

A week later, and it is clear to me that by 'home' dad really meant 'prison'.

"I can't have you running around pack territory," dad had explained. "You're still bonded to that freak of nature, so gods only know what he could order you to do. I can't have you endangering my pack."

"Does mom know I'm here?" I had asked.

Because for some reason, that had seemed important. I was home. Jamison was dead. Dad was locking me away. Summer wasn't mine. Was never going to be mine. And I just wanted my mom to hug me. To tell me everything would be okay, even if it was a lie.

Dad lifted a brow, the harsh line of his jaw hardening.

"What do you think?"

One week on, and I still don't know the answer to that question.

Every couple of days, one of the enforcers brings me groceries. Every day, I can hear the footsteps outside the thick wood door as someone stands guard. Every night, I can feel the unanswered pull of the waxing moon, calling to my wolf. Demanding that I shift and run. Demanding that I return to my alpha. That I return to my pack.

This is my pack, I tell my wolf.

But he and I both know that is a lie. This stopped being my pack the moment Tobias arrived, broken and bloodied at Blackwater, unable to shift into a wolf, and still determined to rescue me.

This is my home, I insist.

But that's also a lie, isn't it? It stopped being home months ago when my own father barred my entry. It certainly stopped being home when it became my prison.

For some reason, my mind flicks back to Lucy. To what Jason had told us about her situation here. She had been locked up too, and I had blamed her for it. Who knows, maybe it was her fault. But now that I'm locked up, with the pull of the moon nearly driving me mad, I don't think I can fault her for wanting to escape.

We are not meant to be confined, my wolf warns me. *We are not meant to be alone.*

And I know he's right. He always is, my wolf. It's me that gets things wrong.

Footsteps thudding outside my door jolt me from the dark cloud of my thoughts. I blink, almost surprised to find myself bathed in the thin sunlight that filters through the grime-encrusted windows.

"Good morning," I call out, my own voice thick with disuse.

I don't expect an answer. They never answer. But I'm lonely.

"Glad that rain finally stopped, huh?" I say, trying to keep my tone light and friendly.

Because whoever these males are, I can't bring myself to see them as my enemies. They used to be my pack mates. My friends.

Whoever they are, I was once supposed to be their alpha.

There's the sound of shuffling, followed by a heavy sigh. Almost like someone is leaning against the outside of my door.

I grin, rushing over, suddenly filled with excitement.

"Look, I know you probably aren't allowed to talk to me," I ramble, pressing my palms and forehead against the rough wood. "And I'm not going to ask you to let me out or anything like that."

I pause, taking a long sniff, trying to catch the scent of the shifter on the other side.

If this was a modern door, the kind that is built to withstand fires or the icy Wyoming winters, I probably wouldn't be able to smell him. But this door was made from several thick pine slats butted together, at a time when hand tools were the norm. This leaves the smallest of gaps between the slats. Just enough that I'm able to catch the scent of my jailor on the next gust of wind.

Anton.

My heart leaps, my wolf careening with barely restrained eagerness, making me feel almost nauseous. I have to bite back the excited whimper that threatens to burst forth as my wolf demands out. Demands to play.

Beta, my wolf urges. *This is our beta.*

Was, I remind him. *He would have been our beta.*

Since we aren't in line to be an alpha anymore and never will be.

But that doesn't matter. Not right now. Not anymore. What matters is that for the first time in a week, I am not alone. For the first time in a week, someone is there. Listening.

I take a deep breath, forcing myself to be calm. Pushing down the frantic, hopeful excitement.

"Hey Anton. I know you are probably under orders not to talk to me. But I'm going crazy in here, man. I really am."

Silence.

"Can you just like, knock or something? Just to let me know you're listening?" I ask, trying and failing to keep the desperation from my voice.

Another silence. It drags on until my heart sinks into my stomach. Until I'm almost certain Anton has moved away from the door.

And then there's a heavy sigh, followed by the faintest of knocks at the base of the door.

Thank the gods.

I press my forehead to the door, relief flooding my system and making it momentarily difficult to speak.

"I'm just going to talk to you, okay?" I say, when the tightness in my throat relents enough for me to talk. "I just – I just need to talk to someone. I'm not good at being alone. You know what I'm like."

I pause, grateful that I don't need to explain myself. Not to Anton. He's grown up with me. We've played together, had our first shift within days of each other.

He knows how much I need to be around other wolves. How much I need to be around my pack.

It's like those humans who are extroverts, who physically need interaction and contact, magnified by the lens of animal instinct and the alpha need to protect.

There's the faintest rap at the door in reply, just enough that I can feel the vibrations in the palms of my hands. Just enough that I know I'm not alone.

And so I start to talk, the words tumbling off my lips without filter.

I tell him about the Liberty pack. How I wanted to help build something big, but then I got caught up in jealousy and fear and longing for someone I was never meant to have.

I tell him about Tobias, and how we couldn't ever seem to agree, even though my wolf still wants to follow him.

I tell him about my betrayal, how utterly stupid I was. How I convinced myself that dad just wanted to help me, even when I really knew better. Because I know my dad. I might love him, but I have never been blind to what he is.

I tell him about Jamison. The other born alpha, who stayed hidden in his wolf form for so many years that he lost the ability to shift. The kind, glorious wolf who had somehow become my closest friend while I had been at the Liberty pack. The wolf who had escaped death from the hands of his pack as a newborn pup, only to be killed by accident. Caught up in dad's attempt to free me.

I tell him how I miss my mom, but that confession is cut short by the tightness pressing at my windpipe. By the stinging pressure building behind my eyes. So, I stop, letting the silence fill the space between us, heavy and impenetrable as that thick wooden door.

Finally, there is the faintest knocking at the base of the door, followed by a heavy sigh and the sound of shuffling as Anton rises to his feet. His footsteps thud, fading into the distance, letting me know he's leaving. Probably changing places with another guard.

Still, I keep my hands pressed to that door for a long while after he's left, grateful for the momentary respite from solitude.

Hoping he will come back.

Chapter 8

Lucy Stone

The two weeks that follow the pack meeting pass in a blur of frantic activity.

From dawn till dark we work. Training with Orrin – usually in human form, given the proximity of the human builders during the week. Helping on the job-site. Digging the seemingly unending number of holes along the territory's perimeter so that we can install Jason's gods-damned movement sensors.

Jason has even enlisted Ross Slade's help with setting up automation for several ridiculously expensive drones. Like all the humans in Buffalo, Ross thinks Tobias is some crazy young entrepreneur setting up a sustainable, exclusive resort. Given how popular this part of Wyoming has become for rich people as a rustic getaway location, it's a believable story. So when Ross queried why the drones needed to be calibrated to pick up birds over a certain size, it didn't take much for Jason to convince him we want to monitor the comings and goings of rare and endangered birds of prey, to help guests spot them in the wild.

I know Jason hates keeping Ross in the dark about what we are, but I suppose it's not that far from the truth. Bird shifters are the rarest of the birds of prey – much rarer than any natural Golden Eagle. And every member of the Liberty pack has a very keen interest in bird watching. At least, when it comes to making sure bird shifters aren't sneaking onto our territory.

"How is it that everyone managed to eat more than a thousand dollars' worth of meat in less than a week?" Danny gripes from his seat at the kitchen table in our RV.

He's painstakingly typing something with fingers too thick for his small laptop keyboard, a frustrated frown plastered on his usually cheerful-looking face.

Papers are spread out between him and Summer, covering the entirety of our small dining table, held down in places by half-empty coffee mugs. Aires sits perched beside Summer, idly scrolling on his phone as he sips his own cup of coffee. Even dressed in jeans and a t-shirt, he looks out of place here, with his overly styled hair and mannerisms that seem better suited to a corporate boardroom.

Summer flicks her long ponytail over one shoulder, letting it slap against Aires' face, before looking up dazedly from her own laptop.

"I'm sorry, what did you say?"

"I said, we ate more than a thousand dollars' worth of meat," Danny exclaims. "How is this even possible?"

"Well," Summer begins, giving Danny a pointed stare, "since you're the one in charge of setting meal plans and making the cooking rosters, I would think you would have a pretty good idea of where that all went." Her eyes drop back to her laptop and she frowns. "What I want to know is how I'm going to keep this build on schedule when the electricians are wanting to do their work a week later than planned, and the dry-wallers are saying they have to start this week or else we'll need to wait until mid-August."

Danny shrugs. "Just let them come when they can, right?"

Summer snorts. "Yah, okay. Maybe we can get the painters in before the drywall goes up too. Heck, why not just start laying the carpet. That'll work fine. No problem."

I shake my head, blinking sleep-crusted eyes as I make my way over to the coffee machine. Only to find it empty. Again.

I round on the group, crossing my arms over my chest. "Okay, who drank the last cup?" I ask, glaring at each of them in turn. Of course, they don't even bother to look up from their devices.

I look at the clock on the microwave. Six in the morning. Unbelievable.

Morrigan give me patience, it's six in the morning and these jerks are already taking up space in our RV and drinking all the coffee. It's bad enough that I've had to start sleeping in the bed with Tania and Summer to give 'the betas' space to work. Now I don't even have coffee to make up for getting a bad night's sleep.

My first instinct is to shout at them. Maybe throw something at their table of carefully arranged papers. It's a plan my wolf fully supports, since the taciturn animal would like nothing more than to chase these intruders from her den.

But then I notice the deep circles under Summer's eyes and the way Danny's broad shoulders slump forward. It's not like they're trying to get on my nerves. There really is nowhere else for them to work. Most betas would have an office, a couple of underlings and at least ten years more experience than these two. If anything, I should be helping, not making things harder for them.

Except I don't really know how to do that either, apart from making them food or something. And Tania does that.

All I know is what I've been trained to do.

I sigh, slipping on my shoes before heading out into the crisp morning air. Already, the sun is peeking out over the horizon, casting the forest in purples and golds, gilding the dust covered RVs with a sheen of magic.

I pause on the steps, considering my options.

There's the mould infested lodge that is thankfully being torn down in a couple of weeks. I'm pretty sure there are a few mini fridges in there, as well as a coffee maker. There's also a high chance I'll catch some sort of mould-induced respiratory infection if I go in there. So that's a hard no.

My eyes land on the RV that Tobias and Jason share. Normally, Danny would be in there too. Asleep. Like any sane person would be at this time in the morning. But of course, he's in my RV with Summer.

I hesitate, contemplating. Jason is probably still asleep. Especially since he's been up late every night for the past two weeks getting the perimeter secured.

It could be a good chance to have some time with Tobias. Alone.

Butterflies summersault in my stomach at the thought.

The past two weeks have been so busy, the only moments we've shared have been the briefest brushes of our hands or shoulders as we've worked side-by-side digging holes for perimeter sensors. Of course, we've spoken between mouthfuls at hurriedly consumed dinners and seen each other at Orrin's daily training sessions. But there has been no chance for real conversation.

And definitely no chance to repeat those wonderfully sensual kisses we shared that night in the rain.

My cheeks heat at the memory and my feet are moving before I can stop myself, as if my limbs are fuelled by the warmth coiling in my stomach.

I open the front door of his RV without knocking, then slip off my shoes before padding silently to Tobias' room. As I suspected, Jason is in his wolf form, stretched out on one of the bench seats that converts into a bed, tongue lolling out as his ribcage rises and falls with the rhythmic breaths of sleep.

My heart thunders as I slowly, carefully, open the door to Tobias' room and step inside. The scent of him in that small confined space is almost overwhelming, and my wolf lets out a low whimper that I barely keep from slipping from my own lips.

And then my eyes land on him.

He's lying on his back, bare chested with the blankets tangled around his waist, hands tucked behind his head in a way that expertly showcases his biceps. His chest rises and falls with the gentle rhythm of sleep, his lips are half-parted and there's the faintest furrow between his brows, as if he's worrying even in dreams.

I can't explain why, but my chest aches watching him. There's something utterly vulnerable about seeing him like this, tangled in those worn, threadbare rose patterned blankets, and I get this strange urge to protect him. To watch over him and keep him safe.

Of course, it's completely ridiculous. He's a born alpha. He doesn't need anyone's protection, least of all mine.

Suddenly, I'm hit with the inappropriateness of my being there. I cringe, a completely different type of heat flooding me as I realise how embarrassing it would be to have him wake and find me there. Watching him sleep, like some sort of unwelcome stalker. Carefully, I step backwards, edging the door open when his sharp intake of breath tells me I'm too late.

Golden eyes meet my own, blinking dazedly before a slow smile spreads across his face.

"Lucy."

The one word is throaty, almost guttural.

"Hey," I say, toeing the carpet with one bare foot. "I – um – we ran out of coffee in my RV," I offer lamely, resisting the urge to trail my eyes over the golden expanse of bare skin.

It's bad enough he's caught me watching him sleep. Now I'm openly gawking at him.

He sits up, gathering the blankets across his lap.

"Okay," he says, smile widening as his eyes glint knowingly.

I flush, realising how ridiculous my excuse sounds when the coffee machine is in the kitchen behind me. When there's a perfectly workable coffee machine in the mouldy lodge. When there is absolutely no reason why I should be standing in Tobias' bedroom at six in the morning watching him sleep.

As if sensing my embarrassment, his gaze softens, his smile losing its mocking edge.

"Come here?" he asks, tentatively patting the space on the bed beside him. "Hang out with me for a bit?"

Wordlessly, I nod, pausing only briefly before crossing the few steps between the door and his bed. Heart racing, I crawl across the covers, pulling myself into a cross-legged position beside him.

"Hey," I say again, barely able to meet his eyes with my own.

Despite our heated moment in the forest, there is something dangerously intimate about being in his room with him, alone and surrounded by his scent.

"Hey," he chuckles, before tentatively wrapping his arm around my shoulders, and pulling me close to him in a one-armed embrace.

I almost sigh in relief as our bodies make contact, at the feeling of rightness that always comes with being near him. At the way my wolf rumbles in unabashed contentment.

I let my body relax, my head resting against his shoulder, my arm encircling his bare waist. Then, without warning, he's tugging me backwards, so that we're both tumbling back into the mattress. I let out a nervous laugh at the move, the sound foreign to my own ears.

"Can I kiss you?" he asks, turning to face me, his fingers trailing gently up my bare arm as his gold eyes bore into mine.

I nod, swallowing hard. This is what I came here for, isn't it? And still my heart is hammering in my chest, loud enough that he must be able to hear it.

Some of that frightened anticipation melts away when his lips meet my own, quickly replaced by another sort of emotion. Something thrumming and electric and dizzying. Something that makes my breath catch in my throat and my hands clench around the blankets.

Without thinking about it, one of my legs slips over his and then he's gripping my hips, sliding me across him so that I'm practically draped over him. My breath hitches because even the thick quilt between us does little to disguise the effect this closeness is having on him.

"Jason?"

The sound of Ross Slade's voice in the RV snaps through the haze like a whip.

I sit up abruptly, my hands flying to my mouth to muffle the bizarre squeaking sound escaping my lips as I stare at Tobias in horror. I can feel the blood draining from my face and I swear to Morrigan I've never been more embarrassed in my life. Because the door to Tobias' room is wide open.

I turn to look over my shoulder just as Ross peers down the hallway, his eyes meeting my own for one horrifying moment. He blinks, as if trying to make sense of what he is seeing, and I watch as his eyes flick down to Tobias laying beneath me, then back to me before his face turns crimson and he looks away, holding one hand over his eyes.

"Oh my gosh, I'm so sorry. I totally should have knocked. I didn't think."

He makes to back down the hall, hand fumbling blindly for the handle to the door behind him, when the sound of a wolf's low growl stops him in his tracks.

Jason is standing between Ross and the door, the gentlest of warning growls rumbling in his chest as he tries to push Ross back into the RV.

For someone familiar with wolf body language, it's clear there is nothing threatening in Jason's behaviour. It's more of a playful 'I would rather you didn't leave' than anything else.

Of course, Ross isn't familiar with wolf-speak, and even though Jason isn't the largest of our pack, he's still much bigger than any natural wolf.

"Oh shit," Tobias hisses, sitting up so abruptly his head nearly hits my own. "Jason."

Oh shit is right.

I scamper off Tobias' lap, leaving him free to throw back the covers and sprint down the hallway before following after him.

"Down boy," Tobias orders, snapping his fingers at Jason, like he's a common dog. "Bad dog. On your bed."

Tobias points to the bench where Jason sleeps, the upholstery coated in brown fur. Jason casts Tobias and me a woeful look before slinking morosely over to his bed and leaping gracefully up. Then he plops down, resting his chin on his paws with a dejected whimper.

What on earth were you doing? I practically shout at Jason through the pack bond. *Have you lost your ever-loving mind?*

Pot, kettle, Jason retorts, giving a pointed look towards the bedroom at the end of the RV.

Not the same, I argue silently.

"Sorry about my dog," Tobias tells Ross, stepping back to affectionately ruffle Jason's ears.

To Ross, it probably just looks like Tobias is patting his dog, but I can see it for what it is – Tobias putting himself between the wolf and human.

I just wanted to be close to him, Jason argues, glaring up at Tobias with a look that I highly doubt any self-respecting dog would give their beloved pet-owner. *He was going to leave and you know what it's like, when you're in your wolf form…*

His voice trails off, leaving behind it the traces of uncomfortable longing trickling across the pack bond. I can feel the need of his wolf to protect, to be near his mate, to keep him close. I roll my shoulders, wanting to shake off the feelings.

You were scaring him, I silently chide him. *Being a complete idiot.*

Jason's wolf huffs, the sound feeling very much like grudging acknowledgement.

"All good." Ross gives a nervous laugh. "That's one seriously massive dog. What is it? A hybrid? Malamute?"

Jason's ears perk up as smug, animalistic pride crashes over me though the pack bond, his feelings so much stronger now that he's in wolf form.

I recall the night of the run, when Jason had stopped Tobias from descending the foothills to Clear Creek pack territory. The feelings of the pack had been charged then too. Almost unbearably strong. I had thought it was because everyone's emotions were heightened from loss and sorrow and the blood-lust of revenge.

Maybe it was because they had been in their animal forms.

"No idea," Tobias says, giving a lazy shrug. "He's just a mutt. Barely housebroken, really."

I snort, then clamp my hand over my mouth to stifle the laughter wanting to bubble up. Jason lets out a discontented rumble, glaring at Tobias and me from his bed.

"Oh, okay." Ross flashes a tentative smile, blinking warily at the wolf. "Well, like I said, sorry to bother you. I was just looking for Jason. Wanted to tell him I got the programming finished last night for the drones and that it's ready to be tested out."

"That's great news." Tobias' words are full of genuine warmth and Ross' smile widens in response, his shoulders visibly relaxing.

"Yah," Ross beams. "I managed to work it out a lot faster than expected, actually. It's state-of-the-art tech you guys have got here, so it's not exactly like setting up a camera drone, you know what I mean? But I guess the basics are the same." Ross cocks his head to one side, considering. "Pretty amazing what you guys are doing. I know a lot of the folks in town might say they're against these sorts of tourist operations, but we all know it's good for the economy…"

He trails off, eyes landing on Tobias' bare chest, the boxers hanging low on his hips and then at me with my rumpled shirt, dishevelled hair and swollen lips. Ross' cheeks flush again, probably recalling what he interrupted only minutes ago.

"Well, I'm rambling now." He gives a nervous chuckle, raking one hand through sleek, chestnut brown hair. "Do you know where Jason is? I'll just go find him."

Jason's wolf lets out a 'yip' from his perch on the bench seat, making Ross jump.

"He's probably at the lodge getting breakfast," Tobias says smoothly, making to shove his hands into his pockets, only to remember he's just wearing boxers. He opts for crossing his arms instead. "You should check there for him first. If you don't find him, come back and I'll help you track him down."

"Okay, cool," Ross says, looking almost eager to have an excuse to leave. "Thanks."

When the latch clicks shut and the sound of Ross' footsteps have faded, Tobias rounds on Jason with a glare.

"Shift," he says, his tone falling short of an alpha command, but ringing with authority.

With a growl, Jason leaps from the bench, his body rippling and contorting mid-air before he lands on bare feet, rising from a crouch.

"What were you thinking?" Tobias asks, echoing the silent question I had asked moments earlier.

Jason gives him an inscrutable look before shucking on his pants and pulling a rumpled t-shirt over his head.

"Jason." There's warning in Tobias' voice now.

"You know what I was thinking," Jason sighs, stalking stiffly towards the coffee machine. "You going to tell me you've never had a momentary lapse in judgement before with Lucy?"

"That's not…"

"Don't tell me it's not the same," Jason snaps. "I'm sick of it, okay. So Ross is human. So he doesn't have a clue about what we are. Big freaking deal. He's mine. I'm his."

Jason lets out a pained groan, bending forward until his elbows are resting on the linoleum counter, his forehead pressing against the palms of his hands.

"I can't take it, okay. Being around him every day, it's killing me. And when I'm in wolf form?" He gives a dry, mirthless laugh. "Gods above. Maybe you've got more control than me, but I'm losing it."

I look away, biting my lip against the discomfort rising in my stomach. I might have known Jason his whole life. We might have shifted together, played together as children. But there is something utterly vulnerable and private about seeing him like this. I have to fight the sudden urge to race out of the RV.

"I get it," Tobias admits, sinking back into the seat Jason vacated and drawing one hand across his face. "But you need to keep it under wraps. The whole wolf thing, I mean. Anything else – the whole, um, relationship thing, that's cool, obviously. Just, um, keep things safe…"

Tobias' face flushes, and there is this incredibly awkward moment where both he and Jason stare off in opposite directions, like neither of them can believe they are having this conversation.

I snort, unable to contain the mirth bubbling inappropriately in my chest.

"Are you seriously giving Jason the birds and the bees talk?" I ask Tobias incredulously. "You know he's older than you right? I'm pretty sure he knows about all of that."

Tobias looks at me with eyes so wide, the whites are fully visible around gold.

"No. No, that's not what I'm talking about." He rubs his cheeks with the palms of his hands, as if to hide the heat growing there. "I mean marking. You know. Mate stuff. Wolf stuff. Shit. This is so awkward." He shoots Jason a pleading look. "Can we just forget this whole conversation?"

"Yah," Jason rubs the back of his neck with one hand, his own cheeks heating. "Maybe just stop talking now."

"Yep. Good plan," Tobias nods in agreement before clenching his lips shut, like he's afraid more random words will just start spilling out of their own volition if he doesn't hold them in.

I press the back of my hand against my mouth, attempting to stifle another laugh.

Boys are so weird.

Chapter 9

Tobias Finch

"You sure you want to do this?" I ask Lucy, my finger poised over my grandparent's doorbell.

"Obviously," she retorts, giving my hand a squeeze. "I mean, it's a little late now. I'm here, aren't I."

I nod, swallowing hard around the anxiety clogging my throat, then push the button. Moments later, the door swings open, and I'm blinking past the smell of stale cigarettes and lasagne rushing over us like a wave.

"Tobias!" grandma exclaims from the doorway. Her eyes are fixed on Lucy though, and there is no ignoring the giddy smile stretched across her wrinkled face as she pulls me in for a hug.

"Hey grandma," I wheeze, momentarily breathless in her vice-like hold. "Dinner smells good."

It's a lie. I mean, I'm sure it would smell good if it wasn't for the smell of grandpa's cigarettes.

Grandma finally releases me, then turns to Lucy, ignoring her outstretched hand and folding Lucy into a hug. Lucy visibly tenses, then casts me a wide-eyed look of reproach over grandma's shoulder. Like maybe I should have warned her, or fended off my grandma or something. I bite back a smile, because good luck stopping grandma from doing anything.

"So, aren't you going to introduce me?" Grandma asks, as she ushers us inside, one arm draped around Lucy's shoulder.

I shoot her an incredulous look. "You met Lucy earlier this year."

It might be my imagination, but I think Lucy pales slightly at the mention of that last meeting.

"You know what I mean," grandma retorts, raising one dark brow. "This is different. Now you're bringing her over for dinner."

"Leave the boy alone, Susan," grandpa grumbles, brow furrowing as he looks up from his seat at the kitchen table.

A cheerful floral cloth is spread over the round table, a steaming lasagne placed in the middle beside a basket of warm garlic bread and a large green salad. The usual plastic dinnerware has been replaced with the delicate rose patterned china that grandma normally keeps stored in the cabinet in her living room. She's never used it when I've come over for dinner before, not even when Cody used to come with me.

I've only seen her use it once before, and that was at Christmas.

"Wow, this looks great," I say, forcing a smile.

Because there's something about the sight of that rose-patterned china, and grandma's beaming smile, and grandpa's dark glower that makes me want to take Lucy by the hand and haul her back to the safety of Liberty pack territory.

Grandma bustles around the table, practically shoving us into our seats before serving up plates of lasagne. All the while, she's talking relentlessly about how wonderful Half Moon Ranch is, and what a great rodeo-man Jeb used to be when he was younger, and how respected the Winslows are in Buffalo.

I watch wide-eyed as grandpa's glower deepens with each word that spills out of grandma's mouth, and even though there's a good space between Lucy's chair and my own, I swear I can feel her stiffening.

"I'm so glad you've gotten to know the Winslows," grandma tells me, oblivious to the tension thickening the smoke-stained air of the kitchen. "And now you're dating Miss Stone! Well, isn't that something. Maybe we can have your parents over for dinner one evening too, Lucy. Wouldn't that be a treat?"

Lucy nearly chokes on her water, and I cast her a worried look. I haven't told my grandparents that Lucy and I are dating yet. I mean, maybe grandma just guessed that because we were holding hands on the doorstep, and because Lucy agreed to come over for a family dinner.

I open my mouth to say something that will make grandma stop talking when grandpa beats me to it.

"I seem to recall hearing that the Winslow and Stone families were both part of the WSGA in the Johnson County cattle wars."

Grandpa's statement comes out soft and conversational, but his words have the effect of someone cocking a loaded gun at the dinner table. Grandma lets out a horrified gasp, her fork clattering to her plate. Lucy drops her glass on the table hard enough that water sloshes over the sides, the faintest of growls rumbling in her chest.

I glance around the table, confused. When nobody says anything that would explain why everyone is so upset about what grandpa said, I ask: "Um, what cattle wars?"

This question is met with unified looks of disbelief. Like I'd just asked what the internet was or something.

"What?" I say defensively, staring down at my plate. "I didn't grow up here, remember."

"I thought you would have learned about that in Mr Paine's history class," Lucy teases. But her voice is hollow, and the smile she flashes doesn't spread to her eyes.

"Maybe," I admit, frowning. "But if I did, I sure don't remember it."

Grandpa chuckles, a cold mirthless sound that feels like ice on my bones.

"The Johnson County cattle wars happened back in the late eighteen-hundreds," grandpa begins, fixing his cool amber eyes on Lucy.

She lifts her chin, meeting his eyes with her own.

"Back when homesteaders were making their mark across the country, taking over territory, fighting over grasslands for their cattle. A bunch of rich ranchers formed an association and started taking out anyone they saw as competition. Accusing them of cattle rustling and then gunning them down, right on their home territories."

"That's just one side of the story," grandma says, wringing her hands and looking anxiously between grandpa and Lucy. "There's always two sides, who knows what the truth really was. And it was so long ago now, does it really matter?"

"Who was it that set up Half Moon Ranch alongside the Winslows?" grandpa asks Lucy, ignoring grandma's pleas. "Your great-grandpa? Or his father before that?"

"My great-grandfather."

"And do you know if they legally acquired that land?"

Lucy doesn't answer, but I don't miss the way her fists clench on the table, the way her jaw ticks. Grandpa doesn't either, because he gives a low chuckle.

"That's what I thought."

"John Leeland Vance," grandma warns.

"I'm just saying, it's important to remember the history of things, that's all. To remember that even the great and mighty Winslows might not have gotten where they are with clean hands." Grandpa shrugs, but the movement is stiff, as if his ageing body is full of coiled tension. "But you're right. Who cares if they grew their empire from soil watered with the blood of innocents? As long as they donate to the local community center and pay for a pretty bronze statue to go up in town, that's all that matters."

Oh. Oh, I see where grandpa is going with this.

Confusion gives way to anger and I lean forward, resting my elbows on the table as I silently demand grandpa meet my eyes with his own.

It's an order he obeys because he can feel it. His wolf can feel it. I might be his grandson. I might be a sixteen-year-old kid. But I'm still his alpha.

"Lucy isn't to blame for anything her ancestors might have done," I say firmly, letting enough of my wolf come through that my eyes are probably close to glowing. "Whatever her family did, that has nothing to do with her."

I hold his gaze for a long moment before adding silently through the pack link: *Don't you go blaming her for Jamison's death.*

The look grandpa gives me in return is so full of agony, I can feel the sorrow in the pit of my stomach.

We should have attacked, grandpa silently argues. *The Clear Creek pack need to pay*.

Unfortunately, my psychotic wolf agrees. The animal wants vengeance. *Blood for blood*, he says. *Soul for soul.*

I grit my teeth, pushing the wolf down, refusing to reply. Because I gave my word to Lucy. Because my pack deserves better.

"I made chocolate cake for dessert," grandma announces weakly, her gaze flitting from me to grandpa to Lucy, no doubt trying to make sense of the silent tension that has fallen over our meal like a shroud.

"That sounds lovely, Mrs Vance." Lucy turns to give her a polite smile, tucking her hands under the table as if to hide their trembling. "I would love a piece."

"Same," I say, trying and failing to keep my voice even. But I don't take my eyes off grandpa. And he doesn't take his eyes off me.

Lucy Stone

"I'm so sorry."

It's probably the tenth time Tobias has apologised since leaving his grandparents' house. In fact, he pretty much just said some variation of the same thing the entire car ride back.

"Honestly, it's fine," I assure him, grabbing both his hands with my own. "It was a nice dinner."

We're standing on the trampled grass outside the steps to my RV, close enough to each other that his every expression is visible in the bright moonlight.

He lifts a brow, disbelief written on his face.

Okay, I'm lying. It was one of the worst dinners I've ever been to.

"The food was good," I offer lamely, but even that is only half true because my stomach had been so knotted up with anxiety that I had hardly tasted any of it.

"I won't let him say anything like that again," he starts to say.

I cut him off, pressing my lips to his own before he can offer up another apology.

"Stop," I say, breathing against him before pulling reluctantly away. "It doesn't matter. Your grandma likes me at least."

He nods, looking unconvinced.

"See you tomorrow," I say, pressing one last kiss to his lips. And then I'm leaping up the steps to my RV, pausing to give him a girlish wave before turning to let myself inside.

Only when the door clicks shut behind me do I let the smile fall from my face.

"That bad, huh?"

I blink into the dark, eyes quickly adjusting to take in the suave, annoyingly chiselled features of my least favourite dragon shifter.

"What are you doing here?" I snap, not bothering to answer his question.

"Just keeping an eye on things," he answers vaguely.

"Well, do that from outside my RV."

"Oh, don't worry, I will," he chuckles, leaning back and resting booted feet on the bench seat that used to be my bed. Before I started sleeping in the room with Tania and Summer.

The dining table has been tucked away, but no doubt it will make an appearance first thing in the morning when Summer and Danny get back to work doing beta things.

"Now that you're here, I can rest easy knowing my mate is safe and protected."

I narrow my eyes at him, because I'm pretty sure he's being sarcastic.

He raises his hands defensively. "I mean it. I'm glad Summer has you as a friend. I saw how you looked after her back at the lair." He pauses, dragging one hand through his perfectly coifed hair. "It's hard, you know. Not being able to be around her all the time. The need to protect. Keep her safe. Especially when she keeps pushing me away…"

He lets out a low hiss through his teeth, a pained expression crossing his face that reminds me so much of Jason. And just like with Jason, I can feel the bitter pulse of anguish through the pack link, full of longing and hunger and guilt. It's jarringly unexpected, since I honestly doubted his capacity for any emotion at all. I almost feel sorry for him.

Almost.

Until I remember that if it wasn't for a biological fluke, Aires would have been quietly complicit in sending me and Summer to whatever fate awaited us at Drake's lair.

I give a curt nod, biting back the angry retort sitting ready at the tip of my tongue.

Summer said not to be mean to him. Fine, I can do that. But she didn't say I had to be nice to him either.

"You can go now," I tell him, making sure to keep my voice low enough that I won't wake Summer and Tania up.

Aires rises from his seat, but doesn't leave. Instead, he crosses the small kitchen in two long strides, until he's standing in front of me. The taunting mask is gone, replaced by something dark and unreadable.

"John Vance gave you a hard time, I take it," Aires muses, folding his arms over his chest. "Probably painted you with the same brush as the rest of the Clear Creek pack. Blamed you for his brother's death."

I open my mouth to deny it, to tell him to leave and stop lurking in our RV, but he continues.

"Don't tell me otherwise. It was written all over your face the second you walked in the door. Trust me. I know that look. At least, I know the feeling. We're the same, you and me. We're both tainted by our fathers." He gives a harsh, mirthless laugh. "Isn't that what you all have been doing to me since the moment you met me? Blaming me for whatever my dad did." He pauses, then gives a little nod, as if silently agreeing with his own train of thought. "And yah, I know what dad did was messed up. Huxley too. But honestly, I didn't even know you and Summer existed until an hour before I met you. I had no idea what dad was doing. No idea at all."

"And if you had known?" I ask, unable to help myself. "Or if you hadn't felt the bond with Summer?"

Aires shrugs. "I don't know. I guess we'll never know." His expression darkens, lip curling up in disgust. "But I'd like to think I wouldn't have stood by and let him sell you off."

His words taste of truth, clean and pure. Guilt starts to crack my resolve, spreading fissures across the wall I've built up against this male. It's a wall made of anger and resentment, and maybe those feelings are misplaced, but they're necessary.

"Well, like you said, I guess we'll never know."

Aires just nods, like he expected that much from me. Then he adds: "For what it's worth, I'm sorry. For what dad did. For what Huxley did." He waives one hand dismissively. "For whatever my part was in all of it."

I stare up at him, doing my best to keep my face expressionless.

Behind the mask, my mind is racing. Remembering all the times I helped dad and Cooper interrogate someone. All the times that, looking back on it, things seemed off. All the times that I did nothing.

Sure, I helped Tania escape. And the guy after her, Ben. And sure, they're both safe and part of the Liberty pack now.

But what about the other times? What about the other shifters?

"I'm not asking you to like me," Aires says, a cold teasing smile edging the corners of his lips as his own mask slips back into place.

"Actually, I don't think I really want you to like me. But you do need to tolerate me. Because I'm not going anywhere. I'll be wherever Summer is. Whether you like it or not."

"Oh yah," I say, crossing my arms, widening my stance defensively. "And what about what Summer wants?"

"Oh, don't you worry about that, little alpha she-wolf," Aires smirks, shouldering past me as he makes his way to the door. "She wants me. Trust me on that. She's just making me work for it."

And with that, he's gone, slipping out into the night.

I stare at the closed door for several minutes after he leaves, mouth agape.

Aires is an arrogant jerk. Summer deserves better. And yet somehow, fate matched her with him. It's enough to make me believe that maybe there is nothing more than biology behind the magic of mates. That maybe mates aren't really twin souls destined to be together as much as they are biologically compatible beings.

I frown, because that theory doesn't hold up when you look at Jason and Ross. Or the number of true mates who struggled to conceive, like Cody's parents.

I stalk over to the bench seat, scrubbing my face with my hands as I rest my elbows on my knees, closing my eyes against the darkness.

The unkind words of Tobias' grandpa come back to me then, his harsh amber stare boring into me through the empty darkness. It had been naïve of me to think he would like me, accept me. After everything that my pack has done, after what happened to Jamison, I should have known better.

And still a childish part of me wanted to be liked by him. Imagined that he'd dote on me, treat me as some darling grand-daughter. That he would stand in the place of the grandparents I never got to know.

We're the same, you and me.

Aires' words ring in my head, echoing against John Vance's accusations. I shake my head, but there is no clearing the thoughts. They rattle around, noisy and wild as caged starlings.

If only my gift gave me the ability to makes sense of this all. To see people's hearts instead of just taste the truth or lie of their words. To see more than uncertain glimpses of past, present or future.

Instead, I feel like everything is muddled. Like my head is full of emotions that don't belong to me.

I squeeze my eyes shut against it all.

Chapter 10

Tobias Finch

"You sure you want it up that loud?" Arlo asks, practically yelling to be heard over the rhythmic beat of the speakers. "Last time you said old gramps didn't like it."

I give a curt nod, not bothering to raise my voice to answer. After grandpa's performance at dinner last night, he can deal with the music.

"Sweet."

Arlo's answering smile is all mischief as he refocuses on his laptop screen, no doubt putting the finishing touches on the night's playlist.

When *No Bad Days* by Bastille comes on, I shoot him a querying look. It's a little heavier and slower than his usual drum and bass.

"I thought we could start the night slow," the owl shifter says with a shrug, not meeting my eyes. "Nothing too peppy, since no one is really in the mood for all that."

I don't know much about music, but I do know what he's not saying. It's only been two weeks since Jamison. We might be ready to come together and celebrate the full moon. We might feel the need to shift and run and be together. But it's still likely to be a night laced with sorrow.

As if on cue, grandpa emerges from the shadow of the pines, pausing on the edge of the meadow before lowering himself to sit on the fallen log Danny and Samson dragged over there so many months ago.

Seeing him sitting there without Jamison, it's like finding Jamison's lifeless body all over again. I stare at him unseeing for a long time, the sound of the music thrumming with my anger.

"You good, alpha?" Christopher asks, shoulder-checking me playfully as he moves through the clearing, arms full of folded blankets.

"Yah. All good," I say, forcing a smile.

But my eyes don't leave grandpa's, refocusing on the dark circles under his eyes, the relentless sorrow tugging down the corners of his mouth. Then I remember the harsh way he spoke to Lucy at dinner, and my hands ball into fists at my sides. I wish I could clamp down the pity I feel on this male's behalf. Instead, I'm left with a strange mix of guilt and pity and anger that I don't know what to do with.

"You going to shift tonight?" Christopher's tone is light, but there is no missing the focus in his pale stare.

I shrug. "Haven't decided," I lie.

Given my wolf's track record, I'm pretty sure shifting would be a bad idea. Who knows what the deranged animal would try next?

"Uh-huh," he says, lifting one blond brow.

He doesn't say anything though, and is soon interrupted by Tania calling him over, showing him where to put all the blankets. Like usual, Tyrone and Samson are close by her side, shadowing her every movement.

Farther away from the speakers, Danny and Summer stand huddled together, both staring fixedly at the same tablet. Danny, with a pouting sort of frown on his face while Summer talks rapidly, her hands fluttering expressively.

All around, the smell of barbecued meat and hot chocolate mix with the scent of pine and smoke and earth and pack. My wolf stretches contentedly, delighting in these comforting scents as the last rays of sun dip behind the foothills.

As if in response to the setting sun, strobe lights flash in reds and blues across rocky outcrops and pines, pulsing in time to the music. Another one of Arlo or Theo's great ideas. Only now we have real electricity, so there is no hum of the generator that used to be required to power everything.

Grandpa frowns disapprovingly at the flashing lights, but says nothing, watching in silence from his log at the edge of the clearing.

The rest of my pack mates mill around, paper plates in hand, laughter mingling with the music. Everyone filling up on grilled meat and sugar as they lounge on blankets under the darkening sky.

I grin. We're just getting started. I can feel the hum of anticipation rising off my pack, thrumming through the pack link. Anticipation and contentment.

Because in an hour, the moon will rise. And then the real party will begin.

HE REALLY DOESN'T LIKE *me*, Lucy comments idly through the pack link.

She's stretched out in wolf form beside me on one of the blankets, her pale fur glistening in the moonlight.

"Who? Grandpa?" I ask out loud. Even though I know the answer.

She nods, the movement decidedly un-wolfish, before resting her chin on her paws.

I sigh, uncertain of what to say about that. There is no point in apologising, because for once it's not me at fault. And there really isn't anything I can do about grandpa.

"He'll get over it," Jason assures her.

He's sitting on her other side, in human form, his eyes flicking between the bonfire and his phone. No doubt checking the constant feedback from the newly-installed perimeter sensors and drones.

"You just keep being your friendly, warm, cuddly self and I'm sure he'll warm up to you in no time," Jason deadpans, giving Lucy's head a consolatory pat. She tosses her head at the contact, nipping irritably at his hand.

"Touchy, touchy," Jason chides, but there is laughter in his voice. Like he knew patting the she-wolf would annoy her, and that's why he did it.

I smile, unable to resist sliding my own fingers into the scruff of fur around her neck. My wolf chuffs smugly when she closes her eyes at the contact. Accepting my touch.

Jason rolls his eyes. "Can you guys not, please?" he asks. "It's bad enough I had to hear all about Ross walking in on you two."

At Lucy's low growl, Jason throws up his hands in mock surrender.

"Don't get me wrong, Luce. I'm glad you stopped trying to kill Tobias. It just weirds me out to see you all affectionate and stuff. It's a little out of character for you."

We going to run? Noah asks, his voice ringing out eagerly across the pack link. The way it carries, I know it's spoken to everyone.

There's a murmur of responses as everyone answers, some out loud and others through the pack link. It's no surprise when the cats and bears give a resounding 'no', preferring to lounge by the fire.

Beside me, Lucy winces.

"What is it?" I ask her, keeping my voice low.

I'm half afraid that it will be another vision. As far as I'm aware, she hasn't had one since that time in the slot canyon back in southern Utah, weeks ago.

Nothing, she replies. But I can tell that is a lie, even if I don't have her abilities.

"Really?" I say, lifting one brow.

She huffs, gracefully rising to her feet and giving her thick coat a shake as Jason mutters under his breath about her getting hair everywhere.

It's nothing serious, she assures me, ignoring Jason's complaints. *Just... well...* She pauses, looking nervously at grandpa. *Ever since I joined this pack, I've been able to feel people's emotions. Like, their excitement and anger...* She gives another shudder. *Honestly, it's all a bit overwhelming.*

"Oh." I frown, at a loss for what to say.

I can feel my pack members through the link, can even see what they are seeing, if I put the effort in. I guess I can sort of feel their emotions, but it's more like I get a sense of what their feelings are in the same way I would if I was standing in a room with them.

I give Jason a quizzical look, hoping he'll have some insight.

Jason throws up his hands. "Don't look at me," he says. "I've never heard of that happening before."

"It sounds like an omega thing," I say, feeling a bit stupid as it dawns on me I don't really know what being on omega means exactly. Like, I know they're supposed to be empathetic, and understand other's feelings, but that's about all.

Jason snorts. "If Lucy is an omega, then I'm an alpha."

Summer choses that moment to pad over to our group, tilting her brown wolfish head thoughtfully as she looks between Jason and Lucy. Lucy gives her a welcoming nod before shooting Jason a glare.

"Don't look at me like that." Jason points one finger at Lucy, his lips still quirked into a grin. "You know it's true. When was the last time you actually cared what other people were feeling? Like, have you ever almost had an anxiety attack because the people around you were arguing? Ever been unable to sleep at night because your friends were sad?"

Jason looks over to Summer for support.

"You live with Lucy," Jason tells her. "Has she ever displayed any signs of being an empath? An omega?"

Summer's laughter flows across the pack link as she gives Jason a look that can only mean "are you serious right now?" Lucy narrows her eyes at the pair, lifting one lip in a mock snarl.

I press my lips together, resisting the urge to laugh.

However much I like Lucy, the thought of her acting how Jason describes is unimaginable. Sure, she's loyal. Protective of those she cares about. But worried about how other people feel? Nope. Definitely not.

"Point made," Jason says knowingly. "You're not an omega. Not even close to an omega. Even if you are feeling other people's emotions, you would have to be driven to help others, make other people happy, to be an omega. Which, let's face it, you're not."

He pauses, wrinkling his nose thoughtfully as he reaches across to ruffle the fur on the top of Summer's head. Summer closes her eyes, leaning into the touch with what almost looks like a smile.

"I'll look into though, okay?"

Run, alpha? Noah asks, the brown wolf butting me playfully, distracting me from Lucy and Jason's conversation. From the feel of Lucy's warmth beneath my hand. *Run with us?*

I shake my head. "Nah, I'm fine," I say out loud.

The brown wolf whimpers in dismay before crouching down, his body wriggling in an almost puppyish manner, pleading with me to play. To run. My own wolf stirs, wanting to stretch his legs, feel the light of the moon that is just starting to show above the foothills.

Leave him be, Ollie reprimands, nipping reproachfully at his brother's ears, just as Summer says: *Run with us.*

Well, I'm running, Lucy announces, rising to stand in one fluid motion.

Something flashes in her eyes as her pale wolf looks at me – disappointment, maybe? The thought sends an unpleasant ache jolting behind my ribs.

Show her, my wolf demands slyly. *Show her you're the alpha you promised you would be.*

I scowl, because he's blatantly using my feelings for Lucy to manipulate me. The animal knows no bounds.

You promised her you would do your best, my wolf reminds me. Mercilessly throwing my own words back at me. *How can you do that if you sit here in your weak human form?*

I feel my shoulders stiffen, irritation prickling across my skin. My human form is not weak. I might only be sixteen, but I've grown a lot in the past eight months. Filled out, my grandma said. I might not feel like it most of the time, but I look like a grown man.

Sort of. Mostly. Okay, at least a little.

Come on, alpha, Noah pleads, giving me one last nudge with a cold, wet nose.

Yes, run, Summer urges.

Gareth saunters over, unbuttoning his worn plaid button-down as he lifts one brow expectantly.

"Okay, fine," I grumble, rising to my feet, heat rising to my cheeks as I start to undress.

No one cares, I remind myself. *They grew up with this.*

Still, I keep my eyes averted from where I know Lucy stands, doing my best not to imagine that I can feel the heat of her gaze trailing over my bare skin. Because that really will make this situation embarrassing.

Instead, I focus on the feel of the moonlight, on the mysterious pull that demands that we give in to the beasts within us. Demanding that we run.

I focus on the feel of the shift, the pricking and snapping and pulling, the almost painful unmaking of my being, followed by the liberating freedom of becoming something wild.

Power, my wolf rumbles, digging his paws into the dry earth, lungs filling with the scent of forest and pack and night and … *Lucy*.

Around me, the sound of the music is amplified to an almost unbearable level, but I like it. I can feel the warm contentment of the cats and bears as they lounge, now mostly in animal form, loosing themselves in the music. I can feel the frenzied flutter of the owls, the more tentative flight of the diurnal avians – Hamish and Ben – who, despite their preternatural shifter vision, still feel better flying during the day.

And the wolves. I can feel the wolves. Can feel their need to run and sing and play.

Run, my wolf demands of me, an urgency coating his voice. *Run*.

My eyes land on Aires, sitting in his human form beside Danny, a mixture of adoration and jealousy on his face as he watches Summer with the wolves.

"I'll slow you down," he tells me in response to my unspoken question, his mouth tipping into a frown.

However difficult my relationship with my wolf might be, at least I can usually shift if I want to. I mean, I wouldn't exactly waltz around Buffalo's main street in my wolf form, but at least I can let my wolf run under cover of night, in the shelter of our territory's trees and rocks. A large wolf can be explained away, should a human happen to see me. Not a dragon though.

"I'm going to stay here and keep an eye on things," Jason announces, drawing my attention back to him. He lifts his phone, tapping the screen by way of explanation. "I just want to see how the sensors react, check that the drones are working. It's all new tech and we haven't really tested it yet…"

His words become the rushing of wind and pine and dry summer grass as my wolf takes over.

Good, my wolf assures him through the bond, not concerned with the details. We trust Jason to watch the perimeter. To help us keep the pack safe.

Pack, my wolf pants, feeling along the bonds that connect each soul to my own, as if he's drawing in power from them. *Pack, pack, pack.*

Run.

This time, it's Lucy's voice flowing across the bond, the one word an order and not a question. My head snaps up, looking to the pale wolf standing mere feet away from me. The other wolves look between her and me, uncertainty flowing over them, as if they aren't quite sure how to react, their desire to obey her mixing with their fear of me.

Good, my wolf chuffs to himself, like a complete psychopath. He's not at all concerned by Lucy giving orders. No, whatever problem the animal has with other's exerting authority apparently doesn't extend to her.

Run, my wolf agrees.

And so, we run. Paws pounding the earth, tongues lolling, pupils dilated to take in every detail of the pale moonlit forest. We run the trodden paths of our territory, cautiously keeping within the perimeter, avoiding stepping too close to the underground sensors. Because even my deranged wolf understands the need to keep his pack within these limits now.

The thought of anyone harming my pack sends a sudden surge of anger pulsing through me and my wolf growls, demanding that I protect what is mine. As if in response, Lucy pushes up against me, knocking me hard enough that I stumble before briefly righting myself.

Hey, I say, the human part of me offended by this sudden attack.

She fixes me with cold, silver eyes. *You need to calm down*, she tells me, and I'm amazed at how her voice is just as much wolf as Lucy. Like, there really is no difference between her animal and her.

I'm struck with a flash of envy as I wonder what that would be like. To be able to co-exist peacefully with the deranged beast raging inside of me, instead of having to fight him every moment of every day.

Calm down, she says again, and this time the silent words are laced with a wolfish snarl as she nips at me.

Nips. At. Me.

My wolf lifts his head in surprise, taken aback, stopping in his tracks. No one has ever dared to nip at me like that. Like I'm a pup in need of reprimand. Instead of a born alpha nearly twice the size of most wolves in my pack.

Lucy looks almost as surprised as myself, but then she tosses her head, as if shaking the emotion off.

Your feelings are pissing me off, she says by way of explanation, as she comes to a stop beside me, circling me. *I can feel them. It's too much in this form.*

Ahh, right. That must be the whole feeling others' emotions thing she was talking about. For some reason, it hadn't dawned on me that this would include my own feelings. I stare at her sheepishly as the rest of the pack circle around us, their eyes full of uncensored curiosity. No doubt wondering why we stopped.

Sorry, I tell her honestly. *I'll try to tone it back.*

My wolf agrees with the sentiment, offended by the very thought of our own feelings making her uncomfortable.

Alpha? Christopher asks, pushing up beside me. I can feel the unspoken question, wondering why we've stopped. But he's looking at Lucy, just like I am. Taking in her bold silver stare and fearless stance.

Alpha, my wolf agrees, eyes fixed on Lucy as a rumbling warm sort of pride fills my chest.

The pale wolf cocks her head, looking between me and Christopher with confusion.

Please stop staring at me like that, she says primly. *It's creeping me out.*

Christopher's grey wolf chuffs, then lunges towards her with a playful yip. Despite her smaller stature, Lucy lifts her chin haughtily, and the grey wolf draws up short, fore-paws lowered, tail wagging.

Soon Noah joins in the play, then Ollie, quick to take an opportunity to bowl his sibling over when the younger wolf isn't watching. Summer joins in, taking Lucy's side, nipping playfully at anyone who gets too close to her friend. Gareth darts tauntingly between the larger wolves, the coyote faster and more agile than the larger canines. Above us, owls call, the distinctive teasing hoots of Arlo and Theo as they swoop down, dipping toward the wolves before pulling back up to the trees.

Playing. My pack is playing.

And Lucy is playing right along with them, baiting and nipping, silver eyes flashing with a mixture of amusement and annoyance, like she doesn't want to stoop to their level but just can't help herself.

My wolf huffs contentedly, settling down to rest his head on his paws. Even in the fray of teeth and claws, the others are respectful of Lucy. Backing down when she pushed forward.

The observation pleases my wolf.

Alpha. Alpha.

The murmur comes from them, from the wolves and owls, and this time it is not directed at me, but at her.

Lucy's wolf shakes her head, the human gesture incongruous with the wolfish form.

No, I hear her tell them firmly. *No*.

But they are right, I realise with only a small amount of surprise, seeing it all through the eyes of my wolf. She is just as much the alpha as me, somehow. Even though no bond runs between us, save for the pack bond and friendship, and the newly planted seeds of something more.

Mate, my wolf rumbles, reminding me of one very important fact.

The wolf isn't surprised at all. Somehow, he's always known. Or at least, that is what the megalomaniac creature wants me to believe. Probably for his own nefarious reasons.

Of course she's an alpha, my wolf scoffs derisively. *What else would she be?* Like I am the idiot here for not realising it.

Gods help me.

Chapter 11

Tobias Finch

Um, guys, we have a problem.

Jason's voice rings through the bond, faint with distance but full of alarm. Instantly, everyone freezes, tensing. The wolves' ears prick and noses lift, as if trying to sense some danger on the wind. Arlo and Theo glide to the ground, feathers cresting on their heads aggressively.

What is it? I ask, trying to tamp down the sickening sense of dread as my mind races, imaging every possible scenario, recalling every horror I've witnessed. Mom and dad and Jamison. The red on the snow at Blackwater. Cody's betrayal.

Vaguely, I'm aware of a warm body pressing against my side, of reassurance and calm flowing through the pack link. Lucy, I realise.

We have a security breach, Jason replies, and my stomach drops.

Around me, growls rumble in unison, their own fear and anger feeding my own, like gasoline to a fire.

Who? I ask, the question low and vicious, coming more from my wolf than from me.

I don't know, Jason admits, unease fluttering alongside his faint response. *The underground sensors indicate that it's just one person... so far. I'm still trying to get a visual with the drones...*

Where?

My wolf doesn't care so much about who it is. Or why they are here. To him, it is simple. The pack must be protected. The trespasser must be destroyed.

South-west, close to the road. I'm heading there now. With some of the others.

Good, I agree. *We'll see you there.*

Actually, we'll beat him there. Because I'm faster, and we're already at the Southern end of our territory.

Run, I say, but dirt is already flying out from under my paws and my wolves are already close on my heels.

Run, they agree. *Run. Run.*

Trees and boulders blur, shadowed grey by night and moonlight. Soon there is only the cool night air on my fur, the faint thudding of paws, the scent of pine and dirt and ... human.

I pull up short, claws scraping against dry earth as I bring myself to a stop, pausing to draw another lungful of air through my nose and take in the intruder's scent. Yes, definitely human. And familiar, very familiar.

As my mind races to place the scent, my wolf is prowling, hunting. Moving forward with measured steps, like the predator he is.

Destroy. Protect. Pack, my wolf rumbles, ignoring my silent urging to wait.

A shadowed figure comes into view, hooded and bulky. Like he's carrying some sort of large backpack. The wind flutters, bringing the intruder's scent right to my nostrils.

Ross. Ross Slade.

And the acrid scent of gun-powder.

My wolf's hackles rise, even as relief courses through my system. It isn't someone from the Clear Creek pack. It isn't another rogue shifter for hire.

Danger, my wolf warns. *Danger to your pack.*

I want to disagree with him, but the deranged animal is right. A human sneaking onto pack territory in the middle of the night, during the full moon, and armed - it can only mean trouble.

Stay, I warn the others, even as I stalk forward, moving deliberately along the shadows of the tree-line. Gareth and Christopher rumble their discontent at being left behind, but they know better than to argue.

My wolf notes their compliance with smug satisfaction, and for once I'm thankful for their obedience. Because I'm not risking any of my pack. Not after Jamison. Never again.

I watch Ross trudge along the gravel road that leads to the heart of our territory, completely oblivious to my presence, and I deliberate on what to do.

I could scare him. But letting him see an unnaturally golden wolf that's about the size of a Shetland pony would probably not be the smartest thing to do.

I could take him out. That is obviously the move my wolf is urging me to make. But even the psychopathic animal acknowledges Lucy wouldn't like that, and Jason would never forgive me. Plus, I like Ross.

So, I wait, stalking him like a deadly shadow as he heads slowly but surely into the heart of my territory.

Meanwhile, I can feel Jason and some of the others approaching. Orrin and Red, I note with relief.

Good. Orrin will know what to do.

I hear them before I scent them, the faintest snapping of twigs under paws the earliest sign of their approach. Probably Orrin, since the bear always has a harder time moving silently through the forest than the rest of us. The sound is loud enough that Ross must hear it too, because he stops, shuffling nervously as he stares into the dark forest on the side of the road opposite to me.

"He-hello," he says tentatively. "Is someone there?"

When only silence answers him, he lets out a nervous chuckle.

"Creepy forest," he murmurs under his breath. "Probably just a wild animal."

His back is to me, so it's impossible to read his expression, to judge whether his face is contorted in disdain at the thought of some wild creature interrupting his midnight trespassing. Or maybe his cheeks are pale with fear. Still, my wolf bristles at his words.

This is our forest. It's not creepy. It's beautiful and wild and home.

He pauses for a moment longer, staring into the darkness, then there is the sound of rustling as he tugs at something under his jacket, followed by the faintest clicking of metal.

A gun.

Before I can stop it, my wolf is letting out a low growl, the sound reverberating through my bones and into the very forest floor.

Like a marionette pulled by invisible strings, Ross jerks around, arms flying out to point the gun wildly in my direction. Even from here, with the darkness and at least twenty feet between us, I can see his hands trembling.

When my eyes land on his face, I freeze.

Half his face is so swollen with bruises, it's barely recognisable. The one eye not swollen shut is wide open, whites fully visible, the pupil darting erratically as he stares into the dark. A faint breeze ruffles his hair, carrying with it the scent of blood and fear.

My chest aches, the instinctual need to protect Ross from whatever hurt him warring with the need to protect my pack.

Before I can decide what to do, how to act, there is the distinctive sound of bones and tendons popping and cracking as someone shifts in the trees across the road. Ross spins around again, gun swinging to face the new sound, hands trembling so much, it's a miracle he's still able to hold the thing.

A low, rumbling growl erupts from the trees. Orrin. The sound quickly followed by Jason's angry whispers.

"Let me go, you brute. He's not going to hurt me."

The words are spoken so low, that I doubt Ross can hear them. Still, the human tenses, likely hearing something.

"Is someone there?" Ross asks, his voice a choked whisper.

Orrin growls again, and I can see them now through the trees, my preternatural vision letting me see what Ross cannot. Jason, recently shifted into his human form, grappling with a large bear in an attempt to get to Ross, while Red's bobcat looks on warily.

The faint click of metal on metal followed by a bullet chambering makes my blood run cold. Instinct and fear propelling me, I lunge out of the trees.

Take him down, my wolf demands. *Protect the pack.*

I've barely taken one step when the gun fires, the sound so loud I swear it's going to shatter the night sky like glass, and everything slows down.

As if in slow motion, Jason breaks free from the trees, hurtling himself towards Ross. Orrin's roar of furry is echoed by Red's warning hiss. Then the sound of my pack erupts all around the forest - the calls of beasts filling the air as very human thoughts of fear and anger flood across the pack bonds.

The questions come too, so many at once it makes my head spin.

What's happening?

Who is it?

Was that a gun?

That was a gun.

Are we under attack?

I squeeze my eyes shut, doing my best to block the questions out, dim them down to background noise as I urge my legs forward. But I'm too slow. Too slow.

Everything is too slow except that bullet, moving straight towards Jason.

Until it hits, and then time speeds up again, the world moving in disjointed flashes.

Jason crumpling to the gravel road. And his chest – red. So much red. Orrin standing protectively over him, spittle flying from his muzzle as he bellows out a roar. Ross falling back, the gun clattering against rocks.

My wolf is mid-air, flying towards Ross' back when in a last-minute flash of genius, I decide to shift back into human form. I'm not sure why exactly. Maybe I'm thinking I can still salvage this, keep what we are hidden. Somehow explain away the presence of a bear and bobcat just hanging out.

Whatever my thinking, the shift happens almost the instant I think of it, and I watch in horror as Ross turns around, his eyes meeting mine as my body morphs from wolf to human. A very naked human.

I hardly have time to appreciate the complete disaster that I have single-handedly created when I'm slamming into Ross, my body colliding into his with enough force to knock the wind from me.

I scramble up, lungs aching, and move towards Jason. Vaguely, I'm aware of Ross' incoherent curses, of the warning growls of the wolves I left in the woods behind me, of the sound of the rest of the pack approaching.

"Jason," I say, ignoring Orrin's rumbled discontent as I shove the bear aside.

Jason's face is contorted in pain, teeth bared, back arching. But he's breathing. He's alive and he's breathing. Thank the gods.

I take a deep breath, smelling blood and gunpowder and dirt and pine but not silver. Not silver, and I send another prayer of gratitude up to the moonlit sky.

Gently – so gently – I roll him to his side, just enough to see the exit wound near his shoulder blade. The bullet tore clean through him, but at least we won't have to get Theo to dig it out.

Another mercy.

"Shift," I order, the word catching in my throat.

Something wet and hot tickles along the sides of my cheeks, but I brush it away.

"Shift," I say again, this time letting the wolf free in my voice, momentarily embracing its dark power.

Jason's eyes snap open, a keening wail leaving his lips as the shift takes him. The sound tapers off to a pitiful whimper, a brown wolf laying in his place, eyes glassy but conscious, sides heaving. Red coats his fur but already I can see the wound is closing, knitting shut with the magic of the shift.

Warm fur brushes up against my side, the familiar scent of lavender and fresh cut grass filling my nostrils as Lucy pushes past me. Without hesitating, she presses her nose into Jason's side, tongue lapping at the wound.

Part of me – the part that grew up as a human in New York - wants to wrinkle my nose in disgust at the gesture. Because, gross. The wolf part of me gets it though, understands at an instinctual level that this is Lucy offering comfort to her pack mate and friend. And gross as it is, her saliva will reduce his pain and speed up the healing process.

"That's enough, pup," Orrin tells her after a couple minutes. At some point he must have shifted into his human form.

"I'm going to take him back to the lodge," he says, before scooping Jason's brown wolf up without preamble and striding up the gravel road, calling out over his shoulder for Theo to join him.

"Jason. Oh my God, Jason."

Ross scrambles to his feet, as if the sight of the brown wolf being carried away has roused him from whatever panicked stupor he'd been caught in. He doesn't so much as look at the menagerie of animals that have gathered around, as if his brain can't handle all the layers of crazy that have just been unleashed around him. Nope, he just hobbles after Orrin, like getting to Jason is the only thing he cares about.

He's barely gone two steps when I grab him by the shoulder, spinning him to face me.

"Finch," he whispers, his one good eye staring up at me, wide and wild and full of tears. "I shot him. I shot him. I… I *shot* him."

His voice cracks at that, features crumpling, his usually handsome face almost unrecognisable. Pity sears through me, dulling my anger until it's a banked fire simmering in my chest, instead of a raging inferno.

"What were you thinking? A gun? Really?"

Ross doesn't answer, just stares after Orrin's retreating back and the long limbs of the wolf in his arms, now barely visible.

"He's a wolf. A wolf. How is that even possible?" Ross asks, turning to look back up at me. His one good eye blinks rapidly as he takes me in.

"You were a wolf." He says, his voice laced with suspicion and accusation. Like even though he's saying the words, he isn't sure if he can believe them.

For a moment, I contemplate lying to him. Trying to convince him he's crazy, that he's made all this up. But I dismiss that plan pretty quickly when I realise that he's also seen Jason shift. And Orrin shift. And he's probably figured out that the twenty-odd animals lurking about aren't exactly acting naturally.

Like the arctic fox that is draped across the back of a massive panther. Or the hawk that is standing on the gravel road next to a coyote, casually preening its feathers.

Yah, that is all pretty impossible to explain away.

I sigh, releasing his shoulder and drawing my hand over my face.

"Um, yep. I was a wolf."

Ross nods, face paling beneath the bruises.

"Okay," he says, breath leaving him in a whoosh. "Okay. This is real. Cool. Uh-huh."

He starts to sway on his feet and I grab his shoulder again in an effort to steady him.

"Look," I say, when his good eye starts to flutter shut. His breaths are coming in quick, short, pants now and it's seriously looking like he's about to faint. "I get this is a lot to take in. But trust me when I say Jason is going to be okay, alright?"

Ross nods emphatically, then takes a long, shuddering breath. I release his arm, hoping he's not going to faint after all, when he turns, doubling over to retch noisily at my feet.

And I'm pretty sure I just felt something splatter onto my legs.

I turn my head away, stomach churning – only to catch Red's gaze as he chortles merrily at my discomfort. I narrow my eyes on him, and he just laughs harder. Like the fact that a human just found out shifters exist and is now puking at my feet is the best joke ever.

My life sucks.

Chapter 12

Lucy Stone

"Guys, I'm going to be fine," Jason insists, pulling the worn yellow blanket up under his chin.

The colour only serves to highlight the pallor of his skin and the dark circles under his eyes. Still, they're the only visible reminders of the events of the night before. Now, with the sunlight filtering through the dirty windows of the RV, it would almost be easy to forget everything happened.

I should take comfort in that. Should be thankful that Jason is finally back in his RV, stretched out on his little couch-bed beside the compactable kitchen table, compulsively checking his phone to monitor the perimeter.

"Put that thing down."

Summer snatches his phone in one fluid motion, then tucks it against her, out of his reach.

Jason rolls his eyes. "I told you, I'm fine. I just want to check the feed from the drones. They weren't as responsive as I thought they would be and…"

"Ross can do that," Summer snaps, thrusting Jason's phone into Ross' hands.

The human takes the phone without argument, but he looks as pale as Jason. Like he was the one who took a bullet and lost more than a quart of blood.

"Yah, sure. I'll check them," Ross assures her, staring dazedly at the phone. "I can do that."

"What did you and Tobias talk about anyway?" Jason asks.

His tone is casual, but I don't miss the way he watches Ross intently, studying his reactions.

I find myself watching Ross too, wondering how much he will say of the private conversation I know he and Tobias had earlier. When Tobias all but cornered Ross outside. Will he be honest? Now that he knows what we are, will he try and run?

To my surprise, Ross' face stretches into a smile, his default expression pulling at the swollen and bruised side of his face.

"Oh, you know, just the expected. Like how I'm not supposed to know about shifters because I'm a human, and that normally shifter law would demand permanent 'silencing' of humans who find out about you guys," he says, making air quotes with the word 'silencing' before giving a low chuckle.

Like death threats are just one big joke to him.

"Look," he adds, throwing up his hands, "I'm not going to tell anyone about you guys, okay. I mean, first of all, who would believe me? They would be like 'oh, there's that Ross kid, he's clearly lost his mind'. That would be beyond the level of spouting conspiracy theories. I would be like one of those people who think that aliens and bigfoot are real." Ross shakes his head, then winces at the movement. "No thank you. I would prefer not to be a social outcast."

"Okay, good." Jason quirks a grin. "And you're not going to try and shoot me again?"

Ross' smile instantly falls, the blood draining from his face.

"God, I'm so sorry Jason."

He leans forward in his chair, pressing his forehead into the palms of his hands, elbows resting on his knees.

"I could have killed you. I'll never get that image out of my head. Never. You're my best friend and I almost killed you."

Ross lifts his head, tears glistening in his eyes.

"I'm so sorry, man. So, so, sorry."

Jason gives a pained smile before stretching one trembling hand out to pat Ross' knee reassuringly. I can tell even that small movement still hurts him. It will be at least tomorrow before Jason is able to move without pain, even if the bullet wound has already healed.

"It's all good," Jason assures him.

I resist the urge to scoff. If somebody shot me, I definitely wouldn't be so quick to forgive them.

Ross takes Jason's hand in his own, leaning forward to mutter more apologies, which Jason will no doubt accept.

Summer gives me a pointed look. When I lift a questioning brow, she looks meaningfully at their joined hands, then at the door.

I roll my eyes. This is hardly a romantic moment.

With an impatient huff in my direction, Summer stands, brushing her hands on her jeans.

"Well, I'm going to get some breakfast, and then take a nap," she says, with a dramatic yawn. "Lucy, are you coming?"

I frown. I had been waiting for Tobias to come back to his RV, but who knows how long he will be out checking the perimeter. Also, watching Ross and Jason together makes me feel uncomfortable. Like I'm intruding on some private moment.

"Yah, I'll come," I say, following her out the door. I could use some breakfast. And I have questions I'm hoping she can answer.

I'M SITTING at our kitchen table, back warm with the late morning sun streaming through the window, a plate full of toast, bacon and eggs laid out in front of me, and I still haven't figured out how to ask Summer what I've been meaning to ask her.

"What is it?" Tania asks, annoyingly picking up on my emotions. "What's bothering you?"

Of course, I can't really snap at her, because she's right. And because she did just make the three of us breakfast.

I frown, wondering best how to word this.

"Well," I start, looking between Tania and Summer, "it's kind of awkward…"

Summer instantly lights up, leaning forward in her seat, traces of fatigue momentarily wiped away.

"Ooh, are you thinking of making things permanent? With you and Tobias? Because I've never done the whole mate-marking thing myself, obviously, but my mom told me everything about it."

Oh, gods above.

I blink at her, not sure whether to be embarrassed or amused.

"You'll want to know if it hurts, right?" she asks, then continues on to answer her question in the same breath. "Well, apparently it does, but only for a short moment. Because teeth. Obviously, that is going to hurt. But there is something in the saliva – I know, I know, gross – that takes away the pain almost instantly and makes you feel good. Like, really good."

A light blush spreads across her cheeks, but she ploughs on, oblivious to the growing looks of amusement on mine and Tania's faces.

"Things can sometimes happen then, but they don't have to. Like, if you were having a formal mating ceremony then it would probably have to wait until after the party, obviously, but if you guys are doing things privately, then it could happen whenever. Or not at all. It's just the claiming bite that does it really, the rest is just, you know, extra…"

Tania bursts out laughing, then covers her face with her hands. My eyes feel like they're about to pop out of my head, and I'm pretty sure I must be redder than the coffee cup Summer is holding in her hands.

Summer stops, looking between Tania and me.

"What's so funny?" she asks, sounding mildly put out. "I'm just telling you what I was told. And it's a natural process. Nothing to be embarrassed about."

"Stop. Please, please, stop," Tania laughs, tears flowing down her cheeks as she chokes on the sip of orange juice she unwisely tried to swallow.

Summer glares at the fox shifter, but Tania holds out both hands in a gesture meant to appease as much as silence, a broad smile on her usually serious face.

"I'm a hundred percent sure that Lucy was not asking you about the logistics of formalising a mate bond with Tobias, okay?"

I press my head into my hands, unable to look at either of them. Honestly, who would have friends? They are the worst.

"No?" Summer asks, the one word heavy with confusion.

"No," Tania replies. "Definitely not."

"Lucy? Really, that's not what you were asking about?"

I lift my head, shooting her an incredulous look.

Tobias and I only just started dating. Sure, we might be fated to be mates, but I'm not about to go entering into some unbreakable bond. And I'm certainly not ready for the other things she was alluding to.

"I think the sleep deprivation has affected your judgment," I say with a decisive nod, because that can be the only explanation. "No, that was not what I was asking about."

"Oh." A sheepish smile spreads across Summer's face. "Oh. Okay. Sorry?"

Tania scoffs. "No, you're not. You're just disappointed to be wrong."

"Well, whatever," she tells Tania with a shrug. "Now she has the information. It's not like they're not going to get mated eventually anyway. I mean, they're dating. And clearly very into each other."

"Hey," I say, waving my hand between them, "I'm right here. And can we please stop talking about me and Tobias?"

"Fine," Summer says with a huff. "What were you wanting to talk about then?"

I resist the urge to roll my eyes, opting instead for taking a long drink of coffee.

"I wanted to talk to you guys about the pack run," I say, and suddenly I don't feel at all self-conscious about discussing this. I'm pretty sure Summer's rant has had the effect of dulling me to all embarrassment. "When you and the other wolves were calling me alpha. What was all that about?"

Tania shoots me an irritated look, then shakes her head. Summer presses her lips together, clearly resisting the urge to smile.

"What?" I snap, narrowing my eyes at the pair of them.

"What?" Tania echoes, a sharp edge to her usually soft voice. "What? I have been telling you for weeks that you are an alpha – the alpha – and you keep brushing it off."

"Tobias is the alpha," I say, brow furrowing. "It just doesn't make sense."

Summer snorts, finger tracing the rim of her coffee cup. "That's because your brain has been sufficiently filled with the propaganda of the shifter patriarchy."

She squares her shoulders, tilting her chin in that irritating way she does when she's about to tell you all about the things she knows that you don't.

"Unlike you," she continues, "I have taken the time to question the misinformation I've been spoon-fed by our old pack. And let's just say there are a quite a few things they haven't been telling anyone."

"Not just your pack," Tania murmurs, rubbing her hands nervously on her jeans. "Other packs – and dens – and lairs…" she trails off, expression darkening, as if she's fighting off memories she'd rather forget.

"Exactly," Summer says, resting one hand on Tania's shoulder in a silent show of comfort.

I watch their interaction with no small amount of envy. It's not the first time I've wished I was better at comforting others. At connecting with others.

"So what am I missing, oh knowledgeable one?" I ask, my voice laced with sarcasm. "What little gem of feminist theory do you have for me today?"

Summer's eyes narrow momentarily, but then a softer, almost pitying expression quickly takes its place.

"You're an alpha," she says simply. "Wolf packs are designed to have two alphas. That's one of the reasons we have mates. Whether you guys formalise the bond, your souls are connected. Which means you are both alphas of this pack."

"Like Cindy and Cooper?" I ask, recalling how we always referred to the pair as the alphas. But Cooper was always the alpha. The one in charge. The one making the decisions.

"Not even close," Summer says, wrinkling her nose in distaste.

"And what, everyone knows this but me?" I ask, recalling the way Christopher and Tobias and all the other wolves referred to me as alpha, feeling suddenly like the kid in class who has forgotten how to spell their own name.

"I doubt it," Summer says, giving a dismissive wave of one hand. "I only know this stuff because I've looked into it. The others are probably just acting on instinct. I doubt they've given it any thought at all."

"Oh," I say, staring down at the now luke-warm coffee in my hands.

In some way, that almost makes it worse. Because for wolves – for all shifters – instinct is everything. Our laws, our stories, our very religion - they are all designed to coincide with our instincts.

If what Summer and Tania are saying is true, and the leadership we've all been under conflicts with our instincts, then there is something very, very wrong in the shifter world.

"Yah. Oh," Tania echoes drily.

This time, I can't even bring myself to feel irritated at her mocking response. Or at the smug, know-it-all smile that is playing across Summer's lips.

Because the word *alpha, alpha, alpha* is running through my head on repeat, both a question and an answer.

And the word, it tastes like truth.

Chapter 13

Tobias Finch

I'm having the most vivid dream about Lucy when the sound of my phone vibrating jolts me from my sleep. Eyes squeezed shut against the darkness, my hand flies out from under the covers, frantically seeking the offending item and silencing it before it wakes the other guys.

I should know better than to worry though. Danny sleeps like the dead on a good night, and Jason is so exhausted after getting shot last night, I doubt anything would wake him.

Before I can set the phone back down, it's buzzing again, humming against my clutched palm like an angry, oversized insect. I lift it to my face, squinting my eyes to stare at the screen, brow furrowing when I read an unknown number.

Cautiously, I answer, then raise the phone to my ear.

"Hello?"

My voice is a faint whisper, barely more than a silent exhale.

"Ahh. That must be the famous Tobias Finch."

The cold voice slinks across the line, burrowing itself into my head with all the gentleness of an ice pick and I jolt up, kicking the covers back and nearly dropping the phone in the process.

That voice. That gods-damned voice. I would know it anywhere. I could live to be a hundred and forget my own name and still remember the exact cadence and vibration of that voice.

"Don't answer," the voice says, before I can open my lips to spew the millions of curses ready on my tongue. "Don't speak a single word. If you value your grandfather's life, you'll listen quietly like a good little boy."

My heart stops at those words, the organ plummeting into my stomach when my grandfather's voice comes across the line, thin and pained sounding.

"I'm fine, Tobias, don't listen to a word he says, don't…"

His speech is cut off with a heavy thudding sound, followed by a muffled grunt.

"Let's hope you've inherited the good sense of your father's line, shall we? Because your grandfather's abilities don't speak measures for genetic competence…"

I bite back a growl as my wolf pushes for the surface, rage heating my blood and burning out the icy fear that has only started to settle under my skin.

My grandfather. This monster has my grandfather.

Rip and tear, my wolf vows, *flesh and bone.*

I grit my teeth, pushing the wolf down, down, down. Waiting.

"Good." He gives a low, mirthless, chuckle and the fine hairs on my forearms rise in response. "Enough blood has been spilt on your account. There's no need to add to the tally. You listen to every word I say, and no one needs to get hurt. I want you to leave that little hovel you're holed up in – don't wake a soul, you hear? – and make your way to the eastern edge of your territory. Now, I trust you know where the Castle is?"

THERE'S an old hydropower generation building just outside Liberty pack territory, an ancient edifice that dates back to a time when Buffalo had more money than sense and decided to build what essentially looks like a miniature castle in the middle of nowhere. Now, more than a century after it was built, the place has been half-claimed by the harsh Wyoming winters, its remnants stained by decades' worth of angsty musings.

It's a place I've wandered to more than a few times, occasionally with a few of the pack, but mostly by myself. I've always kind of liked it for some reason. There's something other-worldly about its story-book silhouette, the ornate pressed-lead panels peeling from high ceilings and the giant machinery that fills the Castle's empty halls. The graffiti is also endearing – a strange mixture of inspirational quotes, angry rants and dick drawings.

I've never been here in the middle of the night before. With the moon only just waning from full, the castle's shadow is long and imposing, a dark creature with a life of its own, disappearing into the darker shadows between the trees. Another time, it would be eerie. It would make me think of ghosts and whatever creatures lurk in the untouched corners of the imagination.

Not tonight. Tonight, the Castle is neither curiosity nor haunt. There is no mystery surrounding the monster lurking behind its high walls.

I stare up at the thick stone walls, glaring into the darkness beyond its crumbling entryway. For once, I could care less about this architectural phenomenon. No, all I care about are the two males inside.

One is the only living family member I have left who knows what I am.

The other is the male I've sworn to kill. The male whose charcoal and pine scent has haunted my dreams almost every night this past year. The male who stole my mom and dad from me with tooth and claw.

He must pay, my wolf rumbles as I lift my nose, catching the acrid notes of *him* on the air. I breath against the rising panic, blinking back the shameful tears that prick behind my eyes as memories come flooding back. As if my olfactory system has a direct link to the most painful memories my mind possesses.

The forest at my back is silent, as if even the nocturnal wildlife can sense the presence of a dangerous predator.

I take a deep breath, steeling myself. Readying myself to come face to face with the living nightmare that is Huxley Black.

I'm not really sure what my plan is. But I don't plan on letting this monster take one more person away from me. And I have a feeling that once I walk into that building, only one of us will be walking back out.

Chapter 14

Cody Winslow

There's a knock at the door to my cabin, the sound harsh and hurried, as if the person on the other side is being chased by hell's own demons, and is desperate to get in.

I leap from my bed, fully dressed and wide awake. It's not the first time I've been unable to sleep at night, anxiety and inactivity churning together in my mind to create a perfect storm for insomnia. Tonight, I didn't even bother trying.

"Who is it?" I ask, pressing my palms against the rough wood door as I try to draw in the person's scent through the draughty gaps.

My head snaps back when the scent hits my nostrils. A scent I know as well as my own. The scent of home and safety and love and sadness.

"Mom!"

The word comes out strangled, emotion choking my throat. Mom is here. Mom is here.

I work at the doorknob, frantically pulling before I remember I'm locked inside.

"Do you have a key?" I ask, my voice rising in pitch with barely leashed emotion. "Can you get me out of here."

"Shhh. Anton is bringing it. I just wanted to make sure you were awake."

Gods, her voice. I don't think I've ever heard a sound so sweet in that moment as my mom's voice. Weeks and weeks trapped in this cabin, with only Anton's silence to keep me company, and now my mom is here. Talking to me. Getting me out. She's going to get me out. She's going to talk to dad and make everything okay.

"Take a deep breath," she orders, her own voice surprisingly steady. "I know you're excited sweetie, but I need you to calm down."

A wide grin splits my face at those words, the expression probably completely manic-looking with my gaunt face and teary eyes. How many times have I heard those words from her? Before each football game or test. As a child on Christmas morning. When I had my first shift.

"Okay, mom," I agree, even as my heart races rebelliously.

"I need you to get dressed and ready to go. We're leaving as soon as Anton gets here. I'll explain everything on the way."

I look down at myself. Grey sweat pants and a black t-shirt. They probably smell terrible after weeks of not doing washing, but mom won't care.

"I'll just get my shoes."

"And a jacket. Don't forget a jacket."

Normally, I would have argued that I didn't need it. That I'm a full-grown male shifter and it's the middle of summer.

"Okay, mom," I say through another maniacal grin.

It's not long before Anton is at the door, breathing heavily as if he's been running, the sound of a key scratching and the heavy lock clicking. When the door finally swings open, revealing Anton's sweat-slicked face, bringing in the sweet scent of the night air, I'm so happy I could cry.

"Hey man," Anton says, looking almost sheepish as he takes in my face.

My eyes fly open in surprise, then narrow in suspicion. For weeks Anton has been silent, listening, letting me think that he was under orders not to speak to me.

"Aww, don't give me that look," he says defensively, then tilts his chin over his shoulder, to where mom is standing behind him. "She lifted the ban."

"Mom," I choke out, pushing past Anton, overcome with the sudden urge to wrap my arms around her.

Even though her head rests under my chin, even though I'm sure I could lift her from the ground without the slightest effort, there is something so reassuring and familiar in the strength of her embrace.

"Mom."

I press my nose into her hair, drawing in that familiar scent as she gives me a tight, shuddering squeeze, before pulling away.

"We have to move," she tells me, meeting my eyes with her own. "Every second counts."

Even in the moonlight, it seems like there are more lines around her eyes and at the corners of her mouth. Lines that speak of sadness and days without laughter.

I follow her through the forest, sneakered feet padding almost soundlessly along unfamiliar trails, Anton at my back. I want to ask where we are going, but her and Anton's tense silence tell me that this isn't the time to speak.

After about twenty minutes of travelling away from Clear Creek territory, we reach a gravel road. I stare in surprise at the sight of mom's car.

"You drove here?" I ask, then realise how stupid that question must sound, because of course she drove here.

Still, I hadn't even known there was a road back here.

Mom doesn't answer, just swings open the driver-seat door and starts the engine, motioning hurriedly for me to get in. Even when I'm in the front passenger seat, her four-wheel drive careening dangerously over gravel and wheel-ruts, she is silent for a long moment, her eyes fixed on the dark road ahead of her.

When she finally does speak, it's through a clenched jaw, as if every word costs her.

"Your dad never told me you were on pack territory. Even when I told him I was worried sick about you, he wouldn't tell me a thing. Didn't even let on that he knew you were alive."

She takes a deep, shuddering breath, knuckles white as she clutches the steering wheel.

"It was Anton who told me. Came to me a week ago and told me you were locked up in that little derelict cabin. Told me that all the enforcers knew as well. That Jeb knew. And that everyone was keeping me in the dark."

A low rumbling growl escapes her lips at that pronouncement, the sound distinctively wolf, and I shudder, even though I know the anger isn't directed at me.

"Gods above, I wanted to run up to the cabin right then and get you out, but I waited. I waited because that same night, I got a call from Rachel."

"Rachel?"

The name sounds familiar, like it's one I should know but can't quite place.

More important to my mind is the fact that mom didn't know. She hadn't abandoned me up there. That knowledge nudges away the last remnants of doubt, replacing them with a comforting warmth. Mom hadn't abandoned me. Mom came for me.

"Rachel Stone," she explains, and my eyes widen.

Anton gives a rumbling murmur from the back seat, the inarticulate mutterings sounding suspiciously like profanities.

"Language, young man," mom chides reflexively. "Yes, Rachel Stone. Lucy and Anton's mother."

I just blink at her, my brain still failing to process this information. Everyone knows Rachel Stone abandoned her children years ago, running off after having an affair with a passing rogue wolf shifter, never to be heard from again. And yet here mom is, talking about getting a phone call from Rachel Stone with the same casualness as she'd talk about getting a call from any member of our pack.

Mom lets out a tired sigh, lifting one pale hand to rub at her eyes.

"Look son, there's a lot you don't know. And a lot of what you've been told are lies." She throws me an apologetic look. "I'm sorry for that. I thought it was the best, and so did Rachel. Thought we were keeping you pups safe."

She grips the wheel with both hands again, expertly manoeuvring down the dark, winding road, a look of steely determination hardening her features.

"I'm sorry," she says again. "I really am. I'll explain it all, tell you everything. But first, we need to get to that poor boy. Before it's too late."

"Who?" I ask.

I'm starting to wonder if maybe this is some sort of a dream. Like one of those hallucinations people get after staying awake for too long, because nothing mom is saying is making any sense. I dig my fingernails into the palms of my hands, somewhat reassured by the prick of pain there.

"Tobias Finch," Anton rumbles from the back seat.

The car groans as Anton leans forward, resting his elbows on his knees so that his face appears between the two front seats.

"Dad has reached an alliance with Huxley Black, and they've got a plan to take out Finch tonight."

I turn to gape at him, and see the truth in the barely contained rage that tightens his features.

"But, Huxley Black…" I start, then shake my head, unable to articulate my thoughts on the absolute madness of dad forming an alliance with that monster.

Huxley Black kept me in a literal gods-damned cage for days. Huxley Black tortured Anton. Huxley Black murdered Tobias Finch's mom – a defenceless, human woman – in cold blood, in her own home.

"Is a monster?" Anton offers, echoing my own thoughts. "A psychopath who taints the air of this earth by breathing it? A coward who kidnaps and tortures children? Yah." He gives a mirthless chuckle. "Oh yah. And apparently him and your dad are best buds now."

I half expect mom to reprimand Anton, to defend dad. Instead, she gives a solemn nod, then shoots me a look so full of guilt and apology, I want to reach out and hug her all over again.

"And now that monster has Tobias Finch," mom says. "Or if he doesn't have him, he will have him soon. All so that your father can take over the Liberty pack."

Anton scoffs. "Yah. Like Huxley Black is going to let that happen. Cooper's an idiot."

Mom nods grimly. "Unfortunately, I have to agree with you. I haven't met this Huxley Black character, but from everything you've told me, it's clear he's not going to be satisfied with something as petty as revenge. No, whatever his plan is, he obviously wants more."

I rub my face, pressing the heels of my palms against my eye sockets.

"I'm sorry. I'm not following. Huxley Black has Tobias? How? How is that even possible? And how is that going to help dad take over Liberty pack?"

Maybe it's the insomnia catching up to me. Or maybe I really am slow, just like Lucy always said whenever she'd get annoyed with me.

Mom casts me an exasperated look, before turning her attention back to the winding road.

"I don't know all the details," Anton admits, "just what he told us enforcers. The plan was for Huxley Black to lure Tobias off pack territory while our enforcers move in, taking the pack by surprise while they sleep. Without Tobias there, dad thinks he can force the pack's submission. And once Tobias is – uh – gone and the pack bond is broken…"

Anton trails off, the unspoken words hanging in the space between us. Once Tobias is dead, dad can force the Liberty pack shifters to swear fealty to him. The Machiavellian part of my brain – the part that has watched my dad's careful handling of one of the biggest packs in the country – appreciates what he is trying to do.

It's no secret that the Liberty pack is full of some of the country's strongest young shifters. There is a reason Huxley Black wanted us to be part of his shifter army, after all.

If dad succeeds, he will have the biggest, strongest pack in the country.

And while that thought is honestly horrifying, it's nothing compared to the thought of Tobias Finch being killed.

Alpha, my wolf reminds me. *Our alpha.*

For once, there is no bitter pang of jealousy accompanying the thought. Instead, it's just the heavy weight of remorse. Because I let him down. I betrayed him. And if he dies, it will be as much on my hands as anyone else's.

And the pack. My pack.

Ice fills my veins at the thought of Clear Creek enforcers marching onto Liberty pack territory, taking my pack mates by surprise in their sleep. No matter how strong they are, no matter how much training they've been doing with Orrin, they won't be strong enough to face grown shifters, armed with guns and who knows what else.

And Summer. What will happen to Summer?

"We can't let them do this," I say, balling my hands into fists. "We can't let dad hurt them."

"I agree," mom says firmly, gritting her teeth as the wheels skid precariously on a patch of loose gravel before finding traction. "Which is why we can't let Huxley Black succeed."

"We're going to the Castle," Anton explains. "That's where he's got Finch. Or where he's planning to take him, if he doesn't have him already. So just pray to whatever gods you believe in that we're not too late."

Chapter 15

Lucy Stone

Something isn't right.

That is the first thought I have when I wake, eyelids still heavy with sleep as I strain to take in the darkness surrounding me. But nothing appears to be out of place. Beside me, I can hear Tania and Summer's steady breathing as they sleep, and when I slip out into the kitchen, everything is just as it should be.

Still, I can't shake the feeling of unease. The knowing that something is wrong. It runs like electricity under my skin, demanding that I pay attention.

Listen. Listen.

I close my eyes, straining my ears. The forest outside is quiet. Maybe too quiet, actually. The sort of heavy silence that descends before a storm. Only, when I look out the window, the sky is cloudless as it was when I went to bed, the moon high and blotting out the stars with its light.

I try to open my mind, try to lean into my gift. Unsurprisingly, nothing happens. It's been weeks since I've had a vision. Weeks since I've had even the slimmest flicker of knowing.

My gift is officially the biggest waste of time ever.

I rub my eyes, doing my best to push down the growing sense of unease.

I'm turning to go back to the bedroom I share with Tania and Summer when the sound of shouting erupts. The familiar voices of my pack mates filter in through the open window, just as feelings of surprise, fear and rage bombard me across the pack bond.

I tense, readying to run out and see what is happening, when the door to my RV flies open. It crashes violently against the kitchen cupboards, revealing the black-clad form of a Clear Creek enforcer, masked and armed, yellow eyes crinkling gleefully when they land on me.

"Alpha. The white wolf has been located. Over," he says into the wireless com unit attached to one ear. He doesn't take his eyes off me, just expertly manoeuvres his body so that he's blocking the door.

Panic rises in my chest, fluttering like a flock of birds as I look towards the window, calculating my chances of escaping.

"Don't even think about it, Miss Stone," the enforcer drawls, his tone a mixture of boredom and amusement.

He looks pointedly at his rifle, now aimed directly at me. There is no missing the acrid scent of gunpowder and silver perfuming the tight space of the RV.

"I might be under orders to take you in alive, but I'm pretty sure a shot to the kneecap would keep you from getting far," he muses, lowering the gun so that it's aimed at my legs.

My muscles tense reflexively, but I force myself to meet his eyes with my own, tilting my head thoughtfully as I say: "Oh, come on, Hank.

I've seen you at the shooting range. We both know if you aimed for my leg, you'd probably kill me."

Because even with his face covered, there is no mistaking the sound of this male's voice or his scent. Honestly, there isn't a single member of the Clear Creek pack that I wouldn't know from scent alone.

Hank's eyebrows lift in surprise and he chuckles despite himself.

"You always were a sassy little thing."

I shoot him what I hope is a saccharine smile.

I've known this male my whole life. He's eaten dinner with us, along with many of the other enforcers. I've even babysat his daughter a few times. I want him to remember that. To see me as pack, even if I'm part of the Liberty pack now.

He lets out a heavy sigh, then lowers the gun until it's pointing at the floor.

"Just don't do anything stupid, okay? You know your daddy would kill me if I had to hurt you."

I want to tell him how very wrong he is, but I press my lips together, biting back my response. Instead, I ask him: "What are you doing here?"

I don't expect him to tell me a thing. I just want to keep his attention on me, to give Summer and Tania a chance to hide or escape. Because I can feel them through the pack bond now, awake and afraid, their panic fuelling my wolf's protective instincts.

Don't come out here, I tell them through the bond. *See if you can hide or get out through one of the windows.*

Even as I say that, I realise that the windows in the bedroom are probably too small for them to squeeze out of, and there isn't much space to hide. Even if they did hide, any shifter would be able to sniff them out.

Hank fidgets, jaw clenching as he fights the urge to answer me. Whatever his orders might be, I suspect his own wolf still sees me as a superior in the pack. Part of the beta's family. Someone he is supposed to be respectful to. Someone he is supposed to protect.

Good. I plan on exploiting every bit of that instinct.

"You'll find out soon enough," he finally tells me, and there's a note of solemnity in his voice that I don't like. "Just as soon as alpha Winslow gets here, he'll explain everything."

My heart sinks, dread settling in my stomach. If Cooper is on his way, that must mean every enforcer is here. It must mean a full-scale invasion. I frown. What happened to the drones? The perimeter sensors? All that super-expensive tech that Jason and Ross spent all that time installing.

Jason? I call through the pack bond. *What is happening?*

His response is a quick flurry of guilt and fear.

I don't know what happened. We never got a single alert, and all our phones are dead. Like, not a single signal. I think they shut everything down. Danny is about to lose his shit and I don't know where Tobias is. They've got a gun pointed at us and Ross is here…

Jason's words fade to whimpers as his wolf pushes for supremacy, no doubt demanding that he run.

Tobias?

I reach across the pack bond, searching for him, demanding that he answer.

There is nothing, only the faint pulse of life connecting me to him. The link that I shouldn't be able to feel but somehow can, just like I can feel every member of this pack. Only his is stretched thin, as if pulled by distance.

Tobias, are you there?

Nothing. Absolutely nothing.

I feel the blood drain from my face at his answering silence.

Outside, the sounds of shouting have quietened down, but the simmering rage pulsing across the pack bond remains. Tentatively, I reach out, letting my voice project to the entire pack.

I think we're under attack, I announce lamely. *I've got an enforcer holding me at gunpoint, and so do Jason and Danny. And Tobias is missing.*

The cacophony of answers makes my head spin, everyone speaking at once.

Noah: *We've got an enforcer here too. I think they're everywhere.*

Aires: *Is Summer safe?*

Summer: *I'm fine. Worry about yourself.*

Red: *Oh, we're under attack? I had no idea.*

Hamish: *Where the hell is Tobias?*

Tyrone: *I swear to all the gods, if they touch Tania…*

Theo: *Arlo and I are out flying. They haven't noticed us yet. We can be your eyes. And yah, the enforcers are everywhere. They're practically swarming this place. No idea how they got in without anyone noticing.*

Orrin: *Be careful. They're armed.*

Arlo: *Oh, we know. Kind of hard to miss the big guns these guys are carrying around. It's like they're trying to compensate for something.*

Christopher: *So, what's the plan, alpha?*

The link goes silent, and at least several heartbeats pass before I realise that Christopher's question was directed at me.

I'm not the alpha, I argue. *Tobias is the alpha.*

I could see if we were mated, that they might call me alpha out of respect, just like we would call Cindy Winslow alpha sometimes. But no one would actually defer to her, obey her like they would Cooper.

Tobias is the one they swore the oath to, not me. He's the born alpha, not me. He and I might be mates, but we aren't mated. We've only just started dating.

Let's just say for arguments sake that you are, okay sweetheart, Hamish drawls. *What's the plan? Had any fancy visions lately?*

I grit my teeth, bristling at the question. My first instinct is to ignore it, to tell him to mind his own business. But this is my pack. They deserve to know.

No visions, I tell them reluctantly.

I look up, meeting Hank's familiar yellow eyes with my own. He's watching me quizzically, like he knows I'm talking on the pack link, and he isn't quite sure whether he should try and put a stop to it or not. I give him a little smile.

We wait, I tell the pack. *I'm pretty sure alpha Winslow is on his way here. So whatever we do, we need to wait until he gets here.*

I half expect people to argue, but to my surprise, no one does. My confidence lifting, I rack my brain for everything I know about my old pack's strategy, trying to recall every little thing I've overheard my dad say.

Arlo and Theo, keep watch, I continue. *Let us know if more shifters arrive. The ones dressed in black with the silver cattle insignia, those are the Clear Creek enforcers. But alpha Winslow would never attack without allies, so keep a look out for others. See if you can get an estimate of their numbers, and where they are on our territory.*

You got it boss, Theo answers, and I almost smile at the flutter of excitement and pride pouring across the bond from the owl cousins.

Clear Creek pack have twenty enforcers, but only ten of them are full-time, I tell my pack. *The rest are really ranch-hands with a bit of combat training. But they're all decent shots and will be using silver bullets.*

Orrin's rumbling growl reverberates through the bond, carrying his disgust and unmasked rage.

But I don't think they'll shoot us, I tell them, and gods, I hope it is the truth. *If they wanted to kill us, they would have done that already.*

What do you think they want? Jason asks.

I swallow, bile rising, because I know the answer. I don't even have to guess at it. After years of watching Cooper Winslow, after years of being his little obedient truth-teller, I know what he wants. It's what he always wants.

Power. Control. Domination.

He wants the pack, I say, squeezing my eyes shut as the familiar feeling of knowing sweeps through me. *He wants the pack and he wants me.*

Chapter 16

Tobias Finch

The first thing I think when my eyes adjust to the dim interior of the Castle and land on Huxley Black is that he's smaller than I remember. It's a strange thing to think, everything considered, but it's true.

Maybe I've grown in the months since I saw him at Blackwater. Or maybe I've just built him up in my mind so much that his actual size can't live up to the monster in my imagination.

Either way, the male is diminutive in stature. A wiry build, noticeably shorter than my six feet. His auburn hair is longer than I remember, slicked back from a receding hairline with what appears to be a large quantity of industrial strength hair product. He should be handsome, but there's something slightly off about his features – a jawline that is a little too heavy, eyes that are a little too close together, a nose that's just a little too thin.

"Tobias Finch."

A broad smile stretches across his face, teeth glinting white in the darkness, and my heart nearly stops in my chest. I've studied the photograph of that smile countless times, compared it to dad's smile, noted the comparative shape and warmth of their expressions.

And still nothing prepares me for seeing my dad's smile on this monster's face.

"Where is my grandpa?" I ask, because I'm not here to chat with my mom's killer. I'm here to get my grandfather and leave. Hopefully ending Huxley Black in the process.

"No manners, just like your daddy," Huxley chuckles, a look of mock disapproval pinching his features. "But not to worry, your precious human-loving grandpa is right here."

Huxley steps aside, revealing grandpa, bound and gagged, tied up to a chair in a far corner of the building. Fury courses through my veins at the sight, hot and blinding, and I can feel my hands shaking at my sides. I ball them into fists, a low growl erupting unbidden from my throat.

"Now, now," Huxley warns. "Let's not do anything you'll regret."

He lifts one hand, holding up a slender black device that looks like a burner phone.

"Do you know what this is?"

I just narrow my eyes at him. I'm not going to play his little question and answer game. He'll either tell me, or he won't.

"This, pup, is your grandfather's fragile, insignificant, life in my hands. One step out of line and *boom*."

He makes an exaggerated gesture with his free hand, fingers opening wide in a way that is strangely reminiscent of jazz-hands, and then his expression hardens.

"You're going to stand there and listen. You're going to do exactly what I say. And if you try and use your alpha command, my finger will be pressing this button before the words have left your mouth. Do I make myself clear?"

When I don't answer, he lifts one dark brow imperiously and raises the device.

"Yah," I bite out through gritted teeth, my eyes flicking over to grandpa. Grandpa meets my gaze with his own, unflinching.

Take him down, grandpa urges through the link, his amber eyes burning like coals. *Don't listen to a word he says and take him down.*

I frown. Of course, grandpa would say that. But he's not the one who would have to explain to grandma why he's not coming home.

I tear my eyes away from grandpa, ignoring the bombardment of telepathic shouts, and stare down at Huxley Black.

"What do you want?" I ask with forced nonchalance.

Huxley's answering smile sends ice snaking along my spine.

"What do I want?" he drawls. "What a good question. First, I want you to take a seat. Right there, by the wall. Yep, that's it."

I sit down, the stone wall cold on my back, clouds of dust billowing up from under me as I sit. Huxley makes a show of checking his watch, some hideously expensive looking timepiece that peeks out from behind the cuffs of a green and black plaid shirt.

"We've still got a few minutes, so this is as good a time as any for a little chat. We are family, after all. Did you know that?"

Horrified shock courses through me at his affirmation of what I've long suspected, but I just stare up at him, forcing my face into an expressionless mask.

"No, no, I didn't think so," he muses, half to himself. "Well, let me tell you. Your precious daddy was my older brother. Well, half-brother, technically. Older by ten years. When our mother died, Finneas took over the pack. He was only twenty years old, but he did a good job of it. Turned the pack into something to be proud of."

He gives a sad smile, eyes going distant for a moment before refocusing on me and narrowing to slits.

"And then he met your mother. The human. Claimed she was his true mate, as if the gods would ever match an alpha as great as your father with a being so weak. He'd been alpha for ten years and she came along and destroyed everything. First, by luring him away from pack territory, because she didn't want to give up her studies in Missoula. And then by birthing you."

His lips curl into a sneer, exposing elongating canines.

"An abomination."

Huxley tilts his head towards where grandpa sits in the far corner.

"It turns out your mother wasn't as human as she seemed. Sweet little Marian. Turns out she was a half-shifter, she just didn't know it. And now we know who carried the born alpha genes, don't we? I'd always wondered where it came from."

I dig my fingers into the dry earth at the sound of my mother's name on this killers' lips. I can feel grandpa's anger through the pack bond, burning alongside my own.

"So you killed her," I choke out, unable to contain myself.

Huxley raises one finger to silence me, giving the device in his hand a meaningful look before rolling his eyes.

"Your mother died because she had more courage than sense. And that wasn't a good thing." He gives a dramatic sigh. "I'd been looking for you for years. Your dad abandoned his pack, choosing his human mate and abomination of a pup over his birth-right. At first, I wanted him to come back and lead. But after a while, it became clear that my leadership was the best thing that could have happened to the Blackwater pack. So then I needed to make sure you wouldn't become a threat to that."

I furrow my brow, staring up at this madman in confusion. How could I have ever been a threat to the Blackwater pack?

"I knew you'd eventually come to Blackwater. That you'd think it was your birth-right, just because Finneas had been alpha." Huxley clenches his jaw, red rising along his throat from beneath the collar of his button up. "I knew it, and that is exactly what happened. You came, and you destroyed everything."

I open my mouth to point out that the only reason I came to Blackwater in the first place was because he killed my mom and kidnaped my friends, but he cuts me off with a wave of his hand.

"Silence!"

He shakes the device angrily in his other hand.

"You took everything from me!" he says, voice rising in pitch until he's nearly shouting. The red flush has spread to his cheeks now, making his teeth and the whites of his eyes stand out in stark contrast. "First you took my brother. You took my alpha. And then you took my pack. You killed my enforcers. You took the army I was building and made it your own."

He bares his teeth, the expression a wolfish contrast to his earlier smile.

"You did everything I warned them about. You became everything I warned them you would become. And now he's dead and you're alive and I have nothing!"

Don't listen to a gods-damned word he says, grandpa urges silently. *He's insane. You're not to blame for anything. Not you. And not your mother.*

I let my gaze flick over to grandpa. Amber eyes blaze like fire in the darkness, his wolf pressing close to the surface, demanding to get free. He must have been given something to prevent him from shifting and slipping his bonds, but whatever it is could be wearing off by now.

Maybe if I keep Huxley Black talking, grandpa will be able to slip free and get to safety. I take a steeling breath, letting the fear and anger solidify in my bones, fuelling my resolve.

I can get out of this. We can get out of this.

I look back at Huxley Black, shuttering my expression so he doesn't see the glimmer of hope flickering there.

I know he doesn't want me to speak, and there is a risk he'll make good on his threats. But after listening to his villain-rant, I don't think he will actually hurt grandpa. He and I both know if he does, I'll just shift and tear him to shreds. And I don't think he wants to die.

"I don't understand," I say, forcing a dramatic yawn. "Did you bring me here to talk me to death? Because I think you're succeeding."

Huxley steps forward, looming over me from my seat on the floor. From across the room, grandpa lets out a warning growl, straining against his bindings.

"You think this is funny, pup?" Huxley snaps, spittle flying from his lips. "You think this is all a big joke?"

I shrug, staring straight into his dark eyes, pupils blown so wide they look entirely black. Black as the night beyond the empty windows of this derelict building. Black as Jamison's coat.

"I think you're a joke," I say, forcing the corners of my lips into a mocking smirk, but it feels more like a snarl.

Destroy him, my wolf demands, and for once the desire to give into the animal is almost overpowering.

Because revenge is here, so close. I can taste it. Smell it. And maybe I can get to him before he can hurt grandpa. Maybe the device in his hand, the wires attached to grandpa's chair – maybe it's all fake. Staged. Some sort of ruse to trick me into complying. To trick me into sitting here, listening to his crap.

My body tenses, power gathering under my skin as I ready to shift. Shift, and attack. That's what I'm going to do.

A phone rings, the sound jarring. Huxley smiles, a broad, white toothy smile that cuts through the darkness like a knife, and he reaches his free hand into his pocket, answering the call.

I expect him to bring it to his ear, but instead he turns the screen to face me and I realise it's some sort of video call. I blink, staring in confusion at the grainy image on the screen, my mind trying to make sense of what I'm seeing.

And then my blood runs cold.

"Tobias," Lucy's voice is clear, despite her pixelated features, and there is no mistaking the fear and horror in her voice. "Oh gods, Tobias."

Chapter 17

Lucy Stone

I hate him.

That is the first thought I have when alpha Winslow's face appears in the doorway of my RV.

Sure, I've never been a particularly liking person. I'm not like Summer, or Jason, or Tania. Most people annoy me, and sometimes I can barely tolerate my closest friends. But I don't think I've ever known the meaning of true hatred until this moment.

I watch him. Taking in every familiar detail. The curve of his mouth as he gives me that cold smile. The knuckles of his hands as his fingers flex at his sides. The way his shoulders square as he pushes past Hank, his enforcer. The glinting silver emblem on his black jacket. The spattering of dirt across his boots.

I can feel Tania's fear through the pack link as she takes in his scent. I can feel Theo's alarm as he circles the sky above us, warning the pack that someone new has entered my RV.

The wrongs this male has committed are innumerable. And now he is here. On my territory. In my RV. Threatening my pack.

My wolf stares at him, silent and watching.

Alpha Winslow is in my RV, I tell the pack through the bond, doing my best to mute the noise and feelings bombarding me.

I need to focus.

I need my gift.

I close my eyes, sending a silent prayer to Morrigan.

You gave me this gift, I tell her accusingly.

I never wanted it. I would have given it back a thousand times over. I've only ever been grateful for it once, and that was when it helped me to save Tobias.

You gave me this stupid, horrible gift and now you need to help me.

I know it's no way to talk to a goddess, but honestly, I don't care anymore. If she exists, she deserves my anger.

Show me, I demand, not really sure what I'm asking for.

Show me how to get rid of Cooper. How to protect my pack. How to bring Tobias back to me.

Show me what to do.

I clench my jaw against the answering silence and open my eyes. Cooper is watching me curiously, eyes trailing over my face as if he's weighing up my value.

"Miss Lucy Stone."

"Cooper."

There is no missing the way his jaw ticks at my informal use of his name. At the way I don't call him alpha.

Good. He's not my alpha anymore. And I swear to all the silent gods that he'll never be my alpha again.

"Take a seat," Cooper orders, tilting his chin imperiously towards the low bench seat. A folding chair sits across from it, even though the table has been tucked away for the night.

"I'd rather stand."

Cooper gives an indulgent smile, as if I'm an unruly toddler, unreasonably demanding to have my own way.

"You're a smart girl. Up until recently, I would have said you were a loyal wolf."

He sighs, drawing one large hand through his dark hair before giving a mournful shake of his head.

"It turns out you weren't as loyal as I thought. I can only hope you don't disappoint me further."

He pauses, as if waiting for me to respond, but I just stare at him.

I know this male. Perhaps more than anyone else in this pack. I've watched him extract answers and promises. I've seen his false smiles and tasted his lies. And I know nothing annoys him more than being ignored.

The thought has a smirk playing across my lips, and his eyes narrow.

"Let's get to the point then," he hisses, the veneer of the protective alpha slipping away as he stalks towards me.

Fast as an adder, his hand shoots out, fisting the collar of my nightshirt, hauling me towards him until I'm forced to balance on the balls of my feet. The cool night air whispers through the open door at his back, wrapping icy tendrils around my bare legs.

Behind him, Hank stiffens, and I wonder idly how many times this enforcer has seen Cooper Winslow drop the mask and reveal the monster living beneath his skin.

Probably never.

"You can smile all you like, you traitorous little bitch," he hisses. "This joke of a pack is surrounded. Your alpha is taken. No one is coming to protect you. No one is going to come and give their alpha command."

Cooper smiles, and this time it's the pure smile of a predator, sharkish and deadly.

"Soon, Tobias Finch will be dead. The pack bonds will be broken. His shifters will have a very simple choice. They can swear fealty to me. Or they can die. I could really care less."

He lifts one shoulder, as if the matter of our deaths means nothing to him. I shudder, tasting the truth in his every word. His hand tightens on my collar, drawing my face closer to his.

"But you, little she-wolf. You don't get to chose death. You will be joining my pack."

"Unlikely," I say, voice strained.

I mean, obviously I'm not a fan of dying. I have no plans to be a martyr. But I also know I would rather go down fighting than roll over.

Dark eyes glint dangerously, and he dips his face towards my own. Close enough that I can taste the stale scent of chewing gum mixed with his breath.

"You will," he repeats.

Then to my surprise, he releases his hold on my shirt, letting me thud back to the ground, legs nearly crumpling beneath me at the sudden weight.

Cooper straightens, rolling his shoulders back as he pulls his phone from his pocket, the mask of the untouchable alpha attempting to slip back into place. But the cracks are there. Fissures showing the monster beneath.

"Just in case you forgot who holds the power here," he says, almost to himself as he dials a number, then turns the screen to face me.

I blink confusedly at my own image staring back at me before I realise he's video calling a number I don't recognize.

The call answers, showing the flash of a face I've never seen before. A middle-aged male with his features cast in shadows, teeth glinting.

Then the camera turns and I feel my stomach drop, plummeting like a bird shot from the sky, spiralling down, down, down.

"Tobias."

His name slides across my lips, at once a prayer and a curse.

"Oh gods, Tobias."

Tobias stares back at me, eyes widening as Cooper moves behind me, handing the phone to Hank and angling himself so that both of us can be seen by the camera. I flinch when Cooper rests one heavy hand on my shoulder, fingers pressing painfully against my collar bone.

Tobias notices and lunges towards the camera, gold eyes flashing wildly.

"Get your hands off her."

Cooper chuckles, the sound low and menacing, just as I hear the unknown male at the other end of the call say: "Sit back down or he's dead."

Tobias freezes, expression pained as his eyes flick to someone behind the camera, then back to me, and I wonder briefly who the stranger is talking about. And then every thought and question is driven from my mind by the overpowering scent of silver, and the icy feel of metal pressed against my throat.

"One wrong move and she dies," Cooper says to the phone, almost boredly. "Don't think I won't do it."

Truth, my wolf whispers, and I shudder.

Cooper might want me in his pack, but this matters more.

"Now, do your part, Black," Cooper orders, speaking into the phone again, ignoring the horrified expression on Hank's face as his eyes flick between me and Cooper. "Do it quick and make sure she sees. I don't have all night and I need her to report to the others."

I stare, wide-eyed at the screen in front of me, at Tobias' pale face, cast in shadows, mind racing to make sense of what is happening. Black? Black? That can only be Huxley Black. And do what? What do I need to see?

My vision blurs, world spinning so fast that only Cooper's grip at my shoulder and the flat of the silver-coated blade pressed to my throat are keeping me upright. The RV disappears, replaced by a bombardment of images. I fight it, because this is not the time to have a vision. This is not the time to lose control.

But the gods don't care about any of that, and fighting them is futile.

Feather and fur, teeth and claw. Wolves fighting, shots cracking like thunder through the night. Wolves I've never seen before fighting alongside shifters I recognise, eyes flashing in the darkness. My pack. My pack.

A deep emptiness in my chest. The soul-ripping pain of loss. *Tobias*, my wolf keens. *Tobias, Tobias, Tobias*.

A wall of fire, roaring up the trees like spires of a deadly cathedral, roaring to a smoke-filled sky.

And then the dawn, pale and tired. The flash of gold through pine trees. A vengeful, burning sun.

Unleash the power, a voice says.

It's a voice I've heard before, different from my wolf's voice. The voice of visions and truth and knowledge.

Morrigan's voice.

Unleash the power, the voice says again, just as the RV comes back into focus, and I realise this time the words are echoed by my own.

"Enough of that," Cooper hisses in my ear, and my vision sharpens, Tobias' face on the screen coming into focus. "Stop spouting nonsense." Then to the phone: "Do it, Black."

There's a metallic clicking sound and Tobias' eyes go wide, true fear carving itself into his features. His golden eyes burn, staring straight into mine through the screen, and for a moment it's as if he's right in front of me. I swear I can feel him, smell him. Like his soul is brushing up against my own, comforting me.

Saying goodbye.

I could almost wrap myself up in his chocolate, sage and pine scent.

Close your eyes, the voice whispers, and I obey, lashes heavy with tears.

I obey, just before a sound like thunder cracks through the phone's speaker, ripping through my soul and tearing a crater into my heart.

Chapter 18

Cody Winslow

The Castle looms ahead, its silhouette stark against the moonlit sky.

I've never liked the Castle. It's the sort of place kids come to get stoned and drunk and tell ghost stories. The place you would bring a date just to have her clinging to your arm.

Sure, I've been here once or twice with guys from the football team. I've even climbed up the rusted pipes to the decaying second floor on a dare. But I sure never felt the need to spray-paint my own tag here. It's not the sort of place I'd want to leave a mark.

"Quiet as you can," my mom whispers warningly beside my shoulder, "he's probably armed."

Thanks for the pro-tip, mom. I press my lips together, thankful for the darkness masking my ill-timed amusement.

Wordlessly, I move forward, steps as soundless as if I was in wolf form. Mom and Anton follow behind me, silent as shadows. We're still not close enough to see into the gaping windows, but I'm certain

Tobias is in there. I know if I reached out, I could speak to him mind to mind.

We had talked about my doing just that on the car ride here, but then decided against it. Tobias has no reason to trust me. For all he knows, I could be part of whatever plan dad and Huxley Black have concocted. My talking to him through the pack link isn't going to do any good.

That's okay though, because I'll show him. Anton and I, we'll take out Huxley Black and then I'll show Tobias I'm loyal. That I'm sorry. I'll spend the rest of my life showing him, if that's what it takes.

Even if he never accepts me back into the pack.

I flare my nostrils, drawing in the cool night air, wishing I had Jason's excellent sense of smell. If he were here, he would already know exactly who was in that building.

"There they are," Anton breaths, and I pull up short, eyes straining to make out the figures barely visible through the windows.

One is standing with his back to me, the other sitting slumped against a wall, face bathed in a faint blue light that casts his features in stark relief. Tobias, I realise, though I wonder at the look of stunned horror on his face.

"He's just sitting there," I muse, brow furrowing as I realise the one with his back to us must be Huxley Black. "Why is Tobias just sitting there?"

I've seen Tobias' wolf fight before. The animal is unstoppable. Why hasn't he attacked or used his born alpha command?

The next moments happen so fast.

Huxley Black lifts one hand, whatever he's holding largely obscured by his body, the movement followed by the crack of thunder. Only, it's not thunder, because the sound is coming from inside the old hydro-plant. And Tobias.

Tobias.

Oh, gods, Tobias.

A keening wail erupts, cutting through the night air, piercing the roaring of the blood in my ears, the sound as much wolf as man. Still, I recognise that voice, full of pain and grief.

That's when I see him. Mr Vance, Tobias' grandfather, tied up in the shadowed corner of the derelict building, screaming his fury at Huxley Black.

Beside me, Anton lets out an enraged snarl, shifting so quickly, his black enforcer uniform is left in shreds beside me. He's halfway to the building before my mind can process what is happening, and then I'm shifting too, teeth bared, racing after him.

I'm vaguely aware of the sound of mom shifting and following after me. Of the scent of blood and silver and gunpowder carrying over to us on a gentle night breeze. It's the sort of summer breeze that should be reserved for lovers and romantic moonlit walks. It shouldn't be the carrier of failure and death. But it is.

My legs burn, rage propelling me forward. Rage, and some indefinable power that pulses through my body. Something golden and warm and alive.

Tobias, my wolf whispers, curling around the golden threads protectively, even as their energy radiates through me.

Power. So much power.

I leap through one of the glassless windows of the ruin, claws scraping across the packed earth floor as I scramble to regain my footing. The sounds of snarling and snapping teeth echo off the walls, filling the empty space, but I ignore it. My sole focus is on the old male in the corner, smelling of gunpowder and tears and pain.

Cody, he says through the pack bond, and even though that one word is weighted with distrust and sadness, the comfort of feeling the pack bond is so visceral that my wolf wants to whimper in relief.

Pack. My wolf assures me. *Pack.*

Without wasting any time, I tear into the ropes, biting and pulling. A knife would be better, but I don't have time for that. Instinct tells me that I need to move quickly.

Get him free, my wolf demands. *Now. Now. Now.*

"Get out of here," Mr. Vance says, his voice harsh and raw. "He's got this whole thing rigged up with explosives."

I snarl back my reply, doubling down on my efforts until I'm sure my gums will be bleeding. When the first rope snaps free, I nearly whimper with relief. I gnaw through a second, then Mr. Vance's hands come free, tugging at the knots with surprising agility.

The instant the last of the ropes fall away, Mr. Vance is springing from the chair, sprinting across the room with a speed that would be impossible for someone his age, if he wasn't a shifter. Ignoring the two wolves locked in a death-match in the middle of the room, he kneels at Tobias' side, covering his grandson's body with his own, as if he can protect him from the world.

"I'm sorry," he croaks, "I'm sorry, I'm sorry, I'm sorry."

I look away, unable to bear the sight of his shaking shoulders, wishing I could block out the sound of his racking sobs. Even worse is the sight of Tobias. The great born alpha.

Gone.

All that is left is the shell of his human form, looking fragile as a child.

I turn to watch Anton and Huxley fight, grey and red wolves blurring, teeth snapping, fur flying. My muscles bunch as I prepare to join the fray, but mom nudges me on the shoulder and I meet mom's wolfish eyes, her pale blue gaze mirroring my own.

It's a strange feeling, not being able to speak to her mind to mind. And yet it doesn't bother me as much as it should, not when I can feel the golden tendrils of my pack growing and blooming behind my ribcage. Grief and love and power singing a glorious song in my blood.

Even without words, I can tell mom wants me to stay back. To let Anton handle this. But she doesn't understand.

Fight, my wolf demands, and I surge forward, ready to answer my own instinct – only to snap my head back when a black wolf darts in front of me, joining the fray before I can. Mr Vance.

The sight of the black wolf sends a pang to my chest. How many times had I run alongside Jamison and his brother?

Mom nudges at my shoulder again, pushing me away protectively, and this time I give in. If I joined now, I would only get in the way. Already Anton's grey wolf has the red wolf pinned on his back. The black wolf lunges just as the red wolf starts to kick free, the black wolf's teeth clasping around the red wolf's throat, holding him in place.

I close my eyes. Huxley Black deserves everything he is getting, but I don't want to watch it. Maybe I am soft, like dad always said. Maybe I'm not the male I should be.

Instead, I pad over towards Tobias, the red wolf's death cries a sickening song at my back. The sound fades away, too quickly, and yet not quick enough. I tilt my head back, filling the new silence with wolf song.

With the song of mourning.

A hand rests heavy on my shoulder, and I look over to see my mom in her human form, her pale face streaked with tears, the tracks silver in the moonlight.

"We need to get to the Liberty pack territory. There isn't much time."

I nod. She's right. Whatever dad had planned, this was only part of it.

I look back down at Tobias. Whatever differences he and I had, I can't even remember them now. They weren't important. None of it was important.

I betrayed the pack. I betrayed Tobias.

And now Tobias is dead, and I was too late to stop it.

I let out a shuddering breath, then shift into my human form, embracing the momentary relief of physical pain.

"We're taking him with us," I say resolutely, bending to gather Tobias up in my arms.

Mom's mouth thins, worry written on her face, but she doesn't argue.

I stumble a little under the weight of him. He's heavier than he looks, like every inch of him is solid muscle, and I momentarily question whether I'll be able to make it back to the car with him, shifter strength and all.

But then a fire courses through me, burning through my chest, filling my limbs with renewed strength. The feeling is at odds with the heavy grief settling in my stomach, clouding my vision. A strange juxtaposition of power and sorrow, light and dark.

I take a deep breath, straightening my shoulders before beginning the trek back to the car.

I might have failed Tobias. But gods help me, I will not let my dad take his pack. And I will bring Tobias home.

Chapter 19

Tobias Finch

I had forgotten how much silver bullets burn.

You would think it's the sort of thing someone would remember, but I'm pretty sure my brain blocked out the memory of it until this very moment.

It's a strange thought to have when dying.

Because I'm most certainly dying. The pain is quickly being replaced by darkness, an insidious black dimming the edges of my vision, deafening my ears, numbing my limbs.

Grandpa's shouts, Lucy's cries through the phone, the distant snarling of wolves, the lingering ringing of gunshot – it all blends and fades, as if it's a television in another room and someone has turned the volume down.

Embrace the power.

Lucy's words echo in the growing silence as I recall the eery image of her staring at me with white eyes. The eyes of a seer, I realise.

Embrace the power.

I don't know what it means. I don't know what any of this means.

I'm adrift, floating, laying on the wooden deck of that sailboat my parents rented in Cape Cod. I'm flying, careening through the air off the horns of a bull while storm-grey eyes watch on. The world spins, spiralling as Goliath's face stares down at me in the fighting ring. And then I'm back at Blackwater, red-stained snow stretching in front of me, like a list of my wrongdoings addressed to the shifter gods.

Power, my wolf urges, but even his voice is weak. *Power*.

And then I feel it.

I don't know what it is, but it's familiar. At once warm and dangerous. Beautiful and deadly. It feels like wind and freedom and fire and sunrise. My wolf basks in it, delighting in the glorious chaos.

I should be afraid of it, my fading instinct warns. I'm supposed to be afraid of it.

But I'm already dying, so what point is there in fear?

I reach for it, stretching the last bits of my consciousness towards the wild glow, letting golden heat envelop me. It coils around me protectively, pulling me gently along as my wolf sings, his power pulsing and growing with every brush of light.

Maybe this is death? But if it is, it feels an awful lot like life. Only, more.

It tugs me along, fracturing me along its golden threads. It should hurt, being pulled apart like this, but it doesn't.

And then suddenly, darkness fades away, giving way to colour and light and sound and feel and scent.

I'm soaring above Liberty pack territory, wind singing through my feathers as my eyes scan the moonlit forest for intruders, cataloguing every single black-clad figure surrounding the tents and RVs…

I'm in our RV, looking down at Jason, Ross and a strange male I've never seen before. My hands are balled into fists at my sides as I resist the urge to shift into my bear form and tear the stranger apart. Only the fact that he's got a gun pointed at Ross keeps me in my skin…

I'm outside a tent, standing back-to-back with Samson as we face down two Clear Creek enforcers, the need to shift and race to Tania almost overpowering. I plaster a bored look on my face as I lock eyes with the enforcer, letting him see that I'm not intimidated by his presence…

I'm staring up at Cooper Winslow through blurred vision, pain and fury warring for dominance in my chest…

Teeth sink into my side, Huxley Black's red wolf making one last move to get the upper hand. My bones ache with age and he's stronger. But I'm angrier. My wolf lurches free, spinning and dodging, teeth snapping until my own jaws are locking around his throat, pinning him to the ground…

I'm back in the derelict hydro station, staring down at my own lifeless body, paws red with blood, a wolfish whimper dying in my throat…

I reach along each golden tendril, grasping tight to each bond connecting me to each of my pack mates, relishing the feeling of rightness in each connection.

Power, my wolf sings, his voice stronger and mingling with my own. *Unleash the power.*

I think of Lucy's words as I let the power wash over me. I can feel it growing, expanding, until each golden tendril becomes a rope, strong and unbreakable. I let it grow until it is overflowing, pushing warmth and strength along the bonds into each of my pack mates.

Power.

This time the thought is as much my wolf's as my own, as if whatever separation existed between us has been washed away by the golden light.

Power.

I let it flow into them all. To my pack. I might be dying, but I can give them this last parting gift. I let myself be the conduit and creator.

Because from what I can see, they are going to need it. Every last bit.

Chapter 20

Lucy Stone

Tobias Finch is dead.

The thought circles on repeat in my head, the image of his fallen form looping mercilessly as I stare into space, only vaguely aware of Cooper Winslow's presence.

"Are you listening to me, female?" Cooper snaps, shaking me roughly by the shoulder.

I blink up at him, trying to focus through the tears, the harsh planes of his face blurring in front of me.

He gives an exasperated sigh, as if the sight of my distress is an inconvenience to him.

"You are going to go out there, gather up your pack, and let them know the terms. They can swear fealty to me, or they will die. "

The words rattle around in my consciousness, but I'm unable to make any sense of them. Our pack can't swear fealty to Cooper Winslow. They're already bound. Bound to Tobias. Bound to *me.*

"You're outnumbered," Cooper continues coolly. "We're armed. Trained. With more experience fighting than you have breathing the air on this earth. You know that as well as I do. Between the Clear Creek enforcers and Huxley's little additions, you pups don't stand a chance."

His words lace the space between us with bitter-sweet truth, settling heavy with the misery already twisting behind my ribs.

"So, what will it be, little she-wolf? Will you put aside your pride for the good of your pack? Encourage them to join without bloodshed? Or will you have them join your mate?"

My mate.

Something about hearing those words from Cooper's lips tears at the gaping wound in the place my heart used to be. I glare up at him, baring my teeth, my wolf rising to the surface, clawing to break free. She is all pride. All rage and fury.

She would rather die than give in to this male.

But even she is not willing to risk her pack.

Patience, I urge her. *Patience*.

But even I don't believe there is anything worth being patient for. The battle was lost before it even began, and there is no prince coming to rescue us. No knight in shining armour. We were just foolish children, thinking we could create something beautiful. Believing that the world wasn't waiting to tear it all down.

I tilt my chin up and swallow down my pride.

"I'll go with you," I tell him, my voice surprisingly steady despite the burning behind my eyes.

I blink away the tears, drying my eyes with the back of my hand. I don't want to face my pack with tears on my cheeks. I don't want them to see this weakness.

"Good." Cooper claps one hand on my shoulder, then nods in the direction of the room where Tania and Summer are hiding at the back of the RV, his nostrils flaring. "Tell the others to join us. I'll have every single shifter outside in five minutes."

Panic surges up the pack link at Cooper's words, and I can practically taste Tania and Summer's fear.

It'll be okay, I assure them through the pack bond. But I can taste the lie in the words. There is no way this will be okay for any of us.

He'll kill them, Tania responds, her silent plea pulsing through me. *He'll kill Tyrone and Samson.*

I press my hand to my chest, attempting to ease the building ache there.

"We'll be outside in five," I tell him. "Give us a moment to get dressed."

I look pointedly down at my scantily clad figure and bare feet.

Cooper grunts in reluctant agreement, before exiting the RV, Hank on his heels. There is no missing the almost apologetic, mournful look Hank gives me as he closes the door behind him. I meet it with a blank stare. I don't want his sympathy. I hope he burns with shame.

The moment Cooper and Hank leave, Tania and Summer are at my sides, pressing against me, wrapping me up in their arms, the feeling of sorrow and concern washing over me.

"I'm fine," I lie, shoving them off. "I'll be fine."

"Oh, shut up," Summer sniffs noisily, attempting to brush the tears from her cheeks. It's a futile gesture, since they flow in an endless torrent. "You don't have to be brave. Not now. We know what he did. We heard everything."

These last words fracture with her sobs, and she presses her forehead to my shoulder. I squeeze my own eyes shut, gritting my teeth against the building ache behind my ribcage.

I need to be strong. I need to be strong for my pack.

"You do what you need to do," Tania whispers, pressing her cheek against my own. "Be strong if that is easier. Cry later. We're here for you either way." She gives Summer a pointed look.

The kindness of her words is almost as painful as Summer's tears, but I'm grateful for them nonetheless.

"I think I'll go get ready," I say, shoving out of their grasp. "I have to warn the pack."

FIVE MINUTES later and I'm climbing out of our RV, each step measured, eyes dry, Summer and Tania at my heels.

Cooper waits in the centre of the clearing where each member of the Liberty pack is gathered, surrounded by black-clad Clear Creek enforcers and a motley collection of plaid-wearing enforcers that I don't recognise. Huxley's lackeys, presumably, since only the Clear Creek enforcers are armed.

I barely give them a passing glance. I barely even look at Cooper. Or at my dad standing beside him.

No, my attention is fixed solely on my pack. On the upturned faces of the shifters who put their trust in Tobias Finch. Who, for some unfathomable reason, are now putting their trust in me.

And I've let them down.

I take in their faces.

Danny's expressive features twisted in agony, fists clenched at his side, towering over everyone except for Orrin.

Jason's drawn expression, the dark circles rimming reddened eyes as he keeps Ross protectively at his side.

Tyrone's green eyes glittering dangerously despite his mask of calm.

Red's sneer of disgust as he eyes the enforcers, his cat ear's twitching irritably.

Worst of all is Orrin's tear-stained face, the dampness of his scarred cheeks reflecting in the moonlight.

"Good of you to finally join us," Cooper drawls, hands tucked with false casualness into his pockets. "I've just been giving your pack here a little update on what's happened with Tobias. Such a tragedy." Cooper shakes his head, giving a little tsking sound. "But, with every loss, there is opportunity…"

I look away from him, his words getting swallowed up in the roaring in my ears as I scan the crowd in front of me. And that's when I realise several faces are missing.

Anton isn't there among the enforcers, despite being my father's protégé and one of the strongest males in the pack. Several of our pack are missing too. Arlo, Theo and – to my surprise – Aires.

When I reach out, I can feel Arlo and Theo through the bond, circling high above us in the night sky. Watching. Waiting. My connection with Aires is fainter, muted, tasting strangely of smoke and smouldering embers.

"…a choice to make…"

Cooper's voice cuts through my thoughts, the familiar tone grating.

"…join the Clear Creek pack willingly…"

I squeeze my eyes shut, casting one final desperate prayer out to Morrigan. There must be something. Something. Some way around this.

And that is when it dawns on me.

My eyes fly open, landing instinctively on Jason.

The pack bond, I say over the link, projecting my thoughts so that the entire Liberty pack can hear, but looking right at Jason. *How is the pack bond still in place?*

It should have been broken with Tobias' death.

For a moment, hope flutters wildly in my chest, like a frantic winged beast ready to break free at any cost. Tobias is alive. There can't be any other explanation.

Jason gives me a pitying look.

The bond is still in place because you're the alpha, he explains patiently. *Somehow, you became the alpha alongside Tobias. We told you this.*

They did, I realise. They all did, and I had ignored them. Brushed it off. It hasn't seemed like a label I had any right to.

And obviously you're still the alpha, Jason continues carefully, while somehow managing to sound a just little condescending. Like this was something I really should have figured out by now.

Alpha, Danny agrees stoically, his voice clear through the pack bond despite his trembling lips.

Alpha. Hamish narrows his eyes at me expectantly, his fingertips trailing over what look like fresh tattoos etched on his knuckles.

Alpha. Red gives me a reluctant nod, jaw ticking as his gaze flicks back to the surrounding enforcers.

"… an easy choice," Cooper drawls. "One that I think you'll find Miss Stone agrees with. Don't you Lucy?"

Cooper's teeth glint as he smiles, his eyes narrowing on me as he waits expectantly for my answer. For me to assure my pack that joining with Clear Creek is the best choice. The safest choice.

I shake my head, lips curving down into a frown. I can't betray my pack like that. I won't. And this isn't just about pride.

I stare at Cooper, letting myself see him, really see him. Opening myself up as much as possible to the very nature of him.

Giving up my pack to him would be the worst sort of betrayal. Not just to Tobias. Not just to myself. But to every soul that I would give into this monster's keeping. Because an alpha – a true alpha – would never take a pack by force. A true alpha would protect their shifters with their dying breath. A true alpha would never harm the shifters under their care.

And Cooper Winslow – he is not a true alpha.

But I am.

Warmth coils in me, golden and soothing, feeling like chocolate and sage and pine and love. My gift mixing with something else. Something other. Something powerful. Something that reminds me so much of Tobias, I feel tears pricking the backs of my eyes.

I take a steeling breath, letting the power fill me up as I meet the eyes of my pack. I watch as they straighten, eyes glinting with the same surge of power that I'm feeling.

Do we fight? I ask them.

Because it's their choice.

Almost as one, they nod, murmurs of agreement carrying across the pack bond. A bond that somehow seems stronger than it did moments before, pulsing with warmth and light. Golden and hopeful as the morning sun.

We fight, they agree. *We will fight.*

I open my mouth, ready to tell Cooper exactly where he can put his offer, when Arlo's voice calls across the pack bond.

Someone is coming, Arlo says, voice full of alarm. *At least ten shifters are at the edge of our territory to the south. Plus there's a strange vehicle coming up the main road.*

My heart sinks, the fire kindling in my chest banking. It's likely the rest of the Clear Creek enforcers and Cooper's allies. I should have known he wouldn't be taking any chances. Not with how hungry for power he is.

I've got another fifteen over here, Theo interjects. *They've just entered our territory from the north.*

Hope sputters, like a fire doused in water.

They're moving fast, Theo adds. *But they don't look like the others, this group here. They're wearing brown. And…* he pauses, a cacophony of shock, distrust and anger rushing across the bond.

And what? I ask impatiently.

Because I've got an angry Cooper Winslow staring at me and a pack to protect. We don't have time for hesitation.

And Aires is leading them.

Chapter 21

Cody Winslow

"Turn here," I tell mom, pointing to the gravel road ahead, half hidden by overgrown pines. "It's just up this way. Not far now."

"I figured as much," she says with a grimace. "I can feel them."

"Uh, feel them?" I tilt my head, looking at her with confusion.

She gives an exasperated sigh, frowning as she casts a glance in her rear-view mirror to where Anton sits beside Mr Vance. Mr Vance's lined, weathered face is contorted with rage and despair as he cradles Tobias' lifeless form, and I turn away, unable to look at either of them for long.

"The pack," she explains, turning her attention back to the road. "The Clear Creek pack."

"Oh."

That one word sits heavy between us, nearly drowned out by the crunching of gravel under tires. I'm starting to realise there is a lot I don't know.

"I'm an alpha," she says, chin lifting almost imperceptibly. "Just as much as Cooper."

She pauses, giving me an apologetic look, fingers tapping on the steering wheel.

"I know this is all a lot to take in, and I'm sorry. But it's best you know now. Because you need to understand. Your dad and I, we're true mates."

I nod because that is at least one thing I do know.

"So, if your dad is an alpha, I'm an alpha too. Not just by name. Not even by the blood bond. But because our very souls are linked. And it's not like human royalty. I'm not the queen to his king, or the first lady to his president. I am the president. And so is he. Both of us. Equally."

My brow furrows, confusion warring with doubt in my mind. Dad has never told me this before. In fact, he's always explained that only male shifters could be alphas. That it was the nature of things.

"And… if dad stepped down, or was replaced? Challenged?" I say tentatively. "Then what would happen to you?"

"I would be alpha. Until I was replaced," she explains simply.

"So, you can feel the pack, just like he can?"

Mom nods grimly, reaching to flick off the car headlights.

"And I can command them. Just like he can."

The car slows, creeping along the unlit gravel road. Even in the darkness, I know this road. Know that we are probably only five minutes from the edge of Liberty pack territory.

I stare out the window in silence, watching the trees pass, heart thudding with each minute that brings us closer. My wolf is pacing, anxious to get to his pack. Uncaring that he probably won't be welcome back.

"Why didn't you ever say anything?" I finally ask. "Why didn't dad?"

"At first, I was in love. You haven't felt it yet, the pull of the mate bond. But when you do, you'll understand. You'll do anything to make that person happy. Give them anything. Your dad needed to rule, to lead. I didn't. I was happy to let him, because it made him happy. And then I got pregnant."

She pauses, lifting one hand from the steering wheel to rub at her sternum, as if to erase some invisible ache.

"And then I lost them. Your brothers and sisters. Year after year. I couldn't think around the pain."

I nod, lump forming in my throat. I don't know how many she lost before and after my birth. I just know she always called me her little miracle. The weight of those absent siblings has sat heavy on my shoulders for as long as I can remember.

And I remember the dark times, when mom would hardly leave her room. *She's resting. She's sick*, dad would explain. *Don't bother your mom with that. Wait until she's better.*

"It took almost losing you for me to realise how wrong I was. How selfish I was."

"Mom, you aren't selfish," I argue. "You were sick."

"I was depressed," she concedes. "But then I got better. I got better, and I saw what your dad was doing, the way he was leading. I saw how he was raising you. How he was training his enforcers."

Her eyes flick back to Anton again, and I hear his grunt of acknowledgement.

"But I took the path of least resistance and didn't challenge him. It was selfish. I let the pack down, and I almost paid the ultimate price for my selfishness."

The road snakes and winds, the increase in elevation letting me know we are almost there. Almost at Liberty pack territory. My wolf is doing cartwheels, clawing to break free, to join his pack. Completely ignorant of the building sense of dread coiling in my gut.

"What price?" I ask, fisting my hands in my lap.

"You," she says simply, the faintest trace of a smile ghosting her lips.

I know it should give me a sense of satisfaction. Instead, an all too familiar weight settles on my shoulders with that one word.

The burden has always been on me. It was up to me to smile and laugh to bring mom out of the darkness. It was me who would strive to be the best football player, to make mom and dad proud. It was me who trained every day to be alpha, to be a leader, to protect my pack.

And I failed. Miserably.

"You're going to challenge Cooper?" Anton asks, his voice almost a whisper. Like he's afraid that even now, someone will overhear and brand him a traitor. "You're going to take the pack?"

Mom shakes her head, knuckles blanching as she grips the wheel, manoeuvring the car up the winding gravel road.

"No, Anton. I'm not going to challenge him."

"Here. You should stop here," I say, interrupting mom to point to the shoulder at the side of the road. "Any closer and they'll hear the car."

Mom pulls over, killing the engine.

"I'm not challenging Cooper, or taking the pack from him. I'm just stepping up and taking what was mine to begin with. I'm doing what I should have done years ago."

She turns to give me and Anton a meaningful look, then adds: "I'm being an alpha."

I DEBATE INTERNALLY for a long moment before deciding to move Tobias from the backseat of the car, settling him at the base of a large pine tree. It feels right, somehow, knowing that he is at least on Liberty pack territory. But still feels wrong leaving him behind.

"I really should bring him with us," I muse, staring down at him.

Lifting him from the car, it was easy to pretend that he was just sleeping. Knocked unconscious or something. Looking at him now, it's hard to believe he's really gone. I half expect him to wake up at any moment. To shift into his golden wolf and attack me. Put me in my place for betraying my pack.

Honestly, I would deserve it.

If I lived through it, maybe he'd forgive me.

My chest constricts at the thought. I'll never have the chance to tell him how sorry I am.

"You know we can't bring him," mom says, voice gentle despite the tinge of urgency. "We need to shift and run. We're running out of time."

"Yah. I know."

"We'll come back for him," Anton assures me, resting one hand on my shoulder. "I promise."

I give my alpha one last lingering look before shucking off my clothes, getting ready to shift for the second time tonight. My body shudders at the thought of shifting again so soon, muscles quivering with fatigue.

But now is not the time to rest. Now is the time to fight. Because I might not be able to apologise to Tobias, but I can show the silent watching gods that I am willing to do anything to make this right.

"Ready?" mom asks, just as Anton lifts one hand to his ear, staring intently into the forest.

"Wait," he says, dropping his voice to a whisper. "I hear something."

"What is it?" I ask, lowering my voice as well, shirt still clutched in my hands.

He lifts one finger to his lips, cocking his head. I follow his example, straining my ears.

At first, all I can hear are the shallow sounds of my own breath, the frantic thudding of my heart. And then I hear it. So faint it could be the scratching of mice in the underbrush, or the burrowing of a squirrel in its den. But then it gets louder. Closer.

The distinctive sound of multiple feet thudding against the earth, crackling dry leaves and twigs. The panting huffs of breath.

Wolves.

My body tenses instinctively, fingers curling into claws as my body gets ready to shift.

Beside me, mom lifts her head, nostrils flaring to draw in the faint night breeze. Her eyes widen, fist clenching against her chest.

I step forward, ready to place myself in front of her. In front of Anton. So that I can take the brunt of whatever danger is heading our way.

"Wait," mom says, lifting one hand to stop me. "Wait."

I'm about to ask her why when two wolves emerge from the shadowed tree-line, followed by several more. Eyes glowing in ranges of yellows and blues and ambers, coats glistening in the moonlight. They eye us warily, circling, fangs bared, hackles rising.

"Wait," mom says again. I obey her, even though every part of my body wants to shift and fight.

And then two more wolves emerge, a sleek, snowy white female and behind her, a large male. Every single wolf surrounding us turns their attention on them.

There is something familiar about the female, but before I can place what it is, the male behind her slinks from the shadows. He's at least a head taller than every other wolf present – probably as big as Jamison and almost the same size as Tobias' wolf. Moonlight glints off brown fur, bits of white glistening the only thing belying his age.

"Who are you?" I ask, looking between the female and the large male.

"Rachel," mom breathes, pushing past me with surprising strength, before kneeling down to wrap her arms around the white wolf's neck.

"Mom," Anton chokes out.

I turn to look at him, his face pale as the moon, his bare feet rooted to the earth as he stares at the wolf. Like she is a spirit-wolf instead of flesh and fur.

"Mom," he says again, pressing one hand to his throat.

The pale wolf whines, shrugging out of my mom's embrace, before trotting tentatively towards Anton. She looks up at him, blue eyes pleading, then shifts.

The shift is effortless and I'm instantly reminded of Lucy. She's the only other wolf I've met who can move between her animal and human form with that amount of ease, like their skin is no more than water. Like there is no barrier between the animal and the person. None of the internal disagreement that usually plagues our kind.

"Anton," the woman – Rachel – says, stretching up to cradle Anton's cheek in the palm of one trembling hand. "By all the gods, Anton."

Anton squeezes his eyes shut, lips quavering with restrained emotion as he presses his own hand over hers.

"I'm so sorry, but we need to move," my mom says, looking from Anton and his mother to the pack of wolves surrounding us. "We don't have much time. I need to get to Cooper if we're going to prevent any more bloodshed."

Rachel gives a pained groan of acknowledgement before tearing her gaze away from her son.

"You're right," she says, sorrow lining her face. A face that looks eerily like Lucy's. "Time is running out." She cocks her head, eyes going white and glassy for a long moment before refocusing, then adds: "But blood will be shed regardless."

Mr Vance gives a grunt of agreement, as if this announcement pleases him. I had almost forgotten he was there, kneeling beside Tobias' prone form like a dark shadow.

"I will run with you," he announces gruffly, rising unsteadily to his feet.

He unbuttons his shirt, revealing a patchwork of cuts and bruises and I wince at the sight of them, at the record of what he must have endured at Huxley Black's hands.

He nods at Tobias' body, then looks at me.

"You will stay with him," he says, the tone of his voice brooking no argument. "You will keep a vigil."

"No, he runs with us," mom argues, folding her arms over her chest. "We're safer together."

I look between the pair of them, then down at Tobias. So fragile and vulnerable in his human form. So alone.

He shouldn't have to be alone.

"I'll stay," I agree, my wolf settling at the rightness of the decision.

Mom opens her mouth to protest, but I raise one hand.

"No, it's alright mom," I assure her.

I let myself be talked out of doing what was right once by my dad, and the consequences were disastrous. I'm not going to let this happen again. No matter how good my mom's intentions are.

"This is where I am supposed to be," I tell her, and the truth of those words settle over me, warm as a blanket against the night chill.

This is my place. At my alpha's side. Even in death.

Chapter 22

Jason Alp

I've spent my whole life living in varying states of fear.

Usually, it's just a low-lying anxiety. The drive to make my family happy. Make my friends happy. Make my pack happy.

Shit, I even get anxious about trying to make complete strangers happy.

Sometimes, I get to experience a more acute fear. You know, just to change things up. Like when your alpha decides to lose his mind and threatens to rip your throat out. Or when your true mate accidentally shoots you.

You could say that fear and I are close companions. The best of besties.

And somehow, despite the familiarity of this emotion, I have never been more terrified in my entire life than I am right now in this moment. Because for the first time, I'm afraid for someone else.

No, not just someone else. I'm afraid for Ross. My mate.

"You can join the Clear Creek pack willingly. Or you can die. One by one. It's an easy choice. One that I think you'll find Miss Stone agrees with. Don't you Lucy?"

Alpha Winslow's voice rings out over the crowd, echoing around the clearing, tainting even the surrounding trees with its syrupy vitriol. I resist the urge to shudder, focusing on keeping my eyes down.

Don't let him notice me. Don't let him notice me.

Even as I think this, I'm angling myself in front of Ross, attempting to shield him from Cooper's view with my own body.

I cast a surreptitious glance in Lucy's direction. Her face is pale, eyes wide and rimmed in red, as if she's been crying. She doesn't respond to Cooper's question, instead cocking her head to the side in that way she does whenever she's speaking through the pack link.

Do we fight? she asks, her question reaching out to every member of the Liberty pack. *Do we fight?*

I shiver, hating the answer.

We fight, I say, my voice joining with the silent calls of my pack, our song for blood ringing out over the pack bond.

Because what other option is there? The Clear Creek pack would never let me claim Ross as my mate.

Actually, I doubt alpha Winslow would let Ross walk away from this with his life. He's a human. He shouldn't know about shifters, about our world. Cooper wouldn't take the risk of Ross saying something and outing our kind.

We will fight, I say again, the silent words rubbing against every natural instinct. Because the alternative is a life without Ross. And that would destroy me.

Someone is coming, Arlo tells us through the pack link. *At least ten shifters are at the edge of our territory to the south. Plus, there's a strange vehicle coming up the main road.*

Lucy's face falls.

"Answer me, Miss Stone," Cooper rumbles, but Lucy doesn't seem to hear. All her focus seems to be inward, on the messages Arlo and Theo are bombarding us with.

I've got another fifteen over here, Theo says. *They've just entered our territory from the north. They're moving fast. But they don't look like the others, this group here. They're wearing brown. And...*

"Answer him Lucy," Jeb barks, and I flinch instinctively at the harsh tone.

And what? Lucy asks Theo over the link, ignoring both the alpha and her dad.

And Aires is leading them, Theo admits.

"That's it," Cooper announces, the words snapping out like a whip. "No more games."

He lifts one hand, pointing a finger in my direction. No, not in my direction, I realise with horror. At Ross.

"Nate, take the human. He can be our first example. He shouldn't be here anyway."

Cooper's voice sounds almost bored, but there is a steely glint in his eyes and I can feel the rage rolling off of him in waves. My wolf whimpers at the feel of it, but I force myself to lift my chin, to meet his eyes with my own as I push Ross behind me. Attempting to shield his body with my own.

"No," I say, but the word breaks on my tongue, feeling heavy as the impossible cries for help in a nightmare. I square my shoulders, gritting my teeth against the fear. "You're not touching my mate."

"Mate?" I hear Ross whisper from behind me, the feeling of his surprise and confusion offering a momentary respite from the fear.

Oh yah. I guess I hadn't told him that little detail when I was explaining the whole wolf shifter thing.

Cooper gives a derisive snort, waving one hand dismissively.

"Move, Jason. Let Nate have the human. I don't want to have to hurt you."

I nearly roll my eyes at that because, of course he doesn't want to hurt me. He might not have given me much notice when I was part of the Clear Creek pack, but every pack needs an omega. With me gone, there would be an imbalance. Cooper would never admit it, but he needs me.

"No," I say again, and this time I'm surprised at the thready determination in my voice.

"Are you challenging me?" Cooper drawls, dark amusement coating the rage. "An omega? Challenging an alpha?"

Shit. This is really not how I saw this going. Why isn't Lucy doing something? Why isn't the rest of the pack stepping up here? I can't challenge an alpha.

We did it once before, my wolf reminds me quietly.

Even now the logical, calculating, animal can't seem relinquish his obsession with facts. Like a retriever with a ball, dutifully collecting up all the information and delivering it to my feet.

We challenged Tobias, my wolf continues. Like I could possibly have forgotten that terrifying moment.

But that was different. Tobias likes me. Cooper barely tolerates me. And Lucy stepped in to save me.

I stare at Cooper. At his dark eyes narrowed in on me with wolfish intensity. I feel his aggression and his confidence. There isn't a doubt in his mind that he'll be able to defeat me. My defiance is little more than an annoyance in his eyes.

I feel Ross at my back. The pain from the injuries his own father inflicted on him second only to the fear and confusion about what is going on. And beneath that, the warm hues of affection. Gratitude.

Is that for me?

My heart stutters and a different type of warmth fills my chest. Similar to the feelings I'm getting from Ross, but stronger. Like liquid gold, or honey warmed in the sun. It's sweeter than any praise I've ever received from my alpha, and my wolf wants to bask in it.

"Yes," I say, meeting Cooper's eyes with my own. "I guess I am challenging you."

The feeling of golden warmth grows stronger, trickling down my limbs, filling every ounce of me with warmth and strength and comfort. It reminds me strangely of Tobias, of the safety of being near my alpha.

I could almost smile at the answering look of disbelief on Cooper's face. Because for once in my life, I feel brave. Strong. Like maybe I could fight an alpha and win.

I flash Cooper a toothy grin as my wolf surges joyfully to the surface.

Clearly, I've lost my mind.

Chapter 23

Lucy Stone

I stare in stunned disbelief as Jason faces off against alpha Winslow, the human male tucked at his back.

I had been so caught up in speaking with Arlo and Theo, with trying to figure out the best plan of attack, that I had completely missed the drama unfolding in the clearing in front of me. Until it was too late to intervene.

"Yes," Jason says, his voice uncharacteristically steady. "I guess I am challenging you."

Cooper gapes with an incredulity that mirrors my own feelings. Because an omega challenging an alpha is completely unheard of. No, not just unheard of. Suicidal.

I shake my head, opening my mouth to object, but feel a hand tighten on my shoulder. I look up at Hank's pained expression.

"You can't intervene," he tells me, keeping his voice low. "You know that. It's illegal to intervene in an alpha challenge."

"He'll kill him," I hiss. "He'll kill Jason."

Hank's lips press together in a frown, jaw ticking. It's clear he likes the idea of Jason getting hurt as little as I do.

"You know the rules."

I do. I know the rules. Better than anyone, even better Cody. Because he might have been trained to be an alpha, tucked safely in his daddy's office, but I was the shadow in the dark, watching justice be served. And even before that, I was the child at the table, easily ignored as I listened to my dad and Cooper talk and plan.

My eyes land on Jason. He must have completely lost his mind, because he's smiling, staring at Cooper with an almost maniacal confidence, stripping off his clothes as he gets ready to shift.

"He's really doing it," I whisper, dread snaking its icy tendrils behind my ribs. "Morrigan's heart, he's really doing it."

"Gods above," I hear Orrin rumble as Red lets out a very feline hiss of dismay.

"Go on and back up, everyone," one of Cooper's enforcers announces loudly, his lips quirking up in a mocking grin. "Jason here has given an alpha challenge." This proclamation is followed by a dry chuckle.

"Someone get in there and secure Ross," Orrin murmurs, shaking his head. "That's why the idiot is doing what he's doing, after all."

"On it," Hamish answers, eyes glinting darkly as he snakes his way through the parting crowd.

"What's going on?" Ross asks, his one good eye wide as he looks from Hamish to Jason. Hamish has Ross tucked under one tattooed arm, a grim expression on his face as he ignores Ross' struggles, effortlessly tugging him towards the edge of the group.

"Why isn't anyone helping him?" Ross demands. "They're not really going to fight, are they?"

Hamish's answering laugh is as dark as a moonless night in a graveyard. The sound is quickly followed by the distinctive snapping of tendons and cracking of bones as Cooper and Jason shift, then the murmur of the crowd as enforcers and Liberty pack members alike move aside to form a circle around the two wolves.

Whatever false hope I might have harboured falters at the sight of those two wolves. The reddish-brown wolf is probably half the size of the grey wolf, looking for all the world like a pup facing off against a predator.

Like an omega facing off against an alpha.

The horror I'm feeling is mirrored on the faces of every other member of the Liberty pack, and even some of the Clear Creek enforcers.

Because while they might be following orders, they aren't monsters. Most of them have known Jason since he was a pup. They've watched him grow up. Some of them even stepped in to help in the absence of his father. I'm pretty sure Hank taught him how to ride a bike. And Nate helped him build a treehouse one summer.

The little brown wolf surges forward, gallantly but inexpertly nipping at the grey wolf's forelegs. The larger wolf dances out of the way, circling around with effortless grace, until he's at the smaller wolf's back. I expect him to lunge, to attack from behind, but the larger wolf waits. Giving his weaker opponent time to realise the danger he's in. Letting him have the false hope of being able to recover and attempt a second attack.

The move would be playful, if the stakes weren't so high. If this wasn't a matter of life and death.

I press my palms to the sides of my face. I can't sit back and watch this.

Have faith, a voice whispers, the sound sweet and strong and familiar.

It's the voice of vision and truth. Of Morrigan. It fills my head, momentarily blotting out the dark disaster unfolding before me, turning my attention back to the golden warmth still thrumming in my chest. It's getting stronger, reminding me of heat and life and Tobias.

Gods above, Tobias.

Have faith and be strong, the voice urges. *And fight. Fight.*

My vision clears, the sight before me jarring. The grey wolf's claws are tinged with blood, his mouth lolling open in what can only be described as a lupine laugh. Red claw-marks rake down the smaller wolf's face, one scratch bisecting an eye as he blinks rapidly to clear his vision.

"Do something! Someone, do something!" I hear Ross call out, his voice clear and pained despite the distance.

Fight, fight, fight, the voice inside me urges, now only a faint echo. But the heat in me burns stronger, moving from warmth to fire, snaking down my limbs with an urgent intensity. Demanding movement.

I look at the male standing guard beside me, his weapon trained downward as he watches the wolves battle. At the other Clear Creek enforcers, their attention solely on their alpha as he toys with the smaller wolf.

And suddenly I know what I need to do.

My wolf straightens, shaking her fur in anticipation. Nostrils flaring.

I'm sorry, Hank, I think to myself, unable to stop the momentary surge of guilt. He's not a bad guy. He's just following orders.

Unfortunately for him, his orders conflict with my need to keep my pack safe.

Take out the enforcers, I tell my pack through the bond. *Disable all the firearms. If you can do that without killing, then do. But don't pull any punches.*

Because they won't be.

We might not be able to interrupt the alpha challenge, I explain, *but there are no rules against taking out their enforcers.*

After all, they are trespassers on our territory. By all the laws of gods and wolves, they are the perpetrators. They are in the wrong.

I can feel my pack's surprise at my words, quickly followed by excitement, heady and effervescent as soda bubbles.

They give a few exuberant "yes, alphas" through the pack link.

And then all hell breaks loose.

Chapter 24

Aires Zmey

Leaving my mate behind with those crazed animals who call themselves the Clear Creek pack went against every instinct. I almost couldn't do it.

But the second I felt the fire's pull, as soon as I smelt the distinctive scent of brimstone and cheap cologne, I knew there wasn't any other choice.

I wait, staring up at the stars above the northern mountains, just past the bounds of our territory, my ears trained on the sound of thundering footsteps. My father's men. They move with about as much stealth as elephants in a jungle. I'm surprised that none of the other shifters heard them approach, despite their inferior hearing.

I lean against a gnarled pine and wait, careless for once of the pine sap soiling my suit jacket. No doubt this suit will be covered in more than pine sap before the night is done.

Pity. It was one of my favourites.

The first of my father's men come into view, dressed in brown and crushing the undergrowth with heavy boots, breathing loudly enough to wake every sleeping animal in this forest. I watch them, forcing my face into a mask of bored amusement for a full thirty seconds before one of them finally notices me.

He freezes, reactively drawing his gun with a shout, then paling and quickly holstering his weapon when he realises who he's just aimed it at.

"I'm sorry, boss," the male wheezes, lifting one hand in a placatory gesture. "I didn't realise it was you."

Trent. I think his name is Trent. It could be Tom though. Honestly, I don't really care.

I lift one brow, smirking inwardly as the male trembles, his face paling further.

Good. He should fear me.

"Son. What a lovely surprise."

Drake's voice is tight behind his smile. A smile that shows far too many teeth.

"Wish I could say the same," I say with a curt nod towards his enforcers. "Your lizards aren't exactly the stealthy type."

There are a few angry hisses at the derogatory slur, but no one says anything. They wouldn't dare. Not when they know it's more or less the truth. Just like my father, they are all wingless. Most are unable to conjure up flames strong enough to light a cigar, let alone burn a whole forest. Defectives who shouldn't have the right to call themselves dragons.

Drake shrugs, but there is no missing the way his jaw ticks, or the bead of sweat trickling down his forehead.

"We're merely retrieving our property," Drake says defensively. "There is no need for stealth just to collect two little females."

My dragon hisses, claws flexing irritably at the dismissive mention of my mate, at the thought of my heart's firesong falling into Drake's hands. Into the hands of any of these unworthy males.

Strangely, my dragon is even protective of the little white she-wolf.

Alpha, the scaled beast reminds me. *She is our alpha now.*

I frown at that. I only knew Tobias Finch for a short while. I doubt he and I would ever have become friends, but I respected him. Respected his wolf. His power. I certainly did not wish him dead.

"Your property?" I repeat questioningly, narrowing my eyes at him.

"Don't pretend you don't know what I'm talking about," Drake says with a dramatic sigh. He was always good at that – dramatics. Even if he wasn't good at anything else. "I know you helped them escape. We found the helicopter – eventually. It had their scents all over it."

"Oh, I don't dispute that I took them," I say with a dry chuckle, peeling myself off the tree I've been leaning on. As suspected, I can feel the tug of sap on the fabric of my jacket. "Because I did. What I dispute is the claim that they are yours."

Drake's shoulders stiffen, all pretence of fatherly friendliness sliding from his face.

"They are mine," he says with a possessive snarl. "I found them. I brought them to my lair. By the law of dragons, they are mine."

Now it is my turn to smile. Because father dearest might as well have exposed his scaleless underbelly to me.

"So, you abide by the law of dragons then?" I ask, not bothering to hide my glee. "And you ask that I do the same?"

The old fool nods, looking almost petulant as he squares his shoulders. Probably attempting to look dignified. But if all the tailored suits in the world don't provide that effect, a simple change in posture isn't going to.

"Then tell me, father," I ask, putting emphasis on the word *father*. Because I know he hates his relation to me as much as I do. "What is the oldest of the laws? The most sacred? The most unbreakable?"

Drake gives a snort, waving one manicured hand dismissively. "I did not come here to discuss dragon lore with you, child."

Child. My lips curl at that word. I have not been a child since my mother's death left me with a father too weak to rule. A fact this male knows better than any.

"Do you not know?" I ask, doing my best to keep my anger in check. To resist the urge to shift and burn them all to ash where they stand.

My dragon rumbles merrily at the thought. It would be so satisfying.

"Of course I do," he snaps.

Which means he doesn't. His knowledge of dragon lore is as twisted as his stunted wings and as weak as his undersized heart.

"The rule of mates," I say, my voice rising despite myself, the taste of ash on my tongue as I bite back the flames. I'm tired of this little game. This back and forth.

Drake scoffs. "There has not been a true mating for dragons in over a century."

I nod in agreement because that at least is the truth. It might perhaps be the one piece of dragon lore he does know – besides those laws relating to treasure hordes – if only because my mother always lamented that he was not her true mate.

She thought that was the reason for her unhappiness with him. But I'm quite certain he was enough of a reason, all on his own.

"No true mates, until now," I clarify.

Drake narrows his eyes at me, disbelief etching itself into the faint lines of his face. "Oh?"

"Summer is my mate," I say, and there is an audible intake of breath from the other males in the clearing, even a few murmured prayers to the gods. After all, what male hasn't dreamt of finding his true mate?

"Impossible," Drake counters.

"Improbable," I correct, "but true. She is mine and I am hers and the gods take any who try to tear us asunder."

Firesong, my dragon rumbles within me. *Our firesong*.

"Even so, that does not protect the other little she-wolf."

I grin at that, imagining Drake trying to capture Lucy Stone against her will. The alpha of what is becoming one of the most powerful packs in North America. My alpha.

"It does not," I agree, "and yet you still cannot have her."

"Really? And why is that?"

He crosses his arms over his chest, like he's some capo in a bad mafia movie, the move causing his ill-fitting suit jacket to bunch awkwardly.

"Because the she-wolf is my alpha," I say simply, giving a one-shouldered shrug. "And I am blood bound to protect her. Even against you."

Drake pales at this, staring at me for a long moment, his mouth opening and closing as if he is a landed fish. The silence suits him, even if the expression does not.

At least he is not so dim-witted as to miss my implied threat. If he attacks her, I will destroy him and every one of the would-be-dragons who follow him. He knows better than anyone that he would never stand a chance against me. Against wing and scale and dragon-fire. He would be nothing more than a pile of ashes when I'd finished with him.

Or worse, I would destroy his horde. Once I found it. And gods above, if he took Summer from me, I would find it.

"You are not serious," he finally says, but the words come out in a choked sort of cough.

"Deathly serious," I say.

There is another long silence, punctuated only by the cracking of twigs and leaves as the men standing shift uncomfortably on their booted feet and the occasional hooting of an owl overhead.

"So, what would you have me do?" Drake asks, glaring at me even as he concedes his defeat. "Turn around and go home?"

I laugh, the sound airy and light on the night breeze. The enforcers closest to me flinch.

"Oh no, not that," I assure him, striding forward until I am in his space. Towering over him. Reminding him of how much larger I am than he, both as a man and as a beast. "You and your lizards will walk with me. Perhaps a little more quietly this time. And you will help me get rid of the dogs pissing on my territory."

Drake's brow knits together. "You want me to turn on my ally?"

I snort. The thought of my father having any true allies is unthinkable. Flightless he might be, but he is a dragon. We don't ally ourselves with lesser shifters.

"I want you to do what you do best. Protect your own hide," I tell him. "Besides, what can Cooper Winslow possibly do for you? He can't offer you protection. He can't even offer you the females he's promised you. Because they are mine."

This last word might come out with a bit more of a growl than I intend, and I can feel the prickling of scales flashing across my skin.

I don't care. He needs to see how serious I am.

Drake stares at me for a long moment, eyes flickering as he no doubt calculates the odds. Weighs whatever paltry gains Cooper promised him against the losses that he knows I would inflict.

Finally, he gives a grim nod.

"Fine." He bites out the word as if it pains him. "We will ally ourselves with for you tonight."

Chapter 25

Cody Winslow

It is the darkest hour of the night. That cold, chilling, hour after the moon has set, but before the first tendrils of dawn reach up to dim the stars.

Tonight, I feel as if the stars are watching me. Like they are a million disapproving eyes, glaring down at me through the pines. As if they really are the glowing eyes of all the wolf shifters who came before me, like the old legends say.

I don't particularly believe in the legends. Or the gods, really. But if there was ever a time that I would question that doubt, it would be now. Because I swear I can feel the weight of their disappointment.

"I'm sorry," I whisper into the listening darkness. "I'm sorry."

The words float away on an errant night breeze, only to be swallowed up by the forest.

I look down at Tobias. At the figure peacefully resting at the base of the old gnarled pine. Looking at him now, it is hard to believe he's gone. Like I half expect to see his chest rise and fall with breath. To see him sit up and fix me with that golden alpha glare.

"I wish I could make it right," I tell him ruefully. "I could give you all the excuses in the world. I could tell you I did it for Summer. That I did it for my dad. That I didn't think things would go this far, that I didn't think anyone would actually get hurt because of me."

I drag one hand over my face, jaw clenching, then turn to stare into the trees.

"The truth is, there was no excuse for what I did. I knew what dad planned, and I sat back and let it happen. Because I was jealous. Jealous, and a coward."

That last word comes as a surprise to me. I've never thought of myself as a coward before, but saying it, I know that it's true. I was afraid to stand up to my dad, even when I knew what he was asking of me was wrong.

"So yah. I messed up."

I pause, giving a dry chuckle, because that doesn't even begin to describe the monumental string of disasters my decisions created.

"I messed up but I swear to all the gods that I will do whatever it takes to make things right."

I squeeze my eyes shut against the painful press of tears that surge forth at this declaration. Because there is no way to fix what I did.

But maybe, just maybe, there are ways to make reparations.

"I'll be loyal to the Liberty pack until I die," I promise into the trees. "I'll beg Lucy for forgiveness, since apparently she's the alpha now, if what mom was telling me is true. Though who really knows, because it's not like that woman was particularly forthcoming with information for the first seventeen years of my life."

I rub at my face, ignoring the moisture on my cheeks.

"I'll offer to take the lowest role in the pack. And if Lucy won't have me back, I'll just lurk outside the perimeter in my wolf form. Like a guard dog."

I nod emphatically. Yah. I can do that. I mean, it wouldn't be an ideal life. But it would be better than living a life as a traitor in my dad's pack.

A hoarse, coughing sound has me flying to my feet, head snapping around to identify the source. But there is nothing, just the old gnarled pine with Tobias at its base. I flare my nostrils, and smell only pine and earth and Tobias.

Still, I'm not about to sit back down and let myself be caught unawares. As quietly as I can, I pad barefooted past the old pine, checking the forest beyond where Tobias lays for any intruders.

When I still don't find anything, I take a deep breath. It was probably some small animal. Some nocturnal rodent. Or a tree branch.

"You won't have to be a guard dog."

I spin around, heart flying into my throat, every nerve coming to life, like I've been hit with electricity.

Because *he* is standing there. In the flesh. Gold eyes burning with an unholy fire, muscles taut with barely restrained energy, a shadow of a smile on his face.

I'm not sure if it's a friendly smile.

"Leti's underworld," I choke out, taking a stumbling step backwards, nearly tripping over tree roots in the process. "Tobias Finch!"

TOBIAS FINCH

My world is a golden, swirling, tangle of power. Of too many viewpoints to focus on. Of threads connecting me to each member of my pack as I channel every last piece of myself across the bonds.

I keep expecting the power to dry up, but it is endless. I can see that now.

Also endless is the void beyond. My future once I relinquish my hold on the fragile bonds with my pack. Because it is clear to me now that these fragile bonds are the only things holding me here.

Wherever here is.

And they are thinning. Crumbling. Disintegrating under the weight of grief and despair as I slowly but surely slip closer to the void.

Yes, I guess I am challenging you.

Jason's voice echoes through the darkness, tremulous and uncertain, but full of courage as he stares at Cooper Winslow.

At the sound of those words – so full of bravery and love – the bond holding me to him strengthens, pulling me just a little further from the looming darkness.

Take out the enforcers. Disable all the firearms. If you can do that without killing, then do. But don't pull any punches.

My chest aches at Lucy's words, at her steely determination and resolve as she stares out at the crowd before her.

Fight, fight, fight.

The voices of my pack mates rise up around me, like a battle-chorus, pulling me closer, thrumming life and hope down the bonds.

The she-wolf is my alpha.

Aires voice shimmers against the dark void, tugging me almost forcefully away from the darkness.

I'm sorry.

Cody's voice echoes across one golden thread, and I wince at the image of my own body, laying lifeless at the base of some old tree.

I'll be loyal to the Liberty pack until I die.

Something snaps at those words, the feeling strangely painful in this painless space, and the void falls away. It's like a game of tug-of-war, when one side finally wins, and the other side goes careening helplessly across the line.

Death is painless. It's living that is hard.

That is my first thought as I crash violently into my body, the first breath shuddering with all the gentleness of broken glass in my lungs. I can feel each heartbeat, sluggish and heavy, as if one of those cartoon anvils is resting on my chest. I can feel my flesh knitting back together, healing faster than should be possible, even for a shifter.

"I'll just lurk outside the perimeter in my wolf form. Like a guard dog."

Cody's voice cuts through the fog of pain, the ridiculousness of his words offering a momentary respite, and I chuckle despite myself. At least, I try to. But my mouth and throat are as dry as that gods-forsaken desert in Southern Utah and it comes out as more of a choking sound.

I swallow, then force my eyes to open, squinting against the starlight. My nostrils flare, taking in the scent of pine and earth and Cody and home. I smile up at the treetops as the familiar press of my wolf brushes against my mind.

For the first time in my life, I don't resent it. Don't resent him.

Fight, the golden wolf urges. *Protect your pack.*

I grit my teeth in agreement, bringing myself slowly to my elbows. I expect the bite of pain or, at the very least, a twinge of discomfort from the movement. But there is nothing. Not even the lingering burn of silver from the bullet.

Well, that's a pleasant surprise.

Thrumming with impatient energy, I rise to stand, relishing the feeling of my wolf's own strength coursing through my human form. It's like the barrier between me and the animal was burnt away, and I know instinctively I won't be able to keep the beast caged ever again.

But I won't have to fight him either.

My eyes fix on Cody. On the back of his head as he stares into the dark forest beyond. His dark curls are longer than they were when I last saw him, his athletic frame thinner than I remember. I can practically feel his remorse and sorrow, the strange mixture of warm loyalty and self-loathing burning in my chest through the pack bond.

I recall his words, his fervent promise to protect the Liberty pack no matter the cost.

"You won't have to be a guard dog," I assure him, surprised at the sound of my own voice.

It's deeper, smoother, confident. Like it doesn't really belong to me at all.

He spins around, eyes wide with panic, colour draining from his face.

"Leti's underworld! Tobias Finch!"

He stumbles back, nearly falling, and I step forward, closing the distance between us with preternatural speed, grabbing his arms to steady him.

"Hey. Hey, it's okay," I assure him, giving him what I hope is a conciliatory smile. "I'm not going to hurt you."

He blinks at me, and I can feel him trembling beneath my grip.

"You're alive," he chokes out. "How are you alive?"

That is a very good question. One I don't think I'm qualified to answer.

"Uh, yah," I say stepping back and releasing his arms.

I look down at my body. At the blood still staining my shirt, the freshly-healed skin beneath the hole in the fabric. I look back up at him and give a non-committal shrug.

"Yep. I guess I'm alive."

Cody snorts, then shakes his head, mirth quickly fading as his expression hardens.

"I betrayed you."

He looks away, his profile lit only by silver starlight as he pushes a mass of unruly curls off his forehead.

"I betrayed the pack."

His jaw clenches, eyes squeezing shut. He takes a long, shuddering breath before turning back to face me.

"I don't deserve my place in your pack, and I accept whatever punishment you deem fit," he says formally, lifting his chin in submission, exposing his throat, his gaze fixed downward.

The pulse below his jaw flutters, belying the rapid beating of his heart. There is no missing the way his whole body tenses, muscles bunching in anticipation of an attack. Like he truly believes that, at any moment, I'll shift and attack him for what he's done.

A dark part of me wants to. The part of me that rages angrily about Jamison's loss. The part of me that recalls the burn of the silver bullet ripping through my chest. The part that – only hours ago - watched Lucy cry as I was shot.

But none of that was Cody's fault. Not really.

It was Huxley Black's fault. It was Cooper Winslow's fault.

Cody was just a pawn. A victim in the machinations of other people's plans. And going by the way he looks, by the things he said while I was laying half-dead at the base of that tree, I am willing to bet he has already paid the price for whatever wrong he has done.

Pack, my wolf rumbles irritably. *Cody is pack.*

I resist the urge to roll my eyes at the animal, even as I agree with him. Yes, Cody is pack.

I step forward, ignoring the way that Cody flinches as I rest my hands on his shoulders.

"Look at me," I demand, keeping my voice gentle but firm.

Reluctantly, he lifts his gaze to meet my eyes with his own.

"You are a worthy wolf," I tell him, and it's the truth.

Because I know he tried to protect me from Huxley Black. I saw as he watched over me, as he swore his loyalty to the Liberty pack, even in the face of my death.

"You belong in this pack."

He shakes his head, blue eyes full of disbelief.

"You do," I argue vehemently. "Yah, you messed up. But we all make mistake, okay?"

He gives a derisive snort. "Betraying my pack is more than just a mistake."

"Okay, good point," I say with a dry chuckle. "But that doesn't change a thing."

He gives me a sad smile, like he doesn't quite believe me.

"I mean it," I tell him.

"You can't tell me you forgive me," he says, dropping his chin to stare morosely at our feet. "Seriously. After Jamison. After everything."

I nod, even though he can't see it.

"I do. I forgive you."

He gives a choked sob at my words, his too-thin-frame shuddering. I can see the glimmer of moisture on his downturned face, smell the faint hint of salt in the air from his tears.

"I forgive you," I say again, leaning forward to press my forehead to his own. For some reason my throat tightens around the words. "Sure, you can be a cocky asshole at times, but you're my friend. You're pack. You're family."

Pack, my wolf rumbles contentedly. *Cody is pack.*

"I – I don't deserve it," Cody whispers.

"It's not about what you deserve. It's how it is. You're pack. I'm your alpha, and there's no getting rid of me."

I say this last part jokingly, then cringe because it's true. Now that I'm alive, my pack is stuck with me whether they like it or not.

Hopefully they like it.

"Thank the gods," he murmurs.

I step back, shooting him a grin. "You say that now. I give it a week and you'll be sick of me again."

"Never," he says, eyes widening.

I lift a brow, but don't bother to argue with him. I might not be battling with my wolf anymore, but it's not like I had a personality transplant or anything. And however sorry Cody might be, he's still going to be an insufferable know-it-all once in a while.

Something tells me Cody and I are always going to clash, just a little.

The call of an owl in the distance has my muscles tensing, and I look northward. Towards where I can feel the majority of my pack gathered. To where the chaos of battle has only just started, erupting with zings of anxiety and excitement across the pack bond.

"My dad has invaded Liberty pack territory," Cody says tentatively, nodding towards the heart of our land.

"I know."

Cody looks at me in confusion. Then I realise that he has no idea that I've just spent the last couple hours seeing and feeling every single thing through the eyes of my pack. I inwardly wince at how creepy that is.

That's probably a conversation for another time. Or maybe never. Never seems like a good option.

"You know?" He lifts one brow, narrowing his eyes at me.

I give a nervous laugh, then pull my ruined, bloody, shirt over my head. Yep, definitely not having this conversation now.

"We should go help them," I say, tilting my chin northwards as I start taking off my shoes. Getting ready to shift. "Our pack needs us."

He grunts in agreement, the corner of his lips twitching upwards in the faintest shadow of smile. Like he knows I'm hiding something, and he's not-so-secretly looking forward to getting the information out of me.

Yah, I don't think much is going to change between Cody and me.

The shift into my wolf form is smooth. Effortless as water flowing over worn rocks. My body thrums with energy, each muscle and sinew hungry for movement.

For the first time since I've been able to shift, there is no fear that my wolf will shove me back and take control. Maybe it's because the barrier between wolf and man has been burnt away. Or maybe it's that I am finally strong enough as a man to equal the wolf within.

Either way, whatever it is, being a wolf feels good. Just like it feels good to have the red wolf beside me, to have the earth of my territory beneath my paws and a battle ahead of me. My jaws open into a wolfish grin, and I meet Cody's eyes with my own.

Run, I tell him through the bond. *Let's run.*

Chapter 26

Jason Alp

I'm going to die.

The grey wolf staring me down is a monster. Sure, he might not be quite as big as Tobias' golden wolf, but he's at least twice my size.

Which means big teeth. And big claws.

I force myself to maintain eye contact, resisting the overwhelming urge to whimper, tuck my tail and roll over to show my belly.

Ice blue eyes gleam, reflecting the light filtering from the windows of the surrounding RVs. I can feel the amusement in his stare. Like he doesn't even consider for a moment that I'm a threat. At most, I'm an annoyance.

And that is terrifying.

The grey wolf lunges for me, almost lazily. Giving me enough time to avoid the nip of his teeth before he knocks me over with his paws. My shoulder collides with dry earth, head jolting back.

Alpha, my wolf whimpers. *An alpha. Submit.*

Shut-up, I tell the animal as I scramble to my feet.

Around me, I'm aware of shouting. Of Ross calling out to me, demanding that someone help me. I tune it out, even as my heart aches to go to him. To wrap my arms around him and promise him that it will be okay. That I'll be there to make sure no one ever hurts him again.

But I can't do that. I can't promise that.

A claw rakes across my face, the pain drawing me back to the present, and I lunge away as a *yip* escapes my throat unbidden. The scent of blood fills my nostrils – my own blood, I realise – as the pack bond erupts with shouted orders from Lucy. With answering cries of *fight, fight, fight* from our pack.

I tune that out too, even as I give a shuddering sigh of relief. If they can disarm the enforcers while Cooper Winslow is busy with me, we might stand a chance.

Maybe.

I just have to stay alive long enough.

The grey wolf lunges forward again, all pretence of nonchalance gone, his eyes glinting with anger, teeth bared as a vicious snarl rips through the space between us.

I spin away, barely avoiding his bite, the fur on my nape bristling almost painfully as I dodge his blow.

Again and again he attacks, and I move away, relying on my smaller size to dart behind him with each strike, until I'm panting with exhaustion and he's practically vibrating with rage.

I'm aware of shots firing, close enough to leave my wolf ears ringing. The sound is followed by the brutal screech of some cat, then absorbed again in the cacophony of shouts and growls and cries as the battle rages around us. Like some violent storm, with me and Cooper the calm but deadly center.

As if finally noticing the fight, the grey wolf lifts his head, his cold blue gaze fixing on the disorder around us. I want to look too, but resist the urge. I might have been stupid enough to challenge an alpha, but I'm not about to take my eyes off the predator in front of me.

Ross' voice reaches me through the mayhem, sounding pained and frightened. My chest clenches in response. He's known about shifters for less than twenty-four hours and now he's caught in the middle of this.

The deadliest battle I've ever seen.

Worse than Blackwater.

Protect him, my wolf urges, the quivering fear turning to steel in my bones. *Protect our pack.*

A fiery determination wells in my chest, mirroring the strange golden warmth I felt earlier.

Only this is from me. I know it. I've felt it before.

I felt it when I ran onto the snowy field at Blackwater, blind to whatever dangers lay ahead of me.

I felt it when I lit the fires on Clear Creek pack territory to give Lucy and Summer a chance to escape.

I felt it when I raced down that sandstone slot in Southern Utah, towards the silver bullets of the Clear Creek pack.

Those times, the fire was an ember compared to what I feel now.

As if sensing some change, the grey wolf's eyes snap back to mine, surprise flickering in their icy depths. I lunge forward, moving before self-doubt can weigh me down, leaving fear behind me.

Protect, my wolf urges. *Protect. Protect.*

All the while, the fire rages in me, hot and crackling with urgency. With the instinctual omega drive to *give*, *serve*, *care*, *protect*, *love*, *love*,

love. The instinct that normally demands submission now demanding something greater.

Sacrifice.

My teeth sink into fur and flesh, the metallic taste of blood on my tongue. I don't balk at it, don't hesitate, even as I'm thrown backwards, the thud of the earth at my back answered by the press of claws on my side.

I roll, tearing free from the grey wolf's hold before he can sink his teeth in, rising up with an answering snarl. The grey wolf's eyes widen in surprise at the sound, then he lunges forward, rage coating his own answering growl.

I hold my ground, ready to meet him, no longer able to dodge the blow. I give myself over to instinct, meeting his bite with one of my own, our bodies becoming a twisting mass of fur and teeth and claws and dirt.

This time, by some miracle of chance, my teeth find his throat. I bite down, ignoring the pain racking my body. I can't let go. Whatever happens, I can't let go.

I'm going to die. But I'll do my best to take Cooper Winslow down with me.

Lucy Stone

At my order, every member of the Liberty pack moves, transforming from passive spectator to attacker. Several shift into their animal forms, while others stay in their human form as they turn on the enforcers closest to them.

"What the…" Hank says from beside me, giving me his back as he surveys the mayhem. Momentarily forgetting the threat that I pose.

Because to him, I'm just Lucy Stone. The beta's daughter. The little girl he's watched grow up.

But I'm not a little girl anymore. I'm an alpha. And there is no time for misplaced guilt. No time for hesitation.

I reach forward, my arm snaking around his front as I grab the rifle clutched to his chest. It doesn't come free easily, but to my surprise I manage to wrest it from his grip.

He turns, teeth bared, eyes flashing as he reaches for his gun. I scramble back, hands shaking as I feel for the pin that will eject the magazine, feeling it come loose just as he reaches me.

We thud to the ground, the magazine careening into the dark grass, the now disabled rifle pressed between us, and I'm momentarily grateful to Anton. For all those times he snuck me on to our pack's shooting range without dad knowing. For demanding I learn to take apart a gun before he would teach me to shoot.

"Drop the gun, Lucy," Hank growls out, his teeth close to my ear, his hands pulling at the empty rifle.

He's stronger than me, and with the element of surprise gone, I don't stand much of a chance against him. Not like this anyway.

With a prayer to Morrigan that Hank doesn't have a spare cartridge within easy reach, I release the rifle, letting him fall back with the movement. Then I twist, rolling out from under him, clothes ripping as I shift into my wolf form.

He curses, looking between the empty gun and me. I crouch down, eyes fixed on him with steady determination before leaping forward, closing the space between us with a snarl.

The gun clatters to the ground, the sound of it thudding in the long grass followed by the popping and snapping of bones and tendons as Hank shifts, taking his wolf form milliseconds before our bodies collide.

He is one seriously big wolf.

That is my first thought as I ram into him, my face and teeth colliding with his exposed throat. There is a moment where we are both air-born, me with my teeth at his neck and him with his claws raking my underbelly.

And then we're thudding to the ground. Rolling. Snarling.

My teeth lose their grip, barely nicking his skin with all the thick fur, and then he's rolling me over, attempting to pin me down. Even still, I can tell he's trying not to hurt me – his teeth hold but don't puncture the skin, his claws press but don't rake.

Guilt floods me at that realisation. We shouldn't be fighting. And I don't want to hurt him either.

A roar rents the air above me, the sound so deep I can feel it reverberating in my bones, and then Hank is torn off me. Moments later, Danny's honey and berry scent fills my nostrils just as a cold nose presses against my side, helping me roll to my feet.

Alpha? he asks, shaggy head cocked to one side, yellow eyes gleaming with fury and concern.

Fine, I say, and it's true enough. My body aches but I don't have any injuries to speak of. Nothing more than a few bruises.

Several paces away, a mass of fur gives a pained whimper. Hank, I realise with a pang of guilt. I want to go to his side, to see if he is okay, but around me shots are firing. Only two of the Clear Creek enforcers are down and at least five have shifted into their wolf forms. The rest remained armed, firing with calculated precision into the crowd.

At my pack.

My hackles rise, anger mixing with icy terror as I watch the scene before me.

My pack mates scatter, some shifting as they run, seeking coverage in the tree-line or behind RVs. I recognise Tania's sleek fox heading for the pines while Tyrone stands guard in his panther form, teeth bared at the armed enforcers.

Bile rises as I watch the enforcer lift his gun, lining up his sights with the snarling cat, and then I'm moving. Running across the clearing before I can think, Danny at my heels.

Sensing movement in his periphery, the enforcer lifts his head, and I recognise his face. Nate. The usual kind smile gone, replaced with a determined grimace.

I can tell the moment he recognises me too, because his eyes widen, mouth falling open in dismay at my approach. His eyes flick to the gun in his hands, then back up to me, as if he can't decide whether to use it or not.

I leap towards him, and he drops the gun, shifting into his wolf form to meet my attack.

Good, I think, even as claws and teeth rake into my side, even as rocks cushion my fall. *That's one less gun.*

From somewhere close by, a shot fires, a cat screeches, and answering snarls fill the night.

I can't see what is happening though because I all can see is movement and earth and grass and fur and starry sky.

One less gun. But it isn't enough. Not nearly enough.

SUMMER GREEN

"We're all going to die," Tania whispers in my ear as we hunker down behind a tree.

She's back in her human form, though gods only know why.

"Probably," I agree, tilting my head up to stare at the stars.

They're starting to fade, the night sky bleeding to grey with the approaching dawn. You would think that would give me hope, but it has the opposite effect. With daytime, it will be harder to hide.

"What are we going to do?" she asks.

I look at her, incredulous. How on earth am I supposed to know what to do?

Oh, sure, I went to Orrin's training sessions. But I thought of those more as exercise classes. I didn't think I would actually need to apply any of those skills. I just liked putting on my active-wear and watching Aires get all red and uncomfortable whenever I bent over.

"You tell me, Tania," I whisper-shout. "It was your idea to run and hide in the first place."

Not that I put up much of an argument. It was either come with Tania to keep her safe, or sit out there and let my old pack mates take pot shots at me with silver bullets.

Not a hard choice to make really. I'm a lover, not a fighter.

And, apparently, so is Tania.

The only difference is that her mates are out there defending her, while mine ran off the second he could get away.

Coward.

And yes, I am aware of how hypocritical that is. Given I'm currently hiding in the bushes.

"We could go for help…" she starts, then trails off as she no doubt realises just how stupid that idea is.

The only pack nearby is the pack attacking us. And it's not like we can exactly contact the human authorities for help here.

I open my mouth to tell her just what I think about her idea, when the faint sound of pine needles crunching underfoot has every muscle in my body tensing.

Tania looks at me, dark eyes wide with panic, her skin rippling with the urge to shift as her animal demands she run. I lift one hand, silently urging her to stay calm, stay silent. If she shifts and runs, whatever is coming towards us will definitely hear.

Surely, it's better to stay hidden.

A furry head pushes through the underbrush nearby, and I instantly regret my decision as at least ten wolves rush towards us.

"Oh shit," I say, grabbing Tania's arm. Probably a little too tightly, going by her whimper.

I can feel her glaring at me as the wolves surround us. Like this is somehow my fault. Like I have singlehandedly summoned them out of the darkness or something.

My heart leaps into my throat as the wolves fan out, closing us in. Staring at us with varying degrees of wary curiosity.

Then one wolf gives a yip, and the others step aside, letting her though.

I recognise the female wolf instantly. After all, I've spent my whole life following this wolf on pack runs every full moon. Usually with Cody at my side.

"Cindy," I breath, my eyes widening.

This can't be good. If Cindy is here with reinforcements, we are completely screwed. Like, it was going to be a pretty close thing anyway, since the Clear Creek pack have guns and we don't, but an extra ten shifters definitely tips the balance in their favour.

"Oh no," Tania murmurs from beside me, tucking her face into my shoulder.

Like I have the power to shield her from anything.

My wolf gives a little proud huff, squaring her shoulders as if she will be able to take on any of the shifters before her. Because she is somewhat deluded and tends to overestimate her capabilities.

The she-wolf before me gives a shudder, rising to its hind legs as a naked woman takes its place. I blush despite myself. Not because I'm a prude when it comes to nudity, but because there is just something super awkward about seeing your ex-boyfriend's mom naked.

Well, I guess Cody wasn't my ex-boyfriend exactly. Ex-lover? Ex-fling? My best-friend who I stupidly slept with once?

"Summer."

Cindy's voice is steady. Calm. Full of authority and graceful power. Making me feel like an awkward adolescent. Like a pup who hasn't quite managed to gauge the length of its own stride, so keeps tripping over its own feet.

"Yep, that's me," I squeak, raising my hand like I'm answering an attendance call in class.

Cindy gives a breathy chuckle, shaking her head. Behind us, a gun fires, the sound distant but clear, and the smile fades from Cindy's face.

"It's started," she says, tilting her chin towards the battle-hum at our backs.

I nod. There isn't much to gain by trying to lie to her. It's pretty obvious what is going on.

She frowns, then turns to the wolves behind her. "Come on," she says, urging them forward, "we're already late."

Tania and I watch with horror as the strange wolves file past, my heart dropping to my stomach as I recognise Anton among them. Like we're watching our pack mates doom approach, and there is nothing we can do to stop it.

"Please!" Tania cries out, taking a tentative step towards Cindy. "Please don't hurt my mates."

Cindy's jaw clenches, her gaze hardening as she stares after the departing wolves, then softening as she meets Tania's eyes with her own.

"I'm sorry this happened," she says, reaching one hand out to brush Tania's cheek, fingertips lightly brushing away the tears glinting in the pre-dawn light. Tania flinches at the contact, but doesn't move away. "I'll do everything I can to make this right."

And then she's shifting, paws thudding against the earth as she lopes after the others.

Tania and I stare after her for a long moment, confusion filling the silence left by Cindy's departure.

What did she mean, she was sorry? And how on earth could she possibly make this right?

Chapter 27

Lucy Stone

Danny is at my back, Christopher flanking my right and Tyrone at my left as we target the next armed enforcer. He fumbles with his gun, seeking to reload it before we reach him.

Several paces away, Samson lays prone, his bobcat form half obscured by the long grass, pained growls escaping alongside wheezing breaths.

I know a few others have been hit too. I can feel their pain pulsing angrily across the pack bond. I can feel their fear.

Behind me, Orrin lets out an enraged roar, and I shudder as he takes yet another bullet.

There are so many of them, and they are scattering us like prey. Besting us like children.

The enforcer in front of me lets out a high-pitched wail, his head tilting back in sorrowful agony, the gun slipping from his fingers. His cry is answered by the screams of the other enforcers, the clattering of rifles against dry earth, then a chorus of mournful howls erupts around us.

I freeze, fur rippling with dread at the eerie sound. At the bizarre spectacle before me.

What is happening? Christopher asks, pressing his flank to my side. *What in the gods' names is happening?*

I don't answer, because I have absolutely no idea.

"Alpha," the enforcer in front of us whimpers, falling to his knees.

Tyrone prowls forward, teeth bared at our opponent, but the enforcer merely stares beyond us with wide-eyed sorrow.

"Alpha," he says again, one hand reaching up to clutch at his chest.

Tentatively, I turn to follow his gaze, my heart stopping at the sight before me.

Jason stands panting, his brown fur coated red with blood, head drooping, legs trembling. Laying beneath him is a very still grey wolf. The grey wolf's head rests at an odd angle, the red staining the fur at his throat leaving no doubt as to the cause.

I blink, barely believing what I am seeing. Torn between wanting to cry and wanting to rejoice.

Alpha Winslow is dead.

As if sensing my shock, Jason meets my gaze with his own.

You won, tell him, stating the obvious. *You won. It's over.*

With the alpha dead, with Jason victorious, no one would dare to attack us. Not when shifter law demands respecting an alpha challenge. Not when so many of the enforcers seemed reluctant to attack us in the first place.

Jason sways, paws stumbling as he tries valiantly to keep upright.

Ross, he says through the bond. *Where is Ross?*

And then his legs give out and he crumples to the ground, sinking into the trampled grass, eyes rolling back.

I race towards him, shifting back into my human form between strides before dropping to his side.

"Jason!"

I run my hands over his face, down his sides, across his bloodied fur, noticing for the first time the extent of his injuries. There doesn't seem to be any one grievous injury, just so many, many cuts.

"He's okay," Theo assures me, coming to my side from seemingly nowhere. "He's still breathing." He presses his fingers into the wolf's thick coat, presumably feeling for a pulse at his throat, then adds: "His pulse is weak though. Probably blood loss."

I nod grimly. He's only just healed from Ross accidentally shooting him. We might be resilient, and able to quickly heal, but even a shifter body can only loose so much blood.

"He needs to shift," Theo says, fixing me with a meaningful look.

Of course. Because I am the alpha now. I'm the only one who can force Jason to shift. To help him heal.

I square my shoulders, hands trembling as I ready myself to give my first alpha command. My chest aches at the mere thought of it, like it's one more step to accepting that Tobias really is gone. That I am now the alpha of this pack.

"I contest the outcome."

My dad's voice booms out across the clearing, sharp as a gunshot and just as chilling.

I spin to face him, rising unsteadily to my feet. Keeping Jason and Theo at my back.

"You what?" I say, shaking my head in disbelief, waving one hand to Cooper Winslow's prone form. "What exactly are you contesting here?"

Beyond him, a few of the Clear Creek pack enforcers exchange confused looks, some tensing as if readying for a fight, others narrowing their eyes at their beta.

Except is he even their beta anymore?

"I contest the outcome," he says again, dark eyes glinting in the pre-dawn light. "Your pack interfered by attacking our enforcers during an alpha challenge. That was a break in protocol."

I shake my head, a mirthless laugh escaping my lips. Unbelievable. Absolutely unbelievable.

"Your enforcers attacked us," I remind him, then point one finger to the soil beneath my bare feet. "This is Liberty pack land. Not Clear Creek land. They attacked the moment they crossed our borders uninvited and armed. We were merely acting in defence."

Gods above, he knows this. He knows the rules as well as I do.

"I disagree," he says with a smirk, crossing thick arms over his chest.

He's still fully dressed, the silver insignia with the Clear Creek logo visible for all to see, his shirt clean, his gun slung over his back. How has he managed to make it through the fray looking so untouched?

"Now that Cooper Winslow is no longer here to lead us, I am the alpha of the Clear Creek pack. And I challenge you, Lucy Stone. As one alpha to another."

My mouth drops open, fists balling at my sides. An errant breeze brushes past, bringing his scent to me, and I wrinkle my nose at the acrid scent of lies. Because of course he knows what he is saying isn't true. And of course, he's not about to let truth or rules get in the way of what he wants.

"You're a liar," I retort, then blush because the words sound so childish to my ears. "You're not the alpha and you know it."

I'm not sure exactly who the alpha is - maybe the pack just gets disbanded, like Huxley Black's did after Blackwater – but it sure isn't my dad.

"And you're a child," he says, deftly seeing my greatest weakness and throwing it in my face. "A little she-wolf playing house, pretending to be alpha of a pack. You couldn't stand against even the weakest of our enforcers here."

My spine straightens, even as heat pricks at my cheeks.

We did fight them, my wolf reminds me.

My gaze flits guiltily to Hank and Nate, the two enforcers I managed to disarm. They stand with the other enforcers, Hank with a pained expression on his face as he leans against someone, and Nate with half-healed cuts raking down his chest.

"You certainly couldn't stand against me," Jeb says, stepping closer, so there is only an arm's length between us. My wolf bristles at having the male so close to her. So close to our injured pack mate.

I lift my chin, meeting his gaze with my own. Praying to Morrigan that he can't see the way I'm trembling. That he can't smell my fear.

"I will," I say defiantly, stepping forward. Closing the space between us.

Because if Jason could face down Cooper Winslow, I can face this male. Even if I know I probably won't win.

"And I will burn every tie binding me to you," I whisper, low enough so that only he can hear me.

Tears sting my eyes and for once, I don't bother to blink them back. I let them fall, perfuming the space between us with salt and sorrow. Dad watches them track down my face with a mixture of idle curiosity and disgust. He's always seen tears as a weakness.

"You might be my dad, but they are my pack. And my loyalty will always be with them."

Even if it breaks my heart.

Dad's jaw clenches, eyes darkening dangerously at those words. At my renouncement of him. That is the only warning I get before he lunges forward, hand gripping for my throat, but it is enough.

I step back, barely evading his grasp, then shift, my body screaming with the agony of my cuts and bruises, with the muscle exhaustion that comes from shifting too frequently in too short a time.

My hackles rise at the answering snarl that rips out of him, and then he's shifting too, dropping heavily to all fours as a deep brown wolf takes his place.

Despite his intimidating size, despite his bulk, my wolf gives a sigh of relief at the silence descending between us.

At least in wolf form, he can't fill my ears with his toxic words.

"Take him down," Hamish shouts, breaking the tense silence. "Show him what a real alpha can do."

"You've got this, Lucy," Christopher yells, and then the rest of my pack is joining in, adding their shouts of encouragement.

Warmth and gratitude bloom in my chest, though it's not enough to stay the icy tendrils of dread. Surely, they know as well as I do that the chances of me winning are slim? But maybe, after seeing Jason defeat Cooper, they are willing to believe in the impossible.

The dark wolf lunges for me, yellowed teeth bared, eyes glinting with unmasked fury. I know there will be no taunting game of cat and mouse with him.

I dart left, barely missing his teeth but unable to avoid the reach of his claws. They rake down my face, leaving pain and the scent of my own blood in the air.

Around me, the crowd falls silent and I can feel the watchful tension, the fear and hope and anguish of my pack pouring through the bond.

He lunges again, spittle flying from his jaws as he snarls, and this time I'm too slow. Teeth clamp around my leg with bone-crunching force, the nauseating sound quickly followed by my own lupine scream.

Dark eyes glimmer with smug satisfaction as he releases his hold. He stares at me for a long moment, his muscles tensing as he prepares to lunge forward again. This time he'll go for my throat. And I'll be too slow to get away.

I squeeze my eyes shut, waiting for the blow.

"Stop."

The alpha command flows over me, thick and heavy, but not strong enough to compel me. Nothing like the order of a born alpha.

Jeb tenses before me, lips peeling back in an angry snarl of protest as he freezes mid-stride. And that's when I realise I know that voice.

Cindy Winslow.

"Stop," she says again.

Her voice is softer, sadder, but no less powerful, and I tremble despite myself at the sound of her approaching footsteps.

It takes everything in me not to duck my head and look away when she comes into view. Not because of the calm power radiating from her. Not even because she's always been a subject of awe and respect for me growing up.

No, I struggle to meet her eyes because her mate lays dead in the grass behind me.

She casts me a pitying look before turning back to my dad.

"Shift," she orders, the alpha command squeezing the air from my lungs.

Dad lets out an answering snarl, and then he's standing on two legs, naked and furious.

"You have no right," he starts, but she lifts one hand to silence him, and the words die in his throat.

"I have every right," she says, her cool gaze moving from him to the Clear Creek enforcers behind him, then back to me.

I'm aware of warmth at my side, of the familiar scent of Anton as his grey wolf leans against me, taking the weight that my broken leg can no longer hold. His scent is soon joined with another. A scent I know as well as his. A scent that sings of home and longing and broken promises.

Mom.

I squeeze my eyes shut, body trembling violently with emotion as she leans against my other side, brushing her muzzle against my face.

Mom.

"Enough blood has been spilt tonight."

Cindy's words are full of pain, and she takes a deep, shuddering breath as several of the Clear Creek enforcers give an answering whimper.

My mind turns instantly to Tobias. I had always heard that losing your true mate was like having your soul ripped apart. Maybe it's the shock of everything, but I'm not sure if that is what I feel. My soul still feels whole somehow, even if I'm soaked in sorrow.

"This ends now," she says, voice rising. "No more blood. No more fighting." She casts a long, lingering look towards her fallen mate and adds: "And no more secrets."

"Yes, alpha," the enforcers respond in unison.

I can feel the sincerity of their acquiescence, warm and sweet with truth. They respect her. My eyes meet Hank's, reading the silent apology there as he takes in my broken leg and bloodied face. Maybe they never wanted this in the first place.

Only dad remains silent.

Cindy turns to him, expression hardening, jaw clenching.

"Jeb Stone."

He lifts his chin, giving her a bald, unapologetic stare.

"You are stripped of your status. You are banished from the pack. You leave without my recommendation."

His face reddens, even as his lips curve into a mocking sneer.

"You can't do that. You don't have the authority…"

"I can. And I do. As you well know."

She pauses, cocking her head to one side, a cold smile ghosting across her face as a strange wolf, easily as large as Cooper Winslow, steps gracefully into the clearing. The male stops beside my mom, placing himself protectively between us and my dad as a low warning growl rumbles from his chest.

There is something familiar about this wolf, though I can't place it.

Regardless, there is no doubting that he is an alpha.

"I should have banished you long ago," Cindy continues, guilt momentarily flitting across her features. "When you first proved yourself unfit to be a mate and a father. That should have been enough to make you unfit for our pack." She casts another mournful look towards her fallen mate, then whispers, almost to herself: "But now is not the time to blame the dead for my own weakness."

She lifts one finger imperiously, pointing in the direction of the Clear Creek pack.

"You have two hours to gather your things and leave Clear Creek territory. Justin and Lance will escort you," she tilts her head towards the two enforcers, and they dart forward, eager to do her bidding. "I don't have to tell you what will happen if you return."

I shudder at the ice in her tone. At the implication of her words. The strange alpha beside me lets out low rumble, eyeing dad with a predatory watchfulness. As if there is nothing he would like better than to chase him down.

The two enforcers pull dad away, no doubt dragging him towards one of the Clear Creek pack's waiting vehicles near the edge of our territory.

For all his curses and threats, there is nothing he can do. Not with an alpha order pressing in on him. Not with two armed enforcers at his back.

I should feel relieved. Grateful that I won't be seeing him again. Instead, I just feel sad. A deep sorrow that cuts through my chest like a canyon, overshadowing even the pain throbbing in my leg.

Cindy turns to me, opening her mouth to speak, when the crash of trees pulls our attention northward, the faint scent of ash and sulphur carrying across on the breeze.

My eyes widen at the sight of Aires, flanked by Drake and several others who can only be Drake's enforcers.

Anger wars with the sickening feeling of betrayal, and I quickly scan the area for Summer, knowing she will take the blow of Aires' treachery harder than anyone. But I don't see her anywhere, and when I fumblingly reach for her across the pack bond, I can tell that she isn't close by.

Aires looks around the gathered crowd too, nostrils flaring, green eyes flashing as the pupils elongate into slits.

"Where is Summer?" he asks, fixing his green stare on me. "Where is my mate?"

Chapter 28

Aires Zmey

There are very few moments in my life when I have been afraid, and none that I can recall since I first fledged into my dragon form.

After all, what is there to fear when you have wings and bulletproof scales? What is there to fear when you are yourself the stuff of nightmares?

And yet fear strikes me now. Because Summer is not here.

My eyes narrow on Lucy. The she-wolf alpha of our pack. She is not my favourite shifter in the world, but I had thought her at least protective of Summer. And here the she-wolf is. Bleeding. Trembling like an autumn leaf. And Summer is nowhere in sight.

"Where is Summer?" I ask Lucy accusingly. "Where is my mate?"

I don't know, she tells me through the bond, her blue wolf eyes full of apology.

I don't want her apology. I want my gods-dammed mate.

The strange wolves surrounding her stare at me, and I glare back at them. I don't know who they are and, quite frankly, I don't care.

"Where is Summer?" I growl, eyeing my silent pack mates.

No one answers. Useless cowards. I knew these lesser shifters couldn't be trusted to look after her.

I swear to all the gods that if Summer has been harmed – if those Clear Creek wolves have taken her, or hurt so much as a hair on her beautiful head – I will burn this forest to the ground. And then I'll fly up to the heavens and set the immortal realm on fire too.

Oh yes. Even the precious gods will not be safe from my wrath.

Why are they *with you?* Lucy asks through the bond, tone heavy with suspicion. *What is Drake doing here?*

The rest of the pack are also eyeing the males behind me with wariness, belaying their own doubts about my loyalty.

"Told you he couldn't be trusted," I hear Hamish mutter to Gareth. But his beady hawk-like eyes are fixed on me. Like he wants me to hear him.

"Shut up," Red hisses. "He looks like he's about to shift."

Gareth scoffs. "Let him. We can take him."

Behind me, one of the braver of Drake's enforcers sniggers. I feel my skin prickling in response, the dragon within demanding that I give it flight.

Flight and fire, it urges. *Burn them all.*

My nostrils flare in agitation. Now is not the time to let my dragon lose. Not when I need reason and cunning and the ability to communicate so that I can find my mate. My firesong.

We have cunning, my dragon argues. *And what are words but wind?*

The dragon has a point.

"Where is Summer?" I roar, tilting my head up at the trees.

"Dude, you need to calm down," Christopher urges, stepping towards me with his palms outstretched, his voice annoyingly steady. The wolf should be quaking before me, not speaking to me like I'm a child.

Lucy shifts, a naked female replacing the white wolf. Rising to stand above the wolves flanking her – one white female and one grey male. She leans on the grey male, wincing as her obviously broken leg knits together with the shift.

"Wherever Summer is, you won't be taking her anywhere." Lucy's ice-grey eyes are full of steely resolve despite the colour draining from her already too-pale face. She tilts her pointy chin towards the males at my back, upper lip curling in disgust. "At least, not with them."

I clench my fists at my side, impatient with this little charade. Who cares about Drake and the lizards scuttling after him? I want my gods-damned mate. Now.

My skin stretches, body expanding, vision brightening. Pain radiates down my spine as wings erupt from my back, followed by sweet, sweet relief as I expand them, blocking out the faint tendrils of pre-dawn light. I grin, feeling my fangs press against scaled lips, delighting in the taste of charcoal and ash in the back of my throat.

"Oh shit," I hear Red say as the bobcat shifter backs slowly towards the forest, seeking refuge in the pines.

My dragon chuffs, content to see at least one of our pack mates has the good sense to fear me as he should. Not that trees offer much protection against dragonfire.

My eyes narrow on the wolves before me. On Christopher, standing between me and Lucy and her band of strange wolves. Even my dragon knows it shouldn't attack its alpha. But the male before me…

I open my mouth, letting ether and flame roil in the back of my throat, politely giving a warning rumble. It's more than I've done for most. Christopher should count himself lucky to be receiving such a favour.

Christopher's eyes widen when he realizes what I intend, his sweatpants shredding as he shifts into his wolf form, leaping away just in time to avoid the brunt of the flames. He whimpers pitifully when a few paltry flames lick at his paws and singe his coat.

I stretch my neck out, relishing the lingering warmth coating my throat. It has been too long since I tasted the flames. And even longer since I last took flight.

I stare up at the sky, at the greyish warning of pending daybreak. I know how foolish it is to fly at any time, let alone during the day when some human could see me. Especially this close to civilisation.

Even if that civilisation is a tiny town in the middle of nowhere. The type of humans that live in these isolated settlements are the most dangerous. They are the most likely to trust their own eyes.

And, therefore, the most likely to try and hunt me down.

Still, I will be better able to find Summer if I'm airborne.

"Don't you dare…" I hear Drake call out from behind me. But his threats are as weak as his dragon, and I ignore them, snaking my neck around to gift him with a short blast of dragon fire as I lift into the sky.

SUMMER GREEN

"Is that Aires?" I ask with a frown, peering through the trees, as if I can somehow see through the distance separating us from the center of Liberty pack territory.

"How am I supposed to know?" Tania hisses. "He's your mate."

"Unclaimed mate," I remind her.

She shrugs, as if me exercising my free will is just a small matter.

"Maybe we should make our way back and check on them," I suggest.

We've been hiding out in the forest for what seems like hours now, though without a phone it's hard to tell. All I know is the sky is turning grey with the promise of dawn, and the sounds of fighting seem to have died down. We certainly haven't heard any gunshots in at least the past fifteen minutes.

"I'm not sure…" Tania rubs the back of her neck with her hand, teeth tugging nervously on her lower lip.

I understand her reluctance. There's no knowing what the relative silence means.

"Have you tried asking someone over the pack bond?" she asks and I resist the urge to roll my eyes.

Obviously, that was the first thing I tried, but it's been radio silence. Probably because in our haste to get away from danger, we also left the range for communicating with our pack.

A roar shakes the trees around us, deep and angry sounding, and Tania flinches. I flick my gaze up to the sky, squinting through the darkness. The sound is soon followed by the distinctive *flap, flap, flap* of wings, not directly above us, but to the north. Towards the center of our territory.

"What is that?" Tania asks, her voice dropping to a low whisper as she crouches at the base of the tree beside her.

I pause, listening, mind whirring. I've spent my whole life in this part of the country. I've familiarised myself with the sound of every wild bird, even the largest avian predators, and have never heard anything that sounds like this.

There is only one thing it can be.

"Dragon," I say out loud, not bothering to lower my voice. Because there is only one dragon with the ability to fly, and he would never hurt me.

At least, I hope he wouldn't.

I take a deep breath, squaring my shoulders.

"We need to get back to the pack," I tell Tania, ignoring her look of dismay. "If that is Aires, then I need to be there."

Because I have no idea where Aires disappeared to before the fighting broke out, but I have my suspicions. And if he is back now, in dragon form, it can only mean one thing. He's here to fight.

Hopefully, he's fighting for us. But if he's not, well… Then I might be the only one who can protect my pack from him.

"Do you think he'd turn on them?" Tania asks, panting as she trots after me.

That's the annoying thing about Tania. She's too observant. Picks up on emotions much too easily. Half the time I could swear she is reading my thoughts.

I shrug, the movement awkward with my half-jog. "Maybe. I don't know."

I pick up my pace, a sense of urgency thrumming down my limbs. I should never have let Christopher and Tyrone convince me to run and hide with Tania. I certainly should never have gone this far into the forest.

Stupid, stupid, self-preservation instincts.

"You're going too fast," Tania whines from behind me and I grind my teeth.

"You could shift and run," I suggest glibly.

To my surprise, she does.

Happy now? she says through the bond, as a little dun-coloured fox darts past, nipping at my bare ankles and giving an angry, warbling hiss as she leaps ahead.

Actually, yes I am.

"Isn't that nicer?" I say to her, not bothering to keep the smugness from my voice. "Also, your fox is super cute. Look at your little fluffy tail," I croon.

The fox turns mid-stride to shoot me a death-glare and I smile, because even that is kind of adorable.

"I would totally keep you as a pet," I inform her.

You are the worst, she says.

Another roar, this one much closer, has us both freezing mid-stride, like deer caught in the sights of a hunter. The sound is followed by the distinctive flapping of wings.

Is that smoke? Tania asks, lifting her nose to the air, whiskers twitching.

My own nostrils flare in response, but I don't smell anything. Probably because I'm in my human form and I never had the best sense of smell to begin with. My wolf was never the hunting and tracking type. More of the leisurely nature-walk type.

"Let's keep going," I tell her, not bothering to respond to her question.

We run in silence, moving through the trees. More than once, I contemplate shifting into my wolf form. My pyjamas and bare feet aren't exactly the best attire for a forest run, especially when I would normally need a good-quality sports bra to make running remotely comfortable. But then I'd have to leave these pyjamas behind, and the last thing I want is to end up standing naked in front of Aires.

All the while, the flap, flap, flap of wings beating the air is growing louder, the rumbling roars becoming more insistent. Almost frustrated sounding. As if the great beast is calling out to someone.

You, my wolf assures me, giving a coy blink of her lashes. *He's calling for you.*

The thought has warmth coiling in my belly, but I push the feeling aside, focusing instead on the discomfort of the stones beneath my bare feet.

My wolf is a shameless hussy. A hopeless romantic. And of absolutely no use to me in this current moment.

Oh my goodness, that is fire, Tania says after several minutes, her voice full of panic as it pulses across the bond.

Ahead of us, distinctive oranges and reds glow through the dark spaces between the pines, crackling merrily towards the grey sky. Not close enough to be a danger to us, not close enough so that we can feel the heat, but there is no mistaking it.

We break through the trees, almost stumbling into the clearing. I pause, resting my hands on my knees, lungs burning as I struggle to catch my breath, taking in the scene before us.

Everyone – our pack mates, the Clear Creek enforcers, and a bunch of strangers I've never seen before are huddled in the clearing in the middle of the RVs. I want to run to them, to check which of my pack mates have been injured, to find out what has happened. To see if Jason is okay.

But that will have to wait because one of the RVs is currently on fire, filling the air with the sickening smell of burnt rubber. Meanwhile, dragon wings fan the flames from above, the green beast shimmering in the light of the new dawn as he roars at the shifters huddled below.

Well, shifters and at least one human, since there is no mistaking Ross' battered face, his one good eye wide with terror.

I scan the clearing again, noticing a group standing apart from the rest. A group of strange males dressed in brown with one very familiar, very unwelcome face at the head.

Drake.

My lip curls, anger and devastating disappointment warring for supremacy in my chest.

Aires betrayed us. Just like Cody did.

A string of curses race through my mind, every single one of them aimed at the scaled traitor flying above us, and I tilt my head up to the sky. Glaring at the male who fate decided to deliver to me.

My wolf whimpers at the sight of him, tucking her tail mournfully between her legs, her ears lying flat against her skull.

"Aires!"

I call out to the beast flapping above, letting all my anger out in that one word, as if his very name is a curse. But either he's ignoring me, or the sound is swallowed up in the din of flames and wings, because he doesn't look towards me.

I stride forward, ignoring Tania's whimpered protests, heading closer to the burning RV.

"Aires!" I call again.

"Summer!"

Christopher's voice is reedy, half drowned out by the roaring fire, but there is no missing the pitch of urgency. I spin towards him, furrowing my brow at the look of panic on his face.

"Summer, get away from there," he says, waving his arms furiously, as if he can somehow pull me through the air towards him. "Summer, the propane. The gas. It could…"

His words are cut off, everything around me erupting in a deafening roar of flame and pain and movement. I'm flying, burning and gods above it hurts. It hurts like the sun itself is trying to swallow me whole. And then I slip into it, thudding painfully against the earth, and everything goes black.

Chapter 29

Cody Winslow

He's forgiven me.

The thought races through my head, tumbling around on repeat until I'm practically dizzy, the words keeping time with the thudding of our paws against dry earth.

He's forgiven me.

I open my mouth in a lupine smile, relishing the scent of our territory. The scent of pine and earth and home. My wolf is practically luxuriating in the feel of running with my alpha.

I leap over a fallen log, feeling for a beautiful moment like I could fly. Like the lightness in my body is echoing the lightness of my wolfish heart.

But my feet hit the ground, and my joy is tempered by the sobering reminder of what we could be heading towards.

A battle. My dad. My mom. And gods only know what else.

Smoke, Tobias tells me through the bond, his ears pressing flat against his head as he races ahead of me. *There's smoke.*

I lift my nose, and sure enough, there is the faintest hint of bonfire on the wind. I let out a growl. The smell of fire always makes my wolf tense.

Faster, Tobias urges me, *run faster.*

I obey him, ignoring the burn in my legs, muscles weakened from so many days and weeks of disuse. But no matter how hard I push myself, it's impossible to keep pace with him.

Despite the speed, it seems like we're running forever. Like we're in one of those bad dreams where you run and run but can never get where you need to go. Meanwhile, the sky bleeds from black to grey, the glimmer of the rising sun casting the tops of the pines in a red so fiery, it's as if the whole forest is burning.

By the time we get to the heart of the Liberty pack, my legs are trembling with exhaustion, my sides heaving as I struggle to draw in breath. Tobias trots ahead of me, golden fur blazing in the light of the new sun.

No, not sunlight, I realise as I draw closer. Fire.

The entire meadow is consumed in a fire so bright it rivals the rising sun. Flames lick up along the sides of RVs and pines, hungrily eating the tall dry grass, creating a screen between us and the rest of our pack.

I can see them though. I can just make out the shadowy figures through the wall of flames. I can hear their shouts and cries through the crackling roar. And there is certainly no missing the massive dragon landing to the ground in the middle of the fire, fanning the flames with lazily beating wings.

Someone gives a pained cry from within the heart of the fire and my breath catches, icy dread snaking down my tired limbs. I know that voice. I would know that voice anywhere.

Summer.

Without a second's thought, I race forward, leaping through the wall of flames, ignoring the burn of embers beneath my paws.

Summer, I call out through the bond. *I'm here. I'm here. Where are you?*

The answering silence has panic rising sickeningly in my chest. I tamp the fear down as I search for her, eyes burning as I squint through the smoke. Meanwhile, I'm aware of the sound of shouting, of the hum of helicopter blades, barely audible over the inferno.

And then I see her, lifeless in the burning grass, flames dancing around her. I race to her, shifting as I run, because my wolf form will be of no use when it comes to carrying her out of this. I fall at her side, tears streaming down my cheeks as I cradle her in my arms, muscles screaming as I rise to stand on trembling legs.

Mine, a voice rumbles in the flames, just as a dragon emerges through the smoke, green eyes flashing, teeth bared in an ugly snarl.

I snarl back at him, even though the gesture is probably ridiculous looking in my human form, my blunt human teeth laughable compared to his fangs.

"Get out of my way, dragon," I yell, my throat constricting with smoke.

I hold Summer closer to me, feeling the fluttering beat of her heart against my chest, noting the struggling rise and fall of her chest.

"She's still alive," I scream. "Move out of my way."

The dragon's eyes widen, a flicker of humanity ghosting across the slits of green before he gives a pained sort of rumble, backing away, head lowered.

It's all the opening I need and then I'm sprinting through the flames, choking and sputtering as I escape the clouds of smoke, then falling to the unburnt grass with Summer wrapped in my arms.

"Summer," I choke out, grasping her face in my hands. "Please be okay."

Her eyelashes flutter, face contorting with pain and I sit back, scanning her body for injury. And that's when I notice the burns.

"Get back," I hear someone say. Orrin, I realise. "She needs water. And then she needs to shift."

Sharp fingers dig into my arms as someone pulls me back and Arlo races forward, lifting Summer's head and gently pressing a water bottle to her lips.

"You're lucky I like Summer more than I hate you, wolf," Red hisses in my ear, "Because otherwise I'd be inclined to put you out of your misery right here."

I open my mouth to object, to tell him that Tobias has forgiven me, to tell him I'm sorry, but then Summer's eyes are opening and all I can look at is the expression on her face as she sees me.

"Cody?"

The word comes out in a wheezing breath, her eyes wide in disbelief.

"Don't worry about him," Arlo urges her, helping her to sit up. "You need to shift. Shift and heal."

Summer squeezes her eyes shut, body trembling with effort as she tries to shift.

"Come on, shift," I say, then lift my head to search the crowd for Tobias. He could order to her shift. Use his alpha command.

"Shut-up, traitor," Red snaps, pulling me away. "You don't get to talk to her."

Above us, the whirring of helicopters rivals the roar of the fire, the sound soon followed by the hissing of steam as water douses the flames. I look up to see the familiar Clear Creek helicopters hovering above us, water-buckets swinging empty below them.

"Let me go," I argue, struggling feebly in his arms. It's of little use. Red is all wiry muscle and I'm weak. Exhausted. Barely able to stand.

"Not a chance," Red says dryly. "We'll see what our alphas say."

Alphas. Alphas. But I need to be with Summer.

I glance back over my shoulder at her as Red drags me away. Behind her, the flames are barely more than glowing embers now, doused by water and the work of shovels and fire extinguishers.

"Are those – are those Clear Creek enforcers?" I ask, blinking in confusion at the black-clad shifters shovelling furiously to build a fire break around the dying flames. It's hard to be sure with the thick smoke and the glare of the rising sun.

Red gives an impatient growl, then mutters something about not signing up for battles and manhandling naked wolf shifters.

"Then don't manhandle me," I retort, "I'm perfectly capable of walking."

Though now that I think about it, I'm not entirely sure that I am.

Red drags me through the crowd, toward where Tobias is standing in his human form, just as naked as I am, beside an embarrassed looking Lucy. They are both staring at something half-obscured by the tall grass.

No, not something, I realise. Someone. Jason.

My stomach churns as I take the bloodied brown wolf. His sides barely moving as he takes in shuddering breaths.

"Shift," Tobias orders, the alpha command rolling out with so much power it nearly knocks the breath from my lungs.

And just like that, Jason is shifting, his human form taking the place of the wolf, wounds knitting together before my eyes with the power of the shift. Lucy kneels beside him, stroking his temples softly with dirt-stained fingertips as Tobias looks on.

I look away, nearly overpowered with relief. *If they can shift, they'll live*, I remember Tricia, our pack healer, saying.

"Summer," I say out loud, and both Lucy and Tobias look at me in surprise. "You need to get to Summer."

Summer couldn't shift. She was in pain, and couldn't shift.

"I'll take you to her, alpha," Arlo says, appearing from nowhere from behind me. "I was just coming to get you."

I glare at the owl in irritation. It should be me at Summer's side, not him. Not any other male. And what in the gods' names is wrong with Red? Can't he let me go already?

"Cody."

Lucy says my name with a strange mix of sorrow and pity. She meets my eyes for a brief moment before her gaze flicks away, as if she's unable to meet my stare with her own.

"I'm sorry about…"

She pauses, swallowing, eyes fixed on a spot in the grass. I follow her gaze, eyes landing on a strange heap of grey and red fur. I blink, my mind unable to process what I'm looking at. *Who* I'm looking at.

Dad? Is that – is that my dad?

A strong arm bands around me, replacing Red's implacable grip, the warm familiar scent of home and safety and love and sadness filling my nostrils.

"I've got you," mom says, pulling my head toward her shoulder, turning my face away from the sight before me. I can tell by the way her body is shuddering that she is crying too.

"I've got you," she says again, and I wrap my arms around her, wishing I could lose myself in the scent of home and love and childhood and safety.

But even her comforting embrace isn't enough to blot out the acrid scent of burnt grass and blood.

Lucy Stone

Cody's grief and shock are almost suffocating, bombarding me over the pack bond, overpowering the myriad of other emotions from my pack mates. I watch in awkward silence as Cindy wraps him up in a hug, as they share in each other's grief, torn between wanting to walk away and offer… something. Condolences? Support?

I frown, rubbing at the now healing cut on my face with the back of my hand, wincing at the sharp sting of ash and salt in the wound.

"Let them have their grief," a voice suggests at my side. "Sometimes space and silence is the best thing you can offer someone."

I turn, meeting my mom's eyes with my own. Seeing her in her human form, I'm struck by how little she has changed in the years that have passed. If anything, she looks younger. More full of life than I remember, despite the fatigue of battle coating her skin.

"Mom," I say, lifting my chin, shoulders straightening.

She might have come to my aid when we needed it, and I might have a better understanding of why she left. It doesn't change the pulse of hurt that thrums behind my ribs at the sight of her.

She sighs, dropping her gaze. "I'm going to go get us some clothes," she suggests, "You'll get a chill standing out in your skin. And when you're done seeing to your pack, we can talk."

I nod, then turn to help Orrin carefully gather up Jason, trailing after him to the only RV that managed to escape the dragon's rampage. Squinting through the smoke, I can see Tobias gently carrying Summer towards us, now shifted into her wolf form, with Theo and Arlo flanking him.

"Ah, company," a familiar voice deadpans when we open the door. "Glad to see I'm not alone." I look up to see a pale looking Samson sprawled out on the RV's bench seat, a wide-eyed Tania at his side.

Samson's expression grows serious when he takes in Jason's unconscious form.

"He'll be alright," I assure him, hoping that it is true. "He's shifted and is healing. Think it's just fatigue and blood loss."

"Yah, he'll be fine," I hear Theo call out from the steps of the RV. He's holding the door open as Tobias carries Lucy through, but the owl has obviously heard everything we've said. "Don't worry. I'm more worried about you. You sure you got that bullet out?"

"Yah," Samson grunts, waving one hand dismissively. "I'm fine." His eyes widen when he takes in Summer's lifeless form, the angry burns visible even with her fur. "Gods above," he says.

Theo scowls at him. "Enough of that. She'll have enough stress without you getting her worried about her injuries. She's healing. She's breathing." The owl shifter pauses, pushing his round glasses up the bridge of his nose with one finger. "Put her in the room," he tells Tobias. "You can use my bed. Jason can have the other one. I can take care of them both."

Tobias looks down at Summer's brown wolf with a sorrowful frown. "You sure?"

Theo nods. "Absolutely." He looks between me and Tobias, cheeks reddening. "I've got some clothes you can both borrow. And then I need you guys to get out of here." He grimaces, running one hand through his hair nervously. "Sorry, that came out wrong. What I meant to say was, this RV is small and…"

"And you're taking up all the oxygen with your alpha-ness," Arlo comments drily from behind us. "Just call it like it is, cuz. You need space to work your healing magic, and these two lurking around aren't going to help anything."

Arlo points one finger at Orrin. "Same goes for you. You're way too big to be in here."

The bear shifter lifts his head from where he is currently lowering Jason to one of the beds, yellow eyes flashing dangerously. As if the bear is still sitting close to the surface, and isn't quite ready to leave the pack mate he's been dutifully protecting.

Theo pats Orrin's shoulder, then pushes past him to start pulling clothes out of the compact closet. "Don't worry, big guy," he assures the bear as he tossed me and Tobias a bundle each. "I'll be at his side the whole time."

Mom is waiting for me outside the RV, wearing clothes borrowed from some Clear Creek enforcer, her expression a mixture of hope and dread.

Twenty feet away, the large wolf who accompanied her watches on, his eyes fixed intently on me. There is a warning there, a silent promise that he'll protect my mom from even her own daughter, and for some reason, I like that. I like knowing that someone will protect her. Especially after seeing how vulnerable she was at my dad's hands in those visions.

Tobias pauses, looking between us, silently asking me whether I need him with me. Part of me wants to hold him to me. To wrap my arms around him and never let him go. To feel every part of him right now and convince myself that he is real. Alive. Mine.

But a conversation with my mom is years overdue. And it is one we need to have alone.

"I'll go and sort out Aires," Tobias whispers, tilting his chin towards the male standing in the midst of smoke and rubble, now in his human form. I nod, frowning at the dragon shifter who nearly killed my friend.

After he had a dragon tantrum and set fire to the first RV - and nearly got Summer killed as a result - he turned on Drake and the shifters accompanying him, chasing them from our territory. While that was appreciated, and at least showed that he wasn't a complete traitor, it also had the unintended effect of making the fire spread throughout our campsite.

I can't even begin to decide what we should to about him. Though judging from the guilt I can feel pulsing off him over the pack bond, it seems like he's doing a pretty thorough job of punishing himself without our help.

"Hey, mom," I say, turning my attention back to the woman in front of me.

"Lucy." She gives a tentative smile before stepping forward, arms open as if to hug me.

I shake my head. I'm not ready for that yet. Not yet. Maybe not ever.

She gives a resigned sigh, then tilts her head towards the trees. "Walk with me?"

I follow. Cautiously, because I still don't entirely trust this female. Even if she helped us.

"I'm sorry," she says when we reach a small copse of aspen trees. Their leaves, already tinged yellow with the promise of autumn, whisper in the gentle morning breeze, the sound incongruous with the destruction at our backs.

I cross my arms over my chest and lift one brow, waiting for more.

"I'm sorry I left you and Anton," she explains, sitting heavily at the base of one tree. "I thought I didn't have any other choice. Your dad – well, when he found out about Gordon and me being true mates, he lost it. I thought he would kill me. I thought he would kill the pair of you. I knew if I took you with me, he would try and track us down. And Cindy promised she would keep you both safe."

I stare at her for a long moment, recalling the fear I felt from her in that vision. Recalling the madness that consumed my dad after she left.

"Thought, or knew?" I ask finally.

"Knew," she whispers, and I taste the truth on those words.

"Because of the gift," I say.

It's not really a question. Ever since the seer ability of my gift manifested, I've suspected that it was a gift she shared too. Just like the truth-telling ability.

"Did dad know?" I ask. "Did he know about the visions."

She shakes her head. "No," she whispers. "I never told him. Even at the start, even when I was in love with him, I knew I couldn't trust him with that. He only ever knew about the truth-telling, and even that…"

I give a curt nod. She doesn't need to explain. I served as the pack's truth-teller for a couple of years. She served for much, much longer. Gods only knows what she was forced to see.

"I understand if you don't want anything to do with me," she continues, staring at the patch of bare earth between her feet. "I thought you would be safe with your father. I thought that whatever poisoned him towards me didn't extend towards his pups." She looks up at me, her pale eyes glistening with unshed tears. "If I had known that he would try to harm you, I would never have left you with him."

I can taste the truth in all of her words, and feel my anger softening. With a resigned sigh, I slide to a seated position beside her, close enough that I can feel her warmth.

"Okay," I say, reaching across to take her hand in my own.

It feels so familiar. For some reason, I thought it would feel like holding the hand of a stranger after all these years not seeing her. But in some strange way, it's like she never left at all.

"Okay?" she asks tentatively.

"I forgive you," I say, then frown when I realise the words are not quite true.

She hurt me. Devastated me, and I'm not sure whether I'll ever be able to forget the pain she caused me.

"You know better than to lie to me," she says with a mirthless chuckle.

I smile at that, recalling all the times as a child I'd attempted to trick her. To blame the missing cookies on Anton, or claim that I had done my homework when I hadn't.

"Okay, fine," I admit. "I'm going to need some time. But I want to try and forgive you. I want to get to know you again." I look up at her, meeting her eyes with my own. "I want us to try and have something."

Her answering smile is watery, so full of hopeful vulnerability, that I feel the last walls of resolve cracking around my heart.

I reach out, tentatively and awkwardly wrapping one arm around her shoulders, letting her enfold me in a hug. It's short and fumbling and I'm pretty sure we are both out of practice.

Still, I can't help but feel like it's the start of something new. Something real. Maybe even something beautiful.

TOBIAS FINCH

"You aren't seriously going to let him back into the pack?"

Red's tufted cat-ears are pressed flat against his head as he scowls at me, making absolutely no attempt at looking like an obedient pack member.

Glad to see my death and subsequent re-birth has changed absolutely nothing.

"He's already in the pack," I point out tiredly, closing my eyes against the too-bright morning sun.

We're seated in the usual meeting tent in the meadow, screened away from the scorched earth marking what used to be our trailer park. Sitting here, it's easy to pretend that last night's events never happened.

"The only person he wronged was me," I continue. "He apologised and we're all good."

"You're all good," Red echoes drily.

His look of disbelief is echoed by many of the others. From the other side of the tent, Hamish shakes his head, clenching one tattooed hand into a fist as he glares openly at Cody.

"He saved Summer." To my surprise, it's Aires who speaks up, his voice a hoarse whisper.

"He risked his life to save Summer from the fire," Aires continues, his gaze downcast. An uncharacteristic red flush creeping up his cheeks as he murmurs: "And from me."

Arlo nods, mouth forming a grim line.

"It's true," he agrees reluctantly, casting Cody an appraising look. "I saw it. I was there. If he hadn't pulled Summer from the fire when he did…"

Arlo's voice trails off. I can feel Cody shudder beside me, as if even now the memory of what we almost lost is too much for him to bear.

We got lucky. Summer and Jason are safely convalescing in Arlo and Theo's RV – the solitary RV that wasn't destroyed by the fire. Samson, by some miracle, managed to shift and heal from a silver bullet to the side, after apparently digging the toxic metal out with his own claws. Everyone else's injuries were superficial – if lacerations and broken bones can be called superficial.

Things could have been much, much worse.

For Cody, things were worse. There is no ignoring the fact that Cody lost his father last night, and I can feel how deeply that loss is eating at him.

Even if his dad was a murdering psychopath.

"Fine," Red concedes reluctantly, "but it doesn't change the fact that he betrayed our whole pack. He didn't just betray you."

"Um, no," I say with a frown, shaking my head. "I was the only one Cooper wanted dead."

And technically, Cooper got his wish. I think. I mean, I'm pretty sure I sort of died. I don't really know how else to explain what I experienced.

"Guys, I appreciate everyone wants to deal with the whole Cody situation now," Christopher interjects, wiping one sooty hand across his pale face. His usually blond hair is dark with ash, the scraps of clothes he managed to salvage after shifting are just as dirty. For once, he isn't smiling, and he looks years older than eighteen. "But shouldn't we wait for Lucy to get here? She's our alpha too."

Lucy and grandpa had both lingered behind.

Grandpa had been worried about what grandma would do to him since he had been out all night without any explanation. Grandpa had also mumbled something about needing to apologise to Lucy, though I don't think he'd had the chance, since Lucy had been busy speaking with her mom and Anton.

As if summoned by Christopher's words, the sound of twigs snapping has us all looking towards the trees that separate the meadow from the clearing where the (now mostly burnt) RVs are parked. It's no surprise when Lucy emerges soon after. Even without the wind carrying her delectable lavender and fresh grass scent to me, the almost painful tug in my chest would have alerted me to her presence.

Mine, my wolf rumbles, full of wolfish possessiveness and pride. I resist the urge to smile at the animal.

"I heard my name." She raises one eyebrow coolly as she approaches, but the faintest brush of a smile softens the look, and there is no missing the warmth in her gaze as she surveys our pack.

The warmth fades when her eyes fall on Cody, the smile quickly falling from her face.

"Ahh. Right," she says, lips pressing into a thin line. "Cody."

"We were just sayin' that we think he should be punished," Red announces boldly, crossing his arms over his chest. "Not just let back into the pack like nothing happened." He gives a nod towards where Hamish and Gareth stand side-by-side. "Even those two idiots agree with me."

Gareth frowns, but Hamish just chuckles in amusement.

I shake my head, wishing more than anything that I could have twelve hours sleep and some coffee. A massive steak wouldn't go amiss either.

"I've already forgiven him," I say, the words coming out more sharply than I intend. "It's done."

"And everyone else, what do they think?" she asks, but her eyes are fixed on me. Burning with something indescribable. Something that echoes with the pain I know she felt at losing me.

Her question is met with a long silence. Because of course, everyone has an opinion but no one actually wants to voice it.

Finally, Aires clears his throat.

"I don't think we can blame Cody for everything," he says, his eyes still fixed on the patch of bare earth beneath his feet. "He betrayed us in Southern Utah, but he didn't invade our territory. He didn't shoot our alpha. That was his father. And Huxley Black."

"I agree," Orrin says with a rumble as he leans back in one of the plastic chairs. It gives a loud creaking protest, looking like it will buckle any moment under his weight. "We can't make Cody our scapegoat. Especially now that there is a truce of sorts with the Clear Creek pack."

"He still shouldn't be let back into the pack," Gareth argues. "There is no way of knowing if he will betray us again. For all we know, he's just pretending to be sorry for what he's done."

Lucy and I exchange a look.

Everyone knows about her ability to see the future, since it's no big secret that her vision saved us in Southern Utah. But I don't think she's told everyone about her ability to sense lies.

Lucy could easily tell whether or not Cody is honestly sorry and whether he plans to betray me in the future, but it doesn't feel right asking her to interrogate him for me like that. Especially when I already know the truth, because I've seen it through Cody's own eyes. Felt his remorse. His sorrow and self-loathing for what he did.

I grimace. I hadn't really wanted to tell my entire pack that instead of dying, I somehow ended up inside their heads for a solid couple of hours last night. It seems like a massive invasion of privacy.

"Well," I say slowly, staring up at the ceiling of the marquee-style tent. The originally white fabric is greying and worn after several seasons of Wyoming weather. I doubt the thing will hold up much longer. "I kind of do know, actually."

I look back down, taking in the exhausted expressions of my pack mates. Nearly everyone is covered in soot from Aires' fire-tantrum, and most are sporting injuries as well. Danny's face is covered in enough scratches that he looks like a younger version of his uncle, Orrin. Tyrone is covered in dried blood that I'm almost certain is not his own. Noah and Ollie are sitting next to each other for once, putting aside their usual sibling rivalry as they silently offer each other comfort.

The truth, my wolf urges. *Your pack deserves the truth.*

I swallow thickly, and then tell them everything.

Chapter 30

Lucy Stone

So Tobias Finch has been inside my head.

I give him a wary look, trying to quell the surge of panic rising in my chest.

My head is a scary place, even for me. Gods only know what he thinks of me now. He's probably seriously questioning the wisdom of the gods or fate or whatever it is that makes people pre-destined mates.

The rest of the pack meeting passes in a blur. I'm vaguely aware of Red giving a grumbling agreement not to try and punish Cody, and everyone agreeing that Cody can stay in the pack. I know I should be more engaged in the discussion, especially since I doubt I'll ever be able to fully trust Cody again.

But all I can think about is Tobias.

My mind can't seem to wrap itself around the fact that he is alive. I saw him get shot. I watched him die. And here he is, looking for all the world like nothing has changed.

Okay, that's not true. There is something different about him. A silent confidence that wasn't there before. A steady calmness.

Tentatively, I reach across the pack bond for him. I can feel his emotions, stronger than the constant hum of all the others. There is tiredness there and joy and sorrow and amongst it all, a warm sort of power that reminds me of that golden energy that coursed through me during the fight.

That must have been him, I realise.

"Lucy?"

My eyes fly open, meeting Tobias' warm golden gaze. A tired smile is tugging at the corners of his lips. With the boyish smile and the soot coating his face, he looks like a chimney sweep from a Dickens novel. Only bigger. Like a grown-shifter sized chimney sweep. And hot.

I blink, flush rising to my cheeks.

"Sorry, what?"

He chuckles, and it's then that I realise the meeting is over and our pack mates are starting to disperse across the meadow.

"I was just saying," Christopher says, waving one hand to get my attention, "that Danny and I are going to head into town and pick up some food. Since most of our food got burnt down in the fire."

"Yah," Danny says, giving Tobias a pointed grin. "We lost the lodge. Huge tragedy."

By lodge he means that structurally unsound eyesore the pack tried to build before they realised they would have to hire actual builders.

Tobias runs one hand through his hair, his smile widening sheepishly. "So sad," he deadpans.

"Do you want to come with us?" Christopher asks, looking between me and Tobias.

As hungry as I am, right now I need to be alone with Tobias. I need to hold him in my arms, to prove to myself that he is alive and real and mine.

Claim him, my wolf urges, like the unashamed hussy that she is. *Make him yours.*

"No thanks," I say just as Tobias says, "Nah, I'll stay here with Lucy."

I shoot him an incredulous look, my face heating. Could he be any more obvious?

Tyrone nods knowingly, thumping Tobias on the shoulder. "I'd do the same, if I could," he mutters, eyes darkening with something akin to jealousy as he looks towards the trees separating the meadow from the RVs. Towards where Tania is no doubt sitting beside Samson. Waiting for him to wake up.

"He took a bullet for him," Tobias whispers as Tyrone trails after Christopher and Danny, leaving us alone in the meadow. "Samson, I mean. Tyrone was in the line of fire, shielding Tania and Summer as they ran off to the woods, and Samson took the bullet."

I gape at Tobias, then turn back to stare at Tyrone's retreating figure. As I reach across the pack bond, there is no mistaking the crushing sense of guilt and jealousy pulsing off him.

"Does he know?"

Tobias shakes his head. "No. I don't think so anyway. No one has said anything about it. I just saw it happen when… you know…" he waves his hands dismissively.

"When you were inside everyone's heads?" I ask pointedly.

He rubs the back of his neck with one hand, cheeks flushing. "Um, yah. Then."

There are so many questions I want to ask about that.

"Do you think I should tell him?" he asks. "What Samson did for him, I mean?"

A strange rush of warmth floods my chest at his question. He's asking me for advice about how to handle his pack. A born alpha.

You're alpha too, my wolf reminds me smugly. *Of course he would ask you.*

I consider his question, brow furrowing as Tyrone's figure disappears between the trees.

"No," I say finally, "I don't think you should. What you saw and felt in everyone's heads, that was private. It wouldn't be fair to Samson if you said anything. Even if it made things better between him and Tyrone."

Tobias lets out a sigh. "Yah, okay."

When he doesn't say anything else, a silence falls between us, tension rising like the distant song of the meadowlark, heavy as the August sun beating down on the tent. I shuffle my bare feet in the dirt, feeling suddenly self-conscious of my borrowed clothes and ash-coated hair. Just when I'm contemplating making a run for it, Tobias finally speaks.

"You were amazing, by the way."

His voice is steady, but when I look up at him, those golden eyes are swirling with a hopeful sort of vulnerability.

"I saw what you did out there. Felt what you felt. You were so brave."

"I was terrified," I say, surprising myself with the admission. "I had never been more frightened in my entire life."

Or more heart-broken. I don't say that though. Because I'm not sure I'm quite ready to give voice to those feelings.

Tobias reaches down, gently tucking one strand of ash-coated hair behind my ear, a thoughtful expression crossing his face.

"I felt everything," he whispers, bending to press his face into the side of my neck, taking in a shuddering inhale. I cringe, because no doubt he's getting a nose-full of dirt and blood and sweat and ash. "Everything you felt. And I am not worthy of it."

I squeeze my eyes shut, feeling a sudden rush of emotion at his words. He pulls me to him, pressing my face into his bare chest, filling my head with his chocolate, sage and pine scent until I'm practically dizzy with it.

"You are," I mumble against his skin. "You are worthy."

"I didn't do anything," he argues, practically crushing me to him. "You and Jason, Danny and Samson – you guys did everything. Even Cody. I didn't do anything to protect our pack."

"You were dead," I point out sagely, pulling back from his embrace to stare up at him.

He shakes his head. "I should have done more."

I blink up at him, I recalling that feeling of warmth that moved over me, strengthening my limbs, steeling me for a battle I should never have had to fight. I recall the energy that seemed to pulse from Jason as he fought Cooper Winslow, taking on a foe he should never have been able to defeat. I think about how Danny came to my side, ferociously defending me when I was sure I would fall.

That warmth had felt like power. It had felt like chocolate and sage and pine and love and home.

"I think you did," I say truthfully, the knowledge filling me like one of Morrigan's visions. "When you died, when you saw through our eyes – I felt something. I was stronger. Our pack was stronger. Because of you."

Tobias gives a derisive snort, tugging me back to him. This time I let myself sink into the embrace, wrapping my arms around him, relishing his warmth.

He's here, I tell myself. *He's here, he's here.*

"Maybe. Maybe there was something," he admits reluctantly. "But if there was, it's not like I had anything to do with it. I was just along for the ride..." he trails off, body tensing as if recalling something. When he finally speaks again, there is a slight tremble to his voice.

"Actually, I don't think I would have come back if it wasn't for all of you. You, the whole pack. You guys are what pulled me back."

"How?" I ask.

"I don't know. That's just what it felt like. Like I was being pulled back by my pack." He gives a dry chuckle. "It sounds stupid, right?"

"No," I tell him, before pressing a light kiss above his heart.

The scar where the silver bullet tore through him is still there, an angry red. Maybe it won't ever heal. Maybe he'll always bear the mark. But when I rest my ear against his chest I can hear his heart beating, steady and strong.

"An alpha is only as strong as his pack," I murmur against his skin, reciting the old words I've heard the Clear Creek pack elders say before.

I wonder idly if that had something to do with whatever Tobias felt. If we really did bring him back somehow.

"Or her pack." His voice is rougher sounding, the faintest groan escaping his lips as I press another kiss to his chest. "You're the alpha too."

My wolf preens at those words and I smile against his chest. The animal is apparently a power-hungry creature. For some reason, that doesn't come as a surprise.

Rough fingers trail up and down my bare arms, igniting a fire in my veins and creating a very different sort of hunger.

"I don't care about any of that," I say breathily, tilting my head up to look at him. Golden eyes meet mine, swirling with a desire that matches my own. "Just kiss me." The words come out in a hurried breath. "Just kiss me and make me forget."

TOBIAS FINCH

"Tobias?"

The voice interrupts the blissful warmth I'm wrapped up in, and I squeeze my eyes shut, pressing my face into the source of the most wonderfully intoxicating smell imaginable. Something wriggles in my arms, and I hold it tighter, not wanting it to escape.

"Oh – um…"

There's a nervous chuckle, then a hissed protest as the sounds of arguing drags me from sleep's warm embrace.

"They deserve some time alone, you idiot," a deep voice rumbles. *Danny*.

"They need to eat and alpha," the first voice argues. *Christopher*.

I groan, throwing one arm over my eyes and clutching a now squirming Lucy to my chest.

"Alpha is not a verb," I mumble. "You can't use alpha like a verb. That's not a thing."

"Whatever you say, alpha," Christopher snorts, intentionally using the title he knows I hate.

I open my eyes, blinking against the midday sun filtering through the birch leaves as I stare up at Christopher and Danny's looming silhouettes.

Lucy and I had kissed. A lot. Then we had made our way over to the shelter of trees at the edge of the meadow and kissed some more.

We kissed until my lips were sore and my whole body was on fire.

We kissed until we forgot about war and death and leading our pack.

And then we fell asleep in the tall, ripe grass, piled on each other like wolves, our skin dappled by the sunlight dancing with the leaves above us.

"Summer has woken up," Danny says tentatively, the fresh scars on his face pulling with an apologetic smile. "She's rambling about the building schedule and where everyone is going to sleep now that the RVs are burnt down and, honestly, I don't think the stress is doing her any good."

I grunt as a sharp elbow presses into my ribs. The feeling is soon replaced by cool air fluttering over my skin as Lucy peels away from me. I frown, siting up in an attempt to hold her back to me, but she's already leaping to her feet, brushing dirt and grass off her rumpled t-shirt.

Gods, she looks beautiful. Even coated in ash and dirt and wearing one of Theo's old shirts.

"Come on." Christopher toes my side with one booted foot. Probably a little harder than required, if we're being honest. "You can lay around later. There are things to do."

I sigh, biting back the protest as I rise reluctantly to my feet. Christopher is right, of course. I have a pack to house and feed. And Summer shouldn't be trying to organise the construction of our pack buildings right now.

"Don't worry," Christopher says, wrapping one arm around Lucy's shoulder before flashing me a grin. "We saved some food for you. I'll let you guys eat first. No doubt you've worked up an appetite." He waggles his blond eyebrows meaningfully and Lucy blushes, squirming out of his grasp.

"Leave them alone," Danny grumbles with a frown, before efficiently shoulder-checking Christopher, sending him scrambling to right himself in the knee-high grass.

Christopher lets out a low growl, eyes flashing blue and muscles coiling as he springs towards the bear shifter. Danny just chuckles, moving gracefully despite his size to throw his pack mate off.

"Can you guys not?" Lucy says, but there is no missing the amusement in her tone, or the look of affection as she watches the pair play-fight.

They ignore her, of course. Instead, Christopher reaches up to flick Danny's favourite trucker hat off, laughing as it sails into the long grass before sprinting out of Danny's long reach. Danny mutters a curse, fumbling to retrieve his hat before chasing after the wolf shifter.

Lucy and I follow behind, the scent of burnt rubber and plastic assaulting my nostrils as we approach the clearing. My stomach lurches at the smell. At the visceral reminder of what we almost lost.

As if reading my mind – or maybe, feeling my emotions – Lucy slips one small hand into my own, giving a reassuring squeeze.

"We're still here," she says softly, pressing her shoulder against mine, and I shorten my stride to match her own. "You, me, the pack. That's what matters. We're here. Everything else can be rebuilt."

Epilogue

Three months later

Summer Green

I stare up at the building in front of me, the modern pine façade glowing warm in the light of the setting sun, the massive windows reflecting its brilliance in reds and yellows. The earth around it is bare, like a muddy canvas waiting for spring.

Except it's only November, and spring is a long time away.

The voices of my pack mates filter out through the open doors and windows, excitement as they explore the freshly carpeted halls and newly furnished rooms. I let out a sigh, hoping they've at least taken off their shoes. If I find mud on my new floors, I swear to all the gods…

A warm hand rests briefly on my shoulder before the comforting weight is quickly lifted away.

"It looks amazing."

I turn, staring up at Cody's face. At those bright blue eyes full of guilty longing. I lift my chin, giving him what I hope is a wide, friendly smile. The sort of smile I would have given him before. When we were best friends and I thought I could trust him.

He nods towards the newly constructed lodge. “You made this happen.”

I wave one hand dismissively, even as my wolf puffs out her chest with satisfaction at his praise.

He’s not your alpha, I remind her. *He’s barely even your friend.*

She’s not the best listener.

“You did the groundwork,” I remind him.

We might not have worked together on this project, but I inherited all his notes when I joined the pack and picked up my role as beta. Even full of disgust at his actions, I had been impressed with his meticulous record keeping. It had certainly made my job easier.

“And everyone pitched in to help, especially at the end,” I add.

I glance down at my bare arms, at the faint scars tracing my hands and forearms, recalling those weeks after the fire.

Battle scars, I tell myself. But it’s a lie. I wasn’t even there for the battle. I was off in the woods, hiding like some prey animal when I should have been out fighting for my pack, like a wolf.

Like a beta.

“Have you picked out your room?” he asks as we make our way slowly towards the front door, walking side by side like we used to do, our bodies not quite touching but close enough that I can feel his warmth.

It shouldn’t be comforting, but it is.

“Yah,” I say, smiling despite myself.

Even when I’m angry and hating myself I smile, apparently. Some habits are so deep, they live in your muscle memory.

“I’m sharing a room with Tania and Lucy.”

"Lucy's not sharing with Tobias? They're mates."

I grit my teeth, biting back the myriad of angry retorts that flit at the tip of my tongue. Because I know he hasn't forgotten that Tania and I have mates too. And also, just because Lucy and Tobias are mates doesn't mean they have to move in together and start popping out pups.

Instead, I let my smile widen. Let it stretch my cheeks almost painfully.

"Nope," I say, letting the 'p' pop playfully. Because I'm playful Summer. Sweet Summer. Agreeable, nice and friendly Summer. "It's just us three girls. Like one big sleepover party."

Cody snorts, casting me a dubious look. Like he knows I'm full of it, but he's not going to call me out.

He's just as happy to pretend as I am.

AIRES ZMEY

I watch Summer and Cody talking and smiling at each other in the clearing below. If they can feel my eyes on them from the second-story window, they don't give any indication.

A low rumbling growl rips from my chest as I see them walking side-by-side, close enough to brush each other's arms. Just one small movement would have them holding hands. It was bad enough seeing that wolf touch my mate. Even if the touch was brief.

Mine, my dragon rumbles, and fire churns in my gut. I swallow it down, hating the bitter taste of charcoal and flame. It tastes like fear and loss and guilt.

We don't deserve her, I remind the beast. The truth of that thought sits like an obsidian stone in my chest, even as my talons emerge in protest.

Summer and Cody disappear from view, but I can hear their laughter echoing in the empty halls of my new self-created prison, the sounds of their mirth joining with those of my pack mates.

Pack mates.

I snort at the thought. What sort of dragon binds himself to a pack of lesser shifters? Puts himself under the control of wolves. Even if one of those is a born alpha.

My dragon rolls his shoulder, dismissing my concern. Apparently, he doesn't care that he's under the authority of a couple of pups.

Mine, the dragon rumbles again when my ears pick up the distinctive laughter of our mate.

Of course, my dragon doesn't care who his alphas are. All he cares about is being close to Summer.

I run my fingers through my hair, my black Henley suddenly feeling too tight as my muscles expand, body demanding that I shift. I turn away from the window, meeting my own eyes in the tall mirror at the other end of the room.

A room I will be sharing with Samson and Tyrone. Since apparently no one else could stand to be around their incessant arguing. And no one else wanted to share a room with me.

After what happened with Summer, I don't blame any of them.

I curl one lip at my own reflection, willing my green eyes to return to their human form, waiting until the shimmering scales become weak human flesh once more.

If I was a better male, I would leave. I would let Summer have her life. Let her finish high school and go to Mills. Let her pretend that I don't exist. That the bond between us doesn't exist.

It would be better than the way she looks at me. It would be better than seeing those scars that mark her skin. Not because they make her any less beautiful – nothing could do that. But because they are a permanent, daily reminder of my failure.

"You almost killed her."

The wolf-pup's words echo in my head. Taunting me. I hear them every time I look at her.

"You coming down? It's almost dinnertime."

Samson's voice interrupts my thoughts as his tall, lurching figure fills the doorway. I narrow my eyes at him, lifting my chin to give him a haughty sneer. My mask of choice.

"Of course," I say with affected confidence.

Samson shakes his head, giving me a strange look before turning to leave.

If I didn't know any better, I would say it was a pitying look. But of course, that can't be right. I'm Aires Zmey. A dragon. The only real dragon left, as far as I know. I've got more gold in my horde than any of my ancestors before me. One day, I'll have my father's gold too. The entire shifter world should be envious of me. Should be falling at my feet.

I turn towards the mirror, taking a moment to straighten my hair, squaring my shoulders. I contemplate briefly whether I should change into a suit, since this is the first official dinner in our new home, but quickly dismiss the idea. Now that I've gotten into the habit of dressing casually, wearing suits feels more restrictive than before.

Or maybe it's just because, with my dragon so close to my skin, even the thinnest cotton t-shirt feels like torture.

Summer, my dragon rumbles, as the scaly beast pulls me relentlessly towards the dining room.

To where he knows our mate will be waiting.

Summer.

My firesong.

JASON ALP

The dining room falls silent when Aires enters, casually dressed but still looking out of place among the red and white chequered table clothes and the exposed pine decor. Only when he sits quietly down at the far end of the table, wordlessly filling his plate with turkey and mashed potatoes, does the conversation pick back up again.

"Well, that was awkward."

Ross' words tickle my ear, distracting me momentarily from the discomfort that always accompanies animosity between pack mates. I feel my cheeks heat, though whether it's from his fleeting closeness or the fact that he doesn't realise everyone in the dining room can hear his whisper, I'm not entirely sure. Maybe both.

"Shh," I caution, "shifter hearing, remember."

Ross grimaces, but I can feel the mirth rolling off of him in waves.

"Oops," he deadpans, "forgot."

I roll my eyes.

My mate – well, my unclaimed mate who has no idea what he is to me – did not forget. He has a laser focus on details and an intelligence that outstrips every single person at our high school. He's also acutely aware of social situations, reading a room effortlessly. Which is probably why he's so popular.

No, if Ross says or does something, it's entirely intentional.

Summer slumps down in her chair beside me, the weight of her sorrow pressing in on my skin, conflicting with the hot buzz of her satisfaction. I shift uncomfortably in my chair, every part of me wanting to reach out to her, comfort her, take away her pain. My wolf whimpers pitifully, and I give in to the urge, slinking an arm around her shoulders, pulling her to me for a brief hug.

"Who do you need me to kill?" I tease.

It's not the first time I've made this joke, but the words don't make me feel any less disgusted. Disgusted, and sad. Because now they just make me think of Cooper Winslow.

"Hah," she says drily, tucking a few stray strands of hair behind her ear. "Maybe next time."

Her long sleeves slip back with the movement, exposing the pale scars on her forearm. I wince, remembering those days spent recuperating together in Theo and Arlo's RV. Hearing her pained whimpers as her body struggled to heal from the burns.

I cast a surreptitious glance at Aires. I'm guessing he has something to do with the sorrow I can feel pulsing off Summer in waves, despite her happiness at finally being able to move into the lodge.

She says she's forgiven Aires for that, but I haven't. I don't think most the pack have.

Because of his actions, we were all forced to seek sanctuary at Clear Creek territory while our lodge was finished. Which wouldn't have been so bad, except I let mom talk me into staying with her.

So, while everyone else was staying in the guest cabins living their best life under Cindy Winslow's care, I was cloistered away in my mom's derelict little shack at the edge of pack territory, forced to endure her lectures on the importance of producing lots of grandpups for her with some nice shifter female.

Does she know about Ross? Yes, yes, she does. Does she care? Apparently not.

Then there was the whole matter of having to see Cindy Winslow nearly every single day. Having to meet the eyes of the woman whose mate I killed.

Honestly, it's a miracle I survived the emotional onslaught.

I sink back into my chair, giving a silent moment of thanks to whatever gods are listening that we are finally back on Liberty pack territory.

"So, have you thought of asking anyone to the school dance?"

Ross' voice jolts me from the haze of my thoughts.

"What?" I ask, blinking my eyes in confusion. "What school dance?"

He lifts one brow, giving me an indulgent smile. "The dance in three weeks. At school," he says slowly. Like I need the extra time to process this simple information or something.

My heart races, thundering wildly in my throat. Is he asking me? Or am I supposed to ask him? I swallow, and settle for staring at him in panic.

He turns his attention to his plate, expertly cutting into a piece of steak and popping it in his mouth.

"I'm going to ask Lisa Jones," he says casually, once he's finished his mouthful. "You know, the blond in our math class. She seems cool." He shrugs, then looks at me expectantly. "You taking anyone?"

I freeze, stomach twisting in a bitter knot of – something. Jealousy? Disappointment? I clench my hands into fists under the table, feeling the prick of claws against my palms as my wolf threatens to emerge.

Run, my wolf urges. *Run.*

"I was thinking we could go as a double date," Ross continues, brow furrowed in confusion at my strange reaction. "I mean, if you're taking someone. We could book a table together..."

I know he's talking, but there's a buzzing in my ears getting louder and louder, drowning out his words.

Jason, Summer says through the pack bond, her cool hand grasping mine under the table. *Jason, are you okay?*

I grit my teeth, biting back my response. No, I'm not okay. What kind of a question is that? She knows what Ross is to me. They all know what Ross is to me.

The only one person who doesn't know is Ross, but I'm the only one to blame for that.

I force a smile, doing my best to meet Ross' eyes with my own.

"Sure," I say, but the words feel like sand in my throat. "That sounds good."

TANIA GOODE

"I can't believe we have to share a room with that jerk," Samson grumbles, glaring at Aires at the far end of the table. "He's literally the worst."

Tyrone jerks his head in reluctant agreement, jaw ticking as if even agreeing with Samson on this small, inconsequential, matter physically pains him.

Before the battle with the Clear Creek pack, they had been starting to get along. I had almost thought they were friends. Now, it's like they can't even stand to be near each other and I can feel the tension between them. It prickles uncomfortably against my skin.

Hide, my fox whispers, watching the two males warily.

I don't blame her for the extreme reaction. Years of conditioning have taught her that tension and anger often result in pain.

Samson reaches for a bottle of soda with his right hand before pausing, tucking his arm to his side and reaching for it with his left instead. I frown, eyes tracking his movement.

Samson notices my eyes on him and flashes me a smile, waggling his eyebrows playfully. I shake my head and look away, a surge of irritation rising at his actions.

Can't he just be real with me for once, instead of treating everything like it's a joke?

I let my gaze wander down the table, looking at anything and everything but the two infuriating males seated closest to me, and flinch when I see Red watching me with his pale brown eyes, an inscrutable expression on his face.

What? I ask him through the pack bond, narrowing my eyes at him.

Red just shrugs, reaching up to rub his stubbled jaw before letting his attention drift towards his brother.

I shake my head, turning my attention to my plate. I hate these pack dinners.

I instantly feel guilty at the thought, because I should be thankful. This is the safest I've ever been in my entire life. For the first time in years, I'm able to shift and let my fox run without fear. I'm able to go to sleep at night without fearing the sound of footsteps or the unlatching of a door.

A sad smile ghosts my lips. For so many years, all I wanted was safety. I couldn't think about anything else. Couldn't even begin to imagine what I would want from life.

Now that I have it, I'm finally able to see all the possibilities life has to offer. All the things I could do and be.

I take a bite of the smoked salmon that Orrin proudly brought down from the Bear Tooth Mountains, and close my eyes around the burst of flavour, my fox practically chirping in gluttonous glee at the feast laid before us.

So. Much. Food.

"This is really good," I tell Orrin.

My voice is low, but I know he'll hear me. He always listens, and for some reason, my fox feels safe around him.

The bear gives me an indulgent smile. "It's not bad, eh? Caught that one myself. It's honey that gives it the sweet flavour."

"Hopefully you didn't catch it in your bear form," Red mutters, wrinkling his nose at the fish.

Orrin's deep, belly laugh fills the space between us, easing some of the tension from my mates' silent stare-off.

"You wouldn't be getting anything if I'd caught it in my bear form, cat," Orrin chuckles. "My bear isn't quite so sharing as me. He's more of a…"

"Hoarder?" Red offers. "Glutton? Mindless consumer of everything edible?"

"Yah. All of those," Orrin concedes, shrugging one massive shoulder unapologetically.

"I wouldn't mind learning to do that," I muse, thinking out loud.

"What, learn to eat everything in your path?" Red asks, his strange cat ears twitching.

"No," I say, trying not to laugh at his ears, and doing my best to ignore the weight of Tyrone and Samson's attention as they watch me speak to Orrin and Red. "Make good food, I mean. Work with flavours."

"It's a good thing to learn." Orrin give a nod of approval. "There isn't anything more important than food, in my opinion."

My fox swishes her tail, smugly agreeing with this proclamation. Safety. Food. Those have always been her primary preoccupations.

"Have you thought about going to chef school?" Summer asks from the far end of the table.

Her eyes are dry, but there is no missing the red rimming them. The reminder of her earlier altercation with Aires.

Beside her, Jason is looking unusually pale, and I wonder idly if his omega tendency to feel others' emotions is getting to him, or if it's something more.

"Chef school?" I ask, cocking my head to one side.

The mere mention of school has my heart racing with a strange mix of fear and excitement. I always wanted to go to school, but my old den was one of those closed-off groups of shifters who insisted on home-schooling their kits. And then I got snatched up by Drake's lair.

"Yah, chef school," Summer continues, her face lighting up with excitement at the thought. "One of our old pack mates went to chef school. I don't remember what one, but he said it was really competitive ." She picks up her phone, brow furrowing in concentration as she taps at her screen. "I've got his details – I'll ask him about it. Find out more about it."

I open my mouth to tell her not to bother. I can read and write, and do basic arithmetic, but that's about it. I don't have my GED or any sort of high school diploma. I'm twenty-one years old and I've never even set foot inside a classroom. I doubt I'd get into some fancy chef school.

Not to mention, the thought of leaving Liberty pack territory scares me. Or rather, it scares my fox.

I'm more realistic. I've been in danger my whole life, and being on Liberty pack territory doesn't necessarily promise safety. As we saw three months ago, when the Clear Creek pack attacked us.

Of course, my fox doesn't see things that way.

I give Summer a forced smile. "Okay," I say softly, "Let me know what you find out."

There's no harm in her getting information. It doesn't mean I have to do anything, go anywhere.

I take another bite of salmon, but I hardly taste it now. All I can think about is: *what if?*

What if I did something more? Something that scared me?

What if I was brave?

Thank you!

Thank you so much for reading **The Tobias Finch series**. I really hope you enjoyed the journey.

If you can, I would so appreciate you leaving a review on Amazon and/or Goodreads! Your support is the lifeblood of Indie authors, and provides us with the feedback we need to give you the books you love.

You can keep updated on release dates and progress on my reader group, website and Instagram.

You can also get bookish prints and merch on my website.

About the author

Elisha Kemp is an author of young adult and new adult fiction, who writes in a range of genres, including historical fiction, paranormal and contemporary.

Most of all, she loves creating worlds you can get lost in, and characters you can fall in love with.

She lives with her partner, two human-shaped wolf pups and black cat by the beach in New Zealand.

Her ideal day would be a powder day on the slopes, then relaxing by the fire with a red wine and a good book.

Also by Elisha Kemp

Tobias Finch Series (Young Adult)

Latent Wolf

Accidental Alpha

Wolves of War

Dying Gods Series (Adult)

Drown the Sea

Burn the Stars

Wake the Gods

Minas (planned for 2024)

Endless Winter Series (New Adult)

The Season

The Mountain (planned for 2024)

www.ingramcontent.com/pod-product-compliance
Lightning Source LLC
Chambersburg PA
CBHW070839020826
48982CB00022B/1542/J

* 9 7 8 0 4 7 3 6 9 9 2 8 4 *